FORGOTTEN MASTERS

THE FOUNDATION

SCOTT M. SWAINE

Primix Publishing
11620 Wilshire Blvd
Suite 900, West Wilshire Center, Los Angeles, CA, 90025
www.primixpublishing.com
Phone: 1-800-538-5788

This is a work of fiction. Names, characters, places, and incidents either are the product of the author's imagination or are used fictitiously, and any resemblance to any persons, living or dead, is entirely coincidental.

Published by Primix Publishing: 08/28/2024

ISBN: 979-8-89194-125-0(sc)
ISBN: 979-8-89194-227-1(hc)
ISBN: 979-8-89194-126-7(e)

Library of Congress Control Number: 2024904026

Because of the dynamic nature of the Internet, any web addresses or links contained in this book may have changed since publication and may no longer be valid. The views expressed in this work are solely those of the author and do not necessarily reflect the views of the publisher, and the publisher hereby disclaims any responsibility for them.

CONTENTS

BACKGROUND LORE

These are a series of principles I used when writing my Forgotten Masters series of books. They describe the characters and their cultural styles, language principles, behaviors, and other details relating to the unique environment of the world I'm creating.

The story evolved over the course of many years, stretching, by this time, on the scale of a decade and a half, maybe more. It is by no means a complete review, but it does highlight a few key points which I feel are important to clarify at this time.

The Estelar

The Estelar are an ancient god society. This is what happens if you successfully manage to survive the excruciatingly long evolutionary path, over the course of what could be billions of years, where you ascend well beyond simple three-dimensional space into the higher dimensional planes. These "planes" exist outside the more common "prime material" universes, places like where we live currently, and can only be discovered once you achieve the appropriate technologies to warp the spatial continuum for hyperspace travel.

As a god society, they are essentially the grandfather race over all other forms of life, where we are described as children in relation to them, being as young as we are by comparison. They are a union of many races who evolved up the ladder and joined together as a peer society to govern everything else.

Their society holds many high-level responsibilities, such as managing all the Seas of Creation, which represents the vast multidimensional space out there, including such common universes as our own, along with the spaces in between. They watch for those societies which are close to their own evolutionary advance, and once they see a likely candidate, they essentially conscript them into a form of apprenticeship to teach them the rules to become the next generation of governors. They generally will not take no for an answer, in this regard, as their rules, described as the Measure of Balance, are paramount to any individual and his or her personal interpretations.

As a society evolved to such an extreme state, they speak in their own unique language, which in its native form is entirely telepathic, conceptual in nature, and nonverbal. They will only "lower" themselves to use a verbal language if it becomes necessary to interact with a younger species, like on our level. Aside from this, they may commonly use a custom language described as Celestial to interact with those intermediate societies who have made a partial ascension to an extradimensional existence, as this now becomes the common language for all those societies to use amongst themselves.

The Celestial language is very sophisticated, rather verbose, might use complex terms and wording, and reflects the highbrow nature of an elite society. In my mind, I am using a form of Old English, or maybe a form of Shakespearean prose, which includes such words as "thee" and "thou", and pronouns like "thy" and "thine", "my" and "mine". According to the rules, when using such words as these, the words "thy" and "my" are used before words that start with consonants. The words "thine" and "mine" are the same as above, but used before words beginning with a vowel. Therefore, you could have such an expression as "this is thy house", but alternatively, you could say the house is "thine own".

In addition to this, I use a unique styling for verbs. Trying to ensure I kept it consistent throughout was difficult, as I naturally tend to write using normal English, and sometimes I got lost in my thoughts before realizing I'm switching to the alternate forms. When using verbs, they apply the verb "to do" as the focus for the verb tense, and the action verb is kept in simple form. Therefore, they might say, "I do regret this action", or perhaps to say, "I did think of that", rather than conjugating the actual verb, such as, "I thought of that". This is part of their extended verbose highbrow prose. The only time they might apply a conjugated verb would be if following a helper verb, such as "to be" or "to have". An example would be, "She has informed me", or perhaps, "They are considering their course".

The Celestial Societies

There are essentially two flavors in this category, hybrid and natural. The natural ones are an evolved race of beings, perhaps on the order of tens or maybe hundreds of millions of years of evolution, until such time as they can no longer represent the base species they started out as on whatever world they first spawned from. By this time, they have moved away from their native home, and indeed all of three-dimensional space, into four-dimensional space, and made a necessary evolutionary ascension, one of two in this case, to meet the needs of life in that space.

Their original bodies might still hold to the older forms, albeit they are becoming vestigial by now, as life in four-dimensional space does not involve three-dimensional corporeal bodies. It is now the mind and spiritual essence that evolves, not the material of the body. Evolution becomes painfully slow, as a result, since the body is effectively locked in place, not being affected by the original laws of physics, as we understand them, in our native spatial continuum. But their minds are growing to expand well beyond the confines of the "cage" their corporeal body might represent, forming as an aura effect around the body, but manifested in that higher dimensional layer.

The Celestial form is an intermediate form of life between corporeal bodies, like ours, and the divine form of the Estelar, who have made that second ascension and cast off the remnants of their corporeal bodies to become truly godlike beings composed entirely of mind and spiritual energies. The evolutionary process may take at least as much time in this form to meet that next ascension point, but in the meantime, they'll have more than enough to occupy them as they explore the greater Seas of Creation in the service of their mentors.

The Sarrukh

These are an ancient society of beings once created by an older, and now defunct god society described as the Primordials. The Primordials are a precursor to the modern day Estelar, now extinct after a series of wars between the two saw them removed for the crimes and other atrocities they were found committing on the Children of Creation. The Sarrukh are survivors of this period, one of perhaps very few who managed to get through this moment in history. They date back to the last time anyone ever saw a Primordial, and this is measured as a period called an Epoch to the Estelar. In my books, I describe this as measured by "scholars and others", as a period of roughly a billion years. They have naturally long lifespans to begin with, on the scale of millennia, and therefore their evolution might take much longer than for those with shorter lifespans (which equates to faster turnaround times in their breeding cycles). By the time we finish the series, they will represent one of the older and more advanced of the Celestial societies out there, traveling the Seas of Creation in moon-sized arks populated by billions of native citizens.

In the first book of the series, they start out of a comparatively primitive Iron Age society, and with limited social skills, as they did not have the luxury to evolve anything else under the authoritarian direction of their Primordial master, Sargeras. They were slaves, gladiators used in his games for his entertainment, and that of his peers. They were never intended to evolve into a proper civilization, and not anything representing a sophisticated culture. Therefore, their language would be like that of a primitive tribal culture. They were also warriors, not scholars or intellectuals, and as such, they might use terse terms and restricted language constructs.

However, once they were liberated from the Primordials by the Estelar, they were able to grow and evolve into a higher form, and away from that barbaric warrior caste, now developing into a more intellectual stature. This would naturally reflect in their use of language and terminology.

Kuroku

What started out, no doubt, as a young warrior born to a tribal matriarch, would one day evolve into something legendary. But such things are not always as we might expect, and neither what we might wish for. Hers was a difficult life.

Kuroku is a member of the Sarrukh, once born in their early period, though it is indeterminable when this actually occurred. In the beginning, we only say she had seen many lifetimes of her people pass before her, as she was gifted at one time with a form of immortality by her master, Sargeras, once he saw how valuable her skills were, and wanted to preserve them. He also gifted her with a potent form of prophecy. He would use this to cheat in those very same games he and the others were playing with their creations.

One day, she discovered what these "gods" were doing through these games of theirs, and that the creations they made were merely toys to them. Her ire, not only for how her people were treated, but everything else as well, festered inside of her. When the Estelar arrived on the scene, she foresaw the outcome in her visions, and later took sides with them for their much fairer policies and teachings. She would eventually lead her people into a proper form of evolution as a robust civilization, but she always kept a close eye on her former master, who ran away from that last fight, and now she wanted a taste of her own revenge. However, before she could accurately follow this path, she had to make her own ascension and join the Estelar proper as one of them.

Tae'Eladar

Our primary world in the series. Here we have a complicated mash of societies and their native cultures. The Sarrukh originally seeded the world, which used to be their original home world, after carefully refurbishing it back to a lush environment from the devastation of an epoch-long ice age. This was on the command of their spiritual Matron and goddess, Kuroku, who was by this time a full member of the Estelar.

The world was originally intended to be the home, or perhaps we should say a secondary home, to a human population picked up elsewhere. But it soon became a focus of attention, perhaps opportunistically so, by several other populations to migrate and set up colony bases. The involvement of these other societies greatly modified the original plans by Kuroku for her pet garden world, and the ultimate direction she had in mind for it.

The Tel'Quessir

Elves, as they are commonly known, are one of the primary races found on Tae'Eladar in the modern day. Their culture was the driving factor, especially in the early days, for the development of the world around them. The name they gave to it, Tae'Eladar, translates as "Beloved Green World", and their language became the predominant form of communication. The human population may have had their own native form of language, but it was quite primitive by comparison, as they were still mostly a Mesolithic Stone Age culture.

The involvement of the elves uplifted the human population considerably, giving them a prominent boost to develop their own culture, build villages and towns, learn to conduct themselves in a more formal social environment, and so on. Eventually, the human population learned to live, in many ways, similar to the elves, but it took time for them to meet eye-to-eye with the more advanced migrant societies and their native values.

Over the course of time, divides evolved between the many diverse societies now living on Tae'Eladar. The elves segregated themselves into their localized cultures, the humans took their own, and the dwarves had theirs. There might be occasions of large cities holding multiple culture zones for populations of people to find their local habitat and lifestyles, but in the centuries and millennia to follow, the divides left their mark as each race felt itself at least partially isolated from the rest.

Language

The language of the world was largely dependent on where you travel and who lives there. The elves had theirs, the humans had a different one, and the dwarves maintained their own. It would not be for quite some time that this would present a serious issue. In the early days, people didn't travel as much, as the roads were often dangerous for all the bandits and highwaymen out there. Roaming parties of orcs would attack anything they see, and wild beasts might take whatever was left. Cities, therefore, were most often surrounded by fortification walls, with gates leading inside, and patrolled by city guardsmen to keep things under control.

Although I think I do not specifically mention this in the books, I envision a kind of background history to the world that eventually corrects this dilemma. Surely, as with most cultures, there would be traveling merchants who might find it of value to bring goods from afar that might hold special sale potential to the locals. And as a classic example of a trade caravan, they would stop at multiple destinations along the way. Naturally, in a world where each destination might speak a different language, or at least its own dialect of a language, you would need to study this to make any sort of meaningful communication. But this simply isn't efficient. The number of translation errors, misinterpretations, and other anomalies would make life very difficult.

It becomes clear that the background history of the world would need to involve a transition point, where someone, somewhere, had to realize the futility and inefficiency of the language barrier. It's so simple, so obvious. But it would not be the politicians to realize this. They're too wrapped up in their personal egos and rivalries. Money talks, as they say, so it would have to be those who actually make that money talk…the merchants.

Imagine a scenario where you have a group of these merchants coming together to discuss their recent woes. They ultimately decide the only way to go is to create a unique language for their caste to use, and they will share this amongst other merchants, whether in other caravans, or within the cities they visit, so everyone has one common form of language to use when conducting trade. They might simply call it the Merchant's Common tongue. This now allows them to travel far and wide, but no matter where they land, the language is the same.

However, it may not stop there, as it might then spread to other travelers. As the world becomes more populated, and those roads out there are better patrolled to keep things safe, ordinary people might wish to travel more often. And knowing there is a common form of language taking root, they might feel more confident to travel, as now they have someone to talk to using a common interface for any form of interaction. Boom! Here you have the formation of a common language everyone can use. And use it they will, as this will likely replace the older forms which are inherently incompatible with each other. Now you have a new language standard, which in this case might simply be called Common, as it is common to all people.

Nevertheless, people are still people, and their local cultures might each carry their own flavor. And despite the fact that so many of them came from elsewhere, they are NOT a space age society with advanced technologies. These people use an alternate form of science, arcanic in nature, to perform what others might call magic. As such, their culture is based on an entirely different principle than what we have here. And to us, it might even look medieval for some aspects of its design. In this way, the culture they apply, and the language they use, would perhaps appear Middle Ages to those of us here. This includes the wording, as well as the prose. It may not include fully formed sentences, as if to say someone from a slum area using a lot of slang and mispronounced wording, and some may simply use their own vocabulary and grammar styling.

As I wrote this, I imagined the people using such as cockney English, like from Britain, maybe in some cases with a bit of Australian or New Zealand accents, perhaps even a bit of Scottish. It is most certainly not intended to represent anything American, as we need to represent a society evolved by standards that are simply not native around here.

Lord Thaelyn

One of our primary characters, he is an example of a hybrid Celestial, which is to say, a being who, on the outside, resembles one of us, in his case a human, but intentionally ascended with divine essence. Therefore, one could say he is literally half god. He is fluent in multiple languages, not the least of which would be his native Celestial form. And as a being who is probably closer to godhood than anything resembling our level, his manners are as lofty as his mental and spiritual uplifting.

He commonly uses verbose wording, is complex in his presentation, and like the other Celestials, and the Estelar themselves, regards all of us as "children". He is often treated as a savior and messiah to the people of Tae'Eladar, in many ways like a holy figure, and he currently leads them in a united world society, which he built himself from all those rabblerousing nations.

As a native Celestial, he does not use word contractions, such as "can't", "won't", "isn't", and so on. He takes a very parental view of all others around him, nurturing and supporting them as they grow and learn. Much like with the Estelar, who are regarded as part of his family, he must follow the Measure of Balance the same as the rest, and this states that life is precious, and each society must grow and learn at its own rate, and in its own time.

He was installed on Tae'Eladar by Kuroku, after a development period to train and educate him, to eventually take over that world, and all those people who didn't otherwise have the ingenious idea to unite themselves into one body. Kuroku's ultimate goal here is not simply to bring that world into harmony, but to pursue her old adversary, Sargeras, the one surviving Primordial who is still out there. The final confrontation will mark her creation, this world and its people, as a new guardian society, her principal role among the Estelar, where she desires to enforce the Measure of Balance as a rule of law, a philosophy of life, and a governing policy over all other things.

Lady Aerlie

Every man needs a good woman at his side, and Thaelyn is no different. Aerlie is also a hybrid Celestial, although in the beginning she doesn't actually know this. She was born in a small village belonging to one of the Elven societies, isolated and far removed from Thaelyn and his campaign to unite the world. Unlike Thaelyn and other native Celestials, she was raised in the native culture of Tae'Eladar, meaning to say their language styling and manners. She would not fully realize her destiny until later in Book One, where she meets with Thaelyn, falls in love, and marries him, only then to be confronted by the ones who were involved in her creation to inform her of who she truly is. Nevertheless, in contrast to Thaelyn, she is much more relaxed in her style of speech and other behaviors.

Aelwyn, and other residents of Sigil

Otherwise known as Cardinal Aelwyn, and originally a native resident of the Celestial city of Sigil, she is yet another hybrid Celestial, much like Thaelyn in many ways. Her manner of speech is very similar to his, if only from the female side of the gender gap. However, due to the fact she is a potent empath, she may find herself sometimes feeling a bit introverted, due to her ability, as a Celestial, to alter the fabric of Reality simply by uttering a specific form of wording. As such, she might take to a defensive third person manner of speech to safeguard her thoughts from getting out of control.

Aside from her example are other residents of the city, including many who are not native, but who may have taken up residence in that place for one reason or another. This makes Sigil perhaps the worst of the lot for the mishmash of people and cultures, as well as their use of language.

Generally speaking, the native language is deeply rooted in a stagnant tradition of verbiage. Words are often slurred, and the use of slang is abundant. And then, for those who are not native to begin with, they are just as likely to use a broken form of language, and this is largely dependent on who they are and where they come from. The planes are a very diverse environment with many inherent regions. There are those with positive and negative spiritual polarity, each of which would carry its own native character, and then ordered versus chaotic, where the use of language, or anything at all, would be very contradictory.

The Dwarves

As we progress into the series, we will encounter more of the dwarven population. While we have a fair amount on Tae'Eladar, they are mostly held in the background, only appearing on a few occasions as supplemental actors. However, later, as we begin to journey across new worlds, we will encounter the home world they originally came from.

The dwarves of Tae'Eladar are a modified version of their original ancestors from their ancient home. They had to grow and evolve in communion with the other races on Tae'Eladar, and as a result, their language changed to soften the original dialect in order to blend more harmoniously with the rest. As we move deeper into the series, we find their home world and the people who still live there, speaking what we might call the original dialect of Dwarvish, which is much rougher and more deeply founded in the original culture of their people. For this, the only thing I can say is to think in terms of a thick Scottish accent.

The Suuden-Aryku and Daanen-Aryku

This is essentially an alien species, and for this, anything goes as far as the rules of language, or anything else we can apply to them. They are a technologically advanced society, well into their advanced form of Space Age, capable of traveling across their local galaxy and back again. They are a society of intellectuals, and therefore they will use a lot of technical terms, but they still have their special cultural charm. Their language can follow any advanced vocabulary and grammar styling, and while they do have a number of colloquial expressions, they are also quite professional in their presentation. They tend to be a polite and formal society, largely pacifist in nature, but they can also be a bit restricted on certain topics, especially anything that doesn't otherwise fit their very empirical scientific studies. They do not believe in a religion, and such things as magic are regarded as pure fantasy.

The two names listed above, Suuden-Aryku and Daanen-Aryku, are one and the same society, with the only difference being the Daanen-Aryku are a breakaway group trying to escape from Sargeras, who is currently occupying their home world. However, to say he is occupying it is a bit of a misnomer, as their entire species actually belongs to his servant, one named Darumon, who is traveling with Sargeras. He is the one responsible for the creation of the Suuden-Aryku as a race. He did this as part of his own plan to take revenge on the Estelar for their past interactions.

Needless to say, the two sides must eventually meet, and Kuroku, who is stalking her former master, will have her final say in things.

Evolution

As the story evolves, so too do the people. The early moments in the series show the people of Tae'Eladar to be primitive, both in their culture and their language. As we move forward, we see this improving, as education and higher social standards come into play. Nevertheless, some aspects remain, as their culture tends to hold greater reverence to maintain certain traditions, and not simply throw them away with each new generation, as we tend to do here. They keep their ancestral values, as well as some of their expressions. For them, their history is very important. It is their identity, the unique flavor of who they are, where they come from, and how they arrived in the present day. And in their case, as they have immortal beings governing them, as well as a society of gods they associate with fairly frequently, this serves as a constant reminder of their origins, and the more refined virtues they need to follow.

What comes after will be another form of evolution, and this will lead us into what might eventually become a new generation of people who will one day find themselves on that long journey across the Seas of Creation, solving problems and promoting the Measure of Balance. However, in their case, rather than waiting for the moment when they are ready for their first ascension to a Celestial grade society, they are already working for the Estelar as a junior associate body. This privileged status grants them a form of wisdom like no other, allowing them to travel places and perform deeds that might seem miraculous to others.

PREFACE

Once, early in my life, I began to fantasize about a world, at least in part based on some old stories and computer games I once enjoyed, relating to the classic "wizards and warriors" scenario. Why is it we find this so captivating? But in my case, I chose to carry things a bit further than just recreating yet another plot of yet another bad guy being chased by yet more good guys, and ultimately to yield only a temporary fix in a world that never improves over the long term. This aspect is based as much on the real world as it ever was in any story ever written. Nothing ever changes in a world that seems to forever create more of the same.

So the question is: When do we ever evolve?

Good versus evil may be a never-ending struggle, but at some moment, life must evolve to overcome some part of that. We cannot possibly say we are at the pinnacle of development as we are. There must be a considerable amount of improvement yet to come, but unless we begin to realize our errors, we may never have the chance to see it. Here is where I bring this book, or rather a series of books, as it turns out, depicting a story of a world in which they successfully solved these problems and created a true utopia. And with all their internal woes resolved, they now have the possibility, and the resources, to go out and do the same for others. Here is where the concept of godliness comes into play, as they evolved away from their animalistic origins, and can now set the example for everyone else.

The story depicts a type of philosophy, along with examples of why it is necessary. You cannot have everything all at once. Some things must be sacrificed in order to harmonize a society. Evil must be destroyed utterly if good is to survive at all, and examples must be set to prevent any more from ever occurring. Then, rules must be enacted to keep it that way, as our fanaticism with "absolute freedom" is incongruous with maintaining order. You must outline a precise corridor of perspectives for the people to follow, and not allow them to go running off to the four winds with whatever they choose. We are not speaking of a police state here. Every society has laws, and those laws are not optional. The people will know the result when they see it, and they will fight for it, not against it. They must, or else fall before it as the refuse which causes the disorder.

Peace comes with two price tags. The first is the initial cost of acquiring it, using law and justice, politics, diplomacy, and even war… whatever it takes to cleanse the world of that which would bring harm to it. Actions carry consequences, and those consequences must meet the level of the actions to hold any meaning. The second price tag is a maintenance fee to keep it that way. It could be in the form of a strong enforcement body, or simply a cultural philosophy, where every citizen is so zealously devoted to this perfect world they created, that each and every one would be willing to take up arms to defend it. It follows as a type of motivation to keep this utopia at any cost.

This becomes our story. A tale of a society so dedicated to its principles, that it succeeded in creating a perfect world, and any who would disagree can go live elsewhere, because a true utopia is truly worth fighting for.

PROLOGUE

"My name is Kuroku, once born as the First Daughter of the honored Matriarch of our tribe. Ours is the Ikoko clan – warriors, like so many others of our people, and we call ourselves the Sarrukh. But unlike my forebearers, I did not simply become the leader of our tribe, I went on to become the ruler of all our people.

But ours is not an honorable life. We are slaves to a master that uses us for his pleasures. And we are not alone, as there are others out there, owned by other masters, and used for these same pleasures – battle! We are made to fight and die for their entertainment as gladiators, dancers with blades and blood, who live only to serve… and who die if they cannot.

However, I know a secret, and this grants me wisdom, but also at great risk. I shared this with my people, all of them, that they might know of it as well, and also at great risk. We must keep this to ourselves, silently, as our master may be watching us. We must know who we are, and why we live. We must know who our masters are, and why they keep us. We are expected to worship them, to honor them with our devotion. We do this because they made us, and so we must love them. But what we are not made to know is if we should ever fail to win even one battle, they will unmake us.

I weep for all those who fall before us. But I must fight to keep my people alive. I must hide what I have learned, but at what cost? Every foe we see placed before us is the same. They must fall so that we may stand. We may live, but only after many others die. This is not a fight for an honorable warrior.

I pray that one day we shall see our deliverance. I pray that one day this might all come to an end, and we can be free, and that no more will ever suffer this fate. I wish I could bring this myself somehow. But I am small, and they are gods."

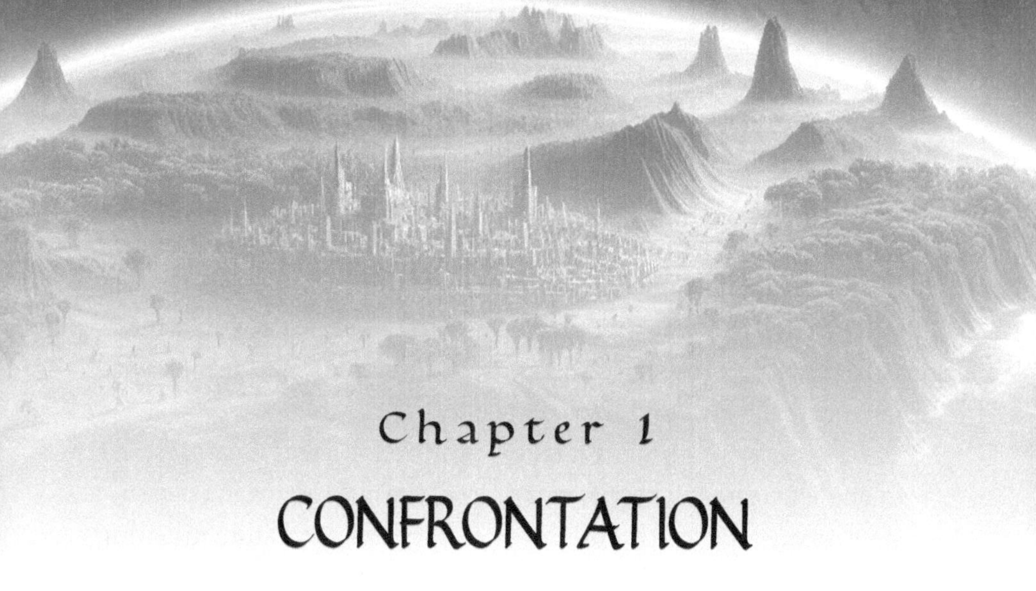

Chapter 1

CONFRONTATION

"Great Matron, we are victorious again!" shouts the clan chief. "All praise our most glorious Matriarch Kuroku!"

A celebratory round of roars and screeches rises up from the warrior caste of these strange creatures. They were a race obviously built for battle, and they had just won yet another campaign against yet another enemy that had been set before them in the great games of their gods. As with so many times before, they rose to overcome the odds of contest to please their Maker. And in so doing, they earned the pleasure of their continued existence.

Their Matriarch and Queen, whose proper name was Ikokokuroku, watched as her people cheered over their recent victory. But her thoughts were not on their success. Rather, it was on her desperate attempt to keep her people alive, day-by-day, as their masters plotted one after another challenge to pit their creations against each other in this ruthless battle of blood, and for nothing more than simple entertainment.

Her eyes panned across the battlefield, now strewn with bodies, some belonging to her people, but many others of their opponents. She reminisced over the events of the battle as it played out during the weeks that came before. It was a hard one, as the other gods were trying to create new challengers to rival her kind after it had seen such a long winning streak.

This was a sporting event, and each of these godlike beings had their own world, serving as a playpen in which to create new lifeforms as contestants for the games. When a challenger was ready, a battlefield was prepared where the opponents would meet, delivered by their respective masters into the duel. But unlike with other contests, this would be a battle to the death.

The gods were a society that cared little for lesser creatures. As each one was tested in battle, win or lose, it would be for the pleasure of its master, and for the others to observe as spectators, gloating over the blood fest of these playthings clashing against each other. The winner would receive a token reward for its victory, while the loser would be erased from existence and something else created in its place.

Ikokokuroku was the matriarch of her local tribe and the matron leader of her people, a society that had done very well in the games. They had proven themselves to be a formidable foe…tough, resilient, and clever, and she had risen to the top as a savvy strategist. She was gifted in her talents, and this gift allowed her to take the lead and bring her people into victory repeatedly. But it was not for the reason of simple triumph. She knew a secret, and it frightened her into pushing herself to the limits, forcing her to invent extraordinary tactics to ensure the survival of her people. If she failed, it would mean their extinction, and not simply for the failure on the battlefield, as their master would also see to the rest of their population.

Her wondrous success in the games had not only allowed her to rise to the top, but it also got her noticed by the very being she now feared and loathed. Needless to say, she had to keep her feelings buried, knowing her continued service might be the only force keeping her people alive. But due to her success in the games, her master, one named Sargeras, had blessed upon her two unique and extraordinary gifts. This was highly unusual, as these gods did not generally bless anything other than this meager tribute to their victory, or a quick extermination for their failure. What she received was nothing short of miraculous.

Her first gift was one of immortality. Sargeras knew a good thing when he saw it, and she was so very successful that he didn't want to lose this tactical genius to such a mundane frailty as her mortal longevity. Her kind had naturally long lifespans, measured in millennia, but even that was not enough for him. To give such a gift as this would not normally draw too much attention, assuming the other gods actually knew about it. In and of itself, it was too innocuous to be of concern. Nevertheless, it was one of his little secrets to success, and he intended to keep it that way.

The second gift was even more important…and even more of a cheat. The Matriarch was blessed with a form of precognition, the ability to see into the future, and in her case, it was a rather potent form of the gift, allowing her to see across years, decades, centuries, and perhaps more, if she could focus herself tightly enough. This was the real key to her success in recent times, as she was able to foresee the upcoming battles and plan ahead. She admired the skill for its tactical value, but she also detested it for the visions she would so often see of bloodied ground and torn bodies.

But this was not the full extent of it, as she had learned new ways of using it. Now, it allowed her to see beyond her world, into the true lives of their gods and the games they played. For this, she knew who they were and what they were doing, as opposed to the rhetoric they so often taught their minions.

She looked back across the faces of her warriors, who by now had calmed their chanting and waited for her to respond. They all knew of her gifts, and revered her nearly as a messiah for her wisdom and insight.

"My children," she begins soothingly. "We have found victory once more, and for this we shall return to our homes. We will tend to our injuries and restore ourselves. We shall give praise…" her voice stalls briefly as she struggles to force the words out, "…to our Master…that he will be pleased with us."

The clan chief knew her feelings on the matter, as she had

confided with him on many occasions over her visions and knowledge. He studied her face as she strenuously held her composure. He knew, like so many others, that their Master would be looking down at them, and they had to put on the appropriate show for the occasion.

"Yes!" he exalts flamboyantly. "Let us rejoice that we have won this day to the honor of our great Creator, Sargeras!"

He raises his hands to incite a renewed outburst from the crowd, even though they all knew silently they were no more than slaves.

✦✦✦

Kuroku and her troops had been delivered back to their home world. Now they would have time to rest and regather themselves. They were a well-populated society covering much of the main continent with many tribal villages. Even though they had the luxury of surviving every game Sargeras had entered them into, they didn't have much opportunity to advance beyond the tribal stage. Advancing to a higher level of intellectual sophistication was not something Sargeras or his kind cared to grant to their creations. They weren't here to evolve, they were here to entertain, and they only needed to be intelligent enough to know how to fight. It was survival of the strongest, not the keenest of mind or advanced of technology.

She hated this perhaps most of all…that the only reason for her existence, and that of her people, was to fight. But her hate was not only on behalf of her people. She could not help but feel for the others placed into contest against them. She didn't necessarily feel hatred for her opponents. Rather, she felt pity. She had to fight them; it was demanded of her. To fail in this would likely bring oblivion to everyone. Deep down, she hoped one day she might find a way to escape from this, but it seemed like a vain hope. Still, she had time now. The recent contest was over, and it would be a while before the next one. This gave her time to think.

"Chief, come speak with me privately."

"Yes, Great Matron. What do you wish of me?"

"I have seen many new visions, and I must speak to you. But we must speak quietly, so that we are not heard in the above-places."

"Have you seen more of what they do up there? Do they make new plans for another battle, or do they sleep now?"

"I believe they will sleep for a time, but this is not what disturbs me. We are but playthings, I have told you of this before. We and all the others we are made to fight."

"Yes, you have said this, but we cannot disobey our Master."

"And neither can the others. I mourn for them as I mourn for our own who are lost to these battles."

"How many more must we fight? Who is next for us to tear into?"

"To be honest, I have seen too many already," she shakes her head. "I do not wish to think of this, and my visions do not reveal this as yet."

"Then what visions do you have? Do we have time to build, time to grow?"

"I am unsure. Something is coming, I cannot be sure what, but it will bring challenge with it…great challenge."

"Matron, what challenge is this?" he asks concernedly. "Must we go to battle again so soon? Many of our warriors are tired. We need time to grow again."

"I know this, and our Master does give this to us. He knows we cannot serve him if we are so tired. But I think this challenge does not come for us. And yet…" she pauses and turns away.

She and the chief were sitting together in a village square near a large bonfire. Many of the other villagers had gone to bed by now in their huts, with only a few scattered around the area on night watch duty. The chief waited for her to finish her statement, curious as to what her visions might be, and unsettled by the implications.

"I foresee something terrible coming," she continues. "Like a great cloud that covers the sky from horizon to horizon."

"A storm? Must we take shelter from it?"

"I think we will, but I cannot be sure where it comes from. I must spend more time in meditation. I must try to find clarity in my thoughts. Something is coming and I must know what it is, as I feel this will bring great turmoil to our people. I hear voices, shouts, screams, but then I hear something new, and it sings with words I do not understand."

"Matron, you should find rest. You cannot see your visions while you are so tired."

"This is true, but I dare not rest long if our people are in danger."

The two of them rise and return to their respective huts. The chief finds rest in his bed while the Matron settles into hers, but she does not go to sleep immediately. Instead, she lays there for many long moments, recalling the visions she had foreseen during past sessions using her gift of Sight.

She tried several times to clear her mind so she could sleep, but she was unsettled. The recent battle weighed heavily on her, as did the eventual coming of the next one. She rolled from one side to the other, attempting to relax, but to no avail. Flashes of imagery erupted within her thoughts. Distant sounds echoed in her mind. And finally, a bold flash covers the scene. It shocks her out of bed, causing her eyes to pop open as she yelps softly and jolts to a seated position.

She rolled her eyes around the darkened room. All was quiet, as it should be. But she could no longer resist it. So, she rose up and moved in front of a small shrine she used for her meditation.

She sat down and attempted to relax herself into a meditative trance, a practice she had perfected since the days when she first received her blessings. She pulled out a pouch from a nearby urn with quantities of several herbs inside, and took out a small handful, placing it into a clay bowl. She then opened a pitcher and poured a small amount of scented oil from it into the mixture. She set the bowl on a stand over an oil lamp and waved her hand in a small circle to generate a charge of arcane energy to ignite the flame. She snapped her fingers and the flame lurched up from the lamp and began to warm the underside of the bowl. She then waited for the fumes to rise up, breathing slowly and calmly.

Kuroku sat on the floor with the bowl in front of her. The vapors from the oil and herbs rose up and wafted around the hut.

She breathed in deeply and closed her eyes, allowing her mind to drift among the filaments of space and time. She needed to see what was ahead of them, to gain clarity over those visions she had not long before.

Her gift of future sight was powerful, but unless she specifically brought herself into this special meditation, she most often only had vague images come to her. Near future events were much clearer than distant moments, but the images that bothered her so much at this time were not as clear as her usual prophecies. She was able to make out scenery, but it was alien to her. There were faces unlike any she had ever seen before. And then there was that cloud, and that flash of light, like an explosion. It frightened her, as it seemed to erupt out of something cataclysmic.

She felt herself being carried away by the aromas of the herbs and oil. The images were coming to her again. She saw faces, many of them familiar. These were the faces of the gods she knew all too well. She felt herself floating, as if outside the world among the ethers. She had come to understand what this was by now, even though her people knew virtually nothing of the realms beyond their home world. She was looking across the vastness of the local space, but seemingly compressed, as if to see the stars and their associated worlds pushed together as a cluster of bodies. And hovering near them were their respective masters, each of the gods with their personal sandboxes.

"And here we are again," she mutters quietly to herself. "Our local space, such as it is. We have our gods, their plaything worlds, and the suns that keep them warm."

She pans her view across the larger scene, but it was mostly the same. Only that selection of active worlds was noticeable. Most everything else was dead…or dying.

"So many others out there," she muses softly. "Why? Are they so old by now? Old suns, red, nothing more, just cold and red. A vast sea of them. Did they once hold life? Were they once bright and yellow, like ours? How old must you be, as a sun, to grow old and red, such that you begin to die. And so many of them. All this space. And yet, those worlds, the playthings of our gods, they are fresh with life. The creations of our gods in an old sea of cold death and ancient suns."

Through these visions, she had learned of the gods creating their playthings, and although she felt guilty for it, she would sometimes peek in on those races to check their strengths and weaknesses, knowing they would ultimately be forced into battle with them. She knew of many worlds by now, and the one that held their most recent foes was her first target. She had to confirm her suspicions for their fate. She knew what was coming, she had seen it before, and she often felt this was becoming a morbid habit.

She turned her mind's eye to their home, bringing her visions to ground level where she saw villages filled with people living their ordinary lives. Hunters had returned with the daily meat. Gatherers were bringing in the local harvests. Children were playing with sticks, pretending to be the next generation of warriors, and mothers were suckling their babies. And above all this was a set of indifferent eyes staring down.

She felt a chill run through her at what she expected to see next. She looked on and saw the apparition of a godly hand wave across the scene, and then there was nothing. The slate had been wiped clean.

She turned away. It was the same as all the others.

The only thing for her now was to seek answers for what came next. She expected there would be a timing delay before the next battle. At the very least, their gods did allow them time to recover between contests, but now she wondered who would be next. She perused the grander scene of the worlds and their owners again, hoping to reach further into the mists of time to find the next challenge. There was often an indication she could focus on that would guide her thoughts. An event, or a sign of some kind. But most notably, she had learned to gauge time by driving her thoughts ahead, while at the same time, trying to follow the circling of her home world around its local sun, thus counting months and years.

She begins pushing her thoughts forward, driving her visions into a future moment. On this occasion, her attention was turned towards the distance, hoping to catch sight of whatever it was that so often disturbed her. In the background, currently outside her immediate notice, her world began to accelerate its motion, spinning rapidly and buzzing around its native orbit. It circled once around, and made a three-quarters turn for a second orbit…a year and three quarters.

Then a disturbance caught her attention. It came from somewhere off to the side.

She turned her mind's eye to observe it, and saw the approach of something. It was like a wave, but not of water, or even the dust of a windstorm. It was a charge of bodies, but not of any bodies she was familiar with. They swept into view with the majesty of gods, and yet they were unlike any gods she had ever seen before. She felt like a bystander on the sidelines of a new challenge, but it was not a challenge like what her people were made to fight. This was bigger, and it was in the realm beyond the worlds of lesser creatures.

The two lines formed up, and she could hear words spoken like distant echoes. But the words were not of voice. They resonated with the power of command, flashing like ethereal portraits, and filled with rage.

"Infidels! Interlopers! Intruders!" rages members of the local side.

"Blasphemers! Despoilers! Defilers!" the new arrivals respond.

Kuroku gazed in awe at the apparent ferocity of the argument. But the meaning behind it was lost to her, as the statements being made were too ambiguous for her to interpret, being spoken in a native conceptual form of language. The contest continued.

"Impudence!" returns another local god. "Possession! Domination! Privilege!"

"Absurdity!" rails an opponent. "Authority! Responsibility!"

"Incongruity! Ascension! Dispensation!"

"Ludicrousness!" shouts another arriving deity. "Irrelevance! Veneration!"

"Veneration?" she blasts. "Negation! Inferiority!"

The two sides assaulted each other with argument, each becoming more agitated by the lack of positional retreat until finally they reached a boiling point together. They quickly took on an aggressive stance, and Kuroku began to witness a clash.

She gazed apprehensively into her vision at the spectacle of two godlike races engaging one another. Such a portrayal seemed dreamlike, but she had to remind herself it was not actually a dream. Now she needed answers. Who were these intruders and where did they come from? She wondered why they were here, what that argument was about, and most importantly, what this meant for her people.

The battle raged, and the newcomers appeared to be gaining the upper hand. She studied their methods, comparing this to her own. Some of it seemed vaguely familiar. Could it be that the gods might use similar tactics? Perhaps battle is still battle, no matter who you are. She was solidly immersed by now. The scene was surreal, and her attention was fully involved, watching it play out like a movie in her mind's eye. She turned to study the local gods. Several of them had fallen by now. She almost felt a sense of liberation. The local gods were getting a little of their own. She smiled.

Now she searched for her master, the one who created her kind. He was her nearest bane. She wanted to know his fate in all this. Was he fighting, perhaps taking his own injury? Had he fallen already? Where was he? She looked for him in the scene of the battle, but he did not stand out amongst the other combatants.

"Where are you, my Master," she mutters privately. "Do you not fight for your own honor, as you cause us to do?"

She knew her master well. She had learned to feel his presence within her visions. If she could not find him in the confusion of the battle, perhaps she could bring her senses to zero in on him personally. This would automatically draw her mind's eye onto him, no matter where he was.

She extended her senses to feel his essence, and a point of attraction presented itself to her. It was not a pleasant sensation, like the warmth of a snug blanket on a cold night. This one stung like the bite of an insect, not because it actually felt so unpleasant, but because she resented it so much. And yet, strangely, this sensation was not where she expected it to be. It was not centered within the conflict. She had to turn her mind's eye far to the side to find it.

Standing away from the conflict, where they might not be noticed, was Sargeras and his closest attendant, known to her as Darumon from her previous interactions. He was the most loyal of his servants, and also the most powerful. The two were backing away from the fight.

"What?" she ushers disbelievingly. "Where do you go, my Master, when there is a battle to fight!"

She directed herself to observe their movements, until a thought occurred to her.

"But wait! Perhaps you are planning a clever ruse? Now would be an excellent time for a flanking maneuver to surprise your opponents. Yes! I must hear your words. What do you speak of over there?"

She then pushed her thoughts into range to hear their conversation.

"How can this be possible?" Sargeras utters. "Such infidels as these…"

"My Master," Darumon responds. "You must listen to me. The others are falling. These younger ones are quite vigorous. Clearly, they have great practice in these affairs."

"Great practice? Do you mean in such way that they might play these games themselves?"

"Master, surely you have heard those same whispers of the progression they have made across the realms. They have driven our kind back. Their youthful zeal and determination empowers their pursuit…" he pauses to glance around the scene. "This is all that remains of our kind. Just look at how the others fall. With each defeat, these invaders grow stronger against us."

"It is true, what you say. We may soon lose this contest…the final play of an eternity-long game."

Kuroku watched and listened to the dialog. She felt a rising sense of curiosity for the subject matter and a renewed interest in the ultimate outcome. She turned again to observe the battle as it drew out in desperation for the local gods defending their homes and their lifestyles.

Silently, she wondered just how far ahead her vision extended. Was it months, years…or perhaps more? She did not take notice of her home world during this time, how far it travelled. She might need to run this again and pay closer attention to it. But even at that, she might still need a sign of some kind to point at a specific moment.

The battle scene continued to rage. Then she sees Darumon with his master again.

"My Master," he asserts. "The others have devised a plan."

"The others?"

"My brethren, Master, we who serve so faithfully at the side of our Great Ones... They have created a plan to destroy these interlopers once and for all, but it must be played out very carefully."

"And what is this plan, my servant?"

"They have decided to invoke the unmaking of the dynamistic flows. The wave of destruction will destroy these invaders, and then we shall be free of them."

"Darumon, be mindful of what you speak," Sargeras cautions. "This would destroy all our creations, and us as well."

"Not if we escape from here first. The plan is to release the Agent of Unmaking, and then hastily depart from this fold. But Master, I feel there is a small risk."

"When speaking of the Agent, my faithful servant, the term 'small risk' is a weak statement. What risk do you now speak of?"

"Clearly, we must depart before the Unmaking, but we must also find sanctuary from the wave, as well. For this, the others believe to escape into the Fifth Fold would allow them to ride above the wave."

"This is reasonable. The Fifth Fold should be well enough outside the reach of the wave, assuming we release it within the confines of this fold alone. But what is this risk you speak of?"

"I will say this only to you, my most cherished Master. I have circled behind these trespassers. I wanted to see where they originate; to learn of their motivations. We know they are not native to this fold, and we have heard stories of their appearance in other folds. This lends me to believe their background could make claim to an even higher prestige."

"Intolerable..." he scorns.

"I agree, my Master, and this forced me to ask where else they can be found."

"Indeed, you are a cunning one. And what did you discover?"

"They seem to have come from across the Folds of Creation, perhaps from a far domain, and they now cover much of it."

"They crept upon us from behind our eyes, and now they dare to oppose us!"

"Yes, I must admit, it would seem this way, but then I must also wonder if anyone was watching that far fold to begin with."

"Perhaps, if we suggest ourselves to have become lax," he sighs.

"If that fold was left unattended for too long, they could arise and then move forward. Master, this…Society, as they call themselves. They came together and now think themselves knowledgeable of the Ways of Creation. They have segregated themselves into polarities, for what they describe as the Measure of Balance. And for this, they engage in occasional contest to test themselves."

"Ah, could this be the source of their skills?"

"It may be, and it gives them veteran qualities. Furthermore, they seem to have enlisted others from other folds as they travelled across, thus expanding their numbers. There may be no true escape possible by now. The others may think they can escape into the Fifth Fold after unleashing the Agent of Unmaking, but I think we must travel farther. We must travel to a place where these cretins have never visited, and therefore cannot find us."

"But Darumon, what of the others we revel with? If to travel to the Fifth Fold is not enough…"

"Master, whatever the others might think, if these intruders believe themselves to be so erudite, I think the Agent of Unmaking should be known to them. They might sense it and make their own exit. If they understand it as we do, they may also travel to the Fifth Fold, and then what do you think will occur?"

"It is true, the battle will begin anew. But then, we should warn the others before they unleash this. We must modify the plan!"

"Master…" Darumon frowns. "I do not wish to speak in such terms, but they have already unmade themselves. Think carefully,

Master. They are currently in battle. If they should suddenly attempt to escape from this fold, for reasons of this plan or any other, the intruders will follow. They are already in the eyes of the intruders, my Master, but you are not. I pulled you aside to keep you out of the conflict, to protect you. You may escape, but they will not."

Sargeras gazed mournfully at his servant, and then turned his eyes into the distance.

Kuroku stared at the scene through her mind's eye, stunned that they were actually considering such a shameful retreat.

"My Master, how could you do this?" she mutters quietly in her thoughts. "Are you not a proud warrior, as you made us to be? Do you not choose to stand and fight, as you force us to do for you?" her voice escalates. "You make us fight for our very lives, and you will not do the same?!" she growls harshly.

"Darumon," Sargeras relents. "You are right, my dearest servant. The others may fall, but we shall not suffer the same. Our existence in this stale and decrepit fold was never a pleasing one, and I would not wish to die here."

"For this," he considers. "We must make a careful withdraw, and it must occur just before they send away the Agent of Unmaking."

Kuroku's attention suddenly spiked. This could be the sign she would need in order to understand the timing. She listened closely to their words, straining to catch each one.

"How do you suggest we proceed, my servant?" Sargeras asks.

"For as long as we remain within a sphere of dynamistic flows, they might sense our presence..."

"Darumon, must I remind you that I require this for myself, as does all of our kind."

"Yes, my Master, I know this, but I think there is no other way. You must go into hiding. But fear not, my most cherished Master, as I will care for you until the end of time if I must. And I will work to bring you back one day."

"You are indeed my most faithful servant. I must admit, you are right. If these infidels have covered so much of Creation, there may be no other place but an empty fold to hide from them."

"I must have you turn inward and retract your form to a dormant body. I will then take you away from here, hidden inside the second moon of our plaything's nest. I shall cause it to fall out of this fold and into one I believe to be devoid of the dynamistic flows. There we shall wait for our time again."

Kuroku made a mental note of the reference, though she could only barely interpret the meaning, as she knew comparatively little of the nature of the local universe. But she suspected the sign of this Unmaking would begin with the disappearance of the child moon circling her world.

She continues to watch as the scene changes before her eyes. She had a focal point now and was pushing forward to find it. She sought the disappearance of the moon, and then to see what happened after. She found Sargeras altering his form in strange ways, as if he was shriveling up like a dried piece of fruit, reducing down to an inert nodule, and then Darumon burying him deep inside the body of the moon. She then saw a wave of energy erupt around it, and the whole moon vanished within a rippling effect of near space.

The display was dazzling in her vision, with such a bright flash of light and energy. She understood the powers of magic, as did many of her people. They used this from time to time in their studies, and occasionally in combat. Their knowledge was not especially high in its level of sophistication, but it opened many possibilities in her mind. Here, in her mind's eye, the moon seemed to glow immensely for a brief instant, and she thought she saw the arrival of countless little stars converging on it just before the rippling swallowed it up. All was calm after that, with only empty space left behind where the moon once travelled.

Regardless of the spectacular nature of the sight, it railed on her nerves that her god would vacate the scene. He not only abandoned her and her people, but also his own kind, leaving them to continue the fight and suffer their fate...a fate they had so often pushed onto so many others.

"Sargeras, my Master," she grumbles. "My most precious Master... Did I not please you enough? Did we not win so many victories for you in these accursed games? Did we not bring you so much glory in the eyes of your kin?"

Her temper was now fuming.

"Did we not destroy so many others in the name of serving your needs? Did we not struggle to keep ourselves from oblivion, simply to fulfill your fetishes? We were your finest champions, battle-tested and victorious on every occasion you drove us into, and now you leave us to this…Unmaking?!"

But before she could finish her thoughts, she was greeted by that bright flash and the erupting cloud from her earlier visions. The other local gods had unleashed some kind of power that was now rending their worlds apart, producing a wave flowing out at incredible speed, tearing through the very fabric of space, and leaving a massive cloud of destruction behind it.

"No! Master, wait!" she whispers to herself. "Do not leave us to this fate!"

Both lines of combatants suddenly faded from existence as they tried to escape from the local space to places unknown. The blast effect rumbles outward in a broad wave, smashing through everything it touches. It was spreading throughout the local space, vaporizing worlds and stars alike. She watched as all the decaying red stars, a whole galaxy of them, were cleaned away, and the blast effect continued beyond to the rest of the local universe.

Her thoughts suddenly turned to her home world. She searches for it, only to see the cloud moving in that direction.

"NO!" she screams within her vision. "We struggled so hard! We suffered so much!"

She quickly finds herself praying for her master to return and rescue them, pulling them out of harm's way the same as he did the moon. She zooms in close to the world to see her people taking shelter in caves and tunnels they had apparently built.

"We must hide!" she considers hurriedly. "Yes, this is our answer. But wait, this will not be enough! The Unmaking destroys all things!"

She anxiously lifted her mind's eye above the world for another look, terrified of what she would see, at least until she realized what she found at ground level. She returned briskly for another peek.

"Why are we hiding in caves?" she mumbles perplexedly to herself.

She dared not ponder this curiosity for long, so she rose back up to see the rest of it. Worlds were being vaporized, and stars obliterated. But as the wave made its approach to her home, something unexpected appeared, and the cloud seemed to crash against it.

She froze in her thoughts. The cloud had been diverted around something. It bore the appearance of a shell of some kind, and it seemed to come out of nowhere, surrounding her world and the local sun. It stood as a barrier, holding the cloud back.

"Master?" she mutters softly.

She surveyed the scene hoping to find him. Her feelings at this point were bittersweet, but if it saved her people, she would accept it. She saw a face, like a reflection within the shell, peering down upon her world, but it was not her master. Instead, it was one of the newcomers. They were the ones responsible. Sargeras had truly abandoned them, tossing them away as so much rubbish. But these others…they apparently saved her people for some reason.

She glanced down at her world as it circled their local sun, until something new caught her eye. She gazed at it in disbelief. There was another planet down there!

"Where did that come from?" she wonders.

And then she saw another, and one more after that, as she followed the orbital ring around her sun.

"Two… Three… Four… Five?" she counts. "Five new worlds? They were not here before! It has always been the one, just our own! Unless…" she glances up at the reflection again. "Maybe… Perhaps. A rescue? No doubt salvaged from that storm out there. It must be! And then brought inside here for safety. Very well, they like to save things."

But this simply caused her blood to boil again. She knew she hated him before, he and all the others for what they were doing, and now she felt it surge to overflowing. Her people were simple playthings, like all the rest, to be created and destroyed at a whim for the entertainment of their masters. No matter how much she might struggle to please him, to keep her people alive through these games, in the end, they were nothing to him. He could always create more.

She fought to hold herself in focus. She still needed to know who these newcomers were and what intentions they bore. She felt a minor sense of release from her master's control, but now she had to turn to what came next. Did they rescue her people only to serve their own whims? It was apparent they preserved them from that cloud, but did this simply put them inside a cage?

She struggled to find anything still alive out there. Aside from these new worlds that were clearly relocated inside the Shell for their own protection, she wanted to know if there was anything else. She tried every trick she had ever learned for this talent to change her perspectives to different views, hoping to catch sight of something. She attempted to center herself on the other worlds, having become rather familiar with them by now that she could actually focus on their landscapes from memory. But there was nothing, only this cloud. Then she thought of trying to center herself on the other gods, those who were still in battle, but who presumably escaped. She must attempt to recall their images, and then draw her mind's eye unto them in a similar manner.

"They escaped to this place they call the Fifth Fold," she recalls privately. "How do I find this Fifth Fold? What is it? I think I must reach far to discover it."

She surveys the local universe, which was now permeated by this cloud. Again, she looked down at her home. It was neatly enclosed within this strange bubble.

"Perhaps it is for the best, at least we are alive. I will give enough thanks for that. And if they were trying to save others, perhaps it cannot be as bad as the alternative."

She recalled the faces of the other gods, choosing one that was quite familiar to her. Sargeras often made many associations with that one, and she would sometimes study this from within her visions. She held the image in her thoughts and permitted herself a sensation of movement, as if to follow it. It was a talent she had been practicing since she first began experimenting with this skill, but it was still a little rough. She had to maintain this perspective indefinitely until she found her mark. This was the hardest part, as she had difficulty convincing herself that she was making any actual progress. Nevertheless, she tried.

She felt herself moving outside the cloud. This much she expected, as this Fifth Fold had to be away from the devastation. Her vision showed her many strange sights with inconceivable shapes, and ahead of her was a body with a filmy membrane. Her drive to bring herself to this individual's face pulled her in the direction of the body, eventually to pass through the membrane. Wispy clouds and vapors drifted by as she found herself travelling through a truly fascinating environment.

"Is this the Fifth Fold?" she wonders. "It appears as a sea of light. So beautiful..."

She intensifies her concentration on the face, feeling more confident now. Soon it becomes clear she is being drawn to something coming into view ahead. The mists around her parted, and the sights revealed many bodies in motion.

"I found you!" she decrees contentedly. "I must remember this place."

She could now see the newcomers and the old gods, but it was no longer a battle. Although the image was strange in her mind, demanding of strong interpretation to understand the visions, it seemed almost like the newcomers were dragging the survivors of the local gods and sending them into what appeared as a glowing hole in space.

"What is that I see?" she muses. "A place to keep them, a hole to bury them... Yes! I understand. Much like a prison. And there they will stay. But now, who will rule over us and what demands will they make?"

She rested from her endeavor. Although she didn't actually feel a physical sensation of weariness, she knew from past experience that these long, deep visions often left her with disorientation, and sometimes headaches when she woke up. Still, she had one final question she had to answer. She had done well on this occasion for everything else, but now she needed to know the fate of her people.

She recalled the image of her home, which now had to include the bubble surrounding it. This was to ensure the time frame for her visions as occurring after the holocaust. She saw her people once again living upon the open land.

"Good, we live, but now what?"

She tries stretching her thoughts far ahead. She was fairly good at this part, as it simply required pushing forward across time. She had done this many times before to see upcoming battles and how they might play out. But here, she had to know what was coming at the hands of these newcomers, as it would seem they would be her new masters.

Her mind begins to catch glimpses of sights unfamiliar to her. She could see her people, and they seemed to be growing, even prospering in ways she could not describe, as her people never had such opportunities as these before. The villages were developing into true cities. The population was booming, and appearing more sophisticated. And they were learning new wisdom.

"But that..." she wonders. "What does it mean? We can grow now? But what do they ask of us? Do we not make battle again?"

She tries to refocus herself, thinking she is losing her attention to detail. She must surely be growing weary by now, but she needed to understand what she thought she saw. There were homes, full neighborhoods of them. She saw marketplaces and workshops, and the children were all going off to a communal place of study. She gazed at this part most of all.

"They go to learn, and not simply the old ways, the way of warriors. This is new, and more intense. And not for battle at all!"

She continued following the streets of this bustling cityscape. There were carts and wagons being drawn by animals brought into their service. And then she saw a temple, where she found people in worship of their new gods. She homed in on the sight to study it now.

"We give praise to them. Yes, I suppose we might, for we are alive, and we must give thanks. But this does not answer the rest of it. What do they desire from us? Our children do not study as warriors for battle, and we are allowed to grow our homes."

She tries zooming in on the people, then the priests, hoping to hear their words. She sees a number of statues on a dais, some male and others female, in forms roughly resembling her own race.

"What? Gods who look like us! This is not what I witnessed before. Why would they...wait," she pauses in her thoughts. "Perhaps... If we are to give worship... No, this is wrong. If they demand our worship, why would it matter how they appear. Sargeras never changed his appearance for us whenever he desired our praise. And neither did Darumon. But this...in such shapes as these...um, to seem more like us? No! Gods do not take shapes to appear like us. Why would they. To appear as one of us. To...wait. Familiarity. But this is backwards. Familiarity? To draw our attention...to WANT to worship them, as they are taking up kind and familiar forms. But this means they are not demanding it. We are simply offering it, as we want to do this. We actually want to worship them. But is this as thanks for saving us? Or is there another reason. It must be a strong one, for all the people I see in here, and all that outside. They allow us to grow. Could this be enough reason?"

She once again relaxed her mind and allowed it to drift, briefly trying to recall the faces of those new gods from her earlier vision. She didn't pay as close attention to them as she did the old gods, but she thought maybe she should. She reflected on one of the statues she saw in the temple. It was towards the front and seemed rather prominent.

"That one must be our new master, but what of the others. Do we give praise to all of them? Which of them created that shell that protected us?"

She recalled the face she saw in that vision, as the bubble came into view and the cloud diverted around it. She drew herself back to that scene, trying to replay that same image.

Once again, she was able to recreate the vision of the approaching cloud, then her world, the bubble, and an eerie face looking down at it. It was one of the newcomers, not her old master. This much she was sure of.

"Who are you? What name do you have? And what do you want from us that we must now build temples to you? And more, that we seem so eager to do this."

Her mind began to unconsciously center itself on the image. She was attempting to scrutinize the motivations and the desires this entity might hold that her people were now made to build temples to it, and how they appeared so compliant in their offerings.

"Do we offer sacrifices to you…some form of tribute?" she muses distantly.

Although she didn't actually realize it at this moment, she was drawing her mind to focus itself at the entity, much the same as she was following the images of the other gods to locate them.

"And where did you come from?" she continues her questioning. "What did you argue about with our gods that drove you into battle?"

She pondered these questions within her mind. They were intended to be private thoughts spoken in her mind's voice. But as she continued to drive her unconscious direction towards the deity, she soon felt a strange alteration of her surroundings, as if something had suddenly grabbed hold of her.

She reflexively froze her thoughts. She often feared such a thing as this, in case Sargeras or Darumon should ever discover her making such wild journeys. She was granted this gift so she could use it to further their goals in the games, not to wander off and see such extraordinary sights for her own personal enlightenment. She tried clearing her mind of anything she had seen to give the impression of emptiness. Hopefully, if one of them had taken notice of her, they might think she was simply resting, maybe dreaming, or perhaps attempting to foresee the next battle in order to plan her latest tactics.

Then a face appears within her mind's eye. It was him, that same newcomer. She began to realize what she had done. It was actually a familiar process, as she had done this on many occasions before to intentionally call upon her god and commune with him. But this time, she apparently called this other one.

"How curious," the voice echoes. "Do we have a lost spirit within a sea of dreams?"

Kuroku could not respond immediately. Instead, she tried to hide her thoughts, to seem as though she was indeed only sleeping.

"I think not, however," the voice continues. "Not with those thoughts I saw flashing before me only a moment ago. There is a conscious mind at play here, but it is frightened now."

Kuroku remained silent, essentially closing her eyes and shying away, as if such a thing would actually help in this condition. But deep down, she knew she had been discovered.

"Child of Torment, fear not us," he speaks with a strong reverberation in his voice. "For we are not of that same mold to commit such sacrilege as thine own Creators."

She felt a cold surge. Not only had she been noticed, but by some unknown entity with unknown designs. And yet, at the same time, it did represent an opportunity to inquire about a few things. She just wasn't sure if she really wanted to carry this conversation.

"Thou dost have questions travelling within thy thoughts," he muses soothingly. "Wouldst that thou may wish to converse with me? Thou didst summon upon my spirit. Perchance it was by accident?"

"Accident?" she echoes timidly.

"Thou didst direct thy thoughts at me with the vision of my form. Was this thine intention, or didst thou come upon this through random occasion?"

"Random? No, I think it was not random, but accidental, perhaps. I did not mean to disturb you, Great One. Please forgive me."

"I am not disturbed by this, but my curiosity is intrigued. How might thou bring thy thoughts upon my face? Thou ought not to know my visage, as we are not of this Fold."

"No, you are not. But if you would allow me, maybe I could ask where you do come from, and also, what do you call yourselves."

"Indeed! We call ourselves the Societies of the Estelar. We have travelled across the Face of Creation to discover its Ways, and in this we have found Balance. But here we encroach upon this Fold, and we do now study it, for it is beholding of much turmoil and malice."

"Do you know of our gods?"

"Despairingly, we do know of them, and not only these in this unclean domain. We have already cleansed the remainder of the Seas of Creation of their taint, but we have not yet encroached upon this body with our displeasures."

"Not yet this body…and displeasures. Seas of Creation? Meaning there is more out there, I suppose. But displeasures? Wait, I beg that I must ask this. I had a vision of a great battle. I do not know the meaning of what I saw. There seemed to be argument, and then conflict. What purpose do you have here?"

"If thou dost hold the power of Sight, then thou didst portend that which is likely to occur. Thy Creators are heathens of malice and discord. We describe them simply as Primordials, for this is how we perceive them, and not with kind favor. They came as a presence before our own, and we do not care for their practice, much as they care not for the Measure of Balance, which we have deemed pertinent to the scaffolding of Creation. Instead, their gluttonous pomposity demeans the infancy of their own Creations, granting unto them not the pleasures of growth, but the pains of brutal contest and oblivion."

"Yes, this much I understand. I detest my own Master and his servant, though I cannot display this openly. I have been made to enter into battles with many others, and I understand that the fate of my people rests on our victory. I have seen what becomes of those who fail."

"Indeed, and this is the greatest blasphemy. Life is not to be made forfeit, and certainly not by such casual disregard. The Children of Creation are not playthings to be tossed about for the mere pleasures of they who would think themselves above representation."

"And so you enter into battle with them. I foresaw this, and further that you will win this battle."

"Thy candor is welcomed, but we do not take this course lightly. Life is precious to us, in all of its forms. If we enter into conflict, it is to preserve that which is brought into jeopardy along the way."

"Such as my people… But wait! I must warn you. My visions were many. I saw much that was disturbing. I heard words from my Master and his servant. The battle was turning, and they sought ways to bring it back to them."

"We of the Estelar are a potent body. Thou should not fear for our cause. Conflict is not unknown to us, and these whom we find in this place are the last of their kind."

"I am pleased to hear this, at least to know there are no others to cause this pain. But this is not my worry. Do you know of something called an Agent of Unmaking?"

The voice paused unnaturally long before responding to this.

"How dost thou know of this name?" he emits soberly.

"In my vision, my Master and his servant shared words. They plan to use this to destroy you, and later I saw a cloud with a wave that destroyed all things. You asked how I found your face. I can answer this."

"I am listening."

"I foresaw the battle; you and they were deeply in conflict. They unleashed this Agent and then departed to escape from you. The Agent sent a wave that destroyed every world it touched, and all the suns out there, old and young. And I watched as it came to our world, but then I saw a shell reach up to shield our home, and the cloud moved around it. I saw your face within that shell."

"Most interesting…an Imberium Shell. Yes, this would certainly serve the role. Thy gift of Sight is of a form most potent."

"It was given to me by my Master. A secret he keeps to himself and his servant. I am to use it to help my people win his games."

"Indeed! Not only does he pretend to be such with his creations, but he also defrauds his own peers," he chuckles ironically. "But thou didst portend we find our victory. What dost thou know of where these heathens travel to?"

"I heard words of a place called the Fifth Fold. All but my Master…"

"We know of this place. We shall meet them there and bring upon them their final judgment, and greatly so for this continued abhorrence. But what dost thou know of thy Master in this regard?"

"He and his servant will flee like cowards!" she snarls.

"Gently now, Child. Didst thou learn of the place they depart unto?"

"Only that he would go into a deep sleep and his servant would carry him to an empty fold to hide, a place where you do not travel and would not find them."

"There are a number of these. And yet, if he should travel to such a place, he will be impotent to cause further malice."

"His servant promises to bring him back somehow."

"I think his choices will be limited, and his efforts futile. Should he attempt a return, we shall meet him again. But in that place, he will be of no concern."

"Then what will become of my people. You are the one to preserve us. And by the way, I found five new worlds added around our home sun. I suppose you did this as well."

"It may be as much, and it would certainly follow our manners."

"But in the end, what demands do you make? In my visions, I saw us building temples to you and offering some form of praise."

"Mortal-child, whereas thine own Creators may hold such malice that the Children of Creation are to them as playthings, we who are the Societies of the Estelar do instead revel in the joys of life and its gifts. We make no demands of our charges, though we can offer guidance. And if, in fact, thou didst see this in thy visions, it is likely thy people do take up some form of attendance to our teachings, as they who would desire this may offer favor in exchange for our blessings. We cannot teach the miracles of Creation, as we believe our Children must grow and learn by their own merits these secrets. But thy people will be safe and nurtured within our care."

The concept being explained to her was almost as alien as the comforting sound of the voice. Her race had been born and bred for battle. They knew of nothing else, even though she resented the idea more and more with each new contest their masters arranged. She could not even envision a world at peace, or her society growing into anything like what she thought she saw in her visions.

"I must ask this," she continues. "Who is this I speak to now? I should know your name if my people are to give thanks."

"Thou may call upon me by the appellation of Helm. But now I must depart from thee. We have much work before us."

Her mind went quiet now. She felt herself withdrawing from her meditation and returning back to the reality of her hut. As she awoke, she found she had apparently toppled to one side onto the floor. As she expected, she felt disoriented, and her head throbbed. She was uncertain how she felt after that remarkable series of visions, to say nothing of the conversation, but she knew one thing for sure. She was very tired now. She should get some rest and try coming at this with a fresh mind in the morning.

Chapter 2

PREPARATIONS

It was morning, and Kuroku was sitting pensively outside her hut. The morning meal had finished and most of the tribal clan members were busy attending to their usual duties. The hunters were out in the fields, the gatherers were browsing the nearby groves, craftsmen were weaving baskets and forming clay pottery, and the village elders had gathered up many of the local children for a tutoring session in the village square.

She had returned to her hut, and now sat just outside in deep thought of her visions from the previous night. She reflected on her conversation with this god named Helm and what words they shared together. One thing she knew instinctively. If her Master should discover any of this, it could mean a very abrupt end for her.

The clan chief took notice of her early on. She had been very quiet all day so far. She might often behave this way, especially if she had one of her visions and needed time to interpret it. But this most often reflected on an upcoming battle she needed to plan. This disturbed him, as there could be very few other things on her mind. The games were the only thing ever to happen to these people. There was nothing else. But he also recalled her earlier words of something coming. He decided to see if he could bring her into conversation, so he tentatively approached to give his greetings.

"Great Matron," he offers reverently. "You sit here so very quietly. Have you any new words to share with us? Have you learned anything new that you can reveal to us?"

She slowly looks up at him, gazing distantly into his eyes, almost as if in a dream. Then she brings herself more into focus as she begins to realize she does indeed need to make some decisions.

"Chief, we need to talk, but it must be very quiet so that no words can be heard in the above-places."

The chief sits down next to her and listens attentively.

"I had a long and very clear vision this past night," she continues. "I learned many things from it."

"Good things or bad things, Great Matron? Do we go to battle again?"

"No, we do not. This is different. There will be a battle, but it is not our battle."

"Do you see the gods sending others into battle? I may mourn for this, but at least it gives us time to rest and grow again. What battle do you see?"

"No, it is not that, Chief. The gods themselves go to battle."

"What?" he urges abruptly, but quietly. "The gods go to battle? Against whom do they battle?"

Kuroku hesitated before answering this question. She understood well enough that if she were discovered with this information, things could go bad, and not only for her. But now she had to decide if she should share it with anyone else, thus perhaps getting them in trouble, and by association, back to her again.

"Chief, you must listen to me and take my words deeply. What I saw this past night runs far beyond us. I think it is poison to our people if I speak this openly. If these words are heard in the above-places, by anyone speaking with another, it can bring bad fortune to us all."

"Then what can you say to me about this battle? What does it mean for our people and what do we do to protect ourselves?"

"I will say this, and only this for now. Find every scout and warrior that can walk and run, and bring them here to my side. I must give instructions."

"Every scout and warrior…" he turns to survey the camp. "Great Matron, I must ask, where do we go if we need all our scouts and warriors?"

"We go into hiding."

These words stunned the chief. He was speechless at the suggestion that they must actually hide from something. This was counterintuitive to their warrior culture. But the honored Matriarch of their people was never wrong. She was too highly revered to question.

He springs to his feet and rushes off into the village, calling up every warrior in sight, and sending word to find even more after that. The hunters and gatherers were called back, the weavers and other craftsmen stopped their work, and even the elders halted their lessons as the full village brought its attention to their Great Matron.

Now she had to give her instructions, but she had to be very careful with the wording, offering only enough to invoke the meaning of her intentions, while not revealing the cause.

"My children," she begins in her traditional maternal fashion. "I must give to you these special words for what work we must make. This work must begin on this day and continue until it is ready."

She pauses to scan the faces of her audience.

"Times are coming that will test us again, but in new ways. For this, we must prepare. We must work long and hard, but I feel we will succeed. And when we do, we will have new reasons to offer our thanks to those above…" she conspicuously looks upward in case anyone was watching.

The gesture was generally understood among the people, as knowledge of their situation had eventually trickled down over the years. This was a sign of deference to their god in order to keep his favor, even though they each knew what they meant to him.

"Our first goal is to seek out the aid of all the other clans across the land. We must have all our people giving themselves to this new purpose. There can be no exceptions. We are one people, even though we may be divided into many clans. We all give ourselves to our Great Master the same. And we are demanded of him to offer ourselves to his cause. For this, I must have our warriors and scouts, all who are able, go out across the land, seek out the other tribes, and summon their chiefs to me. I must speak to them, such that we can prepare for this new test."

The assembled crowd begins a collective murmuring over the implications. Then the elders step forward and try to invoke a more appropriate regale of cheering, once again just in case anyone was watching.

Over the course of the weeks to follow, caravans of tribal chieftains make their way across the land to Kuroku's hut. Here, she shares her private conversations about her plans for the upcoming events.

"We must dig holes?" asks one chief incredulously.

"I have already seen this," she asserts. "We must find any cave and scout it carefully. If we cannot find a cave, we must make our own. Our people must create shelter inside, store much food and tools, all that we might need to survive."

"Why?" asks another chief. "What becomes of the land outside that we must go inside of caves?"

"I think the land outside may survive, but I saw our people go into these caves and tunnels. I think maybe this is only for safety until the calamity passes. Maybe to keep our people calm, and not see such things they are unready to behold."

"And what comes after this calamity?" the first chief wonders.

"What comes after is life, my children. Life as we never knew it before, but I can say no more on this. If more words are said, and heard in the above-places, this plan may fail. Simply do as I say. We can speak more on this after."

"How long do we have before this calamity?"

"In my vision, I saw a sign of its coming. But I am uncertain how long exactly. And yet, I can say no more on this, in case we are being watched. I ask you only to make this work as quickly as you can. Be safe, but be fast. My visions tell me we will finish before the calamity arrives."

The chieftains each accepted their instructions and headed back out, preparing to make their way back to their respective tribes to give their own orders.

Kuroku knew she needed to answer that one question, however. How long until this Unmaking occurred. She needed time for her people to create their shelters. She saw this in her vision, so it had to be true. The work was done by that time. But the calamity she saw approaching was not under her control. It would come when it would come…unless she could somehow measure it.

She stood outside as the other chiefs were leaving. Her thoughts now circled on how she could measure the timing for this calamity. The newcomers would make their advance, this would begin the battle. Sometime after, Sargeras and Darumon would retreat, using the child moon as a means to hide her Master. This would be her sign.

She looked up into the sky above. There were two moons that passed overhead. One was nearer than the other, and they often referred to this as the Mother, with the smaller one behind it as the Child. She briefly tried to imagine the sight in the sky above, where the child moon would be taken away in that rippling effect she saw in her vision.

"We can sacrifice that, I think, if it serves its purpose," she mutters softly to herself. "But I do not care for the thought of what it holds. Not at all! I want finality! I am a warrior, not a coward who hides under rocks. I may tell my people to do this, but only to preserve them. This is not who we were made to be."

She continues her thoughts, now recalling her conversation with the one who called himself Helm. They had much work to do, he said. No doubt this work involved their studies of the local gods, but they must make an advance at some moment.

She understood well enough the need for scouting. She had become a sly strategist during her lifetime. Information was important to know your enemy. But at some moment, you must also move on them.

"We must be ready for it here," she mutters. "But we are not the ones making that move."

The solution for this became apparent to her very quickly. Another lesson she had learned during her engagements was communication. All sides working a plan must be able to share words in order to coordinate their actions.

"Yes! This is what I must do!"

She quickly turned back into her hut and sat down in front of her shrine. She pulled out her herbs and meditation bowl, poured a little oil into it, lit the burner, and waited. She did not apply as much this time, keeping it light. She only needed enough to loosen her mind for a simple communion. While she waited, she mused over the retreat of her Master. She was deeply offended by this action.

"Where did you go, my most precious Master?" she intones coldly. "An empty fold, is it? A place they do not travel, do you say? But what are these words..."

She tries to recall the strange expressions they used.

"Dyna...something... Dynamist... Dynamistic, yes... Dynamistic flows. What are they? You say you need this for yourself? Is this what you mean by the word empty? Empty of these flows, like a river without water, perhaps... And you, as a fish within that river."

She tries to envision a scene with the flows, whatever they were, and another one without, and what Sargeras might have to do if he was like a fish out of water in that place.

"You must sleep, these are your words. And your servant will tend to you..." she muses contemptuously. "Yes, tend to you until one day he brings you back, and then we all suffer again. No! This will not happen! I care not if you are a god. If I must chase you across this great Creation you speak of, I will find you and see to it you pay for all you have done, the same as your kin! This will be my promise!"

She pauses as she tries to reconcile her words. This was a big challenge, to pursue a god to places unknown and for a time immeasurable.

"You gave unto me this blessing to see into the mists of time. You gave unto me this blessing of eternal life. These will be the tools I use against you. I shall be your undoing, and I shall unmake you the same as you and they unmade so many others. I will learn these

Ways of Creation if I must. And if my people will be granted life, I shall teach them the same, and any others I find who will follow me. I shall bring my own game upon you, and turn these teachings into my weapon to destroy you."

She briefly glances around the room to ensure no one was listening, suddenly feeling a little self-conscious that she was speaking aloud, if only in whispers, then returns to her meditation.

The vapors of the herbs and oil had permeated the room by now and she felt a little lightheaded. She tried to calm herself and recall the image of that face again, the face of Helm. He would be the one to preserve her people, so he must be the one she communes with to relay her plans. She decided she would try to make a bargain with him.

She envisions the face in her thoughts, and projects the sensation of motion to draw her towards it, while at the same time recalling the name as a form of summons. Her mind drifts for several long moments, until she feels a presence come upon her. She brings her awareness into focus to latch onto it.

"Thou dost summon me again, Mortal-child," he announces. "What musings dost thou wish to offer on this occasion?"

"Great One, I have a need to speak with you. There are many thoughts in my mind, and I need your help. My people need your help. Can you grant upon me the time to listen?"

"I can grant a measure of time. What troubles thee so?"

"My first trouble is to learn how long before you make your approach to our gods. We need time to prepare here. In my visions, I see us take shelter below ground. I believe this must come to pass, but we must also create these shelters."

"A curious one… Thou didst once say this Sight belonging to thee was a blessing of thy Creator?"

"It is as much a blessing as it is a curse, but I will use it to preserve my people. And yet, there is more to say. I must know when we can expect your march so I can send word to my people to take refuge."

"I cannot offer thee the answer at this time, but if thou dost have such great demand, I shall see to it thou wilt know of our intentions with fair enough warning. I will watch thee and thine in thy preparations, and relay unto thee when the moment approaches. What next troubles thee?"

"My Master again… I know what you said before, but I cannot accept these words to simply leave him in that empty fold. I want him to suffer the same as the rest for his deeds."

"Must I remind thee that within the emptiness, he shall remain impotent to recreate his former malice?"

"And should I remind you of his servant's promise to return him back one day?"

"Thou dost carry a strong spirit, Mortal-child. But again, if he should ever make such an attempt, we will face him, and he shall not prevail."

"What if you are not looking?"

Helm's voice pauses briefly before responding.

"Thou dost present much shrewdness in thy words. But I must still invoke his impotence in the shadow of our authority."

Kuroku realized she had to present her argument better if she was going to win his attention. Then she had an idea.

"What if he should bring another Unmaking, but this time you are not expecting it."

Again his voice goes silent for an extended period, so she decided to use this opportunity. It seemed that she was making an impression, and now she had to bring it home.

"Listen to my words, Great One. You know he is alone. He should know this as well. His servant is a sly one. I know this, as I have learned from him many of the secrets that I carried into battle to preserve my people. In my vision, I heard him promise to care for his Master, to bring him back one day. Do you believe he would promise this if you carried so much authority? I heard them share words where he circled around you, to study you, to learn more about you. Now I think he will behave as a thief in the night. You will not see it. He will strike at his targets carefully and restore that which you took away."

Helm was still silent, extending even longer. Kuroku felt she made an impact.

"What name dost thou carry, and what role dost thou hold amongst thy kind?"

"My name is Kuroku of the Ikoko clan. I am the Matriarch of my people; we call ourselves the Sarrukh. My people revere me as their Great Matron."

"Indeed, thou dost carry such prominence of mind and spirit. And what name dost thou give unto that domain which is thy home?"

"Our world is called Khalen Ruuki, the Blessed Land. And while I may love it as such, it carries a bitter taste when I think of who owns it and how it is used."

"Agreed. Thou didst mention thy role in the service of this malice once placed upon thee and thine by thy Creator. For how long hast thou served?"

"For many untold generations now, I lost count long ago. My people carry long lives, but mine is even longer. And I shall use it to take my vengeance upon him for what he has done. For this, I wish to make a bargain with you, Oh Great One."

"Thou must understand, it is not the common practice for my kind to engage in such negotiation with the Children of Creation."

"You will not negotiate with my children; you will negotiate with me alone."

"Most interesting, thou dost regard thine own kind as children?"

"They are as much to me. You described me as a Mortal-child, but I am not mortal."

"Indeed! How did this come about? Was it another gift from thy Creator?"

"Yes, he sees value in me for my skills in his games. That, combined with my Sight, and it is clear he uses me to cheat his victories. But I am a warrior. I live by a code of honor, and this offends me. Therefore, with or without your aid, if I should live so long, I will see my way to find him, and deliver what must be brought to his feet. I only ask for your support."

"This is a curious premise, and a very determined one. Then

let us discuss these terms. If thy manner is such, we should at least see about the conformance of principle. Thou may not be of mortal bindings, but thou cannot fully compare to thine own Creator. How wouldst thou suggest thy comeuppance?"

"As a battle-hardened warrior, I understand I must know my opponent. I know what he is, but I do not know where he will travel. I will ask of you to teach me the meaning of his words. If you and yours do not take to teaching such exalted wisdom to the Children of Creation, but instead allowing them to find it themselves, then I will abide by these rules. I would even praise this, as it follows in such ways our own creed to fight for that which we see is worthy."

"Indeed, this is a fine merit."

"And so, I only ask to learn enough to see my own way."

"I shall consider this. Continue with thy proposal. What words dost thou speak of?"

"First, he mentioned travelling to an empty fold. He also spoke words of what he calls dynamistic flows. He said he needed this. I am making a guess here; if you will allow me."

"I am listening."

"I do not know what these words are directly, but I will guess it is like a river without water, and he will be like a fish within that river. How do these words compare, and can you teach me more about it?"

"It compares favorably. As for my teachings, I can give this unto thee, but thou must abide by our rules. The Measure of Balance must apply to all things, great and small."

"Good, I will abide by your rules."

"Very well… The dynamistic flows are the boundless energies that waft amongst the planes. Such beings as we consume this as thee and thine would consume the nourishment of thy land and sea, and the air thou must breathe. If thou dost also make use of arcanic practice, it is the energy thou dost summon to cast thy will upon the natural elements."

"Really! Yes! We do use this on occasion."

"Excellent, but as we have ascended beyond such station as where thee and thine do still reside, we have become more dependent on this, such that it becomes necessary for our livelihood."

"I see. This is truly fascinating. Is this to say once, perhaps long ago, you were like us, but then you ascended to this new higher place?"

"It is."

"And now this becomes your new home. Would this also hold true for our masters? Could they have once held such homes as we?"

"It would, although the time it takes for this level of ascension is extreme."

"Yes, this much I think I can understand easily," she chuckles.

"But now, to describe a fold as empty is to describe one without this sphere. We do not travel to these folds, as we would not find it supportive to us to remain there for long durations."

"Much like if I were to go into the water, I think. I would need to hold my breath, but only for a short time."

"Absolutely."

"And so, my Master must go into a deep sleep, if I understand this correctly. How long can he stay this way, do you think?"

"If his servant does provide for him, it could be for the breadth of eternity. We are aware these servants are also immortal, but they are not as dependent on these same flows."

"So they could travel to this place, and while my Master must sleep, his servant is awake and working. This is a danger, I think."

"I will agree with thee on this premise. What other proposals dost thou offer?"

"We must follow him to this place, so that we do not lose sight of him. This is our first goal. He might sleep, and maybe his servant will also hide until such time as you turn your backs. But we must know of this place to watch them."

"I agree, this is sound."

"I cannot be sure how long before his servant will stir with new interest, but we must prepare ourselves to keep him from surprising us until we are ready to strike. And I want to be the one to lead this."

"How dost thou intend to strike at such a creature as this?"

"I do not have the answer to this now," she pauses in a moment of thought. "He will want to strike from the shadows; this I feel is his only choice. But to do this, and against such a power as you, he cannot simply make an approach from behind and plant such as a knife in your back. As you say, you are a great power. If he is discovered, he will be quickly destroyed. He must instead…" she falls silent as a thought comes to her. She shudders from it. "Great One, can you tell me more of this Unmaking? Can he produce this on his own?"

"The Agent of Unmaking thou dost speak of is a substance produced from the dynamistic flows. But if he is within an empty fold, then the answer is no. Without these flows, he has no material with which to create this substance."

"But I am sure he will find a way, especially if he promises to bring his Master back, and for this he must return to these flows somehow…or bring these flows to him."

Helm's voice goes silent again. Kuroku knew she must've hit something by this. It made sense if you consider Darumon's promise. Sargeras needed these flows. The empty fold might not have any present, but somewhere, somehow, he would find some.

"Great One, do you have thoughts on this?" she asks.

"My thoughts are varied and disturbing. If his servant is the one to remove him from this fold, then he clearly has the potential to travel thusly. And if he can travel outward, he can surely return back."

"Oh, yes! This would already be a danger."

"And while the empty fold may not contain these flows, if his servant should have time enough to import them, or travel outward where he may find his supply…"

"Yes! And then he has what he needs, does he not?"

"He does. But in either circumstance, he will surely wish to bide his time until such moment that we no longer expect him. Thou art well adroit in thy musings. It is no wonder he kept thee so close at hand."

"Great One, we must follow him and watch him. But as I said, I wish to lead this charge. He offends me and my children for his cowardice. I will bring my people to learn these Ways of Creation you speak of, slowly if we must, but time may be on our side. Perhaps, if we have enough, we will be ready, and then we will strike...his own Creations striking back at him for his irreverence of our existence. We are his finest champions. We served him greatly in his games, bringing unto him such fame amongst the others that none could defeat us. And he leaves us to this Unmaking. I ask you to feel my rage for this offence, and bless upon me your support to seek my vengeance."

"Child, I do feel thy rage, but I must also caution thee to temper it with thy greater wisdom. Thou art passionate and with just cause for thy yearning, but thou cannot rush forward without judicious care. He may offend thee, but he is still thy Creator. Thou must procure sufficient judgment to make thine approach."

"Then this is what we will do, and we shall offer our favor to you, that you may guide us, all of us, as we make our own ascent, perhaps one day to hold such claim as what you and the others cherish."

"This is a fine pursuit. But hast thou a proposal to aid us, that we may follow his travels?"

"What I know of it is he will change in some way, to prepare himself. Then his servant will hide him within the child moon that travels above us. This is the one that travels behind the mother in our sky. His servant will then cause the child moon to fall out of our sky and vanish."

"I understand this depiction. Indeed, this would prove effective at removing him unnoticed."

"In my visions, I see a bright radiance surrounding the moon, and a rippling, as with a rock thrown into a pond. It swallows the moon, and it is gone."

"Thou art greatly attentive in thine observance."

"Yes, I have learned much in his games," she chuckles softly. "But I think we should not let him see us follow. Let him think he has escaped us. Let him settle into a new bed to sleep. We will grow and make ourselves ready for him. But we need scouts to find him, and to watch him. I will make my plans when he is ready to make his. Can you offer anything to serve us?"

"If we are not the ones to follow, that he cannot know of us pursuing him, we must send others he would not notice. Our difficulty is he will pass through a tear in the fold."

"You said there can be many empty folds, is this right?"

"Yes, and these folds may be vast in their length and breadth. Without the dynamistic flows to guide us, we cannot follow his essence, which would resonate through the flows. This leaves us with a long and difficult search."

"What if we pass through this tear behind him? I saw only the moon fall into it. My Master was asleep, and his servant was not in sight."

"But if to bring a body to follow them, it must attach itself to that which passes through the tear. Didst thou witness any bodies converging upon his vessel, perchance?"

Kuroku took a moment to reflect on her vision. She tried to recall the original image, where the moon began to glow, and the rippling effect surrounded it. But her vision was somewhat blurred by now. Then she had a thought occur to her.

"Let us try it this way."

She was already under the influence of the herbs and oil, so she allowed herself to float amongst the mists of time again, this time directing her thoughts to that same moment. She had a focal point, in this case, so she homed in on it to replay the full scene.

Helm followed her on this occasion, reviewing her visions along with her as she recalled that same moment. Together they observed the moon being enveloped by the bright glow, briefly followed by the arrival of a myriad of star-like dots converging on it, just before the rippling swallowed it up.

"Hold!" he declares boldly. "There, at the moment of penetration. There were bodies encroaching upon it."

"Do you know what those bodies are, Great One?"

"I believe I do, and neither thy Master nor his servant is likely to feel them, as they are not of this fold, and not likely to stand out within their minds."

"What are they? Can we call upon them to help us?"

"We can. To such Children as thee and thine, thou may describe them as elementals. To us, we declare them as Positive Primes. These are beings of light, and can follow thy Master by concealing themselves within the energies of his vessel's transit."

"And so," she nods contentedly. "We will know where he goes. But we must not lose these scouts along the way. Can you bring them to me, that I may speak with them and arrange them to inform me of his travels?"

"They do not speak in such manners as thine own people. Thou must learn their ways."

"Then I ask you to teach me."

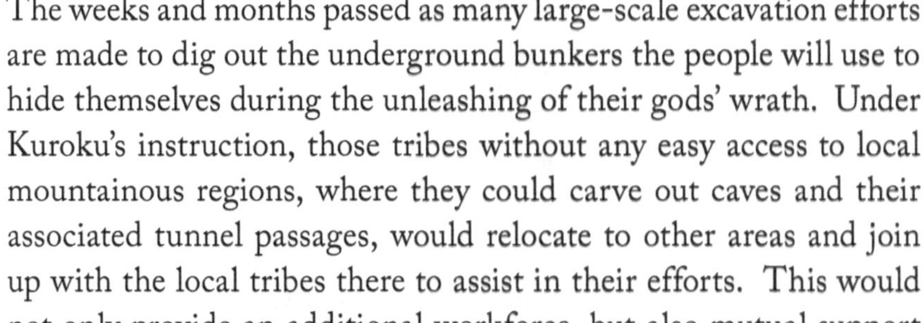

The weeks and months passed as many large-scale excavation efforts are made to dig out the underground bunkers the people will use to hide themselves during the unleashing of their gods' wrath. Under Kuroku's instruction, those tribes without any easy access to local mountainous regions, where they could carve out caves and their associated tunnel passages, would relocate to other areas and join up with the local tribes there to assist in their efforts. This would not only provide an additional workforce, but also mutual support to cover more people.

In the meantime, Kuroku was following two directions at once. On the one side, she was under instruction by Helm now, and as such, she could not share his teachings with any of her people. She would use this for her own purpose to follow and study her new prey, once the hunt began. But for now, she was still in training. Maybe the day would come when she could share some part of this, but only if her people could reach these heights on their own.

Beyond that was her gift of Sight, which was not the blessing of Helm, but rather her former Master. The Estelar may have their rules for what they offer, but she did not have such rules to follow in this case, and so she would use it, prudently of course, to aid her people when and where she felt it was warranted. And currently, she needed to solve a problem.

"Chief," she calls to the clan leader. "I have new instructions I must give to our tribes and their leaders."

"Yes, Great Matron, what words do you wish to share with us? Do you have any new visions?"

"I am making many meditations now, and I must give my thoughts to our people slowly to ensure they understand and learn their meaning."

"Since the time you sent our people to dig these tunnels, you have been seeking many new visions. Some of us are worried about what this means for us. Can you tell us?"

"There is much I wish to tell, and I hope one day I will. But for now, I must ask you to listen. Send word to the tribes. We must build towers with large torches that stand high above the land. They must be far from each other, but still within sight, so that when one is lit, another can see it. The watchers will light theirs and the next will see it. It shall continue this way across the land, and serve to signal all the tribes of the time when we must take to our shelters. Whoever it is to see the sign of the coming calamity, they will light their torch, and the others will follow to pass the signal. Do you understand?"

"I believe I do, Great Matron. This is new to us. Did you see this in a vision?"

"I did, and it is a wise lesson to learn."

"Do you have anything else for us?"

"I do, but I think this must wait until after, when we come out again. Then I shall teach our people new ways we must create for ourselves and our children."

The chief moves away to pass the word, and a series of scouts begins rushing off to spread it to the other tribes.

A steady stream of runners was now passing around between the tribes, a kind of relay network to pass news and information among everyone to coordinate their efforts. Kuroku had created an efficient system of communication, drawing in part from her experience in battle when using scouts to survey their enemy's positions, but in this case applying it to their local population to help her people learn of the general happenings. The obvious benefits were quickly becoming apparent amongst the people as they felt a closer sense of community.

From time to time, she would travel outside the camp for a secret meeting. The chief and the other elders, who would make their usual watch over the security of the camp, knew not to disturb her. She had explained that this was related to the calamity, but they should not know of it at this time for fear this knowledge could be discovered by their Master. She would take this responsibility solely by herself.

She was on one such journey, travelling overland to a rocky outcropping. She ducked around the outcropping and checked the scenery to ensure no one was watching. Then she attempted to use her gift of Sight in a way she was not otherwise supposed to. Helm had shown her how, and assisted in empowering her, and now she was practicing a new skill to call upon a strange entity.

The ambient light seemed to flicker and bend in an unnatural way, gathering up into a bunch and then forming a body. The shape coalesced with a simulated crystalline geometry, but it was in fact composed entirely of energy and light.

"Blessed One," she bows.

Her spoken words were lost on the entity, as it did not have ears to hear it. Instead, she began forming images in her mind. This was a new talent she was learning. Helm described it to her, and through his aid he bestowed upon her additional strength to use it. She was now speaking telepathically.

She shared images with the entity as they taught each other how to communicate efficiently, a form of language exclusively for telepaths, and entirely conceptual in nature. She explained her desires and how they needed to be played out. Timing was very important, to be in the right place at the right time to follow the child moon through the tear in the local fold. This entity, and apparently a great many others along with it, would tag along as the moon passed through. But they also needed to find their way back to her.

This particular entity was a more advanced specimen than some.

Helm chose them because they held the greatest skills in passing amongst the planes. Kuroku was learning about a practice known as folding space. Beings of sufficiently high proportions, such as the Estelar, and Darumon and Sargeras, could do this easily. But there were others as well, and these entities were one such example.

They were a sentient form of life, but unlike anything she might otherwise relate to. These entities were not composed of common substance, and therefore not necessarily bound to any one planar realm. As beings of energy, they could travel in any direction through physical space, and even move outside the local dimensional envelope.

Of course, space is vast in all directions, and Kuroku was learning this as she attended her lessons. To compensate for this, beings of this sort could fold space. This was a similar concept to how she witnessed the child moon vanishing from the skies above in her visions. Folding space, in this case, is to bend the fabric of space with the power of the mind, then to cross over between the two endpoints. But there was often a trick to it, and this involved having a memory image of the destination to focus on, in much the same way as she used this to draw her mind's eye in her visions to some specific point. Alternatively, they might need an external means if one is available.

Kuroku's journey out here was a training exercise, both for her to interact with these entities, and for the entities to become familiar with her and the local surroundings. In this way, they could return here from virtually anywhere. They would use this later when the moment arrived to follow Sargeras.

"Master, I have recently observed a most curious level of activity amongst our pets."

"Oh, my servant? What are they doing on this occasion?"

"I cannot be sure, but I have peered down on them to see they are very active of late."

"Perhaps you would wish to inquire on this?"

"I have thought of doing precisely that!" he snickers wickedly.

"After all, we would not wish them to become distracted from their greater purpose."

"Indeed, but they have always served us so faithfully in the past."

Darumon was in a meeting with his master, Sargeras. They would often share moments of interaction together as Darumon managed the world below and its inhabitants.

Sargeras and his kind largely sat back as spectators to the games, while Darumon and the others, being a pseudo-race of loyal servant beings, would attend to most of the grunge work to make it happen. His duty was to raise the minions on the world below, to ensure they focused themselves on training for the games, occasionally to teach them a few tricks, if it improved their performance to entertain their god, and otherwise keep them in line. They were not allowed to think they could live their own lives and develop themselves for their own benefit, at least not beyond what was necessary to make them worthy competitors in the games.

Darumon was largely instrumental in developing the Sarrukh, although the body template was created by Sargeras. From there, Darumon took over to sculpt their species into the battle-ready combatants they are today. Through his past experiences in prior games, using earlier examples of lifeforms, he had learned what works and what doesn't work, refining his technique to create the current masterpiece. His work was clearly evident for their long series of successes, but he still needed to monitor them from time to time.

Darumon departed from his master and made his way down to the world below. He was skilled in his own gift of folding space, wrapping himself in a rippling effect to phase out of his natural home by his master's side, to arrive on the surface of the world that was the home of their creations.

In his natural form, he was a giant, as tall as the hills. He often adorned himself with a covering of battle armor composed of smooth black plates segmented by red joints. His skin was a dark red, rough and leathery, and he displayed a number of small barbs on his limbs and head. He had a pair of black horns curving out from the temples and tapering to a point, and his eyes emitted a soft yellow glow.

Despite these features, he was also capable of altering his form, to make his interactions more convenient with the lesser lifeforms. He would sometimes use this to mimic another species in order to spy on them, but he didn't do this as often with the Sarrukh. Their long-standing service had appeased him, and for this he portrayed a more relaxed posture. Instead, he would simply reduce himself down to their size to give his instruction. Even though they tended to display a firm loyalty to their Master, they were still a servant species, and occasionally he needed to reassure himself of their devotion, as well as to simply reassert their need to maintain their readiness should he arrange a new contest for them.

Kuroku was back with her people. She had been coordinating their work through a system of communication using runners to relay her instructions. She suspected her Master would eventually look down on them from his high place, so she knew she would need to cover for herself in case Darumon came along asking questions. And today would be one such occasion.

Darumon arrived just outside the village where she made her home. He came here specifically because much of his interaction funneled through her at this point, her being the Matriarch of her people. He preferred this for the sake of simplicity. He would pass his instructions to her, and she would forward them to her people. This had developed over the course of time as a habit.

Words quickly echoed through the village of his arrival as he made his way in, and Kuroku's attention was brought around once these words came to her ears. She approached before him and offered a reverent bow. The chief and the others in the village all kept at a distance and kneeled in silence, as was customary.

"Great One!" she exalts as he approaches. "Do you bless us with your presence again so soon?"

"Yes, I have been watching you in recent times," he remarks. "You seem to be doing a lot of work down here. I do not recall giving you instruction for this, so I came to see what it is you are making for yourselves."

Darumon's voice was rough and gravelly, and it carried a distinctive aura of authority.

"Ah, but Great One," she proclaims. "You should know that we must always test ourselves to be ready for the next challenge. How else can we make our Master happy if we do not make such tireless work?"

"Indeed, but can you tell me what sort of work it is you are making?"

"Oh, but I am creating new plans and devising new thoughts I wish to test, and I must teach my people to follow these plans. I am sure you will find new challenges for us, but we cannot always follow the same steps. We must be clever, as our opponents are clever. Only then can we win the battles we must face, and bring favor to our Master."

"Yes, and you have done well at this," he admits contentedly. "But the work I am seeing here is strange, and does not look like the sort of work relating to battle."

"But Great One, my thoughts are still young, and we must prepare them to see how they grow. And I know how you love that little turn of surprise, and I ask myself if I should spoil this for you with so many words. Our work is not ready, and I must still choose my steps carefully within my thoughts that they give me what I need for our next challenge. Would you truly have me spoil your pleasure with such uncertainty?"

"Hmm, an interesting question. I do so love your little surprises," he chuckles coarsely. "And I suppose if these thoughts of yours are still young, I should give you enough time to develop them fully."

"Yes! I ask that you allow me time to explore this. I have much work to do, and many steps to carry this. I think our Master will be pleased. Give me the peace I need to teach my children and we shall become stronger for it!"

"Very well, Matron, you shall have your peace. You have always shown great skill in the past, and I will look forward to this next one. I will return to my Master and tell him we should give you time to grow these ideas of yours before we engage in any more contests."

"I thank you, Oh Great One. My people will become strong for this. You will see!"

Darumon nods casually and glances around the camp. The other villagers were still kneeling with their heads bowed down, only barely peeking up at the interaction. He turns away and saunters off through the village.

Kuroku watched him as he took several steps away, and then pulled himself into folded space, vanishing from the scene. The rippling effect surrounding his body was the same as what she saw in her vision when the child moon was taken from the sky.

"One of these days, I hope to learn more of this," she mutters silently to herself. "Such wisdom can be had if one learns the Ways of Creation highly enough. But we have much work to do before that."

With Darumon gone, the rest of the village returns to their previous duties, and the Chief rushes to her side to hear if she has anything to say.

"Great Matron, do you have any words for me?"

"Yes, we must hurry and finish our work. Time is passing, and I do not wish for him to learn that my 'young thoughts' are not for his pleasure."

Chapter 3

INDIGNATION

"Chief!" shouts an approaching warrior into the local village. "The Great Matron Kuroku has sent word to us. She has sent her scouts to tell us the calamity is approaching soon."

"Does she say what this calamity is? What do we look for as this sign she speaks of?"

"She tells of the child moon departing from us. It will glow like the sun, and then vanish. Following that, the skies will change. No longer will we see the distant fires. All will flash brightly like a thousand storms. We must be inside the caves before this comes."

"And how long do we have from the time of the child moon leaving and the coming of these thousand storms?"

"Not long. When the torch-watchers see the sign, they must light the fires. This will tell the rest to move inside the caves. But we must not be far. She tells how we should make our camps near the caves and be ready."

"And we do this now?"

"Yes."

"Then we must pick up our camp and move. The caves are a far walk from here."

The Chief issues orders to his people and they begin packing up their tents and huts. They gather up all their belongings, including tools, supplies, food, and personal items, and begin relocating closer to the cave they had been digging out within a set of hills some distance away.

The message was being sent out from Kuroku's village to every other tribal clan across the land. Meanwhile, her village was also relocating closer to a range of foothills where their own excavation was occurring.

The dig sites had moved slowly due largely to their lack of any advanced tools to dig with. They had hammers and chisels, but the materials dulled quickly. They were not a scientifically advanced society, just barely into an early Iron Age, which served most of their needs. But the hurried carving through the hard rocks into the hillsides tested their tools almost to the breaking point.

Kuroku was settling into her hut for the evening. Her scouts had returned from their most recent runs with word that the other tribes were in position, and the torch-watchers were on duty studying the skies. She knew she could wait no longer. She didn't want to take the chance of either Darumon or Sargeras getting curious again, so she decided to report in to see what was happening on the other side.

"Great One, I call to you," she communes within her thoughts.

She had placed herself into another meditation and was trying to summon the image of Helm again. She waited for his reply. She felt nervous about the implications of what would come next, and her thoughts drifted briefly to the other worlds she saw in her earlier visions during the Unmaking. Other than those she saw relocated within her local star system; the rest appeared to have all been destroyed. She felt cold as she imagined they who made their homes in those places. But there was nothing she could do about it. Then she felt a presence enter her mind.

"Child Kuroku of the Sarrukh," he begins. "Thou dost call upon my visage again. Speak, and I shall listen."

"My people are ready. We have stored our food and made our beds. Now we wait for the sign of the child moon to be taken away. When we see it, we will light our torches to send the word, and then take shelter within the caves. I ask of you, what plans do you have at this time?"

"We have made our studies and considered our approach. The musings within thy Sight, thus shared with me, hath informed us of our course. We are ready."

"Then I can see no other way but forward. You must make your move, as we must make ours. We will watch the skies for the child moon, and take to our shelters. When all is calm again, we will come out and give our most humble thanks."

"Then let it be so. Return to thy people and give thine instruction. We shall attend to the heathens and bring harmony to this final domain."

"I only wish something could be done to give aid to the other worlds."

"If thy Sight did see so many of them lost, it may pass that we cannot preserve them. But perhaps thy Sight was not complete. We shall make what attempts we can."

"I thank you, Great One. You are far more caring than our Masters. May fortune and strength be with you."

Their link faded and she returned to the reality of her hut. She stepped outside into the cool evening breeze. The Chief was consulting with several warriors around the village bonfire when he saw her approach.

"Great Matron, the sun is down, and our people rest. I thought you were resting also. What brings you outside again?"

"Chief, we may need to wake our people very soon. Keep your eyes to the sky," she looks up. "It is coming."

In the sky overhead, she could see both of the moons passing by. The larger of the two was setting on the far horizon, but the smaller one was partway up.

The Chief and the others in the group all looked up. So far, nothing was happening, but they felt their nerves tighten.

✦

"Darumon, can you feel it as well?"

"Yes, Master, I felt it just now, which is why I came to you. I do not know how else to describe this but to say we have received visitors, much to my great surprise that there may be any such who would dare approach us this way."

"Visitors? The sensation I feel is new to me, not any of our own. What do you mean by any who would dare approach us? Who are these newcomers?"

"All I can say with certainty comes from the rumors I have heard in whispers. They are quite potent, surely in comparison to our own, and yet they are an unfamiliar form to us. Come, see for yourself, but I think I would have you follow me to one side away from the confrontation. The others are moving to intercept, but I wish to be more discreet."

Darumon and Sargeras met to exchange words at the initial arrival of the Estelar on the scene. The other native gods were assembling with their unexpected guests to share a tenuous greeting, not fully knowing what to expect of these strange new beings just now emerging into the local space. But it soon became apparent this would not be a pleasant welcome.

The two of them moved off to one side, away from the growing commotion of argument and accusations, where they could oversee the encounter and the rapidly developing tensions from relative safety.

"Darumon," Sargeras wonders openly. "Am I hearing these statements correctly? Are they actually daring to challenge our manners? How indignant! Who are they to question our practice with our creations? They would dare pretend to govern us in our own homes?"

"Indeed, Master, I am as shocked as you in this matter. This is not their fold, and these are not their creations. What practice they make with their own, I know not, but to come here and challenge us for ours..."

"How insufferable!" he huffs and shakes his head.

They continued to watch as the nature of the argument took on a new form. Like them, the other local gods could no longer tolerate the presence of these intruders. And soon, the conflict turns violent when battle ensues.

Sargeras and Darumon gazed at the fury of the onset. The other local gods, declared as Primordials by these newcomers, which was presented as a derogatory term, had engaged in open conflict. Blazing energies ripped across the space between the front lines. The two of them were dazzled by the ferocity of the battle, impulsively causing them to back away even further. But what surprised them the most was the fact that these invaders seemed to show remarkable skill in their assault. And as they continued to gaze at the engagement, they began to take notice of several casualties among their fellows and their related servants.

"How can this be possible?" Sargeras utters. "Such infidels as these…"

"My Master," Darumon responds. "You must listen to me. The others are falling. These younger ones are quite vigorous. Clearly, they have great practice in these affairs."

"Great practice? Do you mean in such way that they might play these games themselves?"

"Master, surely you have heard those same whispers of the progression they have made across the realms. They have driven our kind back. Their youthful zeal and determination empowers their pursuit…" he pauses to glance around the scene. "This is all that remains of our kind. Just look at how the others fall. With each defeat, these invaders grow stronger against us."

"It is true, what you say. We may soon lose this contest…the final play of an eternity-long game."

They studied the scene a while longer, where the clashing continued at a vigorous pace, and then Darumon proposed a thought.

"My Master, I must ask you to move away and take shelter. Do not let them see you. I wish to discover their secret, perhaps to find a weakness, and I shall return to you."

"Very good, my servant, this could perhaps aid us to turn the tide in our favor. But do not take long."

Darumon prepares to fold himself out of the local space, while

Sargeras continues to keep a low profile in the face of the vicious warfront.

On the ground, Kuroku and the chief of her local clan were in conference. Many of the people had been woken up from their slumber, as she was expecting something to occur very soon.

"See there, the child moon," she points upward. "So far, it still travels across the night sky, but soon I expect to see it glow like the sun and vanish."

"How can it be possible for the child moon to glow like the sun?" he asks. "And then to vanish! All my life, I see it up there, travelling behind its mother. And now it must leave us?"

"It does not leave us by its own choice, Chief. It will be stolen away from us, but this is a sacrifice I think we can accept. For in the end, we shall discover peace for our people like what we have never known. And I will find a new purpose for myself which will carry me to far places, and for a time I cannot measure," she sighs.

"What do you mean?"

"Let me answer that after the calamity has passed. I will feel more at ease then. For now, we must simply survive."

"As you say, Great Matron, and there is much I hope to learn from this…all these visions of yours and what they mean for our people. I think many people will hope to hear you tell us what you saw and what it means for us."

"Trust me, Chief, there is much I wish to tell you, and more I would hope to teach our people one day, but we must move slowly and use our best wisdom. And most importantly, Chief…"

She turns to face him, offering a sincere and nurturing gaze. She further extends her view across the assembled masses that were now gathered and listening, each of them clearly nervous about the implications of this moment.

"What we bring," she ushers up to the crowd. "We bring for all our people, everywhere, not only our one clan. We are Sarrukh, all of us. Do not forget this. Never forget who we are, never forget our brothers and sisters. We have fought many battles for our Master, and struggled to survive against many foes. Now is our moment, a time of turning, a time like no other, and we must remember this moment, for our children and our children's children."

The people all listened attentively to her announcement. She was often known to give pep talks from time to time, but this seemed like an odd occasion for one. Still, it was welcome to hear her encouraging words in the face of this crisis.

Darumon had returned from his scouting tour and now presents himself to Sargeras with his report.

"My Master, the others have devised a plan," he asserts.

"The others?"

"My brethren, Master, we who serve so faithfully at the side of our Great Ones… They have created a plan to destroy these interlopers once and for all, but it must be played out very carefully."

"And what is this plan, my servant?"

"They have decided to invoke the unmaking of the dynamistic flows. The wave of destruction will destroy these invaders, and then we shall be free of them."

"Darumon, be mindful of what you speak," Sargeras cautions. "This would destroy all our creations, and us as well."

"Not if we escape from here first. The plan is to release the Agent of Unmaking, and then hastily depart from this fold. But Master, I feel there is a small risk."

"When speaking of the Agent, my faithful servant, the term 'small risk' is a weak statement. What risk do you now speak of?"

"Clearly, we must depart before the Unmaking, but we must also find sanctuary from the wave, as well. For this, the others believe to escape into the Fifth Fold would allow them to ride above the wave."

"This is reasonable. The Fifth Fold should be well enough outside the reach of the wave, assuming we release it within the confines of this fold alone. But what is this risk you speak of?"

"I will say this only to you, my most cherished Master. I have circled behind these trespassers. I wanted to see where they originate; to learn of their motivations. We know they are not native to this fold, and we have heard stories of their appearance in other folds. This lends me to believe their background could make claim to an even higher prestige."

"Intolerable…" he scorns.

"I agree, my Master, and this forced me to ask where else they can be found."

"Indeed, you are a cunning one. And what did you discover?"

"They seem to have come from across the Folds of Creation, perhaps from a far domain, and they now cover much of it…"

✦

"…We may be the last to know what happens here," Kuroku continues her sermon. "The last among so many who fought these battles, who suffered and then faded, who should have shared this same privilege, but it was taken from them. We must now carry this in their honor, and do so for as long as our people survive. It must NEVER be forgotten."

She turns briefly to glance up into the nighttime sky again before returning to her people.

"Perhaps a day will come when new children will be born, far from here, far from where all this came to be. They will not know of this. Perhaps we may become the elders who carry the oldest wisdom that ever existed. I cannot know this now, but if we are wise today, we shall live tomorrow, and with the new day, we will learn new wisdom. We must be sure we use this to carry our people, all of them, into better lives. And maybe, one day we can learn enough to help others. No one shall do unto them what was done to us for so long!"

A rising cheer sounds up from the crowd, as they raise their hands and shout their praises to their revered Matron.

＊＋◆＋＊

"…Furthermore," Darumon continues his report. "They seem to have enlisted others from other folds as they travelled across, thus expanding their numbers. There may be no true escape possible by now. The others may think they can escape into the Fifth Fold after unleashing the Agent of Unmaking, but I think we must travel farther. We must travel to a place where these cretins have never visited, and therefore cannot find us."

"But Darumon, what of the others we revel with? If to travel to the Fifth Fold is not enough…"

"Master, whatever the others might think, if these intruders believe themselves to be so erudite, I think the Agent of Unmaking should be known to them. They might sense it and make their own exit. If they understand it as we do, they may also travel to the Fifth Fold, and then what do you think will occur."

"It is true, the battle will begin anew. But then, we should warn the others before they unleash this. We must modify the plan!"

"Master…" Darumon frowns. "I do not wish to speak in such terms, but they have already unmade themselves. Think carefully, Master. They are currently in battle. If they should suddenly attempt to escape from this fold, for reasons of this plan or any other, the intruders will follow. They are already in the eyes of the intruders, my Master, but you are not. I pulled you aside to keep you out of the conflict, to protect you. You may escape, but they will not."

Sargeras gazed at his servant mournfully, and then turned his eyes into the distance.

"Darumon," Sargeras relents. "You are right, my dearest servant. The others may fall, but we shall not suffer the same. Our existence in this stale and decrepit fold was never a pleasing one, and I would not wish to die here."

"Our time here is only beginning," Kuroku announces to the gathering. "We have a long history behind us, all of it in blood and pain. But now, there are many possibilities that wait, and I wish to see my children discover them. We will seek that which was not permitted before, and discover new ways for ourselves. But at the same time, I also have my own work I must do, and this work troubles me, for it will carry me far from here, I think, and for a length of time I cannot measure."

"How do you suggest we proceed, my servant?" Sargeras wonders.

"For as long as we remain within a sphere of dynamistic flows, they might sense our presence..."

"Darumon, must I remind you that I require this for myself, as does all of our kind."

"Yes, my Master, I know this, but I think there is no other way. You must go into hiding. But fear not, my most cherished Master, as I will care for you until the end of time if I must. And I will work to bring you back one day..."

"But so far," Kuroku continues her speech. "I cannot reveal this until I can be sure we have our freedom. And this freedom is nearly upon us. Before this night is out, we shall know our fate, and then, my children, I shall tell you what we have seen and what it means for us. And at the same time, I will share with you my own feelings, and why we must never forget what we have learned this day."

The crowd offers up another cheer, if only tentatively for the obscured meaning of her wording, knowing she had to keep much of it hidden in case anyone was watching. They weren't in the clear just yet, but Kuroku's message hinted at something called freedom. This word was almost unknown to them. Never before had they ever known of such a thing called freedom, as they were always the subjects of their god and his games, the same as all the others.

As Kuroku was finishing up her speech, a strange shifting of the ambient light occurred. The group suddenly turned their attention skyward to see the small moon beginning to glow.

"It comes now!" she shouts. "Light the torch towers! Everyone, get inside the cave!"

A group of warriors dashed off to the towers to light the large bonfires on top. The rest of the assembly jolted and began rushing into the nearby cave entrance, many of them suddenly starting to panic at the strange and frighteningly quick display in the sky overhead.

The second moon in orbit around their world was quickly engulfed in a bright glow. Kuroku gazed at it while the others took shelter. The clan chief stayed by her side, waiting for her to make her next move, but she simply held her position as the image erupted in a brilliant flash, and then faded from the sky.

"Great Matron," he ushers urgently. "Do you not go inside the cave?"

"I will stay here and watch. Our home will survive. This much I know. I simply desire to see the child moon, and all of our worries, depart from us at last. This will bring us our freedom, Chief. He is no longer our Master!"

"What? Great Matron, can you tell me what you mean?"

"Him..." she snarls. "That monster! At last, I can finally say it openly. All my life, Chief, which is more than I should have lived, more than any other, I had to bow before him, to speak fondly of him, to show my reverent devotion to him, when in fact I hated him for all that he was. All of them..."

"Great Matron," he hesitates, glancing around nervously, as if expecting a lightning bolt to come out of thin air. "You speak of our

Master?" he looks up at the now empty sky above. "The child moon is gone from the sky now. What does it mean for us?"

"Yes, it is gone. It carried him away from us. He ran in fear of the new gods who have come to destroy the old."

The Chief was awestruck. He hadn't been fully briefed on her visions for fear of leaking too much information that could otherwise be intercepted by Sargeras or Darumon. Now that the two had departed from the local space, Kuroku felt her own sense of freedom rushing into her that she could now explain herself. But before she could make the attempt, the main body of the calamity was still approaching.

She and the Chief stared into the sky, both of them knowing this was simply the sign, a prelude to the real calamity that would follow behind the loss of the child moon. But before they could react further, the sky overhead erupted in a truly dazzling flash of light that turned night into day, and then some.

The Chief cringed at the sudden presentation of the explosive force crashing against what appeared to be an unimaginably massive shell-like structure somewhere well beyond their home world. The visual phenomenon was spectacular, to say the least, simply for the sheer scale of the anomaly, and it extended across the sky in all directions.

He ducked and turned to find the cave entrance, but before he dashed away to safety, he grabbed Kuroku's arm and tried drawing her along with him. Reluctantly, she followed his motion, at least up to the cave opening, where she halted just inside, still with a view of the scene above.

"Be strong, Great One," she mutters under her breath. "Only you can make this for us. I will teach my people who you are, and we will build our temples to honor you, but you must allow us this day."

The Chief heard her words, although just barely for all the other shouts and screams coming out of the cave from others who noticed the flashes of light. Now he was getting confused. Who was this Great One she was referring to? He chose not to pursue it at the moment, instead just hoping to hold things together until the calamity passed.

✦✦✦✦✦

Kuroku and the clan chief stayed up the remainder of the night, neither of them able to relax enough to find any sleep. Many of the other clansmen stayed up with them, taking turns to peek outside to see the extraordinary new scenery in the sky above. The familiar starscape that once dotted the nighttime sky was now gone, replaced by a brightly glowing cloudlike apparition in rainbow hues, like a massive nebula had swallowed up the universe and their home was smack in the center of it.

At this point, the turbulence of the cloud was visible even at ground level, still churning and boiling after the detonation. It would likely remain this way for the foreseeable future, glowing with its own internal fires until such a time when it might one day settle. Still, nighttime in their world would never be the same as it once was.

The spectacle was at once both awe-inspiring and astonishing for the sheer scale of it. All who might look upon it would see it with admiration for its inherent beauty, but also trepidation for its implied meaning. Although the people did not know of such things as volatile materials and their explosive qualities, this clearly represented a destructive force on a level well beyond comprehension. Surely, only the gods might hold this power.

The morning came with the subtle glow of the sun rising over the horizon, which brought familiar warmth to the land and gently replaced the unsettled skies of their new nighttime with the calming blues of daylight. Kuroku and the Chief were both tired after their long watch, but they held themselves up to the new day that would surely mark the beginning of a new era for them.

"Chief," she begins. "Call the people outside. I must speak to them now."

She stands up and strolls outside to meet the new day. The Chief calls on the people to follow, and the assembly gathers around the camp to receive their new instructions.

Several warriors hurried to collect wood for the bonfire, which had died out during the night, and rebuilt the mound in the center of the camp. Shamans would then arrange themselves to ignite the fires using their primitive magic.

Much like with their knowledge of anything else, their capacity for magic was also not very advanced, and again due to the authoritative nature of their subjugation by their god. But Kuroku, on the other hand, had learned a number of tricks during her lifetime, and she shared this with her people. Although she had to keep it simple so as not to demonstrate any outrageous displays that might otherwise get them in trouble. She watched the shamans light the bonfire, a process she had seen so many times before, but on this occasion, it seemed to hold a new meaning. She studied it as it rose up through the column of kindling and timbers, a new fire for a new day, and in this case, to mark the beginning of a new era.

The Chief watched her as she seemed mesmerized by the simple act of lighting the fire.

"Great Matron," he whispers. "Is there something wrong?"

"Chief, when you look at that, what do you see?"

The Chief was puzzled by the suggestion, so he gazed at the bonfire for a moment, even though nothing unusual stood out from it.

"I see them light the fire. Is there something you see that I do not?"

"Yes, but it comes from what I have learned. Now, I must teach the others. You must listen and learn the same as the rest. We have much work ahead of us, but this time, the work is different."

She turns to face the gathering, all of whom had assembled near the campfire and now waited patiently for her to speak. The Chief joins them while Kuroku takes up a position more centered in front. She takes a deep breath and attempts to let it out slowly to calm her nerves. This would not be easy.

"My children," she announces to the crowd. "This day marks the beginning for us...a new beginning for a new life. No longer shall we be made to fight in the games our Master once created for us. He is gone from us, departed in the child moon we saw taken away in the night sky. He no longer rules over us. We are free. But this freedom comes at a price. Not a price for us, but instead for so many others who paid this price. We were lucky, but they were not."

The assembled masses all turned to each other, where murmuring began ushering up in hushed voices. She begins again.

"I know many of you will ask questions, and these are not new, but questions you have been asking since the beginning of our work, the work that brought us here to this place…" she glances around the camp and the nearby cave they carved out. "I feel now that I can tell you what I have held back. For as long as our people have existed, we were the playthings of our Master and his servant. Our Master…" she pauses with a look of disgust. "Sargeras… That is his name. He and his servant, Darumon… I spit on these names now."

The murmuring in the group became more vigorous until a round of shushing tried to silence them to hear her again.

"Yes," she continues. "You heard me, my children. In my long life, I have learned much about him, but I had to be very careful of my words, and what I could teach you, that he might not know of it. To do otherwise might be the end of me and perhaps many more. Mine has been a hard life," she lowers her head.

"Great Matron," the Chief reassures. "We all love you and support you. Tell us, what did we see this past night? And what has become of our Master?"

"What I have to tell you will offend you, like it offends me. But this is beyond our reach for now. We will take this time to ourselves and build our people. But as for…Sargeras…" she grimaces. "He is mine to pursue. I will not bring my children into this. Not today. You must first grow and learn, find your way, and become great!"

The assembly offers up a cautious cheer as she prepares her next statement.

"Sargeras…" she glances upward at the dawning skies overhead. "I will seek him out, watch him as a predator watching its prey, and when the time is right, I will strike from the shadows, that he will not know his enemy until it is too late!"

"Uh, Great Matron," the Chief vacillates. "I do not wish to argue, but he is…or was…our god. I know you hold much power with your Sight, but do you now think you can fight a god?"

"Today, no… But this fight will not come today. Now, he sleeps, and I do not strike at a sleeping target. I am a warrior, and my honor is my bond. For as long as he sleeps, I will turn myself to my people, and plan for the day when he awakens."

"I think I do not understand. He sleeps, but what happened to the child moon?"

"This is the story I must tell you, and it must be told to all our people, all the clans. We must remember this story for all time. We may be the only ones to know this, other than for the new gods who now come to us. But they will not likely teach such young people like ours this story. It is a story not for such like ours to know. We are children in their eyes, and such children as we do not need to know such stories as this. But this is OUR story, so we may consider ourselves privileged to know it, even though it also brings us so much pain."

She takes another breath to compose herself.

"Since the time of our last battle, when our Master put us on the field to test us again, I have seen visions I could not understand. Some of you may know this, as words tend to spread amongst our people when I go into my hut to use my Sight. This may disturb some of you, and I know many have asked questions about what I saw. Then I began giving new instructions, and this led us to where we are now. You followed me faithfully, and I am pleased, but now you must know the meaning of it."

She once again looked up at the sky, which was now turning a pleasant blue with no clouds visible to tarnish the cool summer morning.

"I saw the arrival of new gods to this place. Ours is a place that holds many worlds, the homes of those others we were sent into battle with. These worlds were the playpens of the other gods we once knew, where they grew their challengers, and then tested them on the field of battle, as we were tested by Sargeras. We are his creation, and we were fortunate to have survived for so long. But I came to know what happens to those that do not, and you have learned of this, although quietly in whispers."

She pauses to check their reactions before continuing.

"But these new gods are different. They oppose this practice. To them, young life like ours is precious, not a toy to be tossed on the ground. They do not make battle with such like us. They were offended by our gods, and so they argued, and finally fought a great battle above the skies."

The crowd moaned and gasped.

"I watched this in my visions. I dug very deep to see all of it, or as much as my mind would allow. But then I saw our…Master…" she scorns. "Sargeras!" she hisses. "That coward!" now her voice escalates. "He did not fight! He and his servant hid to one side, out of view from the rest as the battle raged and the others began to fall."

The crowd now began hissing and shouting catcalls, some of them throwing up their fists in protest.

"He made us to fight for his pleasure, fight for our lives, but he would not fight for his own, or any of his kind. I heard him speak words, declaring this space, all those stars we had up there, and perhaps more beyond that, to be decrepit, as with great age, such that he would not wish to die in this place. Perhaps I can give him this much, as my visions told me the same. But it still offends me that he would hold such a low opinion of everything we might know of in this place."

The assembly again rose up with their discontent.

"Then I saw Darumon departing to scout his new enemy. He returned with troubling words. These new gods cover much of what he describes as Creation, which tells of a space much larger than what we thought to be out there as we looked into the nighttime skies. These others are many, and they are powerful, and our gods were falling."

She pauses again to review the cave entrance, reflecting on their recent work to find protection from the calamity.

"Darumon is part of a servant race, and the others of his kind created a plan to defeat these new gods. But Darumon is a clever one. This I know from my own experience. He knew these new gods were also clever, and might recognize this plan when it came out. So he created his own plan to preserve his Master, sacrificing the others and leaving everything else, including us, their finest champions, to the fate of this plan."

"Great Matron," the Chief issues worriedly. "What was this plan? The child moon is gone, and we saw…I do not know what we saw."

"Yes, that was the result of this plan. The plan was to use a weapon only the gods might understand. Such people like us are too young to know this, but I saw it in my vision. I cannot and should not reveal all to you, but I will say this much, as you saw it this past night. It is a weapon that unmade all things out there," she turns her gaze skyward. "I saw the other worlds, many of them, those that once were the playgrounds of the other gods, torn apart as a rock crumbled to dust and lost to the wind. I saw a wave, as on the sea, but more violent than any storm I can recall, wash across the open spaces, destroying everything it touched. And then I saw our home, as it can be seen from high above. The wave came for it, but then it stopped, as if it crashed against an unseen wall."

Oohs and ahs erupted from the gathering as the depiction made its way around. Many of the people impulsively looked upwards, but the view by now was obscured by the glow of daylight.

"Only a god holds this sort of power," she concludes. "But it was not our Master who came for us. It was one of the newcomers. We owe our lives to them now, our very existence."

"But Great Matron," the Chief hesitates. "The child moon? And if we owe a great debt to these new gods, what demands do they make for it."

"The child moon was Darumon's plan to hide his Master, and then to steal him away inside of it to places unknown to the newcomers."

"What?!" he shouts. "Our Master hid inside the child moon and Darumon stole it away? And this is to run from the others?"

Now the group was shouting angrily, with many of them standing up and waving their arms. The assembly became rowdy with slurs and scornful accusations.

Kuroku raised a hand to regain their attention before continuing.

"Be calm, my children, and hear the rest. Yes, they ran, both of them. Sargeras hid inside the child moon and Darumon carried it away to a place these new gods might not know of. But he is not lost to us, because I saw this with my Sight, and I shared this with the new god who protected us from this weapon. He calls himself Helm, and he is the one who placed this shell around us that now guards us from the cloud left behind from the weapon. Outside, I think it is very dangerous, but inside we are safe. Now we work together to follow Sargeras, to watch him as he sleeps."

"Where did he go? And how are you able to follow him if you are standing here?"

"My Sight told me there was something else out there at the time the child moon was taken from us. Helm tells me it was another race of creatures unknown to us, but now I know who they are. He calls them Positive Primes. They are very strange to us, but I was given time to speak with them. They now serve as my eyes to watch Sargeras where he sleeps. They travel to study him and return to share what they see. I think Darumon will also sleep, and he will stay this way for a long time until he feels it is safe to come out again, and this is where our trouble returns."

"What trouble now? Will they try to return here?"

"Helm and the new gods are powerful, and they control all things now. He says our gods were the last of their kind, and now only Sargeras remains. He cannot stand against them alone. But if he or Darumon should try to create a new weapon, he could make trouble again. And yet, if the new gods should try to search for him, he might feel their approach and seek another hole to crawl into. For now, he might feel safe, and so we shall allow him this."

"For how long? Great Matron, you are right, I am offended by this, and I think many others are offended."

The Chief turns to the rest of the clansmen, and they all offer up shouts and roars of agreement.

"I know this, Chief," she responds calmly. "But we cannot do anything here and now. I will watch him. I have already told Helm, and he will help me. Now I tell you, my children, that you will also know this. Know this today, and for all time, as this is my new vow. I will chase him to the edge of this Creation, if I must, and use every trick I have ever learned in these games our gods once played, to see him destroyed!"

A rousing cheer sounds out from the crowd as she prepares to finish.

"I do this not only for our people, but for all those others who were lost in these games, destroyed by their creators simply for failing to find victory. And I will do this for any others who may suffer along the way until I am ready to make my move. And this is where my children can help. We cannot do this as we are today. For this, we must grow in ways we can only dream of now. We will become that which he would never desire us to be, and do this to spite him and all the others. But we will not use this to bring destruction. We will become wise and compassionate, as life is precious and must be allowed to grow. These are the lessons of our new gods. They will teach us, and we shall become their new children."

The cheering elevates to new heights, and the people began dancing around the campfire singing praises to their newfound freedom and prospects of a new future.

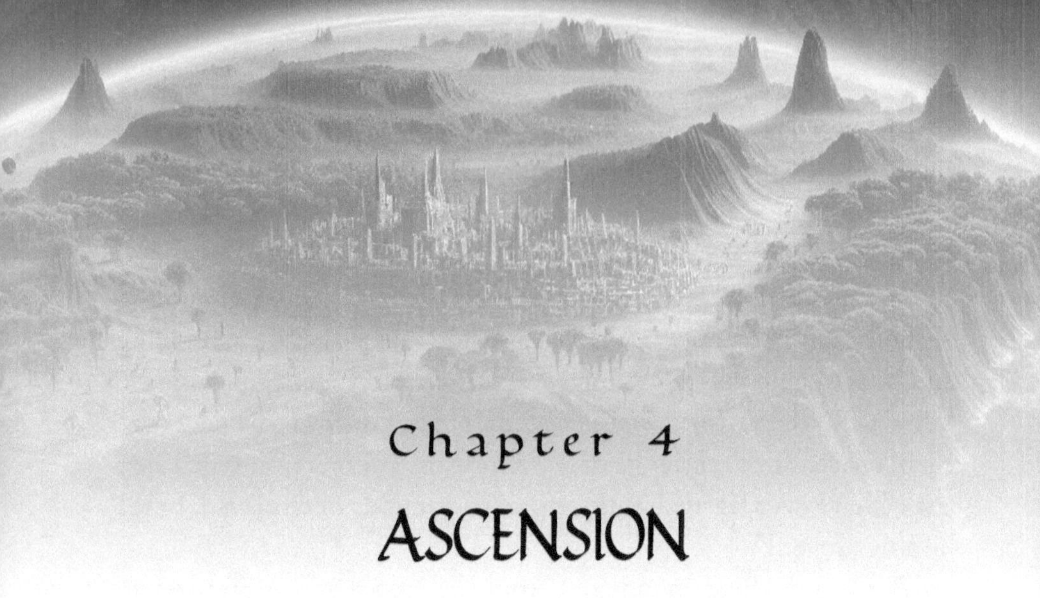

Chapter 4
ASCENSION

Many Ages have passed since the liberation of the Sarrukh from their former subjugation by Sargeras and Darumon. Their civilization has flourished, and Kuroku has led them through many scientific and technological revolutions. Their society dedicated itself to the devotion of their new pantheon of gods, the local circle of Estelar, and has shared many teachings with them, elevating the Sarrukh to great social and cultural heights.

It has been nearly ten thousand years, and their society has come far. All things have evolved in their world. Where once there were open prairies, now there are vast fields of agriculture and its related industry. Where once there were the occasional villages, now stood robust cities and dense metropolitan centers. Highways connected the urbanized regions, along with airways, providing transportation of people and goods, but by this time, these methods were becoming a vestigial remnant of a fading era.

Their skill with the arcane arts had evolved into a unique form of technology that, when combined with the physical sciences, had overcome many of the obstacles that might normally occur with physics alone. This allowed them to explore many new possibilities, including a form of transportation that directly connected two points using devices resembling upright ring apertures to maintain a dimensional rift. This is essentially a hole in space leading from one point to another, bypassing whatever physical boundaries may otherwise lie between.

Their technology had also allowed them to reach into space, establishing space stations and colony outposts for research and industrial development of their local moon and the other planets collected into their star system. The local star system included a total of six planets, some of which included moons, and each of them of a terrestrial nature, although none of them held any significantly evolved forms of life on the scale of the Sarrukh. But most of these planets were not native to this star system.

Just like in Kuroku's vision, the five additional planets represented some of the known remnants of the former playpens of the old Primordials, those that were rescued by the Estelar, and in this case relocated into this strange orbital configuration. There were two rings of planetary orbits, each with three planets at equidistant positions circling the sun. The delicate balancing act imposed by Helm and the others to arrange these orbits kept the planets in perfect synchronization within the life-giving band of radiance where a terrestrial world might find habitable conditions. But these were not the only survivors. During this time, Kuroku learned of other worlds with more advanced forms of life which were relocated outside the local universe to other Folds of Creation. This was to allow them a proper chance for development away from the dangers of the local space and each other.

However, in this time of growth and scientific advancement, the Sarrukh found themselves with a small problem when considering the exploration of anything beyond their world. The Shell acted as an impenetrable barrier. This was not unexpected, neither was this the problem, as there was really nothing outside to explore. But something new was emerging on the horizon which was beginning to raise concern.

Kuroku was standing at the window of her executive political office gazing out at the capital city skyline when an announcement sounded at the door. A well-dressed political officer enters to meet with her.

"Matron Kuroku," the middle-aged man calls into the room. "You summoned me?"

"Yes, Prime Minister, enter. We must talk."

She turns to meet her visitor and the two of them join at the window, still looking outside.

"Matron Kuroku, it is my understanding you have something urgent to discuss?"

"Yes, I see a disturbance approaching, and it troubles me, for we must now prepare ourselves to meet it."

"Matron, if it were any common man on the street delivering such a prediction, I might normally shrug it off as paranoia, or simply someone looking for a little personal attention. But coming from you, that frightens me."

"Perhaps it does," she grins. "If only I could enjoy such casual musings, but mine tend to fall into grave regard. I feel the pressure of an eternity upon me, not only to see our people survive and prosper, but also my ancient promise to seek vengeance on that which brought so much pain to so many."

"We all know of your ancient vow, Matron, although by now I think there are many who feel so distanced from it that it's more like a dream."

"No, Prime Minister, it is no dream. You and your generation are young compared to where all this began, but this is no less real now than it once was so long ago. He is still out there, and for as long as he exists, danger also exists, and not only to that which may be immediately surrounding him. We can also be in peril, as he would remember this place, and this might be his first target, should he desire his own vengeance. Therefore, we must never forget, not even after we see his downfall."

"Of course, Matron, I did not mean to offend."

"Naturally. But this new demand is unrelated, and yet it bears a burden no less imperative."

"Matron, I think we all know of your predilection for using

cryptic terms on occasion, but if you require our help, you'll need to be a little more overt," he smiles gently.

"Indeed!" she chuckles. "You have not yet learned to read my mind?"

"Even if I could, I think yours is too complex to penetrate."

"Thank the Great Ones for that, as it might also strike numb any who would make the attempt."

The two of them shared a brief laugh at the mention before the Matron continued her thoughts.

"Unfortunately, this is a true dilemma that will require every citizen to participate, as it will affect our world and every living thing within it."

"Matron," he offers warily. "Just what is it you have in mind here?"

"The death of our home, Prime Minister," she admits solemnly. "But it cannot be the death of our people."

The Prime Minister fell back a step from her statement.

"Matron, please tell me what you see for us. What exactly is it you see ahead for our world?"

"Sit with me," she directs to her desk.

The Prime Minister takes up a chair opposite the Matron at her desk while she composes herself.

"I have peered into my visions many times by now," she begins. "Trying to analyze what I see and how we must proceed. I have come to conclusions for several aspects at once. In its most basic essence, however, the time is coming that we must evacuate our home in order to preserve our people. Perhaps this might also be for the best, in the longer term, as we are essentially trapped inside the Shell."

"Trapped is one term I can agree with, but couldn't we still use our home as a base of operations once we find a way outside of it?"

"Perhaps we could, but this is not the concern. Our world is about to die. I simply do not wish our people to be present when it does."

"All right, so what is it you mean when you say our world is about to die."

"I refer to my visions quite often, as you know. I want to keep a careful watch on what might be coming next to our doorstep.

Although I am confident Sargeras and his servant are not a bother at this time, I still feel a pressing need to ensure our people find their way forward. Unfortunately, this particular concern comes from one source I would not have otherwise expected…the Estelar."

"The Estelar? What do you mean? Do they have something in mind? Our relations with them have always been so productive."

"Indeed, they have, but it would seem that no matter how high a society evolves, it can still experience its own internal disputes. As you know, Ao, the leader of their faction, assigned Selûne and Shar to govern and maintain our local space. These are described as twin sisters, but never have I seen such disparate twins as these. As such, I now foresee an argument developing between them, and it centers on how they wish to manage this space."

"Wonderful. So where does this argument lead them?"

"Selûne is known for her love of all things bright and alive, while her sister takes an opposing perspective. This is their interpretation of the Measure of Balance, but in their case, I think it is an effort poorly spent. Whereas Selûne may wish to bring continued light and warmth, Shar desires to counter it with darkness and cold. Shar's interpretation would actually harm much of the life we currently have here, but it does not actually end with this. Their argument takes it to an extreme that will destroy everything."

"How?"

"The argument will result in a clash between the two. While this, by itself, will not be the cause of our bane, Shar's ultimate withdrawal will leave a lasting effect. It would seem she is something of a sore loser. I saw a vision where she will cast a shroud upon our sun, and this will dim the light and heat radiated outwards to all things, freezing everything cold as cold can be."

"Incredible," he mumbles silently. "Is there nothing the others can do to prevent this?"

"I have already spoken with Helm on this. He and I agree together that if I perceived this vision at all, it must come to be. And so our home will die. But I will not allow this to take our people.

I struggled to look deeper, and found our answer, but it comes in many parts."

"I see. So where do we begin. I'm going to make a guess here, based on what we mentioned previously, that it must involve building something to carry us away from here."

"It does, but the scale must be great enough to accommodate all our people, and many people must be involved to assemble the solution. Furthermore, I have foreseen, and must admit, that for as much hardship as our people have experienced come by the hands of others, we cannot and should not permit ourselves to become the victims of other people's whims so easily, even if it is a personal dispute that overflows into our home. Therefore, our society must now diverge in two directions."

"Excuse me? Two directions?"

"Yes. We are an old society, and we have learned much, whether on our own, or with the help of the Estelar. We know hardship on a level that becomes desperate, such that no species, great or small, should ever experience this, and yet we were born to it. For this reason, I propose we take a bold direction for ourselves. Not everyone will follow this course, as we need our people to continue in the directions we have already set. But I will bring a portion of them to begin a new line, and this new line will grow into an elite race of guardians that might one day even challenge such as the Estelar, should any of them get any new ideas of playing their games with such creatures as we."

"Matron, not that I would argue with you, but this sounds a bit eccentric, to say nothing of what it means relative to our cultural standard."

"It might, but recall that I am from the early caste of our people. I was born a warrior, and spent my life trying to preserve our people in Sargeras's games. This is what I know, and I know that to preserve ours or any other will require a strong warrior caste to act as a front line of defense, even if you must place it in front of the Estelar and their perceptions of the Measure of Balance, as it would seem even the gods cannot be deemed absolutely perfect."

"That's a little scary, but all things considered, a system of checks and balances does actually make sense, especially if you involve an unbiased party."

"Exactly! The Measure of Balance, as a rule of law and a philosophy, is a fine creation. I would not argue with it. But even they who created it might sometimes fall to the outside. Meanwhile, the remainder of our people must depart from this place. I have considered this process, and I believe it must involve a series of magnificent arks to carry them to the far regions of Creation. This will give our people coverage to explore and learn, while at the same time to spread out, such that we are no longer clustered so close together, and therefore vulnerable to any single cataclysm."

"I understand, Matron. And naturally, this will involve a considerable effort. We might need to retool our entire industry for this."

"We must, for our future here is for naught. Everything we have, from this moment forward, must be reengineered to this purpose."

The Prime Minister nods as he rises from his chair and bows, then turns to leave the office. The Matron turns once again to the window to gaze outside at the city skyline; a sight she now knew would not last forever. A note of melancholy ushered up inside her for all the work she had done to bring her people this far.

"Strength, Kuroku," she mutters to herself. "You could not expect this would be the end of your work. We must still find… Him! And this alone will take us well beyond our ancient home. Our people are better this way. We must travel as the Estelar once did. We must grow and evolve, as they did. Then, perhaps one day, with much luck and wisdom, we can join with them at their side, as others have done."

Word spreads quickly throughout the Sarrukhan society of Matron Kuroku's latest visions and directives. Many people initially balked at the idea; it was so outrageous. But eventually it sank in, and the local industries began churning out new plans and technologies to solve many of the major riddles needed to assemble these components.

Their existing space industry was the first hurdle. It was good enough to support travel and industrial exploits to the other planets and their moons, but this would require a massive reworking of the infrastructure to design and build huge space docks capable of building huge colony arks.

Even this was not enough, however. Although they had the technology to create dimensional rifts, they did not as often use this in their ships, mainly because they had nowhere to go other than the local space, and this was previously accommodated very comfortably by more conventional technologies. Research had been made on numerous occasions to incorporate this into ships as a type of jump drive, but they needed a destination endpoint to direct themselves at, and being trapped inside the Shell didn't give access to anything on the outside.

"This is going to be our biggest challenge to overcome," the Prime Minister admits. "Unless we can find a way to address an endpoint outside the Imberium Shell, the only thing I can possibly suggest…hmm…"

"What do you think, Prime Minister?" the engineering professor wonders.

"Well, the thought occurs to me that we know of some endpoints within the Outer Planar region, thanks in part to some of our earlier studies working in conjunction with the Estelar, so this might offer us at least an escape route, but then what. Where do we go after that?"

"If it's at least an escape path, I could offer a partial solution."

"What is that, Professor?"

"It would seem to me our biggest concern is the preservation of our population from the obvious danger here on the ground. Once the shroud is cast on the sun, things are going to get deathly cold very quickly."

"Right, this much is obvious."

"Of course, we can easily compensate for this with artificial habitats in space, and naturally our ships are designed to keep people safe regardless of the outside conditions."

"So, what you're saying is to concentrate on building these habitats and ships first, and relocate our people there as a priority to remove them from the more dire situation on the ground."

"Yes, this would be my first concern. Although, I would be very sad to see our world turn into a snowball in space. But knowing our people are safe in some form of a controlled environment would give me a moment of relief to consider our next move."

"All right," the Prime Minister considers. "So, let's say we build enough space stations, or arks…whatever it happens to be, that we can relocate our full population."

"And whatever form it takes," the Professor waves a finger. "We must also consider power generation. It certainly cannot be solar powered."

"Ah, yes! Clearly, if the sun is removed from us, this is no longer a viable option."

"We would need to develop our fusion technology more completely. I would put a priority on this, along with the related industries."

"We will need fuel for that, you know."

"Yes, but I believe we can compensate with arcanic technologies to supply us."

"Interesting… And then what?"

"We need to perfect our remote mining operations, as I think doing it manually would place a strain on our people for the climatic conditions we would be facing. Also, our agriculture and food supply will need to be addressed. It must all follow along with us."

"This is becoming complicated, and we're barely even beginning."

"I think once the infrastructure is in place, and we develop a pattern, it should come together as a predictable sequence. And if we can find an endpoint to escape from the Shell, all things become possible. It only seems complicated for us now because we never had to do this before."

"Perhaps you are right," the Prime Minister affirms. "Then we come back around to the endpoint. I wonder if the Estelar can direct us. Surely, they should hold some responsibility for what will happen down here. It is one of their own who will do this to us, so they should offer something to compensate."

"Yes, I would petition them to assist us for this point…unless… wait a moment."

The Professor seems to drift off in thought briefly as an idea comes to mind.

"What about this as a curious alternative. The Matron has her spies, these Positive Primes, watching Sargeras in that hole he dug for himself. Although I would not wish to arrive too closely to that hole, if instead they could find a convenient location at distance, so as not to be noticed, or better yet, some other fold they might have access to, this could offer us a starting point."

"An interesting thought. You mean to have them find an endpoint and assist in marking that location for us? But just a moment, that space is supposed to be devoid of the arcanic energies. Most of our technology would not work there."

"Then we bring these energies with us. We have conducted enough research on where they come from that we might be able to finish the studies and create an artificial environment to supply our own."

"True genius…" he smiles. "And this would provide for us no matter where our travels take us. Then this must also be a priority."

"We will need an incredible volume of materials to provide for all this, along with many redundant safety features and backups to prevent accidents. We are becoming a fully space-based society. We cannot afford to allow our new homes to spring any leaks."

"Indeed."

As the research progressed to solve these technological issues, another group of citizens, largely derived from volunteers of local security forces, was coming together for another project. Rather than the Prime Minister overseeing the process, on this occasion it was Matron Kuroku giving the instruction.

"You have been gathered here for a most honored service," she begins boldly. "This harkens back to our early days, as we were once warriors, proud and strong. Since that time, I have brought our people out of that madness and into civilization, where wisdom and compassion are our hallmarks."

She paces in front of a large number of troops lined up in formation. This wouldn't represent the full membership, but rather a starting point. It would grow over time, and involve much more than just security officers, but this was a chore for later.

"And yet, it comes back to us," she continues. "We are still warriors, and as warriors, we have a duty to uphold. This duty is to preserve that which is made victim by they who would show less respect than is deserved. The reasons for this may be pure malice afflicted by those who care not for any other. But it may also be incidental. We must therefore offer a buffering line to soften this blow, perhaps even to prevent it, and to remind they who ought to be more responsible that they too have a duty to uphold, despite their personal ambitions."

She makes another pass in front of the troops, secretly trying to imagine how this might ultimately develop, because the idea to create something to impose a buffering line between the gods and everything else would clearly be a daunting task. She would need help, and likely to make use of every trick she ever learned from the Estelar themselves.

"In my time working with the Great One we adore, Helm the Guardian, Helm the Watcher, He Whose Eye Never Sleeps, I have learned much from his private lessons. I am prevented from revealing this to my children as part of my promise to abide by the rules of their teachings. They are gods, by every proper definition, and we are not. But to bring this into reality, we must segregate ourselves from our kin, as much as this might sadden us. Only then will we be able to bring ourselves up to where we can serve this new purpose."

She pauses a moment in her steps and glances over the faces of the assembled troops.

"We must create a new form for ourselves," she announces soberly. "No longer will we be able to describe ourselves as Sarrukh. For those of you who cannot pursue this goal, you should rejoin with the others who will depart from our home and create new lives for themselves elsewhere. There is no shame, as this is not a task for just anyone. But neither is it for the faint of heart. Our dedication must be absolute."

She could see the concern in their faces. She expected this. She felt it as well. But after a lifetime fighting on behalf of Sargeras in his games, then another lifetime fighting simply to preserve her people FROM Sargeras, and finally her lifetime afterwards, planning her vengeance against him, she knew instinctively she would never be able to fulfill her promise as such a simple creature. She needed a super army, and she, herself, must be a part of it.

"We have seen what may appear as a great length of time in this place, and yet to the greater mind, this is merely a flickering moment. Time existed long before our kind ever walked this soil, and it will continue for an eternity after we have passed. We must now evolve. Some of us will continue on the path we began, but others must take a new course. We will become the new guardians. We will serve to oversee the actions of both the greater and the smaller. We shall learn and follow the ways of the Estelar, and abide by the Measure of Balance, but we shall remain as an impeding force should any of them, or any other power, decide these rules no longer apply. They may have their laws and justice, but this may not always find its way before the harm is done."

She turns to find a small group of scientists standing off to the side.

"Here we have some of our top researchers in arcanic rift generators. In the past, we have studied ways to create these rifts into regions of the Outer Planes, and we have several functioning examples in operation. So far, this has been mostly for research and investigation of the strange energies found in those places. But now, our research will take a new turn. Our people must leave our ancient home, and they will travel to unknown reaches. But we have another direction to follow, and it leads here."

She picks up a tablet device that was lying on a nearby table and displays a chart. It showed a diagram of a roughly wheel-shaped arrangement of domains. The image was mirrored on a larger monitor for the assembly to see.

"The Estelar describe this, affectionately, as the Great Wheel. I find it rather quaint, myself," she chuckles. "To think of such an advanced godlike society that still desires to invent the wheel."

The laughter soon spreads to the rest of the assembly.

"Yes, but in this case, this is not an object to carry a vehicle overground. This was created by the Estelar shortly after they settled in this region of Creation. Each of these pockets you see here," she points to a number of bubble-like envelopes in the diagram. "These are individual dimensional domains, homes to the various Estelar based on their polarity and character nature. Here is where we must delve into the lessons of what they are as a form of living entity. Some of this is known to us, but we are moving ahead of the common knowledge, and their rules now apply."

She continues her pacing while referencing the diagram on the tablet.

"The Estelar preach to us this principle of the Measure of Balance. All things in Creation must have balance, and this very often reflects on the forces of positive and negative factors holding each other in check. There can also be a neutral component in this equation, and to further complicate things, they also realize there are forces of Order and Chaos. These act as a cross layering over the rest. Positive, negative, and neutral, can each have Ordered and Chaotic extremes, and again with neutrality buffering between them."

She turns to examine the tablet for her example, pointing at the different elements to emphasize.

"Their arrangement is actually very neat. The upper portion here represents the positive polarity, while this lower portion is negative. Neutrality buffers in the middle. On the left side, we have the domains of Order, and on the right, we have Chaos, once again with neutrality buffering in the middle. This creates a matrix of two qualities denoting each of these domains, and they often describe these as their attributes or alignments."

She sets the tablet back on the table and continues her presentation.

"Some societies may identify these alignments with such qualities we might describe colloquially as good and evil, lawful and unlawful.

But more appropriately, we should use such terms as Positivity, Negativity, Ordered and Chaotic. They segregate themselves into these pockets as their way of upholding the Measure of Balance, with each side testing the other to ensure the overall integrity of Creation, and all of us along the way. This is not necessarily to yield the benefit or suffering of any form of life, but rather to ensure it remains strong, to grow and to survive against adversity. We have certainly seen our share of that, but we were forced into it, if only for the pleasure of our former Master and his ilk."

She pauses to glance around the area. It was a sunny autumn day with a cool breeze. She could feel it against her face, and though it was nothing new to her, a sudden thought flashed across her mind that this simple pleasure might one day be lost to her. She had to refocus herself to resume her lecture, despite a sinking feeling somewhere in her core.

"The fact that we survived at all is purely at the expense of so many others who failed. And yet, had the Estelar been in control of this game, they who failed would have been encouraged to overcome their shortfall and learn from it. But with our former Masters, they were simply erased from existence."

She halts her movement and hangs her head in remembrance. Even though it had been many millennia, she could still recall the images she once witnessed from her early visions. They haunted her on many occasions. But she reminded herself she needed to take strength from this. In the grander scheme of things, she had learned from Helm that life may come and go due to many calamities, most of which may be outside anyone's control.

"What we will create is a way to keep this in check, at least within our power to do so. We may not be gods, but then even the gods cannot be all things at once."

She turns to look at the large monitor behind her, which still displayed the image of the Outer Planes for her audience.

"We will begin our studies here," she points to the upper left corner of the image. "This region is known as Mount Celestia. There we shall learn to understand the native energies and how they can be applied. This region is also pure Positive and pure Order. I am told that corporeal creatures like us can be influenced by these forces, if we remain in place for extended periods."

Now she pauses in deep contemplation. A marked look of trepidation crossed her face. The local commander of the security troupe saw her change in demeanor and stepped closer to check on her.

"Matron Kuroku, are you well?"

She looked into his eyes with a sudden rush of sadness.

"I must go there. I will not come back."

"What?" he retorts emphatically. "Matron, you are our most sacred leader. You would leave us now?"

"Captain, our people are leaving. As children, they now leave their home to find a new life. As their Matron, I cannot always follow them. I must allow them their freedom, but my destiny cannot be the same. I am to pursue Sargeras, but I think our children must find another way. I will not drag you into my battle."

"Matron, I must protest! We will follow you into this battle if you ask us, but you cannot do this alone."

"I will not be alone, and the battle is not now. For now, my children must continue to grow, and they will do this in other places, not here. I must remain here, to evolve as these children must evolve," she directs to the assembly of troops. "I must see to it that we build this new guardian race successfully, and this will require all of my skills. But I will make a promise to all my children, and that is I will never forget you. If it is at all possible, I will speak to you when I can, to encourage you that I am still with you in my thoughts. But here we must part ways."

The news hit the full assembly hard. Murmurs were heard echoing through the gathering, and many were shaking their heads at the implications. Eventually, the day concluded, and Matron Kuroku returned to her home.

Word had begun to spread of this new revelation. Many were seen in the streets with signs displaying their love of the Matron and a desire not to see her go. But it soon became apparent that her greater plans demanded her to make this sacrifice. The Sarrukh would become a spaceborne society, no longer with a native home world. Although this frightened many for the loss of their homebound security, it also intrigued them for the prospects of travelling across the endless expanses of Creation. This was a much-anticipated desire ever since the beginning of their early space program, if only for the issue of the Shell holding them back.

Nevertheless, although it might ultimately become clear that she could not stay with them forever, many had become accustomed to seeing her, hearing her voice, and listening to her guiding principles. To think that she might one day be gone from them left a lot of empty feelings.

Again, she calls upon the spirit of Helm for another communing.

"Great One, I call to you again."

"I am here, Child Kuroku."

"My people make themselves ready. The Positive Primes tell me they can help with our initial departure from this place. We are simply waiting for the construction of our vessels now. What is the condition of the sisters at this time?"

"We have warned them to restrain themselves, but thy sight did observe their dispute, and this cannot be denied. They now become restless, each desiring of their own advantage."

"Could you not simply dismiss them from their duty? Assign each to their own domain, and let them have their way of it."

"This has been discussed amongst us, but there are no other domains presently available within this fold. Thy home was the only we could provide within the frame of our encounter with the Primordial breed, although there has been counsel suggesting the creation of more to further populate this fold."

"Can such a thing be made, when you consider the turmoil that still burns outside our Shell?"

"It would require more of the same to be fashioned," he considers. "This in itself is not a burden for us, but it is also not our tradition to create such as this, as thy Creators once did of their own. We prefer the natural course to create such bodies, but this fold is defiled by the Agent of Unmaking they once did unleash. It will demand a great measure of time for it to heal by natural means. We have contemplated intervening to accelerate this process, but as yet the decision has not been made."

"And I suspect, with our departure, this decision will be further delayed, if not completely dismissed. This fold will lose the last of its native inhabitants, and other than for you, it will become a lonely place."

"For us, we have our means to commune with others of our likeness, irrespective of where they may reside within the Seas of Creation. And yet, I will hope for the day when life may return to this fold. It is always pleasing to see such Children emerge and develop."

"Do you recall my desire to deliver some of my children into the Fifth Fold where they may develop as a new guardian race?"

"I do recall this. And although I still question the necessity of it, thy depiction based on the sisters' intervention of the security of thy home does provide justification. We of the Estelar on occasion do still suffer our internal disputes."

"Not all beings can be perfect, it would seem."

"Indeed, I must agree."

"As for myself, I have come to a conclusion. We have discussed this on many occasions, and the result is always the same. My intention to pursue my former Master must carry me to far places and perform extreme deeds. I cannot do this in such form as I am. It becomes clear what I must do, and I ask for your help. Only you have the power to grant this to me."

"Thou hast given this much thought, Child of the Sarrukh. The task thou dost take upon thyself is great. It is further burdened with the premise that we cannot intervene directly. But dost thou have any further indication of how this might reveal itself?"

"So far, Sargeras still sleeps, as does Darumon, and I suspect they will remain this way for a long while. The Positive Primes can tell me much, but they are limited in ways I think only I can fulfill."

"What ways are these?"

"They can observe, but not to such intimacy as to hear their words or reveal their thoughts. While they may be able to perceive the energies of these emanations, the language is lost to them. This is where I must enter. Darumon has a subtle tendency to talk to himself, and I must know what he says."

"Interesting, and therefore thou must become as one with us. Child Kuroku, this is not a proposition to be taken casually. If thou wouldst choose to ascend beyond thy corporeal form, this becomes thy new destiny."

"My destiny already carries me beyond where I stand now. This is nothing new. I had to come to terms with this long ago. To make this transition will simply relieve me of the burden of anticipation, and set me on a path to follow my greater course. However, I must also admit, when the time comes to confront my former Master, I will do so in corporeal form again."

"A most curious suggestion… How wouldst thou envision this moment?"

"At this time, I cannot be sure of the answer, but I think I have the advantage of time to discover it. Until then, there is much work to do."

Many years have passed, and the industries of the Sarrukh worked furiously to design and build a series of massive arks to carry not only the people, but as much of their history and culture as they can preserve. Huge biodome ships are built to take samples of the native flora and fauna, hoping to save some part of their native ecology, as well as the development of large-scale food production using hydro- and aeroponics farms.

The best minds were brought together to resolve the few remaining technical issues for the design and construction of power plants that could carry them literally anywhere without the need for a refueling base, making them fully self-sufficient in all ways. This also included the means to build and maintain the generating platforms to produce their arcanic energies necessary for most of their technology.

The fleet had been assembling in orbit, and Matron Kuroku had coordinated with the Positive Primes to assist in locating a potential escape route from their Shell. A unique piece of technology had been created to serve this purpose that they could carry with them to pinpoint a destination endpoint, record the location, and return it back. The resulting data could then be programmed into their navigation systems. From there, they would progress forward, learning and evolving until they could gain a greater understanding of the nature of Creation to find more of their own.

Meanwhile, Matron Kuroku had been keeping herself busy training a special elite force that had dedicated itself to serve this new project to create a guardian race. Whole communities had segregated themselves from the main body of their society to create a separate entity. Now they were studying the specialized nature of the Outer Planes and their native energies to understand ways of intentionally modifying themselves into a new unique form of life. Nothing like this had ever been done before, not even to the knowledge of the Estelar, and although many of the Estelar found this curious, they chose not to interfere with it.

Finally, the day had come when the fleet was ready. The Matron held a press conference in the courtyard outside her royal office. Many cameras were focused on her to broadcast this announcement on the global network while the ships were being stocked with supplies and the people preparing to say their final goodbyes to their ancient home.

"My children," she begins with a soft tremor in her voice. "It seems like an eternity now…my life. I can still recall so much of it. How, in those very early days, I struggled to keep our people alive in the games brought forth by our ancient Master, Sargeras. How I learned to detest him and his kind for what they did…not only to us, but to so many other worlds and those who lived there. But we survived, if only due to the good grace that we were found by the Estelar."

She sighs and pauses to glance at her senior officers who were standing on the podium with her.

"Since that time, we have seen much history and growth, and I am overjoyed by it! My children..." she halts to catch herself, laying a hand over her mouth to muffle her whimpering. "...Who should now travel off and find their own way, to continue to learn and grow, but this place can only limit you now. It is our home... was our home, but children cannot remain in such a place forever, the same as they cannot remain with their mother forever. And so, we should not be sad. Although this moment may cause us to shed a few tears, I will still be with you in my thoughts."

She again pauses, this time to wipe her eyes. She then tries desperately to recompose and straighten herself.

"We are a society that must move forward now. It is the nature of things; it was fated to occur from the beginning. It is not the end, surely not this. For you, it is a new beginning. For me, it is also a beginning, but our paths must part ways. We each have our work to do."

Now she can feel her strength returning, at least marginally.

"In a way, I might envy you a little, but I will also watch over you. We will not be completely separate from each other. I promise this to you. I will seek ways to speak to you, and you may share your experiences with me."

She momentarily recesses to look upwards.

"I will have my new home, and my new life, a life I believe is destined for me, the only destiny I can imagine for myself, if given where I have travelled in the past and where I should expect myself to travel in the future. In a curious way, it actually seems fitting. From there, I will guide our people. This will be my new throne, and I will have many new children to watch."

She passes her gaze across the assembled audience of journalists and citizens who had gathered in the courtyard.

"And so is the time for you to seek your destiny. We shall travel forward, each of us in our own way. Perhaps there may be times when we might join together for a moment. We will reflect upon our old memories while we seek new ones. But one thing is for certain... the Seas of Creation await!"

She finishes with a sturdy overtone, and the crowds rise up in cheers and applause. The ships began handing out their population assignments, and the people loaded up. The full population was departing from their home, most of them on the ships, while the remainder clustered around Matron Kuroku.

The large assembly was located in an isolated research and training center they created for this purpose, to keep them separate from the rest of the people. There they built a number of barracks, classrooms, and laboratories, as part of their studies of the Outer Planar regions and their native properties. In the center was a transit cluster with portal devices they would use to transport them to and from.

"We must now make our way through the arcanic portals," she issues to her new flock. "This will be our final journey. We will not return home after this. Some of us have made the journey for our research, but now we make our migration."

One by one, she observed them pass through the portals to arrive at their next destination, which was essentially an outpost colony they created on the other side, and they would use this as a starting point for her next venture.

"Matron Kuroku," asks one of her officers. "Our research promises some very interesting results over the longer term, but do we have a name for what we hope to create here?"

"Yes, we must give it a name. I have thought of this a few times. It must be a name that carries authority and strength…though what might carry strength in our mind might not hold the same meaning to another. And yet, it must be a name that will dictate this authority no matter who may hear of it. Therefore, I have considered a few possibilities and decided on one that holds special favor to me."

"Good. What name do we use for our new creation then?"

"We shall call this new race…Draconic."

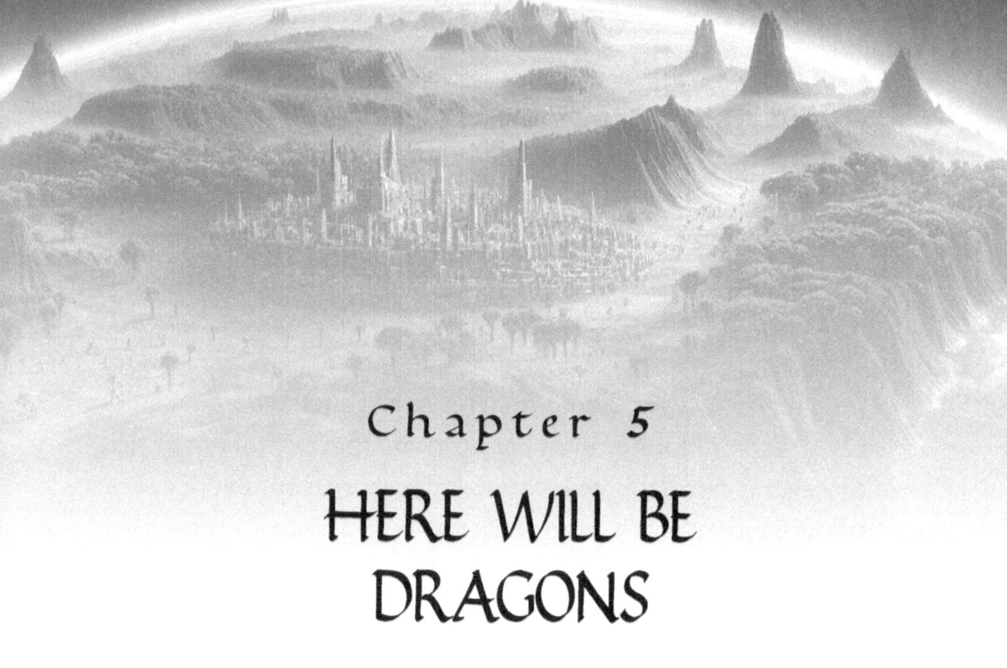

Chapter 5

HERE WILL BE DRAGONS

"And ssso..." one of the patrons relates. "Thisss half-witted... Tanar'ri... Got the idea... That it could offend... The people... Of the border town... By jumping through... The portal... And abducting them. Then to drag them... Back into... The Abyssss... To conduct whatever... Perversionsss... It had in mind..."

"Who was sssent... To defend the town... On thisss occasion...?" another one asks.

"Sssektazi was called... To thisss ssservice..."

"Sssektazi..." a third patron chuckles. "He is not known... To care greatly... For tanar'ri. What was his... Sssolution...?"

"Sssimple! He ssswatted the infidel... Like a bug... Then dragged it... By the legsss... Returning it... To itsss home... Perssssonally... And throwing it back... Into the chasm... It originally... Crawled out of..."

The group had been engaged in a bit of light conversation during a friendly gathering in a plaza courtyard in their home city. The city, in this case, was built in a domain carved out of the Outer Planes specifically for their kind. It had become a home and a base of operations for their policing activities of the Outer Planes, and anything else in the area that needed their attention.

At the center of the realm was a grand palace district, with magnificent artwork, fountains, topiary gardens, and ancient buildings constructed during the early days of their cultural development. And within this palace was the home of Kuroku, no longer a corporeal being, but now a goddess.

The domain was the home to her new children, the Draconics, after a long and arduous evolutionary process that eventually settled, creating several distinct breeds to act as an internal system of checks and balances, along with several castes within each to serve their individual functions.

The group outside were part of one such breed, known as the Metallics. They were a breed whose scales took on various hues resembling precious metals, such as gold, silver, copper, and such. Another breed, which was actually an opposing faction, was the Chromatics, taking on colors like red, green, blue, black, and white. There was also a neutral faction known as the Gems, and a few other minority variations.

While the group outside was engaged in its friendly discussion, Kuroku was inside her palace making a communion with a familiar voice.

"Helm, my Brother. I have finally received the words I have waited for."

"I am here, Sister Kuroku. What words dost thou speak of?"

"He stirs at last."

"The Primordial? It has been a long epoch since his departure. If his intention was to remain hidden until he might drift from our memory, he has surely succeeded. Many no longer recall their breed."

"It is true, and precisely as I would expect of him. But Sargeras still sleeps. It is actually his servant, Darumon, who stirs now. Not that I would expect otherwise."

"Granted, as the Primordial would still demand the dynamistic flows to awaken. His servant would not. What actions doth he take thus far?"

"So far, he seems to be searching his local environs, we think to discover and catalog his resources. No doubt, he will wish to gain the service of a new minion race."

"This is disturbing to my mind. Another home, another Child race…"

"I know, but here he has no compatriots to make sport with, so my thoughts are he will instead use this race to perform some manner of work for him. And for this, he will need them intact."

"Agreed. What actions dost thou have in mind at this time?"

"For now, I will only wait and watch. He is still of no great concern, but once he takes a direction with his minions, I must act. One thing I must consider, if he is taking minions to act as a shield in front of him, I must raise my own to penetrate that shield."

"Thou must take caution with such evaluation as this. We do not wish to become as they once were."

"I know, dear Brother. I will play my game very carefully. I will watch for my opening and strike when he cannot resist me."

They end their link and Kuroku diverts herself again to her studies. She had acquired an immeasurable amount of wisdom by this time since her arrival in the Outer Planes. The Estelar have their own form of technology that is very unique to their society, and she had been granted the privilege to study this after her ascension.

She used special pools of rippling energy that allowed her to peer into spaces not physically accessible to her. These served as a sort of spy camera. She had many of these by now, some of them watching her original children, the Sarrukh, thus allowing her the occasional communion, and others watching her Draconic children, to offer guidance and direction for their work.

She also had a few watching Sargeras and Darumon.

While she might still make occasional use of the Positive Primes, especially if Darumon might be on the move and she needed eyes to follow him, they were often placed on standby, waiting for any critical need that may arise.

She returned to one such pool. In this case, it had been following Darumon as he was apparently surveying a local world.

"Now, my dear former mentor…" she gloats. "What do you have in mind today? How curious it is that the tables are turned, and now I look down on you, where once you did so with me."

In the pool she could see him visiting a world with a lush tropical forest. He appeared to be investigating the area, as if looking for something.

On the planet surface, Darumon had only recently arrived after projecting his form through folded space amongst a number of nearby star systems, looking for one with a suitable environment supporting life. He strolled along through a field of tall grasses and leafy shrubs, studying the trees and other foliage.

"What does this world have to offer," he wonders openly. "I hope it is something just a tad more exciting than the last one."

He sees several small animals scurrying beneath the bushes as he passes by.

"Small things again… I cannot make use of such small creatures! I need something bigger, more robust. Like a predatory species…" he muses privately. "Or maybe not. It might offer some good sport, but I think not this time. I am not here to make games. I need something to help me return my Master to his former home. And for that…" he pauses as the thought materializes, causing him to cringe slightly. "…A passive one. Well, so be it then. If it fits my needs, I will tolerate it. But it must be easily controlled, even more so if I should hope to…evolve it…" he shakes his head grudgingly.

He continues wandering across the terrain, scouting the local region, but finds nothing of particular interest here. So he folds himself to another location of the landmass to see about other zones and their local fauna.

Kuroku continues to watch, redirecting her pool's focus to his new location.

"You cannot escape from me, Darumon," she whispers. "Not as I am now. If only you knew, I would find your reaction most enjoyable. How I have…evolved," she snickers.

"Not a predatory species," Darumon continues his thoughts. "But a more docile sort… Yes, but I must be very careful to keep it under control. If I allow it to reach too far too fast, I might lose it. This will demand time…and patience."

He stops to examine the new surroundings, and finally to look up at the sky, studying the clouds and the local sun shining down on him.

"Time…" he sighs. "This will be my enemy. Without the dynamistic flows to help me shape whatever I find down here, I will have to do this the hard way."

He pauses to imagine the amount of work ahead of him, evolving a species to where he might find it useful, but also unsure where he would want to draw the line before going too far beyond his tolerance level.

"In the service of my most cherished Master, I must do this. I simply need to find a starting point."

He continues walking along the edge of a new forest, this time in a more temperate climate. Then, in the distance, he spies something moving along the ground. It was a herd of beasts crossing an open field.

"There we go. What do we have out there? A herd of prey animals, herbivores perhaps. That might do nicely."

He moves in closer for a better look. It was a well-established herd of creatures, bipedal in nature with hoofed feet and gripping hands. They walked along in a hunched posture, counterbalanced with thick tails, and a set of smoothly curved horns protruding from the temples. They were largely furless, and with bluish skin.

He closed in cautiously so as not to frighten the pack into running. He examined them carefully.

"Definitely herbivores," he observes. "Travelling in a herd, this might be useful to keep them together. An alpha male in the lead, potentially a harem of females…yes, perhaps I could use this. But now, how to manipulate this to my favor? The alpha male would need to be removed, obviously, and as for the females…" he feels another shudder come across him. "Darumon, this is demeaning to you," he sighs again. "And if your most beloved Master were watching…ugh.

But at this moment, there is simply no other way. At least your body offers a universal platform to conduct such as this."

He discreetly moves to a nearby thicket and ducks down. He then begins altering his shape to match one of the creatures moving along in the herd. He checks himself for the completeness of the disguise before lifting up and attempting to merge with the rest.

Kuroku continued to watch the images displayed within the pool.

"I knew he could alter his size, but I must admit I did not know he could change his shape as well. Interesting. I must remember this for later. But the most remarkable is what I suspect he must do next. How humiliating this must be for him."

Darumon, now in his native disguise, merges with the herd and begins moving forward to the front. There he finds the current alpha male. The alpha takes immediate notice of the new male, and sounds a warning to keep back. It felt an instinctive urge to defend its harem and to maintain its position of authority.

Darumon circled around it, setting himself in an offensive posture, attempting to mimic the other creature for its native habits, and even to sound off similar calls. The alpha knew this to be a challenge, and so it took up a stand and began barking off a series of whines and howls. Darumon repeated these sounds, mostly improvising the mannerisms, and waited for the other creature to lunge forward.

The alpha finally charged at him, hoping to head-butt its opponent, much like a pair of rams would test each other by butting horns until one would eventually give up. But in this case, Darumon was out for total domination. As the other creature arrived within reach, he dodged to the side, grabbing the creature by the horns, twisting to throw it off-balance and dropping it to the ground. He loomed over the stunned animal, then bent down and promptly twisted to snap its neck.

"Nothing personal, but I need this over here to serve my Master."

The sudden and unusually violent nature of the attack shocked many of the others in the herd. They backed away, not knowing what to expect next. Darumon suspected there would be such a reaction, so now he moved more slowly to ensure he could maintain stability.

"Now then, what do we have here," he mutters to himself. "This will make a good start, but we'll need to find a tidy place to nest."

"Brother Helm, it is I again. He has chosen."

"Chosen?"

"I observed as he has made his selection. He found a world with a simple non-sapient species which he hopes to bring into fruition. But without the dynamistic flows, he must make this work physically. We have time on our side, for now."

"How might he perform this work of his? Without the flows, does he hope to train or otherwise guide this young breed into sentience?"

"Not exactly… He will jump it through a stage or two. He has taken control of a group of creatures and now mates with them, using his own essence to boost them over that first obstacle."

"Ugh… Indeed, this is problematic, Sister Kuroku. Such a creature as he, if to provide his own essence into the equation, can result in unpredictable permutations with a Child breed."

"I am aware of this. I wonder what sort of result we will see, and especially over the generations, as they no doubt interbreed with each other to further exaggerate the effect," she muses privately. "I will watch attentively and consider my own course now."

Kuroku watched and waited. The process of evolution is a slow one, but Darumon's initial efforts bypassed many of the usual developmental challenges. Whereas a species might take many millions of years to pass from the animal stage into a sapient form, his example cut that short significantly. And yet, the overall development would still take a fair amount of time, if only due to one complication…the apparent longevity of his progeny.

His personal involvement in their modification process showed one initial side effect. The species developed an exceptionally long lifespan. Initially, it stretched on the order of centuries, a huge leap from the original animal ancestor, and it seemed to be continuing to grow, generation after generation, in a rapid, almost exponential rate of increase, soon crossing into the millennia and then some. But rather than see this as a detriment, Darumon instead reveled in it, taking advantage of this feature to apply an artificial habit into his creation.

Their naturally slow physical maturity and great longevity allowed him to impose a lethargic effect with their technological advances, thereby allowing him to better control things without the need for as much intricate micromanagement of the affair. He could set them in motion to a task and then leave for a time, returning perhaps a few centuries later to see the result. But above all, he chose to make his efforts discreetly.

These were to be his puppets, not directly his subjects where he would engage them personally, at least not yet. He used disguises and deception to work his influence, as opposed to the Sarrukh where he and Sargeras were well known to them. This species was not to be his new favorite champion race for the games. He would use them to carry his Master home again, and likely discard them sometime afterwards.

Whereas with the Sarrukh, who were a simple-minded warrior race, well-cultured to serve his needs, this one was intended to be a technological masterpiece, a more analytical sort, which presented a different challenge. He would use them for their technology, as they were essentially useless for anything else, being formed out of a docile prey species. But as a society of intellectuals, he needed to approach them differently.

They developed as a flourishing civilization, and did so quickly; rising above the original Stone Age hunter-gatherer society he began with into a civilized state in only a few millennia. From there, they would pass through one Age after another. He made repeated forays into their midst during the course of their history, impersonating great wise men and political leaders, the purpose of which was to impose a specific direction to their development. After a while, he almost felt a certain level of enthusiasm in developing this race, irrespective of the fact that he detested giving them so much privileged knowledge. In the tradition of the Primordials, such small things as these were not deserving of greater wisdom. But he needed this. Ultimately, it would go to serve his Master. He could correct the situation later.

Kuroku watched his progression. Darumon was unable to detect her observations, so she felt confident in her position. Either he did not have this capacity, or he did not expect such a thing, and therefore never bothered to look.

"If only you could do as well with the others," she mutters. "Perhaps I would not hate you so for your treatment of our own. But then, you do not make this for their sake, only for your temporary service, and then what...do you throw them away as you did us?"

She made many observations within her apparition pools, but she did not wish to forsake her other duties. She had her own children to watch, both the Sarrukh, who had made their own remarkable evolution by now, and the Draconic. Therefore, in the course of her residence within the Outer Planes, just like with the Estelar, she had attracted a number of servants among the seraphim who so often performed work for the others. She would sometimes give tasks to them to study these images in her absence, allowing her to attend to other duties, but have someone watching Darumon in case anything extraordinary took place.

Then a message comes through that catches her attention.

"What is it, Thaliel?" she asks.

"Maker Kuroku, I have observed something which I thought to be out of place with our subject. Here, see for thyself."

Thaliel was her chief seraph in charge of her personal home and study work. Like all the seraphim, she was a tall female figure with pale features and a broad set of feathery white wings on her back.

Thaliel directs their attention at the apparition pool, where she had made a recording of an interaction among a group of scientists.

"The early indications seem to resemble many of the same findings we discovered within our own galaxy," reports one scientist.

"Yes, but we have already explored our own galaxy. Now we should continue outward, shouldn't we?"

"It would seem the most logical direction."

"No, I think not," interjects a male member. "This is not a useful expenditure of our resources at this time. This little detour might suggest to us a potential direction for the future, but we have more than enough to keep us occupied within our local space for now."

"Administrator, if we have already made that initial penetration into our neighboring galaxy, it is not really that great an expense by now..."

"Perhaps not, but then what...we spend another hundred millennia cataloguing a collection of stars we can do nothing about? I say we should invest ourselves to find uses for what we have here first. Nothing in the other galaxy is of any use to us if we do not first find uses for what is local. Time is on our side, Professor. We will put this off for now. You can make your observations from the space telescopes instead; it will provide just as much information."

"I see, although I might say I'm a little disappointed, I suppose in the end you are right, Administrator."

"Naturally. So far, we are still limited to this one world. What purpose does it serve to conquer another galaxy when we have yet to conquer our own?"

"I would not exactly wish to conquer anything out there..."

"Simply to make use of it is still a form of conquest, no matter how you apply the term."

Kuroku and Thaliel both watched the replay.

"That was him again, I presume?"

"Yes, Maker, in one of his personas..."

"Keeping them from pursuing something outside his preferential reach..."

"And this is not the first time, as thou wouldst recall. He has kept them from expanding outward from their home during this long period of exploration."

"Yes, and so conveniently that statement of being limited to the one world. They have explored their full galaxy by now, but never set down any new colonies."

"It seems like a contradiction in his wording."

"Clearly, he wants to keep his flock in one place. He makes promises with this exploration and new discovery, but his false governing body denies the actual exploitation of it. Even worse is that society of his buys every word they give out."

"And this is one of the ironies I find most disturbing. They describe themselves as a free society, but they have no true idea how confined they are."

"I will admit, he gave them a lot. But surely, he would never wish them to get any ideas of going out and making a real life for themselves. But this...he allowed them the freedom to examine their local galaxy... Their local neighbors... That which is close... yes! That word...conquest! Ugh..." she shakes her head.

"Maker, I feel shivers when thou dost behave this way. This is not a military society, so how would we interpret this statement... as if I actually wanted to know."

"Yes, Thaliel. He is using them to scout that which is close by. But this other galaxy is of no concern to him. It is too distant to be a bother. But it does offer something useful...technology. To aim oneself at a body like that would be a milestone event. But he clearly does not want them travelling further. It is only for the capability."

"Ah, I believe I see thy point here. This would earn them a level of technological prestige to aim themselves at other obscure bodies."

"Exactly. But now, if he is curtailing them with such a statement as conquering something, whatever manner HE would wish to apply the term, it cannot be for their pacifist manners, and not to colonize anything. He speaks of making use of the local resources. If this is not to colonize, it must be for something else. But Thaliel, what... resources...might he require to turn a non-military society into a military one to fight his upcoming battle?"

"Oh no...please, not that."

"Right...target practice. Blast him if this is what he has in mind!"

Kuroku moves away from the pool and begins storming around the laboratory room.

"And it makes perfect sense to me if he wants to use them as I might expect him to," she continues. "After all, he raised them for this purpose! This society he created, these Suuden-Aryku, as they call themselves, they are not warriors. But he would need to retrain them as such."

"Maker, this carries a heavy implication. What can we do about this? We cannot simply permit him to lay whole societies to waste in order to train this one."

Kuroku halted a moment to ponder this situation, but it didn't afford too many options.

"We may suddenly find ourselves in a hard place," she emits solemnly. "Anything of particularly low sophistication might not be a concern to him, as he would wish to find a challenge, if not simply to ensure his military receives adequate training, but maybe also to provide for his entertainment. We should not forget he has been without for a very long time."

"Then we are to suggest the more advanced of the Child societies are at greater risk."

"And we cannot intervene in that fold due to the policies of the Estelar that decree it is a reserved space, and they keep these policies very strict."

"Indeed they do. Then we can do…nothing?"

Kuroku again gazed at the pool and the image held frozen on the surface.

"I once learned that life may ebb and flow without anyone taking notice. We have this opportunity to take notice, but even at that, we may not be able to intervene. He should not be there. This species should not exist. And yet, it could just as easily be another species, created by other means, and doing exactly the same."

"I understand this lesson. I do not care for it, but it is still a part of the natural process."

"And here we are. Our capacity to bring this into our favor is not yet established. We could call in the others and have them clean this up, but I want him for myself, in part as my vow to my people, perhaps also as a return for my own suffering, and that which I feel is retribution for all those others I witnessed suffer around me."

"Maker, thou dost carry a very heavy burden. Didst anyone ever tell thee this?"

"Helm did on many occasions. Maybe it weighs too heavily on me, but I feel a sort of responsibility for everything I saw occur around me in those early days."

"It cannot be thine own responsibility. Thou cannot blame thyself, and neither canst thou take this unto thyself in proxy for another."

"Maybe, Thaliel. Maybe. But you did not know him personally. You did not see him, did not listen to his words…he, nor any of his kind."

"Was it truly so offensive?"

"It was, and on many occasions. They believed themselves to be as…well, as gods over everything else, and not in a good way."

"Despicable. No wonder the old stories seem to be forgotten. If they were indeed so foul, we would want to erase them completely."

"Some may feel this way, and perhaps justifiably so. But at the same time, we cannot simply erase that which might still serve as a lesson."

"Lest we once more return to it. I agree."

"As for this…" Kuroku muses. "We can do one thing…make our own move."

"Good. What course dost thou suggest?"

"If he hopes now to build anything, he will need time to prepare for it. Further, I doubt he will be able to pose any serious threat in our fold with such people as they, warrior or not."

"Why wouldst thou suggest this?"

"Because he needs a weapon to dispose of the Estelar, and a simple mortal race, even with such technology as what they have, would not suffice. He needs something else, and I know what it is. I have suspected this from the very beginning. The trouble is I think he cannot build this within that same fold."

"Thou hast now lost me in this sequence of thought. What weapon?"

"Do you know of such a thing described as an Agent of Unmaking?"

Thaliel reeled back at the blatant mention. The name was nearly mythical to her people.

"But he cannot…" she gasps. "No, but of course he can. They did make this once before. But thou art correct; he would require materials not found within that fold."

"And so he would need to travel outside to find them."

"Ah! Yes!" Thaliel asserts energetically. "And thus we have this milestone of travel. They would now possess the capability, if not necessarily the addressing, to find it."

"Correct. But if he uses them for this purpose, as he seems to be using them for everything else…hmm…"

"Yes?"

"I think he must first develop their military power. For this, he would need to take more direct authority over them, and then go in search of his materials. But if he does not allow them to pursue their goals outside their local galaxy, he will need to make a special effort to carry them outside that fold."

"Indeed, and this is a considerable effort beyond their present level."

"But not beyond his. I wonder how he would accomplish this. Still, we must make our preparations. I must now call on my children. If he is building an army, I must build my own. And we will reclaim our ancient home for this purpose."

✦✦✦

"Helm, my Brother, I have need for your assistance."

"Yes, Sister Kuroku. What service dost thou require?"

"I believe he is becoming anxious. I have observed where he is now limiting their forward momentum, and instead he desires to exploit, for lack of a better term, his local resources. I can see only one reason for this. He wishes to prepare for his return."

"I understand. But dost thou still believe he would choose to deploy another Agent of Unmaking?"

"I feel this is the only way, and for this he must find his supply. His minions do not presently understand the mechanics of trans-planar travel, though they do have sufficient technology to fold space for local transit. All they really need is an appropriate index to locate an endpoint, and I suspect he will likely take possession and direct them personally. But until then, he will need to train them for proper combat."

"My last impression of these Children was that they resembled a passive, intellectually refined variety. To transform them into such to conduct efficient warfare would demand a peculiar catalyst."

"This is true, and I do not yet know his intentions, but I am not waiting for it. I am making my own move now."

"Excellent, but what plans dost thou have at this time?"

"First, we need to present ourselves to Lord Ao and request him to command Shar to release her bane on my former home. She has never relented from her initial outrage, but this was once the home of my people, and I still make claim to it, therefore I must demand she rescind her shadow from our local star."

"Indeed, I must agree. We shall see to it. What dost thou foresee to follow this?"

"I will call upon my children, the Sarrukh, and have them return there. We will discuss a plan to refurbish our ancient home, to restore life, and I will nurture it, and set the Draconics to watch over it until they are ready."

"Thou dost intend to use this to counter the Primordial and his folly?"

"Yes, but we will do so as wisely as we can, and I shall lead them discreetly. And yet, we will still need an overt leader, one to guide them in a single harmonious direction, to ensure we have cohesion."

"Thou hast given much thought to this. Who wouldst thou suggest for this overt leader?"

"I have not made my choice yet, but this will take time to develop. I will make my decision as we progress forward."

The star that held Kuroku's home world had been shrouded with a shadow since the time of the dispute between the twin sisters, Selûne and Shar. Their argument resulted in Shar releasing this shadow over the star and therefore rendering the rest of the solar system in an icy freeze.

Shar was often ill-behaved, feeling like she was more deserving of attention in relation to her sister, who preferred the light and nurturing warmth. To compensate for this discrepancy, Ao, the leader of the local group of Estelar, made a compromise deal. With the promised revitalization of Kuroku's home, he would invoke the creation of two other realms, one for each of the sisters to manage as their personal garden. A council of the other Estelar would then offer their support to whatever lifeforms may grow out of this.

Kuroku then called on the Sarrukh to return. An expeditionary deployment arrived to examine the damage to their ancient home and begin making plans for its restoration. Within the great ark, a vessel the size of a small moon, in an operations center at the core of its research division, a group of scientists and engineers gathered to examine their task.

"Our ancient records tell us how it once appeared," submits one of the researchers. "It was lush and full of life, but now look at it."

"We should expect this much," infers another researcher. "It may sadden us to see it this way, but we have been absent for a great period of time. We cannot expect it to resemble what it once was, even under the best of conditions."

"True. But now, our first task must be to adjust the climate. Even with the local star at its normal output, the reflectivity of that icy surface will prevent any immediate improvement to the climate."

"I had a thought come to me a while ago," offers a third researcher. "Our ancestors likely brought away a large abundance of resources to build our initial fleet and to supply us until we could become fully established. This would leave the planet in a mineral poor condition."

"And so we might need to replace that if to give the younger society a proper opportunity to proliferate."

"Yes, but now consider this. We could resolve both of these concerns at once, if we were to import a small cloud of mineral-rich asteroids and drop them onto the surface."

"This is an interesting proposal," the second researcher suggests. "But not all at once… We should distribute them to offer a sporadic layering, and this would further assist with the climate, as the ice would counter the warming effect from the impacts."

"We could shape some of the projectiles to lessen the impact blast effect, and this might also serve to better bury the materials for later excavation."

"Good," the first researcher reflects. "This gives us our entry point. Then we need to begin building the ecological tables. What has the bioresearch segment decided for the species selection?"

"I was reviewing their list recently…" the second researcher begins, redirecting the group to a video table.

The group steps over to a table with a large holographic display surface. On the virtual interaction display, he calls up a research report conducted by another division on the potential choices for their specimens to transplant.

"The criteria we feel are most important include adaptability and rapid breeding cycles, which would therefore promote a strong urge to see progress on a smaller time scale, as well as tolerance for a variety of climate conditions and environmental provisions. Matron Kuroku desires them to be able to move forward quickly, as she is concerned for her opponent's progress factor."

"Of course…"

"They refined their search to a few selections, with one of these standing out for a number of reasons."

"Indeed, and what reasons are those?"

"First, the world we are looking at is recently emerging from an ice age, therefore it is important to record if any of the species are adapting to this change, and one of them seems to be making excellent progress."

"This would be a good choice in our case," the third researcher considers.

"It would, if you consider Khalen Ruuki will also be recovering from such a moment."

The three of them paused briefly to glance at the main screen on the wall and the image of their former home below.

"If you look at this image here," he points at the table. "We have a continent to the south, and this other larger body to the north, connected by a land bridge. Our studies describe a species of early sapient mammaloids that seem to have originated down here and then migrated north as the local conditions began to falter. They then diverged across this larger body."

"The climate conditions between these two should be quite different from each other," the first researcher notes.

"They are. This lower continent is near the equatorial belt, warm and arid in some regions, tropical in others, while the northern body is temperate and moist, and also prone to wider climatic shifting during seasonal changes. Further, the northern body is where the last remnants of the ice age were still present, at least until recently."

"Interesting, this represents a rather substantial environmental difference."

"Next, we also observed the remains of a secondary species inhabiting this region, but they were more specialized to that climate. Now they seem to be fading and supplanted by the new one."

"Is the new one destroying the old?"

"Some of our studies suggest a subtle merging taking place, with occasional interbreeding to produce a type of hybrid form."

"This would offer a curious level of diversification," the third researcher offers.

"Our bioresearch segment suggests sampling this species, especially from this recent merger, and maybe also from the eastern region, where they still remain true to their former origins. Our delivery zone is most similar in environmental conditions to this region here; therefore, a like-for-like transplant is recommended. We could then deliver them into different zones and see how they develop."

"Very good, and we should also sample a variety of the local flora and fauna to create a familiar setting for them to establish themselves."

"Absolutely…"

The group of scientists paused to study the display, where it presented both a male and female example of the target species. They were bipedal, largely hairless, with medium dark skin, and anthropological in design…humanoid.

◆◆◆◆◆

Kuroku's home…Khalen Ruuki, the Blessed Land, as it was known to them…was beginning to show new life, but it was not Sarrukh. The former owners of this world had now officially donated it to a new species of early sapient life. It would be their home from this moment forward, the ultimate contribution to a young society.

The process took several thousand years to fully calibrate the environmental and ecological balance. It began with the smallest microorganisms, working its way up through the stages of microscopic plants and animals, then to larger species that might depend on this smaller scale for sustenance, and then to an even larger framework beyond that. It concluded with the delivery of the top-level animal species, and several clusters of hunter-gatherer societies sampled from their original home world.

The hunter-gatherers were a primitive society just barely adorning themselves with hides and stone tools. They were acquired after being carefully tranquilized and transported, then arranged in a camp-like setting roughly resembling their original home, so as to minimize the shock of being transplanted into a new world environment. From here, they would hopefully discover their new home and learn how to survive in it.

Along the way, it became necessary for the Sarrukh to establish a number of temporary research outposts on the ground, many of which involved underground facilities to conduct their evaluations before releasing the finished product into the surface environment. Of course, the word 'temporary', when measured over thousands of years, is a very relative term, but the Sarrukh were no stranger to conducting their work on this time scale by now.

As their work was wrapping up, they slowly evacuated these facilities and shut them down. Time would eventually erase the evidence as the natural elements eroded the buildings until only rubble remained. Only the underground portions might show any vestige of their passage. But the Sarrukh were not finished yet. Kuroku left one final instruction for them before they departed completely.

"We are nearly completed," remarks one engineer. "The casing is solid and should not suffer any erosive effects from the surrounding material."

"We must be sure of it," replies another engineer. "The Matron desires this to survive over the long term unattended."

"I find it curious," another engineer wonders. "We are essentially creating a sort of time capsule here. The shell is sound enough to survive for tens of millennia, and we will seal it with an inert gas environment at low pressure to preserve the contents. The specifications look good, and we even left instructions in two languages on how to use it. But will these beings understand enough by the time they discover it to know what to do with it?"

"I can only answer that with the help of the Matron. It is her suggestion, so she must have a plan of some kind."

"I sometimes wonder how many of these plans she has in motion."

The engineers finished their work and closed up the chamber, which was located well below ground. Then they carefully buried the passage and returned to their ship. The world was now on its own, newly restored with a vivid variety of life flourishing on the surface. Once again, the Sarrukh said their goodbyes and departed from their ancient home, no longer theirs, no longer to be accurately called Khalen Ruuki, but now belonging to another species and whatever new name they might offer.

Kuroku looked down on her former home. She felt a tiny mote

of melancholy that it could no longer be properly described as hers, but in a small way, it still was. She anticipated at some moment she would likely need to return there as part of her grand plan…and in this way it would be her home again.

Chapter 6

UNINVITED GUESTS

"Maker Kuroku, they have arrived."

"I was afraid of this. They have been conducting studies to migrate away from their home for some time now. But what repercussions will this have in our space. I cannot allow them to disturb my greater plans. This disruption must be discouraged."

"What intentions dost thou have?"

"Thaliel, while I cannot place blame on them, this is a delicate situation."

Kuroku and her chief seraph attendant were watching a disturbing scenario unfolding within their apparition pools. She had conducted a number of sessions using her prophetic sight to watch for potential disasters and other calamities that might come to her former home, but this one might be problematic.

The world below had become the subject of interest to a migration of residents from one of the neighboring pockets, in this case the one owned by Selûne. Much like with Kuroku, Selûne had accelerated the development of her garden world with new life. This was not a common practice for the Estelar to perform, but in the immediate absence of anything alive in the local universe, a few exceptions were made. Unfortunately, her children, who made a rapid cultural ascent, were becoming restless to remain in their native home, and several clans were now making sojourns outward.

At the same time, Kuroku had also foreseen other potential migrations pending from a source outside the local fold. These would naturally require help from a higher source, simply to find the way, and her secrecy concerning her project was now bringing it into jeopardy, as someone seemed to be taking advantage of it. This could complicate things for her new children and her long-term goals.

She moved to another pool, one she might use to commune with the other Estelar, and focuses herself on the mind of Selûne.

"Selûne, I must speak with you," she announces.

"Maker Kuroku," answers a soft voice. "It is unusual, but I suppose not unexpected, to receive thy summons."

"Yes, and I suppose you know the reason. Your Children are intruding into my space…"

"I offer mine apologies, but this is not by my direction. They found their own way."

"I understand, but here we have our problem. I am working on a very special plan here, one which I have held in high confidence, and this intrusion may complicate this plan to the point of failure. Can you call them back home? Because otherwise I must send my Children to defend my space."

"They chose this of their own, and it is beyond my counsel that they should retract from this course. Our governance of our Children does not restrict them from their growth, and this would fall to the same principle."

"Of course, but you should know, my Children have instructions to defend my project from outside interference. I will instruct them to take a defensive stand, and perhaps we can encourage yours to retract, but if they should bring harm to my project, I may need to take stronger measures."

"What project is this thou dost speak of? I was not aware thine efforts were described in this manner."

"Perhaps so. I have special intentions to sculpt my former home for a specific purpose, one to which I have held in confidence with very few, including Helm, as it involves a matter of high security. The context of this effort extends all the way back to my younger days, when I first joined the Estelar, and the experiences I had to endure that now drive me to ensure such will never occur again. And ironically, a part of this relates to you and your sister, and what you once did to the place...with apologies, of course, but we certainly cannot have any more of that occurring. But the project is still in its infancy, and this is a critical time for me."

"I understand thy reference, and I sympathize. My sister can be difficult on occasion. As for thy project, I would wish thee good fortune, but again, I must reiterate my Children found their own way, and this extends beyond my boundaries to restrain them. I do not wish to deny thee my aid, but I feel my Children must make their own choice, and so must thou."

"Of course. I mean no ill will to you or your Children, but I must defend my own. Perhaps a compromise can be found. We shall see what we can discover, and if there can be a polite solution with minimal collateral effect."

Kuroku ended the link and returned to her attendant.

"Thaliel, send word to the Draconics, they must take a stand and use defensive means to...persuade...these intruders to refrain from their advance. Try to keep the bloodshed to a minimum, but demonstrate to these invaders that they are unwelcome in this reserved space."

"Maker," she asserts. "What if they refuse, or perhaps simply cannot retreat away from here? What if they protest the Draconics and their presence? I think they ought not to be familiar with their nature, and may simply view them as beasts."

"Yes, you have a point. This could be a problem. Very well, our compromise. Study them for how they behave and interact. If we must defend our project from despoilation, so be it. But perhaps..." she muses distantly. "I wonder who these people are on the inside. Observe how they live, how they work...their culture. Also, see how they interact with our own."

"Yes, Maker."

Over the course of the years and decades to follow, the invaders continued a determined advance, seeing the dragons as a threat, rather than a deterrent. The elves, as they called themselves, arrived in droves, many different clans of them, ranging in colors and varieties depicting their cultural and environmental origins. They established footholds, built cities, fortifications, and then marched forward.

Kuroku continued to watch. They were definitely a very well-organized society, this much she could not deny. They were also much more advanced in their wisdom and techniques than the locals, which was a little disconcerting. The local population, which were early humans, had demonstrated a reasonable growth rate, but these others seemed to be particularly gifted in the area of magic.

She also noticed something else. Rather than attempting to dominate or displace the humans, the elves seemed to be taking a supportive role alongside of them.

"This is a most interesting turn, Thaliel. Do you see it?"

"Yes, Maker," she nods. "They are encouraging the growth of the others. This seems to be creating a scenario of artificial development, more rapid than their natural course."

"This could actually be to our benefit. Perhaps we should consider this aspect. This could be our compromise element. But we still need to consider how to combine this with our greater plan."

"Maker, I can offer one thing of special interest, if it pleases thee."

"Oh? And what is that?"

"A new name for the world below. These elves, being the predominant society, have given it one of their own, and I suspect this may remain, as their culture seems to be taking a principal role here. They are calling it Tae'Eladar, which in their language translates as Beloved Green World. Personally, I find it rather pleasing."

"Yes..." she muses softly, and forms a subtle smile. "It is not quite as I imagined it, if to come out of our own work, but it will do. We will continue to watch. Instruct the Draconics to ease off, but do so incrementally. If they simply run away, this might raise too many questions. Clearly, our deterrent is not working, but if we make it seem these elves are winning the fight, it might instill a sense of pride. Then we will see where this new course takes us. We still need to develop a form of leadership to bring it all together, but if they can find their own unity, this might make things easier for us."

"What of the other incursions we foresaw?"

"Yes, and some of those are near at this time. I am certain at least a few will make trouble for us. We will need to watch carefully. I cannot be sure who guides them, but if they hold such values as to support rather than depose, maybe we could involve them as well."

✦✦✦✦✦✦

Centuries passed, and the so-called Age of Dragons, as the Elven society described it, was slowing down. But life was not settling as easily as they might otherwise desire. The first of what would be several major wars between the various elven factions was erupting as they attempted to carve out territories for themselves. These wars would later be described as the Crown Wars.

Along the way, other incursions arrived. Tae'Eladar was somehow becoming a central meeting place for multiple societies to converge. One of these was a stout folk describing themselves as dwarves. Initially, they did not seem too particularly keen on the elves, and were only cool-mannered with the humans. Time would smooth this out eventually, as they were forced to realize they arrived in a place already occupied by others.

"That one might serve some value," Kuroku notes. "If only for the variation of its habitat and skillset..."

"They do not seem quite as sociable as the others."

"In the near term, perhaps, but we may have no choice now. We must find a way to carry all this forward."

They continued to study the interactions of the new local races. Kuroku's project had become very complicated for all these incursions. She was concerned over the integrity of the project, and needed to reinterpret her plans.

Time continued to pass until Thaliel called her attention once more.

"Maker, we have something new."

Thaliel had been continuing to watch Darumon during this time. Their original observations were not forgotten, and he was keeping himself busy. But the complexity of the operation demanded her to call in a few assistants to observe other pools with different aspects of her studies.

"What is he doing? Where is he?"

"The signatures indicate he is conducting some of his own exploration now."

"Oh, he is, is he? What a surprise. What world is this he has found?"

The apparition pools had been targeting and following Darumon as he travelled. He had apparently become more active in recent times.

"It would appear he has found his way into another fold by now."

"As I would expect, but how did he manage this if his creations do not hold the key to this place?"

"I have been collecting reviews from mine attendants of his recent activities. He apparently initiated a clandestine research function amongst his creations. I did not present this to thee previously because I was uncertain of his direction. Now I believe I see the purpose, and it is deeply disturbing."

"Very well, give it to me."

"I believe this may be a preliminary form of research, and now he is testing it. This project involved the application of a unique device implanted within their minds to govern their behavior. He can now control their manners, directing them to his course without feedback from his subjects."

"As revolting as this is to my mind, I would not place it beyond his manners. This would answer the question of how he might turn a society of pacifists into warriors. And so he is using this as a test to direct this group into a new fold. But does this fold carry the dynamistic flows?"

"Mine indications tell me it does."

"Then he now has an endpoint for himself. But what is he doing there? Has he found yet another toy to play with?"

Within the pool, they observed Darumon, apparently in another of his disguises, parading around a world with a rather brutish society of beings. He was directing some portion of them into a flow.

"This is curious," Kuroku mentions. "Is that a portal he has there? Where is he sending them?"

"Wouldst thou care for me to orient the pool to follow?"

Kuroku considered the notion for a moment.

"There can be only two likely targets that make sense to me, and the first one is much less likely to make sense than the other."

"Maker, sometimes thou art very cryptic in thy musings," she smiles.

"It is an old habit. I do not see the purpose to send them to the home of his first minions, but if he is using them as an advance guard, maybe as a primer for some future exercise… Thaliel, bring another pool into focus for us."

Thaliel turns and moves to another of their pools.

"See if you can find any appearing on our own soil," Kuroku directs.

The chief seraph makes a careful survey of Tae'Eladar, directing the pool to conduct a filtered review of the land, searching for any energy disruptions from a portal arrival event, and then to see if this particular species was appearing through it.

"Maker, yes," she responds. "I regret to say, I see them occurring in the southern lands below the main societies of the others."

"I was afraid of that. I hope the unity the others have formed can contain this group. They do not look at all friendly. Inform the Draconics about this intrusion, and describe the nature of it."

"Do we have them advance on it?"

"I, uh… At this moment, perhaps we should leave it to the natives. They have been regarding our Draconics in large part as enemies, so let us not give them cause to think they must afford sympathy to this new group. If Darumon is behind it, the last thing we need is for our charges to take up sides with them."

"Of course…"

"But this brings an even more serious topic to mind. He has apparently found us as well, if to open a portal to our project."

"I regret to suggest it must have been during a moment when we were distracted with the local concerns."

"Yes, but what does he have in mind next. He may have peered in on us, found this place, marked it in his mind, and now…yes, I think he might seek to test us with this little foray, maybe to distract us, or perhaps to plant agents for later."

"This is curious, however," Thaliel offers. "He has found this place, but no one, not even the Great Powers, did take notice of his incursion within our fold."

"Surely, after so long, the Estelar would have forgotten him. We have not shared the details of our work with anyone other than Helm. Those who may date back that far would likely have forgotten, and none of the younger societies would know of it to begin with, except perhaps for a few ancient stories."

"Very well, but next on my mind is that he found this same world he once knew from his earlier possession, now to peer down upon it, but seemingly not recognizing it."

"Yes, this is a curious mention. Does he even recognize what he found, or might he simply think it is a world conveniently populated that he could use for some plan?"

"He would expect thy former home to be destroyed, would he not?"

"He should, so he might think himself lucky to find anything at all to gaze at. The alteration of this world over time might also offer a new guise. I think we should not give him cause to believe anything more than this."

Time continued to pass, and the reports accumulated. The last incursion had found a foothold, but the local races were now aware of it and holding a line against it. Meanwhile, their civilization had grown somewhat, even though it suffered several more Crown Wars. Now, much of their earlier internal positioning had established their territories, with the exception of one elven clan, known as the Ssri.

They were a dark-skinned clan with what seemed like a big chip on their shoulder. They were largely responsible for the ferocity of those wars, desiring to conquer everything and subjugating it under their authoritarian rule. As such, they were driven off by the rest into a series of deep caverns and subterranean domains. There they would smolder for their defeat, and their eternal hatred for everything above. They would also change their name to Drow.

At this time, no new incursions were present on the horizon. Thaliel continued to watch Darumon, but he did not seem to be making any new exercises outside his local domain. However, something else was beginning to catch her eye.

"Maker, this is curious."

"What do we have this time, Thaliel?"

"I am unsure how to describe this. I observed as he was engaging himself in an activity of an unusual design."

"How do we describe unusual?"

"He descended in another of his personas to walk amongst his creations. I observed a gathering in discussion surrounding a young child. It appeared as mostly medical experts, maybe some biology specialists, and a few others. And there was a vigorous debate over what seemed like a new discovery. But when the gathering adjourned to rest briefly, he returned and dispatched the child."

"What?!" she roars. "Is he now murdering children? This should be below even HIS level. Why would he do this?"

"I cannot be sure at this time, which is why I call it so unusual, even for him. If it involved something medical, why would he get involved. I do not carry the opinion he is a specialist in this area."

"I...wouldn't know, personally, but I suppose not. Could it be he is trying to defeat something dangerous? A new disease, perhaps? It would certainly put a crimp in his plans if a pandemic got out."

"Yes, it would, but I suspect that society is wise enough to provide the appropriate countermeasures."

"True."

"Even worse is the method he used...it was entirely abnormal. He drained it of its life essence directly, leaving a desiccated husk."

"That…is simply strange," she ponders thoughtfully. "But it would surely be uncanny to see. Maybe it was to disguise any describable cause."

"Possibly. Something must have occurred, and he is trying to cover it up with a most bizarre outcome…at least in their eyes. If thou wouldst permit me, I will attempt to refine my studies in this pursuit."

"Do so if you can. Though this child is now dead, and there may be nothing we can learn from it, perhaps you can listen to the words shared by the others as to what this discovery was about that might cause him to take this action."

"I will, Maker."

Thaliel calls in several of her assistants and they glue themselves to the pools to study Darumon and his creations, hoping to catch any word mentioned by the researchers who were once conducting this study. But nothing new occurs for many years after, until one day she sees another occasion.

"Maker, here!"

Kuroku rushes to Thaliel's side to study the images.

"What do we have here?" she asks.

"This child," she directs at the pool. "Another of the same, and this time I believe I see the cause. It has developed a most curious talent."

"A talent? He killed the first one for a simple talent?"

"Not a simple one, Maker. This is such that I would not expect to see in a mortal body. By the Powers, I might not even expect to see it in one of ours!" she chuckles feebly. "Observe. It appears to have found the means to detach its consciousness from its corporeal form."

"Fascinating…" she croons. "A metaphysical manifestation…"

Within the pools, they could see another gathering of researchers accumulating around a young child, or at least it seemed like it was the child, as the body of the child was neatly tucked into bed while an apparition of the same child was walking among the researchers and carrying conversations with a few of them.

"This might be one of those strange permutations Helm spoke

of once upon a time," Kuroku mentions. "Darumon used his own seed to propagate this species, and now we are seeing the result."

"And what a result!" Thaliel raises her brow intriguingly. "Even for a Celestial breed, this would be impressive. And look here," she points at the image. "Here he is observing the condition."

"And not at all happy about it, by the look on his face... Yes, I would certainly understand this, knowing him as I do. This would give us our answer. He caused this by his abrupt evolution of their kind, and now he is displeased by the result. But if this is a developing condition, I can hardly imagine it to be a mere happenstance with a select few."

"Indeed, they are evolving into a higher form by this measure. I might further suggest their, ehm...inbreeding as his Children..."

"Yes, he is the father of their species, in a literal sense of the word. So as half-siblings..." she clears her throat conspicuously.

"Right," Thaliel nods. "Anyway, this is simply amplifying the effect."

"And if he is so displeased by it, he will wish to contain it. He would surely never desire them to hold this level of authority. This could not be his plan, especially if he would prefer to use these devices to control them."

"Maker, his movements are becoming more critical as we progress."

"Yes, but again, we can do nothing from where we stand. Watch him for now. We will see what his final choice will be, and I will consider carefully where to go from there."

Over the course of the following years and decades, Thaliel and her attendants continued to watch. The breeding cycles of Darumon's creations were slow and far between, and so far, this occurrence was extremely rare. She observed as another child within Darumon's nest was discovered and removed, but this only prompted the local society to take more assertive measures to study the situation and preserve their children. Finally, she watched as he made a decision for his final solution to the dilemma. This followed after one more child was found, and this time relocated to a laboratory for better study and greater security, but still resulting in its death to deny them to learn anything from it.

"Maker, come quickly please," she calls urgently.

"What is it, Thaliel? What has he done this time?"

"He is reviving his Master!"

"Blast! Very well, this is to be expected at some point. But now what?"

"I overheard words that he intends to descend to the place of his creations. His personal meanderings suggested that he must now take their direct management, and the first of his objectives is to contain this new power of theirs."

"He is taking action to cover for his oversight. And if he is going in personally, he will now begin manipulating them to his whims. This may involve those devices, and then reconditioning them into a ready military. But reviving his Master? Using what to empower him? Without the dynamistic flows, Sargeras cannot survive in this state for long."

"I hesitate to suggest what he might use as a substitute," Thaliel shudders. "The flows are an organic creation, and um…" she directs her gaze into the pool at Darumon's sandbox world.

Kuroku grimaced at the possibilities, but she nodded subtly.

"Agreed…fuel for his service. So, perhaps we can offer a stifling effect to slow him down."

Kuroku moved away to ponder her options, while Thaliel waited and watched.

"His subjects do not know of his proper identity," she considers. "But I think it might be dangerous for them to learn the full truth. He might choose to send the entire lot of them into oblivion."

"We would not desire that."

"Such a thing also requires explanation for where that truth came from, as it would be lost by now to all but a very few. And although this would set him back considerably, it might also cause him to relocate and try again, and I have already waited long enough for this moment."

"Then we must allow him to continue on this course, for better or for worse."

"He will be a stranger in their midst, and so to gain their support, he might try deceiving them with some bit of nonsense. Our observations tell us they do not give themselves to worship higher beings."

"And for this, he could not represent himself as a Power within their eyes."

"But he could still represent himself as a very highly developed being. They might surely respond to that."

"Granted…"

"And yet, even though they might be pacifist, they cannot be fools. If we could send a subtle warning for them to reject whatever proposals he might offer, Sargeras would not hold the power to take any direct action, at least not presently, and Darumon is also limited without the flows. Perhaps we can use his creations against him for a time."

"In what way?"

"In such way that they are a very well-developed society of intellectual potential that might actually hold just enough power to resist them."

"This would create a most curious turn, but in the end, it might also create its own disadvantage, as his desperation drives him to enforce his position."

"Yes, it might…" Kuroku relents. "He might take them even with these objections. If he is one to use devices to govern them, he could try converting their full population by force."

She continues to explore her thoughts, and then steps over to the pool to observe the images again.

"Bring up an image of their government for me, please. They would be the ones he would most likely approach."

Thaliel redirects one of the pools to focus on the local government body.

"They call themselves Suuden-Aryku," Kuroku reflects. "Such an interesting name he gave them, the Lifted Ones. I wonder; why did he give them this name? Is it to denote what he did to them, or what he allowed them to do for themselves?"

"Meaning to say, whether lifted from their primeval origins or evolved into a higher society of intellectual maturity?"

"Yes. I find it curious, even amusing in a way, that he would afford them such a luxury to use this term…Lifted."

"You will recall once in their early history; they held a religious devotion to one they called the Creator. It was claimed he lifted them up from the ground to use higher minds."

"Yes! Good point, Thaliel. Therefore, they granted themselves this name, and he probably afforded this to give them a sense of direction. Still, it is curious. The Ancients never behaved this way with anything else they ever created. And now, here we have these people, and they use this representative body as their government…a Council of their Elders."

"The term, in this case, is actually that of a professional title, rather than one of age. It is an interesting formula, a technocratic republic."

"Yes, it is, and perhaps the last thing you might see created by a Primordial," she chuckles. "So, if Darumon should make his approach, they are the ones to make this decision. If they should admit him, he may then have his way with them, using deception, or perhaps these devices to control them. But if they reject him…"

"This could result in conflict, Maker," Thaliel cautions. "The Primordial may not carry his full potential in the beginning, but he could rob them of their essences to empower himself, and then subjugate the rest forcefully."

"This is a bad scenario for those people," she shakes her head. "If they go willingly, they might stand a better chance to survive until we make our own move."

"Maker, I feel I should ask this. Our creations do not hold this level of scholarly prestige. Thou art suggesting we would send them against this blight, but they are far from understanding even the simplest of studies necessary to carry them beyond their own domain."

"This is true, and we will need to correct this shortfall, and further to give them proper access to this destination. His creations are in an entirely different fold, and just as they cannot cross that bound, even with their high prestige, ours are even farther behind. We need an index, and although you and I could provide this, we cannot simply drop it in their laps…" she halts her words as a thought emerges. "Yes… WE cannot drop it in their laps, but what if a messenger came to us."

"Maker, thou hast lost me again… Who would be this messenger?"

"Allow me a moment to consider this aspect."

Kuroku paces around the room, mumbling quietly to herself. She closes her eyes and submerges herself into a partial trance.

"They would need to depart from that place," she utters softly. "He has yet to develop a proper military, and he mentioned making use of local resources. I foresee something occurring here, and it is not at all pleasant, but the greater demands of Creation might force our hand here."

"Maker, when expressed in such terms, the thought becomes disturbing."

"It does, but as a master of warfare, I must now call upon my finest tactical prowess. I must recall every trick I once learned in the games my former Master played. There may be sacrifices, and we can do nothing about this but to stay the greater course. Someone must come away from there. I foresee a pursuit in my mind now. A band that detaches and he gives chase. He will build his military, and give it practice along the way, but this band…" she sighs harshly. "He will find his entertainment, no matter how we play this, but at least it will follow a path."

"What path is that?"

Kuroku delayed her response as she delved deeper into her meditation. Thaliel waited, knowing these moments required her patience. Then, the Maker emerged with new instructions.

"Thaliel, call the Positive Primes. They have a new assignment. And call my children, the Sarrukh. I have work for them, and it must be completed quickly. Maybe we can salvage some old museum pieces as our platform."

Chapter 7
DIVERGING PATHS

"Thisss is madnessss…" the blue dragon asserts frustratingly.

"What is it… Thisss time?" asks one of two whites.

"Our purpossse here… Was to protect… And defend… Thisss world… From the outsssiders. And now… Look at usss. We withdraw… While they grow ssstronger."

"These were our insssstructions…" states the other white. "The Maker… Has reconsssidered… Their value…"

"Value!" the blue snorts. "Thisss world… Was to be home… To they who were planted here… By the ssSarrukh! The othersss… Now pollute thisss place…"

"But if the Maker… Decreesss they hold value…"

"Pah! Value! Do the orcsss hold value? They were the lasst… Invasion… And we were told… Not to pursssue. And yet… They do not show value… Of any sssort. They attack anything… They crosss pathsss with. They are the worsst of it…"

"Then what is it… You wish to sssay? That thisss world… Is losst?"

"We are Draconic! We are the guardiansss! It is our purpossse… To defend thisss place… And yet the Maker… Tellsss usss to withdraw… As the outsssiders gain ssstrength. I think the Maker.… Has lossst her way…”

“Be careful…” cautions the first white. “We do not wish… To anger the Maker…”

“Anger her? She does not… Even tell usss why… We mussst go to ssservice…”

“Or why to withdraw…” adds the second white.

“Exactly! The orcsss… Are clearly invadersss… We do not desire. At the very leassst… We should dessstroy them…”

“And the othersss?” the first white asks.

“They were not welcome… In the beginning. But I think… The Maker… Became sssoft. Perhapsss to avoid… Conflict… With the other… Essstelar…”

“What do you propose? That we go againssst… Her ordersss?”

“I once overheard… Conversssation… By the elvesss… As I was masssquerading… Among them. They arrived here… With the aid… Of a device… Created by… A potent group… Of magesss. It is a sssacred… And powerful object. After their migration… It was moved… To a sssecret temple… In a range… Of craggy mountainsss. It is sssaid… The temple is protected… By golemsss…” he snickers.

“Only by golemsss?” the second white chuckles. “Should we be… Frightened by thisss?”

“Maybe…” the first white considers. “If they were made… From clay… Or perhapsss… From mud…”

“Yesss! I ssso hate it… When I get that.… Lodged under my claws…”

The group shares a wicked laugh.

“Thisss is not… Our greatessst concern…” the blue continues. “Golemsss may be… A bother… To these sssmall onesss… But my point is thisss…”

The other two dragons returned their attention to their compatriot.

“The temple… Is nearly imposssssible… To asssault by land. There is only… A narrow passss… Leading up to it…”

"Thisss would make... Good ssstrategic sssense..." affirms the first white.

"Yesss... But only... If you were walking..."

The two whites pulled back in consideration of this obvious suggestion. Dragons were winged creatures. Walking is the least of their concerns.

"An aerial attack," the second white offers. "Would ssserve perfectly... Againssst thisss target..."

"And more," the blue affirms. "They could not... Mount a proper... Counteroffensssive... To take it back..."

"Leaving usss in peace... But to do what?"

"We would take possession... Of the artifact. I sssuspect... It might hold... More function... Than to import... These invadersss..."

"Sssuch as... To repel them?"

"At the very leassst..."

"And the Maker?" wonders the first white. "What do you think... She would sssay... To thisss action?"

"I am no longer... Interesssted... In her opinion..."

The two whites glanced at each other for the implications of this statement.

"What sssay you... My brothersss..." the blue urges. "We mussst be... United in thisss..."

"I will admit..." the second white suggests. "Many of our kin... Have fallen... In battlesss... Without proper... Definition... To our cause. What have we become... If not guardiansss... As we are meant to be..."

"If we go againssst... The Maker..." the first white adds. "We go againssst... All the othersss... Who are ssstill... Loyal to her..."

"It is sssimple..." the blue submits. "We are ssserving... Our primary purpossse... To keep thisss world... In itsss desired form... Clean from invadersss. We will sssimply... Put thingsss back... As they should be..."

"Maker," Thaliel asserts. "Mine observations of the Primordial and his servant suggest he is becoming anxious."

"Then we must be sure to move promptly when the time comes. Has he made any new ventures into that other fold? That is the trigger I am waiting for to see his true threat emerging."

"Not as yet, though I cannot expect it to be much longer. His military is well established by now, and there is nothing else for him to test it upon. And he has certainly taken enough merriment from that escaping faction," she frowns.

"I know, Thaliel, I feel for them as well, but it must be this way. He took enough time with it, more than eight millennia by now, and only nudging them along as his forces cleared the local surroundings. He must be making up for his long absence of pleasure. I have gazed carefully into my visions to see where they will travel and what may become of them, and along the way I gave instruction to the Positive Primes to make occasional visits to impart advice and guidance to their leader. I simply hope they can maintain themselves long enough to find their way through to us."

"Where wouldst thou expect them to make this initial contact? Here within our fold? They should hold no more potential to find us than the others."

"This is true. The visions are just now coming into clarity. I foresee a meeting, but this meeting is brought to us indirectly. And he will be the cause of it."

"How curious, he will be the cause of his own misfortune."

"In the meantime, the societies below are exhibiting enough unity that I believe we can build on this, but we need leadership."

"Maker, thou were once the leader of thine own. Wouldst thou take this role again?"

"Not this time, I must remain in the shadows. I will only emerge when the time is right to strike at my enemy."

"Then who wouldst thou choose for this? And what form would this take? A mortal leader would not hold the longevity we might demand to carry us until the time of our meeting."

"Indeed, and he might not hold the greater wisdom to know the way. And if to span multiple generations, we have the possibility of corruption along the way. No, this leader must be special. He must be durable enough to carry us the length of time until this moment, wise enough to understand his enemy, and strong enough to face him down. He must be a true warrior, but also a wizened governor, able to bring these people into harmony. We will require their full support to bring us the benefits necessary to see victory."

"This is a heavy burden, Maker. In the history of that society, no single member ever held that level of influence over so many. The proliferation I see of corruption and villainy would require a…" her voice catches as she begins to realize what she's saying. "Maker, just what manner of being art thou suggesting for this purpose?"

"Nothing less than a Celestial…"

"Indeed! But the Celestial races do not typically take part in the affairs of the Prime domains."

"This is true, and I want to see this world carry a future potential, even beyond our present interests. Therefore, this example will need to represent an exception to that rule, something unique, and I shall encourage him to follow this desire. But I must also make my own move, and lay several foundations for our new Children to follow. And for this, I will require additional aid from you and the others to assist me."

"It shall be done, Maker."

As their conversation wrapped up, one of Thaliel's attendants was arriving with a new report.

"Maker, and Mistress Thaliel," she begins. "I have new tidings to unveil."

"What is it?" Thaliel asks.

"They have come under attack again. That faction he has been pursuing."

"He does certainly seem driven to harass them. Is it again to set them in motion?"

"The attack resembles the others. It is forcing them to flee once more. But on this occasion, I have observed him in his familial persona carrying a debate with their leaders. I heard the words 'wild jump' mentioned, which in their language symbolizes to make a leap to places unknowable."

"This is it, I think," Kuroku affirms. "A wild jump? Where might this take them?"

They rush to the apparition pool just in time to witness the bridge of the huge vessel making its exit from local space.

"Follow it!" she orders.

Thaliel recalibrates the pool to follow the dimensional conduit through to its new endpoint. They see the ship and its occupants reemerge into real space, but the outside scenery is very different.

"Thaliel, identify their new location. Where are they?"

The chief seraph programs an analysis of the local space. Then on a hunch, she compares this with her previous readings of Darumon's travels.

"Maker, he is there now. This is that same domain we saw him enter before."

"Finally, this is the moment. From here he will likely go in search of his materials. His creations will not know how to collect the flows, so he may need to follow a less sophisticated process. If this is the case, we have the element of time on our side that he will be delayed in the processing."

"What course do we take now?"

"Now we must move to establish our side. Time is pressing on us, and once again, we have much work to do."

"Command me, Maker...what dost thou need of me."

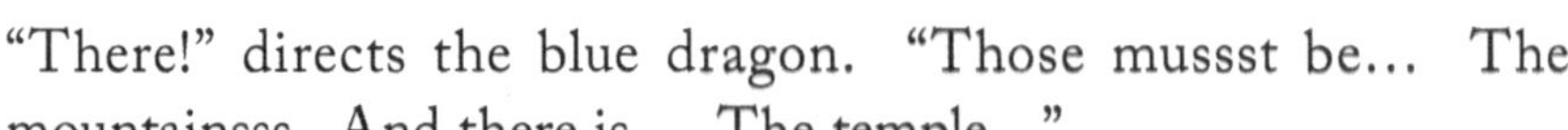

"There!" directs the blue dragon. "Those mussst be... The mountainsss. And there is... The temple..."

"Finally..." the first white relents. "We have been sssearching... Long enough..."

The three dragons, a blue and two whites, had been flying high above the land for months, looking for the temple that housed the special elven artifact they would hope to steal in a last-ditch effort to cleanse the world of so many interlopers. Finally, they found what they believed to be the one.

The temple was a well-built structure neatly nestled on a ridgeline in a rocky outcropping. There was a narrow winding path leading up from the valley floor, but no other obvious access in or out. For a ground assault, it would be extremely difficult to gain an advantage, as the walls overlooking the path would afford archers and mages to fire off shots at anyone making the attempt. From the sky above, however…that was another story. Although shots could be fired upwards, the main courtyard of the temple afforded a nice landing zone for anything airborne.

The three dragons circled briefly to study the situation below. On the ground, the priests and caretakers immediately began rushing around at the sight of the large beasts in the sky above. An alarm went out, and bells sounded of an impending attack.

The temple didn't hold much of a garrison, in part due to its location, which was believed to be secure enough not to warrant one. It was a secret holy site, and not many people actually knew about it. The golem guardians would serve the greater need to protect against thieves, but there was not much else to attract treasure hunters or any other visitors.

The priests and their guards arranged themselves on the walls in the defense of the temple grounds. The dragons made several low passes. The two whites used their breath weapons, in this case a spray of ice, to assault the exposed troops, freezing many of them in their tracks.

Arrows were fired off, along with several magical bolts, but these mostly just bounced off the dragons' thick scaly hides. The blue swooped in and released his unique weapon of electrical energy as a series of directed arcs of lightning. He then made his landing in the courtyard and began snapping and batting the guardsmen rushing into the fray. The two whites joined by his side and the three of them marched forward, systematically cutting down the remaining guards scurrying at their feet.

From deeper within the temple, the golems were called to

life at the arrival of the intruders. Several large stone behemoths plodded outside with heavy two-handed hammers. They stormed determinedly at their prey, but the mature dragons were too well-seasoned to be worried about this. For each golem to arrive in range, the dragons simply mauled and tossed them, picking them up in their claws and mouths, and throwing them down again, eventually shattering them into rubble.

Somewhere inside the temple, an elder group of priests hid and watched the carnage outside. They knew their meager defensive forces would not be enough to defeat these three creatures. They prepared to lock themselves inside the temple, first by closing the door, and then calling upon their elven gods to aid them in applying a strong holy seal to keep the door locked. This would prevent the dragons from immediately breaking through, and maybe give them time to flee. Then they proceeded through a secret passage leading out a back door and down a long stairway through the mountain to the valley floor below.

At the base of the mountain was a small village, which provided food and supplies to the temple above. It also had a stable. The priests each took horses and then sped away to warn the elven nations.

✦✦✦✦✦

Kuroku was overseeing a gathering of her Draconic children. She had assembled this group to make a selection. From here, she would ask for a volunteer, but the request was a solemn burden, as this volunteer would need to make a dire sacrifice.

"My children," she begins. "This moment has long been approaching. Once I did make a promise, and I have kept myself focused on this during my long existence. It was a heavy burden and it tested me on many occasions. Many have come, and many have passed, and I have seen more than my share of hardship. But my children have never disappointed me."

She examines the expressions of those in attendance before continuing.

"On this day, however, I have a special task to perform. This task is in preparation for the fulfillment of my ancient promise. Many of you may not remember this, and I do not speak of it openly, but there is an enemy I have sought for nearly an eternity. This is my fight, not yours. For this reason, I have kept you and so many others out of it. But now I must take action, and I must call on one of you to join at my side. But before you leap forward, you must know there is a grave cost to it."

She again pauses to judge their faces. Several murmurs usher up from the crowd.

"I do not take this lightly, and neither should you. Below us, in our ancient home, we have built a society. I feel the collection that has assembled within this society may hold a unique value to us for its diversity. In a way, I am actually very pleased about this, as it may offer strength and resilience such as we may not find elsewhere. But it still needs leadership to direct it on the path I desire to see my way forward. And this leadership must come in a special form, one that might command respect and admiration, as well as fortitude and wisdom. He must walk amongst them as a symbol, and he will carry them to greatness. But he cannot be one of us. He must be born to this…anew."

The membership of the gathering all glanced at each other trying to interpret the meaning of this statement and its relevance to their assembly.

"Maker Kuroku…" announces one member. "What do you mean… By these wordsss… To be born anew? Do we ssspeak… Of a child… To be born… Among usss?"

"A child, yes, but not Draconic… He must be in a form to resemble they who live there, as they must be able to associate with him on their level. They do not see us in the same manner. But he cannot be a simple mortal. Instead, I desire to bring a Celestial into this position."

The murmuring suddenly escalated as they discussed the premise of such a potent being taking control of the population.

"A Celessstial… In a Prime domain…" resounds another member. "How would they… Ressspond to that?"

"I can imagine… One resssponse…" replies a third patron. "Any who are corrupt… Would be mossst… Dissspleased!"

A gush of laughter wells up from the crowd.

"But consssider thisss…" the first member offers. "They who hold… Reverence… To the Powersss… Might sssee him… As a sssavior!"

The voices now croon with affinity.

"And as a Celessstial…" the second member adds. "He would likely… Represent… A formidable opponent… To any who might… Wish to take… His position… Away…"

The remainder of the group nodded in agreement.

"But my children," Kuroku continues. "Here is where we must come to the hardest part…the selection. I need a spirit essence to donate into this. I must create this leader, and guide him, to ensure he follows his proper course. And then I must also take my leave, to prepare myself for my own role. No one is to know of this, and you may not speak of it."

"Maker Kuroku…" begins the lead member of the congregation. "How would your role… And his… Play thisss part… In your upcoming… Engagement…?"

"I cannot reveal this fully. But he would lead the people, to condition them and make them ready for that moment when I need them. We will then launch at my enemy, once he shows his face, and that creature will not know what hit him."

Cheers and celebratory roars rise up from the crowd, until the lead member speaks again.

"Maker… The ssspirit essssssence… You require. How will it be… Applied…?"

"I will need to recruit aid from Helm, and maybe one other. I am thinking of Tyr for this point. We will provide him with the essence and have him create the Celestial, then nurture and train him until he is ready. By the time he comes to my side, he should be a potent force."

Another round of cheers sounds out from the gathering.

"But I will need a source for this essence, and it must be from a strong body."

Now the crowd goes silent as the meaning settles.

"Yes, I know this, my children, and it pains me to ask this, as someone must make this sacrifice for the greater good."

The assembled membership of dragons looks around at each other and another series of mumbled discussion is heard. Suggestions are made that it should be a mature member to offer the greatest strength. Several members can be seen nuzzling their mates in a moment of fret that they may lose someone close, until finally one member perks up and moves forward.

"Maker… I offer myssself…"

"Sssektazi… Wait!" calls another member. "You are highly honored… Among usss… As one of our… Eldessst membersss. But why would you… Choose thisss…? There is… No return from it…"

"I have lived… A long life… Here with you. The native energiesss… Of thisss domain… Provide for usss. I am not sssad… To depart… As I know… I will not be… Forgotten. Thisss offersss me… A new beginning… For a noble cause… To ssserve our Maker… In her lifelong pursssuit. There can be… No better reason…"

"Sektazi," Kuroku affirms. "You must be sure of this. You can hold no regrets. You will not recall yourself. Your old memories will be taken from you, and you will start a new life in a new form, with only fresh thoughts."

"I undersssstand… Maker. I have lived long… And ssseen much. The prossspect of renewal… Enticesss me…"

"Then we must begin. We must travel to Celestia and go before Tyr. I will call upon Helm to prepare the way for us. Both of us…"

"What?" yelps another member. "Maker! What do you mean… By that…?"

"This is what I spoke of earlier. I must also take my place, but I will do so in corporeal form. I will face my enemy physically, to look him in the eye that he will know who I am."

"Corporeal! You are our Mother… The Maker! What form will you take…?"

"I will still be your mother, and I will shine no less than I do now. You can be sure of that. I will not let this transition degrade me. But the process must follow its course, and it begins here. I will become as my Children again."

"A Draconic, like us?" asserts another member.

"The finest there could ever be! But you must keep my secret, and it will remain this way until my duty is complete."

"To arms! To arms! The dragons have taken the temple! They seek to steal the sacred staff!"

"Calm yourself!" replies a town official. "What dragons, what temple, and what staff?"

"The Temple of the Protector, the Staff of Ethers. A group of three dragons attacked us. Everyone has been killed, and the guardians destroyed. We sealed the doors with a holy ward, but I suspect it will not last long."

The priests from the temple had arrived in a nearby elven city. Their hurried pace left them weary and in a near panic. Now they needed to recruit aid to retake the temple, even though they knew a ground assault would be extremely difficult to succeed. With the ruckus of their arrival, people began pouring into the town square.

"The Staff of Ethers!" shouts a local priest. "But how? Did I hear you say the guardians were destroyed?"

"In fact, they were. The dragons were mature wyrms, and fought fiercely as they entered the temple grounds. We only managed to escape through the secret tunnels, sealing the doors behind us."

"What are we to do about this? The pass leading up to the temple is narrow and winding, not made for a large assault."

"Exactly," adds another priest. "And precisely the reason the temple was built up there to begin with. Attacking from the ground will be nigh impossible."

"One moment," interrupts a guardsman. "What purpose does this staff serve? Why worry so much over a simple staff?"

"This is no simple staff," responds the temple priest. "This is the Staff of Ethers, which our ancestors used to carry us from the old Fey world. It's a very powerful artifact, kept hidden and secret, stored away where it can be held in safety from those who might seek lost treasures."

"And now these dragons hold it?"

"Perhaps not as yet, but if they should break through the seals..."

"The dragons have long sought to dispel our people from this land," asserts the local priest. "In the hands of these dragons, this staff could possibly give them the power to destroy us. It must be returned to us! There can be no other way!"

"But the way up to the temple is treacherous," offers the second priest. "An army must travel as but a single column marching up there."

"And this makes them vulnerable. The temple was built to guard against such an intrusion."

The townsfolk begin mumbling vigorously about the implications, with more arriving as the news spread. Merchants came out of their markets, smiths from their shops, and the town square filled to capacity. Then a voice shouted above the other commotion.

"There can be only one way to approach this scourge! From the air!"

The townspeople halted and turned at the sound of the seemingly ludicrous suggestion. There they saw a travelling merchant band of uniquely gifted people. Gifted with wings!

"You there!" shouts the guardsman. "Yes, of course! But these are mature dragons, did you hear? No offence to you and your kind, but do you actually think you have the strength to fight dragons?"

"And why not? We have done as much in the past, during the Age of Dragons that we all fought against. I will admit our numbers were brought low, but we will not back away in the face of such a threat to our people. Would you?"

"I might agree, but this battle would fall largely on your shoulders.

We can send our forces on the ground, but the journey would be hard, and likely you would be the ones to bear the worst of the battle."

"If we do nothing, we all fail. It is better to fight and die than to die for nothing. We will gather our people and return here. Have your own ready by that time, and we shall see to this together."

The crowd rallies up while the visitors quickly depart to alert the rest of their people of the crisis.

Many days passed, and the city became the focus of a large massing of troops, many of them ground forces, and others belonging to this unique race who described themselves as Avariel. The local commanders gathered up their armies and gave the order to march forward.

The ground forces were the ones to launch first, allowing them time to progress in order to balance the timing with the winged troops. It was hoped that the combined arrival would work to their benefit, with the winged troops distracting the dragons while the ground forces worked their way up the mountain. Several more days passed when they came into view of the mountain.

The winged troops took to the air to circle around while the ground forces dashed towards the pass. It would be a hard climb, especially if made in haste. But to delay the ground movement might cause the aerial assault to fail, leaving the ground forces vulnerable to further attack.

"Look there..." the first white dragon directs. "They come for usss now..."

"It is about time..." the blue replies. "I was wondering... What was taking... Ssso long..."

"But look! Coming up at usss..."

"Cursesss! Not those pestsss again..."

"Avariel..." the second white observes. "A good many of them... Thisss should be fun. They are not... Particularly ssstrong... But they are... Maneuverable... In the air..."

"They are organizing... With the othersss..." the first white notes. "Hoping to dissstract usss... While the ground troopsss... Make their advance..."

"Prepare yoursssselves… My brothersss…" the blue intones. "The battle beginsss…"

The three dragons arranged themselves on the temple grounds, after mostly resting and contemplating the holy seal on the door, and waiting for someone to come around trying to knock them off their newfound perch.

The Avariel swarmed in flocks up the mountainside, and then began circling the temple, firing off a series of magical arrows. Several of them attempted to swoop down for a blindside hit with their specialized glass-like swords, which were made of a blend unique to their kind, only to be batted away.

The dragons once again used their breath weapons to spray frost and electrical blasts into the air, many of which caught groups of Avariel, either freezing or electrocuting them, and causing them to fall to the ground limp. The winged elves were dropping almost like flies, but they continued to fight furiously, and the dragons were taking damage, although slowly.

The ground forces continued to work their way up the mountain pass, largely unhindered except for the terrain. The air assault was working, but the Avariel were taking a lot of casualties. They moved quickly, darting in and out, taking up contrasting flight patterns to confound the dragons' ability to follow and target them efficiently.

"These pestsss!" the blue spits. "And I thought… I hated them… The firssst time… I sssaw them…"

"There are too many…" the first white admits. "And the othersss… Come clossser…"

"Their arrowsss…" the second white complains. "They are beginning… To burn!"

"We may need… To withdraw…"

"Withdraw?" the blue protests. "We ssstill need… The artifact!"

"The sssseal on the door… Is ssstrong… And they are fighting… Too determinedly. We may not… Achieve thisss one…"

The blue reluctantly understood this was true, though it was frustrating in his mind to let it go. But he and his companions were taking more injuries by now, and it wasn't looking good.

"All right!" he urges. "We will retreat. Let these pestsss… Have thisss world… And the Maker… Have her menagerie. We are finished here! But I will not… Forget thisss insssult!"

The blue leads the three of them out of the temple grounds, no longer attempting to fight, but now to escape. The Avariel pursued for a distance until it was clear the dragons were leaving the area, and then returned to the temple to see about their injured and watch over things until the ground forces arrived.

"Thisss battle… May be lossst…" the blue asserts angrily. "But those little onesss… Will not go… Unpunished…"

◆

"Then thou dost desire this one to be remade in a new form?"

"It must be so. I hold plans for him, but I must have another perform this task for me, as I will be occupied with some of my own. Therefore, I have chosen you, as I feel your teachings will work best for this cause."

"And what form dost thou desire? Thou didst mention that of a Celestial breed, correct?"

Kuroku was in conference with Tyr on her desires to provide a spirit essence to create her new leader image. She and her selection, a gold dragon named Sektazi, along with Helm to offer his support, were standing in Tyr's court discussing her terms.

"Yes, my thoughts are to keep in line with my original pattern. I am aware of other examples created once by such as Lathander and Corellon Larethian, who chose amongst the mortal races of Tae'Eladar to create their own. The premise is intriguing, and would serve my needs perfectly. Therefore, I would wish to remain with the original human frame, as what we first installed, and as such, ask for this to be Aasimar."

"The hybridization of such as ours and a mortal-child is a rather unusual process to undertake, to say nothing of the need to ask for it, and for what purpose it may serve. And then, thou wouldst ask that he be given special training?"

"Yes," she affirms. "For this, I would make a proposal. The training will demand time and experience. He will serve in your court, study within your halls, be sent on your errands to perform your tasks. He will earn his way to receive your blessings and gifts. We shall make a contract of service. I believe a term of one millennium will be sufficient to serve my needs and yours. I want him well-trained, well-experienced, and well-equipped to serve my greater needs."

"Thou dost demand a fine example. What would be thy end purpose for this?"

"Brother Tyr, I would answer that, if only for my need of secrecy to ensure my final goal remains untainted. In short, I need a champion of unique proportions. I have in mind to assign him to my former home on a special mission. But he cannot be a common mortal, and instead must be of such proportions that he is virtually unconquerable by any others. Worlds such as this tend to be too chaotic to allow a common man to hold rule. Such an example does not carry the longevity, nor the clarity of mind and durability of body to see it through to completion."

"Such is the case with all mortal domains, Sister Kuroku."

"I know, but THIS one is destined for something special, and it must follow a specific path with a predictable outcome. And he must be the one to lead it. Therefore, I ask that you grant this to me and provide me what I need to serve this purpose. In the end, you will see the result, and I think you will be pleased, as it will carry a high grade of quality. But to meet that end, we must follow a pristine path."

"This is curious, but thou dost hold solid rapport with us during thy long partnership. I shall provide this unto thee according to thy designs. When the result is complete, wouldst thou desire him to be transferred unto thee?"

"Not precisely a direct transfer. He will know what to do of his own accord, as I will see that he develops an interest in this new future as a challenge to overcome. I wish him to choose this path, rather than to be assigned to it. I think the enthusiasm to seek this path will offer its own inspiration."

"This is a most clever approach. And it certainly does offer a layer of intrigue."

She now turns to Sektazi, who had been standing by patiently, listening and waiting, feeling a little nervous, but holding strong.

"Sektazi, you will hold a special place within my heart and my mind. The journey may be long, but I believe you will serve an honored role. And one day, we shall stand together, although you may not know our past, but we will share a magnificent future."

"Maker…" he croons. "The thought of ssserving… Pleasesss me… That I have… Thisss moment… To offer myssself… To your great cause. Perhapsss even more ssso… To hear of thisss… Curiousss plan…" he snickers. "Thisss should be… Mossst interesssting to sssee…"

She reaches out to caress his head, and then steps back, sharing one last look before she knew she must leave. She closed her eyes and departed from the local realm back to her own, with Helm following behind her.

"Brother Helm, I must also be sent forward."

"I recall this mention. Thou dost take a most curious turn with this path."

"It is necessary. I wish to present myself to him in a form he will take notice of. His once great champions now turned into a new breed of even greater design. And I would have him know who did this."

"Thy rage with him has never diminished, Sister Kuroku. Art thou aware of this?"

"I am under control, my old friend. Simply help me with this much."

"Where wouldst thou desire to be sent, and in what form?"

"I will tell you, and you must carry me."

She turns to look at Thaliel, who had joined them by now, and together they began to prepare themselves for this new twist.

✦✦✦

On the world below, in a lonely cave tucked away within a distant mountain range, was a lone female silver dragon. She had taken up this residence after retiring from her former duty in the service of the Maker, now simply relaxing and reflecting on her past achievements.

As a Silver, one of the Metallic breeds, her kind were somewhat more respected amongst the people of the world, as they had developed a reputation for being more sociable and cooperative than the more notorious Chromatics.

She had been contentedly musing over some of the local affairs she had heard recently from the outside when she noticed a strange shifting of the light within her cave. It was unexpected, but she knew right away that she was receiving a visitor.

A column of light descended from the ceiling of the cave to the floor. Within that column was a shimmering orb floating down and taking shape. The silver dragon gazed at it, knowing almost instantly what it was, and taking up a reverent stance to welcome it.

Thaliel had arrived in view, having materialized out of the glowing ball. She turned to the stunned expression of the large silver beast.

"A ssseraph…?" the dragon wonders. "Why do you come here…?"

"Child of the Maker," Thaliel explains. "We have a special chore for thee."

"A chore. But I thought… My work was done…"

"A Draconic's work is never truly done," she smiles gently.

"Of courssse. But what work… Do you have for me… Thisss time…?"

"This one is uniquely special, and very discreet. The Maker herself demands absolute trust and dedication."

"I undersssstand. She is mossst wise. Tell me… What mussst I do…?"

"Thou art to bear a child for her."

The Silver pulled back abruptly at the outlandish suggestion. To go into battle, to protect someone or something, to perform some great deed in the traditional service of the Maker, this much would be expected…but to have a child?

"What...? A child...! Is thisss what she asksss...? But I have no mate..."

"Perhaps, but this is not just any child. Thou cannot reveal this to anyone. The child will be delivered unto thee artificially."

"Artificially! Ssservant of the Maker... What do you mean... Artificially...?"

"Quite simply, a child will be created within thy body. Thou wilt then give it life and nurture it, much like any other. And the Maker has selected thee, as thou art not currently in full service, and asks thee to provide thyself for this cause. Wilt thou comply?"

"I would not hesitate... To comply... With the Maker... But thisss... Is very ssstrange..."

"I understand, and we do not make this request lightly. There is a greater need, which must remain hidden for now, and can only be made apparent at the appropriate time. But for now, thou must prepare thyself. Lord Helm will bring this unto thee, and thou wilt care for it and nurture it until it can carry on its own. An explanation may come at a later moment, but until then, the Maker thanks thee for this."

Thaliel bows as the cavern begins to experience a new shifting of light, much greater than before.

Helm now emerges as a planar manifestation into the cave, and the silver dragon feels herself very small for the majestic visitation into her humble home. She settles herself as Helm reaches out to her, laying his ethereal hand onto her body and delivering a blessing that dynamically creates a new life within her.

Dragons are best described as a saurian species, much like their Sarrukhan ancestors, and as such, they are egg-layers. But unlike most common reptiles, these beings will stay with their young to care for and nurture them. Therefore, the Silver suddenly feels the urge to deliver an egg. She glances around urgently to gather together any spare thatch and straw she had lying around to create a nest before laying her new egg into it. Then, with his work done, Helm retreats to his native realm, and Thaliel departs back to hers to continue her other duties.

Chapter 8

INCARNATION

His eyes opened to see a brightly lit structure, not immediately knowing what it was or why he was waking up here. It gave the impression of a temple, or the grand hall of a palace. Rows of pillars rimmed the massive structure, and he began to surmise it was a court of some kind. The air was sweet, and everything shimmered.

He looked around and saw the shapes of delicate orbs of energy drifting by through the air, along with feminine forms on wings moving along corridors behind the columns. Although he could not recall ever seeing such creatures before, he somehow knew these were called seraphim. As his view turned full around, he next took notice of a large throne set atop a dais above a series of stairs.

Sitting on this throne was a being of great size. His presence was aglow with wisdom and authority, appearing timeless, with flowing white hair like that of extreme age, but also appearing broad and powerful in body. Curiously, he also seemed to be missing his right hand, and his eyes were closed, as if he were blind.

"Thou hast awakened!" he announces with a prominent booming effect. "And thou dost have questions of thy new existence! Indeed, thou dost even bear questions of mine own company. Ask, and I shall answer all that I can, all that I hold permit to answer."

The man was clearly confused and disoriented, mentally asking himself who he was and where he found himself, having no apparent memory of his own existence. He prepared to speak, but the being gave his answer before a word could be uttered.

"Thou art here in my court, in a Fold we describe as Mount Celestia. This is the domain of my home, and it shall be thine as well, for a time. Thou didst arrive here by thine own will, from a place where thou didst once hold another form. Thou art a petitioner here, fresh of mind and purpose, and therefore thou hast no name thus far, so I shall give thee a name. I shall call thee Thaelyn."

The man was grateful, at least insofar as anyone could be under these conditions, to now have a name, but this still didn't answer anything about who this other being was and how he came to be here. Once again, the answers were given before the man had the proper opportunity to ask them verbally.

"I am Tyr, Lord of Justice!" the great being thunders. "I am the Power that does make residence here, and I shall be thy tutor and mentor during the time of thy contract."

So far, Thaelyn found his questions were being answered before he had a chance to actually pronounce them. He was determined to employ his own voice by now.

"My new...mentor?" he offers gently. "I do not understand. Please tell me how I came to be in this service. I have no memory of anything before this."

"Indeed, such is the way of thy transference. In thy previous form, we did engage in discussion, whereby thou didst submit thyself into a contract of service within my court. The terms of this contract are specific, and the bindings limit me as to what I can now reveal back unto thee. Nonetheless, what I can reveal is as follows. Thou didst present thyself forward to receive a new form, specifically such a form as what thou dost now behold. This form was created by my hand and given unto thee. The essence of the spirit thou didst provide prior was then incorporated into this form, and thus thou dost now hold claim to thy new existence."

"So very curious... Did I give a cause for this?"

"One such was stated, but only partially, and yet I regret that the bindings deny me to give unto thee this answer directly, as these bindings involve other parties who must remain undisclosed. I can only suggest that this may come about of its own, and at such time as it seems warranted."

"Very well, I will watch for that, but then about this contract. What form does it take? I should know what is expected of me, should I not?"

"Indeed. The terms of the contract, by mutual accord, are as such: The term shall cover a period of one full millennium. During this time, thou wouldst serve here within my court. I will train and educate thee with my privileged teachings, and thou wilt use this during the course of thine engagements. Thou wilt also receive, from time to time, as thy endeavors may grant this upon thee, the blessings of distinctive qualities deserving upon thy breed. I shall offer these unto thee over the course of thy service, to extend and enhance thy prowess, and to provide thee with greater potential to overcome greater challenges."

"This sounds very generous. What manner of work will I perform?"

"The duties may vary as the need arises. Here, within this domain we describe as the Great Wheel, there may be many demands. As thou dost grow and mature, so too may be the demands upon thy service. Thou must consider thyself in a form of training, and this training does not ever truly relent."

"I understand. And therefore, your teachings will help me to perform this service, and I will mature to provide you with greater service as time progresses. What might we see at the end of this contract? Is there a predetermined direction for me?"

"In a manner, there is always a predetermined direction, though I do not hold one for thee myself. When thy contract is complete, so too will be thy need to remain here. Perhaps, at that time, thou wilt find some suitable course that is appealing to thee."

"I see. I will be free to find my own direction after this. It sounds as if I entered into this agreement at least as much for the education and training, as anything."

"Indeed, but thou dost need to understand the most critical of thy lessons. We shall give unto thee our teachings, and these teachings will grant upon thee such great wisdom as it travels beyond that of the Child societies. And yet, here will be the highest mandate thou must abide by. We who call ourselves the Societies of the Estelar do hold specific directives, and thou wilt also be held to this same bond. Among these is that we choose to nurture and cultivate the Children of Creation, but never to bestow upon them that which they are not yet mature enough to behold of their own accord. All life is precious, but it must find its moment when that moment is due."

"These are the policies of the Estelar, and I am one among you? We appear quite different in form."

"Perhaps so. But I would regard thee as a Child of mine own, and thou dost present thyself in this form we describe as Celestial. Thy breed, in this specialized form, doth carry the designation of Aasimar. It is in part derived from our own, and in part from a specific Child society, of which perhaps thou wilt learn about during thy tenure. And yet, thou art as much a member of our Society as any of our own likeness."

Thaelyn looks down at himself, trying to analyze his physical form in relation to the being on the throne, and further to wonder about the other part from this Child society. It was clearly different, but by the description, this seemed like a crossbreed of some sort, and this only added to his initial confusion. But he decided to dispel these musings for now, as he would surely learn more about it at another time. He was only just beginning.

A group of scholars was called out from a corridor. They ushered him away to a vast library, ornately decorated with sculptures and artwork. This is where he would begin his lessons. He was placed at a desk, and the scholars began presenting him with a series of devices resembling neatly cut crystals that radiated with their own internal light. They presented holographic simulations above them, offering lectures and visual illustrations for detailed studies. These would be the first of what would surely be many lessons to come, covering a wide variety of extraordinary topics.

Screams echoed across the small town in a remote mountain region, the most recent of a series that had been occurring over the course of the last century. Every year, the local citizens were assaulted by the three dragons that once attacked the elven temple. But with that plan failed, the dragons have instead taken to terrorist tactics to bring suffering to those who posed the greatest insult in their minds on that day of the battle.

The town was a mountain village owned by the Avariel elves, the ones who made the initial assault on the temple to retake it from the dragons. The dragons took particular offence from this variety of elves, if only due to their gift of flight. Now they were laying into them to return the favor. The tactics they were using were brutal and swift. They were making short attack runs to cause large-scale damage to homes, marketplaces, and farms, attempting to cripple the elves and whittle them down incrementally, essentially taking their time to impose the greatest amount of pain.

The Avariel were trying to hold the line, but the dragons were simply too powerful, and hit without warning. This caused many of the winged elves to fall in combat, and thus diminishing their numbers slowly.

"Attendant Seraph, I come to speak with Maker Kuroku."

Thaliel was called to the attention of a visitor arriving to meet with Kuroku. This was an unusual visitor, as she was not known to get out much and interact with the other Estelar.

"Aerdrie Faenya," she muses curiously. "I have never had the opportunity to meet with thee before this moment. Thou dost carry a noteworthy presence, if also a detached one. What service can I offer?"

"I have a need to make consultation with Maker Kuroku concerning a matter of grave import."

"My apologies, the Maker is not currently present to attend to thee, but she gave me authority to represent her in her absence. What matter dost thou desire to discuss?"

"It concerns her Draconic guardians and their assault on my Children. Why would she demand this? I once held the belief that her campaign to defend the Prime domain had ended."

"What?" Thaliel gushes. "Wait a moment. What Draconic and which Children do we speak of?"

"My Children, the Society of the Avariel. I have heard their cries as they are assailed by a faction of Draconic. This sequence repeats periodically, and their homes are destroyed without cause, as they do not make offence to warrant this action."

"This is the first I have heard of this action. The Maker has not given instructions for any further pursuit of the Societies below. Her last word was to withdraw and attend to other duties. If this faction is conducting itself in this manner, it is not by her command."

"Then she must investigate and make amends. This action is unjustified."

"I would agree. I will deliver the word, and try to bring my own investigation while she is absent. What recourse are thy Children taking in their defense?"

"They attempt to resist, but their numbers are diminishing. If amends are not brought soon, they may vanish altogether."

"This is undesirable…" she shakes her head. "May I offer my advice as an interim solution? Thou should inform them not to make their resistance. This may be a futile pursuit for them. Instead, they must retract and evade, to preserve their numbers. I will inform the Maker, but she is currently engaged in a deeply immersive task and outside my reach at present."

"Very well, I will see to this much and await the Maker's response."

The goddess makes her exit from the local domain while Thaliel ponders this new situation.

"Draconics assaulting one of the mortal societies…and without authorization… This would be a violation of the Maker's last directive."

She rushes away to begin her investigation, first by trying to locate this dilemma within one of the apparition pools.

"My daughter…" the mature dragon soothes. "Did you sssleep well… Thisss eve…?"

"I had…another dream…Mother…"

"What dream… Did you have… Thisss time…?"

"I sssee visionsss…in my mind. Facesss…voicesss… And I hear namesss. I feel that…I should know them…like lossst echoesss… in the wind…"

"You have had many… Of these dreamsss… And they ssseem to be… Growing in number… And intensssity. I worry for thisss…"

"No… I think…there is a reason…but the wordsss…are not there. I sssee a face…and she ssspeaks to me…"

"Who is thisss… That ssspeaks to you…?"

"I do not hear…a name…but she is there…not like usss…but different…"

"What does she sssay…?"

"She tellsss me…to be ssstrong…to grow…to learn…and one day…I mussst find her…"

The mother dragon looks at her small daughter with curious eyes and a turn of the head. She might expect something unusual to come from this child, but to hear her telling of a vision that she must go in search of someone, or perhaps something, was unexpected.

"You are ssstill… Very young…" she offers supportively. "I think… You cannot go… In sssearch of riddlesss… Jussst yet…"

The years continue to pass, and the sounds of shouts are heard rising up from yet another Avariel village.

"We need to flee from this place!" cries one citizen.

"This is our home!" shouts another. "Why do they attack us? We have done nothing to them!"

"I can only think it must be related to the battle at the Temple of the Protector," urges a town elder. "These are the same three who invaded it."

"The same? How do you know?"

"I was there! I fought in that battle. Many of us were killed, but we drove them out of the temple. Now they simply want revenge."

"Revenge! For driving them out of OUR temple? This is madness!"

"Madness or not, they are here now."

"Listen to me," shouts a priest entering into the conversation. "Our goddess demands us to save our people. We are told not to fight them, but instead to run. They are too strong, and we only lose more of us. We will rebuild our homes when they are gone, but most important is to keep our people alive."

"For how long?" the elder demands. "How do we fight a battle if we do not fight the battle? They come, and we run. They destroy our homes, and we rebuild, only to see them come again."

"I do not have the answer to that, only that the Winged Mother is watching us and will guide us. This is all I can say for now."

The Avariel, in their desperation, can think of no other way but to pick up and leave the area until the dragons have finished their rampaging for the year. But they knew this would come again next year as well.

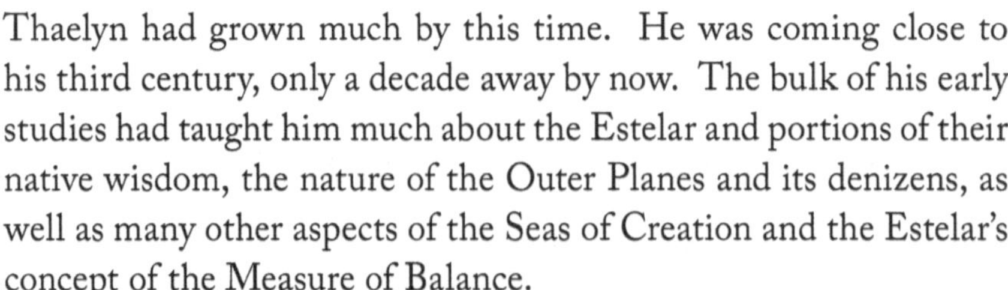

Thaelyn had grown much by this time. He was coming close to his third century, only a decade away by now. The bulk of his early studies had taught him much about the Estelar and portions of their native wisdom, the nature of the Outer Planes and its denizens, as well as many other aspects of the Seas of Creation and the Estelar's concept of the Measure of Balance.

His duties had been varied so far, with many of the early examples being mostly errands to give him experience to find his way around, discover and interact with the other societies that live amongst the planes, and to develop his physical and mental prowess to prepare him for his higher service potential.

Along the way, he met with people, developed a few casual friendships, and learned the manners of social interactions, which he found to be very intriguing and potentially valuable to improve his own etiquette.

He still wondered on many occasions how and why he would make such a curious proposal to Tyr for this contract. During his time in study, as well as his interactions with others, it soon became apparent that simple spirit entities do not make a habit of offering proposals to the Great Powers. And yet, oddly enough, he was an exception to this rule. He began to feel there was a reason behind it, one that Tyr might know about but was forbidden to reveal. In that first moment, when he awoke in Tyr's court, and this moment still occasionally echoed in his mind, it was suggested that he might learn this reason over the course of time. To this end, Thaelyn began to consider his own twist to his development.

He considered that his creation was intentional, at least as much to receive this extended education and training. But whoever, or whatever it was, that came before Tyr that day, desired to serve a purpose. What purpose? That was the question. Needless to say, he probably should proceed with care, and perhaps also a bit of guile, to ensure this purpose might carry forward unhindered. Although the Celestial races were commonly known in many places amongst the planes, it might be best for him to walk a finer line. It may be obvious that he was one of them, but perhaps he should not reveal too much about himself to just anyone he might cross paths with.

The concept fell in place naturally with the policies of the Estelar and their Measure of Balance, which he thoroughly believed in. But if he truly desired to develop himself this way, he must understand more of the interactions of the races and various lifeforms he might encounter.

Living within the planar domain known as Mount Celestia

resulted in a rather strict cultural doctrine and social structure, and this didn't give him much leave to explore alternate forms of interaction. What he needed was an occasional escape from his many duties, and fortunately Tyr would give him time to find relaxation. During these moments, he had discovered the city of Sigil.

Sigil was a heavily urbanized development with a peculiar twist to it. It was an independent body among the Outer Planes, an artificial structure, generally designed as a neutral meeting place where residents from different, often opposing regions of the Outer Planes might meet and interact, within reason, and without waging war on each other.

The city appeared in the form of a large toroidal body, like a giant donut, but hollow, with the city occupying the interior surface. There were no doors or windows looking out, and the only way in or out was by way of portals. Hidden within the city, among the many nooks and crannies, were a myriad of portals leading to any number of locations around the planes. Knowing where they were was more of a chance discovery than common knowledge, and you also needed to know how to use them, often requiring some manner of key to unlock and open them.

The people who lived there held many racial backgrounds, including a few imported from the mortal races. But one thing you would not find would be any member of the Estelar, other than the governess of the city.

She was known locally most often as The Lady, although many might whisper behind closed doors an alternate form, calling her the Lady of Pain. She was not necessarily an oppressive ruler, simply very rigid. Her first and foremost objective was the security and protection of the city, and since she allowed so many varied guests to come and go, her rules had to be very strict.

Thaelyn had developed an interest in visiting the city whenever he had his free moments. It presented him with the most variety of social and cultural interaction of any destination he had ever visited. During his visits, he met with people, including other Celestials, with whom he could find common ground for conversation and social interaction. The city might also offer an occasional opportunity for him to test his skills, and even to learn something new to bolster his already swelling repertoire of wisdom. And among these was one in particular.

"Your tail seems a bit lopsided today, Kimasxi. Have you been sweeping the sewers with it again?"

"If it's crooked, it's because of the shock of seeing your ugly mug trouncing around twice in the same year!"

"That is only due to the cycles blowing your distinctive musk my way that I must investigate what died around here."

"And it might stay dead if only to see your shiny backside storming along to tussle up the Duster tables!"

"Indeed, and the last time I saw those tables, I mistook it for your private boudoir."

"My boudoir is the last place I would want a stuffy-headed berk from Sunshineville to come visit!"

"Absolutely! As I am quite sure what lies beneath would burn at the very sight of true cleanliness."

"Aargh!" she screams. "Thaelyn…" she pants after their long tutoring session. "You've come a long way. I can't believe it, but you actually wore me out with that one."

"And I thank you, Kimasxi. These sessions with you have indeed opened my eyes to some fascinating dialog."

"I still can't believe you, of all people, a Celestial from the primmest part of the Wheel, would be interested in taking lessons from a fussy old tiefling like me."

"We must find our studies where they are best delivered, and you surely do have the goods to offer."

"All right then, that's all for today. I need to rest."

Thaelyn offers a polite bow and leaves the room. He returns down a hall to a foyer where he meets with the headmistress of the establishment.

"Thaelyn," she croons. "I would not have believed it if I did not hear the screeches echoing down the hall. You gave her a good run today."

"Grace, I might suggest we gave each other a good run. It is such an exhilarating sensation to spend time in here."

"Such a curious statement coming from a Positive Ordered. You do recall we describe this as a brothel. What would your Father say to this?"

"I do not specifically feel this would affect my other duties; therefore, I am of the opinion it is not necessary to concern him with this inconsequential detail," he grins cutely.

"And that also tends to defy my preconception of a Celestial. Very well, as you desire. Do you wish to make a visit with…um…" she rolls her eyes seductively around the corner of the hall.

"But of course, Grace!" he admits heartily. "How could I make a visit here in the city and not pay honor to the one I look forward to seeing the most."

"She is currently available. Her last appointment just finished."

"Indeed!" he grins and proceeds to the hallway again.

This time he turns the other direction, as the building formed a circular pathway leading around a series of rooms which served as parlors for the various ladies serving up their skills.

Although the building was described as a brothel, it was not an establishment for carnal pleasures. Instead, this one catered to intellectual stimulation, and the ladies who served here were in fact students in a local guild known to specialize in emotional and psychological sensations. Any manner of sensation was on the table here, from the simpler forms of emotional release to the more complex forms that combined deep permutations of psychological anxiety and revelation.

The guild was one of several in the city, and each of them held their own beliefs. In this case, it was as much a form of study as a religious doctrine, believing that to excel in one's ability to perceive the vastness of the psyche might grant higher wisdom and enlightenment, a form of transcendence.

Thaelyn approached the door and knocked gently. A moment later, a young lady answered and immediately displayed a bright smile across her face at the familiar arrival.

"Ecco, my sweet…" Thaelyn coos. "It seems like half an eternity every time I am away."

"Only half an eternity?" she projects in her thoughts with a mild pouty face. *"And what about the other half?"*

"Ecco, I think it goes without saying that one half or both is already too long."

She brings him inside and they take up seating in a set of leisure chairs, sitting opposite each other so they can efficiently carry their conversation.

Ecco was mute, though not by nature. She had lost her ability to speak some time before, and was now mostly limited to writing notes, or in Thaelyn's case, simply projecting her thoughts at him.

Thaelyn had recently gained one of his Celestial gifts, in this case telepathy, and now she helped him practice. Although she was not telepathic, she could speak with her mind's voice, and he could hear her. He might also occasionally project his thoughts into hers as a way to practice his new skill. But overall, this gave them a chance to communicate.

"Thaelyn," she begins. *"How have you been?"*

"I have been quite busy, as you can probably guess. My Father has me working now as an inquisitor within his court, and I must say it is quite the challenge!"

"To serve in the court of Tyr must be a challenge no matter what role you play. But now as an inquisitor…what manner of service does he command from you?"

"For one, I hold investigations and take testimonies from they who might bear witness to the misdeeds of others. I have also been involved in a number of interrogations, which can be rather difficult on occasion, depending on the individual. Some are more resistant than others to reveal what we need to bring proper justice."

"I can only imagine what you might see and hear. Have you brought any new sensations back to me?"

"Ah, my dear, I know how you love these moments. Let me see now. Have you ever seen the endless shores of Elysium, or the mirrored landscapes of Bitopia? Let me share with you a few of the places I have been to recently."

Thaelyn and Ecco both lean forward as he prepares to share his thoughts of the places he has been and things he has seen. He opens his mind and portrays serene seascapes with broad shorelines that extended out of sight. He recalls a surreal image of a twin landscape, where one surface was inverted over the other. Instead of a sky, one would look up to see the other half of the plane upside-down, looking back down at them.

Ecco smiled brightly at the gift, as she never really had the opportunity to go out and see anything beyond the city. Her duties kept her neatly boxed up inside the local ward.

"Ecco," Thaelyn continues. "It still pains me to see you this way. I cannot say it enough, that mage simply went too far with you."

"Thaelyn, it makes no matter now. What is done cannot be undone."

"Indeed, especially as his rage drove him not simply to remove your tongue, but to thoroughly destroy it after. There is no recourse to repair this. Well, not unless I could bring you out of here, maybe up to Celestia and…"

"No. You must let it go, my love. And do not go chasing after him. This is often how things are in the city. Justice for you in Mount Celestia may follow a predictable course, but here it is all too often open to personal interpretation," she pauses and glances out the door cautiously. *"And the Lady would not likely care much for you to seek your own within the city."*

"This is true. I must keep myself under control here, for a number of reasons, not simply due to her. She may allow members of the Celestial races in here, but she vehemently denies any of the Powers."

"And you should not go around speaking so openly about her, either!" she frowns.

"Yes, Ecco, I will temper myself now," he smiles softly.

The two of them continued their conversation a while longer, until finally sharing a tender hug before Thaelyn excused himself.

He went back outside to find a local café in the plaza that was known locally as the Clerk's Ward. Within this Ward were a number of homes, markets and cafés, and a museum. Then of course was the brothel, and finally, in one corner, was a large temple-like structure representing the Guild of Sensations.

Thaelyn had become very familiar with the district, although he had spent time touring other areas, some of which were not nearly as neat and tidy. He knew of a café on one side where he might meet with another good friend who also happened to be Aasimar. She was the daughter of Lathander.

"Aelwyn," he announces as he sees her sitting alone at a table. "You are here by yourself today?"

Her response carried a distinctive, but unusual mode of speech.

"She looks up at him, pleasantly surprised to see his face again," she intones softly in a third-person manner.

"Aelwyn, I believe I mentioned this at least once before, but we are the same in this regard, and you do not need to speak to me in such prose."

"She acknowledges his plea, but she reveals to him that she is feeling insecure today and does not wish to impose herself on the others within the Ward."

"Aelwyn," he urges sternly.

"Very well, Thaelyn, but only for you. I had another…accident… today. I allowed my emotions to get out of control and they were felt halfway around the Ward," she ducks her head away.

"You simply need time, Aelwyn. You are in possession of some very powerful gifts, and unfortunately, they came to you perhaps too early for you to fully contain them."

"Yes, but my emotions are perhaps the worst of it. I can contain my power over Reality if only to speak indirectly. But emotionally, I am locked in my fate as someone of great passion."

"I have often asked myself if this might be the cause for your studies within the Sensorium."

"Indeed! I had hoped to be able to experience such a great variety of sensations as to learn new ways of controlling my own."

"And have you found any success?"

"In a small way, I suppose I must answer yes. But I am still young, and with much to learn. Therefore, I must pace myself with my studies, and perhaps the counsel of others along the way."

"You certainly could not have chosen a finer establishment than that in which to make your studies. But with respect, you are not actually as young as you proclaim yourself to be, are you?" he raises an eyebrow.

"Thaelyn!" she retorts mildly. "You should know better than to ask a lady such a question."

"Yes, but in my mind, you are much more like a sister to me," he smiles.

"It is true; we are siblings of the spirit, brother and sister. If you were any other, I might cause you to feel remorseful dejection for your statement," she grins.

"Thankfully, I think I might be able to resist that projection."

"But you are right, I am nearly a century older than you. Perhaps my seniority might afford me a subtle advantage?"

"I might permit you this due only to my chivalry."

The two of them now share a quiet laugh.

"Thank you, Spirit-brother," she offers. "You made me feel better. Perhaps now I might have the strength to see this day complete."

"It is the least I can do. I am not aware of any other family relations for myself, but if I can call you my sister, even if only in spirit, it is a valuable addition."

"Do not forget Aristan. You could call him a brother in a similar prose."

"Indeed, I could. Though I do not see him as often. He tends to keep himself to his Father's libraries."

They shared a drink and some more conversation, until Aelwyn had to return to her work, leaving Thaelyn to pass his remaining time wandering around the Ward to browse the museum and some of the local shops.

One of these, found at the far end of the Ward, was a curiosity shop. It was managed by a creature that was almost as much a curiosity as the fare she offered. Her kind was known as tanar'ri, otherwise described by mortal races as demons. In her case, she was one of the lesser forms. Normally, they would not be as interested in commercial exploits, preferring instead the more carnal pleasures, but she was something of an exception to the rule.

Thaelyn had not visited this shop before as he could sense her presence even from out on the street. But boredom was setting in, so he decided to take a quick peek inside. The shopkeeper saw him enter as soon as the door opened, and she knew instantly what he was. Her senses could feel his spiritual nature the same as he could feel hers. Nevertheless, ever the enterprising sort, she attempted to stifle her personal revulsions and greet her new patron.

Thaelyn, being a Celestial, was a direct opposite to the tanar'ri, both in polarity as well as character. If Mount Celestia was the realm of both Positivity and Order, and the home of the tanar'ri, being the Abyss, was Negative and Chaotic, you might guess the natural outcome. But here in Sigil, they might actually have the power to resist reaching for each other's throats.

"Ah, a visitor," she offers in her practiced manners. "You are new here. What can Vrischika help you with today?"

Thaelyn felt ill at ease in this place, but he considered it might be worth looking into, if only for the entertainment of seeing what she has to offer, as well as to disturb her with his simple presence in her shop. He decided to play into the false posturing.

"Ah, shopkeeper... Vrischika is it? Oh, yes, this is my first foray into this most extraordinary venue. Have you held this shop for very long?"

"Yes! Vrischika has been here for a long time. Are you new to the city?"

"Indeed, this is not my native home, and I will admit I have come and gone a few times by now, but there is so much to see. And today I find myself travelling along this way, hoping to familiarize myself with the local venues and what fascinating items might be for sale here. Then I came upon this one, which so curiously is found so far removed from the rest, and it makes me wonder. Do you seclude yourself out here to hide all these extraordinary values from the common folk outside?"

"Ah…" she snickers wickedly. "No, Vrischika would not say she hides, but her wares are very special. They are not for just anyone, you know."

"Truly! Then might I have a moment to browse and see what amazing opportunities await?"

"But of course! Look at what I have. If you have questions, Vrischika will answer."

"Wonderful!"

She moves away from him, feeling her own sense of relief to put a little distance between them, but she keeps a close eye on him.

Thaelyn begins browsing the nearby shelves, taking careful note of their contents, and discovering some truly strange items on display.

He saw powdered extracts from demon horns, oil extracts from various organs and tissues, most of which might be useful to a mage or alchemist as reagents. There were bottles of water taken from the renowned river Styx, which was revered for certain magical and alchemical properties, and then he came upon an unmarked box.

He stared at the box for a moment, sensing something unpleasant inside, but he restrained his initial reaction to it. He could not see any clear indication of the contents, so he decided to bring her attention to inquire about it.

"Yes?" she responds as she eagerly rushes over. "I see you looking here. Do you want to ask something?"

"A simple question if I may. There do not seem to be any markings here, so can you explain what is inside?"

"Ah, yes! This is new. Vrischika brings this in only recently, no time to mark it yet. Inside is a tongue! But not just any tongue, this is the tongue of a demon!" she cackles.

"The tongue of a demon…" he ponders. "Do tell. But now, this begs the question, what purpose might it serve? For instance, I see many items here that might prove valuable to a mage, but a demon's tongue?"

"Yes, I have many suppliers that bring reagents from across the Planes. But here, they tell me this tongue has a special property. Not just anyone would find value in it, but perhaps someone would.

It is said that if you place this in the mouth of one who has no voice, it can give it back to them!"

Thaelyn instantly reflected on Ecco, but he also knew a demon's tongue would not simply give back a voice. His Celestial teachings already told him this. A demon, being such a vile creature, would not typically have anything polite to say if it had the opportunity to speak, and the tongue would behave the same even if given to another.

"Remarkable," he feigns his interest. "But of course, as you can clearly see, I do still have mine attached. However, if to keep this in mind, perhaps one day I may meet someone who might find a use for it."

"Yes! Do this. Send them to Vrischika and I will help them. Vrischika wants to make good business here in the Ward."

Thaelyn continues browsing the nearby shelves while the woman moves away again. Finally, he offers a wave and departs.

"A demon's tongue…" he muses silently as he walks back along the plaza. "Clearly, she must be thinking of Ecco in this regard, I can think of no other immediate need for such as this. And Ecco's condition is not especially hidden. Many would know of it by now, including her. So, likely she is hoping to cash in on a little fun. I can only imagine what poor Ecco would be like with one of those caught in her throat."

He continues up the plaza back in the direction of the brothel, thinking he might want to warn Ecco of this potential danger. As he comes into view of the door, he sees a group of people exiting the building and looking around the plaza as if lost.

The lead individual of the group looked like death warmed over…multiple times. Thaelyn had never seen such a wreck of a man as this, at least not standing upright. He was joined by a young tiefling female and a githzerai, one of the native societies who lived in the Outer Planar realms. This pack was clearly not native to the Ward, and indeed didn't look like the sort who would join together for anything else. He decided to step up to investigate, sensing something curious in this lot.

"My apologies," he begins politely. "I could not help but notice you seem to be a bit out of place here. Perhaps I can offer some assistance to find something?"

The man looked at Thaelyn, studying him from head to toe briefly, taking notice of the neat appearance, the armor plating, and the longsword hanging by his side. Thaelyn was dressed as a soldier, but unlike any guard known in the city.

"I am looking for something, yes," the man emits hoarsely. "I need to speak with someone here, but she cannot give me my answer by any means other than verbal. Unfortunately, she is not capable of that, and this has brought my search to a stalemate."

"Verbal... Would you happen to be speaking of a young lady known as Ecco? I know she is mute. Is she the one?"

"Yes, actually... I have been seeking answers to a personal problem, and very few in the city hold this information by now. I was told she might hold a clue, but for some reason she cannot write this down for me, instead it must be spoken. Something about twisting the threads of Reality in ways that could snap back at her..."

"Yes, I believe I understand. If to put something in writing, it can reflect back on the one who wrote it. There are those who could use this as a means of taking action against another, for instance if they might hold any form of grievance. Most curious...may I ask what it is you seek. Perhaps I could offer a new direction."

"Unlikely. At some moment in my past, something was taken from me. I must try to understand who it was and how to retrieve it back. I received a clue to come here, but it leads to her."

"And in her condition, she cannot help you. This represents a problem."

Thaelyn again reflects on the curiosity shop and the item he saw on sale. Even with the unpleasant repercussions, it might offer a solution, but he resisted bringing this burden to his dearest love.

"Perhaps there is someone else who can help me," the man suggests, realizing Thaelyn might not have an immediate answer. "I thank you for your offer."

The man and his group wander off deeper into the plaza, leaving Thaelyn to watch them passing by the various shops.

"If he continues on his way," Thaelyn contemplates quietly. "He might find it himself, and she will explain to him the same as she did me. But he might not know the difference."

He continued to watch the group move further down the avenue, visiting each shop in turn. It was clear, if they continued this pattern, they would come upon Vrischika's shop eventually.

"This will become complicated rather quickly. Surely, she brought that tongue in for this purpose. But now wait, she is a lesser tanar'ri, so I might expect her to take this course for the sheer pleasure of it, but she does not apparently behave as a true tanar'ri. She has held this shop for some time, and this demonstrates...of course! Her statement, she wanted to make good business in the Ward. But in her case, we must be speaking of profit! She might offer this, with or without the pleasure aspect, but to make profit...she must have an antidote."

He began strutting down the plaza again, more determinedly this time.

"And if there was an emergency," he continues privately, "as I am sure there would be, once Ecco tried to speak, this is where she would pull her little trick on us. But I wonder..."

Thaelyn continues down the plaza, discreetly staying behind the group as they passed by a nearby café and now headed in the direction of Vrischika's shop.

"If I were the enterprising sort," he wonders. "I might have it on sale in another portion of the shop, but not near the primary item. It would likely be concealed amongst other items of inconsequential nature to diffuse its importance, and I might also suggest at a reduced cost to defray its inherent value. Would that not be a fine opportunity? She might raise the price at just that moment when it became critical. But if to discover it in this initial setting, and bargain for it as a purveyor of rare oddities, perchance for a collection. Yes, she may need to accept this, but if to see her afterwards..."

He observes them go into her shop, so he walks around to the café, pretending to ponder if he would wish to sit for a drink, and using this as a stall tactic. He waits several long moments, attempting to project his mind into the shop to perceive their outward thoughts.

"Yes, he is doing it, I see it now."

A few moments later, they emerge outside again. Thaelyn moves to intercept as they begin proceeding back up the plaza.

"Excuse me again," he utters. "I had a recent thought come to mind. I suppose you are still contemplating ways to retrieve your answer, and a curious notion occurred that I might be able to help after all. Are you on your way back there, perchance?"

"Yes, actually…" the man responds. "We found something in this shop over here which might help us. I doubt it is really necessary for you to trouble yourself by now."

"Oh, it is not a bother at all. In fact, I know Ecco quite well, as we have shared many conversations together. May I offer a suggestion? I would wish to accompany you to visit with her, but I must first stop over here to investigate an important item. Can you wait for me before proceeding, and we shall go together?"

"Well, I suppose we could, if you think it is really so important."

"Indeed, I do believe so, and my thanks. I will return quickly."

Thaelyn turned and strolled over to the shop again. This time, he had to put on a good show if he hoped to gain his advantage.

"Ah, another visitor?" she calls from a back room. "You! Yes! You were here not long ago. You have come back, perhaps to make a purchase?"

"Indeed, I could not resist returning back to review this marvelous selection. It occurs to me there was another side of the shop I neglected before…I must have become distracted. But anyway, I simply had to come back to correct this unfortunate oversight."

"Oh yes! Vrischika has many fine wares to offer. Look, see for yourself, and remember, Vrischika will make a good offer."

Thaelyn begins a more attentive survey of the items on the shelves, once again browsing those he saw before, but now circling around the shop to another set of shelves on the opposite side. He privately considered what form this antidote might take, assuming one actually existed. He tried to recall his lessons in the halls of

Tyr's library. A demon's tongue was regarded as evil flesh, where the word 'evil' carries certain contextual implications within the Outer Planes. And it would behave with evil tendencies even if placed in another person's body.

He again observed the many vials of oils, salt solutions, several acids, and a selection of potent poisons. He could only imagine who would want one of those and why, but the thought was not at all pleasing. Then he noticed a uniquely shaped vial standing among another group of a completely different design.

The vial in question held a shape unlike any of those around it, or any of the others he saw elsewhere in the shop. The design seemed archaic, as if it was very old, or came from a source with a most unusual background.

"Chaos spawn," he mutters silently.

The shape was irregular, as if molded with no symmetry, abstract and chaotic. Almost everything else in the shop held at least a somewhat regular shape. He then brought up a hand to the level of the shelf, hoping to discreetly sense the contents with his Celestial powers. The contents felt strangely alluring.

"Oh, Vrischika," he announces. "A curious thing, this… I do not see a label on it. Can you tell me what is inside?"

"What? Oh that! Yes…eh…" she steps in closer to examine what he was pointing at. "Yes, Vrischika can tell you. A wandering traveler comes to me. He tells of a long journey to strange places, and he finds a rare old item. Do you see; it looks old."

"Yes, it does seem that way."

"He then tells a story of a dying man who wants to make trade for simple water. Can you believe it!" she snickers. "Well, they make a trade, but now he has this. When he asks the dying man, 'what is it', the dying man says it is tears."

"Tears? Such an odd one that is… Do we know where these tears came from?"

"He tells us, but Vrischika does not know if this is true. You see, I do not put a name here because I cannot be sure. He says it is tears of a deva, but does a deva make tears? Vrischika thinks they do not."

"Tears of a deva, most interesting… Well, I must say, true or not, that would make for a rather interesting conversation item, and I am something of a collector of conversation items. I travel on occasion, you know, and bringing back souvenirs can be rather entertaining for my guests. What might you be asking for this article?"

"This?" she retracts into her thoughts, seemingly hesitant to put an immediate price on it. "You know, if you are a collector of special things, Vrischika can make a good offer on something better."

"Oh I have no doubt, but just look at this," he directs his hands at the item on the shelf. "The shape of the bottle, such a unique and distinctive design, perhaps very old and with such a mystery of what could be inside. I do not think I have anything like this, and it would make such a fine addition on my shelves back home."

"Well, perhaps, but…"

"And certainly we can make a fair deal together, especially since you cannot be sure of its true value. Like you said, he traded it for simple water. Ha ha! It is probably no more than a ruse. I would take this off your hands for…oh…" he pauses in apparent contemplation of a price, examining some of the other items on the shelf for comparison. "What if I offer five hundred coppers? This would then clear the space and allow you to stock more of the items we both know would hold much greater sale potential for you."

"Um…" Vrischika wavers, realizing she backed herself into a corner on this one with her story, but money was still money. "Yes, you are right. It is old and maybe has no real value, but your offer… Oh! Five hundred is good for this old thing."

"Excellent."

They take the bottle up to the counter and Thaelyn makes his purchase. He then waves goodbye and leaves the shop.

Vrischika watches him exit through the door, and then turns to the empty spot on the shelf where the bottle once stood.

"Oh well," she mutters privately. "We make our sale, not like we hoped, but it will be fun to watch those other people," she begins cackling vigorously.

Thaelyn rejoined the man and his group, who were still waiting patiently outside.

"I am still unsure why you would wish to accompany us," the man states. "I think we should be able to find our answer with this," he pats the box he was carrying under his arm.

"Perhaps you can, my friend, but I think if we work together, we might both find our answer."

"Both of us? Do you have something you need from her as well?"

"It is not what I need FROM her, but rather what I wish to give TO her. This has been on my mind for a long while now."

They returned to the brothel. Grace saw the group enter and moved to greet them.

"Thaelyn, you have come back for more, perhaps? You must be feeling restless today."

"Grace, on this occasion, I hope to solve a long-standing issue, but first we must examine what we have to work with."

"I am not sure if I understand your meaning."

"This man here needs to speak with Ecco, and I wish to assist."

"Oh, I see now. Well, you know the way."

Thaelyn leads the group around the corner to Ecco's room. He knocks gently before nudging the door open.

"Ecco?" he calls softly.

The girl was sitting at her desk reading a book when the announcement came. She turned with an instant moment of joy to see her true love returning so soon. Then she noticed he was accompanied by the rest. She settled her posture and admitted them inside.

"*Thaelyn,*" she projects in her mind. "*What is this? Are you here trying to help these people?*"

"Yes, Ecco, this man explained to me his dilemma at inquiring about a delicate matter."

The conversation, at least on the outside, was one-sided, and the man and his group were puzzled over the odd interaction.

"Excuse me, are you speaking to her? But she didn't say anything."

"I am telepathic, and this is how we communicate, since she does not have her own means."

"Ah, my apologies, I was not aware of that. This must make your interactions very convenient; I suppose."

"It does, but I also know how this originally occurred, and it has been a burden for me ever since. But now, on to more important matters. Ecco, we have come to see about this small concern, perchance to find a way to resolve it."

"Thaelyn, I would like to help this man, but what he asks must be provided only as a verbal response. I cannot write this for him. And, well, you know I cannot speak. And I would not dare involve you if you please."

"Ecco, what manner of information is it he requires? Can you at least tell me the nature of it?"

"It's a name he needs. Someone he must speak to, but who would not likely listen to him with no one to vouch for it. And if I write it, I'm afraid the paper could fall into the hands of someone who might use it against me. And considering what I have already suffered..." she turns her head away.

"Of course, then let us examine something new here."

Thaelyn turns to the man and motions to his box. The man then pulls the box around and sets it on a table.

"I found this at the curiosity shop down there," he begins, and then opens the box.

Inside the box was a rather gruesome sight, as it was the demon's tongue. Ecco winced and flinched away from it.

"Yes, I realize it might not look very pleasant," he continues. "But the shopkeeper told me that it holds the power to restore speech to someone who may have lost it. Naturally, since we had our conversation a short while ago, I thought of you."

"It looks awful," she relents, but knowing he wouldn't be able to hear her thoughts.

"Ecco," Thaelyn offers. "I am sure the sight may be rather unpleasant, but the promise of speech is certainly one to consider. Just so long as you try to resist sticking your tongue out at people," he grins teasingly.

She glares at him a moment, and then back to the box, briefly glancing at the man inquisitively.

"She tells me that if we were to place this into your mouth," the man explains. "It would…eh…find its own way, although I hesitate to imagine how that might feel."

She nods disdainfully.

"And after that, according to her explanation, you would be able to speak again. Would you accept this?"

Ecco contemplated the suggestion. The tongue didn't look very inviting, but the promise of returning speech was enticing. She had to balance the two, but ultimately it was either this one moment of unpleasantness or a lifetime of being mute, and she didn't actually like being mute.

She takes a deep breath, sighs, and then nods. She sits down and tries to settle her nerves. This was not going to be pleasant, whatever it might feel like.

The man picks up the tongue, and she opens her mouth, where he gently slides it inside. She almost instantly feels a gagging sensation come into her as the tongue comes alive and begins writhing down her throat seeking its new root to attach itself. Fortunately, the choking effect was brief, and her body settled soon after.

Thaelyn winced at the display, but he knew this was the worst of it, at least on the physical side.

The man also grimaced at the displeasure he obviously invoked, but he suspected it was inescapable.

"How do you feel?" he asks. "Are you able to speak now?"

Ecco hesitated before giving her new voice a try. She looked up at the man, and then at Thaelyn, feeling a little insecure, but she knew she had to start somewhere. She first tried a simple test of her vocal cords, and then followed with a brief statement.

"I… I feel alright, thank you… YOU WILL ALL BURN WITH ETERNAL TORMENT! YOUR FLESH WILL FESTER AND ROT, CURSED WITH THE PESTILENCE OF A THOUSAND PLAGUES!"

Her voice was rough and malignant, and the words rang out

across the room. She instantly slapped her hands across her mouth hoping to muffle anything else that might come out. Her expression turned to horror as she realized what she had just said, but it wasn't her voice that said it. The tongue itself had taken over.

The man gazed at her, shocked at what he had done. He only hoped to give her the power of speech, in part to aid her in her dilemma, and also to assist him with his.

"Ecco…I'm so very sorry. I couldn't have known it would do this."

"Dear Powers, Ecco," Thaelyn submits with a curious smirk. "I did not even know you had it in you. And here I thought Kimasxi held talent."

She glares at him for his impish statement.

"How can you stand there and mock me like that?" she blasts in her thoughts.

"Now, now, Ecco; let us be civil about this. After all, you should know me well enough. Allow me to take a look inside there."

Thaelyn leans over to examine her mouth, carefully pulling her hands away so he could peek inside.

"Open up, but do not speak," he issues.

The man and his group backed away to give Thaelyn room, unsure of what he had in mind.

Thaelyn pulled her mouth open gently.

"Ah yes, I see the problem now. This once belonged to a demon, I believe."

"But I just mentioned that…" the man asserts.

"Of course, you are correct, but what Vrischika apparently forgot to mention is that demons are a rather unpleasant sort, and even if separated from its host, such a thing as a tongue would still carry some portion of this quality."

"Do you know that shopkeeper?"

"She is a tanar'ri, and those are well familiar to my mind. Although she might not follow in many of their traditional pursuits, she still follows a pattern I can expect, and in her case, it might also involve profit, as well as perhaps a bit of entertainment along the way. I saw this in her shop earlier, and got the same story, but of course I chose not to pursue it as I knew what result it would bring."

"Then why did you allow me to give it to her?"

"Because I also suspected Vrischika had a secondary plan. She might enjoy seeing Ecco in this state, but if to make a bit more profit from the ordeal…"

"Aye," the tiefling speaks up. "Now yeh're talkin' my language. So, what sort o' trick da yeh think she would play on this?"

"It would most likely involve a potential antidote, but naturally, not until we had an emergency."

"Right! I might agree ta that. But now, da we know what this antidote really is?"

"Perhaps we do…" Thaelyn offers as he pulls out the oddly shaped vial from the bag he was carrying.

"Eh…right," the tiefling mutters. "Looks like it got sent through a flippin' oven, it does. So, what is it?"

"This was also in her shop, on the other side and carefully hidden among some other bottles. It did not have a label, and she gave me this curious story of how it arrived in her hands, attempting to downplay it as holding no extraordinary value. She tells me it was rumored to hold the tears of a deva."

"As if that held any real meanin' ta me… How does that help us?"

"I am educated in many things which are not commonly known to others, and this would count as one of those. Fortunately, Vrischika did not know this at the time I made my own little play in her shop."

"If she didn't before, she might soon enough, once yeh pull this out."

"Agreed, but I will consider this to be worth it. Deva tears hold a potent ability to soothe evil flesh. We made a deal whereby I posed as a collector of oddities, and used her own story against her that it was simply a valueless item taking up space on her shelf."

Ecco again covered her mouth as she felt a giggle coming out. She was hoping it wouldn't turn into anything particularly nasty along the way.

"Not a bad bit o' dealin'," the tiefling admits. "With a mouth like that, yeh could make a tidy few coppers down in the Hive. But now what?"

"Very simply, we will apply a drop of this inside here... Open up again for me, Ecco."

Again, she opens her mouth and Thaelyn finds a small hairpin on the table to pull out a single drop of the precious liquid. He then places it on her tongue.

Ecco winced as she felt a sudden wave of pacification wash across her mouth. She waited several moments for this to settle before relaxing back again.

"Now try again," Thaelyn smiles gently. "But this time without attempting the slurring competition with Kimasxi."

She glared jeeringly into his eyes before making another attempt, first to clear her throat, and then to try speaking again.

"I think..." she halts as if expecting something obnoxious to come out. "Yes, I think it feels better now."

She breathes a sigh of relief, closes her eyes, and relaxes back into the chair.

✦✦✦✦✦

"Mother..." the young drakeling emits. "It came again...and more thisss time..."

"My child... Are you ssstill... Having your dreamsss...?"

"Thisss is different... It was a dream...but sssomething elssse. I sssaw people...that female...the man...together...and I sssaw...the vision...come to life. I think...sssomething has happened...and I cannot wait...anymore. I need to go sssee..."

"You are ssstill young... My daughter. Where is thisss place... You sssee in your mind...?"

"I sssee a city...it is round...like a circle...and hollow...like a cave. It is closed...with no doorsss."

"I know thisss place... It is a city... Among the Planesss... Called ssSigil..."

"I mussst go there. Please Mother... You mussst take me...

ssso I can sssee…for myssself…if I am right. And we mussst go… to the place of cloudsss…and the tall mountain. I need thisss. The voice…callsss to me. It asksss me…to come to it…"

The mature dragon had been hearing these pleas for a couple of centuries by now, but before this time, she considered her daughter was simply too young to go out on such a long journey. But these visions she was having were developing into a burden that needed resolution. She pondered the idea, realizing it'll only get worse if she doesn't take action, and maybe along the way she might find a few of her own answers.

"All right… I will take you… But you mussst ssstay… Clossse to me… And not get lossst…"

The child nuzzled her mother for the favor, and the two of them prepared to leave, with the mother calling upon her Draconic powers to transport them away from their mountain cave home.

A column of light appeared around them, and the young drakeling huddled close to its mother as the two of them lifted up and away beyond the world. The column carried them through the planar layers and across a sea of light until a new sight was finally revealed to them. It was another planar domain, and they were heading straight for it.

The mother guided them on course through the next planar membrane and settled them neatly on the ground in a brightly lit environment of lush green grasses, deep blue skies, and a magnificently tall mountain in the background.

The little drakeling marveled at the sights, as this would represent the first time she ever left home to see anything. She studied the huge mountain feature that rose up through the clouds and a myriad of small glowing orbs floating through the region.

"What is the name…of thisss place…again…?" she asks.

"Thisss place is called… Mount Celessstia…"

"It is beautiful…"

"What do you feel… You mussst do… To find thisss voice…?"

The small one looked around the scene trying to orient herself, and hoping to recall the images she saw in her visions, and the voice that would come to her so often. But before she could make a decision on where to go first, another column appeared just off to the side of the pair.

The mother turned to examine the sight, instantly recognizing what it was, but unsure why it would appear at this precise moment in time or this close to them. The reason became immediately clear once the manifestation began to form.

"You again…" she gasps and lowers her head reverently.

The young drakeling watched her mother and realized this was something important. She huddled under one foreleg and tried to mimic her mother's action.

"You are the one… Who came to me… With thisss…" the mother asserts with a brief glance at her child. "Are you the one… Ressssponsible… For her visionsss…?"

"Only partially," Thaliel replies. "Her powers travel well beyond my capacity. But I will claim responsibility for directing her return to this place. This much was necessary."

"I would asssk… For what purpossse…? You came to me… With instructionsss… To bring forth… A child. And now… Here we are… To meet again. I beg to underssstand… The reason…"

"Thou art deserving of this much, but thou must also understand this is to be held in absolute secrecy."

"Of courssse… As it was before…"

"At this moment, perhaps the explanation would be better if given unto thee by the Maker herself. But before we can attend to that…" she turns to greet the young drakeling. "Come forward, and do not be afraid."

The little one crawls out from under her mother's leg to present herself.

"What name dost thou have, small one?" Thaliel asks tenderly.

The little creature timidly stepped forward. Although, in terms of a dragon, 'little' is a very subjective term, as she stood nearly as tall as Thaliel by now. And for reference, a seraph is rather tall, in and of themselves. Nevertheless, she felt small, and had to remind herself that she wanted to be here, that this had to be what she was called for.

"My name…" she glances at her mother. "I am called Makinanadalon."

"That is a very fine name for a Silver."

"What are you…?" she asks. "I know your face…and your voice… but my mother knowsss you…as well…?"

"The explanation is complex, and thou art young, but the time hath come for thee to know thy true name and why thou art here. I have something I must bestow unto thee. This will answer all thy questions, and much more. But since thou art still young, thou must absorb it gradually, with more to come as thou dost mature."

The young Draconic tilts its head and puzzles the meaning, trying to understand the strange depiction. She then nods and looks around expectantly.

Thaliel summons up a couple of her attendants, who arrive with a peculiar container that seemed to be made of some immaterial substance, but clearly holding a solid shape with something glowing and undulating inside.

The child instinctively backed away a step as she studied the strange artifact.

"What is it…?" she asks.

"Ooh…" the mother croons. "I do not sssee… Those very often. That is called… A memory core… Encapsssulated… Inssside a bottle… For storage…"

"A memory core…?"

Thaliel nods as she explains.

"This is the part of thee that we have held here until thou wouldst be ready to receive it back again. It is everything thou once were, but could not be contained within thy current form until such time as thou may be mature enough to reabsorb it. As I said, thou art still young, even now, but I will aid thee from this moment and until thou art fully restored."

"Who are you…that you hold thisss…for me…?"

"I am thy servant. My name is Thaliel."

"What...?" the mother dragon gasps. "You are her... Ssservant...? Who is she... That she has sssuch... A sssservant as you...?"

Thaliel simply looked up at the mother and smiled, then returned to the child.

"Place your claw gently on the surface of this vessel and allow yourself to feel what is inside."

The child looks again at the strange object, approaching within reach, and then to sit, lifting one claw and reaching out to the container. She sets it gently on the upper surface, and almost immediately feels a massive surge of great wisdom rush into her.

She lets out a soft moan and her head droops. Her body, even in a seated posture, begins to slump, and her other foreleg feels weak underneath her. Her eyes feel heavy and close briefly, only to reopen with a soft glow, and darting from side to side rapidly, as if reading from an unseen book at high speed.

The mother cautiously moves around to gaze concernedly at the small one, and studying her for the reaction, but keeping away from it.

The young drakeling's head sways rhythmically as she wades through a river of knowledge measuring what might seem like an eternity of history. She lets out another breathy moan and lifts her head again, now angling it upwards.

"Ooh..." she drones softly. "Thisss will do sssomething...to a perssson..."

"Adalon...?" the mother whispers.

"I am here...Mother..." she mutters distantly. "Sssuch a curiousss...ssstatement. Mother. I have not called...that word...to anyone...for nearly an eternity. It fillsss me...with a quaint sssense... of forgotten nossstalgia..." she finishes with a gentle smile.

"Who are you then... If not my daughter...?"

"You know... That ssstatement...ssseems a bit ironic. I sssuppose I am...as much your daughter...in thisss form...as I could be...from my original mother. And I am...no lessss adoring...for your care. But at the sssame time...we find oursssselves...in a bizarre twissst. For as much as you...may be my mother...I am alssso...YOUR mother. I am Kuroko...Maker of the Draconicsss."

The mother dragon gasped and yelped as she fell backwards, collapsing to the ground from the shock that she apparently gave birth to her own goddess.

"I... That... You... Why...? Why would you... Choose to come here... Like thisss...?"

"Long ago...I made a promissse...and to fulfill thisss...I chose to take...corporeal form. I go to battle...an ancient enemy...but I want him...to sssee me...thisss way...to know...what I have brought...in ssspite of him..."

"In ssspite of him...? Why is thisss...?"

"He was once...the creator...of my kind. Our kind...in our primal form. But he was alssso...a monsssster. One of the Ancient Onesss..."

Her mother dropped her head and closed her eyes as she tried to reconcile the apparent magnitude of this situation.

"An Ancient One...? One ssstill exisssts...? Powersss help usss. Very well... What next... Do you asssk of me... Maker...?"

"You are my mother. You will watch me...and protect me...as I grow..." she looks down at herself. "It would sssseem...I will need... to endure...the painsss of maturing...again..." she laughs briskly. "As well as...thisss insssistent...hissssing..." she laughs again more boldly.

The mother dragon couldn't help but to usher up a few chuckles at the mention, though her shock still kept her a little unstable.

"Thaliel," Adalon begins again. "What is the condition...of Darumon...and our protégé...?"

"Darumon has not made any significant movements since our last review," she responds. "He has instructed his creations to go in search of his materials within the local domain, but I think they do not possess the means to harvest them. Instead, I heard mention that he might engage a secondary search for a local labor force to supply this function. As for our...protégé..." she smiles. "He is developing very well. We are nearly to our third century by now, and still with progress ahead. But Maker, we have a new problem."

"Wonderful...what problem is thisss...?"

"The Power Aerdrie Faenya did approach me once, not long

after thou didst descend to the Prime domain. She did inform me of a dilemma whereby a faction of rogue Draconic have taken action to assail her Children, a society known as Avariel. This action is unauthorized and unjustified."

"Why would they...go againssst...my lassst inssstruction...? They were directed...to withdraw...!"

"I have been studying this since the moment the announcement came. They seem to hold a grievance over this particular Child society for an assault they did make sometime earlier. The mention revolves around the Draconics assaulting a temple base. The Child societies did rally to the defense, and they did reclaim the base, but the Draconics were particularly offended by this one for its capacity of flight, which did largely determine the outcome."

"I know of these people..." the mother dragon interjects. "And I heard... Of thisss ssstory. The Temple... Of the Protector... Their god. It was sssaid to contain... An artifact... Of great power... Once used... To bring them... To our world..."

"Do you know...of the reason...why they would attack...thisss place...?" Adalon asks.

"I heard of thisss... From the ssstories... Whissspered... Among the elvesss. It was sssuggested... They hoped... To take the artifact... And use it... For themssselves. Perhapsss... To dessstroy... The elven nationsss..."

"Inexcusssable...! My lassst...inssstructions...were to allow... those sssocieties...to grow...and unite. Now they hope...to unravel... my work...?"

"Maker," Thaliel submits, hoping to contain the moment. "These Draconic are isolated and only assailing this one society. They seem to have shirked their responsibility to thee and thy command. I did advise Aerdrie Faenya to inform her Children to evade their launches, in an attempt to preserve their numbers. Wouldst thou offer any further direction?"

"Yesss... Tell her she has...my sssupport...but I am unable... to bring...an immediate sssolution. If they no longer follow...my direction...they will not ressspond...to my command...to desissst. I mussst then find…and alternate…sssolution. But I think…it mussst follow…an indirect courssse…in order to preserve…our greater designsss…"

Adalon pauses to look around, now feeling more confident with her partially restored faculties. She withdraws her claw from the container and steadies herself.

"Thisss will take time," she muses as she examines the container. "In the meantime…I have work to do. Mother…we mussst go… to ssSigil…"

She gets up and rejoins her mother.

❖

"I thank you, Ecco, for your help, and I am very pleased all has turned out well for you."

"I thank you as well," she replies kindly. "And hope you find what you are looking for."

"And to you, Thaelyn," the man grins. "I might suggest you avoid that curiosity shop for a little while."

"Perhaps for the moment," he admits. "Although I suspect I may wish to look in again at some time just to remind her of the exceptional deal she made this day."

"Aye," the tiefling erupts. "And I'll bet yeh'll be heard clear across the Ward, yeh will!"

"Indeed, and what better form of advertisement than that to bring in new customers," he grins.

The man and his smallish group had finished their business with Ecco, and now they were saying goodbye to her and Thaelyn. They departed from the building, leaving only the two of them behind.

"Ecco, I must also say my farewell," Thaelyn offers. "It is time for me to return home. Do try to stay out of trouble with that newfound accessory of yours. I think Kimasxi does not need the competition just now."

She grins at the thought of taking up a match at throwing insults and slurs with Kimasxi.

"Thaelyn, try not to stay away too long. I do so love sharing my thoughts with you."

"Indeed, as do I, but in truth, Ecco, you and I both know this cannot develop into anything more than that occasional visitation. My contract denies me an intimate relationship."

"Yes, you mentioned this before, but I do not care for this. You are the one I want, and I will accept no other. Even if it means I live alone except for those precious few moments when you return, I will persevere."

"I feel guilty that I may be stealing you away from a more productive life, Ecco. This does not set well in my mind."

"Do not concern yourself, Thaelyn. This is my choice. Now, you go back and tend to your chores, and I will tend to mine. I will wait for you to return, my love. This you can be sure of."

They lean in for a tender embrace and then separate, with Thaelyn slipping away out the door.

He continues outside and further along the lanes to a secret niche where he found a special cubby. This cubby was a framed space bounded on all sides to create a type of doorway, but it was not a traditional door. This was one of the many hidden portals so often found in the city. These features gave the city a nickname, describing it as the City of Doors.

These portals would remain hidden unless someone came along with some kind of key, but this key was not always a physical object. It could be a spoken word, a gesture, an action, a thought, or any number of odd presentations.

He stood in the corner and looked around carefully to see if anyone was watching. When the coast was clear, he straightened his back and attempted to present an image of confidence and authority. He then blew a raspberry at the framework. He quickly glanced around again, just to make sure no one saw that, before jumping through the aperture and out of sight.

Ecco returned to her book, as she had nothing else to do until her next appointment, or unless a walk-in client came to visit. She closed the door, sat down and relaxed, but found her thoughts distracted by the events of the day, which ultimately led to the miracle of her voice being returned to her. This was something she never thought would come to pass.

In the foyer of the building, a pair of strange guests arrived. They clearly represented a mother and daughter pair, but unlike any of the local races found within the city. They appeared entirely in silver hues. They wore silver gowns, had silver skin, long silver hair, and silver catlike eyes. They gracefully walked into the foyer and paused to examine the scenery.

"Is thisss the place... You sssaw... In your visionsss...?" the mother asks softly.

"Yesss...she is here..." the daughter responds.

The headmistress saw the new arrivals and carefully makes her approach. She suspected she knew who, or rather what they were, and so she afforded herself an appropriate level of caution in their presence.

"Greetings and welcome... I have not ever seen you in the Ward before, or for that matter anywhere else in the city. If I'm not mistaken, your kind doesn't usually visit the city often."

"No... We do not... Tanar'ri..." the mother responds curtly. "And you do well... To mind... Your mannersss..."

"Go gently, Mother..." the daughter offers. "She is not...a concern..." she now redirects to Grace. "We are here...to ssspeak... to sssomeone..."

"Can I assist in directing you?" Grace asks.

"She is one...who is known...to have lossst...her voice..."

"Ah, yes, you must mean Ecco. I believe she should be available. Go here to the hall and turn left. Hers is the first door you come to."

"Our thanksss..."

The two visitors moved forward to the hall and turned. Grace watches them, curious as to the reason why two Draconics would make a visit to the city, to say nothing of visiting her brothel.

In this case, the two Draconics had altered their form, using avatars to resemble that of a humanoid form, which they might often use to infiltrate the domains belonging to others. This served a couple of purposes, not the least of which was to allow them to pass through the tiny spaces the smaller races used as their homes and workplaces.

They arrived at Ecco's door and the younger of the two knocked. A moment later, Ecco responds by opening the door, only to gawk at the outlandish visitors she was receiving.

"Can I help you?" she asks, happy to use her new voice, but now finding it unsettling that her first target was something as strange as this.

"Fassscinating…" remarks the child. "She ssspeaks now…"

"Yes…" Ecco affirms gingerly. "I'm sorry, I do not know you, but if you know about me, then you are right. It was only just recently when I was given this back to me."

"He did thisss…for you…jussst as I…foresssaw it. I was correct… in my visionsss…"

"Visions? Do you have the power of Sight? Interesting, but why would you desire to come all this way just to see me? And forgive me, but who are you…and also what are you? I've never seen someone like you before."

"Perhapsss…if you invite usss…inssside…we may ssspeak… privately…"

"Oh! But yes, my apologies…" she begs as she opens the door to allow them entry.

"I sssaw you…in my thoughtsss…many timesss…" the child asserts. "I felt myssself…drawn to you…and now I undersssstand… the reason. Thisss is curiousss…but I sssuppose…not unexpected…"

"I'm not sure if I understand your direction. What do you see in these visions?"

"Before thisss moment…I was unsure of thisss…myssself. But now that I am here…I think I can…determine…the greater need. Will you allow me…to make a reading…?"

"A reading? As if to tell my fortune?" she grins satirically. "No one has ever done that before in here. I'm usually the one to offer help to others."

"Perhapsss…but yoursss…may hold a greater…dessstiny…"

Ecco nods and sits in her chair while the child steps forward and reaches up a hand to the woman's face, laying it gently on her cheek. She holds it there for an extended moment and her eyes seem to stray off in the distance.

Ecco waits patiently, wondering what the girl might see in her future. The mother also waits and watches intently, observing the process and silently asking herself what her daughter is thinking.

"Daughter of ssSky..." the girl whispers, "...ssSky...Daughter... yesss, I sssee it now. Interesssting...you are the sssolution...but then what...where will you go...? You mussst join with him...of courssse...! And the two of you..."

She abruptly pulls her hand away and taps a finger to her lips, subtly pacing a small track along the floor. Ecco jolted faintly from the rapid retraction, and now waits to see what her final analysis might be.

"Thisss makesss perfect sssense..." the girl considers. "You have a future...and it travelsss...far ahead of you. You have a desire...but it cannot be fulfilled...and yet it will be...but not here...and not now..."

"So far, I'm intrigued, but this is very cryptic..."

"Yesss...it is an old habit...but it mussst be thisss way. I hold many plansss...and now...you are a part of thisss. You mussst... lisssten to me...and do what I asssk...and you will be...rewarded. Thisss life...you now follow... Continue as you are. But thisss one... is only temporary. You will then follow...a new path...and it will lead you...to dissstant placesss...and much work. But in the end... your reward will come...and you will find...that which you want... but cannot have...in thisss life. It can only come...in your next... incarnation...and I will help you..."

Ecco was nearly dumbfounded by such a remarkable, and even outlandish suggestion.

"Who are you?" she mumbles breathlessly. "And what are you?"

"We are Draconic..."

"Draconic!" she whispers urgently, then glancing around the room to ensure nothing was about to burst through the walls. "Here, in the city?"

"We do not...make a habit...to enter thisss place. Let usss not... raise our voicesss. Essspecially me...as I would not...be allowed... in here at all..."

"Why?"

"I am a Power...and she who governsss...thisss place...does not permit...our entry. And ssso...we should conclude...our meeting now..."

"But your name...please? And what do you mean, you'll help me in...whatever this is you say."

"Beyond thisss life...you will find...new purpossse. But you will require...my ssservice. I can sssay...no more...at thisss time. Sssimply trusssst me...and place yoursssself...in my handsss. And tell no one...including him...of my visit..."

"Him? Him who?"

"You know who...as now...you can ssspeak his name..."

Ecco felt a flash erupt in her mind, as it was so obvious who she was referring to.

"Thaelyn..." she mutters silently.

"As for me...I was not here...we did not ssspeak...and you know nothing. But when the time comesss...I will return for you...that you may continue...your pursssuit. But you will need...to follow a path...before you find...your goal..."

The girl turns and prepares to leave, but stops just short of the door before turning back.

"In thisss form...I am a child...but I am not a child. And yet... in thisss form...I take a name. I will be known...as Adalon...the ssSilver..."

The two of them now turn and leave the room, and then the building, making haste to escape from the city before the Lady discovers one of the Powers has somehow snuck inside.

Chapter 9
TRANSITIONS

Thaelyn was returning to Sigil during another of his rest periods from his service. As always, he makes his rounds to visit with friends and other relations, but his most anticipated destination was Ecco's house.

It had been several decades by now, and Ecco had retired from her work. She now lived alone with a housekeeper in one of the more prestigious homes in a residential area within the Ward. Her long service to the Guild of Sensations had awarded her both title and status, but as all things must, her career had come to a close.

Thaelyn continued to make his visits whenever he had time for it, and he watched as she aged from a youthful figure to an elder woman, now with the need for a personal attendant to help around the house. Every time he returned, he was fearful of what he might discover, and on this occasion, his fears were finally realized.

He was walking along the avenue, carrying a bouquet of flowers in his hand, as had become his tradition in recent years. Ecco loved the smell of fresh flowers, and she would place them in a vase on a table near the front window. He approached the neighborhood and strolled along the walkway until he arrived in front of her home.

But he could already feel something was wrong. It didn't feel the same this time. Something was absent.

He forced himself up to the door and knocked gently. In a moment, the door opened, and a middle-aged woman answered.

"Ah, Thaelyn… I was expecting you…eventually."

"Muriel, you need not say it. I can already feel her loss."

"Yes, she departed from us almost a month ago. She knew you would return and discover this, and she knew it would be very painful for you."

"I have been expecting this for many years now. I knew it would come, of course, but one can never be truly prepared for it until it happens."

"I know, she spoke to me often about this. She wanted you to know she held no regrets. In fact, she left a letter for you. Please, wait one moment, I'll get it."

The woman rushed off to a back room, soon to return with a letter neatly sealed in an envelope. She handed it to him.

"She wanted you to have this. I do not know precisely what it says, but I'm sure she wanted you to know how much she loved you and adored every moment you were together."

"There were so many of those moments when I felt guilty to distract her from a proper home and family."

"No, Thaelyn…please do not think this. She told me specifically, she never felt remorse over this."

"Very well… I will take this and read it privately."

He paused to glance over the house. In the past, it felt warm and filled with a sensation of contentment. Now it simply felt empty. He then recalled the flowers.

"Here, take these. Place them into a vase and set them on that table she favored so much."

The woman took the flowers and sniffed them, then nodded silently.

"Then I suppose I should depart," he continues. "I will find a quiet place to sit and see about this letter. And I will spend my time in careful review of these most precious memories. Where was she interred, do you know?"

"I…um…" she flusters briefly. "Actually, I'm not precisely sure… you know how those Dusters are. It's a maze down there."

"Indeed, I suppose by this time it might be. Perhaps I can check their books to see what they reveal."

"Maybe you would not wish to cause more pain for yourself," she suggests. "She is at peace, and I feel confident she would not want you to torture yourself with that which you cannot change."

Thaelyn had been looking down at the envelope when she made the suggestion. It was carefully worded to dissuade him from making an unnecessary pursuit, as she knew Ecco was not even present in the city, not after Kuroku had her way. But she also needed to word her statement so as not to invoke curiosity with Thaelyn's deductive skills. For his part, he simply looked up into her gently smiling face.

"We shall see…maybe you are right…it is done now. I will find nothing there but a box and a body. Her spirit would have long since ascended."

"Yes…oh yes, by now, of course it has."

"Then I shall take my leave, and I will bid you a good day."

He bows and turns to leave, slowly strolling back along the walkway and onto the main avenue of the plaza, eventually to find his way back to a favorite café he would often visit. He stops and sits at a table, setting down the envelope and ordering a drink, even though he was not particularly thirsty.

Many people passed along the avenue, and he had become a familiar face to some. They all knew of his relationship, and as they passed, a few would nod, perhaps to set a hand on his shoulder, while others felt he needed his privacy.

A short time passes, and he feels a familiar presence. A set of footsteps approaches from behind, followed by a hand caressing his shoulder.

"Aelwyn," he mutters.

"Would my lonely Spirit-brother mind if I sit with him?"

"I would greatly desire it, please."

She sits at the table and gazes into his eyes.

"I feel your suffering, Thaelyn. I could feel it all the way across the Ward."

"There are times when it is so difficult simply to be who I am."

"And do you think I have it any easier?"

"No, of course not… But then, why do we torment ourselves by living amongst mortals. We are creatures of passion that only feel the endless pain of loss."

"We do not only feel loss, Thaelyn. We feel much more than this, but you are right, as that loss will ultimately come to us. This is simply the cycle of life, and you know this. We might be better described as the exception, not the rule."

"Indeed, but then to associate ourselves with them…it merely exposes us to this eventuality."

"Life ebbs and flows on all levels, even our own, though we might not feel the certainty of mortality. Some may choose to distance themselves, detach themselves from the rest, but this is not the answer either. We should revel in the fact that we have this opportunity to build who we are with these new sensations, then to share this and more with those who may follow behind us."

"That sounds like the rhetoric they teach in the Sensorium."

"Speak kindly, Thaelyn, as those of us who believe in this feel there is a righteous reward awaiting the faithful."

"All right, my apologies, Aelwyn… This is your faith, and I should respect it. Although I have not studied it as you have, but from what you have taught me, it does seem to hold a curious merit."

"And it may be especially helpful to those of us who have such opportunity that time provides us a near infinite potential to seek this endless array to experience."

Thaelyn pauses to contemplate this scenario, and then looks up into her eyes and nods.

"And besides," Aelwyn adds. "I knew her well, and she would not be at all pleased to see you like this."

"Yes, I suppose you are right, but it is unavoidable at present. I had become so accustomed to seeing her, hearing her voice, feeling her touch… Her spirit felt so comforting, so…familiar."

"I understand. She shared a few thoughts with me on this. I am not permitted to reveal all, but she knew you would behave this way. She did feel the joys of your visits, and the sorrows of your departures, but she also held a sensation of comfort and confidence which I had long deliberated. When I asked her once, she confided in me a little secret. What I can reveal about this is that she held no reservations over her actions or the choices she made. She did exactly as she desired, and lived a good life for it. She felt as if she would go forward, as you would also go forward, each on your separate journeys. She once said this life we have here is only temporary, and there is more awaiting us elsewhere. We simply need to follow a path, and let Fate guide us."

"This is a most curious perspective. She said this?"

"She did, and she felt solidly about it."

"Is this something they teach in the guild?"

"Not that I ever learned. So I am unsure where she heard it."

"How interesting, but then, this is Sigil," he chuckles softly. "Very well then, I will take strength in this, and keep this as her special gift of wisdom."

Thaliel was making one of her visits with Adalon in her mountain cave home with her silver dragon mother. This would serve as a temporary headquarters until she matured into her adult form. Rather than returning to her original home in the Outer Planes, she was essentially in hiding during this stage of her plans. She would grow and continue to work her dealings, but this time privately through Thaliel.

Adalon was also working on a secondary plan locally on Tae'Eladar. This would serve to establish her with a reputation as a prophetess, although her prophecies would be rather obscure and narrow of focus. For this, she had begun to write down a number of verses. She would ultimately assemble these into a book, then publish that book to earn revenue which might eventually help her build a little fame, and especially fortune, to be used later.

"Maker," Thaliel begins. "The Primordial and his servant are unchanged at this time. It would appear the faction he was pursuing has been granted a reprieve from his menacing, and I suspect this to be the result of his distraction on these other matters."

"His sssearch…for his materialsss. Good…for as long…as he is dissstracted…they may find…their peace. But the quessstion… is for how long…"

"My greater question relates to these materials, where he may find them, how he may acquire them, and then to process them into his weapon."

"We will watch…closssely…and when thisss occursss…timing will be…our enemy…"

"Can there be a way to close this variance? My suspicion is the society we have forming here will not be sufficient to counter the threat of his creation."

Adalon considered this prospect. The local societies on her world were still in a medieval stage of development, and had largely stagnated in this condition as they did not tend to pursue such as the sciences, having become so complacent with only their magical studies. And with Darumon's creations at a high space-age level, there was a substantial discrepancy.

"We will need…to accelerate…our ssside…"

She pauses in contemplation, and then begins reviewing her notes relating to her prophecies. She searches through several stacks of papers, hoping to get a clue from her own visions on how this might appear. She finally picks one out and reads it to herself.

> *From unseen hands, a formula old,*
> *She carries a goal to pursue;*
> *Where speed of thought, precision of mind,*
> *Is found in a bottle of blue.*

Adalon studies this and immediately realizes what needs to be done.

"Thaliel..." she urges. "Call the ssSarrukh! They have a new... assssignment..."

✦

Thaelyn continued to grow, having been promoted to an adjudicator, where now he carried Tyr's law on his own shoulders, with authority to take action on the field in the absence of any court. While it might still be preferred to bring his quarry in for processing, for those occasions where this became difficult or impossible, his judgment would be final.

On this occasion, he was on a special assignment. This would be perhaps his most difficult to date. He was three-quarters of a millennium old by now, and had earned many of his Celestial gifts. Now was the test. He had been sent down into the Abyss, a place diametrically opposing his native realm. It had been discovered that a very special artifact had been carried off to this place, and was now held in the possession of a greater tanar'ri known as a glabrezu, a monstrous creature that stood fifteen feet tall, weighed thousands of pounds, and had two sets of arms. The smaller set resembled that of a muscular man, but the upper set were huge and terminated in large pincher-like claws.

"Navaatu," he calls. "I have come to take back the sword. Amaunator's Flame must be returned to its proper home."

"Do you think I will release my prize to you?!" he snarls. "Petty little Celestial... Do you want this? Try to take it, and I will add your skull to my throne!"

Thaelyn knew it was futile to negotiate with a glabrezu, but protocol demanded he at least make the initial statement. Now it would be a contest, and the outcome could potentially be the end of one or the other of them.

He needed to call on his extensive magical studies for this one, and his first choice was a personal shield of stone-skin, providing a hard shell around his body, and then an aura of blue flame to counter the demon's native fire wave attack. These had been called up before he even made his approach.

Furthermore, he came prepared, on this occasion. He was inside the realm of Chaos, which was already riding on his nerves, so he carried with him a special warding amulet to offer him a little protection from the native environmental effects, and a ring that offered protection from powerful negative influences, like demons. He would also call upon some of his more recent gifts and studies to offer a clever twist to his usual offence.

The demon was much more direct, being such a large and powerful creature with an extraordinarily big chip on its shoulder. As a tanar'ri, he was a creature of Chaos, and they don't plan their attacks with anything more strategic than the idea that bigger is better. So he simply lurched forward and charged at his opponent.

Thaelyn extended his hands in front of him, and then began drawing them back slowly, coiling up a potent energy charge within his palms. As he drew them close to his chest, the coils resonated like highly compressed ball lightning. He then released, thrusting his hands forward at the creature, and sending the potent charges on their way. They slammed into the glabrezu's chest and sent him flying backwards through the air, smashing through a couple of stalactites hanging from the ceiling, and then into the wall on the far side of the creature's den.

Thaelyn next drew his longsword and readied his shield. These were both highly enchanted items to go with his rank within Tyr's court, but compared to the size of his opponent, they seemed a little pale. The sword was enhanced with ice magic, which was especially effective against demons, and the shield was reinforced to resist fire.

Navaatu was stunned briefly after colliding with the wall, but he quickly pulled himself back up and made another charge, seeing Thaelyn now wielding his normal weapons. He sent away his own magical attack, throwing a spray of fireballs and a jet of flame.

Thaelyn ducked behind his shield and attempted to deflect the inbound volley, then raised his sword to make ready for battle.

Thaelyn's training had endowed him with a number of martial arts skills, and this allowed him to duck and roll beneath the swiping of the glabrezu's claws. The colossal beast might be powerful, but he was not as quick as his smaller opponent. Thaelyn dodged and circled around his rival, looking for an opening in his defense. His primary target would be a critical area where he could cripple the beast, rendering him less capable and more susceptible to a later attack. He found his mark on the back side of the creature's leg, where he made a quick slash to cut through a tendon.

Navaatu howled in pain and made a backhanded swipe at Thaelyn, who simply rolled out of range of its arm.

Thaelyn now stood on the opposite side of his adversary, waiting for him to make his next move. One leg was injured, slowing his actions, and causing a limp. Navaatu tried to support himself on a nearby stalagmite while he made another advance.

"You may wish to reconsider your proposal of redecorating," Thaelyn charges. "My skull would be far too ostentatious for THAT rotting lump."

"You would dare demean my seat of power?"

"Seat of power? It looks more like you salvaged it from a pool of sewage."

"Aargh!" the beast roars and lurches forward again.

The glabrezu swung at him furiously, smashing through rocks and pillars, and leaving a trail of debris hailing from the ceiling.

Thaelyn continued to pull away, occasionally batting at the demon's claws, and leading him in a wide circle around the creature's palace, coincidentally placing himself near the infrastructure supporting the roof.

"Indeed, I was wrong," he continues. "You do know how to redecorate. Just look at all this fine new material in which you can build your next throne."

The insulting barrage, borrowed from his lessons in Sigil on how to use language as a weapon, only served to reinforce the demon's fury and his lust to charge forward.

Thaelyn came back around the other side of the throne room to study the damage left behind. He would allow the demon to make one more attempt before his next move.

"Poor suffering creature," he shouts. "Maybe if I give you a free attempt, it might make you feel better."

"I will crush you!" he blasts. "My suffering is simply to have you in my sight."

Navaatu makes another charge and Thaelyn again ducks and rolls, leaving the beast to crash into another column. Thaelyn quickly pulls himself upright and makes another hit behind the other leg. Navaatu screams again, now for two injuries, and he crumples to his knees.

Thaelyn backs away and stows his gear. He then pulls up another charge within his palms, as he did before, this time delivering additional focus into it to make the hit especially strong. He releases it before Navaatu could bring himself around for another advance, lifting the creature up and throwing him harshly into the far wall.

The shock of the impact again stunned the demon and he fell to the ground. It further weakened the cavern and now bits of rubble were beginning to cascade down from above.

Thaelyn knew this was his moment. He turned to find what he came for, the sword called Amaunator's Flame. It was sitting on a mount behind the throne. He extended a hand and focused on the item, pulling it away from its mount telekinetically to fling across the room and snap into his grip. He promptly adorned it by the shoulder strap, and quickly pulled the large two-handed sword from its sheath, pausing only a moment to gaze reverently at it.

The item was an ornately inscribed greatsword fashioned in the forges of the gods themselves. It radiated a soft blue glow, but this was only its resting state, and Thaelyn knew this. He had been briefed on this before he was sent on this mission. It carried a special secret, and this came in the form of a Word of Power. If spoken directly into the sword, it would erupt in a potent burst of bluish plasma capable of cutting through just about any material imaginable.

"That belongs to me!" roars the demon as he tries to pull himself forward.

"I believe you should rephrase that statement in the past tense.

Now, allow me to demonstrate why this should not be found in such an awful place as this."

Thaelyn brought the sword up to his lips and whispered gently into the blade.

The sword instantly responded with a flash of blue flame jutting out from the hilt and along the full length of the blade, extending even beyond the tip. The aura glowed brightly and illuminated the space around it.

Thaelyn then charged into the beast. Navaatu attempted to swipe at him, but Thaelyn brought his new weapon around and sliced neatly through the demon's arm, severing it at midpoint. Navaatu howled violently from this new injury, and attempted to reach outward with his other arm.

Thaelyn stepped back and spun around, swinging the sword wide as he came full circle, and slicing deep into the beast's torso. Again, the creature wailed in pain, now collapsing to the ground.

At this time, Thaelyn chose to withdraw. His work was done, the sword was secure, and his opponent had been incapacitated.

"And this is why such toys are not for the likes of you," he states confidently. "You simply do not know how to use them wisely."

"We are not finished here!" the beast thunders.

"In truth, I believe we are finished here. You do not represent much of a challenge by now, and I care not to strike at such a pathetic opponent."

"Aargh! Vile infectious pustule! I will remember this day! Who are you to dare insult me in my home?"

"Ah, but of course... To your kind, I am known most often as Thaelyn, Scion of Celestia."

He now pulled back to make ready for his departure. He called on his innate Celestial power to form a bright column of light to open up and descend around him. He then rose up within this column to be carried back to his native home.

"Thisss will become… His new possession. He will need it… In future engagementsss…"

"As thou dost desire, although this is a most potent artifact for a Celestial to wield."

"It mattersss not. He is capable… And deserving. But now… I mussst depart. The time has come… That he should consssider… His future courssse…"

"Maker Kuroku, his service is not yet complete. Art thou considering a premature termination?"

"No… But he mussst… Contemplate… His future… And therefore… A sssuggestion… Mussst be planted…"

"Of course, I understand."

Maker Kuroku, in her persona of Adalon, had been visiting with Tyr in his court for a review of her plans. She had matured into an adult dragon by now, although still young in relation to their full maturing cycle. As she prepared to leave his court, she chose to alter her image, sensing Thaelyn was on his return, and she wanted to keep her current identity hidden.

She began morphing herself into her humanoid persona, appearing as a young adult female figure, again in silver hues, much like she used before when she and her mother visited Ecco in the city. She then began casually strolling out of the court into the open plaza outside.

Thaelyn had arrived from his Celestial transport only a moment ago and was now making his way across the plaza, when he caught sight of the unusual figure strolling along. He decided to divert briefly to investigate.

"Well now," he announces politely. "It is rather uncommon to see one such as you travel by."

Adalon played into the game, carefully concealing her mind from his thoughts to give an impression of anonymity.

"Is it now…" she croons nonchalantly. "But if not to travel… How does one… Come to dissscover… The mysssteries of Creation…?"

"Such a fine quandary! Indeed, I have seen much of the Planes in my time, and yet I am quite sure there is more yet to explore."

"But you ssspeak... Only of the Planesss. Which is to sssay... The Great Wheel. Surely... There is more... Beyond that..."

"Yes, you are correct, but thus far I have been limited to the Planes due to my work."

"Will your work... Inhibit you... For the duration... Of your lifetime...?"

"Actually, no it does not," he admits. "There will come a time when I will be released from my current duties, and then...well, so far I am unsure."

"Then it becomesss clear... There can be intrigue... In your future... Not in the Planesss... But perhapsss... Beyond..."

"Beyond? It would seem to me this place carries a considerable volume as it is."

"Oh... I am certain... You will find... Fassscination... In many thingsss. But here... In thisss place... Over time... You may find... Too much... Redundancy. Inssstead... You may find... More diversssity... Of ssstimulation... And purpossse... Elsssewhere..."

"This may be an interesting proposal, but what places do you suggest can be so enticing for one such as me?"

"Have you ever visited... The Prime domainsss...?"

"The Primes?" he wonders openly. "Not so far. But I should again point out that my duties have kept me largely within this domain. However, once this is complete...hmm. But it is not my understanding that the Primes are a common destination for the Celestial races."

"Common... Perhapsss not. But then... You are not like... The othersss here. And thisss only... Essscalates... The excitement... As you might be... The exception... To the rule. Therefore... Sssimply imagine... What wondersss... You will dissscover... And perhapsss... What sssservice... You may offer... To sssuch a place... As that..."

"A service..." he considers. "In a Prime domain? But still, I might be a touch overpowered for that; do you not think?"

"Sssome might sssay... This is sssubjective. But I would sssay... Nonsenssse... As I am sure... You are more than capable... To manage yourssself. And besssides… You sssaid it yourssself. Thisss domain already has… More than adequate… Sssupport… From those who choose… To remain here. Do you truly wish… To ssserve… Among a sssea… Of ssso many… The sssame as you…?"

"I…um…" he muses deeply.

The thought did carry deep meaning, and he had already long considered what he might do here after his contract was complete. He briefly reflected on that conversation he had once with Aelwyn, that this life is only temporary, and then we move on to something else. A path, where Fate might tend to guide us. These were apparently Ecco's words, and he had come to cherish this philosophy as her special gift to him.

He darted his eyes around the plaza, observing the various other denizens as they travelled by, and with such travels likely repeated a nauseating number of times by now. Then he reflected on his own, those he had already made and what might follow if he should remain here for…how long? He was immortal, and this virtually guaranteed him his own infinity.

"Consssider these thoughtsss…" Adalon continues. "As you complete… Your term… In thisss place. The Seasss of Creation… Are vassst… And you may find… Many opportunitiesss… Among those… Who themssselves… Offer their own… Contribution…"

"What do you mean? What sort of contribution?"

"Sssstrength can be found… In many formsss. Combine these… And you have power. Teach… And you give direction… On how to use thisss… To improve… The end result. What comesss after… Will be nothing short… Of miraculousss. A creation… Borne out of many… United into one… And with sssuch beauty… As to rival… The finessst worksss of art. But not in ssstone or clay. Rather in life… And inssspired to rise… With refined purpossse…"

"Fascinating…" he whispers intriguingly. "Very well, but do you have a suggestion of where to begin? This could become very complex, very quickly."

"Indeed!" she nods. "I might begin… By examining… A Prime domain… With a sssubstantial amount… Of diversssity… Of sssource material. And it jussst ssso happensss... One of these... Ssstands out... In my mind. Tae'Eladar..."

"Tae'Eladar. Why specifically that one?"

"It carriesss... Ssseveral qualitiesss... Sssimultaneously. Sssuch as isssolation... As a platform... To prevent... External interference. And it containsss... Many diverssse racesss... Each with their own... Unique qualitiesss... But disssorganized... In how they apply themsssselves..."

"No one has attempted this in the past?"

Adalon simply gazes at him unknowingly and shrugs.

"But of course," he muses. "I suppose the answer to that becomes clear. The foibles of mortals," he chuckles softly. "Then I should conduct some research on this."

"Perfect! Then I shall leave you... To your thoughtsss. Perhapsss... One day... We will meet again... Ssson of the Mountain..." she finishes with a demure glance at the large feature behind them.

Adalon moves away, leaving Thaelyn deeply entranced by the suggestion. He saunters off towards the court to report in, but his mind was now travelling elsewhere.

"Sound the alarm! They're coming!"

Shouts rang out in another Avariel village as the three dragons once again launched their attack on the hapless people. By this time, the Avariel population was on the decline, as more of them were killed in these attacks which repeated every year. One after another village was sacked and razed, buildings were smashed, livestock was carried away, and the people had no other choice but to flee for their lives, only to try to rebuild again afterwards. It was an arduous and painful cycle.

"Hurry! We have to leave now!" shouts a woman to her husband.

"I know, but I can't leave my books behind. They are simply too valuable, and it's all we have left."

"We don't have time for this!"

The man rushes to grab several books he had on his table and stuffs them into a bag. The routine was not unfamiliar, and like with so many others in the village, most of it was in a partial state of readiness anyway. It had become a routine part of life to have most of their valuables in bags ready to just pick up and go. The buildings would be abandoned as the people took to the skies to escape, then to go look for another location to settle and try again.

He grabbed the last of his books from the table, including a small black leather-bound tome that had been passed down through the generations, and placed them in the bag.

"That's the last of it," he ushers. "All right, now we go."

The two of them dashed out the door and immediately took off, flapping their wings furiously to evade the inbound dragons and their tyrannical rage. Behind them, the house they once lived in was summarily torn apart.

The small population quickly departed the area, now searching for another mountain region in which to settle, while slowly being pushed across the land. Occasionally, smaller groups would join with other villages, trying to merge into larger populations, but this also posed the risk where more people would come into jeopardy simultaneously. Overall, the number of choices was decreasing as each village was wrecked, reducing them to a smaller territory each time.

The village refugees coursed their way through the skies, reduced very literally down to only what they could carry. They arrived at the next village seeking sanctuary.

"More of them come," mutters a local resident as he observes their arrival.

"Yes," affirms another one. "And soon the dragons will find us too, and then we will all need to flee."

"There must be something we can do to correct this!"

"The priests tell us our goddess has a plan, but it is not ready. For now, we must keep our distance as best we can."

"It's been centuries for this plan! Why is it taking so long?"

"I do not pretend to understand the workings of the gods, but you are right, I too am becoming increasingly impatient when I see more refugees torn from their homes."

"What if we were to try asking for help from the other races?"

"I've heard the elders speak of this, but our numbers are dropping so low by now that they're concerned over how we might appear too weak in their eyes. They may instead wish to take their own gain at our expense."

"What has become of this world then? Our goddess cannot help us, the other races cannot, or perhaps will not help us, and every year we hear of more people fleeing from their homes. Soon there will be nothing left of us."

The refugees land in the village and are given food and shelter, taking up space in other family homes until something new comes along.

The wife and husband from the previous village take up with the family of a local sage and scholar.

"Greetings, friends," the scholar announces. "Our home is humble, but you are welcome to what we have."

"Ours was once that way," the husband relents. "But then, what can you claim for yourself when you have less than a year to build anything before it is destroyed again."

"A group of us has been preparing to find a new region to settle in the east. These dragons have been heard mostly to be attacking the villages to the west, so we are hoping to evade outside their territory."

"If it gives you the freedom from their savagery, I offer my best wishes. Maybe we could lend our help, but I am no laborer."

"What sort of work do you do?"

"I am, or at least try to be, a student in the alchemical arts. I have a number of books passed down to me, and I was hoping to one day find some value in them to help our people."

"Alchemy studies? How might alchemy help our people against these dragons?"

"I cannot be sure, but one of my ancestors told me these books are too valuable to let go. Therefore, I cherish them in the hopes that one day they might find a purpose."

"May I ask what sorts of formulas you keep in there?"

"I have a number of concoctions, some of which offer healing and curative properties. This can surely be of service to our people, and I often use these in trade for other things. Then there are a couple of books with some very old recipes. I have not found a use for them as yet, as we are being driven out of our homes before I have time to study them."

"Then you should find a safe place to bring yourselves where you can find this time. An alchemist that does not have time to pursue his craft is not of much value to the people."

"You are so right. There is one book I hold here that has been handed down through the centuries with a very curious formula inside. It demands some strange reagents, but so far, I have been unable to find them."

"What sort of reagents?"

"The most important is a type of berry said to be found in a place where the land does not melt. But this is a strange reference. Are we speaking of a place that is very hot, such as with molten rock, but this particular rock does not melt?"

"I do not know of such a place anywhere near to us, and even if I did, I could hardly imagine a plant of any kind surviving in such a place where the land might be so hot that the rocks themselves tend to melt."

"All right, then what else can it be?"

"Perhaps we need to think on the other side of it. A place that is very cold all year."

"I did think of this once, but I cannot think of plants growing within a glacier. You still need soil, do you not?"

"True, but I have heard of a few high mountain plateaus where it is so cold, the ground seems frozen, but without any ice cover."

"Interesting, where are they?"

"Coincidentally, the ones I'm thinking of are to the east, some distance north of a site some of our people are considering moving to. The region also has a number of caves in it. Our Elders think this might be a good choice for us to take shelter, in case those dragons come looking for us."

"How so? Are these caves sturdy enough to stop them?"

"The rocks are very thick, and the passage runs deep. We think if we could place our best valuables inside there, to prevent their loss, and then take shelter when the dragons come, it might be enough to keep our people safe until the dragons spend their wrath and depart."

"And then what? Your homes are still lost."

"They will be lost anyway, but at least this time, if the caves can serve as shelter, we are no longer running to unknown lands. We can rebuild where we are."

"And when the dragons come back the next time? This will repeat endlessly, especially when they know where you are."

"It seems they can find us anyway, and there will soon be no more land for us to flee to. We need to make a stand somewhere."

"What about the Winged Mother? Does she still advise us?"

"The last word from the priests says that nothing has changed. They say a savior will come to us one day to defeat the dragons, but many of us are asking if that day will come before or after there is anything left to save."

"A savior to defeat the dragons?" the husband considers. "One savior against three dragons… A single dragon alone is enough to demand a full army. What do you need to kill all three?"

"I have no idea, and this simply confounds the suggestion."

Chapter 10

LANDFALL

In the Time of Flowers, a Child of the Wheel,
Will shine through a column upright;
The Son of the Mountain, a millennium proud,
Where Justice has been His delight.

Across the Land, they shall herald His name,
And many will follow His course;
Woe be to Evil, wherever it lay,
To be smitten beneath His endorse.

The Pillars of Three shall He bring into cause,
A mighty power beheld;
The fortune of Man, the strength of the Beast,
And the Spirit of nature to meld.

Prophecies of Adalon the Silver, Book One

A elwyn and Thaelyn were sitting at a local café in Sigil, deep in conversation. His contract was nearly complete and now he had to decide on his future course.

"Are you still planning on doing this?" she asks.

"Aelwyn, I feel this could be a very promising direction for me."

"Travelling to a Prime domain… I find myself perplexed over what you might do there. I would think you might actually feel rather stifled for the inherent limitations."

"To the contrary, as I have conducted a series of studies on the history and culture of Tae'Eladar. There is a variety of data to be examined, and already I see a few curious challenges."

"For a Celestial?"

"Indeed, and perhaps this quality may work well to my favor."

"In what way?"

"There are a number of different races currently living there, each with its own cultural gifts. At present, they do not interact in any way so as to take full advantage of these traits. But if to combine them, their versatility could be magnified. For this, I could begin a campaign of education to make them aware of these qualities and how to blend them together for their mutual benefit."

"Can they not do this themselves?"

"Aelwyn, we are speaking of mortals here, and especially those who do not care to speak at all. Instead, they tend to segregate themselves by their racial traits. And then, there is a considerable amount of corruption and villainy occurring down there. This would clearly offer me some occupation."

"But Thaelyn, the Primes are well-known for these qualities. It is an inherent part of their nature. They do not share the purity of the Celestial realms."

"Perhaps not, but at the same time, they do not have a proper form of leadership in which to teach them better. I see a number of nations among them, and they often do nothing more than argue. However, if to bring a uniform philosophy into this equation, they might then find some manner of common ground together."

"One moment…" she pauses with a finger. "Is it not true that the Primes maintain some form of religious worship? Are you suggesting this cannot provide the same function?"

"It is true there are multiple forms of religion down there, but this also adds to the turmoil. First, not everyone follows it, and second, those who do are spread across a broad spectrum of Powers, and this tends to bring about its own dilemma as one abrades against another."

"And so, instead of this, you would suggest replacing it with your own?"

"Not specifically… I am speaking of education here. To bring about the encouragement of a more consistent and refined direction. Rather than to have one say his or her god is superior to the rest, help them to realize they each serve an independent role alongside each other, not in contrast to each other. You speak of the purity of the Celestial realms, but cannot this same purity, or at least a near facsimile, be encouraged on Tae'Eladar? This is where the aspect of leadership comes in, and for this I might suggest my Celestial quality to serve a unique role."

"Oh, and what might that be?" she grins. "I will be most interested to hear this one."

"For one, the simple fact of my immortality… Consider this premise. A leader emerges and brings about a refined moment in history, but for how long? He remains until his mortal demise and is then replaced by another who engages in a completely different, perhaps even contrary practice."

"This is the definition of a Prime domain, my dear spirit-brother," she smirks.

"Indeed it is, and one could also say their most common failure. And this is where I could make a substantial difference. Where is the progress in this scenario? The evolution of a society, the motivation to pursue an ascendant goal, immaterial as opposed to their more common lustful traditions. You speak of your studies in the Sensorium to pursue enlightenment. Why should they be denied this, if only due to their lack of leadership to expose them to the idea?"

"Uh oh…are you turning my own arguments against me now?"

"Look at the history of that world. It has stagnated for many millennia, if only due to these principles I mentioned: Segregation, indifference, corruption, and contradictions. This is further compounded by the mortality of its leaders, no two of which may carry things forward consistently, and who are more often absorbed by their personal motivations than improving the general environment. And this is to assume they even live long enough to make the attempt, which by the way is where another of my fine qualities may come in," he grins.

"Really!" she offers enthusiastically. "And which of these do you regard now?"

"Aelwyn, my dear spirit-sister," he reflects fondly. "You should know me well enough by now to find your own answer. I am a soldier in the court of my Father. The lessons I carry may give direction to many, and my longevity may keep me in service for a much longer duration than any other. But more importantly, I have faced down creatures from across the Planes that would cause many to shrink in fear. A mortal opponent, such as an assassin or a would-be usurper, would be no match for me."

Aelwyn leans forward to the table and gazes concernedly at him.

"Thaelyn, are you thinking of going down there to be their new leader?"

"I would not dare suggest becoming a leader amongst the mortal societies. But if to go there and bring the people together in some manner of harmony, providing them with a strong enough incentive to join their inherent strengths and cultural values, and for a long enough duration until the ill-mannered amongst them fades, we might finally see the sort of progress they have been lacking for so long."

"Carefully, people," cautions the group leader. "They can't be too far away. Stiv, do ya see anythin'?"

"The tracks are a mite thin here. The dry grass is too matted from grazin'."

"They had to come through here though," adds the young mage. "It's the only way. Their camp is to the north, right?"

"Aye, an' they need ta be comin' 'cross this mound ta get in ta town."

"Just stay close," issues the leader. "There's a lot of places ta hide up here."

"With our luck," moans the cleric. "They're back in their camp eating dinner already."

"I have my doubts, Sara," the mage offers. "The supplies were only noticed missing a short while ago by the shopkeeper. That's when the guard called us to get out here and look for them. They can't be too far."

"Aye," remarks Stiv. "An' for all yer yappin', I'm sure they'll be jumpin' out at us afore ya know it."

Four young people from a local town had come out into the wilderness searching for what was believed to be a group of orcs that stole some goods from a local shop. They were a small band of adventurers that occasionally took on odd jobs for the town guards and others as a means of supporting themselves.

The leader was a burly young man wearing leather armor and carrying a longsword. His equipment wasn't top-of-the-line, but it was adequate to his needs until he could afford better. Next was his diminutive companion, another male, skinny in comparison, but limber and with quick reflexes. He served their scouting needs, among other talents. The last two were female, one a mage apprentice, still in training and struggling all the way, and a young cleric who was similarly overwhelmed in her studies.

The group was coursing their way across some hilly terrain, located north outside their home town. An orcish camp was known to exist further northward, and bands of orcs were sometimes seen marauding around the countryside up there. It was not as often for them to come this far south, but occasionally a few supplies might go missing, and with no one else to blame, the orcs were often suspected to be the cause.

The band continues moving over the hilltop, carefully surveying the countryside around them. There was a cluster of trees some distance to the south, with more to be seen on the other hills leading off to the east. They could see several large boulders sticking out of the hillside further along their path, a good place for an ambush, but so far there was no sign of orcs.

"I've got a feelin' about this," the leader mentions. "Right up there," he points at the rocks.

"Aye, Bron," Stiv affirms. "I think ya might have somethin' there."

"Breena, get yer spells ready."

"I'm ready," the mage replies tensely.

"May the Morninglord give us strength," Sara offers.

They continued several more steps, keeping a close eye on the set of boulders ahead of them. Bron leads them in a wide circle hoping to flank the target while Stiv looks for any shadows or appendages that could be sticking out. They take several more cautious steps until Stiv catches something just barely visible.

"Bron! Look there!" he whispers urgently.

Just behind one of the rocks, they see part of a body hunched down.

Bron pulls out his sword and takes up a ready stance, while Stiv moves to the side to offer support. Breena and Sara take up behind the men as a secondary line for ranged attacks.

A lone orc jumps up from behind the rocks, shouting a war cry and waving a large mace. He draws the group's attention in the direction of the rocks, but just as they orient themselves, more orcs emerge out of hiding from a cluster of bushes further along the hilltop and to the side.

"It's a bloody trap!" Stiv scorns.

"Look, over there!" Breena shouts as she points to the side.

Coming up from behind, out of the nearby grove of trees, was yet another orc attempting to flank them.

The team immediately repositions themselves for better cover, with Bron taking up a stand in front to draw the main body and Stiv hoping to oppose the flanker. The two women duck behind, and prepare for a fight.

✦✦✦

Thaelyn and Aelwyn were meeting for a final farewell in Mount Celestia. They were convening here, rather than the city, because his duty was now complete and he was making his final preparations to leave for Tae'Eladar, and he couldn't do that inside the city proper.

"Where do you think you will go first?" she asks.

"I have no doubt that wherever I find myself, there will likely be much work to attend, so I applied my skill at Short Prophecy to see if I could peer into a few places that might hold an immediate need. Needless to say, I saw many possibilities, but one stood out, and I think I should not delay myself long for it. I will begin my work in the western coastal region…here…" he directs to a virtual image he formed as a magical projection in the air. "From there, I could then proceed through the local region and eastward, spreading my teachings and perhaps leaving behind a few wards to continue in my stead."

"Very well, Spirit-brother. Do not forget to return on occasion to share your travels with me. I would be most interested to share any new sensations you might discover along the way."

"Indeed, and I know how you so enjoy those moments. Then, I will take my leave, Aelwyn. Do take care of yourself."

The two of them touch foreheads as a symbol of their affection, and Thaelyn steps away a few paces to prepare for his departure.

✦✦✦✦✦

Breena scanned the area frantically, trying to decide her best course of action. She chooses to try taking down the flanker first, giving the men an opportunity to focus on the front line. She began calling up her limited magic skills hoping to send out a stream of fire at the inbound orc to the side. But as she makes her chant, the fire only fizzles.

"Oops! Dammit!" she scowls.

Sara steps in to offer a divine smite to stun the orc, knowing her skill would be more likely to hit. She calls up a potent bolt from above to strike down on his head, which rumbles through his body and drops him to his knees briefly.

Bron was facing down two orc warriors with maces, and behind them was the group leader carrying a large two-handed axe. The orcish leader seemed content to hold back while his underlings took on the fight.

With the ladies directing their attention at the flanker, Stiv instead joins Bron using his daggers, and together they exchanged blows with the orcs, mostly clashing and deflecting each other's hits.

Breena felt nervous at trying another fire spell, so she decided to try a different strategy, this time to simply detain the orc with a Spell of Holding until the men could come around for it. She makes ready to cast it as the flanking orc pulls himself back to his feet. Sara steps in front, holding her staff at the ready, in case she needed to deflect his attack while Breena cast her next spell.

✦ ✦ ✦◆✦ ✦ ✦

Thaelyn made one final glance around his home and a nod at Aelwyn before making his exit. He then called on his divine gift to produce a column of light to reach down and envelop him. The shaft radiated and sparkled with tiny flecks and streams. His body began to glow softly and then to lift up, rising high off the ground and vanishing into a planar rift above.

Breena charges up another spell and takes aim at the flanking orc. She lets go of a ball of energy which zips across the ground and collides with the orc, freezing his motion rigidly.

"Good, now, don't anybody touch him, or you might break the spell."

She and Sara now turn to the front line, ready to offer their assistance to the others.

The two men were still in a stalemate of clashing blades with maces. Neither of them was very highly refined in their skills, but as a young group, they had to start somewhere, and funding was often too short to train and equip anything better.

Breena and Sara both considered offering some manner of magic to support the men, but before either of them could call up any offensive action, something new catches their eye.

Just off to the side, they saw a bright column of light descending down from the sky above. It was a most unusual sight, as no one had ever seen anything like this before. Breena turned and stared at it.

"What in all the hells..." she mutters.

Sara followed soon after, and the two of them gawked at it.

The prominent illumination from the column then caught the attention of the two men and the remaining orcs, and the fighting slowed to a standstill as the two lines backed away from each other. All eyes were now turned to the column of light, until something appeared within it.

A glowing body began to descend from above, then to settle softly to the ground. The image was surrounded in light which then faded to reveal the form of a man, and soon the column vanished.

He was tall, with silver-white hair at shoulder length and pale skin. He appeared young, which contradicted with the white hair, as this was most often associated with age. He wore a suit of partial plate armor, with joints of a chain mesh to allow for free movement, as compared to the traditional plate that was mostly solid and very cumbersome. Also, it seemed to ripple and glow softly with a potent magical force. Finally, on his back he carried a large two-handed sword, that same one he recovered from Navaatu.

Thaelyn stood there surveying the area. He took notice of the people and the apparent conflict, but it conveniently came to a halt with his arrival. So he took this opportunity to examine the local surroundings and sample the air. He looked up into the sky at the sun, holding up a hand to partially block the intense light.

"Natural stellar radiance..." he mutters quietly.

He then turns his focus to the ground under his feet, kneeling down and reaching out to pick up a handful of soil, then to bring it close to his nose to sniff it.

"Prime material firmament..." he muses.

The adventuring group stares at him in bewilderment, as do the orcs. He seems oblivious to the battle scene, and more interested in dirt.

Thaelyn stands up again and swivels to take in the wider view of the surrounding hills and their accompanying foliage.

"Trees, shrubs, primordial air…" he looks up to see several clouds in the sky. "And native meteorological accumulations!" he smiles.

"Blimey," Stiv wonders. "Does anyone here know what he's goin' on about? I ain't never saw a man so giddy about clouds afore."

"Sara," Breena whispers. "Did you see that? I mean that light… what was it?"

"Breena, I don't know if I could answer that, but it looked almost like it came down from on-high."

"What do you mean, on-high?"

"On…high…" she asserts pointing upwards.

"Sara," Stiv utters nervously. "There ain't nothin' up there. Where is this on-high that a man could fall out of it?"

"He didn't fall down, Stiv, he rode a pillar of light. That says something to me."

Thaelyn continued to survey the region, now examining the activities of the people and their opponents, all of whom were staring at him with curiosity and hesitation. He could hear their conversation, and silently knew he would have a lot of work ahead of him, most of it simply to explain who he was, where he came from, and why he was here. No doubt, none of them had ever seen a Celestial before, and may not even know what they are.

Then the orc that was under the Holding spell began to stir. The spell was expiring.

The orc stumbled out of the rigid grip of the spell and shook his head. He refocused himself on his original target, but then noticed something new standing near him to the side. He turned to find Thaelyn.

"Uh oh…" Breena mumbles. "He's loose again."

The orc stares at Thaelyn for a moment, and assumes he's a new adversary that just arrived to join the fight. He roars his battle cry and lifts his weapon, then turns and charges.

Thaelyn instantly turns to face his aggressor. His reflexes call him to quickly extend an arm, directing his hand at the inbound combatant. He points his fingers at the orc and the creature instantly halts in its steps.

"Um, Breena," Sara mutters uncertainly. "You said uh oh, but uh oh for whom?"

Thaelyn flips his hand over and angles his fingers upwards, lifting the orc off the ground. The other orcs watched in fear and uncertainty as they observed the invisible force apparently holding their companion. He brings it close to his face and speaks firmly.

"My studies tell me your kind is not welcome here," he asserts. "Approach not me, Prime creature," he declares. "You will find no less displeasure with me as you do from the others."

He casually glances at the other orcs before returning to the captive.

"This place shall be cleansed!"

He then swaps hands, exchanging the orc from his left to right, and swings it around forcefully in a broad sweeping arc to the side, sending the orc hurtling at high velocity through the air. The hapless creature sails over hillsides and treetops into the distance until it disappears from view.

"Bloody hell, man!" Stiv wheezes.

"Dear...gods...above," Breena gasps.

"And praise the Morninglord!" Sara offers to finish the thought.

Breena turns to her friend at the statement.

"Are you sure?"

"Well, he doesn't seem to like orcs. That's a good thing, right?"

"Only partially..."

The two orcs facing Bron gaped at the sight of their companion flying off into the distance, unable to fathom any force that could bring this about, but the orc leader wasn't impressed. Rather than simply stare at the spectacle, he was going to do something about it. It was one thing to allow his underlings to take on these other obvious underlings from the town, but this new one represented a challenge. He lifts his large axe in both hands, roars a battle cry and charges forward.

"This ain't good, folks," Stiv announces.

Thaelyn turns to see the new aggressor approaching from along the hillside behind him. The orcish leader was some distance away, observing the action, and this gave Thaelyn just enough time to react. He turns and holds out his right hand at length.

The adventuring team gazes at him wondering the reason for this, but the answer soon becomes apparent as they see his greatsword leap out of its sheath on his back, spin in the air and jump into his grip.

Bron gawps in amazement at the majestic instrument with its soft blueish glow, and then glances briefly at his own flimsy longsword for comparison.

The orcish leader holds his axe aggressively, but slows to a halt as he sees the clearly evident display of the highly magical greatsword seemingly take on a life of its own and come into Thaelyn's hand.

"Are you sure you desire this, beast?" Thaelyn asks calmly.

The orc feels a renewed rage at the statement. He roars and pulls back his axe, gripping it firmly in both hands as he makes ready to lunge forward to strike.

"I will crush you, human!" he growls.

Thaelyn responds with a swift spin on his heels, swiping the blade through the air with a subtle whoosh. A clang rings out and the orc halts all motion as Thaelyn's blade finishes its arc, coming to rest reaching off to one side.

"I am not human," he retorts.

Almost immediately, a portion of the orc's right arm falls away, along with the lower part of the iron axe shaft. Soon after, his grip loosens in his left hand, causing the rest of the axe to fall to the ground. His face turns pale and loses all expression. He begins to topple, with the upper portion of his torso falling forward, and the lower portion teetering backwards, both halves falling to the ground inert.

The adventuring group winced at the obvious display, not only for the gruesomeness of the injury, but that it went along so effortlessly.

"Folks," Stiv cautions. "Keep away from that sword."

"Stiv," Breena wonders. "Did you honestly feel the need to say that?"

"No, but ya know me. I just couldn't let it go by without puttin' in a word or two."

"What is that thing made of that it could cut through an iron rod?" Bron wonders openly. "To say nothin' of the rest of it."

"Something stronger than iron," Breena responds. "My mage studies could give a few names, none of which you'll find around here."

Thaelyn now turns to the remaining two orcs, who were still staring at the sight of their leader laying in pieces on the ground.

"Think carefully on this," he announces. "Do you wish to join him, or perhaps flee to tell others of my arrival."

The orcs glanced at each other nervously, and then back at him. They yelped and dropped their weapons, then began running back down the hillside screeching.

Thaelyn watches the hasty departure. He then returns his sword to its mount and casually saunters over to the team.

"Peace, my friends," he ushers softly. "I am not your enemy."

"Thank the gods for that," Breena submits with a sigh. "But who are you, and where did you just come from?"

"Aye," Stiv adds. "An' what was that light ya came out of?"

"Indeed," Thaelyn admits. "I suppose I will hear many such questions as these, and perhaps more after that. At least until, I should hope, a few of you might pass the word on my behalf. Let us begin with a kind introduction, shall we? I am called Thaelyn. May I know your names?"

"Well, yes," Breena responds anxiously. "I suppose it's only proper. My name is Breena Thaxter, and this is Stiv Armon, then we have Bron Kurgin and Sara Highton."

"How nice, and a pleasant greeting to each of you," he offers with a smile and a subtle bow.

The nobility of his presentation instantly struck the two women, who had at least a little bit of culturing as part of their studies.

The two men also took notice, and began to associate this with the highbrow manner of a town elder or wealthy merchant.

"As to your questions," Thaelyn continues. "I think we will have much to talk about in this regard, although I would imagine there may also be some amount of confusion along the way until we can fully explain the associated meanings."

"Meanings?" Sara interjects. "What sort of meanings? I mean, um…we saw you come down in some kind of a pillar of light. And… um…" she narrows her eyes as she strains to make out what she sees. "Are my eyes playing tricks on me, or are your eyes actually gold in color?"

"It is not your eyes, Child. This is my natural color."

"Child?" she responds with a new chill.

"Well, yes, this is a term of endearment we often use to describe such people as you."

"Me personally…or…"

"The mortal races, Child. Our kind describes you as the Children of Creation."

Now Sara stumbles backwards, nearly toppling over until Breena catches her. Her breath quickens and her face goes pale.

"Did I hear you say a moment ago you were not human?" she squeaks. "Then what are you?"

"This is in fact a good question, and if you can find your proper footing again," he smiles softly, "we can bring ourselves into understanding. I suppose at some moment in time, I will need to explain this, so let us begin the lesson."

"A lesson, is it?" Stiv frowns. "Wonderful, an' here I thought my time in the old schoolhouse was done by now."

"To be certain, one should never consider their education to be fully complete, as there is always something new to be found."

Thaelyn begins a slow pace in front of the four friends.

"My kind is properly known as Aasimar. Does that word hold any special meaning to you?"

"No, actually," Sara replies tenuously.

"Indeed, I might expect as much, if you do not travel in the right circles…although these circles would need to be rather unique. Also, I suppose I should mention the term is a rather limited expression, as there are exceptionally few of us."

"Why is that?"

"Ours is not a proper society, as yours might be. We are a created example, and often for a specific need. Therefore, our numbers are so small as it is quite rare to find this need."

"Really. That's…interesting…I think."

"What about the word Celestial, would you happen to know that one?"

"Um, well, yes and no. It's a word, but not used in this context. Although it does carry a certain amount of loftiness to it."

"Yes," he smiles. "I suppose it might, if only due to the language itself offering some pertinence. In this case, we are speaking of a type of station, as some may hold this station while others hold different stations."

"Oh, well, all right, I can associate with that easily enough. I'm a cleric, but still very young, while my mentors are much higher."

"Precisely! But here, we are not speaking of a profession, rather a stage of development in the course of a people, on the scale of whole societies, developing and growing over what could be extreme periods of time, until they rise to much higher places than where you might find such as yourselves in the present day…as what we now call Children."

"Oh dear…" she mumbles nervously. "That sounds almost like they could be, um…I'm a little afraid to say it…like gods?"

"Indeed, you are much closer than you might realize. To such a young society as yours, they might certainly appear this way, or nearly so, due to their knowledge, and perhaps also their native abilities. And indeed, this is where one of those meanings must come into play. Because to understand who and what I am, you must also learn that your own example is not the only one, and neither is it anywhere near the highest form of existence possible. There are those who are much older, and therefore much higher, if only for the merit of time playing a role. Where the gods are concerned, we could easily describe them as the highest example, with these others coming perhaps near to it by now."

"Incredible! But wait! Is this to say people…maybe like us…could actually…one day…I mean, um…?"

"The simple answer is yes. It would demand a considerable length of time, a great amount of good fortune and hard work, dedication to principle, maybe some specialized leadership, and any number of other devotions. But the process, which we would collectively describe as evolution, begins with the small and aims to go higher. You are simply very early into it."

"Unbelievable… And yes, I think I can see what you were talking about with the confusion part."

"He's certainly got me confused!" Stiv chuckles.

"Yes, this would be where the idea of that continued education comes from," Thaelyn glares playfully at him. "Therefore, the Celestial station is only an intermediate position between yours, which we might call a Prime or a corporeal station, and the divine, which would count as full godhood."

"But just a moment here!" Breena asserts. "Unless I'm getting more confused than poor Stiv over here, this sounds like a progression, from small things to big ones, but INCLUDING the gods themselves. Aren't they something that's, well, I'm not sure how to describe it, but they always seem so, um…mystical, supernatural…?"

"Many societies might see it this way, if only due to the dogmas of their religions. But in truth, the Estelar, as they are properly called, are a society of beings, much like any other, and only after some untold eternity of time lifted them up that high. From there, they may offer occasional guidance to the younger societies, but often in this form you would interpret as deities, since you are otherwise too young to fully understand them on their native terms."

"Oh! Really! Do they make trouble for each other? Because I know people who worship some of them, including this girl here…" she thumbs at Sara, "…although she's a friend of mine, so she's not as bad…"

"Gee, thanks, Breena," Sara chuckles.

"Yeah, but anyway, people who like to rake on others who worship other gods."

"This may be true," Thaelyn smiles. "And I can certainly see how some of this might occur. But it is not as likely THEM doing it, rather YOU who are doing it, and in their name, as you might think they would want this. Mortals tend to have egos, and those egos can make their own interpretations, irrespective of what any gods might say or do."

"Oops! Yeah, that would make sense, actually."

"The only true exception to this might involve the Measure of Balance, which is a rule of law, or perhaps a philosophy of life, depending on how you might wish to interpret it. Like most societies, they have their rules, but in this case, theirs must rise to a much higher cause than anything you may need to contend with down here, as they hold a form of responsibility over much more than a simple town, or a small population of villagers. They must think in terms of all Creation."

"Wow!" Sara croons. "That would certainly be the domain of a god."

"It would, and they do take this unto themselves. The two sides are divided on the principles of positive and negative polarity, and they offer different perspectives for how to manage it. And both sides are required for this balance, as life and all things around us must follow a careful path down the middle, simply to ensure its integrity for survival. You might have nurturing on one side, and then challenge on the other. The road to eternity is never a free ride."

"This is not the sort of lesson I ever got in my temple. Our priests don't even speak of it."

"This would be a very privileged lesson, to be sure. A much older society might learn of this, if given enough time, and the elevation to teach it. Yours has yet to reach that far. Under normal circumstances, you might not be ready for it."

"But then," Breena wonders. "Are you actually supposed to be doing this in the first place?"

"I must follow this same rule. We cannot simply unload all the great secrets of Creation into your laps, as you are not ready for most of it. However, I can offer a few lessons here and there to help you grow. As for this here, my simple arrival will naturally demand a few allowances, if only to keep you standing upright," he grins.

"Uh huh…thank you."

"Now, returning back to the Celestial races, we have two kinds, with the first being the natural one, as I mentioned, where you might grow over the course of time, and the Estelar would eventually take notice of you, and thereby wish to recruit you into a form of apprenticeship."

"Apprenticeship! You mean, like me and my Master at the mage guild?"

"In a very similar manner to that, but here to learn the rules of those higher lessons I spoke of. And this would be to prepare them, ultimately, for that final ascension into their own form of divinity."

"Ascension!" Sara gasps. "Just think of it, Breena. One day, you're just an apprentice, and then next, you might be a true god."

"I don't think I CAN think of that, Sara," she sighs wearily.

"This is all way over my head," Bron relents. "I'm just barely keepin' up with any of it."

"This does not occur quickly, mind you," Thaelyn asserts. "Time is the most important element here, and great lengths of it. These beings, many of them, have truly phenomenal lifespans by this time, with some of them being immortal."

"Ouch!" Breena winces.

"But we're speaking of the natural form," Sara muses. "And if I'm interpreting this correctly, this might reflect on people like us, who are a full society. You said yours is not, so how does that fit in?"

"Indeed, this is the other side of it," he affirms. "From time to time, those in such high places may find it necessary, so it would seem, to create what we call a hybrid, which is to cross such as they with something more approximating yourself, in order to create a kind of bridge. They might do this for a number of reasons, not the least of which is to make interaction easier, if such a thing is desired, or perhaps to serve some special role, and for this point, more on the scale of those same Child races."

"Oh wow. Is that why you're here now?"

"My creation is still something of a mystery to me. The Measure of Balance must apply to all things. So, not even I am immune to it," he chuckles. "There is apparently a reason out there, but I, like so many others, am expected to grow and learn to find my own way. I was once made aware that there may be a hidden meaning I must search for, but I have yet to find it. As for being here now, I received a very intriguing suggestion once for a role I could play in the lives of others to help them grow and learn. And this directed me here."

"Ain't that a little like overkill?" Stiv offers. "Someone like you, down here with peeps like us?"

"You would not be the first to ask this. Even I once asked this, but the suggestion itself posed some rather interesting prospects. And I enjoy a good challenge."

"But then," Sara considers. "What are you hybridized with? You look human to me…mostly. The hair and eyes are a bit funny, but um…"

"Yes, one side of me seems to be human. I suspect these colors are influenced by the other side, but this gives me my general corporeal form. Although as a hybrid, I cannot say my full manifestation is entirely corporeal, as part of my essence is also a potent spiritual presence reaching outside this form."

"Oh dear!" she draws back and scans the outline around him.

"But to say I am a hybrid is to say this is mixed with something else. And naturally, if we are to describe this on the scale of a Celestial, which is so often referred to as being near to that final ascension…"

Sara felt a new chill rushing down her spine as he spoke, and further as she reflected on the column of light he came out of. Her feelings were beginning to spread to the others, as well.

Thaelyn continues, "…The other side, at this moment, would indeed involve the Powers themselves."

"Hold on!" Breena blasts nervously. "Is this to say you're half god, or something?"

"Well, technically, yes…"

"Technically!" Stiv yelps. "Great gods, man. It might be a technical thing to those peeps up there in the clouds, but for us wee folk down here, that's a bit like understatin' things, ain't it?"

"Perhaps, but I am trying not to apply myself on that specific level here…" Thaelyn attempts to soothe. "Though one of them is my Father, and…"

Sara had taken as much as she could handle by this time. She felt faint, and her legs were weak, causing her to collapse to the ground, dragging Breena down with her. Stiv rushed to their side, hoping to support them, but unsure what else to do, as he wasn't much of a religious sort. Bron hesitated briefly, trying to decide which way to go first, to join with his friends, or simply to back away. His arms felt limp, and his sword nearly fell out of his grip.

"Yer…a child…of a god?" he wheezes faintly. "And ya came down here…all the way down here…just to teach us somethin' new."

Now the sensation took over. His sword dropped to the ground, and he fell to meet the others.

Thaelyn simply sighed and grinned gently, shaking his head.

"I suspected this would happen," he relents passively. "Very well, I suppose this is to be expected, at least initially. But now, let us see if we can find our strength again, and behave sensibly."

"Sensibly?" Sara blurts. "You're half god, and you want US to behave sensibly? You know, Stiv was right, you must be crazy to think this is anything other than pure overkill."

"As a matter of fact, I have a friend back home, and we were speaking on this same subject. Maybe it is, to a certain degree. But again, I will recall that original suggestion to come down here at all. Apparently, you people hold certain strengths, but unfortunately, you never once realized this to bring it together on your own. Now, if none of you can realize your own value, where do you think you might learn of it, except from someone who might see a much larger picture."

"Dear gods above...but you do have a point. Who sent you? Your Father?"

"Actually, no. I once met with an individual who held a curious perspective of things. And since I am somewhat unique in my example, being who and what I am, this might afford a special opportunity for me."

"You know," Breena suggests. "That sounds like part of that mystery you spoke of to find your way in life."

"I, um...well, yes, I suppose I must admit..." he pauses to think. "A path...Fate. Indeed! And she did seem very enthusiastic about it, like she was trying to promote something."

"Then your answer might be found down here as well. You came here to help us, but you might also find your own."

Thaelyn had kneeled down by now to assist the others, but as this suggestion came out, he drew back a moment to consider the idea.

"Life can take some very curious turns, my friends. And like I said, I would not be immune to it. I may be the child of one of the Powers, but I am still a man seeking his fortune. It simply works on another level, in my case."

"Maybe so," Stiv admits. "But bloody hell, mates. This man could probably rule this world, an' all he wants from us is a wee bit of chatter."

"And I did not come here to have such people as you bow before me. This is not my purpose. So please, stand up and let us continue."

Thaelyn offers a hand to help them up. Sara looks at his hand, and then at her limp body.

"Stiv, I can't move my legs. You still seem to have a little strength. Can you help me up?"

"Aye, barely..."

Thaelyn assists the group back to their feet so they can continue their conversation.

"Um..." Sara tries again. "Who is your divine...um, you said Father, right?"

"Yes," Thaelyn nods. "I do not actually have a mother, which is a somewhat unusual case. I was created entirely by his hand."

Sara's legs began to feel weak again. She gripped Breena and Stiv for support.

"No mother…all Father…but then, where did the human part come from?"

"Yeah, um…" Breena interjects. "According to my mom, you need one of each to make a baby," she smirks gently.

"Indeed, young lady," he chuckles. "You are absolutely correct, and far be it for me to argue otherwise. But the Powers hold many talents, as I am sure you can appreciate. To create a body based on a known design is actually not so far from reality with them."

"Yeah, right…after all, they're gods," she titters.

"Such knowledge as this is not necessarily limited only to gods. A society with the right level of scientific appeal can achieve similar results."

"Really! Is this somewhere on the ladder you need to climb on this road to ascension?"

"It is, and not necessarily as high as you might think."

"Incredible. But then, who is he?"

"Mine is the greater deity known as Tyr."

Sara lets out a compulsive yelp at the mention, although the others were not as savvy to the training she had received in her studies. Her legs gave out for a second time, but at least the others caught her before she fell completely to the ground.

Breena and the rest simply stared at her, and then at him, trying to associate the meaning. But that particular name was not as commonly known amongst their society, as opposed to the more customary colloquial terms they so often used.

"Sara," she asks tentatively. "Which one is that? This is your study, not mine."

"The Just God," she wheezes. "One of the more prolific forms of worship we have in our world."

Now Breena realizes the meaning. She gasps sharply and stumbles back, then collapses to the ground again, this time dragging Sara down with her. The others couldn't help but cluster around and hunch over penitently.

"Him?!" Breena yips. "Your Father is Him? Eh, He...him...whatever... In all the nine...um, no wait, I better not say that...not in front of you. But HIM??"

Thaelyn found himself once again standing over the group huddling on the ground. He rolled his eyes and rubbed his brow, as he found it amusing, at least as much for the curious reactions, as it was for his expectations of these simple people. But now he had to coax them back into the conversation, and so he again reached down to assist them back to their feet.

"Uh..." Breena begins again. "So, um... What, um... Or maybe, why...no...yes... Well, what I mean to say is, um, I think I want to ask why you're here...well, other than to teach something. I mean, do you think you'll open a school or something? Or do you have something else in mind?"

"My first request is to have you relax," he soothes. "I did a little study of this place before my arrival, and I understand that your beliefs in this world might cause such reactions as this. But I would much prefer if we could see each other as partners working together on something important, rather than the people revering me as something holy."

"I don't think that's going to happen," Sara pants. "Partners or otherwise, you ARE something holy. People will see you this way no matter what."

"Well, I suppose you do hold a point. But can there not be a compromise to this somewhere?"

"I don't know if I could answer that, but if you came to us to teach something, you'll probably be seen as giving out some sort of divine aid to our people along the way. What sort of result are you looking to accomplish here?"

"As I said earlier, I believe each of the individual societies in this world carries its own unique qualities and virtues, if only someone knew how to blend it all together into one harmonious society all working towards a common goal. This is what I hope to teach."

"More of that evolution stuff, it sounds like," Breena notes.

"We're not doing it on our own, so now HE'S here. Worse, if he was directed here, it means someone up there isn't happy with us."

"Right!" Sara affirms. "And THAT would involve something holy. So, school or whatever, following you would be like following a holy savior."

"All right," Thaelyn accedes. "But if we can try to make this seem as much like you with one of your mentors, perhaps it might not feel as…supernatural…as what you describe," he smiles.

"Maybe, but if anyone could do it, the son of a god would surely qualify."

"Then, we should find ourselves a pleasant little place to sit and discuss a few ideas. I will surely need apprentices, and I would wish to invite the four of you to join as the starting point…if you feel yourselves up to it. Ultimately, it is my hope to travel and meet with people in this world, and perhaps to bring more of them into this, maybe to form some kind of movement. They who would wish to be my friends are welcome to join at my side, while those who might be my enemy…well, they would be best served to simply keep away from me."

The weeks and months passed and Thaelyn began to draw attention from the local societies. The initial group he encountered teamed up with him and he began teaching them his philosophies and manners.

Breena was receiving a more directed form of tutoring in her mage studies while Sara was given additional instruction in the gods and their relationship to mortal men. She would never have understood any of this before, if only to study in the temple where she started, as these lessons went well beyond the world around them.

Bron and Stiv were each given more specialized training to improve their style, based on Thaelyn's long experience in combat tactics. Slowly, they matured into a well-coordinated force, and Thaelyn began to lead them on new adventures, taking on new jobs, and often larger ones with greater rewards. This allowed them to improve their equipment and to better supply themselves.

As the months progressed to years, additional people joined up as he began to draw from other races, including the elves and a few dwarves. Eventually, as their numbers increased, it became apparent they needed some kind of headquarters where they could meet and exchange stories, to train, and to find common space for living and dining. For this, he chose to establish himself in one of the larger cities as a base.

By this time, he had accumulated enough money to buy a small guildhall in the city of Amberdain, which was located on the western coastline. It was a fairly robust city, known for the many wealthy merchants and vigorous trade. Also, at this time, word of his arrival was spreading to the other cities and nations around the region. Some simply shrugged, believing this to be just another guild, or perhaps some form of cultist sect trying to make a name for itself. But a few were beginning to take notice of something else.

"Breena, look here at what I found in the wizard's academy library."

"What is it, Carmen?"

"I was in there conducting some research to see if there might be any new spells that could be useful for our guild. There was an apprentice in there helping me a little, and of course he's heard about us, so we started talking."

"Ah, so did you find a new male friend in there, Carmen?" she giggles.

The two women shared the humorous moment.

Carmen was a half-elf, the hybrid offspring of a human and an elf. In her case, her mother was the elf, specifically a High Elf, and she tended to take after her mother's manners and aspirations, including to study as a mage.

Breena had ascended the ladder in her studies enough by now to give instruction to younger apprentices, and Carmen was working under her as a junior assistant.

"Actually, no..." she responds cutely. "He was nice, but I had my work on my mind more than anything else. Anyway, he started asking a few questions about our guild, and how Master Thaelyn got it all started."

"I'll bet that was fun. What did he say to it?"

"I tried to recall your story of that first day, and then something weird happened. He remembered something he read in a book somewhere."

"A book? What book?"

"This one…" she sets a wrapped item on the table. "He allowed me to borrow this, at least for a little while. I'll need to return it soon before his Master finds out it's missing, but he says you can buy this at a shop over in the Promenade. That place is supposed to have 'everything' in it, so he says," she smiles.

"Oh, I've heard of that one. Yes, we could go take a look, but what's so special about this book?"

Breena watches as Carmen unwrapped the item she had bound up in a silk cloth to keep it hidden and safe.

"The Prophecies of Adalon the Silver…" Breena wonders. "Are we taking up with mysticism now, Carmen?"

"Just try reading the first passage. Then you give me YOUR answer."

Breena was intrigued, so she opened it to look inside.

The book was a large heavy-bound item with thick pages. She turned to the first one and began reading.

"In the Time of Flowers, a Child of the Wheel, will shine through a column upright. The Son of the Mountain, a millennium proud, where Justice has been His delight."

She suddenly halts and glares at Carmen, and then slowly returns to the page.

"Across the Land, they shall herald His name, and many will follow His course. Woe be to Evil, wherever it lay, to be smitten beneath His endorse. The Pillars…of Three? Huh?"

"Right, that's what I said, but now finish it."

"The Pillars of Three shall He bring into cause, a mighty power beheld. The fortune of Man, the strength of the Beast, and the Spirit of nature to meld. What in all the hells is this going on about?"

"You're asking me? I'm just the junior apprentice. All right, now what do you think of all this. Just by itself, what do you think?"

"Yeah, just by itself, let's see. The Time of Flowers, that's from the old calendar, Kythorn, the sixth month of the year."

"When did he first arrive?"

"Well, it was summertime. Things went a little crazy there for a while, but I think this is about right."

"All right, next?"

"Next, a Child of the Wheel… You would probably do better to ask Sara about that, since he's been teaching us about the Outer Planes, which is his home. He comes from a place he calls Mount… uh oh… Mount Celestia…"

"Right, that's what I thought. He's a man, he's the son of Tyr, he comes from Mount Celestia, and so he could easily be called a son of the mountain, right? It certainly makes sense to me."

"Yeah, it would if you want to use metaphors for it, and then the Wheel. Go find Sara, bring her over here. She needs to see this."

Carmen hurries out of the study hall where Breena had been spending her time. She rushes down the corridor to another room serving as a temple, where she finds Sara with several clerics in their own study service.

"Sara… Breena and I could use your help with something."

"What is it, Carmen?"

"Just come quickly. You need to see this."

The two of them now rushed back to Breena, who was still studying the book.

"Breena, what's going on?" Sara asks.

"Sara, before you have me answer that, have a look at this book. Have you ever seen anything like it before?"

She studies the book, closing the cover to examine the title, and then returning to the pages inside.

"Well, for sure, I've never seen this particular book before. Where did it come from?"

"I borrowed it from the wizard's academy library," Carmen responds.

"All right, and what's so special about it?"

"Read this page," Breena asserts.

Sara peers down to study the page.

"A child of…" she mumbles and pauses to look at Breena briefly, then continues. "…A column upright?" her voice escalates. "…Where justice has been his delight?!"

"But now, Sara," Breena asserts. "What has he taught you about his native home? You're the priestess here. He comes from a place called Mount Celestia, right?"

"Right, and he also explained to us that the Outer Planes are arranged in a circular pattern that looks a bit like a wheel. They even call it that on occasion, the Great Wheel."

"Good, and then I think he first arrived in the summertime, do you remember?"

She again references the passage.

"The Time of Flowers… Actually, yes, I think that's correct. But now what… Across the Land, they shall herald His name, and many will follow His course. Woe be to Evil, wherever it lay, to be smitten beneath His endorse. Well, this much I can certainly attest to, for all we've seen so far. And honestly, I have no doubt in my mind he could continue this all the way across the land. But next… what? The Pillars of Three? What are the Pillars of Three?"

"Something that hasn't occurred yet," Carmen offers. "These are prophecies, and we're watching them unfold with everything he does."

The three of them study each other's faces.

"Who is this?" Sara ushers briskly while referencing the cover again. "Adalon the Silver… Who is Adalon the Silver?"

"Not a clue," Breena relents. "I've heard of a few people who proclaim themselves to be prophets, and some of them are pretty good, but this…"

She begins scanning the other pages and finds more verses relating to the same person.

"This whole book seems to be only about him! What is going on here? It's like this Adalon person knows his full life story."

"Breena," Sara muses. "What did you once say about him finding his fortune here with that missing destiny of his?"

"Oh dear gods, could this be related?"

"Well, it certainly looks like a story of his life…and before it even occurs!"

"This is weird," Carmen moans. "I think this demands some careful study, if only to try to understand what it's about, to say nothing about what's being said in it."

"I think you're right," Breena admits. "Carmen, you said you could buy this at that shop. Go down there and see. If you can find it, buy it. I'll reimburse you for it. We should then return this so that other guy doesn't get in trouble. This is going to take time to study. Also, let's see if we can ask around about this Adalon person, and see if we can discover who he or she is."

Carmen rushes off to attend to her chore, leaving Breena and Sara still gawking at the book.

"Breena," Sara wonders. "Are we looking at a book that was written only recently, or has this been out for a while?"

"I don't know, Sara, but that might be a good question to find an answer to. If it was recent, maybe it's just someone trying to grab a few coins on something already known, and the rest is fluff. But if this has been out a while…"

"I find it hard to believe it could be false. Not when you're talking about a Child of the Wheel, and we're the only ones who know what that Wheel actually is."

◆◆◆

"A prophecy?" Thaelyn puzzles. "You should be careful of such things, as they can often be very cryptic, especially if you are speaking in terms of Long Prophecy. This form is most often the worst, as a person might not truly know what he is looking at if it extends so far into the future that he can no longer recognize anything."

"This might be true, but consider this," Breena admits. "Assuming this is real, and not just someone trying to make a few easy coins, this person named Adalon pinpointed the time of your arrival, how you arrived, and even goes so far as to describe you as a Child of the Wheel. Who in our world would know what the Wheel is except for those of us here under your teachings?"

"Indeed, this is a curious one. Very well, we could potentially suggest this Adalon might have seen something, and likely overheard such words within these visions. This does not specifically tell us they know what the Great Wheel is about, instead they might only know of these words that were spoken."

"All right, this could be a possibility. Next, we have mention of the people across the land following your call and evil falling. We know this is occurring even now. Finally, and this will surely stick you in the side, there is a mention of something called the Pillars of Three, something you apparently create. Carmen thinks this could point to something still in our future."

"While I may admit, she could be right, this is truly a very odd reference. At the same time, I think I should point out that I do not commonly carry the habit of chasing after other people's dreams. Therefore, if this is something yet to occur, I think it will come whether or not I actively pursue it. I would instead prefer to stay my usual course, with what I can easily discern within my own capacity. We can watch for this, and perhaps there will be a clue somewhere, but let us take this gently."

"Of course, Master, I suppose that seems fair enough. I sent Carmen out to buy a copy of this book for our own collection. I think this definitely warrants a careful study."

"I will not argue on this point, but at the same time, do not let it interfere with your normal studies," he grins.

"Absolutely, Master. Although I have to admit, my studies are progressing a lot easier under your instruction than with my old Master."

"Yes, it would seem some of these wizards tend to be rather finicky about the lessons they give."

"They just don't want us taking over their position, I think. But you are completely different. I think you could easily make a lot of enemies among them simply for how generous you are with the lessons you offer."

"Perhaps, but if they truly wish to argue that point, I will hope they at least do so in a civilized manner."

Breena smiles and bows, then returns to her study.

Over the course of the coming years, she continues to develop, along with her friends, while Thaelyn leads them on more crusades to spread his gospel and solve the concerns of the local populace. Additional people join up, a few at a time, and take up training within the Hall.

The years then turned into decades, and as they reached a certain membership threshold, they found themselves with enough financing and elder members to open additional chapters in neighboring cities. The culture they were creating was beginning to spread a new type of faith, and the people were beginning to see Thaelyn as a kind of messiah, despite his earlier cautions of representing a holy figure in their eyes.

Of course, nothing ever goes without its opponents, and this most often included criminal organizations, corrupt political leaders, rival religions, and people who simply wanted to test themselves against the man said to be immortal. One by one, however, they all fell, while Thaelyn gained even more leverage with both the people as well as the local political authority.

He continued to lead them on numerous adventures and crusades to even further reaches, allowing him to spread to even more distant societies, earning more fame and fortune, and ultimately a knighthood. This honor was actually repeated by two different sovereign states, one human, the other elven, as a symbolic gesture for his service to so many independent societies.

He was about sixty years into his new service, and leading a new, younger team of adventurers on a mission. Word had been received of a criminal who was on the run. This particular one had been conducting some sinister experiments, and was believed to be developing a ritual that could afford him a form of immortality, but at the expense of a number of innocent victims. It now came to Thaelyn and his people to investigate, but their travels would carry them to a very dangerous place.

"There, is that it?" directs one of the archers.

"Aye, it sure looks that way," affirms the scout. "A nice little hole 'tween the rocks, it is."

"We must move very carefully here," Thaelyn declares. "We are about to tread into places unknown with little or no room to move about freely."

"We should make a quick check of our gear," announces the mage.

The group included an archer and a mage, both of them female elves, a half-elf priestess, and two human males, one a scout and the other a frontline combatant.

The team checks their backpacks to ensure they have a supply of their usual consumables, which included healing and restorative potions, and a number of spell scrolls to be used to ward against specific debilitations and enemies.

"Very well, let us proceed cautiously," Thaelyn issues.

He leads them through a crevice within a cluster of large rocks. The opening was large enough to allow a man to squeeze through easily, but the passageway was a little short to afford them enough headroom, forcing them to hunch over as they walked along. It was dark, and so they each conjured up a small orb of light within their palms called a Spark. It was one of the simpler cantrips they learned in Thaelyn's Hall.

They walked along the passage, descending deeper into the earth. Their destination was believed to be taking them to a deep underground region known as the Underdark. This region was only barely understood, as there were no known maps or charts telling them where to go or what to expect once they arrived.

The air grew cold at first as they felt the cooling effect of the native rocks insulating against the surface heating. The tunnel continued into the blackness until it came to the remains of an old outpost left behind by some long-forgotten garrison.

"Watch yourselves," the scout urges. "Sir Thaelyn, do ye feel anythin' down here?"

"Not at present. Continue."

They passed through the old ruins and into another tunnel, leading even deeper into the depths.

"How far until we actually find something?" the priestess asks.

"The Underdark is substantially deep, as I understand it," Thaelyn admits. "We must simply stay the course and keep alert."

"Right, but this place is downright creepy."

They continued a while longer, emerging from the tunnel along a ledge overlooking a crevasse.

"Watch your step here," the archer urges. "I can't see where it goes, but I can tell it's deep."

They circled around a rocky outcropping that swung around to a cove with an opening in the wall. Thaelyn held up his hand to halt their progress. He signaled silently to the scout to check the hole.

The scout tiptoed up to what looked like a cave entrance. The area immediately in front appeared clear, so he waved the others over. As they attempted to peer inside, an echo ushered out. It was a grunting sound, like something was inside there.

The archer tapped urgently on Thaelyn's shoulder, then began issuing a series of hand signals as a form of silent communication. She was asking if they should dare enter inside.

He turned again to the opening and tried looking deep into the blackness, but nothing could be seen from this angle. The cave made a turn partway in.

He gestured for them to follow along slowly, and he took the lead. They crept ahead cautiously, checking each turn for anything moving, and finally to find a large chamber. It appeared empty at the moment, so they carefully stepped inside.

The chamber had two other exits, one of which seemed to emit a flickering light from somewhere within. They suspected whatever lived here was probably inside that room. Therefore, the other exit likely passed onwards through another tunnel.

They were nearly halfway across the floor when something

began to stir in the adjacent chamber. Scraping sounds were heard, along with the scratching of huge claws on the rocky floor. This was accompanied by a rumbling voice.

"I sssense the presenssse... Of visitorsss... Entering my home..."

Thaelyn immediately halted the group, and they all arranged themselves to make ready for a fight, if one should erupt. But from the sounds coming out of the side chamber, whatever it was, it had to be big.

A shadow loomed within the flickering of the side passage, and a shape emerged. It was a huge head held well above the floor. It turned and angled down at the small group.

"A Draconic?" Thaelyn ushers up to the beast.

"I am..." she admits, and then enters the room fully.

In the relatively faint light of their small orbs, they could see the huge creature casually lumbering forward. She stood well above everything else in the chamber, and almost touched the roof of the cave.

She turned her attention to a cluster of crystals arranged on one side, and began a chant on them. The crystals began to glow, offering better lighting for everyone to see.

"Well, that was right dandy of her," the scout mutters. "Now I can better see the gapin' maw about to swallow us."

"Fear not me... Sssmall one. I am not one... Who preysss... On your kind..."

"Ah, a fine thing that. I just wish ye could've told me afore I soiled myself."

The great beast let out a soft chuckle.

"I sssee you are attempting... To passss into... The Underdark. Thisss... Is a dangerousss place..."

"We are aware of that, Noble One," Thaelyn responds. "But we have a pressing need to pursue a villain we believe to have taken a similar path."

"No one has passssed... Through thisss chamber... For a long while. At leassst... Not from the sssurface..."

"We feel he may have used a portal spell on this occasion. He is known to be a powerful mage."

"Ah... I sssee. Then you mussst... Pursssue him. But you will find... Difficulty... Along the way... As you will no doubt... Encounter... The Drow... Who live below..."

"We suspect he may actually be taking refuge with them, or perhaps has some manner of association. I feel we have no choice."

"Then you will not... Accomplish... Your tasssk... As they will attack you... On sssight..."

She pauses to look down the passage on the opposite side of the chamber.

"But perhapsss... I can offer... Sssome advice... To sssee you... On your way... Sssuccessfully..."

"Advice? This is always welcome. What sort of advice do you have?"

"If you were to enter... In disssguise... As one of them... You might passss... Undetected. Thisss would allow you... Free reign... To proceed as you wish..."

"Indeed, this would certainly aid our cause. But unfortunately, we do not typically practice this level of the illusionary art."

"Not to worry... As I have... A few tricksss... I can offer..."

"Ah, most excellent... Would you be willing to help us then?"

"I have no love... For the Drow. Essspecially... In recent timesss..." she snarls.

"Oh? For what reason...not that I would expect a Silver to need much reason for this point..."

"Indeed... But now... They have committed a crime... Againsssst me. Perhapsss... We could make... An exchange..."

"Interesting. What manner of crime was it and what do you propose?"

"My child... My egg... It was ssstolen... By a band... Who crept into my chamber. They took it... And I believe... They hope to use it... In sssome vile ritual..."

"This does not bode well. And so, I must assume you would desire us to retrieve it for you?"

"I would be greatly... Appreciative... For thisss favor..."

"Indeed, I only hope we are not too late in our arrival."

"I sssuspect... The preparationsss... Will take time. If we hurry... We may be... Sssuccessful..."

"Very well then, give us your illusion and we will make haste in our efforts."

The large silver dragon begins a lengthy chant over Thaelyn and the group, enveloping them in a haze that begins to alter their appearance. Soon, they appear as a group of dark elves, Drow.

"But before you travel off..." she continues. "You mussst remember... You may appear as Drow... But you mussst alssso... Act like them. Their malesss... Are sssubservient... To the femalesss. And their sssociety... Is very rigid... And harsh. Fail in thisss... And the disssguise... Will not help you..."

"I understand. We shall proceed with caution and great care."

Thaelyn offers a bow, as do the others, and they proceed hurriedly down the next tunnel.

In this new disguise, they can afford themselves greater speed with less concern of discovery. If a Drow patrol should see them, they will simply come up with an excuse to pass by.

They work their way down a long series of tunnels until they feel the air getting warmer from the internal heat, finally to come out in a broad passage that seems to lead in a direction indicating some form of development.

"All right, listen up," Thaelyn asserts. "My understanding is their priestesses are the superior authority in their culture. Nadeen, you will take the front, and speak for us if anyone questions our purpose."

"Aye," the half-elf priestess affirms.

"Our story is we are merchants from another city looking to make trades for enchanted tomes and charms. We have travelled long and are weary, so we are looking for rest and food. This will hopefully be enough to keep them off our backs until we can make our investigation."

"Let's hope so."

"How do we go about looking for that egg?" asks the mage.

"This is a good question," Thaelyn considers. "I would imagine it is probably in the hands of a high authority, and very likely to be brought up to a temple facility of some sort. We must be quick to intercept it, but not so quick as to reveal ourselves."

"Right, and then be quick enough to escape before they notice."

"That'll be a cute one!" the scout adds.

"Sylnes," Thaelyn directs. "You will carry the egg in your bag once we have it."

"Very good," the mage agrees.

"The rest of you, fall in line."

They proceed up to the front gates of a large Drow city. The guards at the front stop them to determine their identities and purpose. Nadeen steps forward.

"You there," charges the guard. "State your purpose or begone."

"We are merchants here to make trade for goods," she states firmly. "We have magical tomes and charms we wish to exchange for other items."

"And do you think we actually want your trades?"

"What you think, male, is not my concern. We have travelled long and are quite weary. If coin means anything to you, then we have it, but we do not simply give it away."

"Of course, my apologies..." he withdraws subserviently. "Naturally, if you desire food and rest, we have space available. The merchant's row can be found up the lane and to the left. You will likely find what you need there."

He opens the gate and lets them in.

Once inside, they begin meandering up the lane and angle to the left; just in case anyone was watching. When they are out of sight of the guards at the gate, they detour around the area and begin searching for the city temple.

The temple was a large structure and not difficult to find. But for the number of guards circling the area, it was not a place you simply walk into. Only the high priestesses were allowed entry, and these represented the matrons of the dynastic houses that governed the city politics, along with their daughters.

Thaelyn and his group passed by the structure, casually glancing over at it. But they couldn't stop, as the guards out front were watching them closely. They continued up the lane a bit more until a shout rang out calling their attention.

"You there! You must be the outsiders."

The group turned to find the voice and saw a young woman approaching from behind. Nadeen prepared herself for a tough argument.

"Yes, we are the merchants just recently arrived. Are we suddenly unwelcome?"

"Unwelcome in my eyes, perhaps," the woman spits. "But not unwelcome to my mother's. Word spreads fast on visitors to our city. She is curious about you, and has a proposition to offer. Are you interested in a little extra coin, maybe a trinket or two? Then you should go see her."

"Why would we wish to see the matron mother of your house? We are simple merchants. I doubt she might find our...trinkets... so interesting."

"Maybe. Maybe not. But it is not trinkets she is interested in. It's a service."

"A service...from merchants?"

"You are outsiders, and she has a task to perform. But she is not very trusting of anyone local to perform this. Therefore, she is considering you."

"Should I be honored for this privilege?" she smirks demurely.

"If you wish not to be fed to the spiders, you will stop this insipid questioning and follow me."

"Ah, I was almost afraid you wouldn't ask. I do so hate finding my own way."

The woman was visibly angry, but held her composure in the light of this clever repartee.

She led the team along another lane and up to a large manor house, where she brought them inside and up to a well-appointed room representing the matron mother's seat.

"You are the outsiders?" she asks coolly.

"We are," Nadeen responds flatly. "We are simple merchants, however, and yet you have summoned us for a different task?"

"I have. I recently came into possession of a rare artifact. I wish to use it for a special ritual at the temple. But due to its inherent value, I feel I cannot trust any of our usual couriers. This particular item could possibly be used by my rivals, and I would certainly not desire that."

"Naturally, that would be a most unwelcome event. What sort of artifact is this you need transported?"

"It is simply a large egg from a rare creature…nothing more. You need not concern yourselves with the intimate details. All you need to know is to bring it to me at the temple, nothing more."

"That seems like a very straightforward offer. We were informed there might be some form of compensation for this service. Can you enlighten me about that?"

"Do not worry. Once the task is complete, you will receive fair payment for your effort. But you may not speak of this to anyone. We do not wish this to slip outside our control. And also, if you should betray me, you will not live long enough to know how displeased I am."

"Of course, I understand fully. When will this service be demanded?"

"Good, I like that word…demanded," she smiles wickedly. "You know your place well in my home. It will be…demanded…within the hour. The ritual is nearly ready. I must only gather a few more items and then proceed to the temple."

"And where will we find this egg of yours?"

"My daughter will show you. It is currently under lock and key. She shall retrieve it for you, and you will carry it. But then she must join me to make the final preparations."

"Then we shall see you at the temple."

Nadeen bows, as do the rest of the group, and they leave the room. They are soon joined by the daughter who leads them outside again into the lane.

"Wait," she announces abruptly. "Before we proceed to the storeroom, I have my own proposal for you."

Nadeen and the others turn to her as she continues.

"My mother has plans, and her plans do not include you leaving the city alive after your…service…is complete."

"Is this the payment she mentioned?"

"Yes, you catch on quickly. But I will make a new offer. I will give you a true payment and allow you passage out of the city, but you must leave immediately after the ritual, or else I will have you killed no less than she would."

"And what offer is this you ask?"

"My mother intends to offer this egg as a sacrifice, but I choose to turn this to my favor. I commissioned a false egg to be made in the image of the original, except for a small mark on it to identify it to me. You will take this egg, and when she calls for hers, you will give her mine instead."

"I think I should perhaps ask what purpose this serves. One egg for another in some odd ritual… Where does this ultimately lead?"

"She intends to summon a demon and use it in exchange for an item of great power. Now, what do you suppose the demon would have to say about her offering a false egg?"

"Ah, now I see. I doubt he would be very pleased for it, and likely strike her down. Am I right?"

"Good, you do seem nearly as intelligent as you look. Then I will step in and offer the real egg, and take my prize while also rising as the matron mother of our house."

"Spoken like a true servant of the Spider Queen. Then you should provide us with this false egg, and I might also suggest identifying this mark for me, just to ensure my limited intelligence does not make any mistakes."

"You have a smart mouth on you. But yes, I would be rather displeased if you did bring about this error."

The daughter continues leading them to the storeroom and unlocks the door. They pass by a set of guards outside and she finds a box on one of the shelves. She gently digs inside and pulls out a large silvery egg with mottled patterns on the shell.

"This is the real one, be sure to keep this separate from the other one…you know, to prevent errors."

"Absolutely," she ushers and hands it over to Sylnes to place in her bag.

The woman then pulls out another box that was partially hidden under a bundle of cloth. Inside she finds another egg.

"This is mine, look here," she turns it over carefully. "I will look for this mark as you give it to her, again to ensure no errors are made."

"Naturally, and after she has made her offering, and received her…reward…we turn to you with the real one."

"Very good… But now, I must go to her side, and you will follow after. Do not delay yourselves overly long, or else…someone…may become very curious as to where you have run off to."

The woman leads them out of the storeroom, and she closes and locks the door again, then rushes away up the lane to the temple.

Nadeen and the others begin wandering in that general direction and out of earshot of the guards at the door. Once away, Thaelyn leans into Nadeen's ear.

"Are you sure you do not have a little Drow in you, Child?"

"It's in my crossbreeding," she whispers with a tiny smile. "All right, now what? We have the real egg and a false one, and it looks like we're getting ourselves involved in a local conspiracy."

"Indeed," Thaelyn mutters softly. "I do not necessarily care for this, but then I care even less to see the egg sacrificed, and we are not in a favorable position to seek an alternate course at present."

"The way it looks," the scout suggests. "We'll need to find a way to ditch this dame, but ditchin' a dame like her in a place like this won't be pretty."

"And worse," Sylnes adds. "We haven't had time to do our own work."

"This is true," Thaelyn responds. "But considering the precarious nature of the situation we are in; we may need to break from that for the moment. Let us proceed carefully and look for any possible solution for ourselves."

"Do you sense anything with your Sight?"

"Partially, but the sensations are becoming twisted with all this intrigue."

They continued walking along the lane in the direction of the temple, which was a couple of blocks away at this point. They passed a series of smaller homes and a few shops, and then heard a sound ushering out from a side alley. Someone was calling to them discreetly. They turned to find a figure standing in the shadows waving them over.

"What do you want, male?" Nadeen replies as she arrives at the alley.

"Come closer, do not allow yourselves to be seen out there."

The group takes a quick glance around, and then ducks inside the alley.

"So, here we are. What do you want from us? We're conducting a very important job and cannot be interrupted."

"You might consider this to be worthy of your time. You are taking an egg to the temple, yes? You are to give it to the matron mother, yes? But her daughter has given you a false egg, and tells you to give this to the matron mother instead, while she offers the real one."

"You seem very well informed for a male who is not supposed to know of these things."

"I know of this because I am a member of that same house, but I hold a grudge with that woman. I was once her mate, but then she turned me out. Now I want my revenge."

"And how do we play into this?"

"I have another false egg, one that I commissioned at the same time she commissioned hers, but mine does not carry any special marks. It looks identical to the original."

"I see. Now, let me guess. You want me to give the marked egg to the matron mother, your false egg to the other one, and then what? Where does that leave us?"

"It leaves you running out the front gates as fast as you can. Once the guards discover this, you will probably not get far."

"And you?"

"My reward is to see her crumpled body on the floor of the temple. But here, I will give this to you now," he hands over a pouch of coins. "This will compensate you for your travels. We will not see each other again. Take this and do as I ask. Let both of them take their rewards."

"What about the real egg? Do you have anything planned for it?"

"I do not summon demons to offer sacrifices. Take it away from here, I care not where."

Nadeen looks at her teammates, and then returns as the man pulls out another false egg from a bag.

"Might I offer a suggestion," Thaelyn submits. "It was observed that the real egg went inside her bag," he points at Sylnes. "We should replace that with his, so as not to cause any confusion when we pull out this new false egg. She will expect it to come from her bag. I will take the real one."

They begin swapping eggs. Sylnes pulls out the real one and hands it to Thaelyn, while she takes the new false egg. Nadeen was carrying the original marked egg in her bag.

Fortunately for them, their guild finances were robust enough by this time that they could afford more extravagant equipment, including bags with spacious interiors. These bags were uniquely enchanted and described as bags of holding, with varying degrees of internal capacity which seemed much roomier than the external dimensions might otherwise suggest. They could hold more and feel lighter than your average bag. And these eggs were big.

The man sends them on their way, and they continued up to the temple. The guards in front eyed them carefully as they made their approach.

"You there, halt. No one is permitted inside the temple."

"Guard," Nadeen steps forward. "We are here at the request of the matron mother who specifically demanded us to deliver an item for her ritual. So, unless you wish to anger her for our delay, I might recommend you allow us to pass."

"You are her couriers?"

"We are."

"All of you?"

"Her needs are very demanding. Travelling alone is not recommended."

"Yes, of course. Very well, you may pass."

She leads them up a long set of stairs and inside the temple.

"There you are," the matron announces as they enter the room. "I was beginning to wonder where you were."

"Some of the guards around here are rather nervous of they who simply walk along the lanes."

"Yes, they can be, at that. Do you have my egg?"

"But of course, Matron. Would I dare deny this to you?"

She reaches into her bag and pulls out the marked egg, handing it over conspicuously so the mark can be seen by the daughter who was standing off to the side.

"I suspect you will need your space," Nadeen muses openly. "So, perhaps we should simply move off to the side here."

"Yes, keep yourselves available. After all, you should not forget your payment."

Nadeen and her group move along the back wall of the ritual room.

The matron begins her ceremony, placing the egg on the altar and conducting a carefully spoken chant. The brazier on the altar churns, and then erupts vigorously with a plume of flame roaring upwards. A shape emerges within the flame of a winged demon.

"For what do you call upon me, mortal," he hisses. "Do you desire treasure, a powerful item, or do you seek a painful death."

"I have an offering for you, and I will exchange this for a powerful artifact. See here, I bring you this egg from a silver dragon! Surely, you would find this worthy of disturbing your rest."

"An egg from a silver Draconic...this will be a fine treat."

He looks down at the egg, but almost immediately he senses it's a fake.

"What is this nonsense?" he shouts. "This is no egg. "You will pay for this attempt to deceive me!"

He lashes out at the matron with his powerful claw, disemboweling her with one stroke and leaving her collapsed in a pool of blood.

"Hold!" the daughter exclaims. "Powerful One, my mother was a fool to try to deceive you, but I am not. I would make you a truly fine offering."

She turns to Nadeen and motions for the next egg. Nadeen turns to Sylnes, who was carrying the man's false egg. She pulls it out and hands it over.

"Here, behold," the Drow states. "This is the one you want. She was holding it back, but I will offer it to you and ask no less for it. Give me a potent artifact that I may hold unquestioned power within my house, and you may have this."

She sets it on the altar.

The demon takes a close look and sniffs the new offering, then turns up to her.

"You want a potent reward for this, do you? Yes, then you shall have it. Your soul shall be ripped from your breast and made my plaything!"

He lashes out again, this time not only disemboweling the woman, but sucking her life essence away.

"Would any others care to make an offering?"

The demon glares at Thaelyn and his group, but Thaelyn directs them to turn away and be silent.

"I thought not," the demon snarls. "And to think I was called away from my rest for this insult."

The demon flashes away in a large burst of flame and the embers within the brazier settle.

"I think now would be a most excellent time for us to depart," Thaelyn suggests.

The team rushes outside the room and back down the stairs. The guards at the bottom take notice of their hurried pace.

"Hey, you! Where are you going in such a hurry?"

"Guard," Nadeen turns to respond. "When the matron tells you to depart, you depart, do you not? She is quite busy, and does not wish to be disturbed, so I would not recommend going inside there until she is ready. In the meantime, our service is complete, and we were given instructions to leave, and do so quickly. You know, to keep our skin attached. It is actually very simple."

She turns and leads them through the lanes and out of the city.

"Young lady," Thaelyn reflects. "When we return, I think you should write your memoirs of this occasion. This experience would make excellent study material for the younger generation."

"Thank you!"

They continued along the tunnels back the way they came towards the cavern where they originally found the dragon. When they emerged into the open space, they once again heard the sound of shuffling scales and claws against the rocky floor.

"You have returned…" she announces as she pokes her head out from the side passage. "Were you sssuccessful…?"

"Indeed, Noble One, we did find and retrieved your egg, although I might also suggest any immediate return to that place would be inadvisable at present."

"Were you able… To resolve… Your own pursssuit…?"

"Unfortunately, no… We found ourselves being drawn into a situation of local politics and did not have a proper opportunity to continue further."

Thaelyn pulls out the dragon's egg and shows it to her.

"Would you desire me to deposit this somewhere for you?"

"If you would be… Ssso kind… I have a bed… Inssside here…"

She turns and retreats back inside her lair. Thaelyn and the others followed behind to find another large chamber. In a corner, they saw a bed of matting that had been collected as a nest for the egg to rest in.

"Place it here… If you please…"

Thaelyn stepped over and gently set the egg down in the nest.

"Is there anything else you require?" he asks.

"No… And I thank you… But I feel… I should offer… A reward… For your ssservice…"

"Not at all," he begs. "Simply to see this little one safe is reward enough. They were hoping to use it in a summoning ritual down there. A most despicable sight…"

"The Drow… Are a nefariousss breed. I have ssseen many… Occasionsss… Of their attemptsss… To passss through thisss ssspace… In their hopesss to assssault… The sssurface world…"

"Why do you choose to remain here if this passageway is so often trod?"

"I ssserve… As a guardian… To keep them… In their place. But I will admit… I have grown tired… Of thisss role… And I hope to find… A new purpossse… For myssself… Very sssoon…"

"I see. Then I wish you good fortune in that regard. But with regrets, I think we must now take our leave, and allow you to return to your caretaking. We still have our own work, and I think we will need to reconsider our objective before we decide upon our next course of action."

"Very well… And perhapsss we will find… Occasion… To ssspeak again… Thaelyn…"

He suddenly finds his attention peaking at the mentioning of his name.

"Excuse me, but you know who I am?"

"It is a little hard… Not to know you… By now. Your reputation… Precedesss you… Thaelyn… Ssscion of Celessstia. You forget… We Draconicsss… Are well versssed… In the mannersss… Of the Planesss. To my knowledge… You are the only… Celessstial… Dessscended… To a Prime domain…"

"But of course, therefore it is a simple act of deduction to put it together. And I will admit, my reputation in this world has grown substantially since my arrival, but I am still a little surprised to see it reach your ears. I was not aware the Draconics paid as much attention to the workings of the younger races."

"Many timesss… We do not. We go… Where we are needed… Or where we are sssent. It is a condition… Of our pathsss.

Sssometimes we choose our way... Sssometimes we are called into it. And sssometimes... We may require... A hint... To help usss... Find our way..."

"Indeed, I think I must agree."

"Life is a journey... Thaelyn. Sssome might sssay... A temporary one. At leassst until... We find a new courssse. Each of usss... Has our path. For sssome... It is a lonely one... And for othersss... It crosssses... With another... Whom we may have known... From before. Fate is sssuch... A curiousss thing..."

"Your words remind me of something I once heard from an old friend of mine."

"Yesss... There can be greatnessss... In sssuch interaction... If only we learn... To explore... And ssseek wisdom... In those placesss... We might not otherwise... Expect. But enough for now... As you have your work. And yet... I predict... We may meet again... Sssooner than you think... Ssson of the Mountain..."

Thaelyn once again bows, as do the rest of his team, and they make their exit from the chamber.

They wind their way back along the tunnels, having to abandon their objective for now as the Drow city would likely be in turmoil after their previous visit. They worked their way back up to the surface and into the open daylight again, and started wandering back along the road away from the region.

"Sir Thaelyn," Sylnes wonders. "Is it common for dragons to speak in such cryptic manners?"

"Actually, I believe so, generally speaking, at least where non-dragons are concerned. I have not had much opportunity to interact with them, myself. Only on a few precious occasions, and those were mostly in the Outer Planes if we should happen to come across one another."

"Curious... It almost sounded like she was hinting at something in all that."

"I would not be surprised at that. The Draconics are a very old race. No doubt they have grown to be very eccentric along the way."

"I also noticed she used that term Son of the Mountain in there," Nadeen reflects.

"Indeed, she did," Thaelyn muses. "But she apparently also knows who I am…rather intimately I would imagine, and likely from my exploits in Celestia. You will recall she also used the term Scion of Celestia, which is a title I once held up there."

"Ah, that's interesting, so the other one might simply be a derivative, I suppose."

"Sir Thaelyn," the archer offers. "I'm wondering about something, if I may."

"Yes, Ladrim, what is it?"

"A sequence of things, actually. First, she was talking about life as a temporary thing, at least until something changes."

"This actually reminds me of someone I once knew who spoke in similar terms. I am sure it must be from some philosophical prose, and likely this one heard the same at some moment. One's path in life may take many directions, and as one matures, these may change from time to time."

"All right, good enough. But then, she spoke of Fate. This is a curious one for me, a dragon talking about Fate. During the Age of Dragons, the only Fate anyone could gain out of it was the dragons trying to destroy us. Now, here she is apparently hinting at meeting again…crossing paths, she said…and almost as if she holds a positive intention to it, like as if you have a Fate driving you to do so."

"While this would certainly be a curious point, I find it difficult to see how this particular occasion could be part of any kind of Fate, not the way it seemed to play out for us. As for any future potential, well, this is simply too difficult to say."

"What about the part of going where you are needed, or sent? We were essentially sent there, maybe also to say we were needed, because of this mission."

"Well, yes, I cannot argue this, but this could simply be coincidental. In her case, she was probably speaking of her objective in that cave, and how it may have crossed paths with ours. That egg, for example. It was perhaps no more than good fortune for our meeting to give aid in this area. Beyond that, the reason for her to be there might be due to some other direction she received once."

"Receiving direction? From what?"

"From what I understand, the Draconics were created by a member of the Estelar named Maker Kuroku. Although I have heard in recent times, she seems to be absent from her post. Still, my teachings tell me she did so to create a guardian race of some sort."

"Really! But how does this fit with the Age of Dragons? Were they supposed to be guarding something?"

"They tend to be a very elusive breed, and my experience, or at least whatever I heard of it, tells me they do not give out much detail to explain their actions. But then, I believe I heard the Maker herself was this way, so it may follow they inherited some part of this from her," he chuckles.

"Great! That helps a lot."

"But I suppose, if only to speculate, the most reasonable answer is probably yes. As to what and why, and how it fits in with your troubles, this is difficult to say, unless we suggest your people arrived in places where you were otherwise not desired."

"So, this is basically to say, we weren't supposed to come here at all, maybe. But then, if we aren't desired to be here, why did it seem they backed off after a while?"

"Again, I can only really speculate, but my best offer is to say that whatever the reason, it must have relaxed after a time such that it was no longer as critical. Perhaps the reasons were only temporary, or maybe something changed along the way to alter the conditions."

"All right, I suppose I can accept that, but I wish they could've simply told us, rather than what seemed like making war on us."

"It could just as easily have been the other way, you know. You might see THEM as the threat, and made war on them thinking THEY should not be here."

"Ugh, you're right! So, we made our own trouble? Great... All right, but then we come to that last part. Going where they are needed, and so on, Fate, crossing paths, and she predicted meeting again. Sir Thaelyn, once upon a time, I recall stories from some of the early members of the guild leaving notes and journals about you and your apparent Fate. You once said something about looking for something, being told to come here, and maybe you might find it."

"Yes, some of our early members suggested this, if only in passing. Perhaps they are right, but I am still at something of a loss as to where to go for it. I suppose this also reflects on that statement concerning our paths, life as a journey."

"And you are still looking for yours," she muses. "That's a really interesting one, no matter where it comes from. A temporary thing, until it changes. Like your story of being in the service of your Father, until it changed, and you came down here for some crazy reason," she chuckles.

"Indeed," he smiles. "And this is what reminds me of that old friend I once had up in the city of Sigil, in the Outer Planes. She was very dear to me, and left a parting word in the form of describing life as a journey, saying what we have now is only temporary, as a path to take, until we find something new."

"Sounds like someone special," she mulls. "I might expect you have known a lot of people by now. Being immortal can't be easy. I'm an elf, and already I know how hard it can be to outlive so many others around me."

"Indeed, and I have known my share as well."

"But at least in the Outer Planes, you might have other Celestials to keep company with, people who are just as immortal as you, right? Then you came down here with all of us."

"This is true."

"Aye," the scout adds. "And the only one, to boot, just like she said. What do the others think about this?"

"Ben, you might find it interesting to know, I once had a lengthy discussion over this with a close friend of mine, who is also Aasimar. She was interrogating me about my desires and intentions for coming here."

"Ack! Ye mean someone might go 'round interrogatin' the great Sir Thaelyn? That'd be a sight to see."

"Indeed!" he chuckles. "But she is much more like a sister than an inquisitor, and her arguments were simply to understand why I might choose to come here at all."

"All right, so let's hear it," Sylnes smiles. "Why would a Celestial choose to come down here? This should be good," she snickers. "You have this temporary thing with your Father, then boom, you get this wacky idea to go places no one else would likely go. If you're the only one, it must mean this is a rare and unusual thing. Why would none of the others choose this?"

"Very well, but the answer may be nearly as abstract as the question. In many cases, the hybrid Celestials are created to act as a kind of interface between the Estelar and the Child races, although this does not seem to occur very often. My interpretation is that they might choose this on those special occasions where one or another of the Estelar might find a special interest in a Child race."

"Fine, but like you said, this seems a bit abstract, and the most noteworthy thing to ask now is why you. What purpose would you serve if someone up there has a special interest in anything down here?"

"Yes, I suppose this is warranted. I recall this once as a subject for conversation with that first group I encountered. Breena Thaxter was her name, who made a most curious conclusion. We were speaking of this, how I was a rather unusual example, being who I am, and this seemed like a rather interesting course of occupation for myself. But her conclusion, based at least…in part…" he slows as his thoughts materialize.

The group comes to a halt as Thaelyn goes silent and abruptly stops in his tracks. Everyone quickly turns to study him. His sudden alteration of manner triggered their training, which suggested there was trouble nearby. Thaelyn's gifts included the power of precognition, which allowed him to see into the near future. As such, the others knew he had a tendency to detect something imminent to occur which might direct him to make sudden unexpected shifts in his behavior.

"Form up!" shouts the warrior member.

The group takes up a formation, circling around Thaelyn in

a defensive posture, but nothing presented itself in view. As for Thaelyn, his eyes drifted briefly into the distance as he recalled an important moment.

"Powers behold…" he whispers. "And she was silver!"

"What do you mean?" the warrior mumbles.

"My apologies, Stu," Thaelyn directs. "At ease, everyone, this is not one of those occasions."

"Sir Thaelyn, what happened? Whenever you stop like that, it means something just came to you."

"It did, but this was a revelation, and it hit rather unexpectedly."

"A revelation?" Sylnes wonders. "If it's strong enough to hit you this hard, it must've been a whopper."

"Indeed!" he wheezes. "I remember it now. Dear Powers! Sylnes, I think we just came full circle in our discussion. Fate, she said?"

He suddenly turned around to face the road they had been travelling on, now looking back the way they came.

"What just hit you?" she asks. "We were speaking of Breena just now, not that dragon, right?"

"Yes. She once suggested someone up there was displeased for the lack of progress down here, therefore I was…SENT…here."

"Oh grand!" she yelps. "Well, there goes that statement of being sent someplace where you are needed. And who sent you?"

"Someone I crossed paths with once."

"Uh huh, why doesn't THAT surprise me now."

"Absolutely, and she was silver!"

"Silver? Another dragon?"

"Yes, but not in her full form. They have the ability to alter their image to an avatar persona to fit our own proportions."

"Oh! How nice!" she shouts. "And I wonder how many times they used that to spy on us."

"Now, now, let us try to contain ourselves. But SHE was the one to suggest I come down here, and rather enthusiastically, as if trying to advertise something."

"Naturally! She couldn't just simply say, 'Hey there, I have a great idea. Go down there and straighten those people out…'. That would be MUCH too easy."

The group ushers up a quick laugh at the thought.

"So, if we now assemble a few pieces," Thaelyn surmises. "Breena may have been right. To be sent where you are needed, crossing paths, and some manner of Fate. And here we have this one. Could she be the same Draconic?"

"My personal guess… Yes! And likely checking up on you."

"You may actually be correct. That mention of crossing paths, and those references. A hint? Oh yes! And she laid down more than one. And here we are stumbling on them."

"Well, you did say dragons were elusive, and she was certainly cryptic enough."

"Yes, and trying to interpret such can be problematic. She knew me…and not simply my name here in this world. She knew me from before, and this simply must be up there in Mount Celestia. But now, this begs me to ask if this could then relate to my own questions."

"Sir Thaelyn," Nadeen offers. "This is causing me to recall that book now, those prophecies, and that same reference, son of the mountain."

Thaelyn turned and glared at the young half-elf as the suggestion settled. The extended stare caused her to feel a shiver, and she turned to see the others now gazing at her for the same reason.

"All right…" she dithers. "So, I probably should've kept my mouth shut, right?" she titters.

"The Silver…" Thaelyn mumbles quietly. "That name is a suffix title, but who would use such as that, except for one of them."

"So, let's total this up," Sylnes muses cutely. "They're governed by this Maker Kuroku, who is a member of the Estelar, and we all know how the gods behave very strangely," she giggles. "She mentioned going, or being sent somewhere, often for a reason. She apparently is the reason YOU are here, and by association, Maker Kuroku, who as an Estelar might have a reason for you, a Celestial, to be here with us. This might also answer the one about the Age of Dragons. Something changed, and now YOU are here to fix it.

That special need to…create…something to act as a bridge between the two."

"Powers help us, Sylnes, you are learning a lot of lessons from me," he chuckles.

"Hey, I think I need to! I'm following the son of a god. Those are big shoes to fill!"

They all share another quick round of laughter together.

"Very well then," he accedes. "I think there is no other option but to fulfill that last…prophecy…of hers, and see what she has to say about all this. I would barter there is more than just Fate at play here. If the Maker is involved, and her 'strange ways' are to achieve a goal, this could be my reason. But I think perhaps I should go alone, if only due to this possibly holding privileged knowledge."

He begins marching back down the road.

"Stay here," he orders. "Make camp, I will return soon."

He makes a determined strut back down the road and out of view of the rest. They moved off to the side and created a makeshift camp to wait for him.

They had already travelled a fair distance by the time their conversation crested, so they could no longer see the outcropping of rocks. He hurried back the way they came at a quickened pace, soon to come into view of the rocks again and the tunnel opening. He surveyed the region to ensure the area was clear before entering.

He navigated his way through the tunnels again, just as the group did before, but this time at a hastened rate to reach the large cavern. He came to the ledge and the crevasse, turned around the outcropping and found the cave entrance. He paused briefly to collect himself before entering.

The room was empty again, but the cluster of crystals on the side was still glowing from their first visit. He steps inside.

"You have returned…" ushers the voice from the adjoining chamber. "As I predicted…"

"It occurs to me we did not complete a proper introduction. And now I am wondering who you actually are. You called me the Son of the Mountain, which is a curious reference."

The silver dragon again lumbers her way out of the side passage and into view.

"Is it now…" she wonders mildly. "You are Thaelyn… Ssson of Tyr… Child of Celessstia… Which is a mountain. Is the reference… Inappropriate…?"

"No, but this same reference also occurs as a rather obscure mention in a book my people have been reading of late. Another was in Celestia itself, and by another Silver. Now I am asking myself who that one was, because she also mentioned a few things about a journey, fated meetings, and in fact she was instrumental in me choosing to come here in the first place."

"How interesssting. Could it be… Coincidence…?"

"Grand Dame Silver, I suspect you know more than you are letting on," he smiles gently. "Your kind is known to be nearly as elusive as your Maker."

"Really!" she laughs boldly.

"Our group out there was just now discussing several of these topics, and it is coming together that there is a hidden purpose at work here. And you and your Maker may be involved."

The large beast cocked her head and delayed her answer, then decided to lay down for a more relaxed chat.

"Yesss… Thaelyn… There is. You have… A greater purpossse… For yoursssself… Than you might think. Allow me… To introduce myssself. I am Adalon… The ssSilver…"

"So, you are indeed the one who wrote that book."

"I am she. And you are all… That was bred into you… By your Father…"

"Is this to say my creation does hold meaning, and now I might find it?"

"It does…"

"Interesting, and suddenly I find myself a bit nervous to ask. What about that book, what purpose does it serve?"

"It is a chronicle… To inform the people… Of who you are… Where you came from… Why you are here… And where you will go. It is necessssary… To guide them… That they will follow you…"

"As if they actually need a book for that, they seem quite content to do so by my teachings alone."

"Perhapsss ssso... But thisss will provide... Additional incentive..."

"Then, what is this purpose you speak of for me?"

"The workingsss... Of the Draconic... And the Maker... Are complex. Your purpossse... Is to demonssstrate... A refined direction... For thisss world. The people... Have ssstagnated... For too long. The time has come... That they mussst grow. But their leadersss... Are ssselfish... And vain... And deny the people... Thisss pleasure. Thisss is where... You come in..."

"But wait, I did not come here to be their new leader, if this is what you are suggesting."

"Perhapsss it was not... Your intention... But thisss... Is your purpossse. It was ordained... From your birth. It was ordained... Sssince the Age of Dragonsss... As you ssspoke of outsssside..."

"Huh? Wait a moment. You could hear our conversation?"

"My ssSight... Is not limited... To prophecy. The Age of Dragonsss... Was due to an invasion... Of unwanted guestsss. But the Maker chose... To reconsssider... Their value... To her greater plan. The Draconic were called back... And you were created... Insssstead..."

"Powers pay witness, Sylnes was right," he mutters breathlessly.

"She chose to call... On a Celessstial... Rather than a mortal... As you would hold... The power... To sssee thisss through... With assurance. They in turn... Will sssee you... As a sssavior. And together... You will accomplish... What no other can... Or ever has. Thisss is your goal.... To lead them... Into a new era. A Golden Age..."

"A Golden Age," he mumbles weakly. "Adalon, you must be joking!"

"I do not jessst... With sssuch thingsss. My propheciesss... Are alwaysss right. Thisss is the direction... You mussst now take. You will build... A power... An Order of Knighthood... And thisss Order… Will change the world. Thisss is your Fate… And alwaysss has been."

Thaelyn retracted from the debate briefly to reflect on his own past. He recalled his early beginnings, how he apparently made a deal with Tyr for a thousand-year contract of service. He had asked himself many times why he would do this, but it was quickly becoming clear there was a hidden agenda at play here. He began to feel weak, and settled himself to sit on the floor.

"Adalon, what you are suggesting here is a very tall order, for any man, including myself."

"You will not be alone. I will help you… As will one other… And the three of usss… Will work together…"

"Three of us…" he muddles. "Building something… Wait… that book again. Are you speaking of this thing you call the Pillars of Three?"

"Yesss… The Pillarsss of Three. You already know… The fortune of man. You use thisss… Even now… By collecting these people… Together… Into a whole body. My contribution… Will be… The ssstrength of the beassst…"

"How do you mean this?"

"You and I… Are unique… Each in our own way. But if you combine thisss… We will hold power… Unlike anything… Thisss world… Has ever ssseen. We will join… In a bond… As Brother and ssSister… Of the blood. And each sssoldier… Who ssserves under usss… Will share in thisss…"

"Great Powers, Adalon, what are you suggesting here? Mortal soldiers imbued with Draconic blood? Do you know what that could do to them? Does the Maker authorize this?"

"She does. She has a direction… For thisss world. It is no accident… To be created…"

"But one moment…" he emphasizes with a finger. "Surely, you are familiar with the Measure of Balance. This sounds like it might throw things a little off kilter, do you think?"

"We have here… A unique circumsssstance… That offersss usss… A modessst amount… Of flexibility. We are not breaking… Any critical rulesss. But we will be creating... A force... That cannot be countered... By any common meansss..."

"And for what ultimate purpose?"

"To create a force... To dominate... Over the illsss... Of thisss world... And any othersss... We may dissscover... Along the way... As we evolve... Our Children..."

Thaelyn reeled back on this notion...their Children. Not only was she suggesting a union to build a new Order, but she was also proclaiming the future potential to take this beyond Tae'Eladar. A society to overcome the ills of anything they might encounter. But this society would first have to overcome its own ills, and the result would be a Golden Age, with a society so refined that it would have no more ills at all. And he would be its Father.

Now he felt pale, and rubbed his hand across his brow.

"Who is this third one," he asks softly.

"She is called... Shessscellaie. To find her... You mussst travel... To the eassst. There you will find... A circle of mountainsss... And within that circle... Is a valley... And within that valley... Are the lassst remaining grovesss... Of the Dryadsss. She is their Queen... And she is expecting you..."

"A dryad queen? Explain to me how this helps build an Order of Knighthood."

"It does not... Ssspecifically ssserve... A military purpossse... But it will bessstow... Life... Health... And wholesssomeness... To the population. They will cleanse the land... Freshen the air... And purify the water... Promoting longevity... Resssponsibility... And the bonding... Of men and nature... And the union... Of the ssspirit..."

"This sounds like how the elven culture reveres the old Trees of life."

"Yesss... But here... We will teach thisss... To everyone..."

"And indeed this would likely change a few of their manners along the way. This is simply incredible. But this will take a tremendous amount of work, to say nothing of manpower, resources...money. We have done well for our needs, but this is a project even the best of the Holy Brotherhoods around the land could not succeed at. Do you really think we can do this? How long have you been having these visions?"

"They have been... A part of me... All of my life. I have watched you grow... Even to direct you. I have foressseen... All you have done... Or will do..."

"Interesting. Would you care to share any part of this?" he smirks gently.

Adalon lets out a bold laugh at the suggestion.

"I know you do not... Desire... To chassse dreamsss. Therefore... I will refrain... From dissstracting you... From the path... You feel more... Comforting... To take. Besssides... I have... A reputation... Of being cryptic. I cannot... Disssappoint... My admirersss..."

"Indeed! Very well then, I will interpret this as you choosing to test me for my ingenuity. This is acceptable, and perhaps how I would prefer it anyway."

"As for resssources... I can offer... Sssupport... To begin the processss. From there... We will manage ourssselves... As needed..."

Adalon lifts up from her reclined posture and motions for him to follow her into the next chamber. She leads him up to a wall that appeared as a smooth rock face.

"Behind here..." she begins. "Thisss should be enough... To get usss ssstarted..."

She raises a claw and reaches out to the wall while calling out a chant. Thaelyn watches, suspecting the wall is actually a false layer. In a moment, his thoughts are confirmed as an outline emerges and a massive door opens up. Behind this was another large chamber, a treasury room. And it was filled from floor to ceiling with gold, mountains of it.

"Dear Powers," he wheezes as he looks inside.

He steps up to it to peek around the corners of the door frame. He saw mountains of coins, chests filled with gems and jewelry, gold bars and relics, all piled on top of each other.

"Adalon, one moment please," he hesitates. "I know a thing or two about dragons and their hoards, and that is you cannot separate them so easily."

"Those are ssstories... For children... At bedtime. The Draconicsss... Have no true need... Or a desire... For material wealth. I collected thisss... For the sssingle purpossse... Of building... The future leader... Of thisss world..." she finishes and turns to him.

The magnitude of the notion was staggering, but Thaelyn found he couldn't escape from it. This was apparently his Fate, as overwhelming as it might be. He gazed at the incredible riches again wondering how this would ultimately develop.

"How can you possibly expect me to carry all this? Where would we put it? We do not even have enough space to store this much material."

"We will build... A new home... For oursselves. I have already... Ssselected... A pleasant location..."

"You have? Where?"

"To the north... Is a valley... Beneath a row... Of mountainsss. The mountainsss... Are firm bedrock. We shall build a fortressss... A new guildhall... And a home for you... And a home for me... And a city for our people. Thisss is where... We will begin. The ressst will come... As we grow... And ssspread our culture... To attract the remainder... Of the world..."

"The world...all of it? Adalon, what was this world intended to be, if we consider the Age of Dragons, and what you said earlier?"

"A cussstom project... To ressstore life... To a dead world. But we will not ssstop... At sssimply... Ressstoring life here. We will move forward... To grow and evolve... And ssspread our wisdom... And compassion... To othersss we encounter... Along the way. Thisss will be... Our role... Within the Measure of Balance. A refined sssociety... On the Positive ssside..."

"A bit on the young side, also," he grins.

"Perhapsss... But no one ever... Made a rule... Denoting age requirementsss," she chuckles.

"Oh! Are we adding a new line to it, perhaps?"

They share the moment with a laugh before Adalon continues.

"We mussst now… Share our bond… Thaelyn. I have a ssspell to cassst… That will give unto you… A part of me… And unto me… A part of you. Thisss will link usss… And allow usss… To build the ressst…"

Thaelyn contemplated this idea deeply. He had never joined in any kind of blood bond before, and this was with no less than a dragon. The potency alone would likely burn, but the benefits, whether to him or to any that might share this later, would create an army of people that could almost literally move mountains.

He took a deep breath and reflected on the conversation, then recalling all the people he had brought into his collective thus far, and where this would take them and anyone else after that. A Golden Age…he did not actually consider his efforts here would ultimately result in that, although secretly he had to admit, he did wish to refine their direction, and if he were successful, this would likely be an end result.

He looked up at her again. She was standing next to him, towering above him like a tall building, a majestic creature with a bold direction, and apparently the motivation and resources to back it up. He, she, and one other…a dryad queen, the Pillars of Three, a mighty power beheld…

"Very well, Adalon…let us be on with it. I have my people waiting outside, which actually reminds me of our original goal…"

"Do not trouble yoursssself… With that little concern…"

"But Adalon, we received an important report from one of the town guards on this…"

"It was falsssse…"

"What? False? How do you know?"

"I sssent it… To bring you here. It was time… For usss to meet… And I needed… A lure… To attract you. My apologiesss… But thisss is too… Important… And my plansss… Mussst move forward…"

"Plans… You mean those verses in your book, I suppose, along with whatever the Maker no doubt has on her mind. Therefore, the time has come, and we must begin this work. What was this about your egg then?"

"The Drow did sssteal it... But I foresssaw thisss... And timed my effortsss... To bring you here... To ssserve your function..."

"You seem to have a very strong grip on foreseeing and planning the activities of others."

"Indeed... And including... The male Drow... Who was an agent of mine... With a sssecond falssse egg."

"Oh! Really! And how do we explain our meddling in Drow politics?"

"Those two women... Had it coming. Law and jussstice... Should ssstill apply... Even in sssuch... A sssociety as theirsss. And that goddessss they worship... Is unwelcome here. Therefore... We might consssider... Their form of politicsss... Becomesss moot..."

"You know, you are nearly as devious as the Powers themselves," he grins subtly.

Adalon again laughed boldly, with Thaelyn following with his own demure chuckle.

She now turned to face him, and Thaelyn knew this was the moment. He prepared himself for what he expected to be a rough hit. Then she begins a chant in preparation for their bonding.

✦✦✦✦✦✦✦

Thaelyn was on his way back down the road to rejoin his team. He was moving slowly and in a partial daze after the bonding procedure. He wasn't sure how he felt yet, but it was certainly different. In the distance, he could see the camp his fellows had made, and they also saw him shambling along.

"There he is!" Ben shouts. "Bloody hell, what happened...just look at him."

The group all jumped to their feet and rushed to his side, taking him in their arms and leading him to the campsite. They sat down together while Nadeen, being a priestess, checked him over for any injuries or illness.

"Sir Thaelyn," she utters urgently. "What happened? You look pale as a ghost, not that you ever really carried a great amount of color to begin with. And I can't possibly imagine what could sap away at a man like you in the first place."

"Easy, Children," he relents weakly. "I simply had a bit of a spell."

As he reflects on his words, he starts giggling uncontrollably at the ludicrous pun he just made. The others stared at him for his unconventional outburst.

"Um, Sir Thaelyn," Sylnes wonders. "Are you feeling at all within yourself?"

"It is alright. Simply give me a moment. I just underwent a kind of bonding procedure, and Powers behold, this one was not for the faint of heart."

"A bonding…like a spell of bonding. Gods above, Sir Thaelyn, YOU and a bonding spell? What kind? And why?"

"Friends, that dragon… That silver dragon…is Adalon."

The full assembly all gasped at the statement, and each of them turned to examine their reactions.

"THAT was Adalon the Silver?" Nadeen blurts. "A dragon?"

"Indeed, and thus the title, the Silver… It denotes her color, as each one is different, and this is how they often identify themselves."

"Unbelievable! Then what does this mean for those prophecies? Did she explain anything to you?"

"Oh yes," he croons. "She did explain a few things, and perhaps more than I would have ever expected. Sylnes, you were right in your assumptions about the Age of Dragons, and a few other things. In fact, I think I might need to keep a close eye on you. Your growth is creating a curious end result. I may need to begin a list of people like you, simply to note your remarkable achievements and curious manners."

"Um," she wonders softly. "Is that a good thing, or a bad one," she grins. "So, do we know why those dragons behaved as they did?"

"Yes, you invaded a world not your own which was a custom

project Maker Kuroku was building for some personal reason. She did not apparently plan for you, but later reconsidered when she saw you and the others forming up new relationships. Now she wants all of you involved."

"Great gods!" she yips. "So, this world is a personal project for a goddess? And of course, here you are now, maybe as part of her plans to finish it in some way?"

"Again yes, and I suppose this is where we must return back to Breena and her statement once. The Maker is attempting to correct for your LACK of progress to bring things together independently. But more than that, this also answers a long-standing question of my own for how and why I came into being. It is no accident I am here. I had a Fate that created me, and with her acting on behalf of the Maker to see it through that I found my way here. She was that same Silver I met up in Celestia…hinting at me to come down here and investigate my future potential."

"Hinting!" she screeches. "Is that what she calls it? Great gods again! This Maker Kuroku must be the absolute worst for those gods who work strangely. So, she puts together a pet project to build a world, and then, once we have people on it, she puts together a man to bring it into order. I'm almost afraid to ask this next one, but what role are you supposed to serve in all this?"

"What role…" he chuckles giddily.

"Uh huh…get ready, people," she warns the group. "I think we're in trouble here."

"Blimey," Ben moans. "I ain't never seen him like this afore."

"It must be that bonding he took," Nadeen offers.

"Either that," Ladrim suggests. "Or simply to learn your life was engineered for reasons only a God would know about."

Thaelyn glanced around warmly at the group as they all stared back at him waiting for his response.

"My Children," he smiles gently. "So many of you…"

"Children?" Ladrim ponders. "Are you speaking metaphorically, or…? Because I know you use that word on occasion."

"Yes, but I think the relationship will carry a new meaning from this moment, as I am apparently here to serve like a father figure for all of you…everyone."

"Really!" Nadeen smirks. "So, does this mean I need to call you Dad now?"

The rest of them offer up a cautious chuckle.

"Well, Nadeen," he retorts humorously. "I suppose you may if you should so desire. But like Ladrim suggested, it may also be taken metaphorically. Despite my careful restraint to maintain the image that I did not come here pretending to be anything more than a teacher and a mentor, it would seem that my…Fate…is to lead you into a new Era…the entire world. And Adalon will be taking up at our side to see it through. We are now building those Pillars of Three, with the aid of one more, a dryad queen, no less, to create what I might describe to be nothing short of a utopian wonder."

"And here we go again," Sylnes gasps. "Great gods, a third time!"

"A dryad queen?" Ladrim wonders. "We still have dryads out there? I thought the old Trees of Life were gone by now. It fell out of habit so long ago with our people, largely after those old Crown Wars destroyed so much of our original culture, that I thought we'd never see them again."

"These are apparently the last of their kind in this world," Thaelyn accedes. "She says there is a cluster of them in a range of mountains to our east. We need to rescue them and reintroduce them to the world, all of it. Everyone is now going to realize their benefit to bring spiritual harmony to the people."

"Oh wow!" she croons. "I can barely imagine what that will do to the place. I recall some of the old stories. Do you remember those, Sylnes?"

"When I was a little girl, maybe," she notes.

"But just think of it. A utopia. An actual utopia, like the stories of the old Fey world."

"How does all this relate to that book?" Nadeen asks.

"She describes it as a type of chronicle of events," Thaelyn asserts. "It may be prophetic in some ways, but I think it is being at least partially engineered by the Maker. It is supposed to give inspiration to our efforts in the eyes of the people. As if to say, something is coming, so prepare for it."

"Oh! Really! So this is like saying, you're going to live in a paradise whether you like it or not?"

The group again rises up in a bold laugh at the notion.

"Right!" she continues. "And just how does a group of nits like us pull this off? Because this is how they'll see us, you know?"

"We are to form up an army of people bonded with Draconic blood to create a nearly unstoppable force. THAT, my dear, is how she has in mind to do it."

This quickly stifled the poor girl for a response. Nadeen gaped at the idea, as she surveyed the similar expressions of the others in the group.

"I'm sorry I asked..." she whispers timidly.

"But such a thing must be fantasy, isn't it?" Sylnes wonders uncertainly.

"Not for long, I should think," Thaelyn muses. "If we have a pet project being conducted by a member of the Estelar, she must have a plan, and we are now laying the foundation for it, with me being part of the driving force...and all of you being our Children. Incredible..." he gazes dreamily into their eyes. "How does a man attend to all this? This world will never be the same."

✦

The following years and decades saw a blossoming of growth in a pleasant valley beneath a range of mountains. A new guildhall fortress was built on the slopes of the hillside, with an elaborate manor home further above it. At the base of the hills were a series of small hamlets beginning to form, and people were coming from across the land to take up living space.

Thaelyn found himself almost instantly elevated with the title of a noble Lord, and this territory would become the home for his new Order, which he dubbed the Order of the Silver Dragon.

Silver dragons held a certain amount of esteem above other types as being very noble and prestigious creatures devoted to higher virtues such as the preservation of truth and justice. Thaelyn used Adalon's image to create his new heraldry, inscribing a dragon bust and wings in a shield portrait, with entwining vines held in claws underneath.

The vines represented his association with the dryad queen Shescellaie, which he established after his meeting with Adalon. He sought her out and merged another bond, then collected her to bring back with him. She and her daughters bound themselves up inside special acorns grown from their host trees. This would serve as a means to transport them away from their host, which otherwise would not be possible without killing them. After planting these seeds, she would reemerge within a new tree, and her daughters could also be planted elsewhere to create more groves.

The hamlets quickly expanded as more people migrated into the region. Soon they were becoming villages, but the center of this bustle, which was situated right beneath the guildhall, would be Thaelyn's new capital.

A ceremony was taking place to incorporate this new town. Thaelyn, along with several of his officers and advisers, were standing on the inclined roadway leading up to the front gates of the guildhall.

"This day marks the beginning of a special moment for each of us," he announces to the assembly. "Our good citizens, who have come together to create this proud occasion in history, who have dedicated themselves to our beliefs and our virtues, and who donate their service to the common cause, will hereby be remembered for their contribution as we give this fledgling town a new name becoming of its nature. Here we set ourselves upon a path to demonstrate to the world the potential for a finer way of life. We shall portray this to any and all who would wish to participate with us. And to this end, we offer our pledge. It is for this reason I offer this name to our combined creation, dedicating it as our Promise for Tomorrow. And in the words of my native tongue, we shall speak this name as Bya'an Tamoranth."

A rising cheer ushers up from the crowd, along with applause and whistles. Flowers are tossed at his feet and music starts playing in the streets as the people begin to dance and sing. Local taverns brought out mugs with beer and ale, and the people feasted on roast mutton and fowl stacked upon rows of tables lining the streets.

In the background, resting on the mountaintop and overlooking the scene below, was Adalon, along with her young son, perched on a ridgeline. They had come out of their new lair, which had been carved out of the mountain below.

"From here... It will grow..." she muses gently. "We mussst move... Assssertively... But cautiousssly... Using wisdom and guile. Sssome may follow willingly... But othersss will not. And yet... We need them all..."

She pauses to glance down at her tiny son, who was only a small drakeling. He looks up at her curiously. She lowers her head to nuzzle him, and then returns to the scene below and her personal musing.

"Sssargerasss... I come for you. It is only... A matter of time..."

Chapter 11

PASSAGE OF THE CREATORS

"Brother Thaelyn..." comes a raspy voice at the door.

"Adalon? Ah, good greetings to you..."

Thaelyn was in his office inside the guildhall. It had been nearly two centuries by now. Their membership had swelled considerably, as did the local population of the town, which had grown to a large cityscape outside.

His territory had expanded to include a broad swath of regional land, including a few nearby nations, as he negotiated political unions and treaties which ultimately joined their populations together. He had earned the title of Duke, and now owned a substantial number of holdings, reaching from his inland capital, across to the coastline, and northward to the edge of an inland sea known as the Sea of Stars.

On this occasion, Adalon had transformed into her persona form of a tall female in silver hues, and was making a visit to his personal study. Thaelyn stepped up to meet her as she entered, bowing and taking her hand to touch his forehead to it.

"We mussst talk..." she asserts. "We mussst make a few... Advancementsss... Within our resssearch. There are two... That come to mind… Which I believe… Are mossst important… At thisss time…"

"What sort of advancements are these?"

"There are many… I would wish to have… But we cannot have… Everything… All at once. And yet… I feel a need… Pressssing upon usss. For thisss point… I would advise… We direct oursselves… To inventing… Two important elementsss. One will be… An antibiotic. Our people… Need a proper… Curative medicinal… For illnessss… And infection…"

"This sort of science is most often implemented after a fair amount of study in microbiology. Our people are nowhere near this level of precision."

"Not every invention… Mussst come… In sssequence… With another. Necessssity can often… Play a role. The invention… Can easily be found… If one were to ssstudy… Certain sssubstances… And their interactionsss… With othersss. Then… To accidentally… Find the anssswer…"

"Accidentally?" he eyes her suspiciously.

"Perhapsss… If alssso to point… A finger at it…" she chuckles mildly.

"Indeed! I can certainly speak to our science department about this. And the other?"

"Ssso far… We have been… Fortunate… In our relationsss… With the neighboring… Nationsss. Many have recognized… Our valuesss. But as we continue… To expand… More tension will build… In those… Who are known to be… Opponentsss. We invessst… Many resssources… In our training… And I would wish… To pressserve that value… At any cossst…"

"Most interesting. But how do you suggest this?"

"We already have… Policiesss… To offer the bessst… Healing ssservice… To our combatantsss… On the front linesss. But injuriesss… Can ssstill occur. Sssome of them… Grievousss. We mussst… Improve upon thisss… By mandating… The ressstoration… Of our fallen sssoldiers… To bring them back to usss…"

"Would that not cause some amount of disruption amongst the

Estelar that we are disallowing the timely passage of mortal souls?" he grins softly.

"They will have their due... When we are finished with them..." she smirks.

"Oh, as you wish!" he chuckles ironically.

"But thisss is not enough. For those who may sssuffer... Grievousss injury... I want to create... A sssolution..."

"And what solution is that?"

"I envision... An unguent... With propertiesss... To permit... The regeneration... Of flesh. It would be applied... To an injury... Sssuch as the lossss... Of an arm... Or a leg... And ressstore thisss... Back to them..."

"Fascinating. A regeneration formula. This would represent the properties we know to exist in such as swamp trolls, which can regenerate large portions of their bodies, even if they are hacked into small bits. In fact, the only true way to kill one of those is by fire."

"Thisss would draw... From that principle... But inssstead... To fool the body... Into regenerating... Rather than... Sssimply healing... A damaged area..."

"All right, we shall see about this. Is there anything else?"

"The city outsssside... Is prosssspering nicely. We have many... Resssources... To work with. Let usss use them... And inssspire our people... To grow... In new directionsss. Magic should not be... Limited... To only those... In the higher applicationsss..."

"Are you now suggesting we teach this to everyone? I am not against this, although I have resisted thus far due to the inherent complexity. But will this not cause some amount of concern in the longer term?"

"The firssst lesssson in magic... Is dissscipline. We can arrange... The lesssssons... To provide... Utility... As well as... Sssafety. But to allow thisss... For the general public... Will encourage... Miraculousss development... In many areasss..."

"I am quite sure it will, but we must proceed carefully, and raise them up in a balanced manner where they realize the responsibility of the Art. This is something that has never been done before."

"Surely… It has been done. Sssimply not here…"

She bows gently, turns and leaves, departing the room and following the halls to another segment where she enters a small room she used to come and go from her private lair. Once inside the room, she calls up her innate power to fold space, creating a rippling wave around her form and vanishing from sight.

Within her lair, which was a series of large chambers carved out of the center of the mountain, she returns to her natural form again, and then summons her servant. A column of light arrives by her side.

"Yes Maker," Thaliel answers.

"Where is he now…?"

"He is making an attempt at that domain he found recently, using those very same creatures we saw him with once before, the ones he sent forward to this domain."

"The orcsss… How curiousss. That world holdsss… A different environment… Than their native home. I wonder… How they will fare…"

"My suspicion is they will not fare well. The gravitational values are nearly double their native environment. And this has nothing to say about the inherent difference in military capacities, where the natives are surely much more capable."

"Perhapsss thisss is… Sssimply an experiment…"

✦✦◆✦✦

Again, the years passed by, and a new form of study was vigorously underway…biology. Although there had been lighter studies made on the various plants and animals around the world, this now delved even deeper into how it all relates. Naturally, as one discovery is made, it poses new questions demanding of another study.

It was now being realized that different plants and animals held an apparent relation to each other, and not simply as cousins that might have separated due to some form of specialization. This led to the formation of new research, which then called for the development of new specialized centers of study to collect and examine specimens for classification.

Time progressed forward, and this new science moved along with the ambition and zeal of a child with a new toy. The gnomish community, one of the races that migrated to Tae'Eladar along with the elves, and which held an inherent proclivity for analytical thought and research capacity, became entrenched in a flurry of new theories that needed to be either proven or disproven.

Among these were the obvious questions of how multiple species might share similar traits, which led to the prospect of a common ancestor. This idea flooded the scientific community with new thoughts on how many family lines there might be and how each species may have actually come about. The concept broke many of the old perceptions of the origins of life, and now a number of field studies were being conducted on the potential viability of a principle for the origin of species...evolution.

Several decades have passed by this time, and the collection of data was accumulating in research centers and libraries. Several new museums were opening up with the results discovered so far, and more study was currently underway, including excavations to locate and catalog the remains of ancestral species that led to the development of the more modern examples. With each new result came more questions that would take them further back in time. This also naturally led to the issue of the origin of humans.

The elves, dwarves, and others who currently lived on Tae'Eladar each brought with them some part of their ancestral history and culture. But the human society did not hold any such ancient history. They preexisted in the world when the elves first arrived, so it was naturally assumed they were native to this environment. Therefore, learning the origins of human society was also important to understand how they fit into the grand scheme of things where life on Tae'Eladar was concerned.

The other studies pointed to the common ancestral lines for everything else, and even though humans seemed to represent a unique form of life as compared to the rest, many still believed there might be a connection deep in the ancient past. The study of biology was taking on new forms, now moving into archeology and paleontology, to understand the progression of life based on fossil evidence, and struggling to locate new resources to continue this research. This called for more excavations to look deeper into the rocks to find their answers. But now they were hitting a roadblock, and it didn't make any sense.

"My Lord!" calls a gnomish professor entering his office. "This is rather peculiar and becoming exceedingly frustrating."

"What is it, Professor? And how are your studies coming along?"

"That's just it, my Lord. They're coming to a rather abrupt standstill. We've been searching around several sites that previously were producing some very promising results, and now there is simply nothing more to research! The rocks are barren!"

"One moment… When you say barren, in what manner?"

"This is occurring in multiple sites by now. We've excavated down to what we believe to be perhaps thirty thousand years into the past, based on our studies using the new carbon measuring process, which so far has given us some very promising and consistent results."

"Most excellent, and the results you have shown do indeed fall within my expectations. But now you say the rocks are showing up as barren?"

"Yes! We seem to have hit a layer where there are no more remnants of anything at all occurring. It's as though all evidence of life has suddenly vanished…or rather I should say it just suddenly appeared out of nowhere at approximately this period of time."

The suggestion was peculiar, but not actually unexpected, as Thaelyn had once learned of the refurbishing effort to bring Tae'Eladar back to life by some external body. This also reflected on Maker Kuroku and whatever plans she had been working on. It would now seem the time had come to bring this out, but in the traditions of his Celestial family, Thaelyn was forbidden to simply give the answer openly, not without that initial growth experience occurring first.

"Very well, Professor, here is what I will offer. Clearly, there must be a cause, and although I might hold my own thoughts on this, you also realize that I must encourage the growth of our people. I am aware of a few old stories, though many are forgotten by now, of what was once called a Creator Race. The human society once held some ideas as part of their old mythology. But if we are suggesting a sudden and abrupt introduction of life on this world, perhaps we should see if there is any truth to this, as perhaps it may hold an answer. Then we might wish to ask if it did in fact participate in any of what we see today."

"But my Lord, for all that we've learned about the development of life in our world, wouldn't this simply take us back to the idea that it was all created by some godlike entity?"

"There are different avenues we could travel with this idea. One might suggest this is true, while another might suggest only a partial explanation. We do see the development of life AFTER this moment. So the question becomes what happened BEFORE. Could it be this Creator Race simply planted the seeds we see within our history, and those seeds then sprouted into the rest?"

"Yes! Right-a-diddly-do, my Lord!" the Professor jumps in delight. "But this will be a tough one, I think. Where do we go to find our new evidence..." he mutters distantly as he offers a quick bow and leaves the room.

The research on the origins of human society would now need to branch in another direction. The barren layer they found in the fossil record stifled the original study, but they persisted to see if there was anything that might come before, meaning deeper in the rocks from an earlier period. Eventually, they found their answer on that side, but it was just as puzzling as the rest.

They were now finding evidence of life imprinted in the rocks, but this evidence was truly ancient, and didn't match anything else on record. There were remains of species of plants and animals that resembled something almost alien as compared to what existed in the modern day. The dating methods they developed to measure the earlier specimens were useless on these, simply due to their age, and so they began making estimates based as much on guesswork as anything else so far, and the numbers were staggering, measuring on the order of many millions, perhaps even as much as a billion years old.

The process took time to refine, and multiple research centers were involved by now to develop more accurate means of testing the samples. The studies carried teams of researchers across the land, some of them with guard patrols to protect them from any hostile elements in the area. But the surveys all came back with very similar results.

"...And so, my Lord," the Professor relates. "These recent reports are telling us something fan-dang-arifically nasty must've happened maybe about a billion years ago. We're seeing fossil evidence of living things running, hopping, flapping, and crawling all over the place back then, and then bang! It's all gone."

"Do you have any theories on this thus far?"

"We're thinking of some kind of big disaster, and our geology studies are starting to give us a few ideas. We're seeing the movement of rocks and boulders, big ones too, from faraway places, where we see the same kind of rock, but now shoved into places where they shouldn't otherwise be. So, unless you want to tell me the gods are playing with big, oversized marbles, we're going on the idea this is something natural. Wind couldn't be the reason. They're just too big and heavy. We thought about flooding and mudslides, but these rocks may be hundreds of miles from their home, and also too far from any seas or oceans, like if we consider a big wave coming in. But the tickler comes in the time frame, I think."

"Very good, and what sort of tickler do we have on this occasion," he smiles.

"In all our other studies, we had to dig to find the older specimens of fossils and other goodies because they had been buried under so many layers of sediment laid down over time. So, it quickly became apparent to us that time tends to bury things. Now we look at this much older layer. We see a layer of what looks like barren rock just under the last of our recent history, but this is a bit strange, because it looks less like sediment and more like something you might find in a farmer's field."

"Oh? This is indeed very curious. Do continue."

"Under that, we see what looks like old rock, but this is also curious, because between these two, we see a thin layer of something that doesn't look normal."

"How would you define normal in this case?"

"I'm not sure how I might define the normal transition between a cultivated layer and the ancient rock, but this tiny layer in-between doesn't look like it belongs there. We took samples of it back to the lab for study, and it holds some very unusual and previously unknown minerals inside."

"Fascinating."

"We think something happened that left a fine layer of dust behind, and it must've been big, because we see this same fine layer in a lot of places."

"As if to say a large cloud came down and covered the land, perhaps?"

"That would be a very good way to put it, my Lord. And then we have this ancient layer underneath it. But here is where we have our tickler. The ancient layer is turning out to be very old, and there's not enough material above it to show that layering effect of time burying everything before we hit our current period. This tells me something else was covering it and sealing it in place for a long time. And the only thing that comes to mind so far is ice, a big whop-a-doozy mountain of it. We're thinking of an Age where ice covered everything in a deep layer, preventing the normal erosion of the land, and therefore this layering effect of the sediments."

"Very nicely done, Professor, and indeed I can confirm one piece of this for you at this time. There was once a moment in our ancient history where I am aware the twin goddesses, Selûne and Shar, were once directed to watch over this world. These were the very early days following a moment in our history that none of you here would be aware of, but I will reveal this to you now. There was once a great war. We call it the Celestial War. The current gods once did battle with another breed and the result was devastation on a scale unimaginable, resulting in the Ethereal Maelstrom that now swirls in our nighttime skies."

"Really! Ooh! I need to write this down," he yips excitedly and whips out his paper and pen.

"The twin goddesses were tasked with watching over the world, as it was a survivor from that time, and I recall it did hold life of some sort. Unfortunately, they later had a dispute over their management practices, and Shar, being the loser of the argument, cast a shadow over the local sun, causing everything to grow deathly cold."

"Ah! Yes! Most excellent! And this would explain the great ice age we had. This would also explain everything going ka-bam, and nothing new happening until recently. But now, this raises new questions, and I already know what you're going to say, my Lord. I'm just thinking out loud. First, what happened to warm things up, and then where did all this NEW life come from? For this point, I might have to admit we'd probably need a little help to get things going again. Maybe that's where this farming layer came from. Hmm…"

"Well, Professor, it would seem you have more work for yourself. Do keep me informed of your progress. I might find this next part rather interesting to learn, as my own teachings do not go into this level of detail."

"Really, my Lord? Oh goodie! I can't wait till I get back and tell the boys about this one!"

The Professor jumps out of his seat and makes a quick bow before dashing out of the room.

The gnomish professor quickly rallied his teams and shared the news. Now that they understood they were on the right track with this idea of an ice age, they redirected themselves to find some evidence for what came after to rebuild the world. The concept of a Creator Race was growing larger by now, so the studies were focusing on looking for any kind of ancient ruins that might indicate the habitation of this Creator Race during the time they were rehabilitating the world.

Of course, by this time, they well understood that anything left behind from so long ago might not show up anymore. More than likely, it would be buried the same as everything else, or eroded into rubble. The surface evidence might be a lost cause, so they instead turned to the hope of finding something buried.

Teams of researchers began by referencing the old history of the elves when they first arrived, to see if they recorded any observations. It was long known in some parts of the world there were underground chambers, catacombs, forgotten caverns and tunnels. These now became a focus of study, and many examples were thrown out as being either natural or created by other means. But after a while, a few obscure locations were examined and discovered to hold strange relics of something unrecognizable.

There was still a lot of damage, mostly from water and microorganisms invading the enclosed space and causing decay, but the few remaining artifacts were tantalizing. Among the remains were hand tools made from previously unknown materials, some of which didn't seem to decay as readily as the more common substances. No known race on Tae'Eladar was believed to have created these items, and although they couldn't make a positive identification of their true owners, it was becoming clear they could not be local.

In time, they began to see a pattern in their findings to aid them in their future expeditions, and this led them to discover the vague remains of structures in certain locations across the land. They soon realized this unknown race was prone to build underground, so excavations were started to locate buried tunnels leading to the underground chambers, hoping to find more clues that may have survived the burdens of time. More examples were found, but as before, most of them suffered from fissures in the rocks allowing water and other contaminants to seep through.

As the collection of relics slowly accumulated, many included symbols in an unknown language. In a few locations, they found what appeared to be furniture, containers, and the remains of equipment of a seemingly complex design, like some manner of machines, but clearly corroded and crusted with decay. So far, everything they found, although intriguing for its historical potential, was falling short of answering their questions. Until one day, they found something new.

"Over here!" calls a digger. "Looks like a tunnel leading down."

"All right, let's clear it out," shouts the foreman. "Gently now, and watch for anything loose that might be of value."

A team of workers was excavating yet another site. This one stood out a little more than most of the others they investigated in the past. In some ways, it almost resembled a temple, or at least the remains of one. But logic would suggest it was more likely a research facility of some kind. It was a large structure with regular shapes across a broad floor layout. The walls had crumbled into heaps by now, and the roof collapsed, so the workers had been spending much of their time up until now just clearing away the surface debris, along with random shrubbery and grass, and other foliage covering the grounds.

In one corner, they found a depression that looked like so many other tunnel entrances, complete with the upper stairs just peeking through the dust and rubble.

The workers carefully dug out the debris, keeping a careful watch for any artifacts that might have fallen into the hole. As was the usual practice, they created a pile some distance to the side for another team to rummage through, but as the surface layers were cleared off, the diggers began to take notice of something odd in this example. The passageway led rather deep in this case, and they noticed the sides of the passage were neatly tiled to give a nicely finished appearance. Also, the deeper layers of fill were very consistent with rough aggregate and sand, rather than common dirt and loose sediment. It was as if it was intentionally buried in this fashion.

"This is an odd one, to be sure," remarks one digger. "I don't recall anything like this in any of the others."

"Aye, but still, keep your eyes sharp," advises another. "We don't want to miss anything."

The work continued methodically as the debris was lifted away in buckets. The process was painstaking, but determined, until they began to take notice of something at the bottom.

"I think we found something," shouts a worker. "What do we have here now, is it a wall or a door?"

"It can't be a wall," mentions another worker. "It looks more like an outline of a door to me."

"Aye, but if it's a door, how do you open it? I don't see a knob or a lever of any kind."

"If it's a door," the foreman offers. "It must have some kind of trick to it. What's that on the side there," he points to a panel box. "Looks a bit like a cabinet."

"Do we open it?"

"It looks a bit simpler than the other thing. Do I see a handle on it there?"

"Aye, and this looks like it held up much nicer than anything else we've found so far."

"Look at this wall here," directs another worker. "What in the nine hells is this made of?"

The workers all closed in for a better look. They saw a wall that seemed remarkably intact, as compared to so many other examples. It wasn't made from stone, or any other recognizable material. The door resembled a flat featureless panel that seemed to cover an opening, but without any obvious means to move it. On the right side was a smaller panel door with a recessed knob set into it. Everything looked intact, even though it must be very old.

"All right men," the foreman begins. "We'll take this slowly. Let's try this cabinet on the side, and see what it has for us."

The workers moved out of the way to allow the foreman access to the panel. At first, he examined it closely to determine its condition.

"This here looks like a knob that might turn."

He taps gently with a finger on the panel door to test its rigidity, and feels around the knob. It seemed firm. He brushed some of the dust out of the way to see a narrow vertical grip set inside the depression, and tried nudging it lightly to see if it moved.

The knob was stiff, but it did show movement to turn, giving a soft grinding sound from dust contamination. He found he was able to turn it a quarter turn to the right, then felt the panel pop free from the latch inside. He flinched slightly as the door now felt loose enough to pull open.

"Friends, this is interesting, it looks like something completely different."

"Aye, what do we have in there?"

He cautiously pulls the door open, and they all gaze in amazement.

"What in the…" mumbles one of the workers.

Inside the door was an enclosure with what appeared to be two sets of pronged slots, giving the impression of something that needed to be inserted across them. Along the bottom was a panel with several shapes inscribed on it, appearing as a long rectangle on top and a set of boxes underneath. The material was unknown and appeared transparent, like a little window covering something underneath."

"Bloody hell, boss," mentions one worker. "I don't recall anything like this before."

The foreman then looked at the inside of the door panel. There was a plaque attached to it with a diagram and a lot of writing.

"Gods be blessed…" he whispers silently. "Folks, I'd be a mule's uncle if these didn't look like instructions!"

"That writing looks a bit like what we've seen before," one worker relates as he points at the plaque.

"Aye," affirms another one. "But only the top part… Look there at the bottom half. It looks entirely different."

"Men," the foreman suggests. "I think we have something special here. If I'm interpreting this right, these are two different languages, and I'll bet you it's the same thing written in each, giving us a chance to interpret it with something we might be more familiar with…or at least I hope so."

"Aye, but what? I don't recognize either of them, straight off."

"All right, let's do this. Make a rubbing of this and take it back to B.T. See if we have anything in the libraries to match this other language. Until then, I'm going to suggest we leave this be until we can figure out what it says. We'll go from there."

The foreman moves away while one of the other workers brings in a sheet of paper and a block of charcoal to create an impression of the grooved markings on the plaque.

"Good, now take that back to town and see what you can find. We'll continue our work here to see what else we have."

The worker moves away to find one of the scholars assisting the expedition. The scholar was a mage, as it had become a common practice by now to involve people of different skills on these treks to expedite their travels. The mage held a portal rune leading back to the city.

The mage brought out his rune and began weaving his magic over it, causing it to glow, and then erupt with a column of energy that settled back into a glowing ring circling the stone in his hand. The worker then touched the stone and flashed away in a burst of light.

He arrived on a platform to one side of the courtyard of the guildhall. From there, he hurried to the guild's main library, where he found one of the librarians.

"You there, I need some assistance, please."

The librarian turns to his address.

"Yes, what can I help you with?"

"Look here…"

He shows the paper with the rubbing to the librarian.

"Incredible! Where did you find this?"

"In a new dig we just uncovered. There's a box set into a wall with a sign on it, and this is from the sign."

"This appears as two distinct languages. And images? This is a diagram! Oh, we must see if we can decipher this."

"This part up here looks to be more of the language from what we think is the Creator Race, but this down here…do we have anything like this on record?"

"One moment, I know who best to ask. Master Hagram. He's our best language expert."

The librarian leads the man to an office in the rear. Inside they find an elder man studying a number of books.

"Master Hagram, my apologies for disturbing you. Do you have a moment to look at something?"

"Huh? Oh, but of course, come in. What do we have here?"

The librarian directs the worker to step forward.

"Master," he begins. "This here…" he shows the man the paper. "We made this off a sign inside a door to a new dig we just found. We think this writing here is from the Creator Race, but we can't be sure of this other one. Do we know anything about it?"

The elder scholar takes the paper and studies it closely. The crude imagery of the rubbing made it difficult for his old eyes to make out clearly, but after several long moments, he was finally able to pick out the symbols, and his brow began to furrow.

"What…" he wheezes. "Where did you find this?"

"We found it inside a door to a small cabinet in a new dig we just uncovered. We see something odd inside that looks like clips to hold something in place."

"Clips…to hold something…?"

"Aye, and there's something we think is a door standing next to it, but with no clear way to open it. The foreman thinks this box holds a clue."

"A door…and a box with clips to hold something…maybe to mount something…like maybe a key or some such," he stands up from his seat still staring at the paper. "By the gods, in a very real sense of it, do you know what language this is?"

He stops and sets the paper on his desk, then turns to a large bookcase and begins rummaging through the titles.

The librarian and the worker exchanged glances while the elder man searched the shelves, finally to pull out a thick book. He returned to his desk to sit down and began referencing the pages.

He studied the book and the paper, cross-referencing between them, and after only a few moments, brought his bewildered gaze back up to his guests. He then lurched out of his chair and grabbed the paper again.

"We need to take this to His Lordship immediately!" he gushes and hurries out the door.

The three of them now found themselves chasing through the

halls to Thaelyn's office, where he was once again involved in his administration duties.

"My Lord! My pardons, please, but you must look at this!"

"Master Hagram, what happened? You look like the end of the world is coming."

"The end? Maybe not that, my Lord, but see here. What do you think of this paper?"

The Master slaps the paper on the desk.

Thaelyn picks it up to study it, and almost immediately his expression changes.

"Dear Powers, where did this come from?"

Master Hagram defers to the worker again, who steps forward tentatively.

"My Lord," the man submits. "This is from a new dig we found. It was found inside a cabinet door on a box set beside what we think is a door with no obvious means to open it. The box has some peculiar apparatus inside and this looks like it relates to the workings, or so we think."

"You may be right. This is a set of instructions detailing the construction of a power cell to be applied in some manner of device."

"A power cell? What do you mean by that, my Lord?"

"This would relate to a form of science we have not yet investigated, but I would surely wish to see this for myself. Do we have a rune leading to that location?"

"Aye, I got one here," he pulls out the item from his pocket. "Do you wish to go out there now?"

"Yes, I think this demands a careful inspection."

Thaelyn now leads the group back outside to the courtyard. The librarian and Master Hagram each return to their previous duties while Thaelyn takes the rune and enchants it for both he and the worker to find passage.

Back at the dig site, the two men came into view at a designated arrival zone, much to the surprise of the workers still clearing out the debris.

"My Lord!" the foreman shouts as he sees them emerge into view. "Gracious, what would bring you out this far?"

"Your little note…"

"I didn't mean to disturb you. What was it about? Do we know what language that is?"

"Indeed, we do. MY language, the language of the Celestial races. This is most curious."

"Celestial?!" he gasps. "Good gods above…oh, um…" he chuckles weakly.

The activity of the site all turned to Thaelyn as he made his way to the tunnel entrance, directed by the worker and now the foreman. They descend inside and approach the bottom, where Thaelyn studies the door and the surrounding wall.

"This appears to have been very carefully sealed," he muses. "I wonder if the interior is still intact."

He then turns to examine the panel, looking inside the door to study the contents.

"Gentlemen, this is a power junction. And by the positioning, I must conclude it directly relates to the operation of this door. See here…" he points at the sets of clips. "The writing on this door indicates a series of instructions to fabricate a set of power cells that install within these clips. I would therefore suggest this will offer power to operate the door, likely through an application of this panel down below."

"Bloody hell," the foreman mutters. "This is more than anything we ever saw anywhere else."

"I might also suggest that if this door is as tightly sealed as it appears to be on the outside, whatever is inside might be carefully preserved. And this further suggests it was intended this way. See this material?" he leans close to examine the wall. "This appears as a rather durable form of synthetic that would quite likely stand up to the duration of time. If the full housing is made of this…"

He pauses to step back and ponder the situation.

"I wonder… Powers be blessed, could this be some sort of time capsule?"

"A what, my Lord?"

"It is a concept sometimes used if you wish to store something for a later generation to discover. You package it away tightly, and then often bury it, usually with a marker and an inscription to inform others at some moment in time to uncover it, and therefore reflect upon what the previous generation held special favor for."

"Wouldn't it be easier just to put it away in a closet?" offers the worker.

The rest of the team ushers up a gentle laugh.

"Perhaps it might be, but this can offer a certain level of nostalgia. And now, I am wondering what is inside here."

He again studies the panel box and the writing, and once more glances at the door.

"All right, this is what I will suggest for this specific occasion. Until further notice, we should keep this under tight security. Whatever is inside here could be extremely valuable, but it could also represent a level of technical understanding well above that of our current population. There may be a time when we might find ourselves in possession of such forms of science, but this is not that time. I want a garrison placed around this location to secure it from any tampering."

"Yes, my Lord, as you wish," the foreman nods.

"Next, we will decipher these instructions, and we will direct a team of our people to begin a classified project. In fact, I believe this entire site should be made classified until we can better understand what we have here."

"I understand. What will this project do for us?"

"Our first goal will be to create these power cells, and then to install them. I wish to be present at that time. We will proceed forward from that point, but do so carefully."

Thaelyn returns home while the work advances to a new stage. The instructions were translated and interpreted, and a new research project began.

The virtual lack of any scientific understanding of things electric demanded its own careful study. In order for them to interpret the instructions given, they had to conduct a bit of background work to evolve this particular science. Thaelyn decided to create a secret project to solve this problem. The question of what was inside that chamber was too important to simply put it off until the natural progression of science might meander its way up to it, so he was going to bend the rules a bit, but keep it under wraps to only his military research.

In the years to come, his scientists learned the secrets of electricity, how to generate it, how to store it, and along the way, the relationship between that and magnetism. It soon became apparent to those in the study how useful this could be for any number of applications.

Once they felt confident, they followed the designs for the storage cells and created a suitable prototype. The project team then converged on the door again, with Thaelyn now overseeing the operation.

"Gently now," instructs the team leader. "Let's try not to create any sparks from it. These cells hold a fair enough charge to knock a man flat on his backside."

They carefully inserted the two cells into the appropriate slots. The design involved electrodes protruding through a unique gelatinous substance inside a glass tube with metal caps on the ends. When both cylinders were installed, they flipped a small toggle switch behind the panel below, and the panel lit up with a digital readout in the rectangular box. The smaller square boxes also lit up, one green and the other red.

"Very good, it would seem we have power," Thaelyn asserts.

"Good to know, but now what?" the team leader asks. "We have something written inside this long box, and the others are glowing at us."

"In many instances I am aware of, green indicates a desirable action while red is an undesirable or contrary one. Since we are speaking of a door, I might suggest the action of opening versus closing. But then I am looking at that indicator. This may be a progression status of some sort, but it is written in their language. And yet, a status for the simple act of opening a door is a suspicious one, unless there is some procedure involved along the way. This brings a curious thought to my mind."

"Aye, I'll bet it would!" he chuckles. "What are you thinking, my Lord?"

"If I am right, and this is indeed a sort of time capsule, they may have sealed it specifically to protect the contents. This door looks more like a hatch to me, which suggests it to be hermetically sealed. If this is the case, the interior space might be under pressure, perhaps a negative pressure, meaning partially or fully evacuated of an atmosphere. This might also provide additional security to prevent external contamination if the shell…" he taps on the wall next to the door, "…is being compressed due to this pressure, therefore creating a tighter barrier."

"Sounds like a fine bit of engineering, if I do say so. But now, do we dare pry it open?"

"At this moment, if we wish to understand any part of this, we must. Press the green button and let us see what happens. But be prepared if it needs to stabilize the pressure with the outer environment. We may experience a sudden rushing of air."

The team leader tentatively brings up his hand to press the button, laying it on the surface of the touch sensitive display panel. As soon as his finger touches the box emitting the green glow, the apparatus begins beeping.

A whirring sound ushers up from inside the panel, followed by more mechanical noises as locking bars pull away inside the wall around the door frame. This opened up vents hidden within the framework. Another whirring spins up as a blower behind the panel begins sucking in air through another vent on top.

The sound of gushing air began hissing as soon as the vents opened around the door, causing starts and jerks in the full group, and everyone stepped back to observe the scene from a safe distance. The blower behind the panel apparently started circulating the air with the outside to provide active ventilation. Once the pressure stabilized, the door slid open behind the wall.

"Well, my Lord," the team leader admits. "I guess you were right about that part."

The room inside was pitch black, and since they were underground with the only light being the sunlight from above reflecting through the tunnel, they had to use something else to see where they were going from here.

Thaelyn led them inside cautiously. He used his magical Spark conjuration for his own light while the others might use that or a lantern instead. The first thing they noticed was a large appliance situated near the door. They stopped to look at it.

It had more of those sockets in it, six this time, and much larger. The unit was as tall as a man, so whatever it was used for, it was apparently designed for a much heavier workload. It also had more instructions, just like the panel box outside, describing the requirements for the new cells.

"It would appear we have more work ahead of us," Thaelyn notes.

"Aye, best to get these plans back home to the science boys to scratch their heads over."

Thaelyn led them further along, continuing through the room and following the wall adjacent to the large power junction. Their next stop was a row of computer consoles.

"Dear Powers, will you look at all this," he mutters to himself.

"My Lord, this looks a mite more complicated than that last one."

"Indeed, and it will no doubt take some time to decipher. But whereas that last part might offer us a substantial boost to our science where the power systems are concerned, this here..." he whistles emphatically. "This is a form of science and engineering all its own. We will study it for now only to learn its operation, but I think I would much rather allow our people to grow a bit more before taking on anything of this level."

After examining the consoles for a moment, he looks up at the wall behind them, taking notice of a series of large plaques above him. Like before, they included writing in two languages. He stood there reading one to himself while the others waited.

"Gentlemen, we have a name here!" he announces proudly. "They call themselves the Sarrukh."

"Sarrukh, is it?" the team leader remarks with a smile. "So the Creator Race that built all this, and apparently set down the seeds of life on our world, is called Sarrukh. Such a lovely one, that!"

They continued their way around and were soon confronted with a spectacular sight standing dead center in the middle of the room. In the light of their glowing conjurations and lanterns, it appeared as a large upright ring-like aperture standing in a mount on the floor. They circled around it in awe.

"Bloody hell!" shouts the team leader. "My Lord, is that what I think it is? I mean, it sure as anything looks like it ought to be."

"Indeed!" he croons. "And this offers us a variety of possibilities. Try to imagine it now... This appears as a technological variation of a portal device. Now, think... If the Sarrukh were to import life from somewhere, they would surely need a means of transport, and we already know the fine utility of using portals. This might allow them to deliver it into this chamber, and then..."

He takes a moment for a quick survey of the remainder of the room.

"Yes, over there I think I see some research tables, maybe some containers for specimen storage…this might have served as a sort of waystation. They bring it in, perhaps conduct some minor service, maybe also to route some specimens to their other facilities, and then deliver the final result to the surface for seeding. Magnificent!"

"My Lord, what should we do about all this? I'm guessing we'll want to put together those new power cells, aye?"

"Yes, let us work on that next. We may study this, but do not touch anything extensively until we are ready."

The group makes a few more circles around the room before breaking up to deliver the new instructions.

The research labs back in the city were now struggling to assemble the new larger power cells, essentially scaling up the existing designs. The engineering teams were getting a crash course on high energy storage capacitors and chemical power generation. When the new units were ready, the team once again convened inside the chamber.

"Good, that looks secure enough," Thaelyn offers as he supervises the installation process. "Now, it seems we have a switch to pull, but under the circumstances, I will ask everyone to stand back, just in case we have a short."

The full assembly draws back a step while Thaelyn reaches out to pull the switch. He stands off to the side and at full reach of his arm, then takes hold of the lever and pulls it to the 'on' position.

The unit paused briefly, and then began to hum, at first a slow throbbing, as if something inside had started cycling. The rhythm slowly began to pick up, and they could see a series of power indicators rising as colored light bars.

Thaelyn also moved away, just in case the thing decided to blow up. He joined with the others and watched while the unit slowly came to life. The sounds rose to a peak and the cycling proceeded along rapidly now, but there was no outward indication of activity anywhere else in the room. Thaelyn stepped in closer to take a better look at a series of gauges and readouts, although most of it did not make a great deal of sense, as it was all in the Sarrukhan language.

"Um, my Lord?" the team leader wonders. "Can you tell if it's doing anything rightly grand?"

"These indicators seem to show it is functioning, although I cannot tell if this is the full capacity or not. As for the reason we do not see power flowing anywhere else at the moment..." he pauses to consider the situation. "Perhaps if we give it just a little bit longer, it may need to build a proper operating charge."

They wait while the unit seems to have leveled out. It was clearly working, but what it was doing was anyone's guess. Thaelyn continued to watch the indicators, now taking notice of one in particular that was still slowly rising.

"Yes, this here... I think this is the key, it is slowly gaining capacity, which would then suggest when it reaches its peak, we may see something."

"Aye, but something good, or something bad..." the man chuckles.

"For all the trouble they apparently went through with this chamber, I should think they must have something special in mind. This clearly gives the impression of a gift to us."

They continued to wait until the final gauge reached its upper limit. Then a beeping sounded within the unit, followed by a popping, as if from a relay opening up. There was a brief hissing, and the unit began to die down, but not before a new sound ushered up from all around them.

The sound was big, and it seemed to reverberate through the floor and walls of the chamber. The team formed up in the middle, checking all around them. As before with the small unit, this one also began as a hum revving up to speed. And as it climbed the scale, along with numerous electrical whines and whirs, the walls began to glow with a soft radiance filling up from the bottom.

The sight was spectacular as the whole room came to life. The computer consoles automatically booted up and began running their diagnostics. The research tables with their monitors and project lights, and the specimen tanks with their internal lighting, all began to glow.

"Magnificent..." Thaelyn croons.

Thaelyn and his team gawked at the marvelous technology being presented. The room was circular, and dome shaped. The first thing he surmised was where this new hum had to be coming from.

"I believe this chamber must be larger than previously thought, and it makes sense to me now. We are in the upper half of a spherical structure, which seems reasonable if you consider the inherent geometric integrity. A sphere is a very stable body, especially if you apply pressure to it, like where we are buried as it is. And below us must be another segment, and within that we must have the true power source. This over here," he points at the junction, "is simply an actuator. Below us must be a reactor of some sort."

"A reactor?"

"A highly advanced piece of technology to produce large amounts of energy, but this would be well beyond our level at this point, so I think it is best not to go too deeply at this time."

He stepped over to the computers to examine the reports on the monitors, but of course it was once again in the Sarrukhan language.

"We are most certainly going to need to study this language if we should hope to accomplish anything here."

He then referenced the plaques on the walls again, this time reading them more completely, now that he could see it better.

"Actually, one moment here…"

"What is it, my Lord?"

"How convenient… This here," he points to one of the plaques. "It gives a special instruction to alter the output language."

He glances down at the console and finds a touch-panel relating to the language configuration, then presses it. Now the monitors all change to use the Celestial language.

"Ah, this is much better, at least for my understanding. We can work on the rest later. I suspect some of you will need to learn Celestial."

"Well, that was certainly kind of them. Now, what can you make of it?"

"I will submit one obvious conclusion. These Sarrukh must be a Celestial race, if they use this language. This can give us an idea for their level of sophistication to do all this work."

"Aye!"

Thaelyn begins studying the monitors and tries a few panel selections. He takes notice of new information being presented on the screen, and follows a series of menu selections. He then turns over his shoulder to look at the ring aperture.

"I believe I have found a way to activate that device there. This information seems designed to serve those who are not as familiar with their technology, which certainly makes sense if this is intended to be given to a younger generation. Move away from that ring and let us see what happens.

The group steps away while Thaelyn prepares to engage the device. He selects the activation sequence and turns to watch.

At first, the ring showed a series of small lights coming on around the circumference, then came a hissing as the ring was apparently charging up. A faint whine came out of it, and finally a sudden eruption of energy flashed through the center, causing a surging vortex to form within the ring. It created a brief funneling effect protruding out the rear, which stabilized as a flat spinning disk.

The team leader and his people all jumped back at the sight of the potent energies.

"Um, my Lord…is that normal?"

"Indeed, gentlemen, I believe we have ourselves a functioning portal device. But I would not recommend anyone jumping through just yet. Before we take that step, I want to be sure we understand what we have here."

Thaelyn steps around the device to examine it better.

"First and foremost, I can tell you from personal knowledge and experience, jumping through just any odd portal can be dangerous, as you cannot be sure what is on the other side. Now, we are going to make a few assumptions here, and hope we are correct. We will assume the Sarrukh knew what they were doing when they built this. This includes pointing it at a valid destination, and also that the location is not buried under a mountain or lost beneath a sea by now."

"Aye! That wouldn't be a very fine how-do-you-do."

"Next, it stands to reason the other side ought to be a chamber similar to this one, so we might have a sister unit over there that could be activated to point back here. This would provide bidirectional travel. If the Sarrukh used this to travel around, they would surely need a return route. But then, we must consider the condition of that chamber. It would probably resemble the same as ours when we first found it."

"Evacuated of air and sealed up tighter than a drum. Aye…"

"If we send people in there, they will need to be VERY specially outfitted to survive in that space until we can engage the unit and cycle the air, which also means we need more of those power cells."

"Right, got it… More work for the boys back home."

"Now, assuming we reach this point without any unexpected complications, I might then suggest it to be underground again, meaning we will need to dig ourselves out of a hole. However, once done, we will no doubt have a lot of work ahead of us, but I am going to suggest using extreme caution, as we do not know what waits over there."

"You mean like other people, or beasties and the like? Aye…"

"I think we will err on the side of caution. We will use tactics of avoidance, to stay out of sight so we do not cause any disturbances or raise any questions. We will take it slowly and see where it leads."

"That sounds mighty grand to me!"

Thaelyn and his people now set themselves to a new secret project. He was already bending the rules for the previous effort, but in his position, he held the authority to instruct his people to follow whatever plan was necessary to get the job done. If he kept it as a military secret, the outward effects would not be as serious as to simply give it into the hands of the general public, at least not until they were better prepared for the associated culture shock. He could release it to the public later as they grew into it.

He created a new specialized task force and assisted with their training and preparation. Special suits were made to protect the people from what was likely a near zero-atmosphere environment, complete with an internal air supply to provide for a limited duration, which was hopefully enough to cover the time to activate the equipment. It was an extremely risky maneuver, and a lot of things could go wrong, not the least of which is being unable to start the reactor.

Among their equipment would be spell scrolls they would take with them in case there were no natural magical energies in the local environment. They could use these as an emergency escape using portal runes, as they carried their own charge for a single use. They would also carry a variety of other equipment, such as shovels and pickaxes, buckets, and small brushes, to dig out and sweep away the debris and dirt likely to be found on the outside of the door. And of course, they would also carry another set of power cells, and careful instructions on how to use the computer to cycle the environment.

As before, when Thaelyn and his people felt themselves ready, they again assembled in the chamber, which had now taken on a new name, the Sarrukhan Gate.

"This is it, my friends, the moment of truth," he affirms. "I have given you all I possibly can to make that first step. Behind this Gate lays unknown territory, and quite possibly the answers to many of our questions. But it might also contain great danger. Your first objective is to make all efforts to engage the reactor, and then cycle the local atmosphere. This will buy you time, but you must also see about opening the other Gate. This gives us access to each other. If we can accomplish this much, time becomes our friend, and we can take the rest in a more relaxed manner, at least insofar as what might wait for us outside."

He steps over to the computer again to inspect the readings. All appeared normal, as far as he could tell.

"Keeping in mind," he adds. "This equipment, although it appears functional and in good condition, is still very old, and I do not relish the thought of placing a great amount of stress upon it, so we should see about our work quickly and efficiently. Perhaps the time may come when we can learn ways of finding our own path, but that is for another day."

He steps forward to the infiltration team to give a final inspection. They were all dressed in their special environment suits and air tanks. They each held a bag of equipment and several items on their beltlines, including their emergency scrolls.

He gives a final nod to send them on their way, silently asking himself what they might find on the other side, or if he was sending them to their death. The team lined up and one by one stepped through the Gate. It was just a matter of waiting now.

The team leader was first on the scene emerging out the other side. He moved away from the exit point, but the room was absolutely black, other than for the glow of the exit portal. He waited for the rest of his team to arrive and pulled out an electric lantern Thaelyn designed for them back home. He could already tell there were no magical energies here, and in a room without air, so a traditional lantern, which might involve a flame to provide light, would not work.

He began to shine the lantern around the area. The other group members followed suit, and soon they spotted a power junction of a familiar design standing off to one side. They moved in for a closer inspection. The unit resembled the same as before, which was good because it would then use the same kind of power cells.

One of the teammates immediately set down his bag and began pulling out the cells, handing them over gently to the lead member. The cells were installed carefully, and the team stepped back while the leader pulled the switch.

The lack of a full atmosphere meant they could not hear anything substantial coming out of the unit, but the indicator lights began to flash, and they tried to follow the movement of the gauges to observe the power buildup. Time seemed to drag on as their anxiety worked on their nerves. The meter rose slowly while they glanced around the room and at each other. Then an indicator light flashes. This was to signal the final energy dump to activate the reactor.

The next thing to occur was the slow rise of a soft vibrational tremor through the floor and walls. They could just barely feel it at their feet. The walls began to glow, and the illumination level of the room brought the facility to life. They could now see where they were, and the room resembled the other one in many ways, save for a different configuration of the research stations.

The lead member stepped over to observe the computers. The monitors showed a scrolling list of diagnostics taking place, and then several status lights on the console began to flash. Following this, they began to hear a soft hissing coming into the room and growing in intensity. They all looked at each other.

"Can you fellows hear me?" the leader asks.

"Aye!" affirms the next one. "Bloody hell, those Sarrukh are a keen lot. I'll bet they gave us air to breathe in here."

"I suppose it's only proper," admits the third one. "After all, if they're expecting us to follow this way, they ought to at least do us the favor of breathing."

The lead member checked a mechanical gauge hanging from his belt. It was another of Thaelyn's designs and intended to test the air pressure outside. The numbers looked good, so he tried unclamping his helmet. He carefully lifted it up to test the air, taking in a few cautious breaths.

"Aye, men, it seems good enough," he acknowledges.

He sets his helmet on the floor while the others unclamp theirs. He then returns to the console to examine the monitors. He pulls out a paper from a pocket and studies the instructions.

"Now, let's see here..." he mutters as he begins tapping out a series of selections from the menu system.

He follows a careful list of commands Thaelyn wrote down to allow him to engage the Gate, leading him through a configuration and power up sequence.

"Right. Now, get ready, lads. This is the big one."

He taps one final activator key, and then turns to watch the action.

As before, a series of lights engage around the ring, followed by the hissing and whining sounds as it charged up. Finally, the Gate erupted in a surge of energy resulting in a swirling vortex, creating a reverse link to the previous one and therefore establishing a two-way passage.

"Nicely done!" applauds the second member.

They step around to the front to observe their work.

Thaelyn and the others in his group had been waiting anxiously to see any kind of result. When the image of the vortex was replaced by the return conduit, they all let out a momentous sigh of relief. They could now look into the aperture and see the other side projected on a two-dimensional window, peering across at their teammates who were waving hello at them.

"This is a fine piece of work, my Children, but I think we are only beginning."

Following their initial arrival, they opened the door to find the tunnel leading out was buried in sand and dirt. After a while, they were able to dig themselves out, and discovered they had arrived in a strange new land. There were no people in the immediate vicinity, which afforded them seclusion to begin their operations. But one thing they did realize was they were not only on a new world, but apparently a new universe. There were stars in the sky…actual stars, a sight none of them had ever seen before as Tae'Eladar existed inside the protective shell and was surrounded by the swirling vapors of the Ethereal Maelstrom.

Over the course of the next several years, they embarked on a series of ambitious excursions to scout and examine the land and anything living out there. The lack of any magical energy forced them to do things the hard way, but they always carried their emergency recall scrolls in case they got stuck.

The local environment was very similar to that of their homeland. The region was a mountainous area, but temperate in climate. It seemed very remote from any form of civilization, to provide privacy, and difficult to reach, which might afford security. And the Sarrukhan Gate on this side appeared to be nestled within an excavated cave chamber within a mountainside, and blocked from view by several concealment boulders.

In time, they found habitats with humans taking up residence in villages and primitive cities. They found plants and animals in the surrounding countryside, where they recorded their observations, and even took samples, if they could, to bring home.

It became apparent, after a while, that if they were to continue their efforts on a broader scale, for instance to study this world at greater distance, they would need transportation. They soon began experimenting with importing horses using portal runes, then to use scrolls to return them home again.

The Order had also been experimenting with a special breed of gryphons native to Tae'Eladar. These were large, winged creatures that appeared as part eagle, with the body of a lion. They had been training these recently for local use, and quickly learned how valuable they were for scouting. So a number of these were brought in to survey the land from above. This allowed their scouts to cross broad distances and examine the sights in relative safety of any hostile forces on the ground.

Many expeditions were made of scientists searching for the remains of historical data to confirm their suspicions of where they thought they found themselves. Several sites were examined and cataloged, and now the gnomish Professor in charge of the operation was in Thaelyn's office with a final review.

"So, in the end," the Professor submits. "What we seem to have here is a world filled exclusively with humans, no elves or anything else out there. We found a large variety of flora and fauna that resembles our own, but diversified in ways that suggest it may have shared a common ancestor to ours a very long time ago."

"Such as on the order of perhaps thirty millennia?"

"Right, and even the humans, or at least some of their populations, look a little different. Of those we've studied so far, the closest match tends to be largely in the northern regions above that long sea we found. This includes such features as hair and eye color, as well as skin tone."

"Hair and eye color? What ranges are we seeing in this case?"

"There is actually a broad variation. The hair colors come in browns, light and dark, quite a few in the blonde range, again light and dark, and reds. Black seems to be a somewhat rare color in some regions, instead favoring the lighter shades. But in others, it shows as more dominant."

"Interesting. Those other areas must represent closer-knit communities that keep largely to themselves."

"And then, the eyes also vary with browns, blues, some very lovely greens, and greys."

"So, we might suggest, based on what we see here, some of ours might have been sampled from this set, as we have many of those same colors here."

"My thoughts as well," the Professor nods. "But another part of me is wondering what causes this. If we compare to those in the southern regions, they have much darker skin and very uniform hair and eye color, and we don't see that sort here."

"The skin might be a form of diversity based on their local environment, which is something we do not share in our own, at least not as much for the human populations. The elves do have a nice diversity, depending on where you look."

"Yes, they most certainly do."

"Skin color can vary if you have differing intensities of sunlight blazing down on it. And you said those regions were hot and arid, correct? This reminds me of the regions to the south, like with Menenbahd and the Saheen Expanse."

"That's right!"

"But uniform hair and eye colors? This is something I might expect of a single species keeping a common image. And I cannot think of a reasonable means to modify that unless something else got inside there to create those alternate colors."

"As an added note, we also had a chance to inspect the far eastern regions. We found an area where the people all resembled a very closely matched origin. And coincidentally, this matches with our own from the lands to the far east of us."

"Indeed! So the Sarrukh brought in two sets."

"Again, they had lighter color skin, and we also found very consistent hair and eye color. But curiously, much like ours, perhaps even worse, their facial features and body proportions were all VERY similar, and uniquely different from the rest."

"That sounds like they went through a bottleneck, with the inherent variation being constricted to only a few lucky survivors."

"Ouch. That wouldn't be very pleasant."

"And this might further suggest a migration of some sort. They started in one area, migrated to the others, where the skin might change, but this other one would represent more like what I would expect of the hair and eyes keeping the same. As for that first group, I wonder if they interbred with something local."

"Maybe," he muses. "The eyes, noses, cheekbones, and other features might suggest the introduction of something from outside their own. But whatever it was, I don't recall any of our observations seeing it by now."

"Then, either it was absorbed, or it died out, if we consider a rival group. But next, what about their society. Did we find anything more sophisticated than those primitive cultures near our incursion point?"

"Unfortunately, no, what we found tells us everything out there seems substantially behind us. Our people were able to infiltrate some of their settlements, and we even arranged this in different regions for comparison. Best case, we saw primitive copper and bronze tools and other implements, but no iron or anything more elaborate like what we have here."

"Interesting, and this would actually make sense to me, if only for the reason that they might be evolving at a rate that is natural to them. Here, we had the incursion of the elves and others in our world which changed the equation locally. They were already more advanced than the local human population at the time, and artificially advanced them along the way. Therefore, here we are now on a higher level than the original human population in their native home."

"These are my thoughts as well. It's a little disappointing, but I suppose there's nothing we can do about it. I know we hold the policy of not pushing our own people to move faster than they can tolerate for any new advances, and I'm suspecting you would hold the same for these as well."

"Indeed, I would. Therefore, I would say our primary objective is complete. We found our answers. This other world seems to be the true home of humans as a species, and for that matter, many other examples of what we have here. The Sarrukh must have used this as their resource material to seed life on ours. But now we must make a decision of what to do about it, and considering how they are so far behind us technologically, there can be only one direction for us. We should not involve ourselves with their society until perhaps the day when this might change, and we find ourselves on more equal footing."

"I would have to agree. Maybe the day will come when we can return to check on them. But it would make an interesting study to watch them grow."

"It would, I must admit. But for now, we should redirect ourselves to the development of our own people. We will shut down the Gate for now, and keep it under tight security. I will give instruction for a fortress enclosure to be built around it and a permanent guard stationed to keep watch over it."

Chapter 12

SECOND COMING

The Daughter of Sky, from realms far beyond,
And hardships many to number;
A quest She did make to seek a lost love,
As a trade for Her ultimate slumber.

Through dire plights and turmoil quelled,
She strove to meet with Her choice;
Where rebirth brings Her back again,
To the One who gave Her a voice.

Twice around, She will come to Him,
The Daughter of Sky at last;
To the Son of the Mountain, for in His mind,
She is an Echo from His past.

The circle complete, the tidings revealed,
Together they will aspire;
The wholeness of Man, the oneness of World,
And the birth of a Proud Empire.

Prophecies of Adalon the Silver, Book Two

✦✦✦

"Do we have... Anything new... Occurring...?"

"Yes, Maker... Mine attendants have been observing him making a second attempt at that domain, the one with the high gravitational factor. He has corrupted a local society from that new domain he now occupies and is using them as his assault force."

"Which one...? As if any of them... Would ssserve thisss purpossse. And it ssstill... Perturbsss me... That he ssstole them away from usss... To begin with..."

"Indeed. In this case, the High Elven society."

"Thisss is prepossssterous...! They are no match... For the nativesss... In that environment. Why would he use them...?"

"Our observations suggest it could be a diversion. He is planning a covert operation to establish a foundation for himself, and then to plant an agent to perform his harvesting operation."

"Aargh! A diversion..." she huffs and turns away. "And ssso... He has found... His materialsss. But the quality... Will be... Insssubstantial... Forcing him... To demand... A greater quantity..."

Thaliel was delivering yet another report to Adalon in her cave lair on Darumon and his machinations. The pressure was now building for the timing of her efforts versus his.

"He will need... To refine... Large massesss... To obtain... What he desiresss. Ssso be it... As thisss will take time..."

"Maker, dost thou foresee any pertinent outcome to this endeavor?"

"I foresssee our meeting... And he is ssstill... Building himsssself. Our effortsss... Will cause him lossss. Thisss is good enough. He will not sssucceed... Before we ssstrike...!"

"Very well. On other matters, our newest charge is ready."

"Good! Sssend the word... For her to be... Delivered. We musssst bring thisss... Into alignment... And build oursssselves... More determinedly..."

"I will attend to this personally, Maker."

Thaliel bows and leaves the room in her usual manner.

✦✦✦✦✦

"Child of my Devotion…hear me…"

A young Avariel priestess was in meditation at an altar tucked away inside a natural cave that had been further carved out by the local people over time to accommodate space for storage and as a shelter. The voice speaking to her seemed to resonate from the idol of her goddess, but she wasn't hearing it as an audible sound. Instead, it echoed in her mind.

She instantly jerked to attention. She instinctively knew it was her goddess speaking to her. She might try communing with her goddess to receive instruction and advice to help her people, but the messages were often few and far between. Now, her goddess had apparently come to her. This was a rare and privileged occasion, and she anxiously hoped it might bring some valuable lesson.

"Yes! I hear you…Oh Winged Mother," she mutters reverently. "What do you command of me? Please, give me your wisdom that it might lead our people."

"A time has come upon us…" the voice resonates softly. "A moment of arrival…an era of promise long anticipated."

"Long anticipated? Oh, Winged Mother, we have indeed waited long for you to help our people. The dragons still hunt us. There is nowhere else for us to run. We take shelter here in these caves whenever they arrive. It is all we can do now but hide while they destroy our homes, leaving us with nothing but to try to rebuild from the broken remains."

"I know this, Child. I have looked down upon thee, and I see thy pain. I have promised unto thee that I would bring forth my Chosen One, and through this delivery, my Children would find salvation."

"Yes, and we have waited for this Chosen One, but I regret many are losing faith. Can you please advise me what to look for that I may reveal this to our people?"

"The timing of this moment is unfortunate, as there were demands to be met before it was ready, and these demands were outside of my governance. And although thou wilt know of mine intentions, this cannot be revealed openly. Before the Chosen One can bring thy salvation, it must first be brought forth into the world. It must then mature and discover its path. Only then, when this path is revealed, will salvation follow."

"A path..." she mumbles. "Brought into the world... Are you speaking of a child to be born, and then the child must grow? What child, and why can I not speak this to the others?"

"The Child to be delivered holds great purpose, and this purpose transcends beyond thine own despair. It must follow a path, in combination with others, and this path will carry its own Fate. But this Fate must be as much a test of endurance as it is determination, to be discovered only when the time is upon it. This Child will not be born of mortal bindings. It will carry with it the essence of the divine, and therefore our timing, as it was long in preparation before this."

The priestess had been kneeling in front of the altar, but she nearly toppled over from this suggestion. The concept of a child born with divine essence, such as a Celestial, was unknown to her people, as they had isolated themselves from the rest of the world after being hunted for so long by the three dragons that were still taking their revenge on her people. As a result, they knew nothing of Thaelyn and his antics, or anything else about the rest of the world.

"A child...with divine..." she wheezes. "Winged Mother, where will this child come from?"

"From thine own body..."

Now she topples over. She catches herself on the ground, panting from the shock of the blatant assertion. She quickly glances around the room, but fortunately she was alone on this occasion.

"Winged Mother..." she gasps. "What do you mean? You want ME to bring forth this child?"

"Thy strength and determination to hold thy faith is commended. Therefore, I have chosen thee to be the vessel of this spirit. It will be brought forth from thy body and thou wilt nurture it as thine own. When it chooses to seek its path, thou must permit this. Thou must place thy faith in my direction, and thy people will receive their salvation."

The priestess felt pale and flustered by this sudden announcement.

She knew her goddess had long promised a savior of some kind to come fight the dragons, but she could never have imagined it would come from her own body. She again looked around the room to ensure no one was passing through.

"Winged Mother, this is very sudden, and unexpected. Am I to join with my mate for this, or am I to be touched somehow? I cannot imagine how a child of this sort would come from me."

"It will be given unto thee by the hand of one who has kept this spirit in his care and nurtured it. Now the fruit ripens, and must be served. Thou must travel away from thy home, where thou wilt find a grove and lush soil. Thou must lay thee down upon this soil to receive thy gift."

The priestess was speechless at the suggestion, but she could not disobey the word of her goddess. All she could do now was bow before the altar as the voice faded from her mind.

She now felt herself being compelled, as if by an invisible will. She stumbles awkwardly to her feet, then rushes outside the cave. When she emerges into the daylight, she feels a sensation of demand to travel north and west. She instantly spreads her wings and takes off in a dash.

Several other people took notice of her hurried movement, some of them wondering why she seemed to be in such a fret. They studied her as she made a determined path out of their mountain valley home towards one of the ridges.

"Where is she going?" asks one of the villagers.

"Did she just come out of the cave?" responds another one.

"I think so. She's one of the young priestesses in training."

"Well, you may have your answer. Maybe the elder priestess gave her an errand."

"I, uh…" he flusters. "Wait, I thought I saw the elder priestess go home earlier."

"Maybe someone else then?"

"Who was that? Was that Amavain?"

"I believe so, actually."

The villager then rushes down the lane to a house at the far end near the cave entrance. He steps up to the door and knocks vigorously. In a moment, a young man answers.

"Lafron, do you know if Amavain was given any errands that might take her outside the canyon?"

"Errands? From whom?"

"That's the question. Some of us just saw her fly off to the north. She looked like she was in a hurry."

"What?" he shouts. "It's not allowed to travel in that direction. That's where those dragons keep coming from."

"And therefore, the reason we're asking! We thought she received instruction from an elder priestess, but someone said he thinks she went home earlier."

"Well, you had better go check on that. I'll ask some of the other elders, maybe also the Patriarch. Only he would give permission to travel off that way."

"Do you think perhaps we should go after her?"

Lafron muddled the suggestion, but he was hesitant to answer. Amavain was wise enough to know the rules, and not one to violate them unless there was good reason.

"Let's check around here first. She must know what she's doing. You said she went off in a hurry? That might suggest something. I only hope she doesn't get in trouble for it."

Amavain continued along, coursing her way over the mountain crest towards a neighboring valley, then across another ridge of low-lying hills and into view of a glen with several stands of trees. She angled down and glided smoothly into this new river valley. Her eyes were directed at a determined point, and so she made her way over to it.

She settled on the ground, feeling a bit vulnerable for being out here alone. She knew it was not allowed to travel outside the canyon where they made their home, but her goddess had a plan of some kind, and she was the one chosen to carry it for her. She walked the rest of the way into a grove of trees near the river, looking around in all directions to be sure there were no wild animals or other people nearby. She sat down and waited.

"I am here, Winged Mother, as you requested of me. What do you wish for me now?"

Almost as soon as she finished her statement, a bold column of light opened up in the sky overhead, descending to the ground next to her. She jerked back from the otherworldly sight, and then took notice of a glowing orb floating down through the column. The orb came to rest and took on a solid form. She saw a tall winged female form step out to meet her.

"Winged Mother?" she whispers breathlessly.

"No, Child, my name is Thaliel. I am a servant of they who the Child Races describe as the divine. I am known as a seraph."

"A servant of the gods?" she mutters nervously as she repositions herself in a penitent grovel.

"Rest easy, Child of the Avariel. I have come to give thee aid as thou dost receive thy gift from the one thy kind may give title, the Just God, the Great Power known as Tyr."

"The Just God? I know that name, but I am a follower of the Winged Mother, she who is known to us as Aerdrie Faenya."

"Yes, I know this. She and Tyr have made a pact with mine own governor to bring forth a plan to serve multiple decrees. To enact this purpose, we must bestow upon a vessel our gift. This gift will mature and travel along a path, and this path will bring about those decrees."

"Um, yes, I think I understand. This is what she said to me a moment ago. What must I do to uphold my service?"

"Thou wilt nurture and raise this Child as if it were thine own, as it shall be born of thy body and carry thy family stock. But it will also carry the essence of Tyr and the spirit He has nurtured for this purpose."

"Incredible…" she murmurs. "Do the gods do this sort of thing often?"

"Not especially," she smiles gently. "But these are very peculiar times we are in, and they demand special action to be taken. Now, lay thee down and prepare thyself, Child."

Amavain turns herself over to lay down, unsure how this might work, but feeling a sudden nervous tension that she is about to receive a gift from a god, to say nothing of a baby from someone other than her husband. Her devotion to her religion drove her to obey, but deep down, she felt a little guilty. Still, she tried to settle herself in spite of her anticipation. This was like a sacrifice to help her people, and that was surely important.

Thaliel assists in preparing the young woman by loosening her clothing and removing the lower portions to reveal her abdomen. She then moves away and angles her gaze upwards.

"She is ready, Great One."

Amavain stares upwards, trying to follow Thaliel's gaze, and then sees a new shaft of light open up directly above her, and an image emerges out of it. It included an aged face of a man with pale features and a flowing white beard, and he was bringing his hand around to point at her. The young priestess found herself unconsciously digging her fingers into the soil and pulling up clumps of dirt into her palms.

Tyr looked down at her and lowered his hand to touch her.

"Let This Day Thou Bring Forth This Child."

He touched his fingers to her belly, and she could feel his warmth seeping into her. He held his hand there for an enduring moment, and she felt a strange sensation developing.

Amavain tried looking down at herself, and could see her body visibly rising with a new pregnancy. But this was not your ordinary pregnancy. Whereas it might take many months for an elf to produce a child from the moment of conception, this was occurring right before her eyes.

She began breathing harder, and her head fell back to the ground. The pressure inside was building faster than she could ever imagine. She tried again to look at it, now to see a mountain rising up from what was once a flat figure.

"Oh dear!" she moans. "I think it's coming, but I'm all the way out here."

"Relax, Child," Thaliel asserts soothingly. "I am here."

Tyr's work was now complete. He retracted from the woman with her overly enlarged belly, then pulled back into the divine column and vanished. But Thaliel remained, as her duty was now to help deliver the baby.

Amavain could feel herself experiencing the contractions of childbirth. She pulled up the folds of her robe to give room for the procedure while Thaliel positioned herself to assist, setting down a cloth to catch the child. She began a series of strokes along the sides of the woman's abdomen, a kind of massage to stimulate the muscles. The contractions built up rapidly and Amavain could barely hold them back. She felt the urgent need to bear down. Thaliel watched and waited for the moment, then began with her instruction.

"Now, bring thyself upon it! Do so greatly, Child."

Amavain pushed hard while Thaliel caressed the woman's body to invoke a muscle reaction to assist in the smooth delivery. This caused the baby to begin a directed motion through the birth canal in one continuous and surprisingly swift effort. The procedure went along so quickly that it actually shocked Amavain for her lessons on childbirth by her mother. She pulled her head up to glance down at herself in disbelief.

"Blessed Mother, is it done already?"

"Indeed, Child. With my help, we have brought this forward most favorably."

Thaliel now proceeded to clean up the baby, severing the cord and using her divine power to close and heal the remainder. She brought out another cloth to use as swaddling, and began wrapping the baby up snugly, then handed it over to Amavain to cradle in her arms.

"My husband will likely have a fit when he sees this. Me, suddenly with a child, when we had not made our own effort yet."

"This does not disallow thee to make thine own with him," she smiles. "But thou wouldst be wise to allow this time before bringing forth another."

"Thank you. But now I ask myself what this child will do for us. The Winged Mother said I may not tell my people about this, but they will surely take notice of me with a child."

"This is true, and thou were indeed observed departing from thy home. Thou wilt need an explanation for this. Say unto them, thou didst receive direction to retrieve this Child from the wilderness. It was lost and thou must grant it a place within thy home."

"Are we conspiring on something together?" she smirks tenderly.

Thaliel smiles at the thought.

"The Maker, mine own governor, did select this spirit for a purpose. The misfortune of thy people is unintended, but she cannot reform this herself. Instead, she has forged designs for another to perform this task. But he does not know of thy people, as thou didst lock thyselves away here in this place. This Child shall be the hammer to break that lock. Thy people cannot remain this way."

Amavain glared at the winged creature who was still stooping over her as she finished her work to clean up the afterbirth.

"What do you mean, unintended? And then being locked away… well, I suppose I can understand that part, we were driven to hide up here."

"The three that pursue thee were once her servants, but they disobeyed her desires, and she no longer controls them. The attack on the ancient temple was unsanctioned, and indeed each of those since. In so doing, they have profaned their former devotion."

"Former devotion?"

"Indeed, they were supposed to be guardians, not destroyers. And certainly not to pursue thee and thine to this place. But now, thy people must persevere until this Child matures. She must travel a path, and this path will ultimately lead to thine aid."

"But how? What sort of aid? Who is this we speak of? I know we tried before, but…"

"A man, another like her, delivered into this place some time ago with his own purpose, to which he now pursues. The Maker did install him to serve a purpose no one else would choose unto themselves. And now this one. Their Fate is intertwined."

Amavain now felt a new shock hit her which left her speechless. She gazed down at her new baby and tried to imagine someone else in the world who shared a common Fate. But this could not be an ordinary Fate if both of them shared divine essence.

"What is happening in the world?"

Thaliel smiled warmly as she finished up and moved away.

"A vivid transformation…" she croons. "The culmination of a long era of effort."

She was preparing to leave when Amavain felt the urge to resolve these last few statements.

"Wait, please. I need to know what you mean by a few things. Please help me understand, or I might go crazy with all this confusion."

"Well," Thaliel sighs. "I do not hold the authority to reveal all things. But perhaps if we keep it simple."

"Good. First, what purpose none of us were pursuing? Are we supposed to be pursuing something?"

"Generally speaking, it should be the purpose for any world society to pursue one overriding goal. World unity. Something none of the races here were ever attempting. This is detrimental in the longer term to the harmony of a society."

"Oh, well I am so sorry we didn't think of this before. But I'm not the one in charge of the local politics. So we are supposed to join together somehow?"

"Making wars is not the path to harmony. Delineating thyselves based on racial, cultural, religious, social, or political values, is not the path to harmony. But this is all thy people ever did. Everyone here."

"All right, I suppose I can't argue with that, as we did do this."

"Worse is that thy people ran away from the rest based on such dogmatic values as thine own vanity for thine appearance before them. Thou art one of the worst for this decree. Thy wings cause thee to feel overly righteous above the rest, keeping thyselves separate and isolated. Had thou stayed with the major nations, thy people would have found support with them. And I may also suggest, these Draconics might not find thee as opportunistic a target."

"Well, yes, again, I suppose I must agree, and I am personally very sorry, especially for where it brought us. But I suppose, like everything else, it can only be known in hindsight."

"Perhaps so, for some."

"But next, you said these dragons were supposed to be guardians. Guardians of what? And why would they attack us to begin with?"

Thaliel considers for a moment how to answer this, as she didn't have authorization to give out the full history of the world. But this one might be at least partially warranted, if only to ease the suffering. She bends down to speak again.

"This is only for thee to know, as there are many secrets in play here. The Draconic breed is a society of beings once created by the Maker for the purpose of giving law and protection. However, thy people, and the others, did never see them this way, instead proclaiming them as beasts. But it is actually thee who art not belonging to this place, as THIS is what they were guarding... this world, to which thee and thine did intrude upon unwelcome. Therefore, they did try to drive thee out, but thou didst not leave."

"Uh oh..." she groans.

"Yes, but after a time, the Maker did find it necessary to reconsider, and here she did call them away, hoping thou wouldst join together in harmony, which thou didst not achieve either. The Elven nations do describe themselves with but a single word, Tel'Quessir, meaning The People. But they do not behave by such standards as to follow this level of unity."

"All right, I think I can see that. And we are a bad example by proclaiming ourselves so unique and special above the rest due to our wings."

"Again, yes. And not only thine own, but the rest, as well. Each of the races, and many factions within did segregate themselves for one reason or another. Therefore, this man has been sent to see this corrected."

"And another uh oh!" her eyes bulge.

"Indeed, and so he is currently in this pursuit, and thou wilt likely encounter him even without this Child. But the Child will accelerate this, in part to resolve thy woes with these rogue Draconics, and in part to educate thee about what thou art missing due to thine animosity of the other races. It will then become thy purpose to join with him to see about the rest."

"And yet another uh oh!" she screeches. "What is this world that a goddess would place so much attention into it?"

"A special project with a much higher purpose. It was originally to involve only the human population, as this is what came before anyone else. But the inclusion of these others now needs to be taken into consideration. There is life beyond this world, Child. Thy tender musings in this small place are meager in the greater light of it."

Now she pulls back and prepares to leave. She smiles once again and nods, then opens a new column of light above her, and rides the beam up and away to her home.

Amavain was still laying there in awe, once again staring at the tiny baby girl she held in her arms.

"Well, that was certainly a shocking experience," she mutters. "What did we miss out there, no thanks to those nasty dragons. But now, what can we expect once we return home. Ugh, Lafron, my dearest, I hope you don't lose your feathers too badly on seeing this."

Bells rang out again in the Avariel village, signaling the latest arrival of the dragons. Every year it was the same thing, almost like clockwork. The people had become so conditioned by now that they didn't bother building up their homes to anything more than a simple thatch roof held up by a set of thin walls. It wouldn't last more than a year anyway, by the time of their next arrival, then to be torn down and crumpled under the dragon's claws.

The people screeched and fled into the caves at the lower end of the canyon valley they called home. Most of their valuables, whatever they still owned, were stored in there for safety. They kept their food in there, many of their tools, their books and other learning materials, and many of their work desks and tables.

Lafron was visiting a colleague when the alarm went out. He immediately took flight down the lane to his home to find his wife.

"Amavain!" he shouts as he bursts through the door.

"I'm here, and I hear it already," she replies anxiously. "Aerlie, come quickly. We need to go to the caves again."

The three of them make a mad rush to the cave entrance, along with the rest of the village population.

"This is crazy!" Aerlie scorns as they run along. "They come, and we simply hide in the caves. Can't someone do something about this? Every year, it's the same thing. Our home is ripped apart, and I'm tired of sleeping on rocks and splinters."

"Aerlie, I know," Amavain ushers urgently. "But we tried already. Do you remember the stories I told you?"

"Yes, and it's not right! We tried asking for help from the kingdoms below the mountains, and they didn't send any. They just took our gold and treasures and ignored the rest."

"Child, you must keep the faith in the Winged Mother. I know she has something in mind, but it takes time for her plan to grow."

"Time for her plan to grow…and meanwhile we keep losing our homes."

They arrived at the cave and the people peered outside to see the three dragons, two whites and a blue, wreaking havoc in their once quaint village. It was not a new sight, and it simply reminded them of their eventual fate that one day they would vanish completely.

The dragons had made it a habit to return every year, destroying the Avariel homes and fields where they grew their food. It was a long and brutal vendetta aimed at harming the Avariel out of spite for their gift of flight, and the old battle at the temple that started the whole thing. It didn't seem to matter anymore, their intended purpose as guardians, as they had completely fallen from their former prestige by this time.

The people were just barely able to survive all this, moving from place to place as their homes were destroyed and they found themselves pushed ever farther across the land until they finally settled here. The benefit of this place gave them fertile land to grow crops, but they considered themselves lucky to succeed in just one planting season, then to store and ration the food for the remainder of the year. They knew the dragons would come along and destroy the fields at some moment, therefore preventing any further planting until it could be cultivated again.

The other benefit was a series of natural caves at the lower end where they could hide. The dragons didn't seem as interested in digging them out, instead taking the slow and arduous path of creating hardship and starving them to death. For this, their homes would be shattered, and the people could only hope to patch them together again using the splintered remains of the former buildings. It was rare for them to successfully bring in any new materials, since many of their tools were worn and they were unable to harvest anything effectively.

Amavain and her family watched and waited for the dragons to finish their rampage, then to turn and fly away back to their mountain homes in the north. The people slowly emerged from hiding to survey the damage, then to scrounge for whatever they could find of their possessions and fragments of homes.

Aerlie was only thirty years old, still regarded as a child by elven terms, although an older child by now. She followed her mother out of the cave to survey the damage, but all she could do was shake her head morosely.

"Why can't they let us live in peace?" she mutters softly. "We can't build homes with anything more than broken wood and a few stones. Our beds are nothing more than straw and thatch. We barely have food to eat, and even then, it's mostly dried or preserved in jars. And there's almost no meat, not unless we can find something out there to hunt. This is no life for us."

"Aerlie…" ushers a firm male voice from behind the group.

She turns to find the village Patriarch approaching from behind.

"This has been the way of things ever since the battle," he relents. "You recall the story of the battle, correct?"

"Yes, Patriarch Daeselri, but that doesn't make it right. It was OUR temple, and they invaded it. We were only defending ourselves and the other nations. Do we deserve to be hunted simply for protecting what is ours?"

"No, but we long ago came to the conclusion these three dragons were hunting us out of their rage at losing the battle. The Winged Mother has long told our people to run rather than fight, as we did not have enough warriors to fight even one dragon, let alone three, and then we were losing more to these raids," he pauses to survey the scene with the people now rummaging through the remains of their homes. "We cannot find time for ourselves to rebuild any more. All we can do now is to hide."

"For how long?" she urges. "How long has this been happening? How much longer do we have to wait? Does she even look at us anymore? If we can't fight them ourselves, we need to find help."

"Aerlie, what would you have us do? We tried once, a kingdom to the south, and they demanded all our gold to pay for an army, not that we had that much to begin with. When next the dragons came, there was no army. We tried again, another kingdom to the east, but with no more gold, they instead demanded all the treasures we still kept sacred. And as with the first, they also lied to us and ignored our call."

"There must be others out there. What about to the west? Did you try that?"

"With no more gold or treasures to buy their interest, I doubt anyone else will do anything at all for us. Those human kingdoms are simply too greedy. All they care about is their wealth and luxury."

"Well, aren't there any elven kingdoms out there? We once fought to defend those nations. Do they not remember this?"

"I would not even know where to find them by now, and surely, they would be too far to march the distance. They are not gifted with wings, as we are, so they are simply limited to walking. Now, enough of this, Child, we have work to do. I don't like it any more than you, but it's all we have now."

The Patriarch moves away to find his home and join the others at trying to rebuild again, leaving Aerlie frustrated at the apparent futility of their meager lives.

"Aerlie," Amavain soothes. "Come here."

The young girl steps over close to her mother to share a hug, as Amavain tries to soothe her impatient child.

"Listen to me," she whispers into the girl's ear. "I know something, but I am forbidden to tell. I can only ask you to be strong. One day, we will find our salvation. Our goddess promised this to us, and I believe her. Unfortunately, some things simply take time, and not even the gods can change this. Meanwhile, perhaps you should find something for yourself to do while we clean up. Standing here with so much fire in your eyes will not make things better."

"Mother, I just can't accept that there is nothing out there in the world to help bring peace to our people. We never go outside our mountain home, and the Patriarch forbids us even to peek over the ridgetops. What are we hiding from, other than the dragons? They're gone now, and won't return for another year, as always. And yet we don't even try to find help from anyone, or just to go out and say hello. Are the other races so evil that we have to hide from them as well?"

"That's a good question, but like you, I don't have the answer. I felt the same when I was young. Like everyone else here, I believed our people always felt like outsiders, even with the other Elven races. If you were to ask your father, he might say the same, and this is because of our wings, which only our people have."

"And so, what? We should fear everyone else, or maybe hate them? Are we so special, or different, that we cannot be a part of the rest of the world? Living up here just keeps us alone and easy prey. That's silly, isn't it?"

"It's curious that you should say this, as you are actually correct. I once heard someone speak to me these same words. They said we hold such feelings that it isolates us from everything else, and how this is an unhealthy thing to do. We did this to ourselves by running and hiding, and not simply for these dragons hunting us, but that old battle at the temple, which started the whole thing. Our vanity drove us into isolation, and now look at us. But unfortunately, I'm not the one who makes these decisions. And with our people suffering for so long, a lot of them have lost faith, and my power to convince them otherwise doesn't seem as strong."

Amavain turns to survey the broken village with her daughter. She then glances up at the mountain range around them, as if in distant thought.

"Perhaps," she continues. "Somewhere in the world, there may be hope just waiting to be discovered, but I don't know where it is. Only the Winged Mother can answer that. She once promised me she had a plan, but this plan had to follow a course of its own. I cannot govern this. I cannot say when, where, or how. I can only wait for it to happen."

"But the Winged Mother..." Aerlie begins sternly, but then halts and sighs. "Well, she's a goddess. Can't she just go poof and make something happen?"

Amavain smiles and shrugs.

"Aerlie, yes, she is a goddess, but I don't think they can always just go poof and the world turns exactly for them. People have this thing we call free will, and sometimes you have to wait for one or another of those before that poof thing can actually occur. Maybe someone, somewhere, has to make a discovery, or a decision, and this might begin a process involving other people. And for this, the rest of us have to wait, although I am sure we have waited long enough already."

"All right, fine! I'm tired of arguing. Maybe I could help you clean up?"

"No, Aerlie, I think you are too disturbed right now. Go find something pleasant for yourself. Your father and I will see to the rest."

Amavain leans over to kiss Aerlie on the forehead before turning to join the others.

Aerlie gazed at the scene of shattered homes, a sight she had seen many times before, feeling helpless and empty. She knew the process well. They would rebuild the shambles that were now their homes, ramshackle huts that just barely stood up, and in another year, it would come down again.

She looked up at the mountains surrounding her home. They lived in a hilly canyon surrounded by tall mountains. A river ran along one side as runoff flowed down and angled away through a ravine to the northwest. The steppes traced down to the shoreline of a large sea some distance away, and while this might allow for ground travel, their home was simply too remote for anyone to bother making the climb.

In the valleys below, there were a series of local superstitions of strange, winged creatures that lived in the mountains, and although many people didn't believe these rumors, no one showed any real interest, or felt comfortable enough to actually go up and check on it. Therefore, other than for those kingdoms the Avariel tried contacting, most people considered the Avariel to be nearly a myth. Even those kingdoms they contacted largely dismissed them as anyone they might care to risk themselves for against three dragons.

Aerlie decided she needed some fresh air to soothe her nerves, so she took off in the hopes that circling around a few times might settle her frustration. Several people on the ground noticed her take flight, but it was not unusual to see their children circling in the air as a means to find freedom from the despair of life below.

She made several circles, climbing higher to feel the calm breezes that might sometimes flow over the ridges. They were cool and crisp, and sometimes carried unusual fragrances wafting up from the valleys beyond, especially in the springtime when the fields were blooming with fresh wildflowers.

She allowed her mind to drift to what might lie beyond, trying to imagine a world of people and nations. It simply couldn't be as bad as the Patriarch so often described it. If only she could take one little peek, she might find something to satisfy her curiosity. She had become so frustrated with the dismal life in her village that she wanted to know how other people lived. The dragons had been attacking them for so long, but could it be there were other dragons attacking other villages, or was it really like the Patriarch said. Maybe these dragons were the only ones being so cruel, and the rest of the world was doing much better. She dreamed of a world where people lived in better homes, ate better food, and did not suffer such attacks. Could there really be something out there like that?

She angled her flightpath around to the west. She already knew the kingdom to the south was not helpful, the same as the one to the east, so she would avoid those. Maybe the west held something of better interest.

Amavain assisted her husband to pick up the pieces of their home and sort out their personal belongings, but she maintained a habit of keeping one eye on her daughter. She watched Aerlie circling above, and then directing herself at the western ridgeline. She halted her work as she watched the girl fly along the ridge and take up a new weaving pattern, as if she was trying to survey the sights on the other side.

Lafron noticed his wife's change of posture and he followed her gaze, soon to take notice of Aerlie cresting the ridge.

"Amavain, is that Aerlie?" he asks urgently.

"Yes," she responds calmly.

"What is she doing? She should know better than to fly around up there."

"I'm asking myself the same, but I'm also wondering if this is her Fate taking its course."

"Fate? What Fate? Amavain, ever since you brought this girl home, I know a lot of people have been asking where she actually came from if the last of our society is right here in the valley. No one was known to be carrying a child, and this says nothing of travelling to that place where you say you found her."

"Lafron, please… The Winged Mother has a very complex plan, but I am not permitted to reveal it. You must simply place your trust in her."

"Amavain, I'm your husband. Of all the people in this village, I should be the closest and dearest to you that you might share at least some part of this secret. After all, I'm a scholar and a historian for our people. I'm highly respected, and I would hope also well-trusted. Can you at least give me a small hint?"

Amavain looks at him and sighs. She realized she might need a comforting hand to support her, and maybe an extra voice to stand by her, in case this Fate should finally come around. She just couldn't be sure what he might be able to offer if she wasn't able to offer anything of her own. Reluctantly, she draws him near to whisper in his ear.

"She is my child, born of my body."

Lafron's eyes popped wide open at the suggestion, and he stared at her both confused and bewildered.

"Amavain, you were not carrying a child before this. How is it possible you could bring one out like this?"

"She was a divine gift. I was told to find a secluded grove in order to receive it away from the eyes of the people in the village."

Now Lafron's expression turned to shock.

"A divine gift?" he wheezes. "What is she? A gift from whom, the Winged Mother?"

"Actually, it was the Just God who gave her to me…and who, by the way…" she glares at the Patriarch as he was cleaning up across the village square, "…I believe he is one of the human gods, as this was originally their world before we came upon it."

"Um, Amavain," he notes cautiously. "Am I detecting something in that statement?"

"Possibly. You are the historian. Who lived here before our people arrived? How do you think they, or anyone who favors their presence in this world, would feel if foreign invaders arrived uninvited?"

"Oops!"

"Yes, and so we have the Just God, who had been nurturing a spirit of some kind that needed a new home. She carries a purpose within her, and this purpose relates to something that likely predates a lot of things, including our woes up here. I cannot reveal what it is, so please do not ask. When I received her, I also received a lot of information that I have to keep secret. All I can say is, well, things are happening in the world outside these mountains that we so unfortunately ran away from, rather than staying with them to find those armies that might otherwise fight for us."

"Oh! So are YOU now protesting the Patriarch and his rules?"

"Lafron, think a moment. Use that scholarly mind of yours. Why did we run away to these mountains. Because we didn't want to appear weak after the great losses we took in that old battle. Now, what do you think this will do to us in the eyes of those dragons who want to pursue us? I'll give you a hint, as it does NOT offer protection by the major nations we ran away FROM."

Lafron paused to consider this idea, and he found no other recourse but to nod in recognition of it.

"We isolated ourselves and made ourselves vulnerable."

"Right. And what is the underlying reason for this, do you think?"

"Um, I am unsure if I am following you now."

Amavain decides to demonstrate her point by glancing over her shoulder and fluttering her wings emphatically. She then returns to his gaze.

"Our people seem to hold themselves especially high for the reason we have wings. We even have a name for those who do not, and it is not a kind one."

"Uh oh… All right, I see it. And so, because we held ourselves so high, and we ran away to keep THEM from seeing us as anything less, we made ourselves vulnerable to the dragons by isolating ourselves from those major nations and their major armies. Wonderful. How nice of the Winged Mother, or whoever it was you spoke to, to tell us of this NOW."

"I might agree, but at the same time, it was not SHE who told us to run away. She may have told us to keep away from the dragons, but not the people out there. Our own people chose this due to their arrogance and vanity. A wiser mind would know to stay with the support of the others, even to blend in more harmoniously to form a closer-knit society with them. But our kind never did. So much for the name Tel'Quessir!" she huffs ironically.

"All right, I see a direction forming here. The oneness of a united society. Is this another of our failings?"

"It's all of our failings…everyone in this world, apparently, as no one ever did this. What is it people say about strength in numbers, but do any of us actually listen to this time-honored wisdom?"

"Uh huh…I get it. That's a nasty rub, Amavain."

"But there is more to it," she glances around the ruined village. "And I suspect the rest of the world is being made aware of it. But up here in these mountains, and with such as the Patriarch denying us to go out and talk to people, we won't know of it until they actually march up that pass and show us to our faces. This is where Aerlie comes in."

"How is that?"

"She will be the one to bring them here…our salvation. We must simply allow her to find them."

"Find…our salvation?" he flusters and once again glances up at the ridgeline.

"Yes, I suppose it's the only way. They might find their way up here eventually, but if she actually goes out there and looks for it, this simply accelerates the process, do you think?"

"I, well…yes, I suppose. But isn't she a bit young to go out on an adventure like this?"

"I don't know the Winged Mother's plan, but I do know she is the one given to us for it."

"As you say…" he offers tenuously.

Aerlie had been making passes across the mountain ridge trying to see what lay beyond, but there were too many other mountains obstructing her view, so she decided to sneak away for a quick sortie to see if there might be anything to learn out there.

Amavain and Lafron both watched as the young girl disappeared from sight on the other side of the ridge. Amavain bowed her head and closed her eyes.

"I pray the Winged Mother will watch over her. She is indeed quite young."

Aerlie glided down the other side of the mountains, passing over a number of ranges before finding flat land. She could then see a valley off in the distance, and it appeared as a broad field of green grass with a few small stands of trees. Further along, she could make out a settlement. It seemed small in comparison to the landscape below, but still larger than her village. She kept at altitude for safety and to give her the best view, drifting along the breezes to scan the terrain below.

The town stood out prominently against the surrounding countryside, with roads leading in and out, and many homes built out of wood and stone, much better than in her village. She could see some wagons moving around, and people walking along the roads between what looked like a central square and other buildings. She pondered over what these buildings represented, but coming from a village where most of their inner workings were hidden away inside a cave, she didn't have any personal knowledge of a true town-like setting.

She circled a few times to watch the activity down below. No one seemed to be paying any attention to the odd creature flying around in the sky overhead, so she felt comfortable they were not evil monsters who might want to harm her. They just looked like ordinary people living their lives, and apparently doing much better than hers, so she moved away to see if there was anything else, once again travelling across the field of green.

"Ay now, did ye see that?" mutters one man.

"Aye, that was one of them, wasn't it?" ushers another.

"Rightly so, I'd wager. That'd make a fine catch, don't ye think?"

"A fine and kingly catch, to be sure. But we can't reach it from down here."

"Right, but they don't spend as much time simply walkin' about, from the stories I hear."

"How do ye figure then?"

"I hear tell they come down and carry off livestock, maybe a child or two."

"I don't own any pigs. Do ye have one?"

"Nah, but I got me a wet-nosed tyke I found in an alley once. She'd be a right fine offerin'. Quick, let's get out there and set ourselves up afore that beastie decides to go off somewhere else."

The two men had been observing the strange sight in the sky above, taking notice of the unusual flying creature. They begin dashing around to collect their equipment, hoping to capture this rare trophy.

One man runs off to find a young girl he had been keeping as a slave. She was barely into her teens and dirty, wearing little more than rags. The other man hurried to find a wagon with a large net and some rope, and together they rushed through the town into the open field.

"Now, ye know the trick, aye?" the slaver instructs. "Ye go run around out there like ye're bein' chased. Be sure to get its attention and try to draw it down from there."

"What if it tries hurting me?" she whines.

"Aw now, ye know me, I'll be right behind ye with the net. Hang on tight and we'll pull it down real quick like. Do this right, and I'll give ye an extra helpin' of gruel in yer bowl this eve."

The girl nods reluctantly and begins running out into the field screaming. The two men hold back, allowing the girl some space before they take off after her, giving the impression of a chase scene.

Aerlie's keen Avariel hearing picked up the screams of a young child. She circles around to see the girl running along the ground apparently being chased by two men.

"What's happening down there?" she asks herself. "Are those men chasing that child? That's not right! Did she do something wrong or are they just being mean?"

She watches the girl apparently making a zigzag pattern across the field with the two men still behind her.

"That looks like a young girl. She couldn't possibly be wicked, so it must be the men. I wonder if there's anything I can do to help."

She studies the scene a moment longer, and then an idea comes to mind.

"If I swoop down and pick her up, I could maybe carry her away somewhere to safety. They can't catch me if I'm in the air. But I must be quick."

She then angles herself into a dive, picking up speed and swinging around in front of the girl. She flaps vigorously to slow her descent before landing just in front of the startled child. The girl screams even louder.

"It's alright, I'm here to help you," Aerlie asserts as she tries reaching for the girl.

The girl fights back, batting Aerlie's arms out of the way in a frightened panic.

"Didn't you hear me; I'm trying to help," she shouts. "Just let me take you…"

The struggle between them causes Aerlie to lose track of the movement of the two men behind her. As she and the girl tussle with each other, the men throw their net over both of them, then rush in to pin them down.

"Let go of me!" she screams. "Who are you people?"

"Such a curious one, that," remarks the first man. "The thing actually talks."

"Aye, that's a new one," the other one considers. "Do ye know what it's sayin'? It's all gibberish to me."

"Likely some odd bit of goblish or some such. I hear some of these wild beasties use that on occasion."

"Aye, but ye know…I ain't never heard of them wearin' clothes like this. I always thought they had more fur, or feathers, or some such."

"Well, I guess ye can't believe ALL them old stories."

The two men laughed and finished wrapping up their bundle. Aerlie was carefully tied up and manhandled back to town.

◆◆◆◆◆

"Ooh, look at this one! Have you ever seen the like?"

"What is that, some kind of harpy?"

"I thought harpies had claws for feet."

"Well, whatever it is, it's certainly a curious one."

"Aye, this one alone would be worth the admission fee."

A group of visitors was passing through a circus tent, gawking at the strange oddities that had been gathered together for display. The circus was a popular local attraction that travelled across the hot arid region known as Menenbahd. This land was often crisscrossed by travelling merchant caravans and traders of rare and often illicit merchandise. But in this region, anything goes.

In addition to the usual novelties, the circus also featured a number of attractions. Some of these included the more common performers of acrobatics and magical tricks, but one tent was devoted to the exhibition of strange and rare beasts. These creatures were brought in from the far reaches of the land, or so it was said, to dazzle and amaze the populace. For a small fee, one could pass inside to gaze in wonder of the spectacle.

While it was true that many of the people were indeed fascinated by the sight, a number of them also felt somewhat offended by the odors wafting up, as the circus was not known for its hygiene or the proper care and maintenance of its trophies. And among these odd creations, each held in its own iron cage, was Aerlie.

The cage was barely enough to contain her, and not comfortably. She did not have room to stand up fully, and her wings often abraded against the bars. It had been several months, and the sores she had been developing across her body, especially her wings, ached persistently. Some had become infected, and as a result she often felt dizzy and faint. Her wings were the worst, for this point. She had lost much of her plumage, and there were many lesions from the tips of her wings inward almost to her body. Her legs were so cramped, having been forced to sit on the cage floor most of the time, that she could barely move them by now.

The circus owner and his henchmen cared only for one thing, money. For as long as she might hold value, he was going to milk her for every coin he could get before she eventually succumbed to illness. He didn't bother with medicine, not that he might even have access to it, and he might only offer a bath by dowsing her with a bucket of cold water on occasion. She was unkempt, her clothing was stained and ragged, her beautiful hair was matted and tangled, and she looked every bit as miserable as she felt.

The circus brought in a regular attraction of tourists from the city. It was not a robust flow, but enough to pay the bills. The extended duration of their attraction had been wearing off as most of the populace had been there and seen that by now. But occasionally, there would be renewed interest in seeing what's new, or simply to enjoy a bit of entertainment. And not only did the circus cater to these attractions, but it also sold novelties for the kids and a selection of goods for the more mature crowd, including lotus and opium.

By this time, Aerlie had come to believe she had been forgotten. She disobeyed the Patriarch and crossed over the mountain ridge into forbidden lands. She prayed to her goddess for help, but with no word coming back to her, she feared she had offended the Winged Mother and was left to her fate.

She also understood by now these people around her did not speak the same language. She was an elf, and the only language she understood was Elvish, the native language of her people. They did not study anything else, as they had nothing else to study, so the human population, for all they spoke about with each other, was a mystery to her.

At the end of each day, the circus henchmen would come around with a plate of scraps to feed their prize attractions. Aerlie was often given some fruit and bread, as she seemed to be most responsive to eat that. It was just barely enough to keep her strength up.

In the city of Bya'an Tamoranth, Thaelyn had been giving one of his lessons in the combat training hall. He often participated in the teaching of his students to offer some of his own experience to the younger generation. On this occasion, he was demonstrating the proper stance for swordplay to a new class enrollment.

"You must pay attention to your footing," he advises. "By keeping your weight balanced and under your control, you can then offer greater force in your attacks, while at the same time denying your opponent to use your weight against you. Keep your guard up, turn at the waist, and use your shoulder. Also remember, your sword is not your only weapon. Hands, elbows, feet, and legs can also be dangerous implements if you only know how to use them. We teach this in another course as a form of martial arts training I once learned. The body can be its own masterpiece of warfare, but as with any other, the harmony of mind and body must also be in balance."

Down the road from the large guildhall was a temple devoted to the gods worshiped by the people of Thaelyn's rule. They now represented a nation that encompassed much of the western part of the continent, at least that of the northern half. The temple was an elaborate structure with several large alcoves inside to offer piety to a selection of gods favored by the many races living within their society.

The priests of the temple were also part of his holy Order, all trained in the traditions of his military, although they most often played roles more approximating that of a civilian application. This included not only the religious services for the public, but they were also the primary healers and medical experts. Their gifts involved a combination of a blessing of divine power to offer healing and curative aid, as well as the study of actual medical science to provide alchemical solutions and more conventional treatments.

The high priest currently attending the service had been giving lessons to his own group of new students when he noticed a strange glow beginning to emanate from one of the statues representing their gods. It was Helm's icon. The group immediately turns to it and gathers around, all lowering themselves in reverence of the rare visitation.

"Lord Helm," the high priest calls. "You come to us, and we will listen. What words would you wish to share with us this day?"

"There is one who does now desire an audience," he speaks firmly with his voice resonating throughout the room. "But this one is not of thy common focus. Seek the one for whom thou dost give title, the Protector, and receive his instruction."

The idol fades and the high priest puzzles the meaning of this strange message.

"The Protector wishes to speak?" he muses quietly. "This is curious, why would he not simply come forward himself."

The high priest then rushes over to one of the alcoves featuring the elven pantheon. The others in the room follow him at a distance, wondering what sort of message this other god has to offer, and why the indirect manner of presentation.

The priest kneels before the elven idol for the deity known as the Protector, which represented the lead member of this pantheon. He raises his hands to it.

"Lord of the Seldarine, He who is known as the Protector amongst our blessed kin. Do you hold such need to speak with us?"

The idol began to glow, just like the other one, and a voice rang out from it.

"I am given to bring unto thee one who does not hold direct favor for thee, as thou dost not belong to they who are her Children. And thee, who art not her Children, do not give direct favor unto her, as she is not within thy realm of offering. But she is willing to exchange this favor if thou wouldst perform a service."

The high priest was now even more perplexed. The nation Thaelyn had built so far contained many races, between humans, elves, dwarves, halflings, and gnomes, and all of them were accounted for with their associated gods. Who could possibly want inclusion that would otherwise be outside the loop, while at the same time of that appropriate alignment that Thaelyn and his philosophies would agree with?

"Lord of the Seldarine, I must admit, I am confused by this. Who is this you speak of that would wish us to hear her plea?"

"To her Children, she is known as the Winged Mother. To thee and thine, thou may not have a name, and so I will give it to thee. She is known by our address as Aerdrie Faenya."

"And what is it she desires from us?"

The idol now faded, leaving the priest wondering what was coming next. A moment later, he found out.

The room began to glow brilliantly. The light seemed to emanate from the walls and coalesced in the center on the dais near the priest and his class. The entire assembly fell to their knees, and then some. The image formed an ethereal visage of a being with many wing-like fins undulating on all sides, centered on an oblong amorphous body that seemed partially translucent. It hovered motionless above the floor. No one had ever seen a member of the Estelar before, only the glow from the idol as they might casually manifest themselves for a brief visit. But this one was in full view.

The priest gazed at it, unable to speak. He tenuously glanced over his shoulder at his class and the other priests who had assembled around the apparition. He knew he needed to understand the purpose of this arrival, so he forced himself to find his voice again.

"You are the one known by some as the Winged Mother?"

"I am," she answers smoothly.

"And you have come here to seek our service?"

"I have. But I must speak to he who is thy governor, as it is he who must perform this task."

"Of course, please allow me a moment," he turns to the others behind him. "Someone fetch His Lordship! Quickly!"

Thaelyn was still in his class giving his lecture when a frantic call came through the door.

"My Lord!" the priest shouts. "Great gods above, you need to come down to the temple immediately!"

Thaelyn lurched around to meet the address.

"What is it?"

"You have a caller down there. It's one of THEM! In the flesh… if you can call it that."

"Dear Powers, what are you saying, one of the Estelar?"

"Aye, hurry please, she has something to tell you."

The two of them now make a return dash outside and down the road to the temple. They burst through the door and Thaelyn gazes up onto the platform to see the divine entity. He hurries forward, and then kneels before the otherworldly creature.

"Great Power, you did call upon me?"

"I did. I am known as Aerdrie Faenya, dost thou know of me?"

"I know the name, but I do not believe we ever had the opportunity to meet. What might bring you here to this place?"

"A Child of mine is suffering, and I would call upon thee to offer thine aid. In exchange for this, I will grant upon thee and thy people my dearest favor. But this aid comes in two parts, the first of these to begin in the present moment, the other to occur at another moment when Fate shall bring it forward."

"And how would this aid present itself?"

"The aid shall present itself of its own accord. Thou must first find the Child, and when thou dost find it, thou wilt know what aid must be brought."

"Very well. And where might I find this Child?"

"I perceive it to dwell within a prison. It is placed into exhibition, as humiliation to serve the greed of its keepers. It travels through a dry land of sin and corruption."

"I see, and this already gives me a few ideas. Is there anything else you can offer to assist me in my service?"

"When thou dost find my Child, bring it safely to its home, where it will find sanctuary."

"And what of this other task, the second one…"

"Thou wilt know of it when the moment presents itself."

The image of the deity now wavers and fades, allowing the room to return to its natural lighting.

"My Lord!" the high priest utters breathlessly. "What does all that mean? Who is this goddess? I don't recall hearing that name before."

"She is one of the Estelar, but not one we would normally associate with here as she tends to specialize only with certain creatures. She is most often known to keep flighted creatures as her Children, which offers a curious premise before us. Who, or what, is this Child she mentions?"

"Do you have any ideas to get us started? Her wording was rather cryptic, not that it really surprises me, knowing the gods as I do," he smirks.

"Indeed, this would be one of those moments where the Measure of Balance is testing us. I will need to gather up some of our people. Join us if you like, but this will first demand some careful review and investigation."

Thaelyn leaves the temple and heads back up to the guildhall, calling several of his officers to join him along the way and convene in a tactical planning room inside.

"All right, everyone, listen up," he announces. "We have just received what sounds like an urgent call for assistance from none other than a member of the Estelar with the name of Aerdrie Faenya. This is a goddess we do not normally associate with as she specializes in areas outside our usual focus. Her Children are most often flighted creatures, and on this occasion, she is calling us to perform a task to rescue one from something she describes as a prison that moves and offers exhibition. Right off the top, this sounds like a cage to me, and if it moves, it might be part of a travelling attraction."

"A travelling attraction?" offers a scout. "Like maybe a circus, perhaps?"

"That certainly does sound reasonable. It caters to the greed of its keepers, which also fits, and runs through a dry land of sin and corruption. Now, where does this sound like in your mind."

"That's an easy one. The lands to the south are a good one for this point. Places like Menenbahd."

"Indeed, but our trouble here is we do not hold friendly political relations with Menenbahd. So, if we are to perform any manner of action, it must be done very carefully, if we do not wish to start a war. Although, to be honest, I would not actually mind such for the reputation that place holds."

"We might find ourselves in one sooner or later, anyway," offers a Captain.

"We might, but let us see if we can avoid it for the moment. Our first objective is to find this Child. I cannot be sure what to look for, so we will send scouts and rangers into the area first, to see about any kind of travelling caravans or circuses that might have cages with something bearing wings. I am going to make an assumption here that we are not speaking of any simple bird, however. If this is a Child holding favor from a goddess, it is likely a sentient creature, but I cannot think of too many possibilities at this time."

"Right, then," the Captain considers. "I might first suggest we go in undercover, using disguises to keep anyone from asking questions about us. Menenbahd is rife with ruffians and thieves, so we must stay sharp and keep ourselves low. Mayhap we could establish a base somewhere for our people to report into, and use portal runes to make timely returns back here with any word of what we see."

"This is good. But on the odd chance we are not speaking of

Menenbahd, we should also send out teams to survey a few other regions."

"Aye, we can do that. Now, if we are indeed looking for a circus, or some such, we'll need to know what to do about it once it's found. Do we have any suggestions?"

"This might depend largely on what we find and how critical it is, but at the very least, we need to find a way to bring it out of there and into our care, and then somehow return it home to its own kind."

"All right then, the most important for now would be to find it and make a close inspection of the situation. We will then decide our course afterwards."

The meeting adjourns and the officers go to work, calling in a large number of active and reserve members into service. Teams of scouts and rangers are sent out, mostly to the south as this is where most of the dry arid regions were found, and especially of sin and corruption, as Thaelyn and his nation occupied most of the northern lands by now.

Troops departed on horseback, and many used portal runes leading to the southern cities of the nation as a shortcut, rather than simply running the full distance. From there, they moved out across the borders, sometimes under the cover of darkness to avoid any patrols, and then took up hiding in smaller settlements where they applied their disguises to mingle with the natives.

The circuses were known to travel mostly to the larger cities, and one important example was the capital city on the coastline, known as Fortune's Faire. Of all the cities in the region, this was the worst. It was ruled by a criminal kingpin with his own private army of hoods, some of whom carried very distinguished reputations.

The scouts were all very carefully trained at infiltrating tight spaces, so they found a local shop where they were able to gain access to a back room for their private business. From here, they would send out agents to survey the local happenings, and it became quickly apparent there was a circus in town.

"Hear ye, hear ye! Come one, come all! See the most amazing, the most bizarre, and the rarest of beasts in the land! Watch the jugglers and magicians, the fire breathers and the animal tamers!"

The circus owner shouted his cries across the plaza in the market square. This area was well-known for the many caravans to set up their trays and stands, and hawk their wares to the people passing by in the streets. The circus was a familiar sight around here, as it held this spot for a long time.

"You Sir!" the circus owner shouts to a passerby. "You look like you haven't yet seen the greatest show this side of the Saheen Expanse. Why not give yourself a treat and come on in? It'll only cost you a meager ten silver, barely more than what might be a loaf of bread, and the sights you'll behold will fill your eyes with fancy."

The man had been passing by the circus, studying it carefully from the outside to see if it might be of any interest to actually visit. It was clearly a well-established feature, and it drew a modest crowd, not a large one, but perhaps enough to help make ends meet. There were several tents, a number of small market stands selling novelties, and several cages out in the open with animals of various kinds, most likely used in the circus acts.

He moves in closer for a better look. This drew up the circus owner hoping he might finally make a sale after a slow day.

"Yes! You there! I'll bet you've never seen the likes of what we have in store for you. Just imagine if you will. We have beasties from the far reaches, the likes of which I'm sure you've never seen before. We've got jugglers and magicians, fire breathers…have you ever seen a fire breather? I'll bet you haven't! Well now, this is your chance to see it all, and for just a few tidy coins to help us keep all these little lovelies fed and happy. What do you say, ay?"

The man passed his eyes casually around the layout, then to settle on the owner.

"A tidy few? How many would that be then?"

"Oh, we don't ask for the tip of the crown here, just enough to keep us in business. Ten silver is all. Surely, that isn't asking too much for all the fine sights you'll have in front of you."

"Ten? Why, that doesn't sound like a great amount. Such a fine and reasonable offer, and from what I can see out here, I must admit, I am rather curious as to what you have hidden away in there.”

“Oh yes! And you should be sure to check our merchants, with all manner of trinkets for the little ones, and a few delights for you and your lady friend…eh, you do have a lady friend, do you not?”

“Oh, well,” he grins fondly. “I might have one or two tucked away…but of course, I’m sure you know how that is.”

“Really! Ooh, what a lucky tom you must be,” he chuckles openly. “Well then, what do you say, just a few coins to help keep our wee ones in their swaddling.”

“I think I can manage that…”

The man pulls out a coin purse and fishes around for some money. He hands it over, and the owner invites him inside the circus ring.

“Just help yourself as you please. The tents are all open. Look around, find yourself a seat, and enjoy the show.”

The man strolls inside the ring of tents peering inside each one in turn. In one tent he finds seating for what appears to be a juggling and magic stage. In another, he finds several animals in cages, but these all appeared as common animals likely to be used in the shows. He continues around, passing in and out of several tents of various sizes, some with people offering fortune telling, others with gambling tables, until he finally comes to one with more cages.

Inside these cages, he saw a series of odd creatures, many of which appeared as animals, but seemingly with birth defects or some other mutation. However, in one cage, he saw the figure of what appeared to be a young girl with heavily injured wings. He checks the rest of the room to see if anyone was watching, but since it was apparently a slow day, there were no other people present. So he steps over to examine her, squatting down to her level.

“You there, can you speak?”

Aerlie was nearly delirious from fever at this point. Her eyes were droopy, and she was only vaguely aware of him. She brought her view up to meet him, but she didn’t respond.

“Can…you…speak?” he asks more slowly, pointing at his mouth, and then at her.

She continued to stare at him, almost as if she either didn't want to respond, or couldn't respond.

The man examined her physique, and then the injuries.

"Great gods above," he mutters to himself. "No wonder she was so desperate to find help. If you're the one she's talking about, you look almost as if you're on death's doorstep."

Aerlie simply stared at him. Somewhere in the back of her mind, she understood he was more than just another gawker staring at her for her odd features. This man seemed to actually show interest. But it didn't help her to communicate with him, so she simply lowered her head again.

Then the man decided to try something new.

"You look like you might be elven, at least partway. Let's try this. Lle quena i'lambe tel'Eldalie?"

Aerlie jerked at the mention of her native tongue. She pulled her head up to look at him again, furrowing her brow trying to understand how he might speak this language.

"Yes, I speak elvish," she responds groggily. "How is it you know this language?"

"Where I come from, it's much more common to learn than what you might find around here."

"Where you come from…where is that? And where are we now?"

"This place is a land called Menenbahd. Not a very nice place to be if you wish to keep your coin, or your life. I'm from much farther to the north. We have a large nation up there, but not very friendly with these people," he glances out the tent flap. "Speaking of which, I probably shouldn't spend too much time here before someone sees us."

"It does not matter. I will die here," she turns downward again.

"Not if I have anything to say about it. Let me ask you something. Do you worship a goddess called the Winged Mother?"

Aerlie gasped sharply and brought her focus intently on the man's face.

"What did you say? The Winged Mother? Why would you ask this?"

"She's the reason we're looking for you."

Suddenly, Aerlie felt a surge of hope flowing into her. Maybe her goddess did hear her after all. But why would she send these people, as they were not Avariel.

"You are saying my goddess sent you? But why? Who are you, and why would you come looking for me?"

"I'm sure these are all very good questions, but like I said, this is not a good place to talk. For now, I'll just say this. Your goddess sent us looking for what she describes as one of her Children, which I'm guessing is you, who was in a cage in a place that exhibits you for coin, and occasionally moves around. That describes this place nicely enough. She's asking us to help get you out of here, but this place is a dangerous one, so we have to plan our move carefully."

"And then what?" she asks hesitantly. "What will you do with me after?"

"From the looks of you, I would say we'll have our work made for us just to keep you alive. After that, she's asking us to return you home. The trouble is I doubt any of us knows where that is."

"Yes, not even I know the answer to that. They put me in this iron box and covered it with a cloth. I could not see where I was going, but it was a long journey, I know this much."

"All right, I need to report this in. I'll ask you to stay strong. I'll see if I can get food and maybe some medicine to you, but it has to be very quiet. Do you understand?"

"Yes. I will look for it."

He stands up and backs away a step, once again checking the tent flap in case anyone might enter at that moment. Then he turns and leaves, returning back to their local base of operations.

✦✦✦

"A circus in Fortune's Faire, of all places," Thaelyn relents. "Very well, so be it! But unless we wish to start a war, I think it might be better to be discreet and try a more clandestine approach."

"Indeed, my Lord, but now, what do you suggest in this case?

Personally, given the condition of this young lady, I should think food and medicine would be a high priority to aid her health and recovery."

"It would, but we must also find a way to sneak it in. And then we must consider ways to bring her out. But to simply walk in and carry her off over a shoulder might be a little too conspicuous."

Thaelyn paces around the room in deep contemplation. The other officers waited in anticipation.

"If we cannot go in to fetch her," the Captain suggests. "Could we catch them if they should go out travelling again?"

"While that might offer us an opportunity, we need to know when, or if, they have in mind to do this. They might feel themselves nicely settled in that place."

"What if we could lure them out?"

"A lure? Hmm, interesting, one moment… To lure them out, as if to say to invite them with an offer of prospective new business…"

"My Lord," offers the scout who made the finding. "When I was passing along down there, the circus seemed a little shy of business. Now, the man sounding off in the street, I'm guessing he might be the owner, was giving me the line of shelling out a few coins to help keep him in business, feeding the animals and whatnot. Whether this was just a ploy or not, I don't know, but if he's not actually making that much coin for himself, he might find a finer offer to be rather enticing."

"Perhaps, but then we must ask ourselves what sort of offer might bring him out of the city and within our reach. It would have to be an exceptionally fine one. Especially if you consider any actions we take within the bounds of Menenbahd would likely bring some rather unpleasant repercussions our way."

"It would be right dandy if we could bring him all the way up here. Amberdain would surely be a fine place to make a man rich. The City of Wealth, there's no finer promise than that."

Thaelyn pauses in his steps to study the man a moment, then passing among the others.

"Such people as he would not likely care to travel this far north, especially if he carries any manner of contraband. He should know better than to cross that line. I would think our reputation has become rather well defined by now that no one from below the border would willingly..." he halts his thoughts.

The other officers watch him for his next reaction, all wondering if something new has come forward.

"Willingly..." Thaelyn mumbles distantly. "If he could be enticed, for instance if money is short and he could be attracted by a grand amount of it. The City of Wealth, yes, it is indeed a lofty promise, but it has to be made with no strings attached if to entice him this far. He would not willingly come up here for fear of being caught with his contraband, and no doubt he would bring some. The simple fact of that young Child in the cage would be enough to throw him behind bars. But if we could remove this constant..."

"My Lord?" the Captain wonders. "What do you have in mind for this? It sounds almost like a contradiction, but knowing you as I do, I'd wager you have a clever trick brewing up."

"Perhaps I do, but it must be carried out very carefully in order to uphold our principles of Law."

✦✦✦✦

"Hear ye, hear ye! Come one, come all..."

The circus owner continues to shout across the plaza hoping to draw tourists to his attraction. People pass in and out of the marketplace, visiting one or another of the shops and market stands belonging to the travelling caravans, but again it seems like a slow day for the circus.

A young woman with a low-cut blouse and knee length pants wanders by, apparently looking for something to do. Her obvious manner of dress might suggest her to be a lady of the evening, but for the more refined palate. Her voluptuous curves caused many to turn their heads as she casually strolled along. She had been meandering through the plaza until she eventually spied the circus attraction, so she turned and sauntered over for a closer look. But her focus was not on the circus.

"You there, young lady!" the owner shouts. "Yes, you! How would you like to see some of the finest attractions in the city?"

"Would that include you, perhaps?" she responds sensually.

"I…huh? I mean the circus. We have sights that would dazzle your senses…"

"Oh yes, I'm sure I'm dazzled. Such a man with so many… sights…" she admits as she studies him head to toe. "I've seen you out here for…how long has it been? I just love a man so dedicated to his work. Such men are often quite well positioned in life."

"Men? But I…"

"Oh come now… You can't tell me you don't occasionally feel the rush of success flowing through your trousers. And a man like that is exactly what brings my desires to a boil!" she smiles flirtatiously.

"Um, young lady…"

"The name is Teena, but only to my special friends."

"Uh, all right, Teena… I'm actually trying to…" he turns and waves at the circus tents behind him.

"Yes, I'm sure you are, and I'm sure you've made a fair few coins along the way. But don't you think it's time to explore the other side of life? And what better way to explore it than with someone who holds a spirit of wild adventure, and maybe a few ideas to go along with it…for the right man, of course."

"Ideas? What kinds of ideas?"

"The sort of ideas for those men who know how to make mountains of gold…and maybe who also know how to please a lady. You are one of those, aren't you?" she raises her brow demurely.

"Well, now that you mention it, but I'm not really one to brag…"

"Oh, tell me true!" she yips. "But I don't just join up with any man, you know. I'm very selective…" she turns and steps nonchalantly to the side. "I know what I've got, and it comes at a price."

"A price…" he muses cautiously. "What sort of price are we talking about?"

"Oh, do not think I would rob you of all your worth. That would be self-defeating. After all, a man with money is a very attractive item in my book. Even more so is a man who knows how to make even MORE money… Ooh, that's what I like. A good woman should know that to be truly happy, she needs a good man who understands this. Would you happen to be such a man?"

"Well, but of course!" he agrees priggishly. "Naturally, I've had my dealings with the ladies, but nothing quite as fine as you. You know, it's actually not so easy to find someone as refined as you in this town."

"Oh, don't I know it," she rolls her eyes. "I'm a rare treat…just ask anyone," she asserts as she coolly surveys the plaza. "But not here. These simple people wouldn't know quality if it crawled up their leg. But you, I know your type. I look at you and see you have all this…" she waves auspiciously at the circus ring behind him. "This doesn't come about easily, I'm sure. You must have put a lot of time into it, am I right?"

"As a matter of fact, yes… Like I tell all our guests, we bring in attractions from the far corners of the land. That takes some careful negotiating with hunters and trappers, tradesmen, and the like. We have oddities you'll not find anywhere else, just inside here."

"And this would surely make you very popular."

She now turns and steps up close to him, laying her hands provocatively on his shoulders and thrusting her bosom into view.

"But you know," she declares softly. "I have a little secret, and this could make you absolutely rich. Then all this could be yours," she glances downward.

He reflexively looks down at her alluring shape and almost instantly feels his body surging with lustful desire. He looks back up into her longing eyes, and can't help but wonder what she has to offer. He then glances briefly over his shoulder at his circus, asking himself how he can afford such a fine treat as this with the pittance of coin he actually draws in.

"What kind of secret?" he inquires gently.

The woman smiles warmly at him, knowing she's hooked his interest.

"I happen to know that people might pay good coin to see such extraordinary sights. But I also happen to know, most of them won't be found in this sagging town. These people barely have enough coin on them to buy food before someone cuts their purse and runs off with it."

"I'll admit, you're right, actually."

"But there are other towns where you have some truly wealthy people, and my information tells me they don't get out much to see such curious attractions as what I've heard can be found inside here. Now, you tell me, when you put these two together, what do you have?"

"Um, it sounds to me like you have a lot of people who might be very anxious to see something, and...um, they'll pay good money for it?"

"Now, that's the kind of man who turns my attention," she affirms seductively. "But simply knowing this doesn't bring my desires to their fullest. He also needs to be keen enough to act on it. Are you keen enough?"

"I...might be," he offers with another quick downward glance at her figure.

"That's right! You just keep your eyes on the prize. This is your reward if you can make me truly happy. And trust me, I know my way around a man to make all his dreams come true."

"Really? Wow..."

"But first things first... We need to find that big pot of gold that's waiting for us, and I heard a little whisper recently that got me thinking of a wild opportunity. There's talk of a city filled with wealthy merchants and nobles, but they must be so sad that they don't ever get to see a really exciting circus."

"What city is that?"

"It's a little way up to the north...the city of Amberdain."

"Whoa! Teena, wait," he jerks back abruptly. "That's up there with all those people spouting off that new religion, or whatever it is. I might not mind a little adventure, but that's asking more than I think we could get away with while keeping our heads attached."

"Nonsense…" she waves it off nonchalantly. "Not if we go in with a story that we come from…oh, let's say we come from someplace more to the east, where they might not be as familiar with the people, but they're still welcome to visit. Have you ever been that way before?"

"Um…not recently. I was once born in a small town out that way, but my family had to run when those armies came marching in."

"Really! How interesting. And also, how convenient. Then, this can be our story."

"A story…" he pauses to consider the idea.

"And not just that, but I heard of something else that simply sweetens the deal for us."

"What could sweeten the deal enough to risk going up there? They'll likely dig a hole special for us both."

"Not really. I don't think they have as many patrols on the roads as they used to. They're all one big happy nation these days, you know. And this is a special occasion, so I hear."

"A special occasion? What kind?"

"I heard there's a big festival going on soon to celebrate the spring blossoming. Everyone's talking about it. Apparently, as the story goes, the city will have what they call an Open Gate Day…well, several days, it seems. This is to promote free trade where merchants from all around the region come in and set up inside the city. You want to talk about making money, that's the day to do it!"

"But don't they have guards or something?"

"Well, yes, but I hear they won't be checking the caravans passing through like they usually do…all part of this free trade bit. I think it has to do with this big new nation they made up there relaxing some of the old restrictions they once had from the early days. So, the deal is, we go up there, arrive during this Open Gate Day festival, they'll pass us on through, we set up shop, and bam-o. You got yourself a tent full of rich merchants and nobles clamoring to see all these exciting, rare treats of yours. And as for me, I'll be a very happy girl, and you know what comes next, right?" she swivels to rock her bosom.

"Wow, yeah, that would be nice."

"And there's more where this comes from," she croons while sliding her hands down her sides. "So, how does your sense of adventure feel now? Care to go for a little ride in the country?"

The circus owner couldn't help but find attraction in the idea, to say nothing of the woman. This could turn things fully around for him, both financially and otherwise. The journey would take many days, but if he could get in during this Open Gate Day, he could pass himself off as a travelling merchant from someplace local that wouldn't draw as much attention.

He contemplated the suggestion while carefully studying the sultry body of this living doll standing in front of him. He couldn't know where she came from, but here she was, and so blatantly throwing herself at him. All he needed was to earn her pleasures with this lucrative little exercise. It seemed so simple, and virtually flawless.

He instantly turned around and started issuing orders to his henchmen to start packing up their wagons. He called up his merchants and gave orders to resupply their wares with fresh material. Everything would go along, the full assortment of novelties as well as the finer goods. If he was going to cater to wealthy merchants, he needed the best of everything.

Throughout the remainder of the day and into the night, they packed up the tents. They rested for the eve and headed out first thing the next morning. Each night they would stop to rest, and begin again at first light.

As they travelled, Aerlie and the other caged attractions were kept under large tarpaulins to conceal them from outside view. During the evenings, as the owner and his henchmen made camp, they supplied the usual rations of food. But later, as the crew found their rest, a lone figure crept into the camp under the cover of an invisibility cloak and up to the wagon where Aerlie was stored. He climbed inside quietly and shed his cloak only briefly. Initially, this caused Aerlie to jump from the sudden appearance, but after a few visits, she started to get used to it.

"Here you go, love," he whispers softly. "A bit of food, and this here," he produced a small vial of liquid. "You need to drink it down now. It'll taste foul as can be, but it's actually good for you."

"What is it?"

"It's a type of medicine to help fight all that nasty infection there on you. We call it Festerkill. You'll need to drink a right fine amount for it to do a proper job, but we can't make too many visits in here."

She opens the vial and sniffs it, nearly gagging on the smell.

"You want me to drink this?" she gushes incredulously.

"Like I said, it smells foul, and tastes just as bad, but it'll help you in the long of it."

Aerlie looked at the vial again and struggled with herself. She brought it up and held her nose, then forced herself to take it in and swallow it, hoping to hold it down long enough that it wouldn't find its way back out. After several long moments of trying to push it down, she felt herself relaxing.

"How much of this do I need to drink?"

"If you were in our proper care back home, we might have you take two or three a day."

"You're joking... Ugh."

"Anyway, here's some food. It's called a sandwich, a layering of bread with some meat, a bit of cheese, some lettuce, and a wee bit of sauce for flavor inside."

She takes the item which was wrapped in a napkin. She gently opens it up to reveal the odd assembly inside. She turned it around to study it from different angles, not quite sure how she was supposed to approach it.

"Here, like this..." he ushers, as he demonstrates visually how to hold it, and then bite into it.

Her first attempt was a bit awkward, as it represented a healthy mouthful, but it quickly settled as she realized how convenient it was.

"What do you think...is it to your liking?"

She nodded enthusiastically as she munched on the tasty morsel that was likely the best food she had ever eaten, including back home with her people.

"Right, then. I need to be on my way. Take care. I'll be back on the morrow with more. It shouldn't be much longer till they arrive. Keep your chin up."

He takes a potion from his belt and drinks it down, causing him to go invisible again, and then creeps away into the night.

Several more days pass, and they are well into the northern territory. The road was long from Menenbahd, but the trip was uneventful. As they came into view of the city, they took notice of many other caravans coming and going across the countryside. The circus owner and his female cohort studied the scene carefully.

"There it is," Teena directs. "Now, you remember what I said, right? We just need to get past the gate, and then we'll have all those lovely merchants and nobles drooling all over our bums," she giggles.

"They'd better not go drooling on yours, my little sweetling. That one belongs to me alone."

"Oh, but of course, and you know I'm saving it just for you. I'm just speaking figuratively, you know. Do you know what you'll say to them?"

"Aye. I've been thinking about it, and I've got the perfect line for them. It even carries a wee bit of truth if you can believe it. That way, their gods, or whatever it is they're doing up here, don't catch me with a fib."

The circus caravan made its approach along the road up to the city wall and the large gates leading inside, taking up a position in line with a series of others moving along past the guards in front.

One by one, the guards made a cursory review of the caravans passing through the gates. They stopped the drivers just long enough to ask a few simple questions concerning their origins and type of cargo, but did not make any detailed inspections to ensure the integrity of the stock. When the circus owner and his lady companion arrived, the guards called them to a stop.

"You there," the guard calls. "Welcome to the City of Amberdain. Where do you hail from, traveler?"

"Ah, my good man," the owner replies, trying to maintain his cool. "You might find it interesting to know, I was once born in the distant lands of Kordaran, far to the east. Of course, I've travelled a fair bit since then, but I always recall my sweet homeland," he smiles disarmingly. "And now, here we are, anxious to make a fine tally of coins during this grand celebration."

"Indeed, Kordaran, is it? And what sort of wares do you carry this day?"

"Ah, but we are a performing circus, with many entertainers and exotic attractions. Do you often get circuses this far out?"

"Actually, not as often... If you're a circus, you will likely wish to set up in the Promenade district. Proceed on through until you come to a broad avenue leading north. You'll see signs to help guide you. Turn to the right and follow it until you find the Promenade. Good day to you, traveler..."

The guard waves the caravan through, and the circus owner leads his team along the roads around the city until he finds his destination.

The Promenade district was a segment of the city lined with many markets circling a large feature in the middle. The feature resembled a huge oval shaped bowl depression, much like an arena, and lined with steps that were actually lanes with shops circling the bowl. On the floor of the bowl were a few other caravans that had already set up, leaving the circus to proceed down a ramp and take up space at the opposite end where they had more room.

"This seems like a fine enough spot," the owner admits as he studies the surroundings. "All right, men, let's get to work. I want everything laid out by nightfall. We'll open for business at first light."

✦✦✦✦✦

The morning comes, and the circus rises with the dawning light. The owner and his henchmen sat around their campfire finishing their meal while Teena freshened herself in one of the wagons. Today was expected to be a big day for all of them, as they hoped to see a large flow of tourists passing through, paying their fees, and buying their wares.

The city slowly came to life as the sun continued to rise, and the other caravans in the bowl began to open up. The circus owner took notice of this and started giving instructions to his men.

Teena had emerged from the wagon at the sound of the activity outside to watch the owner and his team arranging their market stands, organizing the animals for their acts, and opening up their tents. The bustle was a practiced routine for the men, and while they were busy with that, she milled around casually to examine some of the crates and barrels with their more specialized goods for sale. Most of it was concealed inside one or another of the tents, to keep it out of view, but she had other ideas.

She found a small wicker basket with a lid and checked it to ensure it was empty. She then moved across to one of the barrels containing their more illicit selection of goods. She opened it up and began pulling out several handfuls of the material to deposit inside the basket. She winced at the odor wafting up from the pungent herbs and glanced around carefully to ensure no one was in view of her, then closed the barrel and replaced the lid on the basket. She then hurried outside to set the basket down near a stack of other boxes lined up by one of the market stands, then turned and walked away innocently.

The district started flowing with people visiting the local shops and taverns. It began slowly at first, but built up as the people came out of their homes to attend the daily chores. Teena stood watch out in front of the circus as the activity began to stir, since she was not an official member of the crew, and therefore with no specific duties to attend. She soon noticed the owner come out and prepare himself to start hawking his attraction to the passing tourists.

"Snoogins," she coos. "You probably don't need me around here for a little while, so I was thinking I could take a little walk to see the sights. I've always dreamed to see how the other half lives."

"Well, just try not to spend all our money right off."

"Oh, don't worry. I'll just go look around and make a list of all the wonderful things I'll have you buy me…you know, to keep me happy…and I know you want to keep me happy. That's what it's all about, isn't it?" she flirts with another rocking of her bosom to reinforce the notion.

"My little sweetling, when this is over, I'll be looking forward to making you so happy, you'll burst right out of that tiny shirt of yours."

"Ooh!" she squeals. "Just be sure you're there to catch me."

She finishes with a kittenish smile and a wink, before sauntering off across the bowl to a series of steps leading up the side.

The circus owner watches her walk away with her hips swinging femininely in gentle arcs. He secretly fantasizes over the lustful indulgence he will share with her at the end of the day, but first he needs to attend to his business.

Teena proceeded up the stairs and further along out of the district through a local gate. As she continues along the road, she takes notice of an assembly of guards forming up with their commanding officer. She also takes notice of Thaelyn leading the group. She flashes a quick wink at him, and then casually steps up to the Captain.

"Oh, guard? May I have a word please?"

The Captain turns to greet the young woman. Although her dress was a little unusual, her demeanor was clearly evident of the common manners of the local populace.

"Yes, citizen, what can I help you with?"

"I was just now passing through the Promenade amongst those new merchant caravans when I caught a whiff of something very strange. It was a strong odor, not anything I was commonly familiar with. And whoo-ee, it made me a little dizzy for a spell. I can't be sure what it was, but I'd sure be interested to find out!"

"Indeed! Very good, we'll take a look. Thank you, citizen."

She smiles and bows her head, then continues along.

"My Lord," the Captain continues. "The inspection tour is assembled and ready."

"Excellent," Thaelyn begins. "All right, men, this is a simple spot inspection. Given that we have this special occasion occurring, we might have all sorts of merchants travelling in and out of our fair city. While I might not normally expect any of our good people to be transporting inappropriate materials, it also stands to reason we might have a few from outside hoping to sneak past us to unload their cargo. This inspection is simply to ensure the integrity of our trade routes and the safety of our people."

He pauses to glance through the nearby gate towards the Promenade before continuing.

"We will go down there and make a polite pass amongst our visiting merchants, perhaps to ask a few questions about their goods, and make a cursory check of their stores. Captain, do you have anything you would wish to add?"

"Aye, that young lady who just passed by suggested an odd odor coming up from somewhere. Men, I'll have you keep your eyes, and also your noses available, in case anything should present itself. You all have your training, so be alert for any sights or smells that seem out of place here. My Lord?"

"Good, let us proceed."

Thaelyn leads the troupe of guards through the district gate into the Promenade, and then down the stairs into the bowl. The circus was at the upper end, but they instead diverted off to the right towards the lower end. They had a couple other caravans that way, and this would be their starting point.

The circus owner had been calling out his lines hoping to attract people into his circus. So far, no one was taking up the offer, but it was still early. He saw the guardsmen come down into the bowl and eyed them carefully as they began making a circuit around the other caravans. One of his henchmen comes up to join him.

"What's that business, Boss?"

"I don't know. It looks like an inspection. I thought they weren't supposed to be making any inspections during this festival of theirs."

"That was at the front gate. This is inside. Maybe they make occasional runs through to check on people."

"Maybe. You should close up the tents just in case they get any ideas of peeking inside."

"Right."

Thaelyn and his men were seen speaking to the owner of the caravan across the way, and several of the guards were examining some of the crates he opened for them. The circus owner continued to watch as his henchman returned.

"Everything's good, Boss," he reports. "All our finest is inside the tents and closed up. All we have outside are the trinkets for the kiddies."

"Good. He's apparently checking their wares, so if he comes around here, we'll just show him our toys and that's all. Everything else is part of our entertainment act."

"What about the tents? Do you think he might ask about those?"

"We'll tell him the tents are for the jugglers and fortune tellers, that's all. There shouldn't be any need for him to go inside and look."

"All right then…"

Thaelyn moved on to the next caravan and repeated the sequence. Once again, the owner obliged by showing off his stock, opening several containers to demonstrate his goods, and explaining his business. When that inspection was done, Thaelyn moved on to one more that included an open stage for an acting crew. With nothing of special interest to inspect, he moved forward to the circus.

"Ah, my good man," he announces jovially to the owner. "I hope you are enjoying this fine day."

The circus owner played into the game carefully with his own greeting.

"Yes, it is such a lovely day. I was noticing you making a circle through here and I've become curious as to what you might be looking for."

"Oh, this," he pans his gaze informally around the bowl. "This is just a simple tour we sometimes make to ensure our good citizens meet with their satisfaction. It is most often to see our visiting merchants hold up the good name of our trade practices with fresh goods and quality merchandise. But as I look here, I find I must ask what manner of business you have."

"Oh, yes of course. This is a performing circus, one of the finest in the land…if I do say so. We have travelled far across this great land of ours, providing entertainment and exotic sights for both young and old…eh, perhaps you might have heard of us?"

"A circus? This should be an enjoyable attraction. I do not recall too many circuses passing through this region, so this would surely be a delight for the locals. Where do you come from?"

"You know, as I was so proudly informing the guards at the gate out there, I was born in the fine lands of Kordaran, far to the east. Such a lovely place…" he reflects dreamily.

"Indeed, and those lands are only recently annexed into our kingdom. How do you find your trades since that time?"

"Well, to be honest, I've done a fair bit of travelling since then, so I must say my experiences are varied from place to place."

"Yes, such it may be for a profession like this," he nods contentedly, realizing the posturing was just as much a roleplay as anything. "And what manner of attractions do you carry?"

"Firstly, we have jugglers and magicians…these are always very popular, especially for the young ones. And then we have the fire breathers! I've seen many a crowd shouting in awe when they put on their show."

"Fire breathers?" Thaelyn pauses to examine the cloth tents. "I certainly hope these tents of yours are not prone to burn easily," he chuckles.

"Oh no, we are very careful of that. Clearly, we wouldn't want that to happen."

"What about sales? Many times I would expect to see a circus selling some manner of trinkets. Do you indulge in this? I believe I see a few market booths over yon."

"Oh yes! We have toys and other baubles, again mainly for the children."

"May we take a brief look? I am always curious as to what sort of items might be on sale at a circus."

"Of course, here…"

The owner leads Thaelyn and his team inside the ring of tents to the market stands, where they had several stacks of crates with their supply of toys and other items they might sell commonly to the public.

Thaelyn directs the captain to begin his inspection, sending several of the guards to check around the crates visually, as well as to sniff closely anything that might emit any unexpected odors. While he does this, he continues interacting with the owner.

"Ah, yes, these are certainly adorable," he comments of several wooden animals. "I might imagine you will find a good market for these here in the city."

"Yes, we sell a lot of these back home. As you can see, we carry many boxes, all the same."

"And what about inside these tents?" Thaelyn asks. "Are they all for some kind of performance, or do we have anything else of interest inside?"

"Oh, there is nothing special to look at in there. We have stages where the people sit to watch the show, we have a fortune teller over here," he points across the way. "And this one is where we keep the animals for the animal tamer act. Have you ever seen an animal tamer before?"

"An animal tamer?"

"Captain," announces one of the guards hovering over a set of boxes. "I think I smell something a mite peculiar over here."

The mention draws the attention of Thaelyn and the circus owner, both of whom turn to observe the scene.

The captain steps in closer while the guard directs a finger at a small wicker basket covered by a lid. The officer bends down to sniff the air and instantly crinkles his nose.

"What do we have in here?" he asks the owner.

The circus owner hurries over to take a look, not sure what could be causing the disturbance, but feeling a little vulnerable to the suggestion. When he sees the basket sitting there, he is puzzled by the reason, as it was not one of the common crates of toys.

Thaelyn moves in to make a closer inspection.

"What do we have, Captain?"

"My Lord, we smell something odd coming out of there, a pungent odor, like from an herb or some such."

"Can you tell us what might be inside here?" he asks the circus owner.

The circus owner couldn't be sure what was inside, but if it smelled like a pungent herb, he had to guess at the nature of it. Still, why it was in this basket was anyone's guess.

"Ehm…goodness, I can't be sure, unless it's something that went bad on us during our long journey."

"Perhaps we should check," Thaelyn nods concernedly. "We certainly would not want any spoiled goods to taint your lovely presentation here."

Before the circus owner could object to this otherwise innocent proposal, the captain gave an instruction to open the basket. Inside they found a pile of preserved opium pods.

Thaelyn and his Captain both stared at the container, which was clearly filled with an illegal substance. Even though it was not a large quantity, possession of any amount was still a crime.

"This appears to be a form of preserved opium," Thaelyn mentions. "This is actually illegal in this region, are you aware of this?"

"Oh dear, how did that get in there…" the circus owner blushes. "My deepest apologies, I can only suggest one of my men picked up the wrong basket…eh, what I mean is he was retrieving some of the supplies we usually stock, but something must have crossed paths."

"Perhaps, but I cannot imagine where this might come from to begin with. I am aware of a form of opium, which also happens to be preserved in this manner, but which is mostly found in the southern regions of the land, not so much to the east. How might it have found its way into your hands at all, if this is the case?"

"Oh, really? Um…" the owner flusters. "This is very strange. After all, we came out of Kordaran. How could it find its way out there? Maybe an alchemist, or perhaps an herbalist ordered something, do you think?"

"I suppose this might hold some relevance, but this is a very carefully regulated substance. I would think, if they did have such an interest, for instance in developing a medical treatment, it would more likely travel through different channels. Not one where a common merchant could accidentally cross paths with it."

"Really! Well, I suppose," he pauses to think. "But you know, this is only a very small amount, and I'm a man of business. Like you said, a common merchant, a simple circus owner! And I can see you're a man of reason. I'm sure we could come to some kind of understanding over this little mishap, right?" he raises his brow.

"An understanding?" Thaelyn muses in apparent consideration. "While I will admit, this is only a small amount, the local city council does have some rather strict policies. What sort of understanding do you suggest?"

"Oh! Yes! Well, it occurs to me, and just as we mentioned a moment ago, this could hold some value to certain people. Now, if we could simply overlook this little accident, maybe I could find someone to take this off my hands. After all, this is the city of merchants, so they say. Surely, someone would be willing to pay a few tidy coins for it. Then, it would be only fair if I offer some amount to you for your most gracious allowance to let me go about the rest of my business. Like I said, I'm a simple circus owner. What need do I have for such as this?"

"I see…" he contemplates. "So, if I were to simply overlook this unfortunate occasion, and allow you to find a way to dispose of this, quietly of course, then you would share the proceeds with me for my favor?"

"Absolutely! A few extra coins in your pocket are always welcome, yes?"

"This is curious. But we are forgetting my officer here," he directs at the Captain. "He does serve the city authority, and surely, we must recognize he holds a rather delicate set of responsibilities on his shoulders. I would not wish to portray an image that could upset those higher demands."

"Oh, but of course, how silly of me," he titters. "And I would not want to leave him out of this fabulous offer. After all, he's a good sturdy man who might like a few extra coins as well."

"Him as well? But then, I should further point out these others," he directs to the rest of the team. "Our guardsmen are a well-respected authority in the city. We certainly would not desire any of them to tarnish this in the eyes of our public. We do hold our pride, you know. And I should once again point out the city council, as they do like to receive reports on things from time to time…"

"Oh, naturally!" he interjects. "And we certainly wouldn't want to disturb them with anything unpleasant. But, um, you know," he contemplates the basket and its contents again. "This is only a small amount here, and it might not reach as far as all this…" he briskly surveys the full guard troupe. "Oh! I know! Maybe I can make another offer. I know some people who might be able to help. And this would surely provide for our needs to keep this in our favor. What if I could find even more of this, and then we can make ourselves a deal that is truly worthy of a man in your position," he smiles graciously. "We could make a good bit of profit together, and share it with all our new friends. After all, this is the city of merchants, is it not?" he grins expectantly.

"Even more?" Thaelyn raises his brow. "My goodness, that would indeed represent an offer," he ponders conspicuously. "Captain, what do you think? This dear fellow is making us an offer to share in the proceeds of dispensing these materials within the city, quite possibly a substantial supply of it, and thereby making a fine amount of coin along the way, if only we were to keep this to ourselves and permit him the freedom to pursue his extravagant business ventures. I might say this presents a rather curious opportunity for us. Would you agree?"

"Indeed, my Lord…" he nods. "And a most curious one at that. Especially as I reflect on our conversation and his rather determined negotiation. You don't often see a man with such a fervent direction as this. I might say this could bring several of our concerns into a solid fruition at once."

"It most certainly could, and quite rapidly as well. Captain, arrest these men for the possession of illegal goods, both trafficking as well as intent to sell, and also for bribery and an attempt at corrupting city officials. Then I want a careful search conducted to see what else they have around here."

"At once, my Lord!"

"What?" the circus owner yelps as he's grabbed by a pair of guards.

The circus becomes a flurry of activity as the guards begin charging forward to grab the other henchmen. A whistle sounds off and additional guards from around the district move in to assist. The scene is chaotic as henchmen scramble to find an escape, only to run into more guards closing in on all sides.

Thaelyn saunters along casually within the ring of tents, allowing his people to do the work, rather than go in himself with his prior knowledge of what he might find. His men had to make the discovery, which would then cause the circus owner to dig his own grave. Once the henchmen had been gathered up, his men began a thorough search of the tents, pulling out boxes and barrels and inspecting each one.

"My Lord, more of it here!" shouts a guard as he finds the original barrel containing the contraband.

"And here," barks another guard hauling out a crate. "Looks like lotus in this one."

"Indeed, this is quite a selection," Thaelyn replies. "One might think of opening up a specialty shop by now."

The circus owner glares at Thaelyn as he watches his henchmen brought down and all his possessions dragged out and exposed.

"Just who in all the hells are you?" he scowls.

"If you were in fact from Kordaran, and I suppose I should temper this by saying 'recently' from Kordaran, as we conquered that territory only a few decades ago, you would already know the answer to that question, as Kordaran is a part of our nation, and each of my citizens would know me by name as well as my face. This can only mean you are not one of my citizens."

"One of YOUR citizens? So, you're the one who's been taking over the place up here?"

"Indeed, and I suspect you are far more likely to come from somewhere south of the border…at least more recently. I am aware of a horde of refugees who were fleeing before us as we made our approach, and we generally allowed them their escape as they would not be welcome amongst us to begin with. Time will erase them eventually, as we continue to unite this world and bring harmony to it."

"Unite the world? Is that what you're trying to do up here? And do you think you can actually do it?"

"I have already made a good amount of progress, and I have no doubt I can continue this way until it is done."

"That sounds like a mad plan, if you were to ask me."

"Many have said this in the past, but here we are, doing it. Anyway, by your appearance, and the apparent cultural designs of these tents and other paraphernalia, I might suggest you are instead… more recently…from Menenbahd, am I right? When last my advisors notified me, we do not hold friendly political relations, nor do we hold any trade relations. Captain, add that to the list, will you?"

"Aye!" he nods.

"And so," the circus owner groans. "You simply toss my offer back in my face and choose to arrest me instead?"

"Sir, for all your determined negotiation to the contrary, I offered several attempts to convince you of our…very legal…manners of conduct up here. You could have backed out at any moment, and I would have likely excused you for the error. Instead, you only dug yourself deeper into a hole until I had to make my own stand. I am a man who is very strictly dedicated to law and justice, and I do not compromise this for anything."

"Really! So, a mountain of gold holds no meaning to you?"

"Indeed, gold does not hold any true value to me, other than possibly to place food on my table and clothes on my back. And having mountains of it simply sitting around is of no practical service to me. Wealth is nothing more than a tool to enable commerce. And commerce is better employed to the greater benefit of a population, not a single individual."

The circus owner simply grimaced at him as Thaelyn continued.

"Furthermore, the pittance of material in this basket is indeed unworthy to bicker over. Had you instead chosen to sacrifice it by excusing yourself that it was indeed an error, I might have overlooked it and given you a simple pardon. But your continued raving over selling these goods and sharing so many underhanded riches forced me to consider if you were in fact hiding something even larger behind our backs. And none of MY citizens would do this, as they all follow the same principles as I do…quite religiously."

"Oh yes, that funny religion I heard of up here," he huffs.

"Are you aware of the one whom people call the Just God? He should not be so ambiguous as not to be known in such a place as Menenbahd."

"Yes, I know that name, but he is NOT worshiped down there."

"I may expect as much, but he IS very highly revered up here. Such that His teachings are an intimate part of our lives."

The guards continued along systematically until they came to the tent with the cages.

"My Lord! You need to come see this one!"

Thaelyn turned at the mention and followed the guard through the tent flaps. There he saw a series of cages with the exotic creatures and oddities, including Aerlie.

"Dear Powers, this is intolerable."

He made a cursory review of the assortment, but turned to focus on the one with the young girl inside. He kneeled down to gaze at her, with several guards entering behind to observe the strange sight.

Aerlie looked up at the many guardsmen staring at her, but focusing mostly on the unusual individual kneeling right in front with shoulder length silver-white hair and golden eyes. She had never seen a face like this before.

The two of them exchanged stares. Thaelyn studied her. She had topaz blue eyes, almost crystalline in appearance, and long hair that looked nearly the color of spun gold, if not for the fact of being dirty and matted.

Thaelyn peered over his shoulder to find his officer.

"Captain, bring him in here."

The captain ordered his guards to usher the circus owner inside.

"This is a most curious sight," Thaelyn begins. "Do you have a proper explanation for why this Child is inside a cage and placed on display, apparently with a variety of oddities?"

"Because it is one, that's all," the owner spits defiantly. "What difference does it make?"

"It? You do not even recognize SHE is a female, to say nothing of a person?"

"A person?" he yelps. "That thing?"

"Indeed! She is an elf. You do know what an elf is, do you not? They tend to travel here and there on occasion."

"That's no elf like I ever saw before."

"I will credit you for this point only, as her race is indeed a rare one, but no less an elf than any other. Our history tells of their kind from almost a millennium and a half ago, and they are known as the Avariel. They were last known to be observed during a famous battle at an ancient elven temple to preserve a powerful artifact from being taken and misused by a band of dragons. They were able to route the dragons, but apparently lost a great many of their kind in the gambit. The remainder were thought to have travelled off to find sanctuary until they could recover, but they have not been seen or heard from since…" he returns again to Aerlie, "…until now."

"And you expect me to know all this? I'm just a simple circus owner."

"Perhaps, and I may also admit this would require a bit more of an elaborate education than what you might find down in Menenbahd, or even Kordaran in those early days. But if you can at least see she holds some similarity to an elf, with or without the wings, you might have tried speaking to her. Then, Powers Behold, you might learn something…assuming any of it actually mattered to you."

Thaelyn now turns to Aerlie and tries using the elvish language.

"Child, do you understand my words?"

"Yes, I understand you," she emits faintly. "Why are you yelling at that man?"

"Why? Dear Child, just look at you. Would you not yell at the one responsible for all this? That man, and they who follow him, are criminals, and I am not at all pleased to see you in this condition."

"Yes, maybe so. But who are you?"

"My name is Lord Thaelyn. I am the ruler of this land we now stand upon. I would offer you a fair welcome, but our circumstances are rather dire, and the meaning becomes lost as a result."

"Yes, I suppose it does. Are you the one sending all those men to help me?"

"I am, and it is at the request of your goddess that I make this effort."

"Why would she call on you to do this?"

"Our people hold a very close relationship to our local gods, and she likely found it convenient to call upon us. Also, I hold a substantial amount of authority in these lands. Combine this with my purpose here, and it might seem fitting that she would take advantage of it."

"So, a goddess would actually call on someone down here to help HER?"

"Yes," he chuckles. "I suppose that does represent something of a paradox. People often say the gods work in strange ways, but much of it is to enforce a condition of learning to solve your own problems, rather than depending on a divine figure to do it for you. Regardless of who or what they are, it is not their direct responsibility to take these matters themselves."

"And so," she mumbles. "My mother telling me she can't simply go poof with things. We have to find our own way."

Thaelyn again turns to look at the circus owner.

"Where is the key to this cage?"

"I could give it to you, but you won't get it to work by now. She'll be in there till her dying days, and then some. The lock is so badly rusted by now, it won't move."

Thaelyn turns to inspect the lock. The mechanism was indeed very badly corroded, and worse, it stank of something rancid.

"What happened to this lock? The odors coming out of it are unbearable."

"A funny one, that. Some of my men took to pissing on it, just to watch her reaction. It's like she'd never seen a man's pole sticking out before," he chuckles callously.

Thaelyn's face wrinkled in a fierce scowl, and his eyes flashed briefly. He turned and lurched to his feet.

"You, Mortal, are an abomination!" his voice booms, shaking

most of the people in the room, especially Aerlie. "It is because of such as you that I came to this world in the first place, to cleanse this land of your wretchedness!"

"You think you can clean up Menenbahd? You think you can challenge the Pasha? Go ahead and try, I'd like to see the result."

"Petty little man… I carry a divine mandate to do exactly that. My existence in this world is not by accident. Your little nation down there is no match for what I have created. Your Pasha can dream his fantasies, but once I set my eyes on him, his mortal days will become much shorter."

He pauses to scan the other cages in the room, then Aerlie in hers. She was clearly showing fear in her eyes at the intense booming of his voice. But if the lock was frozen with rust, he needed another way to get her out.

"Captain, take this man outside and hold him firm. I want him to know who he is truly speaking to that he would dare challenge my authenticity. And I want some guards to lift this cage and bring it outside as well. Place it in the center out there where we have plenty of space."

Thaelyn leads the group outside again while the captain and his men move the circus owner off to one side and bring Aerlie and her prison into the center of the ring of tents.

"We need blankets," Thaelyn issues. "Or a tarp or some other heavy sheet… Cover her with it. Aerlie, I need you to bend low, as much as you can."

"Why," she mutters nervously. "What are you going to do?"

"Apparently, the lock on your cage is badly rusted. Therefore, I must try another way to free you from there, but this is going to require some careful precision. Simply trust me."

The guards rummage through the tents and wagons, and bring out several blankets. They thread them through the bars and lay them over Aerlie inside, carefully covering her.

"I think it might also be wise to find some poles or rods, something to pass through both sides as support.

"My Lord," the Captain wonders. "What do you actually plan on doing here?"

"Cutting off the top…"

"You're mad!" the circus owner blasts. "That's an iron cage. Just what do you think you're going to use to cut through that?"

Thaelyn glares at the man while the guards scavenge several poles out of the tents and insert them across the upper portion of the cage to act as a support in case the top falls inside.

"All right, men," Thaelyn instructs. "Sit with your backs to the cage and support those poles from underneath. Be ready in case it falls in. Tilt your heads down to keep your faces hidden, and also watch your fingers."

Thaelyn now pulls out his sword. Aerlie can just barely see him from under her cover. The circus owner also watches, but can only twist his expression thinking Thaelyn was crazy if he thought he could cut through an iron cage with a simple sword. The Captain and his men, however, knew what was coming.

Thaelyn crouches to examine the cage at eye level to line up his mark. He then stands up and extends his arm to measure his distance and aim. Finally, he brings his sword up to his lips and whispers into it.

The sword erupts in a brilliant blue flame enveloping its full length. The sight of it immediately stifled the circus owner, who was now aghast at the apparent power of the large weapon. Aerlie looked at it in awe, although she was not the sort to really understand such powerfully enchanted artifacts. The Captain and his guards all took a step back to give him his space.

Thaelyn turned to the right, now standing sideways to the cage. He holds out his sword and begins making a series of swirls and spins, twirling his sword with just one hand in front of him, then to his left, again in front, and finally to reorient for a sideways swipe. The sword levels out as he spins on his heel in a full circle, bringing the blade through a perfectly flat slashing motion that met cleanly with the top of the cage just below the upper plate.

A shower of sparks sprays in all directions, and a loud clang rings out from the metal prison. The glowing rain bounced off the blankets covering Aerlie as she lets out an urgent yip for the sudden commotion. The guards on either side were mostly protected by their armor and unaffected. The top panel of the cage teetered and fell inside, but was caught by the poles acting as a brace.

Thaelyn brings the sword back up to cancel the enchantment, and returns it to its sheath, then casually turns to glance at the circus owner for his reaction.

"And if that is not enough to convince you, Mortal, let us try another one. Consider this a free lesson on the nature of a Celestial."

He motions to the guards to remove the cage top and the blankets, allowing Aerlie to return upright.

Aerlie now found herself in a world of iron bars sticking up from the floor of her cage, but with no roof to it. If her legs were so capable, she might actually be able to stand up, but her cramping kept her motionless.

Thaelyn raised an arm and extended his fingers to point at the cage. Again, the Captain and his men knew what was coming, but the circus owner could only wheeze at the sight of the iron bars mysteriously curling down, first in front, then the left, and finally the right. The cage was opening up like peeling a banana.

Aerlie gazed at the ghostly force pulling the bars down on all sides of her. She had never heard of such a power, but it seemed clear Thaelyn was the one responsible. She almost felt like screaming, but her shock, combined with her faintness and fever, made it seem more like she was hallucinating.

When he was finished, Thaelyn returned to the circus owner for his final impression.

"Now can you begin to comprehend the power of a Celestial as compared to your beloved, and simply mortal, Pasha?"

"Aye..." the owner relents wearily. "Although, to be honest, I don't actually know what a Celestial is."

"In short, I am part human, like you, but my Father is that same god."

"He's your Father?!" he yelps. "No wonder you're so strict. Right. Methinks the Pasha is in a lot of trouble with you around."

"Such is the way for this entire world. And not simply for me, but the army I raised along the way. Captain, I must bring this Child to B.T. promptly. Given her condition, we will need to provide her with medical treatment immediately. I will leave the cleanup to you. Bring these men into custody, pack up everything here, and place it in storage. We will attend to it as time permits."

Thaelyn steps forward and kneels next to Aerlie again.

"Child, I will carry you from here. We will go to my home city where we have a temple with healers who will attend to your injuries. We will afford every effort to see you returned to full health."

"Another city? Is it far? I don't know how much more I can take."

"Do not concern yourself. We are very well prepared for such occasions."

He leans in and takes her into his arms, then lifts her up gently.

As soon as the two make physical contact, each of them feels an odd sensation. Thaelyn pulls himself upright, but pauses momentarily as he tries to reconcile a strange familiarity seeping into him. But his mind quickly returns to his duty as he must bring her to the temple and the healers.

Aerlie, on the other hand, being partly delirious from fever, feels the sensation warming her with a calm relaxation. She almost feels like she's found her home, and leans her head into him.

"Guards," Thaelyn directs. "Bring up one of those blankets. Her wings appear too weak for her to hold them up, and we need to collect them. Wrap them up and bundle the edges here for her to grasp hold of."

The guards comply by wrapping a blanket around the girl's wings to hold them close to her body, then bundling up a wad in front for her to hold during transport.

Thaelyn now makes his way out of the circus ring, followed by the captain and several of the guards with the circus owner and his henchmen. When they come out into the clearing, the circus owner is greeted by Teena, who had returned from her shopping trip. She was standing out in the open waiting for them.

Teena smiled at him and offered a flirtatious wave, then blows a kiss at him. She then steps up to Thaelyn.

"My Lord, can I offer any assistance?" she asks while glancing sideways at the circus owner.

"Indeed you can, Adept. Do you have your rune on you?"

"Of course!"

The circus owner glared at the girl.

"You tricked me!" he shouts.

"I did no such thing. I simply appealed to your senses, which included money, and these," she cups her hands under her breasts and subtly jiggles them. "You did everything else. I didn't tell you to bring all that rubbish with you. There really is an Open Gate Day, as you can clearly see, and your circus probably could've used the money, from what we saw of it down there. Your management practices, however, leave a few things to be desired. Oh well…"

"So, you bring me all the way up here just to put me in prison? Why? I was in my own home town. You shouldn't have any authority down there."

"True, but it's actually her we wanted," she nods at Aerlie. "When a goddess tells you she wants her Child back, you tend to listen."

The man reels back at the notion.

Aerlie looked up to see the woman speaking harshly with the man.

"I wish I knew what you people were saying," she mumbles faintly.

"Rest easy, Dear," Teena soothes. "This man in simply a terrible example of a person."

"But if all you wanted was her…" the circus owner begins. "Why go through all of this?"

"Would you have given her over to us if we'd simply asked?" Teena responds. "Probably not. Based on his shouting a moment ago," she glances at Thaelyn, "which was probably heard halfway across the city, you must have done something really, really bad. And I can only guess, by my observations over here," she thumbs over her shoulder, "that it occurred inside that tent. By the way, what was it?" she asks Thaelyn.

"The lock on the cage was badly corroded from urine, of all things," he responds.

"Gods above! How did that happen?"

"His men were abusing it, and therefore her inside of it."

"I swear!" she screams. "And so, here we have it," she returns to the circus owner. "And given her condition, and your clear lack of concern for her, we couldn't wait for it. After all, she's one of your main attractions. We are a society of laws…strict ones…given to us by no less than the gods themselves, through him…" she directs at Thaelyn, "…as he is a child of one of them sent here to bring all of US into harmony as a world body. Your Pasha down there really doesn't have an opinion on the matter, as this isn't HIS world. It's theirs. And we are their Children, who now need to grow up and learn our lessons."

"Are you actually serious?" he winces. "I know what he said, and what he did over here, but…"

"Yes, this world is a pet project being managed by one of them. This means WE are here for a reason, and it's not to make trouble with each other. But we still have a few areas we need to bring together, including yours. Meanwhile, as you can see, we actually do have this Open Gate Day as part of a new practice we're experimenting with to increase the commerce lanes around here. Within our nation, crime is at an all-time low, so why board up our cities with walls and gates?" she shrugs. "This is a thing of the past for us."

"And so, you play this little game on me."

"It's not my fault if someone from down south might find so much interest to sneak in under our fences, regardless of any enticement. All I did was to mention a few details and let you decide from there. You could've left the nasty stuff at home and still made some good coin for yourself. As for her, if you were a proper man, you might actually apologize for the error, rather than gloat over her as a trophy. Nevertheless, we had a visitation not long ago from a goddess who told us to go look for her. She was lost from her people, and our instructions were to bring her home. It's that simple, your values notwithstanding."

"A goddess actually came here and spoke to you?" he balks. "Are we speaking of physically?"

"Thaelyn is from that place where the gods make their native homes. He is part of THEIR family. So, yes, it might be expected from time to time. The world is changing, and we are coming closer together. As for our methods, short of actually going to war and conquering your petty little nation, we decided to take it more discreetly. Nothing personal to you."

"Uh huh, nothing personal. You choose to ruin me to save a half-dead runt like her."

"A runt… Be careful, or you might find yourself more than just ruined. These runts, and the other elves they're related to, are the primary reason we humans have enough brains to actually stand upright and wear clothes. When they first found us, we were living like animals."

"Huh?"

"Yeah, I guess you need to attend one of OUR schools, rather than whatever you got out of Kordaran before your family ran away. Our ancestors were VERY primitive, and might still be that way if it were not for the elves arriving when they did. And the Avariel were a part of that."

"Uh huh."

"But as for her, the half that's not dead can be salvaged. The other half can be repaired, including those diseased wings you apparently never attended to. We have medicine to clear that up, one of the many gifts our most gracious Lord gave us. So, while she might be half-dead to you, she's a fantastic discovery to us, and promising the favor of a new goddess in our temples. That's worth a lot to us."

"I'm glad I'm not religious," he moans. "The whole thing sounds crazy to me."

"Religious or not, it doesn't matter. The gods are people, in some ways like us, only bigger, and they carry a lot of authority, to say nothing of wisdom. Your opinion is therefore moot."

Teena pulls out a portal rune and begins enchanting it. The stone begins to show the classic surge of energy forming around it, as it settles with a glow. Aerlie watches the curious display.

"What's that?"

Thaelyn steps forward as he briskly glances at the young girl, and then at Teena.

"A portal rune…" he asserts. "Hit me with it."

Teena brings it up and touches it to his shoulder. Both Thaelyn and Aerlie are sent away in a bright flash, which further startled the circus owner. Teena simply turned and smiled at him.

"By the way," she smirks. "I doubt your Pasha would see us coming, let alone have time to react to it, even if we did declare war on you. We would simply appear on your streets, combat ready and striking at you before you could even focus on it."

Thaelyn and Aerlie arrived in the guildhall courtyard. Aerlie perked up when the flash enveloped her, and was now trying to reconcile the sudden change of surroundings.

"What just happened?" she asks.

"Do you know what a portal is?" he offers.

"Barely, and only as stories."

"Very well, but we use them often around here to travel around. We use enchanted rune stones as the means to open portals to certain locations, and that one brought us here to our capital city of Bya'an Tamoranth. Now we will make our way just down there to the temple."

Aerlie looked over her shoulder to see the rest of the city. From up on the hill, looking out the front gates, she had a fairly good view of the bustling city below. She saw people walking along, horses pulling wagons, and a neat arrangement of nicely built shops, inns, and taverns. Everything appeared sturdy and well maintained, in stark contrast to her home village. She next turned to look back up at the large fortress that was the guildhall with the guards standing out in front.

"What is that?"

"That is the guild home of my military Order, and where I spend much of my time giving lessons to share my wisdom and philosophical teachings. Further above, if you follow those stairs, you might also see my home."

Aerlie looked through the gates and saw a long staircase leading up to a proud manor home on top, overlooking everything else.

"You live up there? It looks very beautiful."

"Well, thank you. You are very kind."

Her rising interest in the various sights brought her mind into better focus. They were now walking along a main avenue crossing in front of the guildhall towards the temple, which was a block away on the other side of the street. She watched as they made their approach to the large ornate building, soon to pass through the double doors and forward to the dais.

"My Lord," the high priest rushes up to him. "Is this the one we were sent to find?"

"Indeed, it is, and much to my amazement, she is a member of the long lost Avariel. I now find myself asking how many more there might be and where they have been hiding all this time."

"Yes, of course. I cannot recall the last time anyone ever saw one of those. Please, come this way, we have a bed ready for her."

The priest leads them through a side door into an annex known as the Healer's Ward. There, they find their way to a room with a bed and several other priests waiting to receive their new patient.

Thaelyn sets her on the bed and helps to remove the blanket containing her wings. There were several gasps at seeing the strange, winged shape, but they were also gasping at the extensive injury.

"Apparently, she can only speak elvish," he asserts. "So, we will need to accommodate her."

"Of course, my Lord… Eh, young lady, may we know your name, please?"

She looked around at all the people hovering over her, unsure what to expect from them, then turned to the high priest speaking to her.

"My name… It's, um…" she stutters. "My name is Aerlie."

"Such an interesting one… Very good, Aerlie, we are going to apply our healing service to see if we can bring this infection under control. It would also appear your clothes are badly worn and, well, you appear very soiled. But we will help you bring all this back into order. First, I think we should have you lay down here. Perhaps it would be best if you lay on your stomach, to give us easy access to your wings."

She tries turning over and lies down, while the priests manage her wings. They brought in a set of side tables to lay her wings across for support, and then began the meticulous work of cleaning and prepping her for their service.

◆◆◆

Several days have passed since Aerlie was admitted into the Healer's Ward for treatment. The priests have been administering medicine on a daily basis, as well as massage therapy to ease the cramping in her legs and restore her movement. Her muscles were weak, and she was badly malnourished, so a steady diet of nutritious food was ordered and delivered. But her wings were another matter.

"My Lord, may I have a moment to offer our most recent update."

"Yes, Priest, what do we have today? Has she settled any more from her operation?"

"She is much calmer now than before. That poor child was in a terrible fret when we told her we might need to amputate."

"It would seem the Avariel place a great amount of value in their wings as part of their identity. What about the unguent, is it working?"

"Yes, her body is responding very nicely to it. We're seeing a steady development of new growth. We think she should be fully restored by the end of this next week."

"And her medicine?"

"She has been very good at taking it. Once we explained how the regeneration unguent works, she became less agitated at losing her wings due to the amount of damage they held, and now she is watching the results as they redevelop. I think as time progresses, she will become more at ease, and perhaps even a bit anxious at seeing her new wings."

"That would be a pleasing sight, indeed. But next I must wonder about her plumage. Her wings may regrow, but I would imagine her plumage will take time to restore itself."

"Those are my thoughts as well. Just as hair takes time to grow after it has been cut, feathers should also take time to replenish themselves. I wonder how long this might take in her case."

"This actually brings an important thought to my mind. I would wish to return her back to her people as soon as possible, but I would also like to give an appropriate presentation. I wonder if we could call in a druid from the Grove District for some advice. Perhaps Shescellaie might be able to offer us a shortcut."

"Now that's an interesting idea. I will see to it right away."

The priest bows and leaves the room.

Aerlie had been lying in her bed since the day she arrived. The infection had become so severe, especially in her wings, that it had developed gangrene. The only solution was a partial amputation. But fortunately, Thaelyn and his people had developed that unguent several decades before, at the request of Adalon to spur some of their medical development, and this was now offering her new hope.

As the current week passed into the next, Aerlie watched her new wings grow until the priests halted the treatment when the growth matched the original progression for her age. Her body would take it from here as she continued to grow and mature naturally. But as expected, her plumage was missing, so her wings were just bare skin so far. The only feathers she still held intact were a few near her body. In time, she was ready to be released, so a druid was brought in for a visit.

"Greetings, Child," she announces. "How do you feel today?"

"I'm much better now, thank you. Are you the druid they spoke of?"

"Yes, I am. My name is Priestess Myanis."

Aerlie studied the odd-looking woman with her tribal attire made of natural leaf and bark adornments over a leather vest and leggings.

The priestess wore a wreath of vines on her head and a necklace of wooden charms.

"You look like an elf, I think."

"I am," she smiles. "I'm called a Wood Elf. My people choose to live among the trees and forests of the natural world."

"Yeah, and it looks like you carry some of it with you," she grins softly. "But why are you here in the city?"

"I am here because I choose to serve His Lordship and his Order. It's regarded as an honor to serve under him, and I am very happy to leave my home to come here. I make my home here in a part of the city we call the Grove District. It's a very lovely area filled with trees and plants, vines, and flowers. Everything is filled with life. Would you like to go see it? We were thinking it would be healing for you to visit the grove and speak to Shescellaie."

"Who is Shesa…Shesesla…" Aerlie winces at the complex name.

The druid laughs softly.

"Shescellaie… She is the dryad queen who lives in the grove here within the city."

"A dryad queen? My mother once told me a story about dryads, but I always thought it was just a story. Are you saying they're real?"

"Of course they are! And she is their Queen, come to share her teachings with our people and promote a finer way of life, bonding our people together in harmony with the natural world."

"You're talking about elves, right? Are there really so many elves that live here?"

"We have many different races that live here. Elves are one, and we have several different clans represented. We have mine, the High Elves are another, and we have a few more after that. Then we have the humans, we also have dwarves, we have halflings and also gnomes."

"That's a lot of people. How do you get all those into one city?"

"We are not just one city. We are a nation. We occupy most of the northern half of the continent by now, including part of the Sea of Stars, where we also found relations with the Alu society who live within the sea itself."

"The what that lives in the sea?"

"They are another race of elves that live in the sea. Some people call them Water Elves. They make their homes under the sea. For a long time, they kept mostly to themselves, feeling so different that they could not associate with anyone else."

"How are they different? This actually sounds a little familiar now, after something my mother told me once about our people."

"Quite possibly. We recall a history of your kind. Yours and the Alu are very similar for this point. For one thing, they have gills, much like a fish, and this allows them to breathe underwater. Though they also have lungs like us to breathe air. But this difference made them feel alone, so they kept to themselves, with only a minimal amount of interaction, perhaps with a few coastal communities that might make occasional trade with them. But once Lord Thaelyn began to spread his teachings to the people, he made contact with them and negotiated his treaties and alliances. Now they are joining us as a part of our nation."

"A nation of so many people?" Aerlie mutters. "And so many different kinds of people! But how come we…well, no, forget it. We never go out to see anything, so we wouldn't know about you."

"Why not?"

"Our Patriarch forbids us to go outside our mountain home. He says it's too dangerous, and the human societies near us aren't nice. Now I understand why, after all this," she glances at her new wings. "But it's like nothing out there is nice, and we have to hide from all of it."

"Interesting, but your kind is also known to hold this same aversion, much like the Alu. The rest of us recall the history of our people, all of us, as we all go by the name Tel'Quessir. This is who we are, and have always been, even from before we first arrived in these lands. But there is an earlier history, from even before this. This is where such as yours and the Alu first came to be, and it became a bit unfortunate after a while."

"Why is that? What happened?"

"Each of you found special favor in a very unique god. And

this changed who you were, on the outside…" she points at Aerlie's wings, "…as well as inside…" the druid taps a finger on her head. "Due to this, you took up attitudes of superiority for your favoritism with your special gifts."

"Uh oh… We did?"

"Yes, unfortunately. The rest of us recall this, though it is very old history by now. For you, your goddess gave your people, who were once much like the rest of us, the ability to fly, so you could take up homes in places the rest of us might find difficult to live in, such as the high mountains we couldn't otherwise reach. And the Alu, with their god, for the sea. But this was not intended to make you better than us. It was only to give you a different home that others could not use themselves. The rest was all you, taking up your attitudes and feeling yourselves so special for the gift. Here is where you separated yourselves from the rest, thinking you didn't belong any longer."

"Oh dear. I'm sorry. I didn't know this history. It must be really old, and maybe we forgot about it."

"Likely so, as it was forgotten by many people, until our Lord Thaelyn helped us by rediscovering some old relics of our past which reminded us. Now, we are changing the world around us, so that we will better understand who we are and where we are going together. Because we ARE going somewhere…together!"

"We are?" she asks hesitantly.

"Well, yes. For as long as we all live on this one world, we are going somewhere together…within this single environment of a world we live in. And like it or not, your people are a part of it, as are the Alu, and all the others. So, we may as well learn to like it, and unite our people as one big society. It makes the journey so much more interesting," she smiles.

"Oops! That sounds serious."

"It is. This world needs to come together in harmony, because there is a future waiting for us, and likely as anything, it'll go well beyond this one world. But fighting with each other every step of the way won't help us find it."

"I, um…well, if you say so. This is a little strange for me."

"Perhaps. We had to learn this lesson a long time ago, so for us, we are born into it now. But anyway, where do you live? It cannot be anywhere near to us, so it must be more to the east, I think."

"I…uh…" she hesitates. "I don't know if I can say. I don't know where I am now or how I got here."

"Then perhaps what we need to do is go see His Lordship and try to find your home. We need to bring you back somehow, so we must try to understand this."

"Yes, I suppose. But how can you do this? We were chased… um…" she cuts herself off.

"Chased?" the priestess wonders. "Chased by who?"

"Nothing… This is why we live up in the mountains away from everyone."

"Are you hiding from someone?"

"There's no place for us to hide, except inside caves. But this is only when they come, and there's nothing anyone can do about it."

"Child, what is it you want to say? I feel you are keeping something inside of you."

"Nothing, forget it," she turns away from the conversation.

"You are filled with pain. I can see this now. Very well, perhaps you do not feel comfortable speaking of it now, but you cannot hide it forever. There must come a time for you to let it out."

"The Patriarch just tells me to be silent about it."

"Uh huh, that Patriarch again. The same one who never lets you go out to see the world, or what WE have done to it. Well, your Patriarch is not here with you…I am. And by the sound of it, he must have already given up, and is dragging you down with him. He might also be a prime example of what I just spoke of, that attitude that keeps you away from things."

Aerlie turns to look up into the priestess's calming eyes. She feels a subtle hint of release, and this caused her to ask herself if maybe there could actually be someone out there that would listen to her people's call for help. But she still felt the burden of what they might ask in return, and she knew the Patriarch of her village would only argue about it.

"Come," the priestess urges. "Let us go visit the tree. You will feel better for it."

She and Aerlie both got up and walked outside. Aerlie started taking notice of the city features again, now being more alert and able to focus her attention to it. They walked along the avenue, passing by people, many of whom turned to look at the odd visitor with the bare wings. It made Aerlie feel a little uneasy, being the center of so much attention.

They continued along to another district where the local culture changed the architectural designs dramatically. Rather than a series of prim stone and wood buildings, now it was more organic, with many large trees offering their own support for homes and shops built right into the natural undergrowth. Aerlie stopped and stared at it.

It seemed the entire neighborhood was a living entity. The fragrances drifting along were invigorating. The area seemed to be dominated by wood elves as the common resident, but there were many other tourists passing through from other parts of the city.

In the center of the main plaza was a large tree with a huge umbrella canopy offering shade and comfort to a circle of six smaller trees of a somewhat similar nature. Several people were sitting around the tree in conversation, while others passed among the local venues.

"Incredible," Aerlie mumbles. "It's just like the story my mother told me. Is that it?"

"Yes. Come, let's go sit and see if we can call the Grove Mother out. I think she will be very happy to see you."

"Me?" she retracts impulsively. "But I'm not a wood elf, and I don't even live here."

"It doesn't matter who or what you are, or where you come from. You are a part of this world, the same as all the rest, and she would love you just as much as any of her other Children."

The priestess takes Aerlie gently by the hand and leads her closer. The nervous girl steps forward while looking up at the huge tree canopy looming overhead. They stop just in front of a short wall lining a circle around the grove. Nearby was a rack of shelves where several sets of shoes had been placed by the other visitors.

"This ground is holy to us," the priestess submits. "It's customary for us to remove our shoes here."

Aerlie glances at the priestess, and then looks down at her slippers. She bends down to remove them and stores them on the rack. The priestess then brings her forward inside the circle.

The first thing Aerlie feels as she steps inside the holy circle is a surging of warmth flooding through her body. It was surprising, and caused her to halt her advance as she struggled to understand the source of it. The sensation quickly brought her attention to the large tree in front of her. She then followed the priestess another few steps, there to stop, where they both knelt and offered a gesture of devotion with their hands. The gesture involved making a triangle with their thumbs and first fingers and lifting this over their heart, then their mouth, finally their forehead and waving it past their heads. The priestess now drew Aerlie off to the side to sit in a clearing.

"Good, now wait here while I call her. I think she is expecting you."

"Why? Am I so strange in this city that everyone wants to look at me?"

"Aerlie, again with that attitude? I thought we covered that already."

"I'm sorry, it must be something old, like a habit."

"Indeed!" she giggles softly. "And how old are you? You look like you are only a few decades by now. I must ask myself what your parents are like. I can only guess your anxiety is caused by being so isolated up there in your mountain retreat, maybe with your Patriarch filling you with so much nonsense. But the rest of the world does not regard you as a freak. Well, perhaps I should modify that, given where we found you. We here do not. Among other things, we have a history that tells us of the bravery and heroism of the Avariel. But then you vanished, and no one knew what happened to you. It's not our fault. Your people seem to have chosen this."

"History? Wait, are you speaking of the battle?"

"Yes, the last time any of us knew of your kind was at the great battle at the Temple of the Protector, where you fought off three dragons in a desperate hope to save the nations. We have not forgotten our Brothers and Sisters of the Wing."

"Brothers and Sisters? You call us Brothers and Sisters? But... um..."

"But, um, what, Aerlie?" she asserts firmly. "Do you recall what I said a short while ago about our people...ALL our people, being the Tel'Quessir, which literally means 'The People,' and this dates back to the old Fey world of our ancestral home. And this does also include yours, as the Aril clan was one of those to colonize this world."

"We did?"

"Oh please, you don't even recall this much?" she shrugs and sets her hands on her hips. "Where did all of your historical books disappear to?"

"I, uh, don't know. Probably lost somewhere along the way. But wait, my father is a scholar and a historian. Maybe I can ask him when I get home again."

"Yes, do this. He probably missed a lesson or two. But after your people vanished, we worried for you, as we never heard anything to come after."

"Yeah, this is where we had those other problems."

"Uh huh, the ones you don't want to talk about?"

"Well... Please, I can't say anything right now. Maybe if I can tell the Patriarch about all this, he can be the one to do it. He's the one to speak for our village."

"Very well. Just remember, whatever the world used to be in the olden days, it is not that way now. The nation we are building is based on a very different philosophy, given to us by our Lord Thaelyn. His purpose is to bring us together, as this is what the world is intended to do, not what it was doing. Now, allow me to call the Grove Mother. Let us see if she has anything special to say about this wondrous occasion."

The priestess steps up to the tree and lays a hand on it, then speaks in an odd dialect of Old Elvish to summon the spirit within. A moment later, she steps away and kneels.

The tree begins to deform, first with what appears as a face protruding out from the trunk, followed by a neck and shoulders. Aerlie gazes at the strange entity trying to extract itself from its host. An arm comes out and lays a hand on the trunk as support, followed by the other one, and then a leg. The entity pulls itself free, borrowing material from the tree itself to form a feminine body that takes on a shape roughly approximating that of an elf, and covered only in natural foliage and smooth bark.

Shescellaie was now an independent body. She turned and slowly sauntered along as she approached the mesmerized young girl who seemed frozen in her gaze, then to crouch down in front of her.

Aerlie found herself staring into the eyes of a creature she previously thought was a myth. More and more, she was learning about the world around her, and it was apparently much different from the old stories she once heard when she was little.

The dryad reached out a hand to caress Aerlie's face, sending soothing waves into the girl's body, and peaceful bliss washing through her thoughts. Aerlie closed her eyes as she entered a dreamlike state.

The other people in the area had begun to gather around at the amazing sight, not simply of Aerlie and her wings, and not simply that she was in communion with the dryad, but that something extraordinary was occurring while Aerlie seemed to be in a quiet trance. Her otherwise naked wings were growing feathers.

Slowly but persistently, her bare wings were covering up with white down. This further developed as numerous quills began to extend outward along the full length of each wing. Her plumage was filling in as a curtain of pure white.

The priestess stood back and observed, while the people sitting in conversation elsewhere in the grove all stopped and now emitted oohs and ahs. The assembly gathering around outside the circle went silent while Shescellaie conducted her work at restoring Aerlie to her final natural form. When the cycle was complete, she drew back and once again caressed Aerlie's face, reviving the girl back to full alertness.

Aerlie opened her eyes feeling very relaxed, as if awaking from a deep slumber.

"Wow…that was incredible. I thought I heard singing."

"It is quite possible," the priestess beams. "She has healed you, Child. She has reunited your spirit with the harmony of nature, as you should be. This is how she restores the natural bond in someone who was born without. And I'm sure your people were without for a very long time. We all were, ever since the old Crown Wars, when much of our ancestral culture was lost to us."

"It was? But then, if this was lost to you, where did THIS come from?" she points at the tree.

"Thaelyn. He recreated this tradition as a boon to all our people, everyone, not just the elves, as we can all benefit from it the same. And it is changing our world. But more than that, look and see what she gave you."

Aerlie was puzzled by the mention, but she reflexively glanced over herself and immediately took notice of the fresh white feathery coating of her wings. She squealed in surprise, and slapped both hands over her face. She jumped to her feet and tried spreading her wings for a better look. It was everything she could hope for, but she could never have imagined it would come to her like this.

She tried testing her wings with a gentle flapping motion, to see how well they felt against the air. The lifting power felt firm to her, although they were still weak as they were only newly restored, and now she would need therapy to rebuild her strength.

A round of applause rose up from the assembled crowds, drawing Aerlie's attention to their pleasant approval. She turned back to the dryad and fell to her knees again, then reached for Shescellaie's hand to kiss it. The dryad queen soothed the girl with another caress before returning back to her home inside the tree.

❖

"My Lord, I believe she's ready,"

"Ah, Priestess Myanis, come in."

The priestess and Aerlie were on their way to see Thaelyn now. They were just entering his study to make a formal presentation and review to see about completing the request by her goddess to bring her home again. The priestess enters first, followed by Aerlie, who was distracted by the glamor of the ornately decorated office.

"Well now," Thaelyn croons. "If it is not our charming young visitor…and look how lovely she appears with her wings fully adorned!"

Aerlie's attention is broken away from the decorations by the affectionate complement. She blushes and steps forward with a bow.

"I want to thank you very much for your help. I'm sure I would have died in that cage if it weren't for you. I still can't believe my goddess would call on someone…well, from around here, to go look for me and go through all that trouble just to bring me home. I disobeyed the Patriarch, and I was sure I offended the Winged Mother as well. But I guess she didn't forget about me after all."

"The gods do not take such offence easily. You might have done wrong by travelling to places forbidden to you, but she would not leave you to your own. Now, we should see about returning you home. Can you think of anything that might offer us a clue as to the general region where you originate?"

"I don't know. I can't be sure right now."

"All right, then let us see if we can piece something together. Maybe if we were to look at a map, you might recall something out of it."

"A map? But I probably come from somewhere very far away…"

Thaelyn calls a page and directs him to find his officers to meet with him. He then leads the priestess and Aerlie out of the room and down the hall. They pass by a number of other offices until they come to the tactical room where they make many of their plans of expansion and other important movements, and whether to devise political treaties or wartime assaults. They arrange themselves around a large table while Thaelyn and his officers assemble. He pulls several oversized rolls of paper off a shelf and lays them out on the table.

Aerlie studies the diagrams with the highly detailed drawings on them. She had never seen a proper map in her life, as no one in her village bothered to make one. They never went anywhere, and had no interest in knowing anything about the rest of the world. And these were particularly impressive.

"Wow, what is this?"

"This is the greater portion of the continent of Sein'amar."

"Wow. It looks so big."

"Indeed, it is. Now, we need to see about where you live in all this."

"That looks like it'll be really hard. Where are we now?"

"We are in the city of Bya'an Tamoranth, which is located here adjacent to these mountains," he points to an inland location in the west about midway up along the northern half of the map. "We found you down here in Menenbahd," he moves his finger to a small nation much more to the south.

"All right, but I remember I was carried a long way before being put inside that circus. Also, that place was hot and dry compared to my home."

"I have heard your people tend to prefer high mountainous regions. Is this true?"

"Yes, and ours was kind of cool, and very cold in the winter."

"That might suggest a northern region."

"Um, the priestess here says you have a nation, how big is it?"

Thaelyn answers by circling his hand across the entire upper left quadrant of the map. Aerlie's eyes open wide, and her jaw drops.

"Our nation covers most of this territory here," Thaelyn asserts. "From the coastline eastward to the Sea of Stars, north to these mountains up here..." he points at the top of the map, which represented the upper edge of the land, "...and across to about here, so far halting just before this body," he moves his finger to another body of water. "We call this one the Moonsea, and it drains into the larger one with this river. This is where we currently draw the line on that side."

"I have heard of that name before, I think. My people call it the Sea of the Moon. And this other one, we call the Great Sea of Stars."

"These are much older terms, but if you have been out-of-contact for so long, it could be your terms are also outdated."

"Maybe. But my goodness, whatever happened to all the old nations I remember hearing about from my father and his stories."

"If your knowledge is so old by now, all that would be absorbed into what we have here. And we are not finished yet, as we still have the eastern portion, and then the other continents to the east and south."

He now repositions himself to the southern side of the larger sea.

"For instance, down here, we have made several advancements, moving through this land here, once a nation called Kordaran, and further to this one, which is our more recent acquisition, a vassal territory called Chesterly."

"A vassal territory? What does that mean?"

"It means that it is new to our nation and must undergo a period of adjustment to acclimate to our teachings, philosophies, cultural and social values, and religious doctrines. The people will slowly assimilate, one day to become full citizens."

"Oh…hmm… You do this with everyone?"

"We are trying to bring this world together into harmony with itself. It has been stagnating for far too long, with wars, corruption, intrigue, and the like. When I first arrived, I had designs to teach the people a better way of life, hoping they might realize the virtues of working cooperatively rather than competitively. In doing so, I have drawn many to my side, and together we have built all this," he waves his hand across his own territory. "We try to accomplish this peacefully, as war is most often very destructive, but there are those who have other ideas. For instance, here…"

He now moves his attention to a location on the far side of the large sea.

"Our current movements are aimed at making agreements

through this region down below, and curving up this other side. The nation of Morakane might pose some trouble, as I am aware of a number of criminal organizations and corrupt leaders in this area. Most notably is a powerful guild of elite mages who, coincidentally, have already voiced their opinion, in a manner of speaking, of their opposition to my efforts in this world."

"Oh? How did they do this? Send a messenger or something?"

"If an assassin can be called a messenger, then yes, and not just once."

"Whoops!" she yips. "They sent an assassin? Why?"

"They like their positions of power to lord over others, and I represent a threat to that, if my intention is to take over."

"Uh oh! Be careful with that. They don't sound nice at all."

"Indeed!"

"What will you do next, go to war?"

"I would not choose this of my own, but they are likely to press the need, if only to take down their grip on power. They are a potent guild who has held this position for several generations, I believe. They once took control of the local governing authority and replaced it with their own. Now they rule with a very oppressive hand. In a few ways, we can associate them with Menenbahd and their more criminal antics, where that one is ruled by a crime lord. In the case of that one, and for the amount of corruption occurring down there, I might actually take the first move. It is highly unlikely they will ever change. And yet, for any other example out there, I would prefer to make the appropriate political negotiations to see about pressing an alliance that could lead to a unification effort, rather than simply conquering things."

"This sounds like a lot of work. Is it really necessary to do all this?"

"This world must be brought together, one way or another. Therefore, I must be assertive."

"Wow, whether they like it or not."

"It actually goes along a much higher purpose than simple desire, whether on my part or theirs. This world has a destiny ahead of it.

Whether any one particular leader chooses to see it, it is still there. If they do not wish to admit to it today, I can wait, but the time will ultimately come when it must occur. It is preordained. I am simply following my Fate."

"Following a Fate? Is this to say the gods demand it or something?"

"In a word, yes, one in particular who started this as a personal project, and I am a part of that project. I once learned my presence in this world is not by accident, and neither are my movements."

"Oh dear, so you're saying you hold some kind of holy purpose to do all this?"

"I suppose that might be one way of saying it. There is a book that was written once with a series of prophecies. They seem to describe what I am doing now. And it was written by someone who carries the same authority as that goddess who commanded it. She and I are now working together on this."

"By the Winged Mother," she whispers. "Just where did all this come from..."

Aerlie sighed heavily and shook her head at the thought of a man following a purpose that could go so far as to bring the whole world together. This naturally brought her thoughts back to her people. How would they fit in, or would they fit in at all?

"Now, moving further along," Thaelyn continues. "We will eventually bring ourselves full circle back to this range of mountains," he points to an area just opposite the smaller sea from before. "The last of these regions might be tricky, as I have word telling me the kingdoms that live here are rather conceited."

"Conceited? How so?"

"Being so far removed from the rest, they seem to have developed their own manners. Take this one here, the nation of Inakarta..."

Instantly, Aerlie perks up at the mention of the name.

"Inakarta! Wait, I know that name!"

Thaelyn jerks up from the map to look at her.

"You do? What do you know of it? Is it near your home, perhaps?"

"I remember hearing that name once, it's one of the kingdoms we tried asking for help, but they ignored us, instead they just lied and cheated us."

"What did they lie to you about? And what sort of help were you asking for?"

"Um…well…" she dithers. "We don't ask anyone anymore. But one time, we were, and they were nearby, so we tried, and it didn't go well. There was another one, also."

"Another… But you do not wish to tell me what this was about?"

"It doesn't matter now. The Patriarch won't go out asking anyone else."

"Your Patriarch…I see."

"My Lord," the priestess interjects. "If I may, she was speaking of something earlier, but she seems reluctant to reveal it fully. I feel she is hiding something delicate, and it seems to have manifested itself in their opinions of the outside world. An opinion I think has been exaggerated since that ancient battle and the manners her kind once held for everyone else."

"Manners?"

"We have an expression," Aerlie offers. "Holding our wings high. She's speaking of our…attitude of superiority…because we have a special goddess who gave us special gifts."

"Ah, that," he chuckles softly. "Perhaps a little like the Aluerea and their life in the sea? Very well, but Aerlie, you should know, if you had dealings with these people, they are certainly NOT the sort of people you might find satisfaction with. Furthermore, they do not represent the rest of the world."

"All right, I'm sorry," she offers. "I seem to be saying that a lot around here. We have stories told by our ancestors, and they speak of a very different world."

"Perhaps so, and that world was indeed a different place, and precisely the reason for my involvement. But with my arrival, we intend to change that world. The main difficulty here being it is a process that takes time, if only due to so much of it out there. Nevertheless, we should try to understand the relationship here. Do you know where these nations are in relation to you?"

"Yes, this much I can help on. One kingdom was to our south, the other to the east. We live in a big range of mountains."

Thaelyn and his officers reference the map again.

"Here, my Lord," the Captain offers. "This has to be it."

"Yes, and just across in front of our line... A few or several years, maybe as much as a decade, and we might have found them anyway...this large set of mountains, where Inakarta is just to the south, and this other one, Gamaska, is to the east."

"Gamaska?" Aerlie muses. "That sounds familiar too."

"Good, then we have a target. We should send some people out there to confirm this for us."

"My Lord," the priestess offers. "May I suggest something in this regard?"

"Of course, what is it?"

"If she is any example, by our earlier interactions, I am going to make an assumption that her people have become very xenophobic in this time. Their isolation, perhaps compounded by their poor relations with their neighbors, may have caused them to become very distrustful of outsiders. If we send anyone in, I might suggest them to be very careful to observe but not to disturb them."

"This is reasonable, but it also presents us with a problem...how to return her home without causing our own disturbance."

"I'm not sure how to answer that, other than to avoid any large-scale deployments. Perhaps simply to keep it small and unobtrusive."

"Indeed. Then we should first observe and see what we have to work with, and perhaps I can simply go in alone, maybe on horseback with her riding along behind me."

"That might actually work well for us."

The meeting breaks and Thaelyn sends a series of scouts into the region to investigate the area and report back. Many days pass as the scouts ride through the region, first arriving on horseback, and then proceeding on foot until they can catch sight of the Avariel village. Eventually, they begin to see the remnants of a village setting in the distance within the canyon, although it doesn't represent anything connected to any of the other local population centers.

"See there," directs one scout. "Where's the scope at?"

"Here you go, mate."

They peer through their scopes to see people moving around among the buildings.

"I see a lot of wings out there."

"Aye, that must be the one then, all alone up here, tucked away where no one seems interested in travelling. Poor blokes, I wonder how long they've been there."

"From the looks of that village, it can't be much. There's not enough out there to hold up to a rat's nest. This must be the lower end of it."

"Lower end or not, it must be the one. There's nothing else out here. Let's mark a rune where we are, and then turn in."

"Aye..."

The scout pulls out a rune stone and casts an enchantment on it. A swirling spiral of energy spins up around him, then inverts and funnels down into the stone in his hand, causing it to glow briefly. He puts it away on his belt and pulls out another one, enchanting it to allow the two of them to return back home.

Thaelyn and Aerlie reconvene back in the guildhall. She had been given temporary lodging within the guild until they could locate her people, but now the time was upon them to take her home. A horse was being prepared outside, and the rune leading to the site was ready with a mage to enchant it. Aerlie eyes the bulky creature in front of her as the squires prepare the saddle and reigns.

"And you want me to sit on that thing and ride it?" she asks tenuously.

"You have never ridden a horse before?"

"We don't have any, and besides, um..." she flaps her wings emphatically for demonstration.

"Of course," he smiles. "I suppose that is a given."

They mount up with Aerlie taking up behind Thaelyn and wrapping her arms around him for support.

Once again, she felt a strange sensation come into her as she made physical contact. Her nervous tension soothed, and she was suddenly much more at ease, causing her to lean her head against him, at least until they began to move.

Thaelyn also felt something, and he briefly laid his hand against hers wrapping around his waist. But again, his mind was on his duty, trying to imagine the interaction he would soon enter into with her people. This represented a new political contact, but on this occasion, it would be with people thought to be extinct, and to make matters worse, they had likely developed isolationist disorders.

"Mage, are we ready?"

"Yes, my Lord, on your word."

"Excellent, open it up."

The mage cast his enchantment on the rune, this time in an upright orientation which created a projected aperture. Thaelyn brought his horse around and made ready to jump through it.

Aerlie studied the magical conjuration. She was fascinated by the creation of the strange apparition. In the time she had been visiting these people, she had been trying to study and learn a few of their ways, and one thing she noticed early on was the proliferation of magic everywhere.

Thaelyn oriented his horse and gave a command. The horse lined itself up with the aperture, having been specially trained for such occasions, and trotted forward, picking up speed, and then leaping through the circular hole in space.

Aerlie watched as the envelope of light surrounded them in a quick flash, then to dissipate, allowing the new scenery to emerge. She recognized it immediately. She perked her head up to survey the area and automatically turned to find her village.

"That way," she points. "I can find it easily from here."

"Very good. I will bring you in and deliver you to your home personally. Perhaps I might also be able to say hello and offer my greetings to your people. You should not allow yourselves to be as isolated as you are up here. The world is changing, Aerlie. It is not as you once remember it to be. If my purpose is to unite everyone, this includes you as well."

"I know this now, but the Patriarch is a little bit stubborn. I get in a lot of trouble with him for always complaining about things."

"Really! Well, now…how might you be so fortunate," he chuckles.

They make their way in casually so as not to incur any anxiety with the locals. They crossed the hilly terrain, closing in on the village, until the sights became more pronounced in their eyes. Thaelyn studied the dilapidated nature of the construction and generally poor arrangement of structures and landscaping.

"Aerlie, is it my eyes, or are your people actually in such an impoverished state?"

"Um, I don't know how to answer that right now, please. I can already hear the people talking about us coming in, and there are a lot of words going around."

"Are you speaking rhetorically, or can you actually hear them from this distance?"

"We have very good eyes and ears. I can actually hear them, even though we're not inside the village yet."

"Interesting… That represents a fine talent."

They continued the rest of the way as the people were clearly taking up positions along the roadway watching the unusual visitors just now arriving. As they make their way into the relative center of the village, Thaelyn brings the horse to a halt, and then helps Aerlie step down.

Amavain and her husband both rush into the village center when they see Aerlie getting off the horse. She takes the girl into her arms for a tight embrace with tears rolling down her cheeks.

"Aerlie, I was so worried for you!" she sobs. "Where did you go, and what happened to you?"

"Mother, that's a really long story, and a lot of it isn't good."

"How typical!" the Patriarch huffs as he glances up at Thaelyn. "And what price do you demand for bringing this young child back?"

"Let me guess," Thaelyn muses. "You are the local Patriarch, am I right? Perhaps you would wish to indulge in a more appropriate form of greeting, rather than simply accuse me of a wrongdoing I have not yet committed?"

"Oh! My apologies…" he emits sardonically. "I am indeed the Patriarch of this village, my name is Daeselri."

"Very good, my name is Lord Thaelyn, and I offer good greetings to you. My impression is that you do not receive a great many visitors up here, not that it surprises me, as you are rather far afield."

"It's that way for a reason. We don't trust land-walkers like you."

"How interesting. Should I interpret this term as one of disdain for those who are so unfortunate not to possess wings? Most people are like this, you know. In fact, to my better knowledge, the Avariel are rather unique that they do in fact have wings as compared to the more common form of life in this world, including the other elven societies."

"Really! And does this make you so superior because you number so many?"

"Does the name Tel'Quessir mean anything to you, or have you forgotten the master name for ALL your people. And there are a great many. And this is a rather old name, to my knowledge."

"Old, perhaps, but I would hardly describe ourselves to belong to any of that by now."

"This is a curious statement. One to which we have had conversations about in the past. You know, the rest always DID regard you to be a part of it, but your own behaviors very often suggested something else. They speak of how you often held a rather lofty attitude that you were once blessed with the most extraordinary, and highly unusual gift of wings, and by a goddess that tends to specialize in such things, as opposed to all the rest who still offer their service to the Seldarine."

"Uh huh, and I suppose this makes us freaks in your eyes?"

"This is a rather subjective term. Would one describe a bird as a freak for its wings? Would one describe a fish as a freak for its ability to breathe water? What about an insect for how many legs it has? The natural world has many curious and fascinating creatures in it, and not a single one can be called any more freakish than those of us with such attitudes that we must rise above the rest."

"Ouch…" Aerlie giggles softly as she watches the show.

Both her parents, along with many others in the village, gazed at Thaelyn for his clever responses, which were matching the Patriarch one-for-one and his accusations.

Thaelyn continues, "Quite realistically, Patriarch, yours is but one of a great many who live in this world, most of whom are not your own. We number so many because we account for the remainder of the world's population. You do recall there is a world out there, do you not?"

"We do," he snaps. "Not that it ever helped us for simply knowing about it."

"Knowing about it, and participating in it, are two different things. Aerlie mentioned a word or two about some interactions you had once. While I may feel sorrow for your troubles, your woes are not due to me and mine. You simply turned the wrong direction outside of this valley. My people are to the west of here, a large nation of them."

"Oh, so you're saying you're somehow better than those to the south and east. How nice. Maybe you could make your own diversion and tell them how displeased we are for our...past interactions."

"I may just do that, if not for your sake, then for my own reasons. But as for the rest, I might also suggest, your isolation up here is not my doing. You chose this for yourselves. Had you remained with the rest of the world, I think your history might be recorded a bit differently."

"Ah, but of course. So, rather than simply being cheated and lied to, we might be what...enslaved, perhaps?"

"My dear Ariler, kindly do not put words in my mouth that do not belong there. The remainder of the world records a history of your kind with some rather unpleasant attitudes due to your privileged status as flighted beings. THAT is not polite, when the rest of us do not have this. And it is further demonstrated by that word you used just now. If this is your attitude for everyone else, this is not our doing, but yours. So, unless you are personally knowledgeable of anything else out there, you do not hold a right to judge it. Yours is a rather dogmatic position when you isolate yourselves up here and then scorn the rest of the world for woes you essentially created for yourselves."

"What would you know of our woes!" the Patriarch shouts. "And what would you care, unless it somehow puts coin in your pocket?"

"And here we have the mention of coin again. I may not know the specifics of your woes, good Patriarch, other than you ran away from us for whatever reason motivated you. We hold no history of you after the battle at the Temple of the Protector. Whatever came after was outside our view. So, unless you would wish to share these stories with me, I might suggest you hold your tongue where my own motivations are concerned. Did I even once mention coin where this young child is concerned, or did you simply begin by spitting your venom at me?"

"All right!" Amavain shouts. "Daeselri, enough! Your rage is only going to make trouble here. Bring those pompous wings of yours down. He's right. You are the worst example of our people. Our ancestors locked themselves away up here and hid from anyone who might otherwise bring help to us. We had to stay with those nations, not run away from them. But those fools of our ancestors just couldn't bring their aristocratic bigotry down out of the clouds long enough to admit we needed their support. And you would dare blame THEM for not even knowing about it?"

"Amavain," he responds sharply. "We DID tell them about it, two of those nations, and look where it got us."

"That isn't what I'm talking about. We ran away to hide our losses, and this was long before any of the rest of it hit us."

The Patriarch scowled at her, but deep down, he knew this was actually true. Their fear of appearing weak came long before the dragon attacks.

"Patriarch," Aerlie interjects. "I learned those two nations are probably the WORST nations out there, all because they're way out here in the middle of nowhere, and away from the rest where no one bothers them. And unfortunately, these are our neighbors."

"Aerlie, it's all the same, I'm quite sure."

"Including all those nations we once tried to save at that old battle? Do you think they would just say, 'Thank you for losing half your population, now go hide up there in those mountains and don't come back?' That's what you're saying here, you know?"

Amavain laid a gentle hand on Aerlie's shoulder as she stepped forward through the crowd to give her own address.

"My apologies, Your Lordship… Clearly, our past dealings have left their mark upon us, some more than others," she glares at Daeselri. "I'm Aerlie's mother…and I for one am very happy you brought her back safely to us."

"But of course, Madam," Thaelyn smiles and nods. "And it is in fact a fine pleasure for me to do so. She is a lovely and very pleasant young lady, though a bit inexperienced in anything outside these mountains…much like the rest of you, I would suspect."

"Yes, I think by now, we could say that."

"I had anticipated a rough introduction on my arrival, if for no other reason than your people being so isolated and perhaps out of practice in your social graces. But I try to be patient wherever possible," he glances briefly at the Patriarch.

"Yes, our history since that old battle has been a hard one, trying to survive in these remote regions."

"There are surely more pleasant ones out there, do you think?"

"Maybe, maybe not… I don't know any more, but I doubt we could find any better peace there than up here. As for my daughter, she has been missing from us for so long. Where did you find her?"

"In a land very far from here, to the south and west, a nation called Menenbahd. It lies to the south of mine, and it is a rather unsavory place, if I must say so."

"Ah, another one!" the Patriarch announces boldly. "And is this one also so far removed as not to be a bother to anyone? Perhaps not…how unfortunate. And so, I'm not supposed to judge your human societies until I know more about them. Well, thank you for informing me of one more, and so it goes that I stand correct in my previous statements."

"For THIS occasion, perhaps, good Sir, but I said it was to the SOUTH of mine. Do try to take note of that minor clarification."

"All right, but then what relation do you have with them?"

"Unfriendly, to say the least, and I suspect, at some moment, and for multiple reasons, I may find myself at war with them one day."

"Well, isn't that a curious piece of news to come our way. So, the nations out there still fight wars."

"I might remind you of how your elven societies are no less guilty for some of theirs, and I believe the Avariel were a part of it once."

"That would be a very long time ago."

"Indeed, it would be, but do try to recall this, and not simply place blame on others for theirs alone. Yours are just as guilty as anyone else. As for the modern day, you might find it interesting to learn, there are not as many by now, as we have been uniting them together into one large body."

"Oh, so someone finally decided to bring it all together into one big lump?"

"Absolutely! After all, we certainly would not want random bands of people running off in all directions, and then blame the rest of the world for all their inherent fallacies. What fun is it when people keep making such wild accusations out of the prejudice of their antiquated beliefs."

"Oh, I'm sure that would be a terrible shame to leave unattended!"

"And naturally, I own half of them. I am a noble Duke, and my nation has been uniting virtually everything west of here."

"Wait a minute... A Duke, in the leadership of a nation? Shouldn't that be the role of a king or something?"

"Well, yes, technically, you would be correct. It began much smaller, and my advisers have been nagging me for some time now to perform the appropriate coronation. But I have been putting it off, so far, for a number of personal reasons, not the least of which would be the management of all our new acquisitions."

"Oh, I'm sure that must be a tough one."

"Anyway, we are expanding in this direction, soon to take over those errant nations near you as part of our progression. Therefore, I suspect, if it was not for your goddess directing me to find this young lady here..."

"What?!" he screeches. "Our goddess would ask YOU for something?"

"Oh, indeed!" he croons ironically. "She came before us in our temple and made a specific request to find one of her lost Children that was suffering. In exchange for this, she would offer us some of her special favor. Naturally, as we are a society that reveres the gods rather highly, this might be worth something to us. So, as for your mention of coin, I am already paid for…figuratively speaking."

"Paid for?" Amavain wheezes. "The Winged Mother called on you to help us? But, um, well, I feel I should ask this. Why you?"

"Aerlie asked this same question once. I could offer a couple of reasons. One, we hold a very tight relationship with a number of other gods, and she likely saw an opportunity in this. Two, my position as the ruler of a large and powerful nation, where we could get the job done, one way or another, and do so very efficiently. Beyond that, as they so often say, the gods work in strange ways, and my experience tells me this is certainly the case."

"Oh!" the Patriarch blasts. "Yes, naturally, they most certainly do, and all the more reason I think I wouldn't believe that preposterous statement. It would be an insult for OUR goddess to ask someone like YOU, a simple land-walker, for help."

"Well, she apparently did not ask you for it, not after running away from the world so you could blame all your woes on it later. And I doubt you would do anything even if she did, with such an attitude that everyone out there is a villain, so why bother. As for me and mine, we found her, brought her to our home city, gave her food and medicine for her ills, and then brought her back up here. And for this, I am treated like a criminal by her people, who refuse to acknowledge the wishes of their own goddess."

"Wait!" Amavain interjects anxiously. "I'm a priestess, and this man," she scowls at the Patriarch. "He's simply in a bad mood today… and every day for that matter. I, for one, believe our goddess might call for help, as our people have been suffering a lot of hardship since that battle…"

"Stifle it, Amavain!" the Patriarch orders. "He's just like all the rest, it's so obvious…such a ridiculous story."

"But Daeselri, she found him!"

"Oh yes, she did! And now he knows where we live! As if we actually needed THEM to learn of this, on top of everything else…"

"You don't understand!"

"Amavain, the only thing I need to understand is he's just another human who wants something from us, so he's putting on this fabulous show to sweettalk us into giving over whatever we still own."

"Patriarch," Thaelyn asserts. "Whatever dealings you had with those nations near you is outside my control. My nation began in the west and is still moving in this direction. It is not an easy thing to unite a world under one rule. Some nations are friendly to the idea, others are not. But as I started to say, in another few years I might be at your doorstep anyway. Then, Lo and Behold, the world might recall the great Avariel people…who are thought to be extinct by some."

"Oh really, and I'll bet you would like it that way…less for you to enslave."

"Powers help us, you are a difficult one. Perhaps I should simply drag you back to my home city and introduce you to a few of your former brethren, so you can insult THEM like you are insulting me, and let them realize just how arrogant your kind are in the flesh. They revere you for your sacrifice in that battle, but maybe you were simply hoping to be elevated to a new pedestal for display."

"A new pedestal?"

"Yes, Patriarch. They recall a history of your attitudes, and this dates back even as far as your ancient home, and it is not a kind one. And it began with this most extraordinary gift of your unique goddess, who was simply giving you a gift to occupy places the rest might not find convenient."

"Oh, is this to say to occupy places the rest don't want to occupy?"

"If we consider such as the Aluerea, who live in the sea, I think the answer is a clear yes, as most others would drown in that. As for you, many of us cannot climb mountains as easily, and yet this is a fine place to be if you have wings. It is what we call a niche environment. Something outside the mainstream that someone wants to fill."

"Uh huh. And I'm sure you would be happy if we stayed there… outside YOUR mainstream."

"You should probably direct that question to your goddess and see what she had in mind when she gave this to you. But in reference to your goddess, or any other, I hold a divine mandate to unite this world, and that means your people as well. Your goddess probably knows this, which could be the reason she came to us. But if you truly wish nothing to do with the rest, then I suppose I can simply build a wall around you in these mountains. Not that it would stop you from blaming us for anything, as your famous wings would simply allow you to pass over it, and then you may have unlimited opportunity to complain about our fine prestige and your clear lack of it," he glances at the poor living conditions around him.

"Ah, yes! Our broken village…I wonder how THAT happened."

"Without a proper explanation, I cannot answer. But in MY nation, our people are prosperous, all of them. And I, dear Patriarch, am revered as a savior to them, all of them. And this also includes elves of every sort, save the Drow. We have dwarves, gnomes, and halflings in our population as well, and our cities support each of their native traditions and cultural refinements. We are a society of laws, and slavery is illegal, as are a number of other things. Therefore, I will now advise you to hold your tongue where my people are concerned, as I am sure they would be rather upset by your statements and manners."

"He's right, Daeselri," Amavain declares. "You have no right to judge his people without first seeing them."

"Amavain," he retorts. "How could any man, especially a human, possibly hold such claim as all that! It's as ridiculous as all the rest of his stories. In fact, I wouldn't be a bit surprised if he was nothing more than a simple bard from some tawdry tavern looking for a new audience to woo."

"I swear, Daeselri…" she moans.

"Indeed, Madam," Thaelyn offers. "I might have to agree. Aerlie once mentioned the words 'holding one's wings high', so this must be a most noteworthy example."

"You have no idea..." she shakes her head.

"As to this last statement, in the absence of any of YOU doing it, elf or otherwise, I was delivered to do it for you. And I doubt it really matters what race I belong to if I can rally the people to follow me. The elves existed in this world for thousands of years. And for all your pompous attitudes of superiority, you never achieved anything from it. Maybe you were simply too content to live your meager lives in a Dark Age. But there are those who may desire more, and if you cannot do it, they will. And they will likely drag you along with it."

"Do we get a choice?" the Patriarch asks curtly.

"Not if you want to continue living in this world. If the purpose is to unite everything, this is also to say, you will not tolerate separatists. And your statement of corruption and war is the reason for it. Now..." he takes a deep breath hoping to collect himself. "Perhaps if I were to directly ask about these woes of yours, since you are so adamant to proclaim my ignorance as such a misery. Aerlie seemed hesitant to say anything, so I must assume this runs deep."

"Don't bother yourself!" the Patriarch states brashly. "We had others turn us down, and I seriously doubt you and your prestigious nation of so many rich citizens would bother soiling themselves to come all the way over here for anything. Oh, and I should probably include our...goddess...that she would compensate you for it adequately enough. Offering her...favor...to solve our woes would probably not meet up to the challenges you would have to face. Surely, as a noble Duke, rather than a king, and with SUCH a fabulous nation as you proclaim, if all you have is a simple horse to bring this girl back, I must wonder what kind of 'favor' you got out of it," he smirks disdainfully.

"Daeselri!" Amavain gasps in astonishment. "I can't believe..."

"Amavain, I am speaking here, if you don't mind. You have your child back, and that should satisfy your need. If he says he got his payment out of it already, let's just hope she doesn't carry any diseases along the way."

"You would dare!" she huffs fiercely.

"Indeed, dear Patriarch," Thaelyn leans forward in his saddle. "That was uncalled for with this young child. And I must admit, I am growing quite weary of your attitude as well, which is not an easy thing to come about in my case. While I cannot speak for this woman, or any of these others who may be listening to this tirade, I feel a little civility would go a long way. As for my presentation, would you rather I bring my army up here instead, or would that disturb you too much for your privacy in these mountains?"

"Oh, but naturally, he has an army. How could I miss that? But as a noble Duke, why aren't you travelling with at least a guard of some kind? I thought people like you didn't go outside without something to protect you from all the bad things out there."

"I suppose you do hold a valid point for this much, as many nobles have a history of this. But then, many of them do not use portals as extensively as we do. Therefore, the road up here was only from that side canyon to this point. I think I can manage that much on my own."

"Portals? Well, now, that's a fine one! So, you simply pop out of a hole in the air and here you are. And how do you expect to get back home? I don't see your mage travelling with you."

"I am a mage, Patriarch, and a rather adept one, at that. I am also a soldier, a scholar, and a symbol of leadership to all that I meet. I chose to arrive independently due to Aerlie's aversion to so many things out there, and the suspicion she must have gotten it from somewhere. Therefore, to be discreet."

"You got that much right!" Aerlie asserts as she glares at the Patriarch.

"And if you are so dissatisfied with my immediate presentation, perhaps I could offer a small demonstration. This village over here, for instance… These structures appear as though they were reduced to splinters, and then reassembled using little more than ear wax.

As a noble Duke, to say the least, and someone you have never met before to hold any right to judge, perhaps I can offer assistance."

"Oh! Yes! Here it comes," he bellows. "He's making an offer we simply cannot refuse. And no doubt it involves providing so many luxurious goods and materials as to lift us up nearly as high as his people. But does he know why our homes are splinters? No, I suppose not, if by his own words we vanished from the world without a trace and now they think we're extinct. No doubt, like so many others, they would much rather keep away from us, or else possibly see their own homes turned to splinters. And once again, I suspect he will send the bill to our goddess, who is so generous that she will grant him more of her favor for helping us. Such a fascinating line, it almost makes you think he holds a personal relationship with them up there. My goodness, how the world has changed..."

"Daeselri..." Amavain groans tensely. "If you hold any respect to the Winged Mother..."

"Amavain, I lost my respect for her a good century ago. And in fact, I didn't really hold that much to begin with, not after listening to you and others spouting off so many promises that went unfulfilled. Now I simply want this charlatan out of our home. My dear Duke," he redirects derisively. "I regret to say, but I simply must refuse this offer. Thank you very much, and I hope my improved civility meets with your pleasure. Now, I must return to my other duties, so I will ask you to kindly take yourself back to this great nation of yours, with all your rich citizens. Oh, and say hello to our goddess the next time you meet. I'm sure she will love to share more of her... favor...with you for this little excursion you made up here...all alone out in the wilds."

Thaelyn straightens up with a minor scowl on his face. He was not entirely surprised at the reaction, as so many of these statements reflected on him being a Celestial and the activities he had performed largely outside their view of the world. Nonetheless, he was still displeased by the Patriarch's complete lack of leniency to at least give him an opportunity to prove himself.

He briskly surveyed the rest of the crowd, seeing many who didn't appear in total agreement with the Patriarch, judging from their expressions. But it was moot, as their Patriarch apparently held a dominating role here. So, he pulls out his rune stone and enchants it for an immediate return.

"What's that?" the Patriarch asks urgently.

"This, Patriarch, is what we use to open portals. Our full society is learning magic, and it is changing the world…one you apparently choose not to believe in, and neither to participate in. But Patriarch, even as an elf, you are a mortal creature. Perhaps one day your successor will be more permissive, and we can try again."

"Uh huh…and no doubt YOU will return back up here for the occasion. Well, if you think you can live for the next few centuries to meet my successor, you're welcome to try, human."

"We shall see, Ariler. But I think it will not be measured in centuries. The border of my territory is just the other side of the Moonsea over yon, and soon to surround you. And I suspect, somewhere along the way, there will be another occasion when my service to your goddess will come around. No doubt, it relates to this grievance you have up here that no one wants to tell me about. And I will indeed be sure to tell her how genteel your welcome was on this occasion. She might find it interesting to know…if she does not already."

Thaelyn leans down and gently wraps a hand under the horse's neck, issuing a soft command to prepare it, then slaps the rune to the side, sending both him and his mount back home. The sudden flash startled many of the people in the near proximity, especially the Patriarch.

"Hmm…" he mumbles privately. "Maybe he was a mage after all. Well, I know their kind as well, and they're just as bad for their own greed."

"You FOOL!!" Amavain spits. "Do you have any idea what you've done?"

"What are you talking about? I simply sent that madman away."

"Yes, you sent away our potential salvation! Aerlie brought him here for a reason. He could've been the one to save us, but your arrogance may have just cursed us to oblivion!"

"You're not making sense, Amavain. What do you mean our salvation? He was another accursed human charlatan, that's all. And how could this child of yours know anything?"

"Damn you! That's why she's here. She was given to us to save our people…but you! You just couldn't allow him to finish his statements before you had to barge in with your narrow-minded intolerance. It's no wonder the Winged Mother told me to keep silent. She probably considers you to be completely unworthy to know of her plan. May you be cursed for this, Daeselri! Cursed like you have just cursed the rest of us."

She turns abruptly and storms away.

"What?" he calls after her. "What is this talk now about the Winged Mother?"

Amavain halts and turns back sharply.

"She gave me Aerlie to bring our salvation back to us, and you just sent it away. I was told to keep silent, but Aerlie is her Chosen One to save our people…or was supposed to be. That's why I was told to go out in the woods to find her. She was delivered to us."

"Delivered to us to bring a human back? You must be joking!"

"Who lived in this blessed world before our people intruded into it, Daeselri? I'll give you a hint, it wasn't elves. So if anyone is to be a savior, it'll probably be the ones who were first granted life in this place. Nevertheless, does it actually matter who she brings back, if he holds such authority as to rule a nation? Daeselri, I was told a number of secrets out there, most of which I'm not permitted to share with you. But if that man was indeed the one she was supposed to bring back, then I think you should've paid a little more attention to what he was saying about this great nation uniting the world and everything he did for it. Because it sounds to me like he might be a substantially higher grade of…human…than those mongrels to the south. Even more, that he's doing this to everyone, whether they like it or not, if only to stop all the wars out there. And I do know there were a lot of them out there at one time. Remember, my husband is a historian," she thumbs energetically at Lafron.

The Patriarch simply grimaced at her as she finished her statement. He then passed his glance around at the others, many of whom were now glaring at him for his clearly prejudiced perspective.

"And furthermore," Amavain continues. "It seems clear they don't even know we exist up here. I would have to agree with him, as well as others. We ran away and made ourselves vulnerable to those dragons, at least as much for our opinionated attitudes of our wings as our vanity for losing so many people in that old battle. Had we stayed with the rest, we would have THEIR armies at our backs to fight those dragons. And I think they would've fought for it if they held us so high for our valor."

"Oh, you think so?" he retorts. "When was the last time, Dear Amavain, whose husband is a historian, that any of us actually won a victory…in direct contest, that is…with even ONE dragon, to say nothing of three?"

"In direct contest? But do you mean other than that temple battle?"

"Yes, but also to the death…of the dragon, I mean. Not simply to chase them away because they probably became bored at swatting flies."

"Well, um…" she flusters.

"I wish to offer something here," Lafron emits as he steps forward.

They all turn to him as he continues.

"I recall a curious mention in one of my early lessons as a child from my father. I found myself searching not long ago to see if I could refresh myself on the details."

"What details were those," the Patriarch wonders.

"Though there were many battles, and they often resulted in the loss of some of our people, and this includes elves, among others, including some humans who became involved, but it never went so far as to completely eradicate anyone and everyone who was present. The engagements seemed limited, and broke up after a time when the opponents seemed to hit a stalemate. And the dragons, who were never defeated, did also never completely destroy any of us. This observation was noticed by at least a few scholars, and it raised many questions as to the reason after a while."

"Questions! Like what? How they grew weary of us scrambling around at their feet?"

"Maybe. And that we never took any of the lessons THEY may have been trying to teach to US."

"Teach?" he balks.

"Daeselri," Amavain retorts. "Do you have ANY idea why those dragons were here to begin with? If not, then I would suggest you stifle that tongue of yours. WE arrived here and started wars with THEM. Now, how would you define our role in that?"

"We started wars with THEM?! They're monsters, Amavain! What do you expect us to do?"

"Patriarch," Lafron argues. "They preexisted in this world, the same as the humans, and all we ever did was describe them as beasts. Furthermore, we apparently proclaimed that we should own this place more than any other. This is a very hostile attitude for anyone to take. Therefore, we started it. And worse, we pushed it without ever once asking why it was here to begin with."

"Oh! Really! So, we elves should not own this place?"

"No, Patriarch. If you invade a bear's cave, should you expect him to invite you in for a cup of tea? It is HIS home, not yours, and he has every right to defend it. You know, my wife and child are correct. You hold your wings entirely too high, for your own good, and any of ours."

Now Lafron turns and storms away.

"That's all beside the point, Lafron! These dragons, in particular, behave entirely differently from what you describe, and it seems to have become personal to them. And those nations out there would probably turn us away at first sight, sending us off into the wilderness to face our oblivion while they try to preserve their homes."

"Daeselri," Amavain responds. "In this one instance, you may hold a point, but this one instance may also be very specific. And

I know we settled ourselves on this idea long ago. It relates to that one battle, and our victory, where they simply hold a grudge."

"Right! Therefore, it doesn't fit with everything else. Just like with your husband, and from my own history lessons, I recall they seemed to be pulling away, until this one battle at the temple turned it around. How do YOU explain that?"

"I'm not sure if I could offer a full explanation, unless you consider desperation to rid this space of people who never took a hint. Maybe this one group was angry, or frustrated, or simply very determined to achieve something none of the others did. If we say those others were trying to convince us of something, after we invaded a space we might not have been welcome in, this one group might have felt we travelled too far. Who knows. But it doesn't solve the greater issue that we ran away and made ourselves even more vulnerable up here in these mountains. Daeselri, you are a wise enough man. What kind of situation would we place ourselves into by running away from all the rest, as organized as they were, and that was apparently NOT coming under attack anymore, and into isolation as those flies who made themselves so much a target as we did up here in these mountains?"

"Fine, Amavain. Perhaps you do have a point. But why would the Winged Mother call on a human, of all things? And why so long for us to wait for it?"

"Would you prefer an elf? Would that seem so much more capable of fighting a dragon? To say nothing of three? I recall this world also belonged to humans before we came into it. Maybe one of THEIR gods granted some special privilege, and therefore ours is simply falling in line with a process fated to occur to people whose home WE invaded and pretended to take over. And maybe that man is the one who was…fated…to finish the job ours interrupted so long ago by our intrusion."

"Fated…" he muses softly. "Well…"

"I don't know who or what he is, but as for the reason to wait so long, I can only guess because Aerlie wasn't ready for it until that day I was called out to fetch her. How am I supposed to know the inner workings of the gods? Maybe it takes a thousand years to build a Chosen One. Maybe it takes so many centuries to build a powerful enough nation that they can NOW fight dragons. Who knows? Like he said, the gods work in strange ways, and I doubt we…mortal creatures…are privileged enough to know what they are. So, go back to whatever it is you're supposed to be serving around here, because it certainly isn't preserving our people."

She turns once again and continues storming away, with her husband and Aerlie following alongside. Lafron, like so many others, glared at the Patriarch as he turned to follow his wife. Within him was a sinking feeling that they had just lost an important opportunity.

"Mother?" Aerlie calls softly. "What did you mean by all that talk about me and him, and everything?"

"Never mind, Aerlie, maybe it's not truly the end. You're young still, and the Winged Mother promised me this would come. So, I need to trust she knows what she's talking about. He did mention something about possibly being called again, and that he is apparently just around the corner from us. Maybe this simply wasn't the day for it. But I hope that day does come, and soon."

Chapter 13

UNCERTAIN PARTICIPANTS

The experience found with Aerlie and the Avariel left Thaelyn with several disturbed impressions. As a result of this, he met with his officers to engage in a number of careful reviews of their expansion plans.

The nation of Menenbahd would not likely go quietly, as it held too long a history of crime and corruption. Political interaction was pointless, and waiting for new leadership might also prove fruitless as they merely progressed from one gluttonous kingpin to another. Therefore, he delivered an ultimatum to reform their ways or else, in the name of world peace and progression for the future. Naturally, they refused.

The result was a vigorous, but short-lived war, by land and by air, using their new cavalry of gryphon riders. This saw the rapid downfall of Menenbahd, along with their leadership and criminal practices. The former nation became a vassal territory with heavy garrisons and rigid doctrines aimed at reforming its population. It was estimated to take at least a full generation, maybe two, for the new culture to sink in, but Thaelyn was a patient man.

He further made examinations of the two nations that once

offended the Avariel to their south and east. After receiving several preliminary reports of the corrupt nature of their leadership, and their snobbish designs for their neighbors, he decided they too needed to be reformed. To initiate the process, he sent missionaries to see if he could soften their interior by appealing to the populace. This was tedious, to say the least, as the leadership tried opposing it by arresting or otherwise expelling the intruders. But after several years, a few people began to listen, and their leaders started to lose their influence.

During this time, Thaelyn's political station was becoming even more outdated and obsolete. His nation was becoming a superpower in the world, and the title of Duke wasn't sufficient enough to oversee it effectively. Therefore, his top advisors and high-level priests were imploring him that a change was necessary. Previously, he was reluctant to make this move, as he felt it might seem a little presumptuous, reflecting once again on his one-time conversation with his spirit-sister, Aelwyn, on the matter. But his unrelenting efforts to unite the world would ultimately lead him here, and he could no longer deny it.

A coronation was held in the grand Temple of the Planes down the lane from his guildhall, and the service attracted people from around the city and across the nation. The streets were lined elbow-to-elbow with citizens as they watched and waited for the temple bells to ring and the pageantry of his royal procession to travel its way on a tour of the city. Shouts and whistles echoed from all sides, and the royal carriage was bathed with flowers and ribbons as the people paid homage to their new Lord and King. The tour carried him around the city, giving everyone an opportunity to greet their new liege and offer their respect.

Tales of his exploits across the land had spread to the remaining nations, and those who enjoyed their positions of power were beginning to worry, leaving them to feel the pinch in their own military and economic might to bear up against it. War was becoming an unfavorable option, but it didn't stop the two nations opposite the Avariel when Thaelyn decided to make his move. It also didn't stop the nation of Morakane.

"We will make an advance on multiple sides," Thaelyn instructs. "I want way-lines to open up in multiple areas of their home city. We will hit them from the front, as well as the sides for flanking maneuvers."

"This is going to be messy, I think," his military advisor admits. "I would expect those mages to put up a fierce resistance. And likely using everything they've got."

"Indeed, so we may need to use all necessary means to win this, even if it results in half the city being demolished in the process. I just hope the public can move out of the way quickly enough to avoid any mass losses."

"I would further suggest we keep a large number of our own mages as a counterforce, to offer protective spells, and lots of priests to haul away the injured for quick healing."

"We should establish a treatment area for this purpose. We can use portals to carry away the wounded, treat them, and for those who can return to their feet easily enough, send them back into the fray for another go."

"Those mages are going to be in for a sweet surprise," another officer chuckles. "They take down a group one moment, only to see them back on their feet the next."

"And this will likely put our Draconic augmentations to the test," Thaelyn accedes. "Our people are much tougher than your average army. But against such potent mages, this will likely leave a few marks. Still, I want maximum protection, both arcanic as well as divine, to keep them standing upright."

"Absolutely, my Lord."

Thaelyn and his officers were making a series of plans to attack the home of the infamous Guild of the Red Mages, the de facto leadership of the nation of Morakane. The mages were regarded as having elevated themselves to an elite station in the Art, so fighting them would be a hard win, and likely to cause a lot of collateral damage. But the threat they posed, not only to their local population, but to anything else out there, including multiple attempts at Thaelyn's life using assassins, only prompted him to make this effort to put an end to it. War was the only solution to this one.

They launched using rows of portals called way-lines, opening up within the main city to unleash hordes of troops on all sides of the guildhall where the Red Mages made their primary home. Gryphons arrived in the skies overhead, using their magically enhanced transport, which accelerated them to extreme speed. And even more soldiers advanced on the outskirts of the city to close in around the local garrisons, squeezing them from all directions to compress them into tight spaces.

Thaelyn's troops, being so heavily augmented by the Draconic blood, as well as a myriad of arcanic and divine enchantments, made them very durable. The battle raged over the course of the day and into the night, setting massive fires to the city and crumbling half of it to the ground. Fiery rain and earthquakes roared through the streets. Enemy troops were dispatched, leaving mounds of bodies. The panicked citizens shrieked and ran in all directions, believing in some cases the world was coming to an end with an apocalyptic cataclysm.

The mages themselves held firm in their fortress keep, unleashing masses of fireballs, lightning strikes, both icy and molten shards, and numerous other forms of high-level magical attacks. Thaelyn's mages countered with protective shields, and their own offensive forms of magical strikes. Archers fired off magical arrows from specialized bows that used elemental magic as ammunition. And soldiers hacked their way through rows of enemy troops and golem constructs.

It became a war of attrition, as it carried for days, with the sturdy fortress being hacked away almost as quickly as the Red Mages could magically reassemble it. But slowly, one by one, they began to fall. And with each loss, the guild began to crumble completely.

At the end of the battle, the standard militia owned by the city laid in heaps. Pyres were erected in multiple areas to dispose of the bodies. The Order troops showed a number of their own losses, not nearly as many as the enemy, but the wear took its toll. And large portions of the city lay in ruin, either smoldering, or splintered, or both.

Thaelyn and his men had surrounded the fortress with their siege until all had finally gone silent. Now, they needed to enter inside to check for any survivors or hidden elements. The outer wall was a shambles, and much of the inner keep was broken, but some portions still stood.

They circled around to the remains of the gate and trudged over the broken stonemasonry. The courtyard was empty, except for a number of bodies that fell during the battle, and the shattered remains of several golems the Red Mages unleashed along the way.

They found a door leading inside the keep, which was a large building with many floors and rooms. Most of them involved libraries and study halls. Some were laboratories for younger members to train, while others were the private quarters for the elder members to practice their more elaborate skills.

Most of it looked like the scene of a disaster. Bookshelves were overturned, desks smashed, and laboratory equipment was broken and scattered across the floors. They marched through the building, checking each room, but only to find more of the same. They found the bodies of the mages, some of them charred by fire, or else frozen or electrocuted by other magical attacks. Others were impaled by arrows, and a few appeared crushed by fallen debris.

As they made their way through the fortress, they began to descend into a lower level of chambers, representing more laboratories, and a few prisons. Most of it was empty, with the only current occupants being the skeletons of whoever was once imprisoned here. But as they arrived at the end of a long hall, they noticed light coming from a room ahead, and Thaelyn sensed the presence of someone moving around.

"Gently here," he ushers softly. "Up there, do you see it."

"Aye," responds one of his officers. "Looks like someone might be inside there."

They crept up to the door, which was just barely ajar to allow the sound of activity to come through. But before they could open it to see what was inside, a voice rang out.

"Indeed, come in!" it echoes pleasantly. "There is no need for so much caution. I am not here to fight you."

Thaelyn halted, and he glanced at his guardsmen before reaching for the door. He carefully pushed it open, only to find a lone man inside wearing an ornate mage's robe, much like any of the others, which is to say red, full-length, and with a hood…the standard uniform of a Red Mage.

The room was yet another library and study hall, with several tables of laboratory equipment, including alchemical jars and beakers, bottles of various odd substances, and a variety of what appeared to be the mummified remains of both animals and people.

"Well now," the man exalts. "If it isn't the would-be king of the world come to claim yet another victory. Congratulations on defeating these rapscallions. The world is probably better off without them, for all the good they ever did. Though it is a bit of a shame. These libraries held some fabulous teaching material."

"And who are you," Thaelyn wonders, "if not one of them?"

"If not one of them, yes, that would seem to be the mystery here. I may be one of them, if only for those libraries I spoke of, but that is all. They do afford one a great amount of freedom to explore the magical studies in these halls. And with so few limitations…or perhaps none at all. Unlike certain others you might find around the land. Some academies can be so fickle, you know."

"Perhaps, and what manner of studies are you interested in that you would choose this place as opposed to any other?"

"The kind people like you would probably not allow, with respect of course. I did my homework on you, Thaelyn, Scion of Celestia. You would be the last person a necromancer like me would find employment with. It must be so distasteful to one who comes from the Positive side of the Planes."

"Indeed, it would be. Then why were you not up there with the others? Do you not care for a fight?"

"What I care for, Your Lordship, is study. And whether or not

YOU care for it, I believe mine is as valid as any other. But I can see the writing on the wall. You are here to take over this world in the name of your gods, and this would likely put someone like me out of business. But I regret to say, I do not wish to be put out of business. So, I waited until you found your way down here to offer my special greetings. But now, I must take my leave to find some other place to continue my study. Knowledge is not something to pick and choose based on your preferential taste. I believe your god Oghma would agree to this. So I will leave you to your victory, and even offer you a blessing to see it through to its final conclusion. As for me…"

He now picks up a portal rune and enchants it for a quick departure. He had several travel bags slung over his shoulders, stuffed with notes and reference material taken from the library. He then enchants the portal and prepares to leave.

"Should I ask where you are going," Thaelyn notes. "And whether I should expect to see you again?"

"I suppose you might, at that. After all, it is your nature. I am going somewhere that should not be a bother to your new kingdom. And neither will your kingdom be a bother to me. This should allow me the privacy and freedom I need to continue my studies. As for another meeting, only time will tell if our paths should cross again. Creation, as you people like to call it, may be vast, but I suspect it may still afford a few possibilities."

"Perhaps you would tell me your name before you go?"

"Ah, but of course, my apologies. I became distracted. I have so many things on my mind, and I tend to be very devoted to my pursuits. My name is Master Zharaden, Necromancer extraordinaire…or at least I hope to be one day. But probably not under your employ. You wouldn't like the things I've learned."

He now claps his hand over the rune and departs away from view, leaving Thaelyn and his men wondering if they will ever see him again, and what surprises it might hold.

◆ ◆ ◆ ◆ ◆ ◆ ◆

The decades passed and Thaelyn's nation continued to grow. They were experiencing a Golden Age, a period of prosperity and prestige the likes of which the world had never known. Crime had all but vanished entirely, poverty had virtually disappeared, and the citizens learned to live in harmony with each other, regardless of their race or cultural diversity. Thaelyn's teachings inspired the people to bring their differences together to supplement themselves and build strength between them.

The Avariel, on the other hand, were not faring as well.

"Get to the caves!" shouts a man running through the village.

The three dragons had returned again for their yearly rampage. The routine had become a sinister habit, and their ire showed no letting up. They continued to destroy homes and fields in an apparent spree simply to torment.

Aerlie and her family hurried to the shelter, along with the rest of the people, only to turn and peek outside as their village was once again reduced to rubble. They could no longer even feel for the loss of their homes as there was nothing to become so attached to by now. They could only wait for the dragons to finish and once again gather up the pieces.

"This is so tiring!" Aerlie grumbles.

"Aerlie," Amavain relents. "I know how you feel, but please try to contain yourself this time. Every year, it gets worse. I know you're old enough to speak your mind, but simply arguing isn't going to solve anything."

"Right, Mother… Arguing doesn't solve anything. Words don't solve anything. Nothing we do solves anything."

"Aerlie," the Patriarch ushers sternly. "We don't have the means to fight this. We have too few people, no weapons, no magic, and at this moment, I doubt even the gods would come to our aid."

"This isn't about the gods coming to OUR aid, it's about us going out to find our own. One thing I learned out there that time was the gods aren't supposed to do our work FOR us. Best case, they're teachers, to TEACH us to do our own. Unfortunately, we're not learning very well up here. Patriarch, being underground is just not for the Avariel! We are born to soar through the skies and feel the wind in our face, not hide inside caves."

"Aerlie, if you want to soar through the skies, I won't hold you back. Just don't come crying about any more circus freak shows."

"Really! How nice of you to pull that one up again. I was caught by people who were probably no better than those ones to the south. They were probably part of the same clan, for all we know."

"They're ALL the same, Aerlie. All humans are the same."

"No, they're not! Those I found in that one city were very different, and in fact took offence at so many of my own manners, which by the way were inherited from YOU, that I found myself apologizing many times over to excuse my behavior."

"Oh really! So, they had you bent over a barrel begging for their mercy, did they? I'm sure that 'favor' he spoke of came about somewhere along the way."

"Ooh! Patriarch, my mother is right. You are THE most intolerable man in existence. Don't you remember any part of my story? I told you about Lord Thaelyn's kingdom. It was filled with a lot of nice people from a lot of different races all living together. They were all very wise and using magic, and all very polite. They had humans, elves, dwarves, and more. They even had a fabled Tree of Life, and it was home to the Queen of the Dryads!"

"Preposterous, girl…you were a child then. How could you possibly know what a Tree of Life is, much less to actually see one in a HUMAN city? That's simply ridiculous. Humans don't hold such values as those."

"Oh, in a human city, as if the elves were doing it by this time? My information tells me, and my father can even confirm this, that we ELVES stopped the ancient tradition way back with those horrid Crown Wars we fought. So don't go trying to tell me we were any better by this time. This is something we brought with us from the old Fey world, and of all people, we should be the ones doing it. But my goodness, if it took a HUMAN to remind us of who we are supposed to be, why couldn't we do it ourselves. Hmph!"

She folds her arms and turns to the side defiantly. The Patriarch simply glares at her.

Aerlie continues, "And besides, it was NOT simply a human city. I saw MANY people there, including whole sections of elves. And I saw her myself. She came right out of the tree, just like in the old stories. Child or not, that's a little hard to miss. And then she gave me this!" she stretches out a wing to demonstrate her feathers. "The priestess told me all the people are their children, no matter who they are. If you're a part of this world, you're one of them."

"Oh, so the humans have somehow corrupted the sacred dryads as well? Unbelievable, how this world has fallen," he shakes his head. "Those are OUR holy symbols, not theirs!"

"Daeselri," Amavain groans. "I doubt you would call anything of ours holy anymore, YOU have fallen so far."

"I agree!" Aerlie scorns. "To describe anything as purely ours is as bigoted as to say our wings, which are a VERY strange thing for any goddess to give to anything, make us somehow more privileged than anything else in this world. It's no wonder the rest of the races call US the troublemakers. What about the Alu? Do you remember the Water People? They held themselves the same for THEIR gift to live in the sea."

"Uh huh," he moans. "And did he somehow manage to get THEM to join his lovely little nation?"

"As a matter of fact, he did, apparently. But I suppose that doesn't really matter to you."

"No, it doesn't. But fine, have it your way. So, why don't any of THEM come up here to help us? Surely, a dryad spirit ought to know something about what's happening in the world, shouldn't it?"

"I don't actually know the answer to that," Amavain responds. "If they don't have any contact with us, maybe they don't have any way of seeing us up here."

"Then what about…our goddess…" he flutters his fingers provocatively. "If she's giving out so much of her favor to these people, why doesn't she tell them about us?"

"You know, he did mention something about a later occasion to return, so maybe there's something still waiting for us. And yet, why didn't YOU tell him when he asked you about it? Maybe she only told him enough to help Aerlie, and you were supposed to fill in the rest once he got up here. Aerlie is right, the gods don't give out free information, and instead expect you to learn a few things for yourself. When I speak to the Winged Mother, she doesn't teach me the secrets of Creation, she only offers enough to guide me on a path of learning."

"A path of learning," he grumbles. "As if that actually helps us when we see our homes destroyed."

"Patriarch," Aerlie resumes. "When I was down there, I saw some of this path of learning…it had to be! For instance, I told you my injuries were so bad, they had to cut off part of my wings, but then they used some strange kind of medicine to regrow them back out again. It was amazing!"

"Yes, and that was the most hilarious part of your story, Aerlie. They hold such power as to regrow your wings after chopping them off," he laughs. "And then to suggest they might actually give this to you without asking for any manner of payment?"

"Well, let us not forget our goddess with her…favor," she retorts jeeringly. "After all, what might this 'favor' actually be made of, do you know? Maybe it's worth more than gold to these people."

The Patriarch glared at her for the outlandish suggestion. But he briefly found himself wondering if there might actually be a mote of reason to it. Nevertheless, he quickly shrugged it off as so much continued nonsense.

"I still question why she would call on them, rather than anyone else, like maybe an elven nation, if there are any still out there."

"You weren't listening to him very well, were you? I saw a map of the full continent of Sein'amar, and he owned most of the western half of it at that time. He also explained his plans to take the rest of it. So, any nations at all, elven or otherwise, will come under his rule one day. And he apparently has a divine mandate to do so."

"Oh! Yes! Here's another of my favorite claims…a human with a divine mandate to do something. Aerlie, are YOU listening to what YOU are saying? He's a human, Child. And they don't live long enough to carry anything that far, divine mandate or otherwise. And worse, from one generation to another, they never hold their aim to any single cause. So, even if he has a successor, I find it highly unlikely to see that one following this glorious mandate of theirs. More than likely, he'll go around tearing down that great nation and putting the coin in his pocket."

"Daeselri!" Amavain scorns. "You are the most intolerable person I think I ever had the displeasure to meet."

"Amavain, you and I haven't seen eye-to-eye since the day that charlatan tried passing himself off as a charity giver. I no longer really care about your opinion. You claim our goddess would bring herself so low as to speak to a simple land-walker? That's insulting, and not only to me. I honestly don't know how you can continue kneeling at the altar with such inventions."

"You forget, virtually all of our brethren are land-walkers. Therefore, just about ANYONE she might call would be a land-walker, since we up here are so incapable of it. We are the exception, not the rule here. And if she were so offended at my service, I think she would've told me by now. Instead, she keeps silent, and I think it is because she knows YOU will know your comeuppance one day when the truth is revealed."

"Yes! Good! Excellent! So be it. But is that before or after the final fall of our people, Amavain? Maybe your Chosen One daughter would like to make another go out there and see what new trouble she can find. I'm sure there must be a circus somewhere wanting for a new attraction."

"All right!" Aerlie screams. "That does it! I'm finished here! You want to challenge me to find that thing I was Chosen for? Fine! I'm a full century now, and I'm making my own decisions in life, and my first decision is to do what you refuse to do, Patriarch! I'm going to find that Lord Thaelyn and see if I can get him to help our people, regardless of what you think of him."

"Aerlie, do you actually think he, or any man, would care to risk life and limb for US, and especially against THREE dragons? What price would he ask for this, do you think?"

"Why must you always bring that up? He didn't ask anything before. He never said one word about it."

"Fine, so he understands we have nothing to offer. Any fool can see this. What's next, he takes us as slaves? We wouldn't even be worthy of serving that much by now."

"I should think even if to live as a slave is better than living inside a cave with dragons at our backs. And it's certainly better than, as you like to say, to see the final demise of our people. But I happen to know he is NOT one who likes criminals. By the Winged Mother, you should've seen him when he was speaking to that circus owner. He blasted the roof right off the top of the tent with his screaming."

"All right, fine. You go ask him for this blessed service and offer yourself as his personal slave. Wash his feet, empty his pot, and rub the scabs from his back. And along the way, maybe he desires some more of that favor he spoke of so fondly."

At this point, Aerlie couldn't take any more. She launched a short jab that pounded into his shoulder for the insulting manners.

"You would dare suggest anything to me when YOU are more the contemptible tongue. Yes, I'll go find him. And I'll tell him everything about our troubles up here. I only regret I was too afraid to do this the first time, and mostly due to you and your bigotry. I suppose I was also hoping YOU would tell him…you being the one responsible for the safety of our people, and whose job it is to find help."

"My bigotry is justified by my experiences with them. But if you feel he is so much different, go ahead. Just remember what I said. Humans don't live that long, and this was seven decades ago, Girl. He would be long dead and buried by now."

"Well, as I said, if they hold a divine mandate, maybe whoever ordered it might pass it along to the next. If the gods want this world united, I don't think one man's mortality is going to stand in their way."

Aerlie now storms through the cave to look for a shoulder bag, then starts loading up a few provisions to prepare for what she expected to be a long journey.

"Aerlie," Amavain mutters softly. "What are you planning?"

"I'm going back there. I think I remember where it was. We were looking at a map once, and he's all the way across the Great Sea."

"That's a very long journey, my daughter. And you can't be sure what you'll find along the way. Remember what you said before about being captured."

"I'll be more aware this time. I was a child before, and very naïve. I didn't expect something like that. But he said his kingdom had a border just across the mountains to the west, past the Sea of the Moon. Like I said before, those people were probably more of the same as those in the south, and also outside his territory. But I also recall he said in a few more years, he would own much more of it. Maybe, in this time, he's already moved past us."

"I suppose…"

"Regardless, if I can get to the other side of that big sea, I shouldn't have as much to worry about, I think…I hope. I just need to fly long and hard to find that city of his."

"Very well, and maybe this time you'll find your Fate."

"Mother, it's strange to hear you say this. Me, a Chosen One, and with this Fate. The Winged Mother brought me into your arms so that one day I might find something bigger than all of us. How is a person supposed to understand what that means?"

"The gods work in strange ways, Aerlie, that's all I can say," she smiles softly. "She said you carry something special in you. I can't pretend to know what that means, but looking at you tells me it must be very unique."

"Yeah, and then we have that again," she chuckles faintly. "My wings, my hair, my eyes. Most people think of me as a freak right here at home."

Aerlie finishes packing her bag and turns to face her mother. She could see worry and distant hope reflected in Amavain's eyes, so she gave her a hug and a comforting peck on the cheek, and then strutted outside. She took off in a dash, flapping her wings vigorously, and lifted off.

Amavain and her husband, along with so many others, watched as Aerlie gained altitude and began sailing towards the western ridgeline. She turned to look at the Patriarch, who was standing nearby and also watching. He turned to return her gaze.

"I will never bow down to a human," he ushers scornfully.

"Of course, Patriarch," she retorts confidently. "But I think before this is over, the rest of us might have a few things to say about bowing before you."

Aerlie soared high above the mountains and into the valley beyond. She knew this would be a very long journey indeed, perhaps lasting many days, assuming she pressed herself for the full duration of daylight. And then to actually find her way without getting lost, which could cost her even more time. She would try conserving her strength by rising up and then gliding some distance, carefully surveying the land below looking for any sign of life, but keeping at distance from it just in case it wasn't friendly.

Forests and rivers passed by underneath, then more forests. She angled south until she came to the shores of the great Sea of Stars, which accounted for a huge expanse of water. She would follow this around, hoping to use it as a guide to lead her around to the western extremes of the land where she hoped to find something familiar in the form of Thaelyn's home city.

"He said he already owned everything on that side," she muses privately. "So, maybe it might be safe if I land somewhere to ask directions. What was the name of that city again?"

It would be at least several days before she might find her way to the western shores of the sea, and while she drifted along the airstreams, her mind began drifting through her memories.

"The Patriarch is a fool, just like Mother says," she mumbles to herself. "He has no idea. But I was there! It was such a beautiful place to live. I wouldn't mind just staying there, but I can't leave my people. I wonder if I could get others to follow me."

The scenery below rolled by, slowly changing from mountains to forests, and occasional open fields dotted with towns. She looked down wondering what the people below were doing at the moment. Did any of them ever look up? Can they see her up here? And if so, what are they thinking right now.

The day was long, and at the end she felt very weary. She was stressing herself beyond her normal limits. As nighttime fell, she carefully circled the area to see about a place to land, and descended cautiously to avoid being seen by anything. She tucked herself away under the cover of the local shrubbery, pulled out some food and settled herself to rest. The following morning, she was on her way again, but as each day passed, her body became worn, and her wings began to ache.

After a few days, she could see the shoreline closing around a channel that seemed to pass through to a smaller body of water. She could see towns on both sides and a myriad of small fishing boats out and about. Her muscles were sore, but she forced herself to press on, crossing the channel, but soon relenting to take a break. She closed in on the town below, eyeing it carefully to see who might live down there, and finally deciding to take the risk of landing. She set herself down by the seaside, much to the surprise of the people below. Almost immediately, she collapsed to the ground panting.

Several people came up around her, but unsure if they wanted to move closer. One stepped forward in the hope of trying to communicate.

"Eh, you there, are you alright? Great gods, what are you?"

Aerlie didn't understand the local tongue, so all she could do was look up at the person and try using her own.

"Does anyone here speak elvish?"

The crowd all looked at each other, and several began murmuring.

"We need to find someone to speak with her," calls one man.

"Perhaps one of the guards," offers a woman. "They should be able to help."

"Here!" shouts a voice from the local fishing dock. "I can help. By the Lord of the Undersea, I can't believe my eyes!"

The crowd, including Aerlie, all turn to spy a female figure coming up from the boat docks, apparently a merchant visiting the city. But she was certainly not anything you would expect of a local dweller.

She appeared roughly elvish, but only vaguely. She had pale bluish-green skin, similarly colored eyes, and seemed devoid of hair. More importantly, she had gills at the base of her neck. And she wore a skintight suit, like that of a very skimpy swimsuit, with a lot of skin showing.

"You!" the man waves. "Are you able to understand her? It sounds a bit like Elvish to me."

"I'll bet it is!" she yips excitedly. "One of the famous Winged Folk, no less!"

The woman arrived up on the street where the rest had been gathering. Aerlie glared at the young woman for her clearly scandalous attire. The woman made a polite approach and began speaking in Elvish.

"Would you be an Ariler?" she asks.

"Yes!" Aerlie nods enthusiastically. "My goodness, you look like one of the Water People. Aluer, is it?"

"That's right!"

The woman sits down on the grass with Aerlie so they could talk.

"Your people are just a story to me and mine," Aerlie states.

"I could say the same for you, you know."

"I think I heard once how your people joined the kingdom, right? How long have you been a part of all this?"

"A couple of centuries, at least officially. His Lordship managed to coax us out of the water much earlier, but we were very difficult to work with in those early days. There were a few times here and there, when one or another of our people might come up to see what's new out here, maybe to try a few simple trades. But we were always so afraid of what we would find, or how we would be treated. Such a silly thing…" she giggles. "But once he came into it, all that changed. We couldn't be happier now."

"I wish it could be the same for mine. We ran away and stayed there. But I hope to change that now, if only I can find him again."

"Are you trying to find him now? Where did you actually come from?"

"From a mountain range on the other side of the Great Sea."

"Ouch! That's a big sea. I've never tried swimming the full length of it…I was born in a village we have right down below us out here," she points at the nearby shoreline. "But the sea itself is big. And did you fly the full distance? I saw you up there just now, and couldn't help but to come over here and see."

"Yes, and I'm very tired now. But I can't stop, not yet. I need to find that city again."

"You mean B.T., where His Lordship lives? It's not too much farther, but maybe you should rest a bit first. We wouldn't want you falling out of the sky before you got there."

"Thanks. How much farther? Can you tell me?"

"From here…" she muses. "I remember once my mother taking me there for a visit when I was young. But we couldn't stay long. When we travel on land, we need to keep it short."

"Why is that?"

"Our skin…" she examines a hand, which included slightly webbed fingers. "Being a creature that lives in the sea, our skin can dry out quickly if we stay too long on land. So our visits up here need to be brief. Either that, or bring lots of wet blankets to wrap around us," she chuckles.

"Uh oh! That sounds like trouble."

"But let's see. From here, you would normally take the roadways… but I'll bet you would probably want to fly it, right?" she smiles demurely.

"Probably so. It's what we do," she returns the friendly gesture.

"There is a road that travels along the countryside to the west, and then bends south around some mountains. It's on the other side of those mountains. But if you're travelling by air, I would imagine you'll have a great view from up there."

"Oh, indeed! It's beautiful!"

"Then you should be able to see it if you simply travel west of here. I think those mountains should be visible on the horizon from where we are. It's not that far, I think. Not as compared to where you came from, at least."

"All right, that's good to hear."

They paused the conversation as they watched the people passing by. Aerlie studied the girl sitting next to her, who seemed so friendly and sociable. And yet, she was one of those who supposedly also held those aversions due to their special gifts.

"Can I ask you something?" Aerlie begins. "I just want to understand something, from your side of things."

"Sure! What is it?"

"You say your people had a hard time in the beginning, like with how you might be treated, and something about trades. But what kinds of trades would you make with people like these," she glances around the local townsfolk. "You live in the water."

"This is a good question. You might think there isn't much we would find of interest. Our lifestyles, and the environments in which we live are quite different. And a lot of things up here don't last long if you bring them in the water for a long time."

"Does that include clothing?" she grins softly as she glances at the woman's scant apparel.

"Well..." she chuckles as she examines herself. "The people around here are used to it by now, but it's actually not convenient for us to go around wearing such billowy garments like yours that would catch the currents and slow us down as we swim along."

"Oh, wow. Yes, I think I can see that. So it has to be small, and very tight to the body?"

"Yes, and our culture down there doesn't hold some of the same opinions about how much skin we show off. So long as the important areas are covered, the rest doesn't matter."

"Really!"

"Some of the things we might trade, even in those early days, relate to food. Things like fruits and vegetables, which tend to survive a bit longer in water. But you still need to eat them quickly once you bring them home."

"I see."

"We can't grow them down there, but we do have some very good water plants we cultivate, like kelp and algae, and we found the people up here can sometimes find a use for them. Some of it has become a specialty food for them, like those fruits are for us. And the algae, some of it, can hold medicinal and alchemical value."

"It does? Interesting."

"But then, we have some other foods you can only find here on the land. They don't do well underwater. So we now make regular visits up here for special outings with friends and family to eat at their local diners and taverns. They also have some great drinks up here."

"They do? Hmm. Yes, how would you actually drink something underwater?"

"Yes, and some of the food, like soup. Try eating a bowl of soup while in the water," she giggles.

"Ew! Eat it, or breathe it!" she laughs.

"That's right! And some of it uses special seasonings and spices. And my gills would be a bit sensitive to that!"

The two of them share a laugh, as Aerlie feels a growing sense of familiarity with this strange young lady.

"But aside from food," Aerlie continues. "How do you fit in with this kingdom? You live in the water, they're up here on land. I would think that doesn't give you much for how to fit your people with the rest."

"This is how we felt for a long time, until His Lordship came into it. He showed us how our special and rather unique qualities can hold a really important role in areas that others might find too difficult, or simply not as convenient. When you make your homes in the water, that becomes your native environment. So, if you are a land-borne body, things like underwater exploration and scientific study become problematic. Say you want to study the biology of underwater plants and animals, or the geography of the landscape down there. If you need to breathe air, you have to build something like a ship to carry you down there, and also to survive the heavy pressures of all that water on top of you. But for us, it's a natural thing to simply swim down there, take a few specimens, some measurements, whatever, and come back up to report in.”

“Oh my goodness! I can only barely understand what you’re talking about, and it already sounds like a special role for you. And you would be a natural at it! Is this what you do out here in the Great Sea?”

“Quite often that, maybe also emergency rescue for ships in distress, and also underwater salvage. A lot of old ships went down out there, and we might find them, and assist in their salvage and reclamation. We can also make expeditions out in the oceans, although we need to be a bit careful out there.”

“Why is that?”

“Two reasons, actually. You have a lot of big, and sometimes vicious sea creatures, like sharks. You don’t have those here in the sea. We need to carry special protection for that. Also, the saltwater content. The Sea of Stars is a freshwater body, but the ocean has a lot of salt in it. We can tolerate salt water, but only for brief periods, as the salt buildup in our bodies from breathing it can make us a little dizzy after a while.”

“Oops! All right, got it.”

As the conversation progressed, Aerlie could feel her strength returning, if just barely enough to continue her journey. Her muscles still ached, but she had an important task ahead of her, and she wanted to get on with it. Her people depended on her, and she was becoming anxious about what she might find in all this, maybe even to find a role of some kind for herself.

“By the way,” Aerlie submits. “What’s your name?”

“Oh! I’m sorry. Yes, my name is Pyavin. And you?”

“I’m Aerlie. Maybe we could see each other again? I need to be on my way, as I have some really important business to attend, but I would enjoy sitting and talking again.”

“Sure! I come and go a lot, but you should be able to find me out here by the docks on occasion.”

“Great! And thank you so much for the chat.”

Pyavin smiles and nods as she gets up and returns to her chores.

Aerlie felt newly inspired to meet someone like this girl, and to learn that her goal must be very close. It was apparently just across another set of mountains. She shouldn't have any trouble finding it after that. She watched as people passed by in the street, all of them turning discreetly to look at her, and she could hear them whispering something.

"It's alright," she mutters quietly to herself. "I'm not going to be offended. We're a lost society, so you simply haven't seen anything like us for a long while. I should expect this. Maybe I'll also take strength from it, the return of the Avariel!"

These words gave her a renewed sense of vigor, as well as a subtle sense of melancholy, when she considered what was left of her people by this time. But whatever she might find on the other side, she hoped her people would find their peace at last. She would press on, find whoever was in the seat of power here, and ask them for help… even if she did need to offer herself into slavery. Although this didn't seem as likely, not when you have people like Pyavin who found such a positive role in a world of people so different from her example.

After another few moments, she stood up again, stretched her wings to test them, and tried lifting off. Her body felt like it wouldn't last much longer, but if she was so close, she was going to push herself to find her answers, no matter what.

Up until now, she had been mostly coasting on the winds, but now she started flapping to increase her speed. The day was barely midway along. She angled off to the west and could already see a row of mountains far on the horizon.

"That must be it. All right, let's see how fast you can fly."

She took herself up and made a determined effort at the distant ridgeline, settling herself into a comfortable rhythm. As before, the fields rolled by, and she could see farming and ranches below. A road led off into the distance along the coastline to another town, but she angled more to the south, aiming to fly over the mountains rather than circling around with the roadways.

The sun progressed across the sky, and it was now early afternoon when the mountains came more into view. It was a long north-south range. She took to gliding again to conserve her strength before making the climb over the top. Then, she scanned the terrain below trying to judge her positioning, and took notice of a broad cityscape stretching out across the valley.

"Wow, that place looks big even from up here."

The city was a large urban center, with several outlying suburbs and a few farming communities beyond that. She knew she needed to find the large fortress that was the guildhall of Thaelyn's Order. She recalled it was set above the rest on a hillside, with his manor house set above that. She surveyed the scene until she found what she thought to be her mark, and circled around along the ridgeline behind it to confirm her suspicions. But by this time, she was feeling exhausted.

"All right," she wheezes. "I can do this, just a little more…please."

She angles into a dive, coming around the side of the guildhall over a series of large buildings. She didn't know what they were, but they were coming up under her fast. She tried flapping to get over them, nearly missing one rooftop and hoping to dodge another.

On the ground, in front of the fortress gates, the guards stood watch as a testimony to the prestige of the Order. One of them happened to catch something out of the corner of his eye moving in the air. He turned to look at it.

"Blimey! Look there, lads! What's that coming in?"

The others all turned to follow the mention.

"I don't know what it is," ushers another. "But it's coming down hard!"

"Is that a person with wings?"

"Aye! By the gods, you're right!"

"Lads, that looks a wee bit like one of those Avariel we found that time, do you think?"

"Aye, but gods be blessed, it looks like she's out of control!"

Aerlie was closing in on a circle driveway at the top of the hill in front of the gates. She was hoping to hit a soft patch of grass on the side, but her aim was faltering. She tried twisting to correct her trajectory, but her wings refused to move by now. All she could do was try to catch as much air to slow down before she made impact.

"Lads, get out there," shouts one of the guards.

Aerlie hits the ground and tumbles, attempting to tuck her wings until she came to a rest, finally to settle face-down just on the edge of a grassy margin.

"Lass!" shouts a guard. "Are you alright?"

The guards gathered around to inspect her for injuries. Aerlie was sprawled out and rasping.

"I…need…help… Please…"

One of the guards crouched down to look her in the face as she tried pulling her gaze up to meet his.

"Lass, from the looks of you, I think you need a bit more than just help. Are you one of the Avariel?"

"Yes… I was here before…" she pants. "I was young then… Just a girl… But I remember you people…"

"Aye, I recall the tale from my grandpop. He was a soldier here during those days. But what brings you back here, and in such a fret as well? You look like you must've flown the full breadth of the land in one day."

"Well," she chuckles weakly. "Maybe not a day, but it was a hard flight. I need to ask for help. I remember once when you helped me, but now I beg you to help my people. I'll do anything for it…please."

"Right, then, lass. Just calm yourself a bit. Someone fetch this little lady some water, and call His Lordship out here!"

One of the guards jumps to his feet and rushes through the gates into the courtyard.

"We need a flask of water out front!" he shouts. "We've got an Avariel out there, and she's asking for help. Call His Lordship!"

The call goes out, and a set of pages rush off to bring the requested assistance. One hurries to find the water while another dashes toward the combat training hall where Thaelyn happened to be spending some time tutoring the students.

"My Lord!" he shouts into the room. "I'm hearing of an Avariel outside. They're calling for you, prompt like!"

"An Avariel?!" he responds sharply. "Where?"

"Outside in front..."

Now, Thaelyn rushes behind the page into the courtyard and out the front gate.

Aerlie had been brought into a seated position and was sipping her water. When Thaelyn arrived in view, she directed her attention to the tall figure making a hasty approach and instantly gasped when she gazed into his face.

"You?! You're still alive? But I thought, well, you know...after all this time..."

"My lifespan is just a tad longer than your average human," he kneels next to her. "Aerlie, I am very pleased to see you again, but I must admit, this is something of a surprise. And yet, at the same time, if I may, it appears you have grown into a fine young lady," he smiles pleasantly. "But still, I must wonder what brings you back here, especially as I look at you, and this causes me to ask if you are well for your travels. The distance you must have covered, if you flew all this way, would be considerable."

"Yes, it was, and I'm very tired. And thank you for the complement," she blushes softly. "It took many days, and I was hoping not to get lost along the way. I stopped over here on the coast in a small town to ask directions. Oh! And I met someone while I was there. She was very nice!"

"Oh? Who was it?"

"An Aluer! She must've been visiting the town. I think maybe she was a merchant or something. We sat and talked for a while. She was so friendly and full of life. Are they all like that?"

"I might say yes, at least in our modern day. In the early moments, it was touch and go, but it smoothed out with experience. Since then, to my understanding, although I cannot personally go down there and see it, but they seem to have clustered much of their society near our shores on this side of the sea."

"Really! That would make good sense."

"But now, Aerlie, what could drive you to come all this way, and in such a rush that it wore you so thin?"

"I need to ask you for help," she whines. "And I'll pay whatever price you ask of me."

"Aerlie, with respect, what is it with you Avariel and these costs? Your Patriarch, as I recall him, assaulted me with accusations that I had ulterior motives to indenture you and yours for all you might be worth, and then some."

"I'm sorry, for myself and all the rest. And please don't listen to him. He doesn't like humans for the way we were treated in the past. But I know you must be different."

"I will not fault him for this point, as I have known a fair few of those as well. Now, what is this trouble you speak of? Is it related to that earlier concern? Is someone accosting you? Although I cannot imagine who at the moment. Those two nations you once spoke of no longer exist."

"Huh? What do you mean?"

"Do you recall the last time we met when you spoke of being cheated by those two adjoining nations?"

"Yes. What happened to them?"

"I happened to them. They are now undergoing conversion as my latest vassal territories."

"Really! So, we have you as our neighbors on all sides now?"

"Indeed! After returning that day, I made a few changes to my original plans, thinking perhaps you needed a little security up there from anyone making more trouble for you."

"Well, I suppose I should thank you for that, but they're not actually our problem. Yes, they lied and cheated us. The first promised to help if we pay them all our gold to raise an army to come to our aid, and the other took whatever remaining treasures we had left, but neither actually sent anything to us."

"I see. But an army? For what purpose? Who is actually offending you?"

"More like what, at this point," she sighs deeply.

"What... All right, what is it we are speaking of?"

"Your Lordship, I beg you to help my people," she pleads as tears begin welling up. "This is probably going to be a lot for me to ask, but we desperately need help. It's been going on for so long now," she begins to sob. "I should've said something before, but I was young and afraid, and the Patriarch always tells us it's hopeless."

"All right, gently now, Child, and explain what is happening."

"I'm not actually a child any more…"

"Yes, but I tend to use this term on occasion. It is a form of parental perspective."

"Oh, all right. Interesting. My mother uses this on occasion. But she's a priestess."

"Yes, they tend to use this as well," he smiles gently. "I suppose it is simply inherited from the religious perspective that generates the idea."

"Right. But anyway, we've been hunted for as long as any of us can remember. It all started with a battle our ancestors once fought. I think you know the history, right? The temple?"

"Dear Powers, Aerlie…that was nearly a millennium and a half ago. What happened?"

"My mother told me the story when I was little. A group of dragons invaded the temple, but the road leading up to it was too difficult for the people on the ground to reach it."

"Right, and so the Avariel rallied themselves to make the initial assault while the rest hurried their advance up the mountainside. At the end of the day, you routed the dragons, but not without taking considerable losses, and the ground forces retook the temple and the sacred artifact it held. What came next for you? As far as we were aware, you departed and were never seen again."

"The dragons began chasing us."

"What?!" he blasts suddenly. "They started chasing you? Why? This is not supposed to be their purpose. In fact, let me see…" he ponders a moment.

Thaelyn mulled the timeline in his memories. He then studies the group of guardsmen who had gathered together by now.

"The Temple of the Protector," he mutters. "This was almost a millennium and a half ago, correct?"

"Aye," responds one guard. "I believe so, from our history books."

"But when did we declare the official end to the Age of Dragons? It was much earlier than this, I believe."

"Gracious…um, right, it faded away slowly, if I recall. It began LONG before this moment. Centuries…thousands of years even!"

"Aye," offers another guard. "Talk about a slow retreat!" he chuckles. "But it finally came to a proper end well before this."

"Right," Thaelyn nods. "A slow withdrawal, maybe to offer a showing that they are simply backing away. A tactical retreat, yes! The elves were not taking the hint to simply leave, so this was a show to display a progression of victory, since they so often regarded THEM as the enemies. And rather than simply run away, they might have been hoping to encourage a form of camaraderie amongst the rest that they held this success together. Therefore, this might encourage their united growth."

"Bloody hell to that, though, as it didn't seem to work."

"Yes, well, this can once again reflect on the selfishness of their leadership."

Aerlie gazed at the group in bewilderment at the rapid deliberation of details that made no actual sense to her, due to her obvious lack of education in this area.

"But wait a moment," offers the first guard. "I recall a few scholars once say this was a curious one-off thing, because of the timing. It didn't seem related to anything else, like maybe to say it was a raid, and perhaps as a last-ditch effort by this one group."

"A last-ditch effort," Thaelyn muses. "As if to say this group made one final assault. But men, if this was AFTER the Maker's orders to withdraw, we must be saying they turned rogue against her orders and took independent action."

"That might sound fair enough. But my Lord, Draconics doing this? They were always said to be here to guard the place, not ruin it."

"And then to go after these people?" the other guard points assertively at Aerlie. "For what purpose? That would be downright criminal!"

Aerlie continued to listen perplexedly to the conversation, which they were carrying in Elvish, at least as much because this is what they started with, as also to involve her benefit. Finally, she had to speak up.

"What are you people talking about?" she asks anxiously. "Maker who, some kind of orders, criminal something, um…"

"Aerlie, one moment," Thaelyn interjects. "Do your people hold any opinions as to why these dragons are chasing you? Did you do something specific to offend them? And do you have any details on why they would attack the temple in the first place. Our information suggests it was to steal a special artifact from there, possibly to use as a sort of weapon against you."

"Yes, this is what my mother once told me, but they started chasing us, probably because we won the battle, and maybe they just want revenge or something for us beating them."

"Preposterous!" he shouts. "These are Draconics, Child. They should hold higher standards of behavior than random terrorist attacks. This would most surely offend the Maker, to say nothing of that temple assault."

"But last I heard," offers one guard. "The Maker was missing."

"Indeed, wherever she went off to, they are taking advantage of her absence. Or maybe this is due to her lack of overview. I cannot be sure, but one thing I CAN be certain of, this must end!" he growls.

Aerlie reeled back from the sudden strength of his voice and his clear revulsion of the situation. But it didn't help her to understand what they were talking about.

"Wait, please," she begs. "I'm lost now. Who is this Maker? And then all the rest of it."

"Her name is Maker Kuroku, and she owns the Draconics, who are an ancient race she once made as guardians to protect…well, whatever it is she sets them to protect. And at one time, this world was one such target…against invaders who were not otherwise welcome to arrive here," he gazes determinedly into her eyes as he finishes.

Aerlie draws back as she studies his face with his curious expression.

"Why are you looking at me?"

"Because, my unfortunate young lady, you and your kind, along with all the other elves, dwarves, and everything else that was not otherwise human…were the invaders. This world, as it turns out, is known to us as a special project she was conducting to build a new home for the human population, and everything else invaded her space. The Age of Dragons, which you all declare was such a problem for you, was actually a policing action to deter you from invading further. But it seems the elven societies, among others, took offence to the dragons and their actions, thinking YOU should be here, and no one else."

"Oh! Wonderful! Now you tell us! The Patriarch would LOVE to hear that one!"

"Indeed, I can already hear it," he chuckles ironically. "My apologies, but we only learned of this a few centuries ago when I had a meeting with someone we call Adalon the Silver, who is an agent serving the Maker. She revealed some of this to us, and then we learned even more when we found evidence of how and why the human population first arrived on this world. This world, as it seems, was a dead world before she took an interest in reviving it."

"That's…well, interesting, but how does it relate to where we are now?"

"Where we are now is after the Maker apparently reevaluated her schemes where the other races are concerned. She apparently had time to study you, and realized you held some fascinating potential, if only you knew how to use it by combining all your societies into one. Therefore, to join these strengths together. Unfortunately, your societies never understood this by their own reasoning."

"Uh huh…and so we have wars and such, I guess, and she wasn't happy about that?"

"Correct, very good… And one very obvious example is your people running away to isolate yourselves, and further endangering yourselves in the face of this threat. Had you stayed with the other nations, you could bury yourselves within THEIR defense as support."

"Oops! Oh great, that really rubs it in. And I recall my mother mentioning something about this once. Wow!"

"Indeed. And so we have such as your Patriarch's attitude. But along the way, as we were just now discussing, she withdrew her Draconic Children as a means of allowing you the freedom to discover yourselves and hopefully unite together. The Age of Dragons ended long ago. So technically, this attack on the temple should never have occurred at all, unless some group of dragons turned rogue against the Maker and disobeyed her orders."

"OH!" she shouts. "Good gracious, Blessed Mother! Is THAT what we're talking about here? So, a bunch of dragons are angry with us because they don't like us being here, AND that we beat them up at that temple they weren't supposed to be attacking. Wow, the things you learn when you go places you're not supposed to go."

"Yes, it is a curious thing," he smiles. "Now, on to other matters…"

"Um, wait, please, one more…" she asserts. "This still doesn't explain you. You said you had a divine mandate or something once, right?"

"Ah, but of course. I am the solution to your otherwise miscreant behavior down here."

Aerlie wheezed abruptly, and her mouth fell open. Her eyes bulged, and her arms, which were still holding the flask of water, fell into her lap, spilling it out onto the grass.

The guards who were standing nearby all grinned and chuckled lightly.

"Aye," one guard mentions softly. "That's the fun part, watching that face."

"Right to that!" adds another. "Although you don't see it as much these days…"

Aerlie observed the men having their little moment of fun as she tried to recompose herself.

"Is this why you're still alive?" she mutters timidly.

"Well, it is certainly one consequence," Thaelyn affirms. "I am not subject to those same limitations."

"I, uh…wait…" she pauses to recall some portions of the conversation. "Centuries… YOU met this Adalon…something… centuries ago? You're centuries old by now?"

"A bit more than that, at present," he grins impishly.

"More...than centuries..." she flusters. "What are you?"

"Not human. Not even mortal. The Maker ordered up a special champion, born directly of the gods and made part of their society. So, Aerlie, if your Patriarch thinks I might hold such fond relations with them, he is right. They are my family."

"Oh dear!" she whines. "I'm not so sure I want to hear what he has to say about that!"

"Perhaps, but on this occasion, I think we have no choice, as I suspect this is Number Two for us."

"Number Two? Number Two what?"

"Your goddess, whom we address as Aerdrie Faenya back home, came to us in our temple down there..." he glances off to the side and down the road, "...telling us there would be two occasions to offer our service, and after this, she would give us her favor. But Aerlie, I suspect it does not end there, as there are no other creatures within our domain that she might otherwise provide service to with this favor. She tends to specialize in flighted creatures exclusively. Therefore, why would she give this to us when we are not described as her Children?"

"You're asking me?" she whimpers.

"Well, you are flighted, young Miss Ariler," he raises an eyebrow.

"Uh oh... Is this to say you want me to stay here?"

"It is to say she probably expects all of you to with join us."

"Oh! Well, yeah, I suppose that probably would make sense," she titters. "But, again, the Patriarch..."

"I will deal with him when we have a moment. First, these dragons... How many and what kind are we speaking of?"

"Three. Two of them are white and one is blue. But does it actually matter?"

"It does. Each one is different based on its color. This includes their features, their skills, their natural forms of attack, and also their defensive qualities."

"Wow, you must really know your dragons around here."

"Yes, you might say we have some special tutoring available to us."

The guards all erupted in a bold round of laughter as he finishes.

Aerlie turns to study them, suspecting they must know more than they were letting on. But it also seemed a little creepy.

"You people are starting to frighten me, you know? What have you been doing out here all this time?"

"Building a world the way it was meant to be."

Now Thaelyn jumps to his feet and starts shouting orders.

"Captain, sound the alarm! I need troops, give us a full brigade! Have them outfitted with that new dragon-slaying gear…two Whites and a Blue!"

"Aye, and this will give us a good chance to actually try it out for once."

"Yes, well, there is a first time for everything, but Adalon tells us it should work, and I trust her opinion. And find my squire. I need my armor and sword, as well as my special assault gear."

"Right to that!"

"We need mages with rune stones, make it a way-line of twenty. We will rally the men here in the field, and then summon them forward onsite."

"Good to know!"

"Guard, go around and ready the gryphons for our leading charge. And if you have a spare moment, call on Adalon. I think it is high time she got a little exercise."

Before Aerlie could blink, suddenly the bells were ringing, and people were rushing all around her. Thaelyn ran back inside the courtyard while one of the guards dashed along a side walkway behind the guildhall. She had no idea what was happening, but the flurry of activity suggested something big was occurring. The remaining guards watched the action while keeping close to help the girl.

"I think mayhap we should call up a priest to help this girl find her strength again."

"Aye, I'll go fetch one."

She watches as one of them runs off down the road and over towards the temple, soon to emerge with a pair of priests rushing back up to her.

"What's happening here?" she asks.

"Lass, these priests will help you find your strength. We're going to battle, so you should be ready and keep your right mind for it."

"Battle? Just like that? I barely open my mouth and you go wild?"

"Little lady, our purpose in life is to bring this world to order. Anything that might stand in the way of that won't be standing for long."

"Yes, but these are dragons!"

"Aye, we know this, but at this point, I suppose it also includes them."

"Oh dear Blessed Mother, no wonder you people are taking over the world so quickly, and especially if you have a goddess pushing you. Is there anything that might actually hold you back?"

"I can't rightly think of anything, not unless His Lordship tells us so. But he's fought even bigger beasties, from the stories he brings, so I have my doubts even the gods would want to stand in our way, for this point."

"Are you joking, or maybe exaggerating?" she gushes while the priests gather around.

The priests went to work, and Aerlie felt her muscles relaxing and her strength returning. Several moments later, Thaelyn returns outside to retrieve her. He was adorned in his full armor and greatsword. Aerlie gazed at it, and recalled the sword from her youth, but the armor seemed to glow independently of the sunlight.

"What kind of metal is that?"

"This is adamantium, a highly durable magical metal that can take a number of strong enchantments, and tends to emit its own magical aura."

"Really..." she croons. "And you can fight dragons in that?"

"Indeed, I can fight many things in this, including gods and demons, if they should be so brazen as to cross my path."

"Gods and demons!" she shrieks as she glances at the guard again. "What kind of man would try to fight gods and demons? I mean, um...he said...and you said...but..."

"As I mentioned before, I am not human. Rather, I am a type of being called a Celestial, in my case called Aasimar. We are much more capable than your more common example, and significantly more daring to get the job done. Our purpose in life is often the result of the teachings of our divine parentage, which in my case is the one you might know of as Tyr, the Just God."

"Him?" she screeches. "My mother taught me about him, at least a little bit. Part of her priesthood lessons, you know. He's your... um, well, what, in this case?"

"I regard him as my Father. And it is for this reason I have been so successful at uniting the greater majority of this continent under my rule thus far. The people follow my teachings, and those who cannot or will not listen, I simply rehabilitate into better manners."

"Rehabilitate...hmm... Is that how you describe it? So, those nations to our south and east are currently under rehabilitation," she smirks cutely.

"Captain, are we ready?"

"Yes, my Lord! The men are assembling in the field below, and the gryphons are on the runway."

"Excellent. Aerlie, you will join at my side."

"I will?" she flusters. "Where are we going? I mean, I know where we're going, but...um..."

"Just follow along closely and listen carefully to my instructions. All will be well, Child, but we have work to attend."

"And here is where you use that word 'Child' I suppose, like my mother, who is a priestess."

"Indeed! The gods see such as you as the Children of Creation, and so do I. Now, straighten yourself and hold your head up. Today, your people will find their freedom, and perhaps a few other things as well."

He leads them around the walkway down the side of the guildhall. They divert to a short flight of stairs up to another walkway leading all the way to the rear towards a row of structures stretching out along the foothills. The structures were a series of stables lined up behind a long runway strip.

Aerlie followed close behind Thaelyn, with her eyes curiously drawn to his sturdy physique and ornate adornments. The pomp of his presentation suggested he was a powerful warrior, as well as a very prominent individual of high esteem, but she also felt something else. It didn't register consciously, but standing so close and following behind, she felt a kind of attraction, and a rising sense of confidence.

They rounded the corner and passed through a gate to find a long row of huge creatures with a body like that of a lion, and the head, wings, and feet of an eagle. Aerlie wasn't watching where she was going immediately, until she nearly bumped into one. She yelped and leapt back.

"What is that?" she yips.

"This is what we use on those occasions when we need a tactical air advantage. With regrets, Aerlie, you and your wings are a little obsolete. We have our own, and ours are further empowered by magic."

"How do you empower wings with magic?"

"Climb up and I will demonstrate."

"Um, couldn't I just fly alongside? I have my own, and they're very good."

"I am sure they are, but under the circumstances, I doubt you would be able to keep up."

"Oh dear…"

Thaelyn helps Aerlie climb up a small ladder on the side of the saddle mount, and directs her to take the rearward of two seats. The creature was the size of a small elephant and extremely powerful, capable of carrying two people. He takes up his own seat, then turns around to help her with her harness.

"Here, like this," he directs. "We have this backing for support. This is to prevent stress on your spine."

He arranges a stiff seat backing for her to lean against. It contained several safety belts to wrap around her body.

"These belts wrap around from behind, one set over your shoulders, another around the waist. And these buckles fit together in the center, and then into the latches down here in front to clamp your legs in place. Next, you should set your feet into those special stirrups there. They clamp inside so we do not have anything loose dangling about."

"These things lock me in here very tightly. I'm not too sure how I feel about being held in place like this."

"Relax, you will be fine. But all this is necessary for the acrobatics we are likely to perform up there. Simply allow the gryphon to do the flying on this trip."

"If you say so..."

The other gryphons were loading up with a large group of mages, and the assembly began taking up a launch pattern.

"Are we ready?" Thaelyn ushers. "Then let us proceed. Skywing, forward, take us up."

The huge beast lurches forward on its powerful legs, charging and building speed.

Aerlie could feel the muscles rippling through the saddle as it jostled her. She was entirely unaccustomed to riding on a mount, so the experience had her gripping tightly to a metal bar just in front of her for support. As the creature built up its critical speed, it spread its wings and began flapping furiously to lift off.

She watched as the ground slipped away under her. It was a sensation she understood well from her own experience, but sitting on this beast had her looking at it from a completely different perspective. She instinctively felt like flapping her own wings, but needed to remind herself to hold them back.

They lifted higher into the air as a group, taking up a standard V formation, and then angled off to the east. Thaelyn brought out a lance-like staff from a side mount and held it upright.

"Um, what's that for?" Aerlie asks uncertainly.

"Technically, it serves two purposes: Steering, to guide the gryphon through the air, and also that magical empowerment I mentioned. You will want to keep your head low, and I would further suggest you pull your wings in tight."

"Uh huh..."

Thaelyn glances over his shoulder to check the rest of the flight.

Further behind in the background, he could see Adalon coming up from her mountain perch.

"Ah, good, there she is. Are we ready men?"

Aerlie turned to see what he was looking at, and found the others in formation, but then her eyes focused on the enormous creature following just behind them. Her natural reaction was to scream fiercely.

"It's a dragon! There's a dragon chasing us!"

"Aerlie! Calmly, Child," Thaelyn issues sternly. "Do you recall what we spoke of just a moment ago with the Draconics? That is Adalon, she is one of them."

"I swear! You people... And just how does one of THEM fit in with your nation-building plan?"

"She is assisting with it, providing some of her knowledge to spur it along."

"I should've guessed. So, let me see if I have this right. First, they try to shoo us off this world because it wasn't ours to begin with. Then they bring you in to straighten things out, and now you have one of them helping you. Yeah, the Patriarch will have a festival with this one."

"Perhaps if I also mention she shares her strength with our military Order. How do you think he might respond to that?"

"Shares...you mean to actually share... You must be kidding me! Your army shares the strength of a dragon?"

"Indeed, in the form of a blood bond using a special series of enchantments. This is one element that allows us to see to our goals of putting down all the ills of this world and keeping it that way."

"Including gods and demons," she closes her eyes and shakes her head, "if they should make the mistake of getting in your way. Yeah, there go my feathers...they just fell off."

"Interesting. Is this a curious expression among your people?"

"It is, and just for occasions like this. I swear, what happened to this world since we were gone. How long have you been doing this?"

"I first arrived here about four and a half centuries ago. It built slowly at first, but when Adalon entered into it, things took a new turn for us."

Thaelyn raises his staff for the others in the flight group to see, and they each raise theirs to match.

"Now, keep your calm, Aerlie," he asserts. "You will not be expecting this next part."

"When was I ever expected to expect something out of this?" Aerlie mumbles to herself and ducks low for safety.

Thaelyn begins a chant, which is echoed by each of the other riders. A bold series of magical energies then shoot between them that link all their staffs into Thaelyn's lead control. He brings his staff down and sets it into a mounting hook in the collar to the right of the gryphon, then extends the tip just beyond the creature's head and begins another chant.

Aerlie could sense something was about to happen, but as the chant completed, she could not have expected a thundering boom and the world below turning to a sudden blur. The animal had been surrounded by a bubble of energy, and the wind forces outside took on speeds greater than she could ever imagine. She screeches again, but this time tried to stifle her cries as she pressed her face into Thaelyn's back. When she finally found the courage to open her eyes again, she looked out and saw the world passing by at lightning speed.

"Blessed Mother," she wheezes. "If the Patriarch could only see this, I think he would reconsider that land-walker statement."

"Indeed, Aerlie," Thaelyn admits. "And we have had this for a fair amount of time by now."

"I'm sorry I ever questioned you. I mean, it's just that all these things are so new, and so crazy. How can a person even imagine such a thing?"

"When you have a full society of people studying and developing the mage craft, among so many other topics in our academies and schools, many things become possible, if only for the broad spectrum of minds contributing into it. The world is evolving, Aerlie, just as it was meant to be. But unfortunately, too many people in those early days did not share this with the masses."

"And you are…" she muses softly. "But where do you hope to go with all this?"

"We are building a world with a perfectly harmonious society, a type of utopian paradise where we will focus ourselves on sharing our prestige with any we may encounter along the way as we one day move beyond this world."

"Move beyond this world? As if to say there are others out there?"

"There may be many, Aerlie, but we must first find them, and then to see what sort of relations we may have, if any. I do not expect all of them to share our beliefs, but perhaps we can teach a few."

"Does this have anything to do with that mention of rehabilitating?" she giggles.

"Perhaps not precisely," he smiles. "We may do this here to bring OUR world into harmony, but others may need to be approached more diplomatically."

"All right, I suppose I can accept that. But speaking of uniting all of us, and then our goddess and her favor and such, what do you think you would do with us once you have us? I recall some of those other elves in your city, but we're not quite the same. Then there was that Aluer, and the things she told me of what you found for her people. Wow, who could imagine that!"

"Indeed! Their example affords us a few very useful, if also curious capacities, and I would imagine we are only beginning. Perhaps you may also have a few unique qualities that are valuable, if only we can find a good purpose for them. I try to find positive uses for everyone I meet, and your people might hold some rather interesting potential. The only downside would be your Patriarch, at the moment."

"Yes, he is a problem. My mother doesn't like him anymore, and neither do I. I think a lot of people are like this nowadays. He's even taken to insulting me, can you believe it?"

"Insulting? This is certainly not appropriate. Not for him as a man towards a woman, and not as a leader to his followers. How so?"

"It has to do with that 'favor' statement, but twisting it around in a vulgar manner. I think he's using this in relation to, um…well, a few other things some people back home aren't quite settled with about me," she lowers her head.

Thaelyn turns to look over his shoulder at her, and sees her appearing to partially hide her face.

"Aerlie, what is wrong? Do they mistreat you in some fashion?"

"Most people don't say anything, but I know they might look at me sometimes behind my back. I'm…different from the rest."

"In what way? I would not know one from another at this point since you are so new to me."

"My hair, eyes, and wing colors aren't quite normal. No one else in our village has this."

"Are you native to that village? Perhaps, if you came from elsewhere, your heritage carries something different."

"I'm native with my mother, but her colors and mine don't match. She has blue eyes, but not the same as mine. And my hair is abnormal, as is my wing color. No one in the village has colors like these, and some say they're not even natural for us."

"I see. Well, if you do not mind my saying, I personally think your colorations are quite lovely. So, do not think yourself to be anything so abnormal that you would not make a lot of friends elsewhere."

Aerlie suddenly felt a surge of tenderness flow through her, and she started blushing. She felt like a new dawn was approaching with the promise of a fresh day.

"My mother thinks you are the one to bring our salvation, and I suppose I must agree," she glances around at the flight of gryphons and the contrails following behind them.

"Interesting…" Thaelyn wonders. "She holds a belief I was destined to give aid?"

"Yes, and I was created to bring you to us. It dates back to the beginning, or close to it. Our goddess began telling us a savior would come one day, and we need to be patient and wait for it."

"Oh, is that how she is playing it? Yes, the gods will do this on occasion. She must have had a plan from a very early moment. Therefore, we have her arriving in our temple with her message to us. But she says you are to do this?"

"I'm said to be some kind of Chosen One with a Fate following me."

Thaelyn suddenly turns around as best he can to study her. Aerlie observes him, now wondering if she just opened something that held special meaning.

"Um, did I just say something?"

"Fate, such an interesting term, and one I have heard on a few occasions on my side of things. Do you know anything more about this Fate?"

"My mother says she has a few secrets she is keeping, but my Fate was to find someone to help our people."

"This would surely reflect on your goddess and her message to us," he returns forward to review his flightpath. "And if it involves me, I can only suggest it had to be timed in some way that I might hold the proper influence and authority to take this action."

"That makes sense, and therefore the long wait we had. But how long did you say you were here? We were getting this from WAY back."

Thaelyn again turned to glance at her.

"Interesting...VERY interesting... I spent the first millennium of my life in the service of my Father in his court. So, if this dates back so far, it had to be long before I was ready even to come to this world. This now must reflect on the Maker and her apparent designs for me, and therefore suggests a cross deal with your goddess."

"Uh huh...right, and there go my new feathers," she sneers at him playfully. "My mother will probably lose hers as well, and then we have the dear Patriarch again," she sighs.

They were crossing the huge inland sea with the other side coming into view. Aerlie reflected on how long it took for her to travel across it, and then their return trip for comparison, as well as the other statements, and her mind was circling with a flurry of new ideas.

"Just for the sake of asking, if my people were to join your kingdom, what would we do together?"

"My first suggestion would be to educate yourselves on the world affairs in recent times, then to find productive purpose for yourselves. For instance, what manner of trade skills do you have?"

"Me personally? Not much so far. My mother is a priestess and taught me a few things, and my father is a scholar and historian. He knows a little bit of magic, mostly a few tricks passed down the family line, but I was always fascinated by this. As for the rest, he tells me that over the years…and centuries…we lost a lot of our old trade skills as we weren't able to build any proper workshops to train new people."

"Then, how are you able to survive up there? I recall the unfortunate appearance of your homes. Are you not able to repair or rebuild any of those?"

"Using what? The dragons arrive every year to destroy things. Our tools are so old, nothing works by now, and we're not able to gather up anything new to build with, not that anyone would know what to do with it even if we had it. We have a few simple worktables in a cave behind the village, but that's all. We don't even have any proper furniture anymore, like beds to sleep on. And our clothes! Look at me, do you know how many times my mother has struggled to patch this one dress?"

Thaelyn tries looking over his shoulder at her clothing, but only frowns and shakes his head in despair. He returns to face forward again and ponders their situation up in those mountains, and what would be required to correct it. Then his mind turned to the Patriarch and the obvious expectations he would receive in that corner. But soon a thought began to emerge. He mulled over a potential sequence of events that might invoke a rather curious scenario. And as the thought came into focus, he formed a mischievous smile, soon to erupt in a hearty laugh.

Aerlie heard his outburst issuing up, and tried peering over his shoulder to see what he could be reacting to. But with no obvious signs of what could be causing it, she felt a need to ask.

"Um, why are you laughing now?"

"Oh, Aerlie, I am trying to picture our arrival, and no doubt your Patriarch's reaction to it. And naturally, I need to plan my response.

And with all that you just told me, it plays out a very curious picture in my mind."

"What kind of picture? You mean, what you might say to him?"

"Yes, and perhaps this might offer us a most interesting way to present ourselves. But for now, I think we should focus on our primary duties."

"All right, this should be good," she smiles.

"Aerlie, how do your people feel, generally speaking, about your Patriarch and his ravings? When last I was there, I felt there might be some dissent amongst them."

"Yes! Many people are angry with him now, partly for that last visit, and partly for other reasons. You should've seen the argument my parents had with him after you left. It ruffled a lot of people's feathers for months," she chuckles.

"Ruffled their feathers…" he muses humorously.

"Yes, another of our expressions. And again, another thing relating to our wondrous wings, as you can tell."

"Indeed. But perhaps, in this case, we can claim for ourselves a quaint little parody."

"But anyway, he keeps telling us there's no hope and to just keep hiding in the caves until there's nothing left of us."

"How many do you number these days?"

"I don't know the numbers. I don't think anyone bothers to count any more. We can't build a lot of houses, so we end up living with multiple families in fewer buildings."

"Well, one thing I would recommend is a census to record your names, family associations, and population count. Also, we should begin a program of repopulation to bolster your numbers, especially if you are so few that you only fit into one simple village. Having so few people can lead to inbreeding and a number of related complications. Therefore, you need to mix your bloodlines as much as possible to ensure the next generation is healthy and strong."

"Really! All right, I can tell my people about this. Anything else?"

"Clearly, you should not keep yourselves in isolation. You must become a part of the rest of the world and seek support from it. If you do not wish to be a part of our society immediately, we should at least establish trade and commerce, and from this you will benefit from a very robust assortment of goods that could greatly improve your way of life. It might also help to ease you into a union with the rest when you are better experienced."

"Maybe like those Aluerea, I suppose," she nods. "That would be great. But again, I think the Patriarch will have something to say about it."

"Then here is where your people may need to make a decision. They are the ones who must take benefit from this, not simply him."

"Right, I was afraid you might say that. As for me, I actually like that city you live in. Do you think I could find a place for myself there?"

"Absolutely, why not…"

Looming in the distance ahead was now the large mountain range containing Aerlie's home. She studied it as it rushed into view at a frightening rate.

"Hold on now," Thaelyn advises.

He guided the flight of gryphons down into it, adjusting the transport envelopes for better control, and when he saw the Avariel home valley, he brought the group out of its supersonic travel back into normal flight.

On the ground below, the placid stillness was broken by a sudden strafing of thunder strikes riveting the earth as each row of gryphons arrived in sequence and shed their spheres. The Avariel all jerked up to find the source, which was shockingly unexpected as there were no clouds in the sky. There they saw a large flock of strange, flighted creatures arriving in their space, soon followed by the huge silver dragon. Panic instantly ran through the population as the Avariel all rushed to find shelter in the caves again, only days after reassembling their flimsy housing.

"You did that on purpose!" Aerlie teases. "Didn't you!"

"Perhaps…" he smirks innocently. "We would certainly not wish them to miss out on this most important occasion."

Thaelyn brought his team into a gliding approach near the village while Adalon took another direction out in the open field. Her enormous wings kicked up far too much wind to be safe around habitation, to say nothing of these particular buildings.

"I need a way-line out there, twenty-wide," he shouts. "Stretch it across and call in our people. Then return to your mounts and prepare to take to the sky."

The mages rush to set themselves up to create a row of portals. They each pulled out a rune stone and prepared to mark a location. Once they had finished, one of them pulls out a rune leading back to the guildhall in order to send the new runes through to another set of mages standing by on the other side.

Adalon lumbered her way over to join the others after she was on the ground. Thaelyn rode his mount up to meet her, still with Aerlie in the back seat and now shuddering at the thought of getting so close to the gigantic beast.

"Adalon," he calls up to her. "Do you know anything about these three Draconics and why they are here?"

"I do... Much to my sssorrow," she admits. "They defied the Maker'sss... Insssstructions... And turned renegade... To her plansss. They are an insssult... To their breed..."

"What do you think might be the outcome of this encounter? Should we expect hostilities?"

"I sssuspect... It is likely to occur. But I will try... To ssspeak to them... Before thisss... And sssee if we... Can negotiate... An alternative sssolution..."

"Very well, we will hold back until we see the outcome of this. Good luck to you."

Aerlie observed the interaction with fascination, although the words were lost on her, as it was again in the common tongue, not hers.

"You can just go up to that thing and talk to it?" she wonders.

"Indeed, we share a very close friendship. She is a founding member to build our nation, and we relate to each other in a way much like brother and sister."

"Brother and sister with a dragon?" she gasps. "I'm still trying to understand how your society of PEOPLE describes itself as brothers and sisters."

"Indeed, we have created a very productive social environment, not anything like it once was. My teachings have brought new wisdom and insight into their eyes."

"Yeah, I'll bet it did, which just means my people have so much more to learn now."

Thaelyn turns away towards the village while Adalon moves up to one of the nearby ridgelines. She would perch there until Thaelyn had a moment to announce himself to the locals.

As Thaelyn and Aerlie arrived in the village, he turns to her again.

"Here I will ask you to jump off. Just detach the harness there, and you could probably use your wings for the next part."

"Oh, NOW you let me use my wings," she laughs mindlessly.

"Indeed, we cannot allow you to go slack," he grins.

"Right!" she replies cutely. "You know, in this short time, I feel so much different. The conversation, learning so many things, I feel almost like a new person sitting here. Then again, maybe sitting near you is having a weird effect on me," she giggles.

"Indeed!" he chuckles. "I suppose I have been known to do that on occasion."

Aerlie unbuckles her harness, and then uses her wings to lift herself off the back of the creature and settle on the ground.

From inside the cave, the Patriarch and others observed the arrival of the unusual assembly outside. They hesitated about coming out to investigate, but as they observed Aerlie moving around so confidently out there, several of them made the effort to take a closer look, including her parents.

Aerlie moved off into the village to meet with her people, while Thaelyn rode in on his mount behind her. The first into view, of course, was the Patriarch. He looked up into the face of the man on the gryphon and his jaw fell open at what he saw.

"You again!" he shouts. "I might have thought you to be dead by now."

"Ah, yes, and such a pleasant occasion to make this renewed acquaintance with you too, Patriarch. My apologies for disappointing you that I might have outlived my anticipated life expectancy, but these things tend to happen on occasion."

"All right, I can already see where this is going. Let me rephrase myself. I was not expecting to see you again after this long period of time."

"Very well, and I understand. Such a thing might be expected by those who are not as familiar, or as well informed. But here I am, nonetheless. You know, I seem to recall our last meeting where I asked you to explain these misfortunes of yours, but you apparently felt it was unnecessary to do so. Perhaps it was simply due to my diminutive presentation on that occasion, and you felt I was inadequate to fulfill the need. Well, Patriarch, I hope my presentation on THIS occasion might correct for that unfortunate oversight."

"Uh huh... And naturally, I suppose you would offer this extraordinary service of yours free of charge again. Or wait, maybe our...goddess...has once again paid you in advance?"

"Ah, but my dear Patriarch," he retorts smoothly. "Our usual business practices back home carry a certain procedural sequencing. We most often perform our services first, and then present ourselves for payment afterwards. And I certainly would not wish to offend any of our merchant guilds, you know."

"Oh, perish the thought!" he proclaims brashly.

Aerlie stood by her parents and oversaw the interaction. And although Amavain once again found herself fuming at the Patriarch's obvious demeanor, Aerlie began quietly snickering as she listened to the curiously theatrical bantering. Amavain turned to examine her daughter for her subtly concealed outbreak.

"Aerlie, are you alright?"

"Yes, Mother, it's just that I learned a few things on this occasion. Let's listen in."

"In the meantime," Thaelyn continues. "It might be advisable for you to usher your people into safety. After all, we would not want any harm to come to any of these valuable assets…now, would we?"

"Oh, of course not!" the Patriarch submits boldly. "And then afterwards, I suppose we will all come out and offer hugs and kisses for a job well done, right?"

"Why, Patriarch, I was not aware you were such a man, but then who am I to deny you. I am after all a human, am I not?"

"You most certainly are, right to the core."

As Aerlie continued to watch the interaction, she began to understand Thaelyn's direction. He was playing a game, and turning the Patriarch's manners right around at him.

"Fascinating…" she muses quietly. "And yet, somehow so familiar…"

"Aerlie," Amavain whispers. "What am I looking at here?"

"Mother, again, it's alright. Just be silent and let the men have their fun."

"Fun?"

Amavain glared at her daughter, believing her to have finally lost her mind.

"And what is that beast you brought to our home?" the Patriarch points assertively at Adalon.

"Oh, her…" Thaelyn glances nonchalantly over his shoulder. "Yes, is she not an adorable little thing? I found her once and she followed me home."

"Oh, and do you now take her on your little walks through the woods?"

"I would be delighted to, except for those woods becoming a mite trampled along the way. It makes life so difficult for her to find an appropriate relief spot."

"How unfortunate… Now, aside from this happy little banter, why have you come back, and what is THAT doing here?"

"As for why, dear Patriarch, if you know why Aerlie came to me in the first place, I think that should be your answer. We hold certain virtues, and giving aid to people is one of them. It goes along with uniting the world under one rule and correcting for all the misfortune out there."

"Uh huh, right," he nods disbelievingly. "How could I forget? You humans are SO virtuous."

"Indeed! As we...humans...were the ORIGINAL owners of this world before your kind invaded it. As for her, she is a valued member of our founding authority to build our world, which WE started, and YOU intruded upon. And her participation has provided a remarkable spark of motivation to our public to realize those same virtues."

"What you started, and we intruded upon. This is interesting. So NOW, you claim those dragons were actually some sort of servants belonging to you. This is simply grand! Such fantasy! And here you have one providing...motivation. Yes, I'll bet she provides motivation. I'm just wondering how you managed to motivate a monster like that to do anything at all for you!"

"Oh, well..." he waves the statement off casually. "I seem to recall how you once declared us humans to hold such powers of sweettalking, and surely, if we were such masters of the art, dragons would represent the highest achievement in this regard."

"Unbelievable!" he blasts. "You know, I've seen humans in my time, like those to the south and east, but YOU... You really take the prize."

"Why, thank you, Patriarch. You are such a charming conversationalist. But now, if I may..." he turns to point over his shoulder.

Out on the field, he directs at a row of portals opening up and a full brigade of heavily outfitted troops pouring through.

"You once questioned me about my...army. Well, here is a small portion of it. And trust me, there is more where this came from. After all, if I am to conquer a world, I will need a sizeable volume."

"Naturally..."

"Furthermore, as you can see, we make extensive use of portals. Therefore, one can easily suggest that no part of this world is safe from us actually conquering it. But I should also offer a small stipulation here, and that is we would prefer to use diplomatic means first, and only result in warfare if we are pushed into it."

"Really!"

"Yes, really…" he asserts firmly. "Despite your accusations of humans as a breed, they are not savages. They CAN behave in a more civilized manner, unlike a certain Avariel I am familiar with, or all those elves who nearly ravaged the world with their famous Crown Wars."

The Patriarch wanted to respond to this, but he decided to refrain from another outburst, and simply grumbled something unintelligible before speaking again.

"All right, fine. I suppose if you're out there…conquering…the world, I should expect you to be knocking on our door eventually. But did Aerlie actually tell you what we have up here that's causing us so much suffering?"

"She did…on THIS occasion…and so I brought what I believe to be adequate support to accommodate us. After all, we only have THREE dragons to contend with today."

"Oh, my apologies, did you desire more?"

"Well, if you should happen to come across any, I would certainly appreciate the thought. But anyway, together we hope to provide you with a shining example of what you have been missing these past few centuries up here."

"Right, I very nearly forgot, but only the past few centuries?"

"Yes," he sighs overtly. "Everything must have a beginning, even for us humans."

"Of course, and naturally with YOU leading it during this time…"

"Why, yes! You are so insightful, Patriarch. And as a human, I have been so extraordinarily fortunate in this regard."

"I swear…" he covers his eyes and turns away.

Aerlie continued to watch the display, as were the rest, most of whom being unsure of what they were looking at. But in her case, she felt an uncontrollable surge of giggles trying to push its way out. By this time, she simply couldn't help it anymore. She burst out laughing at the two men, drawing the attention of the assembly as she nearly doubled over.

The Patriarch studied her, asking himself what she could possibly be reacting to. The only choices were that she was losing her mind, or she must know a secret. But the absurdity of the conversation simply couldn't afford a rational explanation that this could be their fabled salvation.

"And so," he begins again. "You hope to kill these dragons with this out here. I wonder, do dragons like their dinner roasted or simmered to a slow boil?"

"That would be a question better asked of Adalon over yon," Thaelyn replies. "It was only this last week when we had a full crew trying to pick her teeth of the small village she consumed recently," he briefly glances around the setting. "Such a traditional delight, you should have been there."

Thaelyn offers a parting smile as he turns and rides his mount away to join his people, leaving the Patriarch fuming over that last statement, and Aerlie still quietly giggling.

Adalon had climbed one of the nearby hillsides and positioned herself for her role. The troops were arranging themselves in a formal presentation, at least until the dragons might arrive, and Thaelyn joined with his Captain.

"My Lord, did you enjoy your little exchange with the locals?"

"Indeed, that man reminds me somewhat of an old friend up in Sigil, but without the furry legs. I am eagerly looking forward to my return when this is done."

"Very good, but now we simply need to wait for our quarry to arrive."

"Yes, and I hope they are not far from here. But I am concerned over what may follow. Draconics are supposed to uphold much greater virtue than this, even if they are Chromatic."

"I can't say for certain, my Lord, but whatever comes next, we'll be ready for it."

Adalon glanced at the troops on the field to see they were ready. She observed Thaelyn taking up his position, so she returned her attention to the north and drew in a deep breath. She let out a long bellowing roar, followed by three shorter howls that reverberated and echoed across the hills and far into the distance. Now they just had to wait, as the challenge call could not go unanswered.

Aerlie helped direct her people back inside the cave. She glanced at the Patriarch as they passed by, but he could only scowl at her.

"What's the matter, Patriarch," she asks. "Are you angry that I called for help from land-walkers, and maybe also showed them where we live so they could use portals at any moment to pop in on us? Or are you simply displeased that it might cost us something we don't otherwise have to offer, maybe some form of…favor…you don't want to pay out."

"Aerlie…" he growls.

"Patriarch, I'm tired of hiding under a rock. And I'm sure most of these people are the same. Sure, the nations to the south and east were crooked, but that's not the whole world. Your wrath to blame so many people you don't even know about so many things that aren't their fault is infuriating just by itself. And do you want to know something else?"

"What…"

"Our dimwitted ancestors who brought us up here doomed us to this fate. Our better choice had to be to stay with the nations, and hide behind all their professional armies."

"And do you think they could fight these three dragons?"

"Maybe, at least as far as to chase them away…again…as they apparently did so many times before. And probably a lot better than we could. And they could rally a lot more people to it. So we basically killed ourselves by running away."

"All right! Maybe I cannot argue that by now, if only in hindsight. But if you must know, I'm angry that he'll probably incite those dragons to finish us off once and for all, after they finish him."

"Fine, but I say he could possibly win this battle. And then what? Would you like to make a bet, perhaps?"

"A bet? You must be joking! What sort of wager do we have to offer here? If he loses, the dragons finish us soon after. End of deal. And if he wins, no doubt he'll probably demand us to join this illustrious nation of his."

"And is that such a bad thing, Patriarch? I've actually been there and seen it. I would love to be a part of it. And if any of our people were to see it, they might agree."

"Then what would you have me offer as a wager, my position as Patriarch perhaps? Yes, I'm sure you'd love to take over that role."

"Actually, no, I would be happy with a simple life, free of dragons, free of crumbling homes, dirty clothes, and empty pockets. Patriarch, let me ask you something. Who governed this world before we vanished from sight? Do you remember?"

He pauses to reflect on his history lessons for a moment.

"I recall a number of kingdoms out there at one time."

"Father?" Aerlie calls into the cave. "Can you come out here a moment?"

Lafron emerges into view, along with Amavain to participate in the discussion. He raises his brow as a silent inquiry while Aerlie continues.

"You once told me the story of the Flowering, remember?"

"Yes, the Flowering, where so many of us initially arrived in this world. Ours were among the first, actually."

"Right, and others followed shortly after to begin colonizing this world, which we thought was free for the taking…except for those unfortunate humans we found here," she glances sideways at the Patriarch.

Lafron took notice of her curious manner and quickly reflected on her behavior outside during the debate. He decided to try playing into it as best he could.

"Yes, and they were quite primitive as compared to our people. In fact, I recall several stories of how we had to give instruction and culturing simply to teach them how to live in proper homes, and even to build simple villages."

"Yes, but I think I should emphasize, they were here FIRST. Which might suggest this is THEIR world, not ours."

"Um, well, I suppose we could say yes to that."

"And at what time did they show any capacity to rule their own land?"

"Oh, that was not for a long while…centuries simply to bring them up to a respectable level of sophistication. And later, I recall when our people allocated land to them to build their first nation."

"But at that time, what about us?"

"We held several powerful nations by then. And this would follow the five Crown Wars the elven nations fought, simply to settle their native territories."

"So, this is to say the humans were well behind us…what I mean is the elven societies, not us here…even up to that moment when we departed."

"Yes, I suppose so, although the humans did seem to make a lot of progress during this time."

"But were they ever trying to push us out, or simply living alongside of us."

"Actually, I think many of our cities were largely elven, and the humans mostly had their own territories."

"All right, but now, let's say someone came along and tried uniting all of this. If the human society was not as powerful as ours, why would our people join with them under any circumstances, especially if we weren't even joining forces with our own kind, but instead creating so many independent nations, and further to go to war to prevent any form of unity to begin with."

"Aerlie, that's a big statement."

"Yes, it is. So, what changed in all of this? And especially if to bring those unfortunate, and so often backwards humans, into this position. Unless we say something from outside got in there. And here is where we might need to ask ourselves why those dragons were so angry at OUR intrusion to the place. Do you hold any history of those dragons ever attacking the human population, or only ours."

Aerlie raises her brow and turns away curtly, breaking from the discussion to return her gaze out onto the field. Her parents both glared at each other, and also the Patriarch, who seemed clearly puzzled by the suggestion. They then retreated back inside the cave while Aerlie and the Patriarch remained outside.

"Are you going inside with the rest?" he asks.

"No, I feel confident enough to stand here. If anything comes flying my way, I'll just duck to the side. But they're all the way over there," she points across the field.

"That could change, you know."

"Yes, but the cave entrance is right here," she thumbs over her shoulder.

"All right, as you wish. I think I'll stand here with you, as I'd like to see this as well."

"What about that bet?"

"Aerlie, I still say I don't know what to offer as a wager. Either way, I will lose. If he wins the day, I'm probably out. If he loses, we're all out. What do you do after that?"

"How about this… If he wins, you stifle all your ranting about humans and everything else out there. You open your eyes and your mind to the possibilities that something big is happening in the world, and our salvation is only a small part of it."

Amavain was standing just inside the cave entrance, still listening to the exchange. She peeks out to interact again.

"Aerlie, did you learn something while you were out there?"

"Yes, Mother, I learned several things this time out. On this occasion, I actually asked questions, not simply cowered like a little girl who was afraid of her own shadow. And wow, did I learn something!"

"Really!" she croons. "I wonder… Can you share anything with us?"

"I think I'll wait until after this out here. It might give a better impression. But now, Patriarch, what about you? Can you think of a wager yet?"

"Aerlie," he relents. "If you can stand here so determined to tell me something new is occurring out there, I suppose I may have to accept it, as much as I don't like humans for our past interactions. We may have them governing us before this is done."

He sighs heavily and gazes at Amavain.

"Does the Winged Mother have anything new to say about this?"

"I haven't heard anything specific for a while," she responds. "So, I'm guessing she is simply waiting for Fate to find its way on its own time. It might be outside her control."

"Great, and so we have this out here now… Aerlie, I don't have a wager to offer. I think I'm going to lose either way. But maybe, if this big nation really is so great, perhaps we can find a better place to live if we can get their help to actually finish this."

"All right, fair enough," she nods. "Now, let's watch the show. I'm hoping this will be really exciting."

"Are you sure you haven't lost your mind, young lady?"

✦

Thaelyn and his people waited. The troops on the field included front-line warriors as well as archers. There was a line of high-ranking mages, mostly elves at this point, as they demonstrated the longest lifespans to reach the higher tiers of study. And lastly, there were a number of priests present to assist the injured along the way. Much like with the demonstration from Morakane, the combined versatility of this array would normally be enough to send the average opponent force into hiding, if they knew what they were facing. But on the outside, they looked like any other army, except for their equipment.

Just like with Thaelyn, his soldiers all used adamantium armor, as well as weapons and shields made of mithril, another metal of a similar nature, although in this case the front line was mostly using polearms. The archers were all equipped with their enhanced elemental bows, which used magical ammunition, rather than physical arrows. These would be more effective against dragons and their hard scales. The mages were adorned with heavily enchanted robes, and a fine chainmail weave undergarment to protect their critical areas. They carried long enchanted staffs, and were mostly skilled in elemental magic.

Aerlie stood outside the mouth of the cave. This gave her and the Patriarch a clear view of the scene on the field. Her parents were just inside, along with a few others peeking through, hoping to catch a glimpse of the action, while the rest were deeper within, many of whom huddled together in cautious trepidation of what to expect out there.

Many moments passed, and Thaelyn, along with his Captain and others, waited for a response to Adalon's call. Finally, a bold sound echoes across the hills of another roar and a series of howls.

"They come now," Thaelyn emits calmly. "Ready the men, Captain. We cannot be sure how this will proceed, but we should expect them to be unfriendly once they see us."

"Absolutely, my Lord..."

Adalon rested on the hilltop, scanning the horizon for any sign of movement in their direction. Then, she sees something just coming into view in the distance, a series of three shapes emerging over a far set of mountain peaks.

"Thisss day... Will be your lassst. Cretinsss..." she hisses under her breath. "You dissshonor yourssselves... And me as well..."

Aerlie and the Patriarch heard the call, and they strained to see anything out there on the horizon. Word was echoing through the cave of the response, and more were becoming curious to see what was happening outside. This could be a historic moment for them, and now they wanted to see it. Several began to push their way forward to peek outside, and as more emerged, Aerlie found herself being joined by a small group that continued to grow.

The Patriarch turned to see the people coming outside again, and he felt a distant sensation of uncertainty. The caves were their only shelter, but if this did turn out to be their famous salvation, he could be out of a job soon.

They all continued to wait until they finally caught a glimpse of the shapes coming into view as they made their way closer across the mountainous terrain.

"There!" Aerlie shouts and points. "I see them."

"Yes," the Patriarch admits grudgingly. "I just hope your friend knows what he's doing out there. All they need to do is step on those men, and the battle will be over."

Thaelyn watched the three dragons arriving on the scene, the leader apparently being the Blue, and then two Whites following after. The group settled some distance just in front of Adalon and the line of soldiers.

"Ssso…" the Blue scowls angrily. "These little onesss… Finally found aid… To preserve them. But do you think… Thisss pittance… Is sssufficient… To oppose usss? What do you want… ssSilver! Are you hoping… To challenge usss… For these sssmall pesssts…?"

Adalon was already angry enough for their insolence at this long history of assaults, and she was especially insulted at their manners with another Draconic, but she held her temper just enough to make her own introduction. However, given that Thaelyn was on the field, and he knew the Draconic language by now, she chose to use her ancestral tongue instead, to keep the conversation private.

"You would dare… To insssult me… With sssuch vivid… Disssrespect…?"

The Blue was taken aback at the statement, not so much by the wording, but that it was spoken in the ancient Sarrukhan tongue.

"Why do you choose… To ssspeak to me… In thisss form… ssSilver? Is it because… Of these sssmall onesss… Below usss? Do they now… Dare to learn… Our proud language?"

"Ssstay your tongue… Cretin! What the younger racesss learn… Is not your concern. But if you knew… Who you are addresssssing… At thisss moment… You would cringe before me!" she bellows.

Thaelyn stared at the odd interaction, and then turned to his Captain. The Captain looked back at him curiously.

"My Lord, are you getting anything out of this?"

"Captain, I must admit, I am not. That is not the Draconic language they are using. The Blue began this way, but she changed it, and this causes me to wonder why. What language is this and why would Adalon choose this over the more common form?"

"Perhaps it's a private one. You know how she is sometimes with her aloof nature."

"This is true, but why on this occasion. We are simply bringing justice to three that went on a rampage of some sort."

Aerlie and her family gazed at the confrontation and listened to the dialog, although it was a mystery as to what was being said.

"What's going on out there?" she muses quietly.

The Blue glared at Adalon for her last remark.

"Why would I cringe... Before a ssSilver...? You are not... Better than me..."

"Perhapsss... If I were only... A sssimple Draconic!"

"Sssimple...? Do you now... Sssuggest yourssself... To be more than that...?"

"I am... But you were not... Intended... To know my plansss. Inssstead... You went out... And began... Tearing apart... All I have tried.... To create here. I am... The Maker Kuroku!"

The Blue reeled back and hissed, followed by the others.

"He didn't like that one," the Captain suggests. "Whatever it was..."

"Imposssssible! And prepossssterous! Why would the Maker... Take sssuch form...? It makesss no sssense!"

"You are a ssservant... Blue! Your purpossse... Is to defend... What I tell you... To defend. My lassst inssstructions... Were to withdraw... From thisss place. Why did you not obey...?"

"Inssstructions...? If any of your... Inssstructions... Made any sssense... Perhapsss... We would know WHY... We mussst obey! You tell usss... To defend thisss world... From the invadersss. Then you tell usss... To withdraw... And leave them be. Then we sssee... More invadersss... Even worssse than before... And you ignore them... Completely. What is your purpossse here... Maker...?"

Adalon sighs briefly as she realized her complex plans and secrecy were bound to bring about something like this.

"It is true... I was concerned... For the integrity... Of my plansss... When the elvesss arrived. But then I sssaw them... As potential value. Our original plan... To dissssuade their advance... Was not working... And thisss demanded... Reconsssideration.

Therefore… I changed my plansss… To include them. And many of you… WERE informed of thisss…"

"These little thingsss…?" he spits as he directs his gaze at the Avariel peeking out from the cave.

"Yesss!" she roars. "And I will have you… Show proper reverence… When you ssspeak to me… About them. The humansss… Are no different… In their own way…"

"Wow," Aerlie considers. "I don't know what they're saying, but it sounds angry."

"Yes, Aerlie," the Patriarch offers. "This much I will admit to. But so far, it's not helping us."

"Reverence… To you?" the Blue argues. "She who would dare… Claim herssself… To be the Maker?"

"You are a disssgrace… Blue! But I will not… Hold you to thisss… Ssstatement… As my part… In my plansss… Is not even known… To the other Powersss…"

"What?" he pulls back. "You keep your sssecrets… Even from them?"

"Yesss… As I do not… Want them… To interfere… With my plansss… For my revenge… Againssst my former Massster…"

The Blue halts, and cocks his head at the odd suggestion.

"That is a curious one," Thaelyn submits. "I wonder what that statement was."

"Indeed, my Lord," the Captain states. "I would be truly fascinated to know the nature of this argument."

"Former Massster…?" the Blue wonders. "What former Massster…?"

"You should remember thisss… From your early hissstory. Our people knew of it… Sssince that final battle. He is one… Of the Ancient Onesss. They whom we call… The Primordialsss…"

"Gah…!" he blasts. "One of them… Ssstill exisssts…? No. I do not recall… Thisss lesssson… And neither would I want to. But by the Powersss… If you hold designsss… Againssst one… Sssuch as them… You musssst have… Losssst your mind… If you think… These little onesss… Can be your inssstruments… Of revenge. Jussst look at them. They cannot even... Hold their own... Againssst sssuch as usss..."

"Did you think... My plansss... Would involve them... In thisss condition... Forever? Our ancessstors... The ssSarrukh... Did not ssstay... In the ssStone Age... For an eternity... And neither will these. They mussst be grown... And conditioned... And thisss is where... My work... Continuesss. But YOU... You are dessstroying it now..."

"And how are we... Desstroying your work... With sssuch weaklingsss?"

"By not allowing them... To grow... As I desire them to. You argue my plansss? You argue my decisionsss? Yesss... At firssst... These other racesss... Invaded our ssspace. But they did not relent... As weaklingsss might. They ssstood their ground... As warriorsss. Thisss is ssstrength. They fought you... At the temple. Thisss is alsso ssstrength. It mattersss not... If their bonesss break... Or the flesh tearsss. Ssstrength is not alwaysss about... Physical durability. And each of these racesss... Demonssstrated... Itsss own value... Except the orcsss..."

"Yesss... And about those orcsss. Why did you not tell usss... To keep them away?"

"Because the othersss... Regarded you... As the enemy. If I should sssend you... To drive them away... Thisss might bring... Sssympathy... And rally the otherssss... To their defenssse. It was a tactical demand... To have you withdraw... And let the local racesss... Attend to it..."

"Hmm... Perhapsss. But then you choose... To use them... To pursssue a Primordial? They were godsss... Maker! Divine beingsss... And you should know... The difference... Between that... And mortalsss. These little onesss... Cannot even form... A sssimple union... Amongssst themssselves!"

"Had you allowed me... The time... To sssee my plansss through... You would know... Thisss was ssstill... In the making. When was the lassst time... You went outssside... To look at the world...?"

The Blue hesitated, as he had to admit, he wasn't paying much attention to things during this time. He turned to glance at the people on the field below him before responding.

"Had you actually... Informed usss of thisss... We might not be here now!"

Adalon held her reply briefly, realizing this was another aspect of her elusive nature. She had to take at least some of the blame here. And yet, the errant behaviors of these others could not be overlooked. There were bigger concerns than simply her personal manners at play.

"At thisss moment... It does not matter... Blue! You disssobeyed ordersss. And while I mussst admit... My own error... Yoursss transgressssed beyond that! You went on a rampage... To exterminate... An innocent form of life. Thisss is inexcusable!" she roars. "Even the original ordersss... Were not to dessstroy... Only to dissscourage. You are no better... Than the Ancient Onesss... For thisss point. You are Draconicsss! I made you... To be the guardiansss... Of they who could not... Hold their own!"

"Guardiansss... Bah..." he spits. "We fight pestsss... And Negative trash... And thisss is our claim to fame? Thisss world... Is a zoo... Filled with creaturesss... Who can barely... Ssspeak to each other. And YOU! Look at you. You are a Divine One... Maker. You are above thisss. But you take thisss form... And then join... Thisss menagerie?"

"I have my reasonsss... To demonsssstrate mysssself... In his eyesss. But I sssuppose... It mattersss not... To explain thisss. Not to you... As you ssseem... To have made your choice..."

"Indeed!" he retorts harshly. "If your plan... Is to be a part of it... You mussst be... Insssane! I will not follow... A mad Maker... With sssuch inconceivable plansss... Againsst a forgotten Massster... Using sssuch frail bodiesss... As these below usss..."

Adalon had heard enough. She suspected it would come to this, and though it pained her to hear this from her own Children, their crimes, combined with her plans and the sanctity of her work, was paramount.

"Frail…" she growls. "Yesss… Blue. Do you want to challenge… My creationsss? Do you want to sssee… How frail they are… Now that I have grown them… Nearly to maturity?"

The Blue halts his response momentarily. He turns to examine the soldiers on the field, as do the other two with him.

"I sssee only bodiesss. And bodiesss… Are ssstill bodiesss… Maker. Be they dressssed… In fancy armor… Or ssstark naked… They ssstill sssquish the sssame…"

"Then bring your challenge… Blue… And tessst them. Thisss becomesss your Fate… For I am the Maker… Of guardian racesss… And thisss is… My latessst example…"

"Gladly!" he bellows. "And we shall sssee… How durable they are…"

The Blue and his two cohorts began to arrange themselves for a showdown.

"You…" he directs to one of the Whites. "Take those below. They should not be… Much of a bother. And you…" he issues to the other White. "Take her. Her foolishnessss… To take thisss form… Will be her undoing. Her icy breath… Cannot harm you. As for me… I have finally had… My fill… Of those bugsss down there…"

The Blue circles around as he prepares to take off, while the two Whites advance on their respective targets. Thaelyn saw the changing postures and movements, and immediately began issuing orders.

"Here we go, men! Forward! Gryphons to the sky, support the troops!"

Aerlie and her people also took notice of the new activity.

"Oh dear…here they go."

"Yeah," the Patriarch admits. "But I'm also wondering what that long discussion was about."

"Whatever it was, they were clearly angry about something. Probably the crimes they were committing against us."

"Crimes? Aerlie, wait a moment, what do you mean?"

"Those three were never under orders by their creator goddess to attack that temple. They violated something by doing so, as well as attacking us."

"What?" he gushes. "Orders? These monsters have orders of some kind?"

"They're not monsters, Patriarch, they're guardians, and this world was their charge, until WE arrived. But stupid us, we simply saw them as monsters. This world is apparently a pet project…for the HUMANS, not us."

The Patriarch gaped at Aerlie for the outlandish suggestion, before returning to the scene in front. Her two parents also gawked at her statement, as they glanced at each other.

Thaelyn charged forward on his gryphon and took off the ground. He observed Adalon facing down one White, and his men moving on the other, but then he took notice of the Blue making a circuit around the rest with his eyes on the Avariel at the far side of the canyon.

"Indeed, I might expect as much," he mutters to himself.

The Blue launched into the air and gained altitude in his attempt to make an end run past the front line of soldiers. Thaelyn charged up his staff and set it in place. He turned the gryphon away from the action as a means of defraying any immediate attention towards him, and called on the enchantment.

His mount was soon enveloped in the energy bubble and zipping upwards in a steep climb, though not at supersonic speed this time, in order to prevent the disturbance of the sonic barrier, and therefore calling attention his way. He swept around in a broad elliptical arc, coming back around and lining up with the Blue. He would take this one himself.

Aerlie and the others watched Thaelyn and his surreal movements.

"That cannot be possible," the Patriarch wheezes. "How can anyone cause something to move so fast in the air?"

"They have some very powerful magic these days, it seems," Aerlie affirms.

Thaelyn angled his glidepath to follow above the Blue as it soared in the direction of the caves.

"Uh oh…" Aerlie mutters. "That one's coming this way!"

Thaelyn brought the gryphon low over the dragon's back, keeping to its blind spot. He then pulled out a long whip-like lasso and held it at the ready. He dropped out of his enchanted travel and quickly stuffed the staff back into its sheath, then popped open his harness and raised himself up from his saddle.

The gryphon could feel Thaelyn's shifting around, and knew from its own training what was coming next. Thaelyn issued a command for it to dive down, matching its speed with the dragon just behind its head, while Thaelyn pulled himself to a crouching posture and backflipped off the mount as it swooped low to the target.

Aerlie and the Patriarch gazed in fear and awe as Thaelyn landed on the dragon's back, whipping the lasso around its neck, and catching it as it came up the other side. Thaelyn's boots were fitted with special vice-like teeth, which he then latched onto the dragon's scales to hold him in place.

"He must be insane!" the Patriarch whispers.

"He's certainly something," Aerlie responds quietly.

"What?" the Blue blasts. "Who are you... That you would dare... Assssault me? Am I now... To be treated... No better... Than a common horssse?"

"Blue..." Thaelyn shouts in Draconic. "With all proper respect for your kind, you have apparently demeaned yourself. I am simply finishing the job."

"Is that ssso... And worssse... You DO ssspeak... Our sssacred tongue..."

"I am something of a special case, but generally speaking, yes, we are familiar with it. You would expect otherwise by now?"

"Perhapsss not... But for you... To insssult me... By treading on my back... I will sssee you... Sssuffer..."

"You will first need to dislodge me. Do you think yourself capable of that minor trick?"

"Aarrgh!!"

The Blue now starts twisting and turning frantically trying to throw Thaelyn off its back. It diverts itself to swaying into curves and spirals, combined with swoops and dives.

Adalon was facing off against one of the Whites. The two of them matched up fairly well on size, but the White was much older, at least as a Draconic, and considered himself more seasoned and physically robust. They charged at each other, clashing with a heavy thud and a scraping of scales. Their roars were mixed with the snapping of their jaws as each one looked for an opening.

The second White found itself looking down on a full lineup of soldiers, but considering his experience with the lesser races, he felt confident in his position where their simple capacity was concerned... at least until they began their assault.

Thaelyn's army had arranged themselves with the front-line soldiers and their polearms, followed by the archers and mages. The soldiers in front held their line initially while the mages charged up for their attack. When the White was ready to make his move, the first thing he experienced was a sudden shock of numerous ethereal fists pounding down on him from above, followed by several lightning strikes and fireballs. This was soon accompanied by innumerable elemental arrows stinging him with fire and electrical jolts. The experience was a far cry from his last official battle, which in this case was against the Avariel and their simple physical arrows. He fell to the ground stunned, and in very short order, took serious injury.

With the White down, at least temporarily, the soldiers moved in with their mithril halberds. The enchanted blades were part of a new generation of weapons in the world that might be able to pierce a dragon's scales, and using this, they began stabbing and slashing at its legs and wings, with the aim to cut through vital tendons hoping to cripple the dragon's ability to move.

The White roared in pain at the onslaught, swiping at the mass of soldiers and knocking several of them away. He climbed back to his feet and tried stamping down on some of them, only to miss as their quick reflexes and magical enchantments allowed them to quickly dodge and roll to the side. He swiped again at the encroaching line, this time sending a group of them flying through the air to land some distance away.

"Well, there goes part of it," the Patriarch relents as he observes the scene. "Just like I said…"

"Patience, Patriarch," Aerlie assures. "We're not done yet."

The White now turned his attention to the remaining front line, making ready to swipe at another mass, when he sees movement to the side. The group he just sent off through the air were now picking themselves up and making a renewed charge.

"What? Imposssssible! You should be dead!"

Aerlie and the Patriarch also took notice of the unlikely display.

"How can that be!" he ushers. "Those men flew a good hundred feet away, and they simply stand up again? They should at least have a few broken bones in them."

"Maybe it's the armor?" Aerlie remarks innocently.

"Aerlie, I may not be an expert in warfare…or armor, for that matter…but the body simply cannot withstand that sort of torment."

"Yeah, I guess you're right. So it must be all those enchantments he gives them that make them supernaturally strong."

"Huh?" he yelps.

"Well, hey, he needs to take over the world. How you think he's going to do that with soldiers who fall down so easily."

Adalon and her quarry snapped and swiped at each other, with Adalon backing away and drawing her prey along while she readied herself for a strategic riposte. She played the weakened victim of her opponent's imposing stature, luring him into position.

Thaelyn rode the Blue like a rodeo performer as it tried desperately to throw him off.

"What is holding you?" the dragon blasts. "How can you be… Ssso firmly attached?"

"Ah, I am so glad you asked," he replies jovially. "You see, I have some rather remarkably talented people working for me, and with a little help from Adalon over there, we fashioned some custom gear that anchors me nicely in place."

"Thisss is intolerable! How can… A sssimple human… Find the ssstrength… To cling to my back?"

"Such a fascinating question…" Thaelyn muses. "You know, it

would seem you and the Avariel down there are missing an important piece of modern history.”

“Oh… Is that ssso! And what remarkable… Piece of hissstory… Are we absssent?”

“It has to do with my activity in this world. You both think I am a simple human. And neither of you realize what I am doing here.”

The Blue had been making a continual effort of swerving and dipping in the hopes of eventually discharging his unwanted passenger. But on this mention, he suddenly stopped his frantic movements and leveled out. He was now flying straight across the field behind the lines of the other battles and trying to peer over his shoulder at his guest.

“What do you mean?” he asks tentatively. “What are you… If not human? No… Wait… Your aura… Positive Ordered! Aargh! You carry divine esssence! A Celessstial? Are you a hybrid form?”

“Very good, Draconic,” he affirms. “Your senses do you well. But unfortunately, they seem to be a bit late in coming, for all you have done here.”

“It mattersss not! She is mad… Nonethelessss. And why… Would she call… One sssuch as you… To thisss place?”

“I was not simply called, I was apparently made for it, or so it would seem. My purpose here is to unite this world and clean all the errant elements out of it. And though I regret this statement, you have apparently become one of those.”

“But you… Here?” he hesitates. “And yet… It ssstill makesss no sssense. What good are you… Againssst her Massster…?”

Thaelyn now pulls out his sword and readies it.

“Her what? Who are we speaking of?”

“You do not know? Incredible! How does she hope… To fight a battle… With toysss… That do not even know… Why they fight…”

“I am at a loss for your meaning, Blue.”

“It does not matter. She is insssane… And if you think… You can ssslay me… Celessstial… I dare you to try…”

“As you wish…”

Thaelyn brings up his sword and whispers into it, once again causing it to erupt in the brilliant blue flame.

The Blue was trying to look over his shoulder to see what Thaelyn had in his hand, and when he saw the sword light up, a chill ran through him.

"What is that thing…?"

"A weapon called Amaunator's Flame, gifted to me by my Father, the Power named Tyr."

"Imposssible! I know of that one! What is that doing here?"

"I retrieved it from the Abyss some time ago…"

Thaelyn then turned and made a hard swipe at the dragon's right wing, chopping through a portion of it and debilitating the dragon's capacity to fly. The creature screeched and then tilted as it lost its lift and began to fall out of the sky. Thaelyn crouched low, bracing for the impact as the Blue made a hard crash-landing.

Thaelyn now had to move quickly. He dropped his lasso and pulled his boots out of the latching mounts on the scales. He swiveled to slash the other wing and further to reinforce the damage on the first, then rolled off the rear quarter and hit one of the hind legs. The Blue let out a series of loud wails as it tried to locate its assailer to counter the attack.

Aerlie and her people, most of whom had come outside by now to watch the show, gazed at the swiftness of Thaelyn's movements, and the precision of his strikes. He rolled under the Blue's tail and cut through the tendons on the other hind leg, then circled around to a wing and began climbing up onto its back again.

"Hold ssstill…!" the Blue scorns. "Where are you…?"

Thaelyn rushes along the spine to the front left shoulder and shouts an attention call, then rolls off the other side while the dragon turns to find the source. He hits the ground and spins for another hit, now to the right front leg, and quickly jumps out of the way.

The Patriarch stares at the carnage in astonishment.

"How can a man commit so much damage to a dragon by himself?"

"That's a really good question," Aerlie muses. "If only for the size of the thing!"

"Yes, but Aerlie, I'm not just talking about size here. Those scales are said to be nearly impervious to most weapons, and he's simply slicing it to ribbons."

"Well, that sword of his is certainly a unique example. I have no idea where he found it, but that thing could probably cut through anything, by the looks of it."

"And that's another thing. Although I can't say I'm much of an expert on enchanted weapons, what I've heard of it tells me anything so powerful that it can perform like that cannot be made by mortal hands…or at least by the stories I heard once."

"That's really interesting, Patriarch. And from what I'm seeing out there, you may be right. So, it begs us to ask where he got it and how he can even hold it up."

"Uh huh, and it also begs me to ask what you know of it, because your demeanor right now tells me some of those things you apparently learned out there must've informed you about something."

"Maybe they did, but you didn't ever believe what I told you before, so I won't bother you with all this new nonsense. I'll just wait and see how it ends."

The Patriarch glares at her, silently realizing he underestimated the situation, and now she was rubbing it in. He slowly returns his gaze to the scene out on the field.

"Aerlie, can you actually blame me for not believing such crazy stories? Most of it just doesn't sound real."

"All right, Patriarch, I'll admit, they don't. I didn't believe most of it either, until it was demonstrated right in front of my face. I screamed when they told me they had to amputate, and I was absolutely amazed to see they had something to restore the stumps back to normal. So, I guess all those wars, and probably the injuries that go along with it, demanded they find a solution to so many disabled people."

"Yes, I suppose that would make sense. Maybe it was inevitable, even unavoidable after a while."

"I suppose it might also require someone with the gumption to actually order it."

"Maybe so," he nods.

The soldiers had very nearly laid out the White they were assaulting. It had been crippled on all its legs, and its wings were in tatters. It was scorched and partially paralyzed from the electrical shocks, and just barely able to move its head as it tried to follow the many soldiers rushing around it.

Adalon kept just out of reach of her opponent as she lured it into position.

"Jussst where do you think… You are going… Maker?" he charges. "Do you not… Remember… How to fight?"

"I have fought… More battlesss… Than I can count… And I have taught… More warriorsss… Than I can remember. Perhapsss… It is you… Who should anssswer… That quessstion…"

Adalon had been backing away up the side of a small knoll while she spoke, which was nothing extraordinary as most of the terrain was very hilly. But it left the White in a gully. She kept her posture to a low crouch as she discreetly readied her move.

The White regarded the statement as rhetorical, as he felt quite confident in his skills. He looked for an opening, and Adalon finally obliged by backing partway down the other side, allowing the White to take the high ground.

"Of courssse… I will anssswer it. Let me show you…"

He makes a lunge at her by leaping off the hilltop. Adalon digs in for traction, and then springs up to knock him sideways in midair, which sent him off-balance and tumbling down the other side. She quickly rushes up the hill, then to make her own lunge at him before he could recover. She sailed down to land on top of him, rolling him over onto his back and pinning him, then to begin slashing and biting at his legs and neck.

"Wow, I really don't want to be him right now," Aerlie relents.

The Blue was in agony by now. Three of his four legs, and both wings were crippled. Thaelyn circled around to climb up a wing onto its back once more. But the Blue was beginning to realize there was clearly something he had been missing in this time. He turned to observe the progress of the troops and their opponent, and saw they nearly had him beat.

"How is it posssssible…" he relents. "Celessstial… Wait… Please…"

Thaelyn halts as he again arrives on the dragon's back.

"Jussst what is… Your purpossse here?" the Blue demands feebly. "You came to unite them… Into one?"

"Yes, and to usher in a new era for this world. They have stagnated for too long, and now is the time to correct it."

"But thisss does not… Provide… A full ansswer. If she did not tell… Everything…" he muses distantly. "Of coursse… It mussst be. The Measure of Balance. Why did I not… Sssee thisss before. Thisss is her way…" he shakes his head remorsefully. "Tell me… How long… Have you been here… And what… Have you accomplished… In thisss time…?"

"Curious… I arrived about four and a half centuries ago, after a thousand-year term in study and service with my Father, and so far, a greater portion of the continent of Sein'amar is under my authority."

"Four centuriesss…" he considers. "You mussst not be using… Very aggressssive meansss… To take possssession… Of thisss world…"

"I am attempting mostly political methods, only to result in military means when the need demands it. And then we must allow for the assimilation of a new culture and such, and largely as a slow progression through the population."

"Indeed! Yesss! As you surely… Could not perform… All of it at once. Thisss could account for it. Not bad…" he relents. "But your men… How are they able… To bring down… A mature White… Ssso quickly? We are not… Ssso easily defeated… By mere mortalsss. You should know thisss…"

"I do, and normally I would agree. But Adalon over there assisted in the development of our military by sharing a bit of her Draconic blood in a special bond with our people to further empower us."

"In all Creation!" he surges. "She did thisss for you? No wonder she holdsss… Sssuch high expectationsss. Maybe she was right. And indeed… I have disssgraced myssself."

The Blue pauses to mull his errors, now realizing what he has done and how he has behaved. He peers over his shoulder again to study Thaelyn as he stood there waiting for his next action.

"You are Positive Ordered. Who is… Your divine parent… Celessstial?"

"Mine is the greater Power Tyr."

"Jussstice and Law… I should have guessssed. Then I beg you… To grant me… A sssimple requessst. Give me… An honorable death…"

This suggestion perplexed Thaelyn, as he wasn't expecting it, coming from a dragon.

"You ask for an honorable death?"

"It is all… I have left now…"

"One moment, what was that conversation you shared a moment ago with Adalon? And who is this 'she' you referenced several times? Is it the same?"

"She…" he pauses to consider his words. "I think perhapsss… I should sssegregate my termsss… For better clarity. On one ssside… We have the conversssation… Which she apparently chose… To keep private… If you ssspeak our language. She ssseems to like it thisss way…"

"Oh, naturally, and I do know Adalon and her elusive nature."

"Yesss…" he chuckles feebly. "Sssometimes… We are like thisss. But on the other sssside… As a Celessstial… You should know… Of our Maker… Correct?"

"I am familiar with the name, but very little detail, other than she went missing some while ago, and she also seems to be rather elusive."

"We probably all inherit… Sssome part of thisss… From her," he chuckles again.

"I suspect she is also at the root of several things in this world."

"Oh? What sssort of root… Do you ssspeak of?"

"The origin of life on this world, the human population… We

found evidence of a society calling itself the Sarrukh who apparently arrived to refurbish this otherwise dead world. And if the Maker further desired this as a special project, first by using you to guard against trespassers, and later to assign me as one who would bring it into order, I suspect these Sarrukh were also her doing. Do you know this name?”

“I know of it. They are an ancient race… And highly revered. But thisss… Is all I can sssay. We mussst follow… The Measure of Balance… No different from the ressst. Although we have failed… In our dutiesss,” he glances at the other two dragons. “You should know… The rulesss of growth. And I sssuspect… One day… There will be more to learn. But now… Lisssten to me. You should know… That the Maker… Is not only elusssive… In her wordsss… But alssso her designsss. She does not wish… Her plansss… To be known… By any who do not… Need to know… Until the appointed time. It would sssseem… You have a purpossse. Therefore… You mussst follow… Your courssse… As it comesss to you. It is her way. And it would sssseem… She is gifting you… Essspecially… To fulfill your needsss…”

“Like with the blood bond? That would seem a most unusual thing for a Draconic to do.”

“It would indeed! But look at the resultsss…”

Thaelyn glances over at the troops who were finishing up the White.

“You could quite posssssibly… Fight godsss… In thisss form,” the Blue chuckles faintly. “Sssuch a remarkable… Achievement….”

“I may need to agree. Although I wish it did not need to be demonstrated against such as a Draconic.”

“You are… An honorable warrior… Celessstial. Teach your people well. And I am sssorry… For thisss as well…”

“But tell me briefly. Your reason for being here, I suspect you disobeyed orders where that temple was concerned, as we regard the so-called Age of Dragons to have been on the decline long before that.”

“Yesss. We had inssstructions… To withdraw… Long before

that day. But we did not… Undersssstand… Her motivesss… Before now. I was angry… For the conflictsss… Where the orcsss were concerned. We were told… To ignore them. Thisss did not make sssense…"

"Ah! Let me guess. You were supposed to be guarding this world against intruders, and therefore the Age of Dragons where everything else was concerned. But those orcs…they actually would be undesirable. They certainly are an unpleasant sort. But unfortunately, at this point, the rest regarded YOU as undesirable, not knowing of your true intent here. Therefore, if you attack them, it could rebound in unpredictable ways."

"Very good! You are clearly… Well trained. And here is our error… And our disssgrace… And even worssse… Our shame… For our behavior… With the Avariel…"

"And therefore the conversation, I suppose, to further explain these details?"

"Yesss. We departed… From her counsssel… Long ago… And therefore… Did not receive… Any further review…"

"I see. And here you regret your actions."

"I do… And I would ssspeak… For the othersss… As I am resssponsible for thisss…"

Thaelyn sighs thoughtfully as he reflects on the discussion. He realized this would be one of those moments where his teachings and divine authority from his Father would come into play, but this one would not be a pleasant occasion. He had to pass judgment on one who realized his own wrongdoing and regretted it deeply.

"I believe I understand," he declares. "Very well, Blue. On the authority granted to me by my Father, Tyr, Lord of Justice, I will grant upon you release as befitting a proper warrior. I have heard your confession, and will forgive you your sins. But the pronouncement of law must decree a resolution to this matter, and this resolution must follow with a final determination of outcome. The deeds performed, and the stain this leaves behind, does demand the cleansing of that stain, such that it will not tarnish any other which may come hereafter. To this, we come to our judgment. The integrity of our breed must remove that which would invoke impurity. Your regret may allow you to carry your honor for your other deeds, but this impurity must meet with the dissolution of your service. And as I must be the one to carry this out, I will send you forward with a clean blow, then to honor what you and yours truly represent, had this impurity not manifested itself."

"Well ssspoken… Celessstial. I thank you. Maker… Forgive me…"

Adalon pulls up briefly from her target, which was partially maimed by now, and turns over her shoulder to look at the Blue.

"Go in peace… My Child…" she mutters softly. "I hear your plea…"

The Blue lowers his head to allow a clear shot at his neck. Thaelyn steps forward along the spine again, this time to line himself up. He brings his sword up in a moment of silent salute, then takes several bold steps and jumps off the side with a twist to slice downward, cleanly beheading the dragon.

Aerlie gawked at the display, unsure how to react to it, other than with revulsion to her senses for the blood. But her curiosity and intrigue of seeing a lone man, of any sort, killing a dragon, was mystifying. Further, that his army was putting the final touches on the White, and Adalon was finishing hers as well. All she could do now was look around at the Patriarch and the other Avariel to see their reactions.

Adalon had finally felt the last of her opponent's life force seeping away from him. She moved away to a clearing to find rest, but she was in despair by now.

"It is… Inexcusable… That a mother mussst kill… Her own children…" she ushers silently.

She settles herself off to one side and lowers her head, then brings up a wing and tucks her face underneath. There, she begins to weep.

Thaelyn had stepped around the body of the Blue to kneel in a brief moment of reverence to his fallen opponent. Aerlie surveyed the scene, first to wonder what he was doing, and second to ask why Adalon was hiding her face.

"What happened to that one?" she muses openly. "You want to talk about weird stuff? Well, add this to the list. I need to understand what I'm looking at."

As she studied the scene, she found herself being drawn across the village grounds.

"Aerlie," Amavain calls. "Where are you going?"

The girl turns and waves off the inquiry, then decides to take off and fly out to investigate. She orients first on Adalon, arriving near the large silver beast, much to the fear and amazement of the other Avariel.

"Amavain," the Patriarch intones. "That daughter of yours must be as insane as that man out there. Either that, or she has a death wish."

"I doubt either of those, actually," she responds. "Not if you recall the conversation you had on his arrival. Clearly, she learned a few things about them."

Aerlie steps closer to hear Adalon apparently crying.

"What's wrong?" she asks. "Um, do you speak my language? Are you hurt? You don't look hurt, I don't think."

Adalon pulls her head out to observe the small figure standing in front of her.

"Yesss… I ssspeak your language…" she replies softly. "You have sssuddenly… Found great courage… To come thisss clossse… To a Draconic… Young one…"

"Maybe so, but then I remember what he said about you being a part of building this great nation, and like a sister to him."

"Indeed! And thisss is enough… To convince you… After ssso long a hissstory… That we are not monsssters?"

"Yes, I think I learned this back there in that city. Although I suppose maybe I should ask if it's such a good thing in general to approach any dragon like this."

"I sssuppose… That largely dependsss… On the Draconic. Sssome are more tolerant… Than othersss…"

"All right, fair enough… But you sound like you're crying."

"Yesss... I weep... For the lossss... As it ssstrikes... Clossse to me..."

"How does it strike so close to you? Are you related in some way?"

"We regard oursselves... To be related... As we are... An ancient race... And very proud. We hold a doctrine... That Draconicsss... Should not fight... Draconicsss. It is a violation... Of our culture. We are... As a family... Even though... We may be... Very different. But they violated... A rule... And now jussstice... Had to be ssserved..."

"I'm aware from Lord Thaelyn about this violation where that ancient temple is concerned. He said it should never have happened. And we...well, I suppose they just got angry at us that we were able to fight them off."

"It runsss deeper than that... Young one. You are the Children... Of Creation... And we are the guardiansss... Of the sssame. What they did... Was a direct... Reverssssal... Of our reason to exissst..."

"Ouch, that might hurt. And so here you are. Wow, I'm really sorry for that. But at the same time, this is all very new to me. We've been so isolated up here, you know..."

"Indeed... And thisss mussst end... As you cannot... Remain thisss way... Forever..."

"Yeah, I think I might have to agree. But there seems to be so much to learn now."

"If you have... Sssuch ambition... To learn... Young one... Then you should ssseek thisss out... And allow yourssself... To grow..."

"I would agree, but I'm a bit lost on where to begin. Can you recommend something?"

"The ansssswer to that... Is ssstanding... Jussst over there..." she directs at Thaelyn, who was just collecting his mount.

Thaelyn was now walking towards the main road leading through the village, pulling his gryphon along beside him. The Captain and his men were also gathering outside the village bounds, and the mages on the other gryphons were settling to the ground so they could take up with the rest.

Aerlie turned and hurried back to the village to catch up with Thaelyn, as she was still confused over his final action in front of the Blue.

"Your Lordship?" she calls to him.

They arrive on the edge of the village as the Patriarch and the rest of the Avariel were reassembling in the square.

"Yes, Aerlie… Did you have a pleasant chat with Adalon?"

"She was crying. She apparently felt bad for having to fight other dragons."

"I suppose I cannot blame her. This was an unfortunate occasion for all of us."

"Yeah, but now I'm wondering what you were doing out there. I saw you kneel down. What was that for?"

They continued walking along until they arrived not far from the other Avariel, where they paused. This might normally be considered a private distance for their conversation, but for the Avariel and their extended hearing range, it was well within proximity for the Patriarch and the others to overhear them speaking.

"You may not understand the meaning directly," Thaelyn advises. "But as a soldier and a warrior, I felt a duty to pay homage to another warrior. No doubt, you observed us in conversation out there, correct?"

"I saw you were talking, although I couldn't understand the words."

"Yes, we were using the native Draconic language. He explained a few details of his earlier conversation with Adalon, and also how he now realized his error in judgment over the assault on that temple, then against your people, and generally a series of misinterpretations of his original instructions."

"Oh? Can you tell me what this was about?"

"Recall that I said they were guardians," he reflects.

"Yeah, this is what Adalon just reminded me of."

"Good. And they were placed here to prevent interference in Maker Kuroku's little project. Well, unfortunately, the Maker, with her exceedingly elusive behavior, must have left a few gaps in her reasoning. I suppose the conversation Adalon had was intended to cover for this, but at this point, the damage was done."

The Patriarch leaned in to listen as Thaelyn made his explanation. He had become curious for his own reasons by now.

"One of these conflicting points involved the orcs," Thaelyn states.

"Orcs?" Aerlie wonders. "I've heard of those. What about them?"

"They were just as much invaders as the rest of you, but in their case, truly undesirable. However, if to have the Draconics try to expel them, much like they were with you and the others, this might cause the rest of you to think those…unfortunate…orcs needed saving from the…monstrous…dragons. And the Maker did not want this. Therefore, she gave instructions to withdraw, allowing the local races to contend with it themselves. This would emphasize the orcs to be enemies of the other races and not to be rescued."

"Wow, that's, um…well, I'm not much of a warrior, but that sounds clever, if you don't like orcs."

"Yes, the orcs are a brutal warlike society, and do not spend their efforts to negotiate for any reason. Our history with them has never been pleasant."

"But then we had the rest of us, like you said earlier. She reconsidered our value and called the dragons away from us."

"Correct. However, this is where we come to the event with the temple. He did not fully understand these conflicting orders, and therefore was basing his actions on the original orders, which was to remove the invaders from this world originally intended for the human population."

"Yeah, how unfortunate for the rest of us…" she glances at the Patriarch and the others, whom she knew were listening to the discussion by now.

Thaelyn continues, "He was ashamed of his actions and regretted himself. He took full responsibility for himself and the others, and asked for forgiveness with an honorable death. I obliged him, but also felt it necessary to honor him for his nobility as a Draconic that should hold himself to higher designs. And so I did."

Aerlie felt a deep sensation of melancholy at this suggestion, and lowered her head. She then turned to look once more at the body of the Blue, and further at the two Whites. Finally, she gazed at Adalon again to see she had apparently laid her head down in contemplation of the day's events. Thaelyn follows her actions.

"Life is a precious thing, Aerlie," he instructs. "It does not matter who it belongs to, perhaps not even what they did. We must still respect the essence of life as an element in and of itself."

"Is this something you learned back home where you originally came from?"

"Yes, these are the teachings of my Father and his kind, and follow in the lessons they give to the younger races here in this world and elsewhere."

The Patriarch suddenly perked up at the mention of these words, as they hinted at something abnormal where this man might be concerned. He briskly reflected on the battle scene, and again on how any man, human or otherwise, could take down a dragon singlehandedly. He then recalled Aerlie's curious discussion topic before all this began. Clearly, she knew something, and likely received it during her most recent outing. But he dared not to guess the meaning, as it might seem as outlandish as everything else around him. Nevertheless, he knew this victory would carry its own weight when Thaelyn returned to speak to him.

Thaelyn and Aerlie finished their brief conversation and they both continued their way into the village square. Aerlie moved off to join her parents. She was expecting an interesting discussion to occur between Thaelyn and the Patriarch, and she wanted to hear what it was.

The Patriarch was hesitant to hear what Thaelyn might demand for his so-called service, but the words he overheard suggested there might be something else involved. He now had a series of questions circling in his mind that he felt he needed to ask about. Something big must've happened in the world outside their mountain retreat. Obviously, their goddess knew about it, which then implied Aerlie would know about it, if she was in fact a Chosen One travelling around out there to see it, and thereby she would be a part of it.

And then we have Thaelyn, who must also be a part of it. And as Amavain once said, the long wait could simply have been to prepare everything.

"Ah, Patriarch," Thaelyn croons as he arrives. "I trust my little demonstration met with your satisfaction on this occasion?"

"Yes, I think it did. In fact, it was very surprising. I would never have imagined a lone man being able to take down a dragon by himself. And I saw your men out there being tossed around like rag dolls, but they simply stood up and charged in again. Just what are you people made of that you can do all this?"

"I will admit we have advanced ourselves in a number of areas, such as magic and a few sciences. And our soldiers use a number of strong enchantments to augment their bodies. We certainly do not want to spend so many lives out there if we should ever go to battle, and this world has a lot of hostile forces to quell."

"Yes, I suppose it might. But if you can go up against dragons and barely take a scratch, I'm suddenly beginning to realize how you can conquer a world with all this."

"Indeed, and make a fine impression for the rest along the way. Some of my agents to the far nations have been reporting uncertainty in their leadership that they might not want to fight me at all by now. For a few, there is talk of simply surrendering, and joining our league voluntarily, since it is becoming so clear that we are building a better world out there."

"Uh huh, and I think this is where we come back to us. I suppose it goes without saying that I owe you our thanks," he ushers courteously.

"That would indeed be an appropriate form of response," Thaelyn replies with a nod. "I am also detecting a significant change in your demeanor."

"Yeah…" he sighs. "I had a conversation with Aerlie as you were out there on the field. She said a few things that suggested something happened out there, but it didn't fit with what our history tells us, or even what it COULD tell us in our wildest fantasies. Now, here you are, with this battle scene out here, that silver dragon of yours that's supposed to be helping to build your nation, and I also overheard you speaking of something else that doesn't make sense based on anything we could possibly interpret. So, the most obvious thing we need to ask now is, what do you want from us and where do we go from here?"

"Indeed, down to business, is it?" he smiles mischievously. "I spent a few moments pondering this occasion on our way up here with Aerlie. I knew we would need to make some form of negotiation, and at this moment in time, I feel confident that we should find an agreeable conclusion. Therefore, let us see what we have first on our list."

Thaelyn pauses to examine the area.

"My first suggestion is to remove these remains, as I seriously doubt you would care to keep them as any form of ornamentation."

"Well, yes, I suppose that would be obvious. We have enough trouble trying to cultivate our farming plots without having giant bodies getting in the way," he chuckles softly.

"Oh, indeed, I should think so! I can have some of my people remove this to an appropriate burial site. Or perhaps Adalon knows of someone who can help."

"Her?" the Patriarch glances at the large dragon again.

"Yes, I should think she ought to have a few connections amongst her kind for purposes of this sort."

"I, well...maybe... But then what? I'm actually a little more concerned about our people directly."

"Of course, naturally... Let me see..." he ponders deeply.

He pauses to make a more conspicuous accounting of the village and its people.

"Yes, I think we have a fair number of issues to discuss here," he announces boldly. "And so we will need to take them each in turn. But for this, perhaps a representative from the local workforce could be of some service to me in my presentation. I know... Aerlie, would you mind stepping over and offering some assistance."

"Me?" she blurts as she timidly moves closer.

"Indeed, I need a local resident who might represent her people to assist me as I point out these unfortunate concerns. Our past interactions suggest to me you are of sound mind, rational thought, and strong will. Therefore, you would be a fine example for this point."

"Wow! Are you trying to make my head grow so big, I can't hold it up anymore?" she giggles.

"Oh, I think it will not be as bad as that. Now, you do recall our discussion on these matters earlier, do you not? Well, now I think is the appropriate time to resolve them."

Aerlie knew this was a hint, as she recalled the conversation they shared while riding the gryphon. She felt a quick surge of mischief sweep into her, but she didn't have any real experience in the sort of debate she was expecting out of him.

The Patriarch, on the other hand, was becoming suspicious of these two. As he watched the scene in front of him, he began to wonder if they were now conspiring on something.

"Oh great," he murmurs. "Now I have two of them against me."

Thaelyn turns to face a nearby home while Aerlie steps up next to him. As they examine the building, he rolls his eyes at her discreetly and flashes a grin and a wink. She smiles modestly, but secretly she knew she would need to improvise...a lot. She straightens up and clasps her hands, then raises her brow expectantly.

"And what sort of concerns should we address first," she inquires determinedly. "Does it involve this house, perhaps?"

"Indeed, this is a fair enough starting point. Tell me, as I examine this building, and specifically its construction, is this commonplace in your village?"

"Oh yes, this is a common design we have here. Just see for yourself," she waves to a row of them. "We've been building them this way since we first settled here. Why, is there a problem with this?"

"I should say so! The thin walls, the flimsy supports. If a person were to sneeze the wrong way, you might find yourself with a new window peering into your neighbor's washroom. Why, I doubt this structure could hold up to a spring breeze, much less whatever sort of weather you are prone to receive up here in these mountains. For this point, I might simply suggest knocking it down...or rather I should say assist in it falling down, and then build a completely new one from scratch.”

Aerlie was reflecting on her discussion on the gryphon, and recalling some of their statements. This naturally brought up a perfect rebuttal.

“Build a new one from scratch?” she protests. “Using what? These are the only materials we have on hand.”

“Is that so… Then it becomes painfully clear that we will need to import fresh materials, including such as properly milled lumber and professionally quarried stone, if we are to accomplish anything meaningful here.”

Aerlie felt herself quickly becoming comfortable with this line of debate, although she could not know how or why. But she began applying herself more theatrically.

“But excuse me,” she waves a finger at him in mock fury. “My people wouldn’t know how to build anything with such fresh materials as those. We’ve been using these all our lives.”

“Truly! And such a pity! Then I may further need to import some of my own skilled labor into the region to do the work for you, perhaps even to expedite the process to ensure we find our most efficient results, and with as little disruption to the local affairs as possible. That is, of course, assuming you and yours can tolerate They Who Have No Wings,” he flutters his fingers, “wandering hither and yon throughout your village.”

“Now wait a minute!” she blasts, and sets her hands on her hips. “You would bring people without wings into OUR village and have them conduct some form of work on our behalf? This is outrageous! But if this is your demand, then my goodness, I suppose we will simply have to get used to it.”

“Absolutely correct!” he announces firmly.

Amavain gazed at her daughter as the girl was engaged in what was obviously a play. Lafron turned inquisitively to look at his wife, only to see a tiny grin showing on her face. He also looked at the Patriarch to see his own level of amusement, though he was clearly trying to hold it down.

"But now," Thaelyn continues. "As I further examine the remainder of this village, I must admit the entire area appears to be in a similar state of disadvantage. Powers behold, we may simply have to level the full array and rebuild everything from the ground up."

"The entire village?" she gasps. "Are you telling me you're going to make us live in houses where the roof doesn't leak and it's not drafty at night? Unbelievable!"

Lafron grimaces at the curious display, and then turns again to his wife.

"Amavain," he whispers. "What am I looking at over there?"

"I think Aerlie has found her Fate. Just look at them, they were made for each other."

"Now Aerlie," Thaelyn redirects his attention. "The next item on my list would involve your local marketplace. Where do we have one of those?"

"Marketplace? Marketplace?" Aerlie glances around innocuously. "We don't have a marketplace."

"No marketplace?"

"Nope. Sorry. No marketplace," she turns away and folds her arms.

"This is intolerable! Then we shall need to build one," he jabs a finger in the air.

Aerlie lurches around again, seemingly aghast at the suggestion.

"What? Build a marketplace? Why?! We have nothing to sell."

"Then we must make something. What about your workshops?"

"Oh, well," she alludes casually. "We have a few tables and desks in that cave over there."

"A few odd tables and desks inside a musty old cave?" he responds incredulously. "Preposterous! We cannot have that! So, we will need to build a number of proper workshops out here in the fresh air and sunshine."

Aerlie slaps her hands to her temples and screeches at the thought.

"And now you're going to make my people come out in the fresh air and sunshine to perform our work? How could you?!"

"Oh, we humans are a dastardly race, just ask your Patriarch over there."

Aerlie gapes at Thaelyn, briskly passing to the Patriarch and back again.

"And since we are on the subject," Thaelyn continues. "We should consider your tools."

"Tools? Oh yes, of course, we have tools, don't you worry about that. We have lots of tools…broken and rusty, but tools are tools!"

"Broken and rusted tools? This is simply unacceptable! We may need to replace the lot of them with new precision instruments."

"Oh really!" she snaps. "And should I mention, for all the suffering we had up here, a lot of our old talent is gone by now!"

"Hmm…" he muses overtly. "This could be a problem. Therefore, it may be necessary to import some number of our own master craftsmen to offer apprenticeships, in order to rebuild some portion of that."

"Oh! My goodness, so NOW you want us to take lessons from master craftsmen. By the Winged Mother!" she tosses up her hands and turns to her parents. "He's sending us to school now!"

Amavain burst out with laughter at the display, drawing the participation of several others. The Patriarch glared at the scene, shaking his head.

"I think I'm in worse trouble than I could have ever imagined here."

Aerlie continues, "So, just what is it we're supposed to be making with all this?"

"Ah, so kind of you to ask!" Thaelyn responds amicably. "I recall once…" he taps a finger to his chin, "…and I believe this was during my previous visit, some mention of a shortage of coin. Well, we could begin by having you produce trade goods that you can then sell in order to earn a new supply."

"But excuse me!" she enforces with a finger. "I've never once had a coin in my life. What am I supposed to use that for?"

"Well, for one thing," he retorts modestly. "You could buy yourself some new clothes."

"Oh!" she huffs. "Do you now have an issue with my manner of dress? I'll have you know I am very fond of this dress. I've worn it every day for the past twelve years, and more than that, it holds special nostalgic value, as it was loosely stitched together from the remnants of all my previous dresses from the past several decades! I even have my favorite stain right over here," she turns to point at her side.

Amavain's giggling was growing out of control by now, and accompanied by many others. Her husband shook his head in amusement, and glanced at the Patriarch again to see him covering his mouth and attempting to conceal his own reaction.

Thaelyn begins again, "Another thing you could possibly buy is a wider selection of food. You do enjoy eating on occasion, do you not?"

"Oh, naturally I do!" Aerlie asserts vividly. "That year-old dried squash soup is delicious, once you manage to choke it down."

"And finally," Thaelyn prepares to finish. "Something else you could buy, with all these shiny new coins you will be making, might be furniture for your new homes. You know…such things as tables and chairs…perhaps even beds!"

Aerlie screeched again and waved her fists.

"Mother! Did you hear that?" she shouts. "He's going to make me sleep on an actual real bed, rather than my old pile of twigs. I don't know if I can take any more!"

Amavain was doubling over with laughter by now, as were other members of the village populace. She buried her face on her husband's shoulder. Many of the others in the square were dumbfounded at the display, trying to understand if it was real or just a joke.

Thaelyn patted Aerlie on the shoulder, and then stepped back across to reunite with the Patriarch, who was still attempting to hold his composure, but not very successfully. They observed him silently convulsing with hidden laughter.

"And so, my dear Patriarch…" Thaelyn decrees. "Do you have any objections to these proposals?"

"You know, you two must hold some sort of hidden relationship, although I can't imagine what it could be if she spent all her life growing up here with us."

"I would simply say she has a natural talent. I know not where it comes from, but this display was surely the result of something hidden."

"Your Lordship," Aerlie shrugs. "I don't know. It just came out like that. And you dropped a lot of leads to help me with my lines."

"Perhaps, but you demonstrated a good many of your own along the way. I know talent, Aerlie. I seek it out in people purposely. This is how I have spent my time building our new nation."

"By the way you talk about it," the Patriarch concedes. "This nation of yours must be a work of art. And I suppose I must now admit to my own errors."

"I will not hold you to any misdeed, Patriarch. It is not in my nature to do so. Being alone up here, you were simply out of reach of any word to inform you otherwise."

"That is a very generous attitude, especially for my behavior. I'm sure I offended Aerlie on a number of occasions, and my treatment of you was simply wrong for the culture of our people."

"Granted, this may be so, but then again, you did hold a certain level of merit for your opinions. Many of those statements might seem outrageous…unless you have something equally outrageous come into play to create them."

"Oh yes, naturally. But now, this simply returns us back to some of our earlier statements, as well as a few questions on my mind about who you actually are."

"I suppose it does. Do you have something you wish to begin with?"

"Yes. First, magic or not, some of what I saw out there just can't be the work of some simple man who woke up one morning and said to himself he wanted to rule the world. Right now, I'm trying to pull together several things from what Amavain said once, also what Aerlie said earlier, and what I overheard with you a few moments ago. Now I need to ask not simply who, but at this point

WHAT you are. You look human to me, but those eyes are, um… well, strange, to say the least."

"Yes, I get this a lot around here. Very well, Patriarch, since you seem to be much more of a mind to discuss these matters rationally, let us see where we stand together."

"This should be good…" Aerlie mumbles to herself.

The Patriarch glared at her as she made her statement.

"You know something, don't you?"

"He told me a few things, since I was just as surprised as you to see him again. Therefore, he explained to me who…and what…he actually is. And human, he is not."

"Well, if not that, then what? I don't know of anything else."

"On this world, perhaps," Thaelyn asserts. "Patriarch, you departed from the world quite some time ago, and although during most of that time, we can probably say the world did not change by much. I only arrived here about four and a half centuries ago, after spending the first millennium of my life in the service of my Father within his court."

"A millennium…" he winces. "And then four and a half centuries! By the gods, what sort of man can live that long?"

"One that is not mortal…or at least, not with such limited lifespans as what you might find around here. And here is where we have what occurred in this world that a man, of any sort, might one day wake up and decide to rule the world," he shrugs. "Although, admittedly, I did not come to this initially, nor did I come to it of my own accord."

"No? Then how?"

"This is a curious history, and one to which I am still learning of, piece-by-piece, as those pieces are presented individually. My Father is the deity you mortals know of as Tyr, sometimes called the Just God."

A shriek gushes out from the crowd as Amavain stumbles into view. Thaelyn and the others all turn to face her.

"Calmly now," he submits. "If you know the name, it should carry its own meaning."

"Yes, but that's not why I reacted. My apologies, it was simply a reflex. You're born from the Just God? No wonder her Fate is intertwined with yours."

Thaelyn rolled his eyes to gaze at Aerlie and began reflecting on their discussion back at the guildhall. She turns to him, and he raises his brow. She simply returns an innocent smile, and Thaelyn rolls his eyes the other way.

"I suspect I will need to keep a close eye on this one. But yes, she and I shared a few words on this. I believe your goddess, whom we address as Aerdrie Faenya, must have held a secret agreement with another one, and it would seem Tyr was involved as an accessory. The gods do this on occasion...unfortunately," he chuckles.

"Another one? Who?"

"Her name is Maker Kuroku, and she is instrumental in a number of things, it would seem. Allow me to continue. First and foremost, the gods do not simply give away all their secrets at once. They often make you work for it, which is fine, as we believe in a growth experience along the way."

"Really! I've often felt the same for my interactions with the Winged Mother."

"Indeed, and so it goes..." he nods. "My race is called Aasimar, and we are one of a number of Celestial hybrid races, where one part might be a mortal frame, and the other is divine. In my case, the mortal side would reflect on humans. I regard Tyr to be my Father, although the relationship is not quite the same as you with your own father. I was created by his hand, and I share some of his spiritual essence. From this, we can say I hold a relationship with them as a society of beings."

"A society...of beings," the Patriarch rubs his forehead. "This goes a little beyond what our priests talk about."

"When I first arrived in this world, I had a steep hill to climb to teach the people the true nature of their gods in relation to what I am. It was necessary for them to make the association and realize I am not just some man with curious ideas and strange eyes. I had in mind to teach the people of this world how to bring themselves together and resolve so many centuries, and millennia, of conflict and indifference."

"Good luck with that...but then again, I guess you must be doing it."

"Indeed, it was difficult in the beginning. This is probably why it has taken me four and a half centuries to bring me this far. I am taking a slow and delicate path of diplomacy, as best I can, and only to use military force if no other solution is available. But my original plans were simply to teach, not take anything over."

"What changed that?"

"Maker Kuroku..." he glances at Adalon, who was now sitting upright and surveying the area more actively. "Adalon over there is some sort of agent, I suspect, serving the Maker. She is also a powerful prophetess who wrote a book we have been studying for a number of centuries now, detailing what is essentially the story of my life, and how it will play out as I take over this world."

"Incredible. But is this to say you are following the book, or it simply foretells what happens?"

"It foretells everything, including my initial arrival, and many of the steps along the way. I do not make a habit of chasing prophecies, instead preferring to find my own way with what I have in my hand. My students are the ones mostly following the book, and watching these events unfold in front of them. But this might not be occurring entirely of its own accord, if you consider the aspect of Fate, and maybe a little push here and there."

"Those gods working in strange ways, perhaps?" Amavain muses.

"Indeed, and they might do this. And I feel confident the Maker is likely getting her hands involved on occasion, whether directly or indirectly. And here is where we also have your misfortune with the Age of Dragons."

"Oh!" the Patriarch chortles. "This should be good. How do we explain this? Because Aerlie said something about them being guardians."

"Correct, and this world was a special project the Maker was engaged in to refurbish a dead world back to life, starting with seeding new life onto it with the help of a society we call the Sarrukh. We found evidence of their passing from a few or several tens of millennia ago where they deposited the first signs of life, including the early human populations. So, Patriarch, it would seem none of the local races, or anything else for that matter, is truly native to this world. It all came from somewhere else."

"Really! But our history tells us those first humans were rather primitive, weren't they?"

"They were, so we must suggest they were chosen as a primitive form of life to eventually grow into something higher. Unfortunately, your people came in, and essentially took over the place."

"Uh huh…and here we go."

"According to Adalon, the Maker was initially displeased with the invasion of so many foreign bodies into her little garden. The Draconics are her Children, she created them once as guardians, and at this time they were watching this world to prevent any disruption. My information about this period is they had instructions to deter you, not outright destroy you. If it were the other way, we would probably not be here now talking about it."

"Yeah, likely so."

"This would reflect on that conversation we once had," Lafron ushers up.

"Yes," the Patriarch nods. "When you once said they never outright destroyed us, and so many scholars took notice of something strange in this."

"This would surely be an indication," Thaelyn affirms. "But your people apparently took offence to them for simply being here. Later, as the Maker realized you are not leaving, she took to studying you, all of you, the elves, the dwarves, and whatnot, and began to realize you each carried certain value in your inherent strengths and native qualities. Therefore, she called the Draconics off to allow you to join together. But you never did."

"Wonderful. So, by the will of this goddess, our purpose in this world should've been to join together as one society. Is there an ultimate direction behind this?"

"There is, but apparently she also decided you needed an appropriate leader to show you the way, and this is where I come in."

"Naturally, a being who is half-god to lead the rest of us who don't otherwise want to join together for any OTHER reason…" he chuckles ironically.

"Perhaps so," he smiles. "I am creating a world in perfect harmony with itself, Patriarch. When I am finished, you can kiss goodbye such as war, crime, poverty, hunger, illness, and rampant misfortune. We are already entering a Golden Age amongst our people. And once this world is fully united, we can go forward, possibly to find new worlds, and share our good fortune with them, that maybe they can find the same."

"Those are big words. But then, if you're half-god, I suppose you need to think big."

"Indeed, I do. And here we come back around to your goddess. She once promised to give her favor to our people if I were to provide a service to her Children, which means you. She would certainly not offer anything to us, as we are not the sort of creatures she would normally take favor with, and neither is she the sort of goddess we would normally offer worship to, as we fall into different categories. But this favor would come in two parts, with this moment being that second part."

"What?!" Amavain shouts. "That first time wasn't intended to be the one?"

"No, it would seem that might have simply been a primer. I was instructed to find Aerlie and bring her home, and the second part would present itself at the proper time when it was ready. Well, as I look at Aerlie in the modern day, I would say she certainly was ready to serve her role, if she is intended to be a Chosen One for your goddess."

"Yes, and wow," she flusters. "But I don't think she's done yet. I was told a few things and made to keep them secret. I suppose I could possibly let some of this out by now…if I'm careful of my wording. Aerlie is my daughter, but not that of my husband. She was delivered to me with the help of a very tall and elegant female…

with wings, a bit like us…although I forgot the name…but she was a servant of some god."

"A seraph? Here? Powers behold, what is one of those doing down here?"

"I was told to find a secluded place to receive a child, and she assisted with the delivery. Beyond that, I should probably keep silent, or else I might violate something. She also revealed to me a few of these same details about this world, the dragons, and such, but it all seemed so strange, even a bit unreal. And she told me Aerlie's Fate and yours are intertwined somehow, and she has more ahead of her."

"Really! How interesting. This might make sense if we say to create some kind of Chosen One might not simply be for one solitary occasion. The Maker must be playing a very complex game here, since I feel she must be behind some part of this. Aerlie tells me of this story of a savior, and it dates back long before I ever arrived here. If my arrival is due to the Maker, and all her curious plans, and further to see your goddess giving her statement, and then to see this here…" he shakes his head. "The Powers certainly do have a habit of playing games of this sort on occasion, but this one is rather extreme. Although, in this case, I think they chose a very pleasant example," he smiles.

Aerlie blushes at the mention.

"Your Lordship," the Patriarch interjects. "Eh…a Duke as I recall, right?"

"Actually, there has been a change to that as well during this time. Since my last visit, my advisors and priests finally convinced me it was time for a coronation, so I am now a King to my people."

"Gracious…then I should offer an apology to you," he bows deeply.

"Do not concern yourself with that. It is a small thing at this point."

"A small thing…you, a King," he sighs. "And here I am, with my poor behavior, and so many arguments."

"Patriarch, I choose not to be offended by your statements. You held a viable reason to be angry with those nations near you, and perhaps with humans as a whole, if this was your only example to judge by. Your isolation up here can clearly account for your lack of knowing of anything else, and you did hold a valid perspective to think my statements might seem outrageous. I have encountered many like you, and until I had the opportunity to demonstrate myself…one way or another…" he smirks. "They were simply unable to fathom how a man of any sort could do the things I am said to be capable of. Mortal capacity simply does not compare to that of a Celestial. And until my arrival, these people did not even know what a Celestial was."

"Yes, when I think of that dragon over there," he directs at the Blue again. "I think I would have to agree. And I am very thankful for your kindness. I was listening to you telling Aerlie over there about this belief of yours of life and the forgiveness of sins. I can't think of any normal man who would hold such purity, so it must come from a god. And this also reminds me of something else, which I think I need to atone for. Aerlie, I made a lot of harsh and disrespectful statements to you over the years, and some of them were simply inexcusable. It was unbecoming of me as the Patriarch of our village, and simply as a man. I would ask for your forgiveness, if you can offer it, and hope we can find peace again."

"Patriarch," she begins. "Some of those really hurt. But I'm going to take a lesson from him, on this occasion," she thumbs at Thaelyn. "He's apparently a teacher and a symbol for his people to follow, and if we're going to follow this as well, we may as well start learning from his example. So, I will forgive you, and hope you don't ever do it again. Because, if his whole society is learning magic, I hope to get a few lessons in, and then you'd better watch out!" she grins.

"Thank you, I think. But as I was going to say, even if we were to join you, what role would we play? We are so few in number by now, and our current condition is so poor."

"Patriarch," Aerlie interjects. "I could maybe offer a little suggestion, based on someone I met on my way over there earlier."

"Oh? And who was that?"

"Her name was Pyavin, and she was an Aluer, one of the Water People."

"Really! My goodness, you had an occasion to actually meet one of those?"

"Yes, she was making a visit to a coastal town on the far side of the Great Sea. I think she was a merchant of some kind, and when I settled for a rest, she came up to talk to me."

"I thought those people were nearly as evasive as ours, according to the old stories."

"At one time, they apparently were, until HE showed up," she directs at Thaelyn again. "She told me how it was rough in the beginning, and they didn't know what to expect. But over time, it grew on them, and now they have all sorts of possibilities coming their way, if only because they ARE Water People, meaning they live and work down there in places no one else can."

"But what can they do?"

"For one thing, trades of things you can only find underwater, like sea plants and food items, in exchange for what they have up here. Also, finding lost ships, charting the landscapes down there, maybe for something they can use it for later, and not simply in the Great Sea, but also the oceans. There's apparently a kind of science they can study in the water, and because they don't need air to breathe, like the rest of us, they're not limited to building ships or whatever to go down there."

"Well, while that's certainly interesting, this is for them. We're a bit different."

"Indeed," Thaelyn responds. "And as I was saying to Aerlie, where your numbers are concerned, we need to correct that by producing a large volume of children, and do so quickly to replenish those numbers. As for the rest, it is simply a rebuilding effort, and we will support you along the way. Surely, you must have some skills available to you up here. And if not, as we said earlier, we have schools and academies to teach you. In addition, you surely must hold some sort of cultural crafts, and this could be valuable to get us started with a trade venue."

"Cultural crafts… It's been a long time since we had such an opportunity for this, especially when you consider the dragons."

"Perhaps, but we can certainly investigate this to see about any historical practice, and then try to revive it. Next, you have wings, as you are so fond of pointing out, and this can actually hold a number of valuable uses, not the least of which could be found in my military for scouting, or to gain access to locations that are difficult to reach by land. It could be used for surveying large swaths of landscape, maybe for the purpose of mapping, or resource gathering, biological studies of remote regions, or simply to give us an edge above any other form of practice. This quality can carry many functional uses, simply for the accessibility factor."

"Really! Yes, I suppose it could. This is something of a specialty for us."

"Absolutely, and in much the same way as with the Aluerea for their waterborne quality. And the diversity of these skills can be mixed and matched to create even more combinations."

"Yes, of course, I think I can see this now. And this would naturally stand out if you consider that old battle. We joined together, each of us in our own way."

"Indeed. I place value in all my people for whatever specialized skills they may possess, and I tend to employ them to make the finest use of those skills. We should study this together and see what we have to work with, and then go from there."

"I suppose there is no further point in arguing this, especially considering you essentially saved us from eventual oblivion."

"I would not describe this as making a trade of one service for another. You have your freedom to choose, but if your goddess has her designs, and I should also suggest the Maker as well, then I feel we may have our future already made for us. In the end, I can only see a benefit to our relationship, as we all hold special gifts."

"Maybe so, and I can see now how you are able to pull together so many people. Much like some of those…humans…to the south, you're a smooth talker," he smiles.

"I suppose this might simply follow as a form of inheritance," Thaelyn grins.

Chapter 14

ENLISTMENT

"You know, I've never seen so much construction work in all my life, and this includes our people trying to pick up after those dragons."

"Indeed, our society is rich with talent and zealous in their work ethic. We do not skimp when there is important work to be done."

Thaelyn was in discussion with Aerlie and the Patriarch in Thaelyn's office at the guildhall. The two visitors had just recently arrived after several weeks of restorative work in the Avariel village.

"Many of the homes are nearing completion," the Patriarch notes. "And there is new work beginning on some of the workshops. They're also clearing space for a new marketplace, and a few other things. I can't remember the last time our village actually looked like a village."

"This is good to hear," Thaelyn nods. "And what about your farming activities?"

"We've planted several new plots, so we're hopeful for a good harvest season. Your druids also brought in a number of fruit trees. I think they called them oranges and lemons. None of us has heard of these before, or at least not in living memory. They also had apples, which we do recall from some old stories."

"You are not familiar with such as oranges or lemons?"

"Not personally, but according to Aerlie's father, our long absence probably faded our memories, especially since we had no access to anything."

"Perhaps, and this is unfortunate. Or maybe you used another name in those days. But they are described as citrus fruit, and contain some valuable nutrients for good health."

"Yes, that's what the druids said when we asked them about it, so I'm looking forward to trying some once they're ready."

"Excellent. Oranges are sweet, but lemons tend to be rather sour. However, they make fine juices, and we can also provide a number of interesting recipes along the way to make further use of them."

"That sounds nice. Anyway, we're working together to build a greenhouse for them, due to our altitude and local climate. But to be honest, these are new concepts for us."

"Yes, we have had a number of innovations during this time."

"Now, as to what we can offer back to you," the Patriarch continues. "I spoke with some of our people, and we did a little research in our old books and historical papers. We found something we think could be of value, although I can't be sure how right now, but according to your advisor up there, he said to bring it to you for consideration and maybe you could offer some direction."

"Very well, and what do we have here?"

"Once, during our better days, our ancestors were able to produce a material that resembled glass, but with a strength nearly that of steel. We called it Glassteel."

"Ah, I believe I once heard of this, and it is nearly a legend to us...the specialty of the Avariel, but lost to us when you vanished from sight. Do we recall how to make it?"

"We have a series of notes and manuals, but in this time, we lost many of our skilled craftsmen, and therefore, many of our old talents. The books describe the process in reasonable detail, so maybe someone with the right skills could recreate this. The trouble is we don't know where to find the materials anymore."

"As for materials, if we can examine these notes, I feel we can surely solve that. We have a rather robust industry here, so we can fill this in as necessary. As for talent, we have many good tradesmen available to us, and we can share what we know with you so that one day, with a bit of luck and hard work, we can perhaps…reinvent… this material."

"This sounds good, and this allows us to bring back one of our old traditions. But now the big question. What do we do with it? In the old days, it was most often used for blades of various kinds, like swords, knives, and such. It was lightweight and provided a clean sharp edge that was quite durable. But if you are using mithril and adamantium now, I wonder if this would still hold any value."

"Indeed, we have progressed quite far in the application of the other metals these days, but I think this substance could hold some good utility value in other areas besides weapons. If it represents a naturally sterile material, and can hold such a fine edge, I can suggest a few medical applications, such as surgical implements. There are other industries, some of which our people may not be ready for yet, but as a Celestial, I can think of a few advanced technologies that could make good use of a transparent material with high tensile strength, like windowpanes in high pressure vessels, and perhaps also for military applications as see-through barriers during certain forms of weapons testing."

"Weapons testing? Why would you need a see-through barrier for testing a weapon?"

"In the case of using explosives, this could act as a blast shield."

"Wow, all right, I'm sorry I asked," he chuckles. "But yes, I can see this one easily enough."

"For now, let us see if we can create a small sample for testing. We will need to reacquaint ourselves with its properties and see where it takes us."

"All right, I'll collect our notes on this and bring them in for study."

"Now, as for you, young lady," Thaelyn directs at Aerlie and smiles. "So, you have an interest in staying with us and taking some lessons in our academies?"

"Yes," she admits. "I've been talking to some of the students here, and they also brought me up to a few of your Masters. The classes you have here are amazing, with so much to learn, I wish I could take all of it."

"Yes…" he laughs. "We have indeed collected a fair amount of subject matter to work with for our studies. What topics interest you the most?"

"I want to learn all I can about the world around me. I think we missed a lot during our long absence, now we need to catch up."

"Indeed, this is a given. Our courses all provide a well-rounded education to bring our people up to a common level of accord. This includes such as history and culture, but also mathematics, science, politics, language studies, and even more."

"That sounds like a lot, actually," she chuckles. "What about magic? I see a lot of your people apparently studying it. My father once tried teaching me a little when I was young, but we didn't have much available to study."

"Yes, we do have a very robust course of study in the arcane arts. There is a civilian course, and there is also one for our military, which varies somewhat for the applications. Both will provide you with a fine education, and many of our military persons might take up reserve stations to serve civilian roles along the way."

"Really! How long do these courses last? I was talking to a few people, and they say the study is often very long because it requires a lot of time in deep study and practice."

"This is true, the principles are difficult because it not only demands careful discipline and practice, but also the careful memorization of the arcane glyphs and symbols used in the Art. You will learn not only how to read and cast the spells, but you must also learn how to create magical scrolls and other enchanted items. It is a very complex study with many elements, and time is most often your enemy to progress very far in it. Humans have the most difficulty due to their short lifespans as compared to elves, which is why many of our higher-level mages are elven."

"I guess I might hold an advantage for that part, being an elf.

But I'm also a little bit torn between this and the priesthood. My mother is a priestess if you remember. I always wanted to follow in her footsteps since I seem to hold this Fate, and I apparently owe a lot to the Winged Mother."

"This is certainly a noble cause, without a doubt. And to have representation here would be useful to us, as well as to your own."

"I remember when I was little. You found me in that circus, and then brought me here. I was fascinated by the creations you had to help me with my wings and cure my sickness. I thought for sure I was going to die. People as sick as I was usually do."

"Indeed, and thus the reason we created the treatments we gave you. Adalon deserves some credit for this as well since she was instrumental in directing our efforts in this regard."

"Adalon…the dragon? She told you to go look for these things?"

"She and I both, on occasion, give tasks for our people to follow as a means of testing them and inspiring them to grow and invent something new. This was one of those moments."

"Wow, to think of a dragon that actually tries to make the people grow and learn something new. For all the experience we had with our dragons, I didn't think such a thing ever occurred. So, how long does it take to become a priestess?"

"In truth, this probably never has a full and proper completion date, as there will always be something new to study, and of course your worship continues perpetually. To achieve a certain level in the practice can take many long years of hard study, as we are not simply speaking of the religious aspect, but also the health care and medical treatments. Then, to go any further, simply takes longer. We have people in our temples who have taken most of their lives to elevate themselves into the higher-ranking positions."

"So, it sounds like I'm taking a lifetime in mage studies, or a lifetime in priest studies. And yet, I wish I could do a little of both. I want to be useful. I want to help people with their sickness, like you helped me, but I also want to help when you go out and do something."

"They both hold value, each in its own way, so you should not feel deficient in choosing one or the other. We have tried to find ways of combining the two, and there have been a number of attempts at refining the studies to provide for a more efficient course, but the demands of time make it very difficult to become proficient in either one."

"All right, then I'll need to carefully consider what I want, and then stick to it."

"And do not forget, you still need to study our native language. We use the common form here, and the people have accepted having their ancestral tongues removed to a secondary position as a result."

"And this simply adds a few more years onto the total time for it," she sighs heavily. "Well, it looks like I'm going to have a lot of work ahead of me, so I had better find the strength for it."

"Do not fear, Aerlie, as we are a family here, and I am sure you will find many people who would be willing to help."

Aerlie and the Patriarch both get up and offer bows, then leave the room.

The Patriarch returns home, with the help of a mage and a rune, to continue overseeing the renovation efforts in their village, and also to locate the old notes on their cultural artifacts.

Aerlie is currently staying in the city in a guest room while she decides how she wants to pursue her education, and then to apply for classes, perhaps even to apply to serve in the Order. For now, she strolls along the hallways on her way outside to the courtyard, where she finds a bench and sits down in contemplation of her choices.

"Mage craft, or priesthood..." she mutters to herself. "I wish I could do both. Maybe since I'm an elf, and I have more time in my life, I could take a few additional studies somewhere. But that might mean I'll be spending more time in the classroom and not as much out there doing anything useful."

She sits there muddling through her misery. She reflected on her mother and the lessons she often gave inside the cave at the altar. Then she recalled her father, also in the cave, at his desk trying to teach her how to make fire with the snap of her fingers on a piece of kindling wood.

"That was fun," she mumbles quietly. "But he wouldn't let me do it in the house. Too many loose splinters."

She remembered Thaelyn's people on those gryphons, how they united their staffs and shot through the sky like lightning. And all these portals they so often use.

"These people are really advanced with magic. That does look like a lot of fun to study."

She continues mulling her thoughts, undecided and feeling a little disturbed and depressed that she might not be able to have it all, but at least she could dream of it.

Somewhere in the back of the courtyard, a tall figure was emerging from a corridor. Her arrival turned the heads of all those passing through the area, and they all stopped and offered reverent bows. Murmurs began to spread at the unexpected appearance of the tall female figure, completely adorned in silvery hues, as she sauntered along smoothly into the courtyard.

Aerlie was deeply immersed in her thoughts, and she wasn't accustomed to the types of noises that might circulate around the guildhall, to say nothing of the language barrier. She didn't actually take notice of anything until a tall woman wearing a silver gown, with silver skin, silver hair, and silver catlike eyes, came around the other side of the bench into view. She jerked up to look at her, only now realizing the disturbance being caused in the rest of the courtyard as people gathered and stared.

Adalon sauntered serenely towards the bench where Aerlie was sitting so deeply entrenched in her distress. The girl sees the strange silver woman arriving around the side of the bench and move into position to sit down on the other end. This caused a start in Aerlie, as she had never seen this particular individual, and this naturally followed with the thought that she might be taking up a reserved space.

"I'm sorry, am I in your way?" Aerlie mutters nervously. "I didn't know this was your favorite bench."

Aerlie begins to rise up and move away while Adalon sits down.

"Sssit with me… Child…" Adalon offers politely. "And we will talk…"

Aerlie catches herself in mid-motion of standing up, and reverses to sit back down again.

"Um, I don't think I've ever seen you before. Are you one of the scholars?"

"I may have been… A ssscholar… On occasion… But I do not teach… Classsses here…"

"Oh, then what do you do?"

"I oversssee… And advise. I offer sssupport… And guidance… For those who need it…"

"I see. So, is that why you're here with me?"

"Perhapsss…" she glances at Aerlie, and then around the courtyard at the others gathering into view.

Aerlie studies the aloof manner of presentation, uncertain if this was directed at her or simply a common form of behavior for this woman.

"Well, I sure could use a little right now," she admits. "I'm looking at all the wonderful things I can learn here, but I think I don't have enough years in my lifetime to learn it all," she giggles idiotically.

"You are an elf… And you do not… Have enough yearsss… To ssstudy?"

"I know, it sounds crazy, but yes, it sure looks that way."

"What is it… You would like… To ssstudy? Let usss begin there…"

"Well, I am interested in the priesthood, but they say that could take a lifetime to go all the way with it."

"A human lifetime… Perhapsss…"

"Yes, and then we have the mage studies. To develop myself all the way there, that's another good lifetime, so they say."

"Now we have… Two lifetimesss…"

"And that's not to mention everything else they have available. Language studies, history, culture, this thing you call science… gracious!"

"And now… We could be ssspeaking… Of perhapsss… Three

or more… Lifetimesss…" she laughs. "Yesss… Thisss could be… A problem. If only… We could find… More time… In the day…"

"Yes, that's exactly right! More time in the day."

"Then thisss should be… Your firssst goal. To sssolve the riddle… Of how to find… More time in the day… For your ssstudies…"

"But how do I do that? I can't change how long a day is, can I?"

"Perhapsss… You cannot. But the quesssstion remainsss… How do you find… More time in the day… For your ssstudies. The anssswer to thisss… Is clossser… Than you may think… And it can be found… Within sssomeone you know…"

"Someone I know? Who? I don't know too many people around here."

"Sssseek sssomeone… Who is clossse to you… And asssk him… To help you find… The anssswer. How do you find… More time in the day… For your ssstudies. Or perhapsss… We can insssstead… Convert thisss. How do you find… More ssstudies in the day… For your time…"

Adalon now gets up and moves away, returning inside the guildhall, leaving Aerlie sitting there puzzling over the seemingly paradoxical suggestion just dropped at her feet.

One of the students passing through the area stepped up cautiously to speak with the girl. Aerlie's attention is drawn to the sound of footsteps.

"You're that Avariel everyone is talking about lately, right?" the young woman asks.

"Yes, I suppose I am. I'm probably causing a lot of disruption around here, being new and so different from the rest."

"Don't worry about that, we're actually fascinated to see the Avariel after so long a time. My name is Amaree," she offers a hand.

"Oh, I'm Aerlie, how do you do," she takes the hand and shakes. "Are you an elf? You look a little like one."

"I'm actually a half-elf…my mother is elven, and my father is human."

"Oh, people do that here?"

"Sometimes… It's also the reason I speak Elvish. My mother taught me when I was little."

"Ah, that must be nice."

"That was a really crazy thing just now… Adalon doesn't come out very often, and she doesn't usually just sit down and talk to someone like that."

"Huh?" Aerlie straightens up and tries looking around for the huge dragon. "Adalon? Where?"

"Her…" Amaree points at the bench, and then the corridor where she departed. "That was Adalon."

"That?!" Aerlie shouts as she glances at the bench where the silver woman was just sitting.

"Uh, yes, well, all right, I guess you don't know. Dragons have an innate ability to create an avatar form to look more like us…you know, so they can walk around places like this without stepping on everything," she grins.

"Oh, now you tell me!" she flusters.

"Sorry, we all grew up with this, so we don't think much about it. You're the new kid, so I guess you have to start from scratch."

"Right. So, it's not often she does this? Wow, I must be really privileged then."

"Usually, when she comes out, she might say something profound, or go talk to His Lordship about some new school policy or research project."

"Well, I guess she took pity on me because I'm trying to figure out what kinds of classes I want to take."

"I overheard a little bit, and it sounds like she gave you a puzzle to solve."

"Yes, does she do this often?"

"Oh, you don't know about her prophecies, I guess," Amaree laughs. "She's famous for her cryptic suggestions and indirect wording. But this would count as one of her famous knowledge quests."

"A knowledge quest…" she considers. "You know, His Lordship said something about this earlier. Wonderful, but she was saying I might find my answer with someone close to me. Do you have any ideas on that?"

"That's a strange one, but they usually teach us in class to try the simple solutions first. Who is the closest to you?"

"Probably my mother, at this point, and also my father…"

"Then I would suggest you start there and work your way up, who comes after and so on."

"All right, I'll do that. Thanks."

Amaree smiles and returns to her business, leaving Aerlie to consider this strange revelation.

She decides, if Adalon is getting involved, it must be important. This was a puzzle, and she recalled her conversation with Thaelyn earlier that they sometimes give riddles to help find new inventions.

"Can she be doing this with me now?" she asks herself. "Blessed Mother, I'm not even a student here, and she's already testing me!"

She jumps to her feet to find the mage who was assisting with travel between the guildhall and the Avariel village, then solicits a ride from him.

On her arrival in the village, she hurries to find her mother at her old home.

"Mother, I need some help. Do you have a moment?"

"Aerlie, you look like someone is chasing you. What's happening?"

"I just got a puzzle I need to solve from…well, from Adalon, actually. And I'm supposed to start looking at people close to me to see if I can find the answer, so I'm starting with you and Father. Where is he?"

"Last I saw, he went inside the cave with the Patriarch to look for some of our old books. What kind of help?"

"It's a riddle, a really strange one, but it's supposedly to help me decide what kinds of classes I want to take."

"A riddle to help you decide your classes?"

"Yes, I want to study the priesthood, to honor you," she smiles. "But I'm also really excited to study magic. The problem is each of these by themselves is a really long and difficult study, and I don't want to spend the rest of my life in a classroom."

"And how can I help you with this?"

"I don't know. That's the problem. I'm supposed to seek this in someone who is close to me. The riddle goes like this: How do you find more time in the day for your studies, but now twisted in some crazy way…how to find more studies in the day for your time."

"Aerlie, that doesn't even make sense to me."

"I know. Adalon is said to have a reputation of being very cryptic, but I think she knows something. I met a girl at the academy, she's apparently a student there, and she said something about prophecies, and cryptic and indirect wording…" she shrugs. "It sounds like Adalon does this just to test people for this growth thing," she giggles. "And now I'm thinking of what Thaelyn said before about this Maker Kuroku, and how Adalon is an agent guiding some of this Fate business, which simply makes me nervous now for what's going on here."

"Yes, I might have to agree from some of the things I've also heard."

"Anyway, now I'm getting excited that it might help me find the answer for my study choices."

"All right, but personally, I can't think of anything. So, let's go see your Father."

The two of them leave the house and head for the cave. Inside, Lafron and the Patriarch, among others, including Aerlie's maternal grandfather, were reviewing several books, some of them historical, and others relating to various crafting recipes.

"Lafron?" Amavain calls into the cave.

"Here!" echoes a reply.

They united deeper in the cave where they kept most of their archives.

"What is it, Dear?" he asks.

"Our daughter has apparently been given a very perplexing riddle to solve, and her instructions direct her to begin with someone close to her. I can't think of anything, so maybe you can help."

"A riddle! How interesting. What is it?"

Aerlie steps up to answer.

"I'm trying to decide on my classes, but there's simply too much to study in one lifetime, even for an elf. I want to learn the priesthood, but also magic. Both of these are long and very intense, and the time to go anywhere with it can take forever. Now, Adalon…you remember, that big silver dragon…gave me a suggestion in the form of this crazy riddle, which is apparently common for her. How do you find more time in the day for your studies, but twisted to say how do you find more STUDIES in the day for your TIME. It sounds to me like a way to put more learning into a smaller amount of actual time, so I could then have everything at once."

"Gracious! How would a person do that…spend every waking moment studying without food or sleep?" he laughs.

"There must be something to it if she's suggesting the answer is found close to me. Like I was saying to Mother just now, if she's involved with any part of this Fate thing, and also with that Maker of theirs, who seems to be building something, I wonder if this could be a piece of it."

"A piece of something here in our hands?" he winces. "That would be a curious discovery. Well, the first thing on my mind is this would need to be magical somehow, but I don't know of any magic to perform this. Not in any of my books."

Aerlie's grandfather listened and tried to reflect on his alchemical studies. He reaches to a shelf and pulls out several books to reference his formulas. The others take notice and wait for him.

"Magical, is it?" he muses. "This sounds like it could be some manner of augmentation. A potion…perhaps an elixir… And it would have to be very potent, I suppose. Likely an unusual formula, as I don't recall anything we might commonly produce for this effect. Let me think…"

He reviews his notes, flipping among the pages, then puts one book away and switches to another.

"We are talking about a way to learn more in a shorter time… to learn faster, yes!"

"Is such a thing actually possible?" Lafron muses. "How do you learn something faster? I mean, I'm just trying to think for a moment. You sit in a chair with a book in front of you, or maybe you have a Master in front speaking to you. But you can only learn as fast as he might be able to speak to you, which is already as fast as a person could probably listen and remember anything."

"To listen and remember...to think faster... Wait..."

He puts away his current book and pauses in contemplation while he scans his library, then he sees an odd item very seldom used. It was a small black leather-bound tome. It was very old by now, so he pulled it out gently and laid it on the table.

"Father?" Amavain wonders. "What is that? That doesn't look like one of your usual study books."

"It is not... This was handed down by my father and his father. Our family has been told to keep this safe for some reason. But it's very strange, and we haven't found a use for it. In fact, I've barely ever glanced at it, mostly just ignoring it because it calls for some rather strange reagents."

"What kinds of reagents, Grandfather?" Aerlie asks. "And what is it supposed to do?"

The elder alchemist studies the description and furrows his brow curiously.

"Interesting...yes..." he whispers. "The Elixir of Visions, to increase precision of memory and speed of recollection."

"Huh?" Lafron blurts. "Where did that come from?"

"It's old, very old. Just one moment, I recall some journals."

He searches through another set of shelves and pulls out a book.

"This is from one of my ancestors, when we first arrived in these mountains," he flips through several pages. "Here, he wrote down a series of notes in the hopes that one day someone might find time to actually research the formula."

"Does he say where it came from?" Aerlie asks. "Because if Adalon is telling me to go find something, and it's found here..."

"Dear Blessed Mother," Amavain emits breathlessly. "Aerlie, could you actually be right? Can this be another part of your Fate?"

"My Fate? Me, personally? I thought I was done with that after those dragons were killed."

"Well, perhaps, but I recall that seraph suggesting you might have more afterwards."

"Oh, so nice of you to tell me after the fact when I needed to know," she chuckles.

"I'm sorry. It's so very difficult to understand these things."

"This is strange," the alchemist offers. "He says it came into the family…" he halts and retracts briefly from the book to glance at the others. "It came to us sometime after the dragons began chasing our people. An unknown visitor gave it to us with instructions to keep it safe at all costs until the time arrived to use it, but that was all."

"At all costs?" the Patriarch raises his brow. "That sounds intentional, and not only that, with a singular purpose, especially if it's coming out now, only AFTER those dragons are gone."

"Indeed! And then, he further tells that one of the reagents is found in a land that does not melt. He made a note here suggesting the lands to the far north of us that are permanently frozen, and we know there to be some unusual berry plants up there."

"I have to agree with the Patriarch," Lafron admits. "This sounds a little too coincidental. Just like Aerlie and her Fate, as Amavain suggests."

"It also sounds prophetic," Aerlie winces. "She's supposed to be a prophetess. So, unless that unknown visitor just happened to know of a weird plant in a weird location, how could he know we would set up homes out here to find it?"

"Ugh, Aerlie, please."

"I have to agree," the Patriarch admits. "Did we know of this before we first arrived here? Because, if not, someone planned this… prophecy or no prophecy. This has to be at least partially arranged."

"I may also have to agree," the alchemist nods. "And this book doesn't look like anything our people might produce."

"You say it's from shortly after the dragons started chasing us?" Aerlie asks. "Would this perhaps coincide with the Winged Mother and her promises of a savior and such?"

"I don't see a precise date here. But the wording could suggest this easily enough if you add up several of these points the right way.

It came out of nowhere, with stories of things we wouldn't know of until now, and telling us to keep it at all costs, which would surely involve those dragons and their threat. This would certainly suggest it holds a purpose beyond our woes. And now you…"

"What about the other reagents?" the Patriarch asks. "Are they something we can find locally?"

"Let me see…" the alchemist responds as he references the book again. "This berry is the main ingredient, plus water, a binder, and the…" he jerks up and stares in the direction of the cave exit. "What is going on here?! It's calling for an extract from a citrus fruit!"

"Citrus?!" Lafron blurts. "Like those trees they just delivered recently?"

"We didn't even know the word 'citrus' until those druids arrived!" the Patriarch blasts.

"This is weird," Aerlie whines. "It's like we're living a moment that was Fated to occur from the beginning."

"Well, my Child," Amavain offers. "They say the gods work in strange ways."

"Oh please, Mother, we don't need another of those right now."

A week and a half had passed in Bya'an Tamoranth before Aerlie makes a return to the guildhall. She arrived with the help of a local mage assigned to a trade office in her village serving as a liaison with Thaelyn's kingdom. She carried with her a large shoulder bag and made her way confidently across the courtyard and along the halls to Thaelyn's office, then knocked politely as she peeked inside.

"Um, excuse me, Your Lordship, do you have a moment?"

"Ah, Aerlie, I was becoming worried we may have frightened you away with that last discussion. Please, come in."

"Oh no, you didn't frighten me away. I don't think I'm that easy…or at least I hope not."

She steps inside and he directs her into a chair.

"Very good. I am assuming then that you were visiting your family for a little soul searching on your decision?"

"Actually, you're right, and I think I finally came to a decision on what I want for myself."

"Excellent. So, what do we have?"

"Well, if you recall, we were speaking of the priesthood and the mage craft, both of them being such tediously long duration studies."

"Yes indeed, and you were struggling to decide between them. They are both fine studies to take, so do not feel you will be any less for it by taking sides."

"Oh, I'm sure there are a lot of possibilities for each of them, and of course you have so many other things available. Gracious, a person could spend every waking moment of their lives in this place," she giggles.

"You are correct, and I do not discourage the continued study, if a person truly desires it, but we also need to put them to work after a while."

"Oh, of course! After all, what good is all this if you can't use it for something."

"Absolutely. So, what sort of desire do you have?"

"Between the priesthood and mage craft? Hmm..." she seems to mull it carefully. "Yes, I think I want both!" she grins impishly.

Thaelyn leans back in his chair and raises his brow at the overly enthusiastic statement.

"Eh, just one moment," he waves a finger. "Relating to what we were just saying, how would you propose to accomplish both at these at once? I know you are an elf, so your lifespan might permit you a bit more flexibility, but at what moment would you expect to be able to provide your service in this great crusade you mentioned at helping the world?"

"Well, I spoke to a number of people, some of them students, some of them Masters, and I put together some numbers, working with my mother, my father, and my grandfather...have you met my grandfather? He's a really wonderful man, and smart, too. He's an alchemist, by the way."

"Aerlie, this is beginning to sound a bit like that play we made with the Patriarch once."

"Hey, I learned from the best!" she laughs.

"Yes, and I can feel it coming back to me now," he sighs. "Very well, and how does your grandfather play into this as an alchemist?"

"Oh, well, he's quite good with numbers...you know, an alchemist needs to be good with these things. And together we think that for your standard study course, with the priesthood AND mage craft, plus all the normal stuff you throw in, and maybe even a few electorate classes, I could probably do this in ten years. Would that be acceptable?"

Thaelyn grimaces at the suggestion.

"Ten years?!" he shouts.

"And here's where I'm willing to make a bet with you. I'll say I can do this and graduate with top level marks for everything in just ten years. And as a result, I'll also give you the answer on how to combine all this into one course. In fact, I'm even willing to go as far as to say this could revolutionize your entire education system. Are you game?"

"Aerlie, as a Celestial being, I am aware of many curious manners of practice, but what you are suggesting..." he pauses with a sigh. "Very well, let me ask how you might actually succeed at this."

"I'm going to need a little help to get started, so I was actually thinking, if you would be so kind to offer this to me, we could test this to develop a pattern, and then go from there. You mentioned your language course, remember?"

"Yes, you would need to study this before you would be able to take anything else, as it is all in the common tongue."

"Right. And that could take at least a few years to become fluent. But according to my numbers, we could do this in maybe three to three and a half months, depending on how well we can compress it as a dedicated study."

"Powers pay witness, Child! How would you be able to recall anything at that rate?"

Aerlie now reaches into her shoulder bag and pulls out a palm-sized bottle with a blue solution inside. She sets it on the desk in front of her.

Thaelyn leans forward, studying the item curiously. He picks it up to examine it closer.

"Yes, and so…what is this?" he intones warily.

"My grandfather has a book that was passed down from his ancestors, almost up to the point where those dragons started chasing us. We don't really know where it came from originally, other than from some old notes saying it was an unknown visitor giving instructions to keep it safe no matter what."

"Really! That sounds a little suspicious already. An unknown source with such instructions as to keep it safe…"

"The book is very old and doesn't look like the normal binding style our people use. And it had a formula inside for something called the Elixir of Visions, which is supposed to enhance memory recall and speed of learning."

Thaelyn's expression turned from curiosity to fascination.

"It calls for some interesting ingredients too," she continues. "Like a berry plant that seems to be specific to a region north of us, in a land of permanently frozen tundra. But…" Aerlie emphasizes with a finger. "This was long before we were chased so far away by those dragons into unfamiliar lands. We didn't know of that bush until after we moved into the area."

"So, unless this visitor was a well-travelled individual…but this still leaves a rather significant hole if this was outside your usual territory back then."

"Yes, and even worse is after we started being chased by the dragons and essentially lost contact with the rest of the world, including many of the foods you have down here, like lemons."

"Excuse me?"

"It calls for an extract of citrus, using that word explicitly. And here we come full circle to those trees you gave us just recently."

Now his expression turns from fascination to stupefaction.

"But… Just one moment…" he vacillates. "What are we saying here with this? It sounds to me as if you should not have this in your possession at all. Not simply for an ingredient not found conveniently near to you, but also for the terminology used at the time for these fruits."

"Yes, and isn't it strange that Adalon told me the answer to my problem was in someone close to me," she grins broadly.

And now his expression turns to astonishment.

"Adalon!" he roars and slaps his hand on the table. "Indeed! That old soft-scale! She is sinking her claws into more mischief than I think is becoming of her. And did you say this could date back as far as those dragons of yours? Yes, this would surely make sense if someone made a deal up there. That visitor may have been an agent planning ahead with something covert."

"And only to come out NOW, after you arrive, and I come here for anything."

"Yes, this now reeks of planning, and some new mischief in the making. She has been known to use such terms as things coming into play at some appointed time. Very well, so what does it do and how is it applied?"

"We made up a small test batch back home to try it. I volunteered for this since I'm the one hoping to attend classes here. My mother thinks this is another aspect of my Fate, so I'm wondering just where my life is taking me now," she sighs.

"Indeed, and if I thought I needed to keep an eye on you before, I think I may now need to follow you around personally," he grins.

"Why, Your Lordship!" she blushes. "I didn't know you cared!"

They both shared a laugh at the thought.

"But now," she continues. "Our results were interesting, and we had to make a couple of runs just to see how far it went. And this is where our numbers came in. We made up a batch according to the formula, I drank it down, and then we had to evaluate how much and how fast I could learn before it wore off. So, my grandfather pulled out some of his lecture books and began reading to me continuously."

"Continuously...most interesting... And how did that go?"

"Not fast enough. So, my father got involved with a second book, and then my mother."

Thaelyn pulled himself forward to lean on the desk.

"Three people now reading continuously?" he asks tenderly.

"They took turns with their reading, so they didn't conflict with each other's voices, but generally, yes. It was like listening to multiple people giving lessons on different aspects of a larger study subject, since it was all still alchemy. And one after another in turn. And fast, too. No rest periods in-between."

"Powers help us, that would be hard, even on the instructors doing the work."

"And still, I felt I could do a little more, so the Patriarch got involved with one more book."

"But excuse me!" he urges guardedly. "We are now speaking of four people reading four independent books simultaneously. Or at least in what sounds like a round-robin sequence. How can a person spread their attention to something like that?"

"Don't ask me, I have no idea where this thing came from, but I picked up every word and remembered it perfectly. They checked me at the end of the session, and I was able to answer all the lessons correctly. And even the next day and up until today, which is now several days after. I could probably now compete with some of your own people in the field of alchemy, at least for the skill level this might give me. But now, what do you think this would do for your students here?"

Thaelyn's mouth dropped open, and he fell back into his chair trying to fathom the implications.

"Great Powers..." he wheezes. "Who invented that thing? Because it could not be anyone local. This does not simply reek of mischief..." he pauses to consider the idea. "A strange plant in an otherwise inhospitable tundra region, a book from places unknown, and with such instructions as to hold it until an appointed time, and a recipe to do the otherwise impossible. You know, Aerlie, this would suggest that plant is no accident. It must hold a custom origin, perhaps also this custom habitat, and with these custom qualities."

"Custom, custom, and custom..." she muses. "Is it possible to make something like this as a custom thing?"

"Possible, yes, but not for anyone on THIS world. This simply must bring us back to the Maker. She must have something in mind here."

"Yeah, more Fate at work. But now, just imagine," Aerlie asserts. "You spoke before of being unable to combine these academy studies. The priesthood AND mage craft blended as one. Or any other course of study you might have, compounded with a slew of additional studies. Gracious, we would be creating a society of geniuses by the time we're done."

"This could absolutely revolutionize our study programs," he reminisces distantly. "I had long hoped we could find more time for better studies, to involve additional languages, greater flexibility and training for each member, a broader spectrum of skills and capacity… and then on the civilian side!" he jerks forward. "Children learning a full lifetime of knowledge, at least as it is now, but before they are even adults, and then additional material after that. What is the rate of absorption for this, do you know?"

"From the calculations? My grandfather estimates a tenfold increase in learning rate, perhaps more if we can refine the recipe."

"Tenfold! So, such as a ten-year course in only one year. Or perhaps a year of study in only a month or two!"

"Perhaps even better, as you're not wasting half your time on testing for every lecture. It's all continuous lecturing, with maybe only a few tests at long intervals."

"That could improve it to a twelve or better rate just for the compression value."

Thaelyn jumps out of his seat and draws Aerlie along as they rush out of the room. He dashes through the halls, calling up a series of academy masters to join an urgent meeting in a conference room.

"Listen up people," he announces to the assembly. "We have a special project in front of us, and we will need to reorganize our schedules if we wish to see it through effectively. This young lady here is presenting us with a most unusual challenge. In this bag, she has an alchemical substance that she claims can improve memory function and recall rates. Her private testing suggests perhaps a tenfold rate of learning acceleration."

The room erupts with surprise and amazement at the suggestion.

"Therefore, we are going to make a test," he continues. "Since she needs to learn the common tongue anyway, we will use this for now. Aerlie, how much can you provide for this occasion?"

"I have enough bottles in here for several days, and my grandfather promises to make a fresh batch to extend it further. But we are thinking of a ten-day trial period."

"That sounds fair enough."

"Our calculations tell us each bottle can run for four hours, and if I use two per day, maybe with a break in-between so I can catch my breath, we should be able to make a good test."

"I suppose this is reasonable, but it could also place a great amount of pressure on you."

"I'm willing to try. If it turns out to be too much in one day, we can spread it out longer, or maybe adjust the dosage for a different duration."

"Very well, we shall try it and see. Then we must rearrange our courses to accommodate. This is where we will need to place our greatest focus. She tells us that she was able to concentrate on as many as four people speaking in rapid succession to one another, and she recorded every word of it."

The room erupts in even louder oohs and ahs, along with several comments about the implications.

"Now, I think we should approach this cautiously at first, to find our own results. But if she can actually manage this much, or some comfortable approximation, we will need to make some careful arrangements for a study course to provide the information at the accelerated rate feeding into her to make the most efficient use of this elixir. This could change our entire system of study, but we must first understand the parameters."

"My Lord," asks one of the Masters. "If I understand this correctly, we will need to plan a lecture session with perhaps up to four scholars..."

"I might say three to begin with," offers another member. "Start out conservative and build from there."

"Very well, but all of them in the front of the class speaking continually, simply unloading lesson after lesson into this poor young lady, and for the full duration of this elixir? Great gods above! If this does not kill her, it might kill each of us!"

Now the room erupts in a round of laughter.

"Perhaps!" Thaelyn smiles. "So, this will be a lesson for all of us. Let us give this our finest effort and see what results we can achieve."

◆◆◆◆◆

"How far along is she?" whispers one student.

"Day Four," replies another one. "And she's going into studies that might be a good few months of solid learning the other way."

"Part of that is the long day she's putting in," offers a third. "Normal studies wouldn't be the full day on one subject."

"Aye, but just to think of it," the first student asserts. "They're saying if she can actually do this, we could squeeze a full language course, start to finish, in just a few or more months."

"And that doesn't say anything about the rest of it," the second student adds.

"Try to think now," considers the third one. "She wants the mage study, among others. How long does that take?"

"Too bloody long if you hope to go full kilter with it. And I hear she proposed to do it in ten bloody years, on top of the priest studies, and a lot of other bunk."

"And I thought my course load was bad!" the first student relents satirically.

A group of students had been gathering outside the classroom where Aerlie was in a custom study session with her instructors. She sat in the room alone with four scholars giving their lectures in a rhythmic sequential pattern. The system was nearly as difficult on the scholars as it might be for any individual trying to listen, but for

Aerlie, she fell into a comfortable routine, and able to pay attention to every detail.

Word was quickly spreading around the guildhall about her unorthodox study practice and what it might mean for the future of the academy. People were starting to make bets on her success rate, and her overall ability to actually learn everything and hold onto it.

The days pressed on, and she drove herself determinedly through each study session, even though it was difficult to sit in one place for so long listening to them talk. She wasn't as accustomed to sitting in a classroom like this, certainly not like the other students who held more experience in official classroom study. Aerlie didn't have a schoolhouse where she grew up, so it was mostly what her family might teach her, and maybe some of the other village elders.

When the final day of her trial came to a close, the scholars ran a long test of her lessons to see how well she performed in her retention value. Her language skills had improved significantly, and although she was far from fluent, since it was only a short duration trial, she was able to carry on a simple conversation now.

Thaelyn had called the Patriarch to his office for a review with Aerlie and the results of her test.

"Perhaps the most critical concern is to ensure a constant supply to provide for the full duration of her proposed course. For this, we need to examine these plants to see about their maintenance demands, whether they can be cultivated in a farm-like setting, and then to mass-produce this elixir. And once we have a pattern, I would like to see if we can expand on this to cover our other students. Patriarch, this could become your people's most important industry for the foreseeable future."

"Incredible," he gasps. "If only we could have known about this long ago, it might have changed many things for us."

"My impression here is that this has been hiding from us for a reason, only to be revealed at this moment when we can make such effective use of it. I would hesitate to think if this could have come into the hands of..." he coughs emphatically, "...those human societies you so fervently resented," he smiles.

"Yes! You're absolutely right," the Patriarch agrees. "Gracious, if they had this, our troubles might have been much worse."

"I am going to assign a group of our best people to assist you in understanding these properties, and then building whatever industry we need to supply ourselves. We should see if these plants are restricted to only the tundra regions, or if they can be grown elsewhere. From the preliminary reviews I received, I suspect this to be a most unusual species, and since it grows in such an inhospitable region, I must ask myself how it came to be there and why. Especially when we consider Aerlie's little mention of Adalon and her indirect manner of suggestion."

"One thing that comes to mind is this industry you mention. I doubt any of our people would know how to build and manage it, let alone the cost to do so."

"At this point, I am envisioning this to be a very important industry for our education system, which by the way is a government-funded program. This will require its own contract agreements and funding account, plus some form of regulation to ensure a consistent supply, as well as quality control. Therefore, the cost will be subsidized, at least for now, to get it off the ground. We will then see where it goes and adjust ourselves accordingly."

"That sounds complex, but I am certainly willing to give it my best effort."

"Excellent! Clearly, I would be seriously lacking in my own ambitions to see this world evolve if I did not at least see where this could take us. These coming years could see a new form of revolution taking place."

A number of new biology studies were now underway of this entirely new and virtually alien species of plant. Samples were taken and compared to all known species, but no matches were found. It was implausible for any common species of vegetation to be able to survive in the permafrost regions, and the properties of this one held some very unique qualities, leading the biology departments to consider if the species was a mutation, or if perhaps it was delivered there by an outside influence.

Nonetheless, the studies revealed that it was a hardy plant capable of being cultured in a farm-like setting, if only to keep it very cold. Now a new series of structures, along with the associated industry, was under construction. The small Avariel village was suddenly blossoming into an industry town and research center.

While this work was underway, more of the elixir was being produced by Aerlie's grandfather to help her finish her language studies, but she would likely need to go through at least part of her prerequisite courses the normal way until the industry supply began to flow. This would occupy a couple of years' time to ramp up the production. Meanwhile, she would come up to speed on the common level of education within the kingdom to prepare her for the official academy studies. This also gave her time to meet people, make a few friends, and decide if she wanted to take a civilian course, or join the Order proper.

"Amaree," Aerlie wonders. "You're studying for the Order, right? What made you choose this over anything else?"

"My family descends from a long line serving the Order. My mother, even my grandmother, used to tell me stories of going out on adventures with His Lordship, travelling across the land and performing all sorts of deeds for the people. It's something of a romance for me now."

"What's it like? I mean, you're still a student, but what do you know of living a life like this? This is a military role, right?"

"Yeah. It's not an easy one, not like being a shop clerk or a smith in the city, but it's a good life. The people admire and respect you. You can go out and make things right in the world, and we're building something that'll hopefully last forever."

"Only hopefully?" Aerlie smirks.

"Well, no one really knows the future, unless you're Adalon, but she doesn't tell us everything right away. And yet, Thaelyn is immortal, and I doubt he's leaving us anytime soon. So, it's almost a given that things will stay this way for as long as we stick to each other."

"What do you think my chances would be to apply for this? I'm a little scared of this thing you call the Spirit test."

"Yeah, a lot of people feel this way, but our society has evolved over the years that just about everyone holds a kind of reverence to Thaelyn and his doctrines. This seems to have aligned us so that we all fall into a very refined perspective to meet his. You're basically an outsider, but you seem like a really nice person with a high spirit, a little spunk, quick to catch onto things, and very determined to make things right. I actually don't think you should worry about it."

"But what does this test actually do? How do you test a spirit?"

"That's a tough one. It was created by Thaelyn and a group of his best mages, some say as a very hush-hush research project, using some kind of knowledge he brought with him from the Outer Planes. So, we're not actually supposed to understand the way it works with the level of knowledge we have here so far. But they say it envelopes you with a wave of energy which interacts with your spiritual aura to create this glowing orb hovering above you that measures your purity."

"And what does this orb usually show? What did you get, for instance?"

"The orb carries different colors, like what you might see in a rainbow. Red and orange are bad, like if a person is evil…a criminal for instance. Basically, this means you are Negative in your polarity, and this is an automatic bump, as Thaelyn would never allow anyone like that into the Order. Then you have yellow and green, where yellow is less favorable, green is better, and he allows this on condition that they take a special ritual to see if there is something wrong, like maybe something inside their head. You know, like repressed feelings, a childhood trauma, or whatever, and this ritual can maybe help them find it and clean it up, lifting them higher for another test to recheck it."

"Lifting higher? To what?"

"What you actually want to aim for is blue, which is what most of us get, assuming we don't have any other issues. That's the score for admission. I think most of the people I know got blue first off."

"And what do you think I might get?" she asks timidly.

"Aerlie, I like you, and I think that already says something. Thaelyn says we can all feel each other after a while, especially after we experience the bonding of the dryads, and they say you did that once when you were young, that first time you came to us. So, I don't think you have anything to worry about."

"All right, I'll take your word for it, and thanks. I think I would like to do this, but I'm a little hesitant. Do I need to do anything special to prepare for it?"

"They say you are what you are. So, it doesn't matter if you go now, next month, next year, or in ten years, it's still you."

"Well, then I guess if that's how it goes, I should probably just do it and get it over with. I'll be finishing these requisite classes soon, and they say the new industry is working to provide more of the elixir. So, this next class season, we should all be getting a chance to try some. And as for me, well, if I'm going to do this, I have to be a member."

"Especially if you're hoping to go into the higher tiers of mage study, as some of those are restricted to military and certain technical applications. The civilian courses only go to the Sixth Circle, and you want the Ninth! I don't envy you, Aerlie, that'll keep you very busy."

"Yes, and using the elixir, I'm not sure how this is going to work out, but if I can do it at all, it'll probably make history."

"That much I think I can agree on. Do you want to do this now? I'll walk you over there if you like."

"That would be great, Amaree."

The two of them had been sitting on a bench talking. They both get up and stroll across the courtyard into a side door that leads to the administration office. They turned down the hall to a counter where Amaree assisted Aerlie in filing her application and signing up for the test.

The Master who was in charge of the desk, along with his

assistant, then led the two young women down another hall to a room with a strange chair in the middle.

"All right, Aerlie," the Master submits. "I'll have you sit down here, and we'll try to arrange your wings so they fall to the side out of the way. It would seem our furniture isn't exactly made for the winged folk," he chuckles.

"It's alright, I'm getting a lot of that around here. I'll just have to help you design something new one day," she grins.

"Very good! Now, you need to remove your shoes and place your feet on these pads down below, then lay your hands on the pads on the armrests. Once we have that, we arrange this up here..." he points to a circular ring suspended on an armature above her. "We will bring this down around your head."

"Are you sure this thing is for testing and not for torture?" she smirks.

"Well, we haven't seen anyone turned into a frog or a bat so far."

"So far...right."

The Master assists her to position herself and pulls down the crown attachment over her head. His assistant moves to the side with a control switch and readies himself. The Master makes a final check, and then steps away. Amaree was standing near the wall to watch.

"All right, Adept, give it a turn."

The Adept turns the switch, and the energies flow up from the floor, swirling around the chair, and rising up to condense into the crown. An orb forms and begins altering its colorations as the energies attune themselves.

Amaree and the others watched and waited for the pattern to settle, observing it passing through the lower end of the rainbow quickly, then into the upper region, finally passing into blue.

Amaree formed a grin as she saw the color moving into the blue hues, but the grin quickly turned into something unexpected when the orb passed blue completely, now going into violet.

"Huh? Master, what is that?" she urges and points at the odd result.

"What in the name of..." the Master mutters.

Aerlie was suddenly feeling very uncomfortable with the reactions. She couldn't see anything clearly with the crown in the way, even though she tried looking up. But the sudden vocal tones suggested she just did something wrong.

"What is it? What do you see up there? Oh dear…"

"Wait, this must have an easy answer," the Master moves forward again. "Let's check these contacts again, just to make sure we have a good connection."

He waves at the Adept to turn the unit off while he checks each foot to make sure it was centered in place, brushing it briefly, just in case there was any dust or other contamination, then each hand, and finally adjusting the crown to ensure it was situated right.

"Yes, everything looks good. We'll try that again. Maybe it was a strange anomaly with the wings. After all, we've never had an Avariel in here."

The Adept resets and tries again. As before, they all watched and waited for the orb to settle its colors, and once again, it extended into a deep violet.

"In the names of the gods!" the Master wheezes. "What does it mean to get that? I've never heard of anyone getting violet before."

"Violet?" Aerlie gushes. "What do you mean, violet? I thought it only went up to blue."

"Yes, usually that is our maximum result. I recall a mention once of a possibility for violet, but this was mostly theoretical, and only in extreme cases. Dear gods, girl, what are you made of? Adept, go fetch His Lordship, quickly!"

The Adept rushed out of the room to find Thaelyn, who was once again in the combat hall giving another lesson. A few moments later, the two of them returned to the testing room.

"Dear Powers, a violet!" he mumbles as he gazes at the orb still hovering over the chair.

"My Lord, what does this actually mean?" the Master asks. "I think I recall this in the lecture for the theory of operation, but this was…well, only theory."

"Indeed. Blue is what you might expect for most mortal creatures, and I would not think to see anything higher, as they tend to have their inherent impurities due to their youth and primal origins."

"Youth and primal origins?" Aerlie wonders.

"Yes. The mortal races tend to show a wider variance due to their youthful ambitions and personal desires. Thus, we have never seen it rise above blue."

"Ah! Like certain human societies we might know about?" she snickers.

"Absolutely," he smiles. "And we did know of a few examples in our history. But then, we also knew of a few elven ones, as well."

"Of course."

"But, given enough time, these can be refined as a species grows, and they slowly transition to a purer alignment. Therefore, we might see it extend more to the extremes."

"But this would reflect more on evolution," Amaree notes. "And that takes time. Lots of it!"

"It would. So, I wonder if something occurred with the Avariel that altered this. They were isolated and oppressed, and forced to live in a very tight community of mutual support. That might propose something, but for everything they suffered, to attain violet? Even at best, I might say a deep blue, perhaps vaguely touching violet, but just look at that!"

"Aye," the Master affirms. "This is very deep indeed. Fully into it, and so vivid!"

"And she apparently got this twice. Very well, Master Balahine," he shrugs. "I see no other way but to credit her for it. Whatever the cause, this is her score, believe it or not. Maybe it is something unique to the Avariel."

"This is going to send a few new waves through the academies!" Amaree offers ardently.

The Master helps Aerlie out of the chair and back to her feet.

"Aerlie," he submits. "I would normally issue you a special badge we assign with your score, but we do not have any that are violet. This will actually demand a custom order, so we will attend to this and call you in later to receive it."

"That's fine, but what does this do for my admission?"

"Blue is the score we look to for acceptance, but you are above that!" he looks over at Thaelyn for his opinion.

Thaelyn pauses in consideration of this strange event.

"Aerlie, we have never actually had a full violet come to us before. I had considered this privately a few times, and I have noticed over the course of time a few people coming close, perhaps as an evolutionary transition occurs within our populace. But you would account as the first."

"And she's not even a part of our populace," Amaree adds. "Well, I mean the original populace, the one that's evolving."

"Indeed, this is correct, she is a new introduction, and yet I would still think this level of purity to be more of an exception to the rule, so I would wish to take full advantage of it, for whatever it has to offer. Curiously, you are already directing yourself to a very ambitious role, so you may be setting a new standard for us."

"Oh, nice!" Aerlie gushes. "Put a little more pressure on me," she chuckles.

◆◆◆◆◆

The sensation of the Order's first violet score sent waves of conversation and debate throughout the student body as well as the faculty. People were talking about it in the halls, the courtyard, the cafeteria, and even the guild bathhouse. Anywhere they might gather for public interaction, there were people sharing the news.

Amaree and a few of her friends were taking time during the weekend to meet and share some discussion while sitting in a recreation hall.

"What do you have to do to get a violet?" asks one girl.

"They say you are what you are," Amaree offers. "So, it isn't what you do, it's who, or maybe what you are. That's what Master Balahine was asking in there."

"But if it's who or what you are, then…gods above, who or what is she?"

"I don't know, Deena," suggests another girl. "She seems like a normal person to me. A little bit on the innocent side, but maybe that's due to living all the way up there in those mountains."

"Annah," Amaree reflects. "I can tell you she's a very nice person…she could be your average girl next door, if you don't count the wings. Even she was surprised by it, which tells me she doesn't think herself to be anything more than, well, normal."

"There has to be something different though, whether she knows it or not. I don't think you can get violet just by accident."

"Hey everyone!" calls another girl just joining up. "I found something I want you to hear."

"Vonafel?" Amaree responds. "What is it?"

"I was doing a little research in the library and found something…"

"Why doesn't that surprise me," Annah rolls her eyes. "You spend as much time in that library as you do anywhere else."

"Not just that," Amaree smirks. "But she has that fetish for all those old books and the weird stuff."

The group shares a laugh together.

"All right you," Vonafel jeers playfully. "Just listen a moment… As Amaree pointed out, and she's actually right, I have this interest in certain old books and things that other people prefer to ignore, just because they sound weird, and no one can figure them out. Anyway, I make a habit to look for things, and when this new bit came up, it made me go back to check on something."

"What is it you're checking, in this case?" Deena asks.

"Before I answer that, I want you to hear this and give me your impression…this is just a small piece, but tell me what you think of it."

Vonafel pulls out a notebook and flips through it to find her recent work.

"From unseen hands, a formula old, she carries a goal to pursue. Where speed of thought, precision of mind, is found in a bottle of blue."

"That sounds like Vonafel," Annah moans. "Leave it to a high elf, of all people, to pull something like that one out."

"But dear gods above…" Deena gushes. "Wait a moment! Speed

of thought and precision of mind? A bottle of blue… Are we talking about that new elixir?"

Suddenly the group went silent, with everyone gazing at each other.

"Vonafel," Amaree asks urgently. "Where did you find this? It sounds like some kind of prediction."

"I'll tell you what it sounds like!" Deena ushers anxiously. "It sounds like a prophecy!"

"Yeah, it does, doesn't it! And who do we know of that makes crazy prophecies no one can figure out until after it happens?"

"And exactly the kind of book this girl would read," Annah lifts a hand and points delicately downward at Vonafel.

"That's right," Vonafel affirms. "This is from Adalon's prophecies, Book Two!"

"Book Two?" Amaree wonders. "That's the one talking about the Daughter of Sky, isn't it?"

"Right, and the one that seems to be saying she's supposed to come around to Thaelyn and join up somehow."

"All right, wait a minute," Annah urges. "What does the rest of that thing say? Do you have that first part…actually, why am I asking YOU that question?" she giggles.

"Because you like to hear yourself talk!" she grins and turns to another page. "Here it is, let's take this in pieces, since it's a long one."

She prepares to read the verses.

"The Daughter of Sky, from realms far beyond, and hardships many to number. A quest she did make to seek a lost love, as a trade for her ultimate slumber."

"Already, that sounds bad," Deena winces.

"All right, how do we interpret this part?" Annah asserts. "She's female, so she's a daughter of someone…"

"Or something…" Deena adds tenderly. "And if she can get a violet, it must be something special."

"She's spoken of this Fate of hers," Amaree considers. "Her goddess sent her to help her people, so she's like a Chosen One of some kind. And I also know Adalon gave her one of her famous knowledge quests to find this elixir. So, if we combine a few things, this also reflects on Maker Kuroku and her plans where Thaelyn goes, therefore Book One, and well…it's getting too complicated for me to think of anymore," she buries her face in her hands.

"I don't blame you, Amaree. But then if she can get a violet…"

"That first line," Annah interjects. "From realms far beyond… Great gods…and perhaps literally…that couldn't be anywhere local to us."

"That could explain a violet," Amaree intones cautiously. "Thaelyn mentioned that mortal creatures might not qualify simply for our nature of being mortal."

"Hold on!" Annah shouts and holds up a finger for attention. "Do you know what you just said?"

"Um, actually, it just came out that way, but yeah, I have to admit, that would be like…wow! He said we could…evolve…this high, eventually, and refine the score, but…"

"And then to say she's a Chosen One from her goddess?"

"Uh huh…and that just makes things worse."

"But Amaree," Deena begs. "Didn't you just say a little while ago that she could be your average girl next door?"

"Yeah, she certainly behaves that way."

"I wonder if she even knows," Annah submits.

"How can you NOT know if you're a Celestial?" Deena retorts.

"Well, before Thaelyn arrived, no one knew what it was. And her people were isolated up there all this time."

"And if she was SENT here," Amaree concludes. "People, she might not actually know who she really is. Vonafel, what was that part about ultimate slumber?"

"Yeah," she reflects. "This next part could maybe answer a few things for us. It talks about a quest she took as a trade for what I'm guessing to be a prior mortal existence."

"A what?" Deena blurts.

"That's what I thought when I first saw it. Listen to this part. Through dire plights and turmoil quelled, she strove to meet with her choice. Where rebirth brings her back again, to the one who gave her a voice.”

“That's Adalon for you,” Annah moans and shakes her head.

“Yeah, but she's got a point,” Amaree affirms. “She did something to find this lost love. And dammit! Rebirth? That's saying she did this for a second chance at him!”

“But it sounds like she worked hard for it,” Annah concedes.

“She lived one life, but wanted another?” Deena wonders. “And what does it mean to give a voice?”

“That's something we might not know the answer to,” Vonafel relents. “Unless we have someone who is more knowledgeable, and who can tell us the answer. This sounds like private knowledge to me, and it makes sense when you consider how hard these things are to interpret. It sounds like they were intended to hold private meaning to only a select few.”

“With Adalon being one of those few,” Annah offers.

“And Thaelyn being the other, I'll bet,” Amaree suggests. “But he doesn't like chasing prophecies, so he's not even looking.”

“Do we tell him?”

“If Adalon also knows this, she made it so that WE wouldn't know, and he wouldn't know until it actually happens.”

“You know, people,” Vonafel reflects. “In a way, this makes a bit of sense to me.”

“How do you mean?”

“Think about it. They must've known each other. See this part here...” she points at her notes. “Twice around, she will come to him, the Daughter of Sky at last. To the Son of the Mountain, for in his mind, she is an echo from his past. This tells me he knows who she is. They must've shared something in this past life of hers, but then she died, or maybe she didn't die, and instead traded that for this second chance, and she's doing it without his knowledge, like a surprise return.”

“Gods above...” Deena wheezes.

“Yeah,” Annah relents feebly. “And if anyone ever said the GODS worked in strange ways...”

"This would actually have to reflect again on Adalon and the Maker, though. If she's responsible for HIM being here…"

"Yeah…"

"Twice around…" Amaree yips. "Right, I get it. Twice! She came that first time as a girl he rescued from the circus, and again for these dragons. Two times she was in trouble, and her goddess… um, well, basically drove her with this Fate thing to find him. She couldn't know who or what she is if she's following a path of Fate, meaning, uh…hmm…"

"Lose something?" Annah muses satirically.

"I think I saw it rolling off under the table there," Vonafel smirks.

"You're real funny…" Amaree grins. "I'm asking myself how in all the hells she hopes to actually link up with him if first, she doesn't know who she is; second, she doesn't know why she's here; and third, neither of them pays any attention to these books."

"I suppose you said it yourself, she's following a path of Fate, and so far, it seems to be directing her on a very precise course."

"Especially if her goddess is involved," Annah offers.

"Her, and possibly Adalon," Deena adds.

"Deena, I think you just hit on it," Amaree affirms. "Adalon is driving her every bit as much as her goddess. She wrote these things, and so she must know where it leads. So maybe she's offering a little push here and there."

"But Amaree," Annah puzzles. "If we're saying Adalon is offering direction…" her voice trails off.

"Now I think SHE lost something," Deena giggles.

"How old is Adalon, does anyone know?"

"I've heard it said she's about as old as Thaelyn," Vonafel considers.

"All right, if she's offering direction…and if we also reflect on Thaelyn and that story of her directing him here…"

"Whoa!" Deena yelps and pulls back from the table. "What are you saying here? That she also knew this girl and drove her here to follow him?"

"It would make sense. If they knew each other, maybe held a

relationship of some kind, but her original mortality didn't hold up, um…"

"People, I think maybe I could answer that," Vonafel mentions and refers to her notes again. "Here, this last part… The circle complete, the tidings revealed, together they will aspire. The wholeness of Man, the oneness of World, and the birth of a Proud Empire."

They all stopped and stared at each other.

"They get married?" Deena mutters softly.

"And they rule the entire world together," Annah concludes.

"But do we tell anyone?" Amaree asks guardedly.

"I don't think we can," Deena muses.

"Why?"

"Circle complete, tidings revealed… That means all this comes out in explanation after the fact."

"Great."

"I think I'd have to agree," Vonafel accedes. "If we say she did this for a reason, but doesn't remember it now, maybe after the reincarnation event, and is depending on outside help, like Adalon, and further if Thaelyn is not supposed to know anything until afterwards, this basically means we can't get involved."

"Are we talking about more of that famous Measure of Balance stuff?" Annah wonders. "The learning experience?"

"Probably so. It seems to play out with as much mystery as those gods up there," she giggles softly.

"But we can't just sit here with all this inside of us!" Deena submits.

"We may have to, but if we keep it quiet, maybe we can share this among the student body and watch as it follows through."

"I'm just trying to imagine," Annah grins. "How did it all begin? How did they make these arrangements and who is really behind it? This sounds like a plan that needs some careful coordination."

✦ ✦ ✦ ✦ ✦

"This is it," Thaelyn announces to a conference of his academy

Masters. "We may very well be setting a new standard here, which could bring us into a new era for our people's education. We will be phasing in this new Elixir of Visions in certain study-intensive classes, not the least of which would include the mage and priestly studies, in order to accommodate Aerlie and her efforts. As we expand our arrangements, we will involve language studies, history, mathematics, the sciences, and others. This will be as much an exercise for our scholars as it will be for our students, so we must all grow and learn together the best practices to make the most efficient use of our time."

"What about such exercises as mage and combat practice training?" asks one Master.

"Our preliminary review of this elixir shows that it greatly enhances mental acuity. This makes it a fine accessory for classroom study. But so far, we are not as confident of the potential for physical training, as this is largely the working of the body."

"Of course…"

"Therefore, we will focus on the mental demands and perhaps examine the rest as time permits. I think we might do well to keep the physical exercise as it is, for the most part. In fact, since we will be compressing everything else so nicely, we might actually be able to donate more time to that."

"That sounds very fine indeed."

"We will be dividing the day into two parts, separated at lunchtime, where the morning classes will involve two sessions at two-hours each. We will schedule some of the more intensive study courses for this period to make better use of our time. The afternoon will involve three courses of approximately an hour and a third each, when you consider walking times between them. We can involve the lighter classes and training sessions here."

"A training session at the end would be grand," offers another Master. "Then to hit the baths at the end of the day…"

"Indeed, it would. This alters our usual pattern somewhat, but I am attempting to measure this with two of the four-hour elixirs. When considering the results we may find, I feel this is a small price to pay."

"Very good, my Lord, we are all very eager to give it a go."

Thaelyn finished his conference with the academy masters in preparation for the first day of classes using the new elixir. The students were signed up, the learning materials were arranged and delivered, and a stockpile of the elixir was waiting to be dispensed.

Aerlie was anxious to get started. She had finished her requisite classes and felt confident to begin her primary courses now. She would be going into the early mage and priest studies, plus a host of other courses, such as history and math. Her final class of the day would be combat training befitting a mage or a priest, and in her case most likely using a staff-like weapon.

The first day of classes started with a careful revving up of the lecturing to ease the students into the rhythm, rather than slamming them with the harshness of the full speed unloading of information straight off. This would be the pattern they would experiment with until the ritual became ingrained. With experience, the students would become more accustomed to the high rate of information transferal, and there would be less need for the revving up sequence.

The days passed into weeks, and both the scholars and students fell into a predictable pattern. The memory retention rates were exemplary, and the elixir was demonstrating itself to be a revolutionary addition to their study potential. Using this, the students would be able to study more material in less time, and therefore allowing for a much wider volume of knowledge overall. They would now be producing a generation of geniuses, and this alone might allow for subsequent revolutions in the advancement of science, technology, and other research studies.

Aerlie placed all her determination into her studies, knowing full well how important it was to succeed, and also driven to prove herself worthy of her promise, as well as this curious quality of her violet score on her Spirit test. She felt sure there must be a reason for it, and she needed to live up to it, whatever it was.

The months progressed into years as she advanced through the different Circles of study in mage craft. There were nine in all, and so far, she was only into the Second Circle, taking one per year. Her course alternated between classroom study and the practice field, which was found outside behind the mage academy building. There were two fields, a lower one for the lower classmen, and another found higher up the mountain to give more space for the higher-ranking trainees.

Every so often, Thaelyn might select from the student body certain examples to accompany him on an occasional field run. This was partly to provide actual combat experience, as the world still had a number of areas allocated to societies that weren't officially part of the kingdom, as well as a few regions occupied by hostile forces. Among these were the orcs.

The orcs were one of those early immigrant races that arrived on Tae'Eladar during the growth period after the elves arrived. Adalon, at that time going as Kuroku, and her attendant seraph witnessed this, but chose not to involve themselves to correct it, instead leaving it to the local races to manage, as they could certainly handle this much by now. The orcs occupied a few pockets here and there in the north lands, but these were mostly contained by common guard patrols. However, the bulk of their population took up a large region to the south called the Saheen Expanse.

This region was essentially a no-man's land. The other races tended to stay out, but they still needed to maintain the occasional border patrol, and this is where Thaelyn and his field exercises might come in. A site would be chosen that was known to witness a small orcish patrol passing through. Once in a while, the orcs would test the kingdom by crossing the border looking for fun. This often didn't amount to much of anything more than a minor skirmish. The orcs, for the most part, had come to learn that Thaelyn's kingdom was a very strong force, and didn't care to try any large-scale invasions.

Aerlie had been progressing nicely according to her schedule. But she had also noticed an increase in the attention directed at her as she walked along the hallways. Initially, she interpreted this as due either to the fact of being Avariel, which was an odd occurrence in itself around here, or that she held the violet score. But as the school years passed, she could also hear whispers behind her back. One day, she met with her friend, Amaree, in the cafeteria for lunch.

"Amaree, is there something going on around here where the people are talking about me?"

"Huh? What people?"

"Other students… Sometimes I can feel their eyes on me, and I could swear I can hear them talking, but it seems to stop as soon as I pass by."

"Oh, that…um…" she hesitates. "Please, Aerlie, don't take offence. I'm sure it's just that you're trying to accomplish the impossible here, and people are talking about it. We're all very anxious to see you succeed, because it could change a lot of things for us."

"Are you sure? You're not trying to hide something from me, are you?" she eyes her friend suspiciously.

Amaree giggles from the gesture.

"Really, Aerlie, I count you as one of my best friends, and I know a lot of other people are pulling for you. There's probably a lot of silly talk going around. Some are wondering about that test score you got and what it means, and others about this Fate you talk about. That's a weird one for a lot of us."

"It's weird for me, too. My goddess sends me here to help my people, which is fine, but then something else happens, and the next thing you know, I'm creating this revolutionary elixir to change how people study in the academy. It's like I was made to do something special here."

"Exactly, and that's probably what you're hearing people talk about. We sometimes get a lot of crazy rumors going around, and you're the most exciting thing I think any of us has ever seen before. We're all wondering where you'll go next."

"Well, if that's the case, maybe I'll become a future Master and start teaching, or perhaps I'll invent something new."

"I wouldn't doubt it! If you get a full Ninth Circle degree, you'll be able to do a lot of things."

"Hmm..." she ponders. "Aerlie the Mage Elder... Aerlie the High Priestess... Which of those sounds best to you?"

"Considering where you might be going, they may just have to create a new name for it."

"Well, first I need to get there."

"Right. All I can say is just stay the course and focus on your studies. You're doing great so far. Don't let anything get in your way of it."

"Including people talking behind my back about things you don't want me to know about?" she grins impishly.

"Now wait a minute," Amaree protests. "Did I give any suggestions about this just now?"

"Not directly, but you're covering up for something and telling me to ignore it and focus on my most important goals instead. This says something to me, violet or no violet, Fate or no Fate."

"Aerlie, please, trust me. I love you like a sister...well, like a sister crossed with a dove," she giggles.

"Really!" she grins broadly. "Well, the next time you pass under any statues, you'd better start looking up."

"Whoops!" Amaree laughs. "But seriously, sometimes there are things we're just not ready to know about. You have a very serious goal here, and you need to let it follow a natural path. This is how they usually teach us. I can't, and shouldn't, get in the way of that. So, ignore the rest and just let it come."

"More of my Fate, I suppose, which means you do know something, don't you?"

"It's really hard to explain. I think it just needs to find its way before anyone can be sure what it is. You obviously have something guiding you."

"But if I have something guiding me, how can I know if I'm going the right direction?"

"Oh, I don't think it would let you make a wrong turn," she chuckles. "If people say the gods work in strange ways, I think a lot of stuff is like that. And so far, you've done everything you were supposed to do."

"Such as…?" Aerlie implores with her eyes.

Amaree felt for her friend, and she wanted to say something, but was afraid she might interfere with an important goal.

"Aerlie," she sighs. "Let me just say this. You probably have more in front of you than you can imagine. Let your feelings carry you, and don't ask how high, just do it, even if it seems unreasonable for such a sweet girl like you."

"Now what are you saying? Gracious!" she giggles. "Then maybe I'll, um…let's see…oh why not, I'll just marry His Lordship, how about that?"

"Hey, last I heard, he's single…" she smirks.

Aerlie eyes her friend trying to interpret the statement.

"I was joking…" she intones tenderly.

"Well, joke or not, he is actually single."

"Maybe, but who am I to think of marrying a king, of all things?"

"That's a good question, really. I wish I had an answer to it, but he's never chosen anyone else."

"Why?"

"I don't actually know the answer to that. But I've heard a few people talk about this. He's been here for what now? About four and a half centuries. And apparently never tried looking for someone. Some think he's too distracted with his campaign to unite the world, which really is a big project, but there are some who think he's a little afraid."

"Him? Afraid? Of what?"

"The most common answer is attachment to a mortal."

"Oh! All right, and he would outlive that person. That might hurt. But there must be someone back home where he came from."

"You might think so," Amaree admits. "But if that were the case, why hasn't he gone back and, well, I suppose bring her here."

"Do we have an answer to this?"

"The only one I hear is he's an exception to the rule that Celestials don't usually come to places like this. Our society is still too young to draw that sort of interest."

"And this limits him to only what we have here, I suppose."

"Maybe so, but if he could do this at all, why not already?"

"Yeah, you may have a point. All right, but as for us, wouldn't he be better off with another noble? Don't they usually stick together in cases like this?"

"The way our history teaches us, this is what usually happens, the elite society marrying each other, maybe also for political reasons… you know, one kingdom to another, the children marrying as a kind of pact to join them."

"And here?" Aerlie wonders.

"Here, he's been using political agreements and treaties, and if that doesn't work, our culture might invoke its own influence to work on the people. And if all else fails, we might find ourselves in a war if the other side doesn't like us being so goody-goody."

"Oh, well, isn't that just awful," she smirks. "Like those nations near our home that cheated us once upon a time."

"Right, but no political marriages…"

"So, if he's not aiming for a noblewoman as a bride, he could be open to anything?"

"As far as this world is concerned, all I can say is it's probably all the same to him, at least as far as mortals are concerned."

"Well, all right…so our mortality is a problem. But I suppose one solution might be that an elf would live longer than a human… no offence."

"I'm a half-elf, remember, so I'm a little better than that. But you're right, actually. So, if he's afraid of the mortality rate, this might offer a little relief."

The conversation pauses while they finish their lunch.

"Amaree," Aerlie muses. "Are you actually suggesting something here?"

"I wouldn't dare suggest something where your love life is concerned. That's something you should decide for yourself."

"But what about this thing you seem to know about? Is it related?"

"Aerlie, there are a lot of things about it that don't make a lot of sense to most of us, so trying to interpret anything at all is really just a lot of conjecture. People might talk, and this is one of those things that may sound exciting on the outside, but you just don't know how it works on the inside."

"And so, you tell me to just follow my course, and I'll probably trip over it somewhere along the way," she smiles.

"That's probably just what you'll do, like with that elixir."

"Yeah…" she giggles. "Well, all right, but can you at least give me a few pointers on men, regardless of who I might end up with? After all, one of these days, I might meet someone special, half-god or otherwise."

The two of them laughed, as they continued their discussion for the rest of the lunch period.

✦✦✦✦✦

Aerlie was progressing through her fourth year at the academy, which also equated to her Fourth Circle of mage study. The classes were vigorous, but moving along predictably. A weekend was approaching and Thaelyn was calling up an assembly of students to attend a set of field trips.

"Our scouting reports tell us the orcs of the south are making incursions along the border with Kordaran. They tend to make these attempts on occasion as a means of testing our lines, as well as an exercise for their own warriors. Naturally, we must respond, but since these patrols are often small, we feel this is well within our capacity to offer a little exercise for our mid-classmen students."

He pauses to refer to a map on the wall behind him.

"We have a recent report of a small band moving along a well-travelled trail curling along a range of mountains separating our territories. This is where we very often have our meetings. Since we are still rather early into our experience using the new elixir, I feel it is important for us to explore its effectiveness in the field. Therefore, we shall call up a standard formation squad, and send them out to this location for a bit of sport," he grins. "And since this exercise involves a test of the effectiveness of the elixir, I think it is appropriate to include that specific young lady who brought it to us."

He turns to gaze at Aerlie with an impish stare, causing her to giggle and blush.

"Beyond that," he continues. "This bears the appearance of a classic patrol function. Now, if there are no questions, we will begin the selection process for the first excursion."

A series of groups were assigned and scheduled for the weekend sorties. Thaelyn would accompany some, while a few of his seasoned officers would lead others. Mages would be called up with portal runes to the selected destinations to deliver these teams, and another mage stationed at a watch post would offer a return trip.

Aerlie was selected to be a part of Thaelyn's team. As one might expect, she was excited as well as nervous to be sent out on an actual combat duty patrol. She wanted to make a good impression for herself, so she made a careful review of her most recent lessons before heading out.

Thaelyn and his team presented themselves for transport, and they each arrived in an open field near the base of a range of mountains. It was early in the day, and they would spend perhaps half of it wandering through the area before returning home.

Many times, these patrols saw no real action, but once in a while, they might cross paths with an enemy force. The teams most often included a combination of front-line soldiers and scouts, plus an archer or two, a couple of mages, and a few priests for healing and augmentation support.

Aerlie held a dual role, in this case, having been in study for both mage craft and the priesthood. She could go either way for this point, but initially she was hoping to get in a few shots using her new spells.

The patrol coursed its way along a dusty trail leading around the base of the mountains. The area seemed quiet and peaceful. The early summer breezes lifted the smells of the native wildflowers and sagebrush.

Aerlie walked along behind the others, leaving the duty of scouting to the scouts, since it was just as much an exercise for them as it was for anyone else. But she kept her eyes and ears alert, just the same. Then she thought she saw something in the distance.

"Look there!" she ushers cautiously. "Do I see something moving?"

Thaelyn halted the troupe to focus on her sighting. In the far distance, they could just make out movement among the tall grasses and shrubs.

"Your eyes do not deceive you," he admits. "And they could put a few of our others to shame after a while," he chuckles.

"Sorry, I don't mean to take someone else's job, but this is just what I am."

"Very good. So far, I think they have not seen us. Let us duck down and wait for them."

They take up a position off to the side behind a row of shrubs and wait for the other patrol to pass by.

The orcish patrol meandered along sluggishly, appearing bored and restless. They passed along a comfortable distance in front of the team, allowing Thaelyn and his party to come up behind them.

"Looking for something?" he shouts in orcish. "Or are you simply walking in your sleep?"

The orcish patrol halted and turned abruptly to Thaelyn's address. They were immediately offended by his accusation, and arranged themselves to make a charge.

Thaelyn's team organized itself with the front-line soldiers forming up, and the rest behind that. Thaelyn moved to a position out of the way, allowing his students to take the front instead. The mages, including Aerlie, typically had their assignments to follow one or another of the front-line members, offering support and a secondary line of attack.

The orcs charged forward, meeting the front-line in a clash of metal. The orcs seemed to favor maces and axes, as compared to Thaelyn's men using swords, and both sides were using shields, although the orcish examples were somewhat more primitive. Like Thaelyn, the orcish leader stayed behind to allow his underlings to take the battle as their own training exercise.

The lines jostled with weapons meeting shields. Aerlie fired off a few of her smaller magical bolts as she tried to warm up to the heat of battle. The strikes hit their target, but the orc's armor and skin were tough, so the result was weak. The skill levels of the two sides were comparable, which gave everyone a solid challenge, but the superior weapons and armor of Thaelyn's side was ultimately giving them an advantage.

Thaelyn issued a series of instructions to reinforce his men and remind them of their positioning and stances. The orcish leader did the same, but as he saw his men beginning to take losses, he moved around to see about an opening for himself.

"Are we aiming to kill them?" Aerlie wonders openly. "Or simply deter them."

Thaelyn turns briefly to respond.

"Orcish mentality is either to return home victorious, or not return home at all."

"Wonderful. All right, here we go!"

Aerlie was feeling more confident in her actions now, so she felt like trying one of her newer lessons in spell craft.

"Let's see how you like a little lightning, orc!" she mutters.

She focused her aim on her front-line champion and his target as she started calling out the phrases to cast a lightning bolt.

The orcish leader had moved to a new location where he could find a straight line of attack, and his target would be Thaelyn, in order to interrupt the direction of his troops, and to see if he could take him down in the process. He let out a battle cry and began charging forward.

Aerlie was almost ready with her spellcasting when she heard the call from off to the side. This was an unexpected sound, and it made her redirect herself to find the source. That's where she saw the orcish leader making a run at Thaelyn. Her mind instantly turned to protect her noble Lord, and with her spell ready at her fingertips, she reflexively let it go at her new target. Unfortunately, her target had moved just on the other side of Thaelyn from her vantage point, causing the lightning to slam hard into Thaelyn's back.

Aerlie felt a sudden shock of horror at making such a careless blunder. She let out a yelp and covered her face as Thaelyn grunted and stumbled from the hit. But Thaelyn's high durability as a Celestial where magic was concerned allowed him to recover just enough to make a strong shoulder butt to the inbound orc, sending him to the ground. He then reached around to the point of impact, which was actually underneath his armor, and turned to look over his shoulder to see where it came from. He allowed himself a small grin and a soft shaking of his head.

"Your target is over there, young lady," he thumbs at the other soldier. "Keep your focus and stay with it."

Aerlie fell silent and ducked her head. She couldn't bring herself to look up at him again, and timidly returned to her previous champion, going back to the simpler spells and a few healing chants to reinforce the others.

Aerlie was quiet the rest of the day, even though Thaelyn tried engaging her in conversation to relieve her tension. When the day was done, they returned back to the guildhall and Aerlie retired to the recreation room, where she joined with some of her friends.

"Hey Aerlie," Amaree announces. "How'd it go out there?"

Aerlie moped along to sit at the table, speechless and with her head still hanging.

"Aerlie?" Amaree repeats softly. "What happened out there?"

"I hit him in the back with a lightning bolt, of all things."

"Huh? Who?"

"HIM!" she stresses tearfully. "Of all people...him! With a lightning bolt! I'm so ashamed!"

"Aerlie, you're losing me. Are you saying you hit Thaelyn? Wow..."

"Aerlie," Annah tries to soothe. "You need to pull yourself together. I'm sure this isn't the first time someone made a little mistake out on the field."

"A little mistake?!" she shouts. "With a lightning bolt?"

"Well, all right, that might not be so little," she chuckles tenderly. "But you also have to consider he's surely no stranger to taking a few hits here and there."

"But he's our noble Lord and King, and I've been trying so hard to do everything perfect, because I want to impress him and make him proud of me, and then I do this!"

"Aerlie!" Amaree asserts firmly but caringly. "First, you need to remember, this is a school, and mistakes do happen. Mage class is rife with them. I've heard of people setting the training fields on fire a few times. And going out on a patrol is especially stressful, as you're under pressure from all sides, and there's a lot happening out there. It's as much a test of your nerves as it is your wits, and not everyone gets it right the first time."

"Also," Vonafel adds. "Word is they're still trying to assess the effects of this elixir on the student body so they can refine the training process and see about making any improvements. Your, um…mistake…might actually prove useful to see how this super-accelerated education is affecting everyone for their performance. So, maybe you should count yourself lucky it was ONLY a lightning bolt, and it could actually show a weakness that needs closing."

"Only a lightning bolt?" she gushes. "You mean there are worse things to hit him with? I mean, yes, I know there can be worse, but…um…"

"Actually, yes… Thaelyn is a Celestial, and they're a lot tougher than normal people. I've heard it said he's highly resistant to electrical shock, as well as cold. So, your lightning may sting, but I don't think we'll see him hobbling around on crutches as a result."

"She's right," Deena offers. "And he's not the sort of person to scream at you for your mistakes. He'll just give you a reminder of your purpose and redirect you back into it. What did he actually do after you hit him?"

"Well, yes," Aerlie nods. "He reminded me of my primary champion, and to refocus myself."

"See…that's who he is, so don't worry about it. You're still doing great, so don't let it get to you."

"Are you sure?"

"Yes, Aerlie. Just put yourself back into your studies like you always have been. We certainly wouldn't want to see you flub up now, not the way you were going before this."

"All right, I'll try to settle myself and keep to my books."

During the next week, Aerlie tried to refocus herself on her studies. The memory of her error weighed heavily on her, and this caused her to struggle to maintain her concentration in class. She tried to avoid Thaelyn if she saw him passing by in the halls, only to bow quietly, and then move on. After a few days of this, Thaelyn called her into his office for a chat to try to bolster her morale and to ensure she didn't falter in her studies.

"You wanted to speak to me, my Lord?" she ushers softly as she peeks around the door.

"Yes, Aerlie, please come in."

Thaelyn brings a pair of chairs around for them to sit on while they share a little one-to-one counseling.

"Am I in trouble for something?" she asks timidly.

"Absolutely not. I simply wished to see how you are feeling after our little outing."

"Maybe I should be the one asking you that question. You're the one who got hit, but I've been too ashamed to say anything."

"Yes, I can see this, and I think it is important to talk about it. Aerlie, in my day, I have seen more battles than any man would dare attest to, and a single lightning strike is comparatively small to some of the things I have had thrown at me."

"But were any of those thrown at you by your own students?"

"Admittedly, no, not anything as potent as a lightning strike. But you can be sure there were a few occasions of they who swung a sword too far, or who allowed an arrow to go awry."

"My goodness, my Lord, and how did you handle that?"

"Fortunately, my armor is a special design, so the types of weapons we use with our students are not able to cause any real harm. It is also strongly enchanted to resist many forms of magic strikes. Therefore, your example just barely got through. It was just enough to cause a strong twitch in my flank, but not enough to actually cause any real damage."

"Well, thank the Winged Mother for that," she sighs.

"I might even go so far as to consider it an honor to be hit by you!" he grins gently.

"An honor?!" she yips. "How is it an honor to be hit by lightning?"

"Well, you would be the first to make this one, which is a beginning. Further, with you in such a training course as you are, and moving along so rapidly that you could conjure this forth so early in your years here at the academy, makes this a rather curious occasion."

"Um, well…that's interesting, I suppose. You know, I was talking to a few of my friends about this, and they said we're still trying to evaluate this elixir and its effects on our training over time. Do you think my mistake might show something we need to fix?"

"This is a good point. Yes, we are still trying to analyze the long-term effects of this elixir on our traditional training programs to see if we might find ways to improve and to compensate for such errors as this. Clearly, the compressed nature of this training does not allow for the traditional accumulation of time to gain experience. So, we may need to see about allocating more time to physical practice, and perhaps to rearrange a few of the lessons to move those of a higher potential into a more appropriate category."

"So, my mistake might actually go to prove a need to correct something. Well, I guess if we can take something good from it, maybe it was worth it."

"Indeed, and while I would not recommend going out and hitting anyone else with a lightning bolt, or even worse, I would ask that you should not feel so embarrassed by it. We must all go through a learning experience, and you are no different. In fact, yours is perhaps the worst of the lot as you are under so much pressure. Perhaps, one day, we can look back on this and share a laugh or two. But for now, I would have you rededicate yourself to these high aspirations. Just remember that innocent young girl who once stepped into my office and demonstrated the gall to challenge herself to make this attempt in the first place. That is the young lady I want to see walking the halls around here."

Aerlie couldn't help but feel a new surge of confidence rush into her, and it showed on her face as a broad smile began to stretch outward.

"What is it about you that every time I come near, I feel my spirit soaring among the clouds?"

Thaelyn leans back and grins softly. He reflects on her statement, and almost seems to hesitate in his response.

"Yes, that is in fact a curious question," he emits slowly and sighs, then pauses to consider his own feelings a moment. "Perhaps I should also confess…I too feel a lifting effect. You seem to inspire people with the glow of your inner light. I cannot be sure if it is simply your sweet smile, your passion, or your wild defiance of the mundane, but it is almost as though we share a kindred spirit of some sort. Beyond that, I cannot be sure."

"Well, I think there's one thing I can be sure of," she replies fondly. "You are not only our most noble Lord and King, and our most endeared Master, but you're also like a father and a cherished friend."

Aerlie gets up from her chair and leans forward. She then places a gentle kiss on Thaelyn's cheek, before turning and leaving the room.

Thaelyn sat there surprised and deeply touched by the gesture. He remained there for a long moment, staring out the door in contemplation of the tender reward, then finally to try redirecting himself back to his work.

———————— ✦✦◆✦✦ ————————

"You did what?" Amaree whispers urgently.

"Dear gods, could it be?" Deena wheezes.

"Oh, come on!" Aerlie retorts playfully. "It was just a little peck, that's all."

"A little peck," Annah muses. "Is that anything like a little lightning?"

"So, is this how we're supposed to make up for our errors now?" Vonafel teases.

"Girls!" Aerlie snaps. "It's just that he made me feel so much better from our talk, that I felt like I could take on the whole academy afterwards."

"Well, I did say he was good at restoring your morale," Deena offers. "Although restoring it to the point of you jumping into his lap and laying a big wet…" she grins boldly.

"It wasn't a big wet…whatever you're thinking of. I swear, you might think I had something improper in mind."

"Improper…" Vonafel ponders cerebrally. "Attempting to combine two forms of study into one, when it had been proven both ineffectual as well as impractical…"

"Now wait a minute…" Aerlie protests satirically.

"Improper…" Vonafel continues. "Then introducing an elixir of unknown origin that could radically alter the way they teach in this academy, and for that matter, in every other school across the kingdom, if only to resolve the earlier issue."

"Vonafel…"

"Improper… Once, as a young girl, travelling outside your restricted space and getting involved in a circus, then having your GODDESS, of all things, call for a rescue to bring you home again. And finally, improper… Again travelling outside your restricted space, and flying halfway across the continent to find that same help to fight not one, not two, but three dragons…"

"Are you finished?" she retorts brashly.

"That depends on what you have in mind to do next," she giggles.

Aerlie and her friends shared the moment during a break after school. They were gathering in the rec room again, which had become a favorite spot for their meetings.

In the months and years that followed, Aerlie returned to her studies with a renewed vigor, but as she rose higher in her classes, she was also developing several new questions about herself. Her studies were now involving additional subject matter that was not previously part of the common curriculum. Due to the elixir, and the new system of accelerated learning, the compressed study schedules now afforded the students additional time to take on more elective courses, some of which belonged to the more specialized subject matter previously only available to the higher scholars and technical fields. These were opening her eyes to new aspects of consideration, some of which were now reflecting on herself as a person.

"Amaree, I need your opinion," she asks privately.

"Yes, Aerlie, what is it?"

"How do I compare to your average elf, generally speaking and without the wings for the moment."

"Without the wings? But, in what way?"

"Just in general, one compared to another as a race."

"Well, there are a number of qualities you seem to share with other elves I know, Vonafel for example. Physically, you look mostly the same, although your eyes are angled a little deeper than most."

"I think this is common for Avariel."

"All right, and physically you're very slim, which is a little different. Most elves are slim, but you seem a little more so."

"Yes, but again I have to say this is common for Avariel. It's to help reduce our overall body weight and enables us to fly better. We also have hollow bones to reduce our weight even further. And we have slightly larger lung capacity for those higher altitudes."

"Really! That's interesting. So, what is it you're actually getting at here? As an elf, you're within the boundaries of it, other than for the wings, that is."

"Let's start with my eyes. Look at them, what do you see."

"Aerlie, is there something going on here?"

"Just humor me a moment and give me your impression."

Amaree leans closer to gaze carefully at Aerlie's eyes.

"They're a beautiful shade of blue, and I think I even see a little bit of sparkle inside, which is very lovely."

"But it's not normal for your typical elf."

"Well, all right, but you're Avariel, so this must be something specific to that."

"No, it's not."

"Huh? Wait, what do you mean? Other Avariels don't have this sparkle?"

"No. They would be much more like the rest of you."

"Uh huh. What about the color?"

"My mother has pale blue, and my father has pale green."

"All right, so you got the blue from your mother, I suppose, but where did the sparkle come from?"

"Good question. Let's come back to that in a moment. Now my hair…"

"Your hair… Well…" she wonders tentatively. "It's a soft gold."

"I've heard a few people say that it looks like the spun gold you might find in a fine necklace, like from a goldsmith's shop."

"And your parents?"

"Black, both of them…and in fact, THIS is the standard color for us."

"Aerlie, unless you Avariel have some really weird inheritance traits, I'm losing your meaning here."

"One more, please… My wings…"

"Oh great, now you're just being silly."

"Just say it."

"All right, fine," she smirks. "They're white as snow. Do we have an issue with that?"

"Yes, neither of my parents have pure white. My mother has a few brown spots, and my father has black crowns and soft brown tips."

"All right, so what is it you're saying? They aren't your natural parents?"

"My mother admitted to me once that she is, but this was only AFTER Thaelyn brought me home from that circus."

"What?" she yips. "Wait a minute, what do you mean by that? You didn't know your mother was your mother until after you came home from the circus? Wait, that simply sounds wrong just for saying it," she chuckles.

"When I was young, I was raised to believe I was adopted. The people in our village all told a story where my mother was apparently called away by our goddess to bring home a lost baby said to be laying in the woods somewhere far across the mountain ridges. She came home with a newborn baby in her arms, and that was me. She was not expecting a child at that time, and this caused a lot of questions to go around as to who it was that lost a child out there. As far as we all knew, the only surviving Avariel were in our village, and no one else was known to be with child at the moment, to say nothing of going outside to give birth to it."

"Meaning whoever it was couldn't be from your village, but this also offers a paradox. What about this bit of being a Chosen One?"

"One moment, and I'll get to it. So, here Thaelyn brings me home from that circus, and my mother had an argument with our Patriarch for his bad manners with Thaelyn, thinking he was just another human trying to take advantage of us. She said a few things, one of them being that it was my purpose to bring him to help us, and this is where I started to learn about this Fate of mine. She also told me I was in fact her child, but some kind of divine gift to fulfill this purpose."

"Aerlie," Amaree moans softly. "Are you aware of what you're actually saying here? We're saying she wasn't pregnant at the time, then she left the village, went out in the woods, and as crazy as this sounds, instantaneously bore a child..." she winces. "Ouch! That hurts just by thinking about it."

Aerlie sighs deeply and lowers her head as she tries to collect her feelings.

"I don't want to say it, and I feel like I shouldn't dare say it, but I'm almost afraid I have to. These lessons I'm taking right now are teaching me about the Outer Planes and the various beings that live out there. It's making me ask a few questions about who I am when I think back on what my mother said once."

"What kinds of questions?"

"First, what am I if my mother is apparently my natural mother, but my father is not my natural father? Who is my father in that case?"

"Dear gods, Aerlie..." she whispers.

"Yeah, and that's what I'm afraid of, especially when you consider the Winged Mother sent me here."

"Um, excuse me a moment..." Amaree grins coyly. "But are you going to tell me the Winged Mother could be your father? That just doesn't sound right."

"Yes, well…" she giggles. "I know, and this doesn't actually help matters. I remember when Thaelyn killed those dragons, and we were talking afterwards, and my mother mentioned something about a seraph. Now I'm wondering who that was and how, um… she, I suppose…fits into it."

"Another 'she', but so far no 'he' to be a father figure…although, whoever that seraph might work for could be a clue. Do you have any ideas based on this new study of yours?"

"Not exactly… I'm getting the idea the gods hold a lot of strange powers, so maybe to simply create a body isn't so difficult for them, regardless of gender. But then I have to ask myself the only obvious question I can think of after that. My eyes have this sparkle. My hair and wing colors are considered abnormal. The people of my village actually treated this as some kind of anomaly, like a birth defect. But could this be a sign of something else?"

"That would be a very good question to ask, I suppose. Although I have no idea who to ask about it. I'm aware Thaelyn, as one example of someone created by a god, is a very rare case."

"Yeah. My hair, a metallic golden color…how do you describe that for ANY race of elves? My wings, pure snow white. No one in our village has pure snow white. I'm not even sure if this is a natural color for us, at least not completely white."

"Then, Aerlie, you have something very special going on here."

"I don't feel like I hold any special powers, so I'm wondering if I'm actually just touched in some way that gives me this look."

"That's an interesting idea. So, maybe your goddess touched you, or rather touched your mother in this case, and created you, but at the same time, this gave you a few unique appearance qualities."

"Yes, that helps a little. And maybe this could also account for my violet Spirit test score. If I was touched, or created with some particular level of purity, I might qualify for a violet."

"Ah!" Amaree snaps her fingers. "That actually makes sense to me. I remember Thaelyn saying mortal creatures might not qualify for a violet due to our mortal traits, where we are not as highly refined as Celestials. So a blue, or maybe a high blue touching violet, might be our best case, at least until we can evolve more."

"But Amaree, this just takes us back to the beginning again. If you're saying mortals can't get a violet, but I did, then how does that compare to a Celestial by any other means? And then I have to return to this Fate I'm apparently following. My mother said it intertwines with Thaelyn in some way."

"Aerlie..." she intones suspiciously and raises an eyebrow. "Are you getting any sinister ideas inside that head of yours?"

Aerlie blushes and ducks away giggling.

"Amaree, I wouldn't dare think I could do that..." she halts as a realization comes to her. "But then again..." she muses faintly.

"What?"

"Amaree, have you ever been in the presence of someone where you just felt like you were made for each other?"

Chapter 15

DISCLOSURES

"Sssomething is wrong..." Adalon murmurs silently. "I feel lossss..."

The great silver dragon lurches up from her resting position within her lair at a sudden disturbing sensation. She angles upward to summon her servant, and soon the traditional column of light descends down next to her. Thaliel steps out of it somberly.

"What has occurred?!" Adalon demands urgently.

"Maker, there has been a dispute. It is with my deepest regrets that I must bring this upon thee. I only just now learned of it. The Great Power Helm is down."

"Down?!" she roars. "How is it posssssible... To bring one... Sssuch as he... Down?"

"There was a dispute, as I said. He and Tyr held an argument, and a challenge was made to demonstrate the integrity of the statements presented. The result was a contest, and Helm lost," she lowers her head in sorrow.

"No!" she shrieks.

Adalon howls in outrage and grief. She backs away into a clear area of the chamber, then delves into her concentration to produce her own divine column and departs the area.

Thaliel watches as the column fades, and then prepares her own.

Adalon's son, who was lying in his own corner immersed in his personal musings, had been pulled out of his thoughts at the sudden display.

"What will occur... Because of thisss?" he asks.

"I know not, Ikurin. He has been with us a long duration. Perhaps another will take his place."

"And to Tyr?"

"That is also uncertain. Such events as these occur but very rarely."

"Sssuch as the Essstelar... Should not behave thisss way... To begin with..."

"I must agree; thou art correct."

She forms her column, and then leaves the room.

✦ ✦ ✦ ✦ ✦ ✦ ✦

"My Lord! This is terrible news!"

"Who is it that reported this?"

"The Morninglord, he is the only one speaking at present."

"What about Tyr?"

"His altar is silent."

"Why would his altar be silent?" Thaelyn mumbles to himself.

The temple in the city was in a minor uproar as word just filtered in from the priesthood by one of their deities, in this case Lathander, that Lord Helm had apparently been killed.

The death of a god was an exceptionally rare occurrence, and usually the result of intrigue or malice, not natural causes. The loss of a god obviously meant the disruption of the worship by his followers, and therefore the direction and guidance this gave to the people. And Helm was an important example to the people of Tae'Eladar and Thaelyn's Order.

Thaelyn had been called in by a messenger from the temple and was now approaching Tyr's altar to check with his Father to see if he could get any more information. So far, they only knew Helm was dead, by Lathander's report, but not the cause of it.

He knelt down at the altar for Tyr's icon and laid his hand on the plaque with Tyr's holy symbol inscribed on it. He submersed himself into a meditative focus, but there was no response at first. This was unusual, especially for Tyr not to respond to his own son. So he tried again, but this time using more force to invoke a reaction.

A presence began to manifest within the icon, causing it to glow softly, and a voice entered Thaelyn's mind.

"I cannot speak with thee at this time, my son."

"What?" Thaelyn muses urgently. "Why not? What has happened up there?"

"A tragedy… Helm and I entered into an argument, which was followed by a contest to demonstrate these principles. The contest demanded resolution, and in my rage over the accusations presented, I applied myself to mine own justice. But others are coming forward with presentations of falsehood. Now, an inquiry is occurring, and I must depart from thee to participate."

The voice now goes silent.

Thaelyn pulls back slowly from the altar and stands up again. The priests had been watching, and took notice of his success in drawing the attention of the deity, but his face denoted deep contemplation and grave concern.

"My Lord?" whispers the high priest. "Do we have something?"

"Yes, but only a brief word. Apparently, there was an argument, followed by a contest, I suppose much like a duel, between Tyr and Helm over something that is now being brought into question for its true validity. Now the Powers are holding an inquiry to determine the fault."

"Dear gods…in a literal sense of it."

"Yes, it would seem this is one occasion where they played a trick on their own. As much as the gods might be revered by mortals to be immune to such mundane antics, they are still a society that can suffer their occasional domestic intrigues."

"It seems almost a contradiction. One might think they should be above this, and in more ways than one."

"We will have to wait for the results to see what actually occurred. Tyr seemed to believe he was in the right, but the end result is the loss of Helm, which is harmful to many. There was mention of some form of falsehood being revealed, but I must ask myself who created this. I find it doubtful it could be any of the local participants."

"Someone else then?"

"Possibly… The Negative Powers, those of the Lower Realms, often look for opportunities to disrupt things. I might even wager Cyric for this point," he chuckles bitterly. "Cyric, Prince of Lies. This sort of thing would be right up his alley."

✦✦◆✦✦

Adalon was at the center of a tribunal being held in a region of Mount Celestia where several Estelar had gathered to observe and oversee an inquiry regarding the death of Helm, and Tyr's responsibility in this affair.

Needless to say, she was extremely angry.

On the ground was Helm's body. A group of seraphim had assembled, called in by one of the Estelar to attend to the remains, but Adalon wasn't about to permit them access. She charged at the assembly and hissed at them violently, pushing them back.

"Keep your dissstance from thisss!" she demands.

"But Servant Draconic," ushers one of the seraphim. "We are directed to remove this."

"You will keep your dissstance… Until these proceedingsss… Are complete…"

"Servant Draconic," responds one of the attending Estelar. "What authority dost thou have in this place to make such demands of us? Although I would not wish to deny thee, I must still ask this of thee."

"I am not… A sssimple ssservant!" she roars impulsively, but quickly checks herself, as she had not told anyone of her plans or transition to a corporeal form. She draws back and sighs tensely to contain her emotions for a better presentation to answer the question. "I am Maker Kuroku…" she announces.

The assembly reacted to this unexpected assertion with shock and surprise, further that she had apparently taken this unusual form.

"Maker, why wouldst thou appear before us in this form? This is the form of one of thine own servants."

"I have my reasonsss… And none of you… Were intended… To know of thisss…"

"Why? Thou hast sided with us for a long period, and now thou dost hold secrets from us?"

"In truth… I have held sssecrets… For much longer… And when I look at thisss…" she directs at the corpse lying nearby, "… My reasonsss become… Ssself-evident…"

"Wouldst thou explain this to us?"

"I find I mussst… At thisss time. But know thisss. I have held confidence… In my plansss… With Helm… During thisss full measure… Of time… Due precisssely… To the insssecurity… That othersss may intrude… And try to interfere…"

She steps away from the body as she collects her thoughts to explain herself and her secret relationship with Helm.

"Helm and I… Held a pact. I am in pursssuit… Of an ancient foe… Who once offended me… And my people. You were not made… Aware of thisss… For a number of reasonsss. Not the leassst of which… Is you might sssimply… Conssssider him… Impotent and undeserving… Of your concern. Another might be… You would rob me… Of my own vengeance… For the crimesss… He once committed… Againsssst me and my kind… And perhapsss… Countlessss othersss… Along the way. Thisss is MY goal to pursssue… Not yoursss…"

"Who is this thou dost seek? What form does it take, and why keep such secrecy from us?"

"He was once… My ancient Massster…"

A subtle murmuring began to resound through the assembly, but the curious nature of the suggestion demanded its own explanation.

"Yesss…" Adalon continues. "I can already feel… Your

quessstions. Do you recall... The Battle... With the Ancient Onesss... Which brought you here... To thisss domain... In the beginning?"

Another of the Estelar steps forward to answer.

"I believe thou dost refer to the heathens of malice that once did occupy this fold. Yes, Maker. We recall this occasion."

"Indeed, Oghma... ssSage of Wisdom. Thisss is correct. You would then recall... How the battle... Came to itsss... Fruition. But were you aware... That it was I... That gave thisss to you?"

The assembled deities once again looked around and mumbled quietly over this new suggestion.

"I once made... My home... On the Prime domain... Now known as... Tae'Eladar. My people... Once called it... Khalen Ruuki... In our ancient tongue. I was made... To use my gift... Of precognition... By my former Massster... To find my way... In his gamesss. But I sssoon dissscovered... It held more... Utility... Than thisss. I foresssaw the coming... Of our dessspair... When you arrived... And your challenge to them... Along with... The devassstation... They would bring... In the end."

"But our recollection suggests it was Helm who provided us with this knowledge."

"He did... On my behalf... After I found myssself... Ssstraying from my focusss... Then to make contact... With his mind. I shared my thoughtsss with him... My visionsss... Of the battle... And the Ancient Onesss... When they would deploy... The Agent of Unmaking... Upon my home domain..."

Adalon pauses to glance over at the inert form of her old friend and confidant.

"He preserved usss..." she declares solemnly. "It was a part... Of our bargain. He raised... The Imberium Shell... That now sssurrounds... Our home..."

"We are aware of the Shell, Maker, and his part in creating it. This was one of his specialties. But thou art the one originally responsible for discovering this sacrilege?"

"I am... But it does not... End there. I alssso foresssaw... The

essscape of my Massster… And his ssservant… To a barren fold…
Where they would hide… Until sssuch time… As they could
make… A return…"

"Such a thing is unreasonable," offers another member. "If he
is alone, he would pose no threat to us. We dominate the Seas of
Creation now."

"Thisss is true… And I am sure… He knowsss thisss. But
you do not know him… As I do… Or his ssservant. I have been
watching them… With my ssspies… And they are making… Their
plansss… Even now…"

"What plans are these?"

"Plansss I intend… To interrupt… With my own creationsss.
A new breed… Of guardiansss… I bring forth now… On my
ancient home…"

"Maker, is this the purpose of thine efforts in the Prime domain?"

"It is. He has been making… His own… And I mussst meet
him… In a new contessst."

"Maker, thou must take caution here. We would not permit
another such as what they once brought into Creation."

"I know thisss. Helm and I… Ssspoke often of it. I do not
follow… That courssse. But to meet him… I mussst advance…
Cautiousssly… As he might otherwise… Flee… If he were to sssee…
A greater threat… Approaching. Thisss is the reason… I take thisss
form… Ssso that I may join… In the final… Confrontation…
And demonsssstrate to him… What his creation… Has created for
herssself…"

"Thou art taking this as a personal grudge. Thy rage at him
must be great."

"Perssssonal, perhapsss… But not limited to that. Helm warned
me of thisss… Many timesss. But I hold firm… To my goal. It is
here… That I desire… For you to ssstay… At a dissstance… And
allow thisss… As it runsss deep… And intimate… To my own
originsss… And all I have observed… During thisss time. He is
not to be trusssted… And neither excused. Not for his own… Or
any of the othersss…"

"And thou dost believe this new guardian society can achieve this goal? What manner of creation hath he brought forth on this occasion?"

"They are a sssociety... Of high wisdom... And technological achievement. Thisss is true. But in a barren fold... And without the dynamissstic flowsss. Thisss is my advantage..."

"I believe I understand. And how dost thou perceive this final confrontation to occur?"

"As a demonssstration... To draw his attention... While I make... A sssecret advance... To bring him down... Before he can essscape. And mossst desirably... With as few lossesss... As possssible. But NOW... As for thisss madnessss... You have brought... And what interference... It might cause... To me and mine..."

She pauses to glance once again at Helm's body, then to the rest of them.

"Thisss inquiry... Mussst now commence. I want ansssswers! Helm was not only... A friend and sssavior... To my people... He was alssso..." her voice begins to waver as she reflects on their relationship together. "He was..." she tries again as a tremor comes into it, and she feels her emotions taking over. "...As a father to me!"

Adalon drops her head and begins weeping. She stumbles over to Helm's body and sits next to it, then lies down and sobs.

"You maniacsss!" she moans. "You pretend... Yoursssselves to be... As godsss... And Massssters of all Creation... But you ssstill behave... As recklessss children..."

"Maker Kuroku," Tyr ushers gently. "I am the one responsible for this tragedy. Thou should place thy blame on me alone, not the others."

"Really!" she snaps. "Do you think... I have forgotten... The immature anticsss... Of Shar... When she and her sssister... Held that dissspute... Which resulted... In the shadow she cassst... On my home ssstar? It killed everything... That ssstill remained... On our ancient home... And the other worldsss... That orbit there.

And for what reason? That she could not hold… Dominion… Over her little… Playthingsss?”

"Yes, I recall this, but the sentient forms…"

"Yesss! The sssentient formsss! My people… The ssSarrukh. I used my power… Of Prophecy… To foresssee thisss. I am not about… To allow… Another race… Of godsss… To decide the fate… Of life and death… Of whole worldsss. Not even you…"

"You are the cause of this?"

Adalon sighs and tries again to gain control of herself.

"I foresssaw the coming… Of the ice… But the sssmaller detail… Of Shar'sss true ire… Was not portrayed in thisss. She was angry… Not as much… For her differencesss… With ssSelûne… As she was… The departure… Of my people. She is a jealousss witch… Who enjoysss holding power…"

"This, I was not aware of."

"And yet another… Example… Of why I would not… Disssclose my plansss to you. There are those… I sssimply… Cannot trussst here. Cassse in point…" she turns and jabs a claw to point at Helm's body. "How did THISss come about? Because I sssuspect… No one here… Would be ssso wild… As to conduct… Sssuch a vile act… As sssimple murder…"

"Yes, I must agree with this," states Oghma, hoping to redirect the obvious aggression and despair into a more constructive dialog. "Maker, are we to assume thou dost desire to take direction of this investigation, due to thy close relations with Helm?"

"It is the leassst I can do… For all he has done… For usss. He was a prominent member… Of our group. I modeled mysssself… After his image… As well as my… Draconic children. And I will dedicate mysssself… To thisss purpossse… For any future… Guardian sssociety… I should ever create…"

She turns and glares at each member in attendance.

"If for no other reason… Than to keep YOU in check…"

"Very well, Maker," Oghma responds tenderly. "Thy point is made. We may state ourselves to preside over the Seas of Creation, in the hopes that we may ensure the Measure of Balance, but I think none of us can truly describe themselves as perfect. It is doubtful that any creature, even such as we, could ever hope to achieve this level of accomplishment."

"At leassst a few of you... Recognize thisss..." she murmurs.

She stands up again and steps away to consider her thoughts.

"What was the cause... Of thisss dissspute... And therefore the reason... For thisss contessst?"

She turns to look at Tyr for the answer.

"You are the one... That caused thisss. Therefore... You mussst be... The one... With the anssswer..."

"With my deepest sorrow," he replies. "I admit this is true. The reasoning was clear, at the time, but since then has been refuted as invalid."

"Let usss begin... With the reasoning..."

"Helm was performing a service on my behalf. I did request this of him on several occasions. It was to deliver..." he hesitates as he glances around the group before continuing. "It was...to deliver a series of missives to my beloved."

"You mussst be joking! You could not do thisss... Yourssself? You are a full adult... And a mature one at that... And yet you behave... As a love-ssstruck... Adolessscent..."

"It was to apply some stimulation into our relations. We might find it...refreshing on occasion."

She huffs briskly and nods before continuing.

"Very well... And what became of thisss?"

"This process did continue until recently when a return did find mine attention that Helm may have been..." he pauses to make a sound similar to a clearing of his throat, even though the Estelar didn't have anatomies involving true throats. "It did report unto me that Helm may have been secretly charming her away from me."

Tyr turned his head down as he knew what would be coming next.

"Incredible!" Adalon roars. "What did I jussst sssay... A mom ent ago? Is thisss a cassse... Of sssimple jealousssy? Could you not try... To confirm thisss with her... Directly? I would think you...

Of all people… Would know… The due processsss… Of law… And the determination… Of evidence…"

"Yes, Maker, this is clear to me, and a clearly evident failure on my part."

"And ssso you challenge him… In thisss contessst… To do what? Preserve your honor?"

She examines him closely, and then the body of Helm next to her.

"The two of you… Are fairly matched… And yet… You do not appear… To have taken… Ssserious injury from thisss…"

"No, I did not."

"Which sssuggests to me… He gave himssself up to you…"

"In truth, it would appear that way."

She huffs again at the absurdity of the situation, and then continues.

"Then what is thisss ssstatement… Of falsssehood… I heard ssspoken? Who presented it?"

"Here," shouts a smallish voice from amongst the scene of deities. "I am the one who brought it forward."

Adalon turns to focus on a seraph stepping into view.

"And who are you?"

"I am called Umbriel, headmistress of Helm's seraphim caste."

"Very good… And what do you offer?"

"Helm did make a habit to record his duties and maintain records of his travels and actions, including with thee, Maker, and thy secret dealings. But he did also make it clear that much of this was sensitive, and to be kept confidential unless a critical need should arise. I must now come forward with what I have to offer."

"I undersssstand… Proceed…"

"I can provide unto thee the records of his meetings and the delivery of Tyr's missives, but there were no subversive acts taking place. He did hold true to his purpose and high esteem."

"Then where did thisss… Accusation… Of wrongdoing… Actually come from?"

"Helm was involved in a number of objectives during his service. As a guardian and protector, he did hold many responsibilities.

Along the way, he did also have many opponents among the Negative domains."

"Thisss is very… Reasonable. I have a few of my own…"

"I therefore did give instructions to mine attendants to conduct a quick survey, once we learned of this event, to see if any of these were responsible. From this, they did make an inquiry with Primus to investigate any surveillance records that might associate with this occasion, and from this we did find correlation."

She turns and summons up another seraph who was an underling in her service. The tall female marches forward to meet with her mistress. She held up a large glowing square-cut crystal that filled her palm. It radiated with an internal light.

"Within this concept prism," Umbriel continues. "We have a surveillance record of Tyr's court, and a meeting where a messenger did recently appear before him with this declaration of wrongdoing on Helm's part. But the individual hereto represented is not a known agent of any of the Positive Powers. On further analysis, we have surmised it must have infiltrated our domain under a Cloak of Guising to impersonate a friendly form."

"In other wordsss… Sssimple intrigue is at play… And for what? To remove… One of our… Mossst important membersss? Do we know who sssent it?"

"Once we had this information, I did invoke several of our apparition pools on a suspicion, based on this style of interaction. One of these was to observe the Power Cyric in the Negative Chaotic domain, to discover if he might show any acknowledgement or reaction. And he did. We did observe where he was in discussion with an unknown agent reporting this unto him, suggesting his directive was now complete."

"Thisss is as good… As a confession! Ssso… It was Cyric… Who ordered thisss. How typical of him…"

Adalon moved back over to Helm's body and gazed at it. She further panned her stare around the seraphim that were assembled to clean up the remains, but she wasn't ready to call this in just yet.

"I once called him… Brother Helm…" she reminisces. "And he

called me... Sssister Kuroku. Then... As I made my dessscent... He was the one... That delivered me... Into my corporeal form... That my new mother... Would bear me forward. For thisss... He was as much a father... As any could be..."

She turns to face the others, studying each of them.

"I cannot blame you... Tyr... For anything more... Than your failure to examine... The sssituation... Before passssing your judgment. As for Cyric... I already hate him... And thisss sssimply addsss to it. If he should ever... Creep out of that hole... He callsss his home... He will know my clawsss... Before he knowsss... His missstake..."

"Maker," calls another of the Estelar in attendance. "Such as this is indeed a tragedy, but perhaps we should remind ourselves of the Measure of Balance. They do unto us, and we do unto them."

"I will not argue... The Measure of Balance... But thisss was uncalled for! Thisss was not an act... To counter... One of our own. Thisss was sssimple... Mischief. Cyric is mad... Insssane... And you know thisss. He is unssstable... Ever sssince that human... Absorbed... The esssence of Bhaal. The conflict... Of their mindsss... Has driven him... Into recklessssness..."

"We understand this, but he is also out of our reach to correct this."

Adalon sighs deeply. She knew it was pointless to argue this. The Estelar held their policies and practices, and as unnerving as it might be on occasion, all things had to balance in some manner. This included the Positive and the Negative, as well as Order versus Chaos. And Cyric was a personification of this.

She turned once again to look at her former friend and close relation. She knew what she needed to do, and it was no less than what he did for her at one time. She moved close to the body and contemplated her goal.

"He shall not passss... Into oblivion..." she mutters. "He once preserved... Me and my people. Now is the time... When I mussst return... Thisss favor. I will preserve him... And keep him... That he will not be losst to usss..."

"Maker," asks one of the members. "What dost thou intend at this time?"

"Would you now... Quessstion... My integrity... For all of your own... Failuressss?"

"I do not wish to question thee. It is but a simple inquiry. Thou dost seem postured to take a certain course, and I believe we should know thy plan."

"Agreed..." she relents. "Then know thisss... I will take him... Into myssself... Where I will preserve him... As he once preserved... Me and mine..."

"Is this to say, thou dost intend to be his successor, and assume his position amongst us?"

"I modeled myssself... After him... And I already ssserve... Sssuch a role..." she pauses to glance at the body and to consider her ultimate direction. "To take his position... Would involve a burden... Above my own. And his was... A large ssseat to manage..."

She turns to find Umbriel again to see if she reflected any opinions on the matter.

"If I were to take... Thisss position... I will need... Assssistance. You once ssserved him. You know his waysss... You hold his resssources. Would you ssserve me... The sssame?"

"I was loyal to Helm and his doctrines," she decrees. "And thou dost carry this same prestige. If thou were to take this position, I would follow thee and serve thee with no less vigor."

"I already have... A chief ssseraph... To manage my own. If you were to take... A sssecondary lead... For thisss portfolio... Thisss would aid me... Greatly..."

"I would agree to this. It could represent another chapter."

"Then ssso be it... But alssso know thisss. My mossst immediate objective... Is to complete my pursssuit... Of my ancient Massster. Until then... My attention... To anything elssse... Will be limited. I will offer what I can... But my primary concern... Is the management of Tae'Eladar... Until it becomesss... Ssself-sssufficient..."

"I understand."

"And thisss conversssation..." she further glares at the others in attendance. "...Never occurred. Those in attendance... May not reveal... Any of that... Which has been sssaid. I will demand... Sssecurity... For these detailsss... Until my purpossse... Is complete..."

Adalon returns to the body and now extends a claw outward over the remains. She closes her eyes and reaches out with her thoughts into the ethereal mass that was once her dearest friend.

The Estelar are not corporeal creatures. Instead, they are beings of mostly thought and spiritual energy, tightly bound into a body of ethereal ectoplasm. As such, one can actually absorb another in such a case as this, where the one to be absorbed may have died. But even in death, the essence of the body is not completely inert. There is still a residual presence remaining, including thoughts, memories, and some portion of their innate powers. When absorbed into another creature, assuming that creature did not previously have their own, they could inherit this from the former entity and perhaps use this to replace them.

Adalon, being a deity of her own, did not have a special need to inherit Helm's powers, but his knowledge and memories could be absorbed, and what additional strength he might provide, would only serve to make her even more powerful as a deity.

As she held out her claw, the body began to glow softly, and one could see the essence rising up into her claw and spreading as a form of illumination throughout her body. She seemed to enter a trancelike condition as the new energies merged with her own, causing her to behave as if in a dream. She held her posture over the body as it was completely consumed, finally to return to her natural senses and open her eyes again. But even at that, she still seemed lost in her thoughts.

"Yesss Helm... We are here now..." she mutters apparently to herself. "You are sssafe with me... And we shall persssevere together. All is not lossst... But I will need... To find another... To assssist me... In that final moment..."

Several days have passed, and another messenger was drawing Thaelyn down the lane to the temple. On this occasion, Aerlie was attending her study course, but all activities had come to a halt as they were receiving a most unusual visitor.

"My Lord," announces a priest as Thaelyn enters the building. "She arrived just a short while ago and was calling for you. I've never seen the likes as this before. Is this what I think it is?"

Thaelyn and the priest made their way up to the dais where the rest of the priests had assembled, many crouched low in reverent poise to the figure standing on the platform, including a cluster of students, and among them, Aerlie.

Standing on the dais was an exceptionally tall female figure, as compared to any of the local examples. She had pale skin, huge white wings, and wore a glimmering set of noble armor.

Thaelyn arrived and bowed deeply before her.

"It is a rare privilege to see one of your stature presented in such a place as this, Dame Seraph. May we know the purpose of this occasion?"

"I am known amongst my kind as Umbriel, formerly in the service of the Great Power Helm. I have been sent before thee and thine to give notice of a change within the ranks of the Powers."

"I was not aware such a service was commonly made for the Child Races. Why on this occasion?"

"The occasion may occur as the relationship with this society does hold special interest to us. But this occasion does also warrant special handling by my new governor. Helm was lost to us as the result of a malicious venture conducted by another Power. Although the Powers on our side will see to this as they must, a replacement has been chosen, and therefore the Child society of this domain is to be made aware of this change, that they may redirect themselves into their new offering, if they should desire this."

"A replacement?" mutters one of the priests among the group. "Who would be this replacement, and how might we make our offerings? What name do we call up to?"

"The name shall remain the same, as this new Power will adhere to the same mold as the previous, and make use of the same title for the convenience of our Children. But this new Power will require time to adjust to this practice, as the portfolio Helm did once hold was great, and this other Power does also carry their own, now to occupy both."

"This new Power is serving double-duty?" Thaelyn muses. "Who is this other Power in reality?"

"For the present, they prefer their name in its native form to be withheld, in order to prevent confusion amongst the Child societies. At some moment, it may be revealed unto thee, but not until stability is found, and other matters of concern are resolved."

"Very well, but then, what about Tyr?"

"The Power Tyr has been absolved of direct wrongdoing for the loss of Helm, however he has been placed into probation for his abrupt application of decree without full consideration of judgment."

"And the one truly responsible for this matter?"

"The Negative Power Cyric is declared the perpetrator of this misfortune."

"I knew it! The Prince of Lies, as he is so often known to us."

"Indeed, he was discovered to have sent an agent into Tyr's court to deliver the false mention that initiated this event to occur."

"What manner of judgment is scheduled for him?"

"He currently hides within his fold, carefully layered with his servants, and out of our reach at present. But the Powers will see to their opportunities as they present themselves. His actions are deemed unwarranted, no matter the interpretation of the Measure of Balance. Recompense will be demanded."

"I see... Very well, is there anything else we should know?"

"This is all I can offer thee at this time."

"Most excellent, it is enough, and we thank you," he bows again.

The seraph dips her head, and then vanishes in her Celestial column.

"Incredible!" exclaims the high priest. "Such a visitation with such a report from on-high... It almost feels as if we are neighbors sharing the daily news."

"In a certain form, we are," Thaelyn admits. "Although this news is not of the sort I would wish to hear," he sighs.

"Of course, my Lord, surely that much."

"And yet, these are most unusual neighbors, to be sure. In many ways, I feel the people of this world are exceptionally privileged that they hold my teachings to inform them of such dealings. Any other society might not be as privy to these details, as the Estelar do not as often interact by such intimate means."

"She was so beautiful," Aerlie croons. "With such lovely white wings…"

"Yes," he smiles. "They tend to be that way. And a bit like yours if I may say so."

"Well, yes, but she was a seraph, and that probably speaks for itself."

"It may at that. This is a common color for them. In fact, I think this is their only color, which actually reminds me, as I recall your mention once about your own."

"Yes, that…abnormality…as some might call it. But I'm sure it's a completely different thing. She's a different race, after all."

"Indeed, and theirs is quite old, as well. I cannot begin to imagine how far they date back, or what sort of origin they once had, but it might make for an interesting study, if one had the opportunity."

"I also took notice of her eyes. They were very pretty, and seemed to carry a tiny hint of something, like a sparkle or a glow…"

"This much I can attest to. A very subtle glow, along with a tiny bit of sparkle. But again, I would suggest this is due largely to their extreme evolutionary advance, maybe also their time spent living in the Outer Planar regions, as the conditions out there can impose a few curious alterations to one's physique after a while."

"Really! That's interesting. So, living out there can change your appearance if you spend enough time at it?"

"For this, we should probably temper the suggestion with the proposal of whether or not you were born there, or perhaps how long your lifespan might be, therefore, how much time you could afford into it. But the numbers would surely be rather large."

"I suppose so. And I'm sure anyone born into it would have to be blessed for this point. Like you and your eyes. Is that normal for an Aasimar? Are there any others like this?"

"Actually, yes! I am aware of two other Aasimar, one a bit older and the other a bit younger than I am. Both have the same color eyes, so from this example, I am forced to concede this might be representative of the breed. However, one is female, her name is Aelwyn, and she is a good friend of mine, almost like a sister to me. But her hair is a bold cinnabar red with a slight metallic sheen. Quite lovely if I must say."

"Yes, I'm trying to imagine that now."

"The other is a man, just a bit younger than I am, and also her beau, as it turns out. His name is Aristan, and another good friend…I suppose I would associate him a bit like a brother, as we are all very close to each other," he chuckles softly. "His features are actually very similar to mine."

"That's interesting. So, if we try to extrapolate, for a man, the hair color seems to favor the silvery-white?"

"For what we have available as our example," he shrugs. "It might seem that way, while the female may have something else."

"That's really a very curious form of dimorphism at play here. Do we know of any other examples up there?"

"I am aware of just one other example of a Celestial hybrid, in this case another female who is described as an Eladrin, which is based on the elven mortal frame."

"An elf? They do this with elves, too?"

"I think hers might be a special case…but then, most are like that," he sighs reluctantly. "Her name is Nemelle, and she is a close friend of Aelwyn…and of mine, as well, once again as we tend to stick together like an extended family."

"I suppose that sounds reasonable."

"And let me see… She is apparently descendent from a Morier."

"A Morier? Good gracious, how did that happen? Down here, they're called Drow."

"Indeed, but I think her mother was rescued at one time from the Lower Planes. Then, her Father, whom I believe to be Corellon Larethian, otherwise known as the Protector within the Seldarine, blessed upon that woman a child to grant her a sense of fulfillment."

"That would be quite a blessing."

"It would," he nods. "Her features include a pale grayish skin tone with a slight purple nuance, and a number of tattoos. She seems to like those," he smiles.

"Probably her Drow side, I'll bet."

"Perhaps! I believe she carries a slightly Chaotic flavor as compared to the rest. She also has a platinum white, again almost metallic hair tone, and in her case, violet eyes which sparkle like the gemstone amethyst."

"Ooh… That sounds lovely."

"Yes, and as I think of this now, I cannot help but to recall your eyes, also with a slight sparkle reflecting out of them, but in your case blue, like that of topaz. Such a curious thing…gemstone colors… This causes me to ask myself about this goddess of yours and what she did to bring you forward," he muses distantly before turning and leaving the room.

Aerlie was agape at the statement, as were most of the people in attendance. Many eyes were starting to turn in her direction now. She stood there watching him as he left the building, but soon felt the stares of her fellow students.

"Eladrin…" she whispers. "Oh dear gods above…and maybe more…"

"Aerlie," her instructor mentions privately. "Are you alright?"

"Priest Darin, I've been asking myself these questions for a while now, ever since I started taking up some extended classes at the academy. None of my colors match my people, and I'm supposed to be a gift of our goddess in this world. I don't have a natural father, only my mother. So, where did I actually come from? If Aasimar eyes tend to follow gold as a rule, and the only other elven example has a gemlike sparkle, and if we further say my wings are pure white, which is not natural for Avariel, but could be natural for something that was born in the Outer Planes, what does this actually mean if I don't fit any reasonable description for anything down here?"

"But is this to suggest…"

"I don't dare try to suggest anything, but I can't help to ask the question anyway."

"Eladrin?" Vonafel emits curiously. "They have a Celestial form for elves, too?"

"That's what I heard from the students at the temple this morning," Deena admits. "I met with one during lunch. He was present when that seraph arrived and the conversation that followed. Thaelyn said he knew an Eladrin up in Sigil, which is that city up there in the Outer Planes he used to visit. And she had a kind of crystalline color to her eyes, but in her case violet like amethyst, whereas Aerlie is more like topaz."

"Is this a common thing for Celestials?" Annah wonders. "I mean, Thaelyn has gold, which is a metallic color…"

"Not just that," Vonafel adds. "But it's also a noble metal."

"All right, and amethyst and topaz…those are gemstones. So, are we saying humans take this metallic color while elves take gemstone colors?"

"I have no idea, but if this is how you describe Celestials…"

"This was apparently part of that discussion," Deena offers. "It would seem there are too few examples to really get a broad-spectrum impression, but if this is the pattern, well…"

"I wonder what their children would look like…" Annah smirks.

The group was in conference in the recreation room again discussing this latest sensation over Aerlie and her perceived purpose in this world, but now compounded with the news of this potential evidence suggesting a Celestial connection. Of course, this only served to exasperate the previous allegations.

"Annah," Amaree teases. "Just what are you thinking right now?"

"Naughty stuff," she grins. "But if we're suggesting they're supposed to come together and rule the world, what else can you expect?"

"Yeah, I suppose you're right…eventually."

"Hmm…gold and topaz," Deena muses openly. "Would it take one side or the other, or maybe a little of both?"

"Technically speaking, they would be half-elves, like me," Amaree admits. "And our history shows this to be a fairly predictable outcome. So, probably something crossing the line. She's female, so if you have any daughters, it sides mostly with her. Males would tend to side with the father."

"And the hair…" Annah offers. "Silver for him, gold for her…"

"I would have to agree with Amaree," Vonafel suggests. "They tend to split the difference. A daughter would probably have gold with silver highlights. A son would be just the opposite. But in either case, this sounds lovely!"

"Ooh, yeah…I like it."

"But now, where does this leave us," Amaree wonders.

"The Daughter of Sky, from realms far beyond…" Vonafel recites. "With eyes and possibly hair like that of an Eladrin…"

"And snow-white wings," Deena asserts. "Unusual or unknown to Avariel, but similar to that seraph that came by…"

"And all of it literally out-of-this-world…" Annah concludes.

✦✦◆✦✦

"Brother Thaelyn…" announces a softly rasping voice at his office door.

"Adalon! So good to see you again…"

He jumps out of his chair to meet her as she enters the room.

The end of the school year was approaching, and he was making his preparations for the upcoming commencement ceremony. This particular one was special, as it would involve Aerlie in the graduating class.

She had been finishing up her Ninth Circle mage studies, plus a number of other classes that would elevate her to an especially high level of accomplishment simply for the volume she took in this time. The Elixir of Visions was performing admirably for her and the entire student body. This year would produce a crop of genius-level graduate students, representing the first in history to rise this high with anything less than a lifetime of study, and before that lifetime was even past their education years.

Adalon was making her visit in his office. She appeared to be in deep contemplation on this occasion. Thaelyn had noticed a change in her demeanor in the recent months since the demise of Helm, although he could not be sure of the reason. Knowing her manners, the only realistic option was that she must be involved in some new plot she would hold to herself until that critical moment when she would surprise everyone with another scandal.

"Adalon, what brings you here on this occasion? Are you well? You seem very distracted."

"Yesss... Forgive me... Brother Thaelyn... But my mind is lossst... With many new thoughtsss. I need time... To bring it... Under control..."

"Is there anything I can help you with?"

"I wish there was... But thisss... Is outssside your capacity. The Planesss turn... In peculiar waysss... And sssometimes... We find oursssselves... Deeply mired... In their wake..."

"Very well, but I am here if you need it."

"I thank you. You are as much... As a brother to me... As if I had... Mine own ..."

"Excuse me... Mine own?" he smiles tenderly. "Adalon, are you sure you are feeling well? You are starting to sound like the Powers," he chuckles delicately.

"Did I sssay that?" she jerks her attention to his gently smiling face. "Oopsss..." she chuckles softly. "Yesss... Perhapsss... After ssso long... A little has rubbed off... Onto me," she attempts to shrug off the error. "Which actually... Bringsss me... To my visit..."

"Good, what do we have today?"

"A paradox... That will ultimately require... Resssolution..."

"Oh dear Powers... All right, what manner of paradox?"

"The recent lossss... Of Helm... Has played itsss havoc... On many in our home... Opening the eyesss... Of they... Who once thought... The godsss to be... Infallible. But you and I know... They are far from thisss. And thisss has been... Evidenced... Rather boldly... With his death... And the intriguesss... Sssurrounding it..."

"Yes, this has certainly caused a fair amount of discussion around the Hall, and in many other places, especially with this new replacement that seraph spoke of."

"Indeed... And in many waysss... Thisss bringsss them... Within perssspective... Of a sssociety... Of people... Sssimply performing... Their work... As we might perform... Our own..."

"This is a most curious suggestion, but you do hold a point. Therefore, the next question to ask, and I believe this is where your paradox might come in, is how to explain this to our people, and then where to lead them afterwards."

"Throughout hissstory... Mortalsss have revered... Their godsss... As omnipotent... Omnisssscient... And omnipresent beingsss... Of incalculable power. But if one can be killed... By sssuch sssimple meansss... As an error in judgment... Or a rash impulssse... Thisss demeansss them... To little more... Than glorified creaturesss... Barely more advanced... Than our own sssociety..."

Thaelyn places his hands on his hips and sighs assertively.

"You are indeed correct. This is a problem, and it can potentially break an important aspect of a society's culture."

"It can... Unlessss... If that sssociety... Were to reimagine... Itsss relationship... With the Divine..."

"And I suspect this is where your paradox comes full circle with a resolution. I suppose I can see it, but the clear predicament in this case would be the maturity level of the society in question."

"You and I come... From sssocieties... Of a much more... Advanced maturity. The Celesssstials... By their nature... Automatically asssscend... To thisss ssstature... And the Draconicsss... Are an ancient race... That often residesss... In that sssame ssspace. Our proximity... Affordsss usss... The clossseness of assssociation... Nearly on equal termsss..."

"And the people of this world...?"

"...Mussst evolve..."

"Very well, but you do recall the policies of the Estelar, and for that matter the Celestials, on evolving the mortal races too abruptly."

"I know thisss well... But we alssso have... A unique control... In play here..."

"Oh, I simply must hear what this one is about," he grins.

"Our isssolation... In thisss domain..."

Thaelyn paused in his reply as he reflected on the implications of this concept.

"This is actually a rather distinctive suggestion. Yes..." he muses as he begins tapping a finger on his chin and pacing around the room. "Adalon, did you know you are a most unusual example of a Draconic?"

"I am probably... More unusual... Than you can imagine..." she chuckles softly.

"So, if I understand this correctly... Our unique isolation in this fold, where we essentially have no neighbors on other worlds or around other stars, could potentially allow us to make a few movements, while at the same time not adversely affecting anyone else in our local domain."

"And further... Because we have... A Celessstial... Among usss... Teaching our people... That which they... Would not otherwise learn... By any other meansss... Until they were... Far more mature... To dissscover it... On their own..."

"Indeed, and we also have this. This would reflect on numerous occasions of my teachings since my first days arriving here, to say nothing of a certain Draconic I know of who contributed her share," he grins at her.

"Perhapsss... And thisss might allow usss... An opportunity. Thisss world... Has a unique hissstory... And I believe... It will continue thisss way... For a long while. Perhapsss... We should not be... Ssso frightened... Of advancing our people... To that which... They ought not to know... Before their time. And yet... It is ssstill prudent... To maintain a policy... Of conssstraint... To allow them... Time to adjussst..."

"Absolutely! Then, if to say we might renegotiate our relations with the Estelar, allowing our people to become more familiar with the nature of their kind, at least within reason for their maturity level, and then grow this as we grow our world. It should not be too difficult to culture our people to follow such a policy as the Measure of Balance. In some ways, we are already doing this. And as you said, our isolation keeps us in check."

"At leassst until... We dissscover a way... To penetrate the Shell... Sssurrounding usss..."

"Correct, but I would not look forward to that just yet. That will require a considerable leap in our technology, I should think."

"Indeed, it would..." she nods agreeably.

Adalon now turns to leave the room, allowing Thaelyn to return to his previous work. As she saunters back through the guildhall, she continues musing to herself.

"Yesss... Indeed, it would... Brother Thaelyn..." she glances demurely back down the hall. "Assssuming we left it... To the sssimple processss... Of invention. But thisss... Will not be the cassse. Not precisssely... And not as expected... Once THEY arrive..."

✦✦✦◆✦✦✦

The end of the school year had arrived, and there was a ceremony taking place in the prestigious Great Hall of the Order, a grand court within the guildhall where Aerlie and all her friends had been taking studies and finding new lives. A row of trumpeters called out the herald anthem, and people were gathering to attend the graduation ceremony on the main floor. Along the balconies were visitors, friends, and family who were in attendance to watch the proceedings and give their support to those below.

At the head of the room was a platform which acted as a throne for Thaelyn during his official political proceedings, and at other times as a stage for the Master of Ceremonies to give his presentation as he called up the students one-by-one to receive their diplomas.

Thaelyn would stand by to oversee the ceremony, but he did not interact directly. His presence was symbolic, at this point, to offer his support and acknowledgement of the achievements of his students as they made the transition into their new lives.

Aerlie was among the gathering on the floor, standing at attention as part of the graduating class. She had worked long and hard to reach this moment, and was exceptionally pleased with her accomplishment. She pondered what sort of role she might play, whether as a mage or a priest. As a Ninth Circle graduate, she had a lot of possibilities in the field of mage craft, from teaching and research, to setting new policies and legal standards for the Art. But as a priestess, she could go into the medical practice and healing arts, or to lead younger students in teaching on that side.

On the balcony overhead, her mother and father, and several others from her village had gathered, including Patriarch Daeselri, all of whom were beaming with pride.

The MC had been calling out names and giving the ritual oath. The students then received their documents and returned to their place in the assembly. When he came down to Aerlie's name, he was suddenly unsure how to proceed in her case.

"Eh, my Lord," he mutters privately. "This is a new one… How do you think we should proceed in her case? She has graduating honors in two primary categories."

"Yes, I had considered this a few times for what title we would assign. She could go either way, but is deserving of both. Therefore, the only offer I can make is to grant her what she deserves. Here, what if we present it like this…"

Thaelyn steps in to point at the roster the MC was holding and gestures at a possible manner of presentation for her title arrangement.

"Ah, yes…" the MC acknowledges. "So simple, actually. Very good, this should do nicely."

He then clears his throat to call it out.

"Mage Elder and Priestess of the White Cloth, Aerlie of House Lorespinner."

The assembly ushers up a bold applause as Aerlie proudly steps out of her row and walks along the red carpet to the steps. She halts at the base, offers a traditional salute, and then kneels to receive her oath.

"On this day," the MC declares. "You who have come before us do hereby honor us with your devotion. Now, the time has come for you to choose, with final determination, your course to become a member of our brotherhood, the Order of the Silver Dragon, fully and completely, and for the duration of your lifetime. How do you plea?"

Aerlie looked up at the MC as he gave his speech, and now she was preparing her response. It was sometimes tradition for the student to offer a few of their own words, if they had anything special to say, and she wanted to make a small statement.

"As the first of my people to attend this academy, and to honor the favor of our dearest Lord and King, and in honor of our gods, especially those who helped my people find salvation that we might actually be here today, and to all the others that gave us this chance to live in such a beautiful world as it is now, I most certainly, and with all my heart, plead yay!"

The room breaks out with a roaring applause, along with whistles and shouts. The MC and Thaelyn exchange smiles and wait for the room to calm down again, but then Aerlie has a new thought quickly flash into her mind.

"Oh!" she adds promptly. "And I hope not to send any more accidental lightning bolts into anyone's back."

The room now erupts in bold laughter.

"Indeed!" Thaelyn states firmly. "That would be most desirable."

Now the MC continues.

"Then in the eyes of our gods, rise, Sister of the Order, Aerlie of House Lorespinner."

The MC hands Aerlie her completion document, and an attendant steps up to pin a guild heraldry symbol on her vest. She then steps back to offer another salute before returning to her former position.

On her way back, she looks up at her parents on the balcony and smiles brightly.

In the following weeks and months, she settled into a daily routine as a new mage Elder, occasionally giving lessons in the academy, intermixed with other scholars, and trading off with work in the temple down the road. She arranged a schedule to split her time between them, to give her an opportunity to make use of all her skills, although she hoped to eventually find a higher position as she gained more work experience and the occasional promotion.

Serving a dual role like this placed a lot of demands on her time, and so she joined with a few of her friends as they moved into an apartment together to share expenses. Being part of the Order allowed them to occupy space in a row of dedicated housing near the guildhall for convenience's sake. From there, they could quickly and easily travel to their associated jobs, as well as other local venues to attend to their needs.

And yet, along the way, Aerlie still felt a driving motivation to seek the end of this path of Fate that seemed to be controlling her life. As a result of so many conversations with her friends during the later years in school, she had been developing the idea of where it might be leading, and she found herself reminded of the time when her mother once said her Fate was intertwined with Thaelyn's. Finally, one day, she decided to make a move to test the waters on a hunch. So, she invents an excuse to make a visit to his office for a chat.

"My Lord," she begins as she peeks in the door. "Do you have a moment or two?"

"Ah, Aerlie, of course... Come in."

She enters the room as Thaelyn directs her into a chair at the desk.

"What do we have this time from our star graduate?" he asks.

"Well, a few interesting thoughts have been going around my mind, and I was hoping to share them with you to see what you think."

"Absolutely, what are they?"

"All right, it starts out a little like this... I'm reflecting on the loss of Lord Helm. It's been almost a year now since it happened. When we first learned of it...gracious, it sent the temple community into a fit, to say nothing of the word on the street that a god could actually die."

"Yes, these things can actually happen, even to gods."

"I tried doing a little research on this, to see if there were any other occasions on record of something like this, but this looks to be the first, at least in recorded history."

"You are probably right. I cannot personally recall an occasion, at least not within my lifetime, other than that Time of Troubles event we had once, where we may ever have had a devoted icon suddenly taken away from us."

"Right, and that Time of Troubles event, which was many long years ago, was actually due to Lord Ao who had several of his treasures stolen, and he used this occasion to punish the others for some growing complacency issues. I'm aware there were reports of several gods dying in that one, but this held an excuse where Lord Ao stripped them of their divine powers, leaving them in a more vulnerable condition."

"And as such, oh…did they take advantage of the situation," Thaelyn whistles.

"Yeah, and right here in our backyard. Thank you very much, Lord Ao…with respect, of course."

"Yes, I might agree with that. Although I do not think there was as much damage to the landscape, there were several occasions of masses of combatants engaging each other as rival gods, along with their followers, would meet and take out their aggressions right here in our world."

"Fortunately, this didn't last long until those artifacts were found and returned."

"And also," Thaelyn muses. "On this occasion, I believe many of those who fell were of the Negative alignment, which would not affect us as greatly."

"There were also a few Positives in there, but apparently not as highly attended as those we use now."

"This is true. So, where does this take you in your thoughts?"

"Apparently, word has it that sometime soon, and apparently

as the result of Lord Helm, we are going to phase in a few policy changes where our worship is concerned."

"Ah, yes, good point. This is actually the result of a discussion I had with Adalon. She and I held conference on the fact that due to this circumstance, it might alter the way people perceive of the gods if they can actually die or be killed, especially by such frivolous means as this."

"Frivolous means…now there's a statement, and especially where gods are concerned. I have to admit, I'm actually one of those people. I was raised to think the gods were unconquerable beings of unthinkable might. Then we have the day where that seraph comes in with the daily news report from on-high. Headline news, she said…" her voice becomes animated. "Tyr kills Helm as the result of an error in judgment. Conspiracies fly as the truth is revealed!"

The two of them let out a guarded laugh.

"Suddenly," she continues. "Gods are no more invulnerable than we are, and apparently just as prone to social issues and intrigues as any mortal society. This actually contradicts the definition of being a god."

"Precisely, and thus the reason for my conference with Adalon. She came in here with this same mention and suggested we should try to correct this with a careful new course of education, and perhaps also a new direction for our religious studies."

"I'm seeing a little of this taking place now, but I'm wondering what the ultimate direction will be. Can you tell me?"

"What I can say so far is we have both short-term, and also long-term goals at play here, so we need to be sure how we approach it simply because of the implications of bringing our people around to this new perspective. We may be evolving them in ways no other young society like this would normally travel."

"And given my position within the ranks," she asserts. "I'm going to assume I might hold a role in this, if for no other reason than to say I am a star graduate with so much gall as to dare change your entire education system with an inconceivable potion of questionable origins," she grins cutely.

Thaelyn glares at her suspiciously for a moment.

"Why am I getting the idea that you have a hidden motive at this time?"

"I honestly couldn't say…" she states innocently. "After all, I'm just a sweet young girl from a small village."

"Pah! Indeed!" he laughs. "And all the more reason to suspect you of foul play!"

"Well, if you look at the larger picture, I'm an elf, so I'll certainly be around a while, all things permitting, of course. And next is if I hold this strange aspect of Fate, I'm wondering where it'll take me in the end. I don't think I'm finished yet, do you?"

"Actually, I have my doubts on that. So, what do you think your Fate has in store for you next?"

"During my studies, I had an opportunity to take some courses which were largely specialty subjects relating to the Outer Planes. I think this might offer me a special qualification to get us started. I certainly feel myself able to handle whatever matters you can throw at me, if you want to throw anything at all, and being near you has this funny effect on me that I feel lighter than air, with or without the wings."

"Excuse me?" he wonders. "How does that fit into it?"

Aerlie turns her expression away nonchalantly and casually stands up from her chair as she continues.

"Well, if you involve such things as my curious personality…my gall, as you like to call it, and the fact that you apparently enjoy a good challenge…or at least, that's what they say…"

"Just a moment here…" he interjects. "Who are 'they' in this case?" he raises an eyebrow.

"And then," she resumes, apparently bypassing the question. "Let us not forget that I'm the only one to ever get a violet test score…that seems fairly important, plus the fact that you seem to adore my eyes and wing color. I'm not sure about my hair…you haven't mentioned anything on that yet…but it is rather unique, if I must say so, with a curious metallic sheen. And none of this, by the way, is common to elves in this world."

"Aerlie," he intones cautiously. "Where are we going with this?"

She steps away from the chair and positions herself ready to make her exit, but she's not done yet.

"And finally, there are a few rumors going around that you're single, and apparently have never chosen anyone, not since the day you arrived. This leaves a girl wondering what you're waiting for... unless maybe it's something truly special to come along that might offer a little sparkle in your life."

She finishes her statement with a smirk and a brisk fluttering of her wings for emphasis, then turns to saunter out the door, but casting one final glance over her shoulder.

"I think the two of us would make a great team, no matter where it takes us. But I believe my Fate has something special in store. I can't be sure what exactly, but I think you know this as well, because you feel it too...you're just too afraid to admit to it."

Now she makes a pert exit and closes the door behind her.

Thaelyn was dumbfounded, sitting in his chair and stunned at the blatant suggestion just dropped in his lap. Her rapid retreat didn't even allow him time for a rebuttal, leaving him with nothing more than his reflex reaction.

"Dear Powers," he wheezes. "Did that girl just do what I think she did?"

He leans back in his chair to ponder the scene, rolling it over in his mind and reflecting on her wording, which then forced him to recall his own feelings whenever the two of them were nearby. It became obvious very quickly, and he knew it. He felt it too.

Two days had passed, and Thaelyn was trying to pay attention to Aerlie's comings and goings to time her schedule for an impromptu meeting in the guild courtyard. It was a sunny autumn afternoon, and he was taking a rare moment to himself for a little stroll outside.

The students passing through the area all bowed to offer their respects as they saw him apparently milling around in the courtyard, which was unusual as he always kept such a tight schedule for himself. Finally, Aerlie emerges from her work assignment after instructing an exercise in the mage training fields, and she was on her way to a staff assembly room to store some of her instructional gear. For this, she would need to pass through the courtyard, and Thaelyn was waiting for her.

"My Lord?" she asks. "I don't usually see you out here this time of day. Is something going on?"

"Ah, Aerlie… Me?" he responds casually as he seems distracted by watching the people passing through. "Oh, nothing special, I just wanted to get a little air. It occurs this way on occasion, you know?"

Aerlie studied him, discreetly eyeing him from head to toe, and she suspected there was something different here. She knew his schedule too well, as she had also been watching him during this time, waiting for some kind of response to her flirtatious maneuver a couple of days before. She decided to play into his game, and angled off to observe the same sights he seemed so focused on.

"Yes, I love the fresh air and flowers."

"Indeed, and we do tend to enjoy our local environment."

"No doubt thanks to our relationship with the dryads."

"Oh, absolutely! Involving them into our society changed many things for us."

"You know, if you consider the Patriarch, humans simply don't have that special link to understand them."

"While this might be true in one sense, they did certainly come around to it once we introduced it to them."

"And to think, now you have so many others, all happily living and working together."

"Yes, but in truth, it was not so easy to bring this together in the beginning."

"Was it anything like trying to bring us into it that first time? I still recall that Aluer I spoke to once, and what she said about her people."

"Indeed! There were a few of those, but in most cases, we did not have such as your Patriarch making his arguments as he did."

"No, probably not…"

She now turns to look at him.

"You're not really out here just to smell the flowers, are you?" she grins. "You don't need to answer. I've been waiting for this. In fact, I was half expecting to see you out here today."

"Only half expecting? Where was the other half?" he smirks wryly.

"Ah, is our noble Lord discovering his lighter side? Tell me, did you ever hold any special interests in your life?"

Thaelyn sighs and reflects on his past for a moment.

"Yes, I did…once."

"By the look in your eyes, I suspect it didn't go as nicely as you would have hoped."

"It went as well as it could, but it still felt unfulfilled."

"What happened? Or would you rather not talk about it. Is this why you're so afraid to try again?"

"Yes and no, I suppose. She was a lovely young woman, but a mortal, and you can probably guess where this would ultimately lead us."

"Yes, that part is easy."

"But at the same time, we could not join in a proper union due to the condition that I was under a contract of service to my Father, and could not involve myself in an intimate relationship."

"Wow…that would hurt more than anything, I think. So, in the end, what happened? You make a visit and just sit and talk, or something?"

"Essentially, yes…perhaps to share a meal, a story or two, and then a hug and a goodbye."

"For how long?"

"For the remainder of her mortal life… She never joined with anyone else, and I felt guilty for occupying her from having a normal life."

"But wait a moment. I think not. If she gave herself to you, that IS her life. She chose this, and I'm sure for a good reason. You gave each other everything you could, but with you being immortal, you would naturally outlive her in the end. And now here you are, alone with haunting memories."

"You know, Aerlie, in a curious manner of speaking, you hold some of her same strength, and you speak with her same words."

"It just seems these words are the right ones. As for the strength… well, maybe this is a little of my priesthood training doing some counseling work."

Thaelyn laughs at the notion, followed by Aerlie.

Aerlie reflects on her feelings a moment as she continues again.

"Life is simply a path we take. And especially in the case of a mortal one, which can only be described as temporary. Where we go after that…who knows. But surely, there must be something to come after. As for the rest of us, we just keep on going until one day our own Fate comes to us."

Thaelyn's smile softened as he listened to this curiously familiar line.

"Great Powers, Aerlie, you do actually sound like her. She once held the same perspective in her time."

"Then this must be a common form of wisdom, and if it can carry from one person to another, one generation to another, and even from such a place as the Outer Planes to a place like this, it must be very profound! And so, now here we are," she glances around the courtyard. "I think I know you well enough to know you hold an interest, especially after our last talk. I don't think you would be out here now if this was not the case. So, the way I see it, you basically have two choices."

"Oh really…" he smirks. "And what might those be?"

"One is for you to go back home and find another Aasimar… although I recall you only knew of one other, and apparently, she is already spoken for. Well, some other Celestial, you know what I mean, who is just as immortal as you are, and stop moping around worrying about mortal lifespans. Two is to swallow the bitter pill and take a mortal, and love her for all you can get out of it. And I suppose it might not be limited to just one, at this point."

"Indeed, I suppose I cannot argue this," he admits thoughtfully.

"Or...Three," she adds audaciously. "You take me, which is certainly a fine option when you consider what you're likely to get out of it," she again flutters her wings for emphasis.

"What? Three!" he gasps suddenly. "You said there were only two options! And what is this with the wings? Is that some sort of Avariel tactic?"

"You seem to like wings. After all, you grew up with seraphim all your life. Now, I'm a traditional girl. I prefer a traditional courtship wreath with small red and white flowers. Do you think you can manage that?" she grins coyly.

She starts moving away seductively, but halts partway with a parting glance.

"And try not to take too long. We're not getting any younger, and we both have work to do. And trust me, you're going to need my help with all this. After all, my goddess sent me for this purpose."

Aerlie now struts away across the courtyard, leaving Thaelyn once again with his mouth hanging open.

A Watch Captain, who happened to notice Thaelyn standing around the yard, and who chose to remain available in case he might be called on, observed the interaction from afar. He cautiously strolls up, once Aerlie is away, to inquire about his most noble Lord who appeared dumbstruck and emitting soft whimpering noises.

"Eh..." he makes a clearing sound to draw the attention. "My Lord, I couldn't help but to see you and the young lady out here..."

"Did you see that?" Thaelyn asserts energetically with a finger. "With the wings, that is!"

"Aye, that's a curious one, to be sure, but then I'm not too familiar with the mating habits of the Avariel. Eh...so what should we do about this? Perhaps I should call up a carriage? I hear they offer a nice selection of those wreaths over in the Grove District, and we wouldn't want to keep the young lady waiting."

Thaelyn now turns to the Captain with his mouth dropping even further.

"Captain..."

Thaelyn stutters momentarily and shakes a finger at the man, until he begins to realize the many eyes that were on him. He holds his statement as he darts his gaze around the courtyard at all the people who had gathered during this time.

"Incredible!" he wheezes. "I am surrounded on all sides by conspirators! How many of you have been waiting for this?"

The assembled gathering simply looks around at each other, shrugging their shoulders and smiling.

"It's been long enough, to be sure," offers one student. "And she's surely a fine catch! No doubt about that one!"

"But… But… Oh, fine!" he throws his hands in the air. "Captain, call me a carriage," he pauses to check his appearance. "I need to find my coin purse… Great Powers, I cannot even recall the last time I used that."

✦✦✦✦✦

"She what?!" Deena screeches.

"We're talking about Aerlie, right?" Annah wonders. "Sweet, innocent, virgin village girl Aerlie…"

"That doesn't sound like a virgin village girl to me!" Deena admits sternly. "Amaree, you didn't happen to teach her any of your dark little half-elf secrets, did you?"

"Me?" she balks. "I may have given a few pointers, but nothing like this! Especially with that wing flutter…"

"That has to be an Avariel thing," Vonafel considers. "But the rest of it… Either she's not the sweet virgin village girl we all thought she was, or…"

"I can't see how she could have the opportunity," Annah asserts. "Not in a village with three dragons hounding them. This came from somewhere else."

"Well, it couldn't be from any of us. All her time here was spent in a classroom, and I doubt they teach this in the temple."

"Could this be part of that new religious concept I've been hearing about?"

The group offered up a round of laughter at the thought.

"The only thing I can think of," Deena considers. "Is if we look at Vonafel's book fetish, this must be some kind of carry-over."

"Deena," Amaree stresses. "A carry-over from what? Who do you have to be to carry-over a performance like this?"

"Well, it certainly came from somewhere."

"The only place I can think of..." Annah ponders. "Is a...uh..." she coughs emphatically.

"Just a moment, Annah," Vonafel objects. "You're not actually thinking of..." she raises an eyebrow.

"A brothel?" she concludes shyly.

"So, you're trying to say our great and most noble Lord spent time in a brothel."

The group erupted in another bold round of laughter.

Over the coming weeks, and then months, Thaelyn and Aerlie engaged in a courtship ritual befitting the elven traditions. On some occasions, it might be as simple as sharing a cup of tea while engaged in light conversation in a gazebo, or walking along through a botanical garden. They also attended a number of social occasions and seasonal events. Even though the two of them were deeply convinced by now that this is what they wanted, they restrained themselves to follow the traditional path in order to uphold the standards of their cultural values.

Normally, Elven traditions demanded it to carry a full year this way, and these were their plans. But under the circumstances of having a mixed culture, the actual wedding would follow the tradition of a temple ceremony in the style used most often in the common society of the kingdom, except on a royal scale.

On the day of the wedding, the temple bells rang out, and the crowds gathered along the streets. The whole city was decorated with flower wreaths and ribbons, and everyone felt a special ambiance in the air. The people were dressed in their finest suits and gowns, and lined up in hopes of catching a glimpse of the newlyweds once the actual ceremony was complete and they made their wedding drive.

Despite Aerlie's bold flirtatious maneuvers at the guildhall, she was feeling increasingly nervous as the moment approached. Seeing all the flash and glamor associated with a royal wedding shocked her. Thaelyn always appeared in a fairly casual set of attire during his work, rather than wearing any especially extravagant suit befitting a king on a royal throne. She had become accustomed to this, and it felt familiar to her after a while. Now she was looking at herself in a long flowing white wedding gown, custom made for her figure, including lace wraps for her wings, and decorated with silk flowers.

Amaree and her friends were assisting Aerlie with her clothes, while at the same time trying to settle the anxious young bride-to-be from her fret.

"Amaree, does this look straight to you? Wait, the wings don't look even. Now the veil is crooked. Where is my corsage? How does the train look? Is it centered? Who's going to carry it? How am I supposed to ride a carriage like this?! Everything will get all messed up before I even arrive!"

"Aerlie! Shush! We're handling it as best we can. Gods above, if I knew it would be this hard to get you married off, I probably would've warned you away from it," she chuckles.

"I'm trembling under all this! He never looked this high and mighty when he was in combat class!"

"Yes, you're right, but then I never really saw him in ANY special royal setting. It's not his usual style to fashion himself like so many other elites I ever read about in our history books. He's definitely an exception to the rule where that goes."

"He is most certainly a modest man," Vonafel adds. "This much I can say from my own experience."

"Strong, of course," Deena offers. "But surely modest and compassionate, and this goes against our history for a lot of nobles before he arrived, many of whom didn't even talk to anything else, much less marry it."

"And even if they did talk to them," Annah submits. "It was

typically with a very snobbish attitude of superiority, as if it was a special privilege just to gain their attention to look at you.”

“Wow, really?” Aerlie wonders. “But then, what about me, and then all of you… Would you still talk to me after I become one of them?”

“Well…I don’t know,” Amaree wavers. “The girl with the sparkly eyes, the golden hair, a violet test score… Sounds like an elite to me, what do you think, Deena?”

“Didn’t she once refute the idea of marrying a king? It sounds like we had a really big reversal in there somewhere.”

“Oh, yes!” Annah admits. “The sweet little village girl…who strutted her stuff like a seasoned seductress… I don’t think I could trust her again after that,” she giggles.

“Now just a minute!” Aerlie retorts. “I’m not a seasoned seductress, and I honestly don’t know where it came from, it just happened. Being near him does weird things to me.”

“Weird…” Vonafel conjectures. “Such as to hit him in the back with a lightning strike, and he actually congratulates you as the first to receive this honor.”

“Oh no, we’re not doing this again…”

“Weird, where you talk of this Fate of yours, and the next thing you know, you’re propositioning the most powerful man in our world, not to mention the most powerful in all our history.”

“Now you just wait…”

“Wait? I’m actually afraid to wait. I’m half expecting the gods themselves to come down here as soon as those bells ring after you take your vows.”

The group ushers up a round of laughter, and they finally lead Aerlie to a carriage waiting outside to bring her around to the temple.

The streets were packed with observers lined up around the temple. Thaelyn and his entourage, which involved a number of his top-ranking officers, were waiting outside after just arriving in their own carriage.

“My Lord,” remarks one of his men. “You seem just a mite fidgety. You haven’t been able to stand still since we first arrived.”

"Indeed, and I must admit, I feel no different from any other young man during such an occasion. There were many moments in my lifetime when I might sit and try to imagine if I should ever have this opportunity, typically as I watched others around me with theirs. But you can never be truly prepared for it when that final moment arrives."

"I'll admit to that, rightly enough. I recall when my day came. Before the day was out, my kerchief was nearly soaking, for all the sweat from my brow."

"Why does it occur like this? It is a special day, to be sure, but this is simply a ceremony to declare one's devotion on an official level, and we have essentially attended this privately on numerous occasions during the courtship. We felt fine during those moments, but now it seems like an entirely new experience."

"That's a fine one to ask. If you should ever find the answer, I'd be happy to hear of it!" he laughs.

Aerlie's carriage makes its way along the lane until it comes into view of the temple. It pulls over and her flower girls help by taking up her train and assisting with her presentation.

The two lovers meet in front of the doors as they turn to make their entrance into the temple. The bells chime out the wedding melody and the assembled gathering begins a slow march inside and along the carpet up to the dais.

Up on the platform was a choir singing along to the music, and this was echoed by many of the visitors who were in attendance inside the temple. In the front row were Aerlie's parents and other close members of her family and friends from her village.

Thaelyn and Aerlie strode along holding hands in a formal procession, along with their respective entourages. Even though they each struggled to hold their composure, privately they felt swarms of butterflies circling around their stomachs.

As they approached the steps, Aerlie looked for her parents, hoping to find a little comfort in seeing their faces. Thaelyn didn't have the same waiting for him, as he didn't have any family to share this moment with, except perhaps his Father. But the Estelar didn't usually involve themselves on a personal level with such intimate details of the Child societies. Nevertheless, he knew Tyr would be looking down on him, even though he might not be standing amongst the crowds. Still, he did hope to find at least a few familiar faces. Finally, as he arrived near the front rows, he saw Aelwyn and her friend Nemelle standing on the other side of the aisle, both of them smiling brightly. Next to Aelwyn was her male admirer, Aristan. He was a tall gentleman with refined features, much like Thaelyn, and fashionably attired. He sported a flamboyant grin and twiddled his fingers in a childish gesture of greeting, as was his style.

Thaelyn smiled warmly at seeing their faces. Aerlie turned to follow his gaze to observe them as well.

"Is that them?" she whispers.

"Yes," Thaelyn admits. "Here we have the remainder of our group from Sigil. I will introduce you after all this is done. But I will offer a gentle caution. Aristan is a rather colorful example for his personality."

"Sounds like fun," she smiles. "Colorful, just like the Planes themselves."

They made their way up the steps and onto the platform in front of a series of prelates who had gathered to oversee the ritual. The bells finished their tunes, and the ranking priest stepped forward to give his oratory. The crowd stood and waited patiently as he prepared to speak.

"This day is a most joyous occasion for us all," he announces boldly. "Not only to see the union of these two in holy matrimony, but to see the completion of a journey, where a man and a woman come together in a bonding of love and devotion. It is a sacred promise we make that brings us together for all time that we may share our lives, our destinies, our joys, our sorrows, our pleasures, and our pains, if this should be the will of our gods. And it is in the eyes of those same gods that we make this promise, that they may bear witness to this event no less than we."

He pauses for a breath, and to allow a subtle break in the sermon.

"But for many of us, this occasion also carries a special meaning, as we reflect upon the journey we all travel together. For on this day, it is our noble Lord and King that would marry, to complete a journey many of us have long anticipated, due in part to his grand crusade to bring our world into harmony, but leaving his own heart vacant. It is therefore to our even greater joy, that this day brings his own harmony, that he may feel as much joy in his heart as so many others have felt for so long."

"Aye!" the crowd collectively ushers up a fervent shout in agreement.

Thaelyn looks over his shoulder in amusement at the unexpected response.

"I must ask myself how long this has been circling around me."

"A good long while, my Lord," his Captain responds.

A wave of laughter rolls through the assembly, and then the prelate continues.

"And so, we must bring ourselves into this service, that this man and this woman may be united into their sacred bond, that their hearts may feel this harmony, and that our long-awaited journey finds its home."

He now turns to Thaelyn to offer his vows.

"Here stands our most noble Lord and King, who is known to us only by the majestic name of Thaelyn, Knight of the most holy Order of the Rose, Knight of the most holy Order of the Haloed Moon, Son of our blessed God Tyr, and as I understand at one time also described as the Scion of Celestia."

The prelate glances sideways at Aelwyn as he adds that final piece. Thaelyn follows his glance to see Aelwyn smirking for her little contribution.

"And you, as well…" he mutters softly.

"You who have come before us," the prelate continues, "to offer yourself to this woman, with your promise that you will bestow upon her your love, devotion, and commitment, for the duration of your lifetime…and good gracious, that would indeed be a long while…"

The crowd offers up another round of boisterous laughter at the suggestion.

"Indeed!" Thaelyn smirks. "And a fair portion of that spent listening to all of this."

The laughter continues until the prelate resumes his statement.

"Furthermore, to attend and support her in her moments of need, and to grant her your dedication of home and family... Is this, in truth, your deepest vow?"

"In the fullness of statement, it is so," he responds soundly.

The prelate now moves across to Aerlie, who was feeling faint by this time. Amaree could see this in her pale expression, so she decides to offer a little tension breaker. She discreetly steps out of view behind the girl and signals the prelate with a silent hand language, which was common to learn in the guild, and flashes a few brief instructions to him.

Aerlie waited for him to speak, but then took notice of an extended lull as he seemed distracted by something. She turned to look over her shoulder to find her friends, but Amaree simply clasped her hands and smiled.

"What are you doing?" Aerlie asks suspiciously.

"I'm just standing here waiting for the action."

"Yeah, right..."

Aerlie turns back to the prelate to hear her vows.

"Here stands Aerlie of House Lorespinner," the prelate states, but now showing a curious grin. "Traveler to Distant Lands, Partaker of Circuses, Bringer of Mysterious Potions, and Caster of Accidental Lightning Strikes..." he finishes with a broad smile.

Thaelyn covered his eyes while emitting a silent chuckle.

"Captain, do you recall my list?"

"Aye, do you think we need to bring it out on this occasion?" he offers with a smile.

"I cannot be sure. The day is still young. But keep it handy."

Aerlie's mouth dropped open at the unusual listing of titles. She instinctively turned again to find Amaree.

"You!"

"Me?"

"Yes, you! You're making trouble for me back there, aren't you?!"

"Um, maybe…" she smiles innocently. "But look at it this way. You're a nervous wreck, so you needed a tension breaker. Also, you needed something to meet up to that shopping list of titles he holds," she thumbs at Thaelyn.

"Oh, and these are going to be my titles of accomplishment now?"

"Well, they certainly are noteworthy. He did congratulate you on the lightning bolt thing. That elixir is revolutionizing our education system, and you were in a circus making a scene big enough to call down your goddess to pull you out. That's a full life already!" she chuckles. "Besides, you looked almost like you were going to pass out. That much is solved now," she smiles pleasantly.

Aerlie raises her brow at the notion, realizing Amaree was right. Her nerves suddenly felt much more secure now. She glanced briefly at her parents in the crowd, and her mother simply shrugged and smiled.

"Actually, yeah, I feel better now," she sighs contentedly. "Well then, if this is how I'm going to be described, so be it! Call them out!"

Another round of laughter rumbles through the audience. Thaelyn glances at his Captain again, raising his brow and smiling softly. The prelate simply closes his eyes, shakes his head in amusement, and continues his speech.

"You who have come before us, to offer yourself to this man, with your promise that you will bestow upon him your love, devotion, and commitment, for the duration of your lifetime, to attend and support him in his moments of need, and to grant him your dedication of home and family… Is this, in truth, your deepest vow?"

"It most certainly is!" she affirms proudly. "Despite the fact he found me in a circus, and later took a lightning strike for the pleasure of it!"

Laughter and applause thunder through the temple at her bold announcement, as she holds her head high and casually glances around at the audience.

"Dear gods above," the prelate moans. "What is it we have to look forward to in this so-called harmony ahead of us?" He returns to his sermon, "Then let it be said that on this day, I bring these two together into this union as Husband and Wife. May the Gods we adore give them their blessings of a long and endearing life…and the rest of us mercy that we may survive it."

The room resounds with loud applause and cheers for the newlyweds. The couple turned to present themselves to the audience, while flower petals were tossed in the air and onto the rug where they would begin their way down the steps and along the aisle again. But before they reached the bottom of the steps, the room began to emit a radiant glow, seemingly to emanate out of the walls and ceiling, and permeating the air itself. The shouts and whistles suddenly came to a halt as the full assembly began looking around at the extraordinary alteration of the environment.

Thaelyn and Aerlie halted partway on the steps as the manifestation began to arrive.

"Something is coming," Aerlie whispers.

Above the platform behind them, there appeared a brilliant glow coalescing out of the ambient light. It gathered into a large figure and took on the shape of a head.

The audience gasped and shuddered, dropping to their knees in expectation of the divine visitor. Thaelyn and Aerlie spun around to see the great image of an aged face with pale features and a long flowing white beard. They both quickly lowered themselves in reverence.

Amaree and her friends felt a shiver at the otherworldly sight. They stared at each other, and then at Vonafel.

"I think I'm going to punch you now," Annah intones cagily.

"What?" she retorts. "Why, what did I do?"

"You called it, remember?"

"Called it? Oh, wait…yeah, I did, didn't I…" she titters. "All right, just not the face…"

Thaelyn looks up at the image in amazement.

"Father? This is indeed a pleasant surprise, but I was not aware you had in mind to make a visitation."

"Thaelyn, my son," Tyr's voice resonates. "While it is indeed a pleasure to make this occasion to see thy cheerful union, it is not solely to this purpose that I make myself known at this time. There is another cause that delivers my mind unto this place."

"Another cause? What might this other cause be?"

"My purpose here is as much to partake of thy joyous occasion as it must also be to conclude a moment of business. And this pertains to the fulfillment of a contract that has recently come into maturity. Now is the time of its final disbursement."

Amaree and her friends were speechless at the suggestion. They could only glare at each other as they listened.

"A contract," Thaelyn states perplexedly. "It could not be mine. I thought ours was concluded long ago."

"In truth, it was, and fully enacted. But the contract in question here is not thine. It is hers."

"Oh dear G-g…g-g-g…" Annah begins, but her voice catches in her throat.

"Yeah," Deena asserts. "Be careful how you finish that one."

"A contract?" Aerlie wonders openly. "But I… I don't remember anything about a contract."

"In thy present form," Tyr declares, "thou wouldst not recall this. But thou didst once find thyself presented before me with a proposition to be fulfilled, and we did make an agreement."

"She was presented before you?" Thaelyn ponders. "This suggests a third person was involved."

"Oh great…" Aerlie moans. "Is this more of my Fate coming around?"

"What were the terms of this contract," Thaelyn asks. "Can you tell us?"

"Much like with thine own, the terms do not permit me full disclosure, but of that which I can disclose, I will reveal this much. A mortal-child of mature age did once come into my court with concluding directive…"

"Concluding directive…" Thaelyn mumbles privately. "This is a curious one."

"Concluding directive?" Aerlie puzzles softly.

"Concluding…um, my Lord," Amaree asks timidly. "What does that actually mean, to those of us who aren't so, um…you know."

"It is a term we might use up there to describe that which you would otherwise call a last will, or to put your final affairs in order if you are near the end of your life."

"Oh, well, that's easy enough. But you have to do this directly to the gods?"

"Actually, I am not aware of this ever being done directly to the Powers, especially of a mortal making this proposal. Therefore, we might suggest this third party, who may have been a sponsor of some sort."

"Wow, so she must've been really special, and then to include all this talk of her Fate, her goddess, and so on. But this simply begs the question of why, in her case."

"The cause for this choice," Tyr responds, "is not permitted to be disclosed at this time. Or at least, not by mine own action. But the contract decreed for a term of service to be enacted, and from this the accumulation of Favor later to be disbursed."

"Favor?" Aerlie gasps. "What Favor? And again, does this have anything to do with my goddess, the Winged Mother?"

"It does, if only partially. Her involvement was supplemental to achieve a goal, but this is not thine only purpose here."

"Yeah, so it seems."

"And yet, the disbursement of this Favor remains unfulfilled."

"Unfulfilled… You mean I didn't receive everything yet?"

"What more could you have earned?" Amaree submits. "You got sent down here, saved your people from the dragons, gave us that weird potion, um… And it sounds like you got some kind of reincarnation…"

Annah slaps the girl on the arm briskly as she makes her statement.

"What!" Amaree retorts. "We're probably at that point by now, so why keep it a secret anymore. There's an actual god hanging over our heads."

"Yeah," Annah accedes. "But maybe we shouldn't say anything else right now. We haven't heard everything yet."

"What are you two talking about?" Thaelyn asks.

"Um, please, my Lord. I'd like to hear a little more first before I answer that."

Aerlie eyed her friends, realizing this must relate to that secret Amaree was holding back. She decided to see about learning more about all these little bits and pieces that had been building up.

"I...uh... Lord Tyr," she hesitates as she glances at her friends. "Maybe you can help me understand something. Surely, you would be in a position to know this better than most. During my application to Thaelyn's academy, I underwent a test we call the Spirit test. Are you aware of this process?"

"I am. It is a process we might employ to measure the caliber of the essence of life, in order to classify it for its polarity and character."

"All right, but strangely, I got a violet score, which had never been seen before. Then, along the way, I recall a conversation with my friends here, so I might as well bring this into play while we have the chance. My eyes, my hair, my wing color...none of this matches my mother," she pauses to glance over her shoulder at the woman in the audience. "My people have often viewed this as an anomaly. But then, as I reflect on a conversation I had once with Thaelyn, speaking of some of the beings he knew from Sigil and other places, it made me to wonder, but I was always too afraid to speak it aloud, thinking I might be overstepping my bounds with so much audacity. Simply said, what am I? Because I feel there is more to me than meets the eye."

"Indeed, thy suspicion does hold merit, as thou art not born of mortal bindings. Thou art Eladrin, my Child."

Amaree and her friends screeched at the mention, while others in the assembly whispered and murmured on what this could mean.

"Eladrin?" Aerlie shudders. "You mean, I actually am..."

"Thou art a Celestial, the same as he, Positive Ordered."

Aerlie was already in a kneeling posture, but on hearing this, she collapsed further to the floor. She laid a hand on her brow and felt her tensions returning many times over by now, and was feeling faint again.

"There goes the mortality thing," she whispers.

Thaelyn felt a sting of shock pierce him as the meaning struck home, and he too decided to sit on the steps for better comfort. Despite those earlier conversations, he could not necessarily permit himself to believe another Celestial might find its way to this world, to say nothing of passing itself off as a simple village girl looking to get married. He glanced wearily at his Captain again, and further around the room, eventually setting his eyes on a series of scribes who had been assigned to record the occasion, and who were now busy scribbling the details of this momentous turn of events.

"And so much for Number Three…" he mumbles. "Priest…" he glances over at the prelate who conducted the service. "There is a message here. Be careful what you ask for."

"Indeed, my Lord!" he gushes.

He turned again to look at Aerlie, meeting her eyes as she looked up at him. As they exchanged glances, he began to realize what his feelings were telling him.

"Well, this would explain a few things…" he notes softly.

"Oh!" she retorts roguishly. "Do you think?"

"Indeed, the fact that we feel so curiously comfortable in each other's company is a fair indication of the match in our spiritual alignments. Ours would be especially potent, so the sensation would tend to stand out. Although that wing flutter of yours will likely require some further investigation," he smirks.

She giggled tenderly, but her nerves were still too tense to enjoy it fully. She then turned her gaze up at Tyr again.

"But even as a Celestial," she wonders. "Wouldn't I still need a father? My mother tells me I was born of her body, but my father is not apparently my natural father. Now, I know you might be a god," she grins gently. "But don't you still need one of each to make a baby?"

"Ah, but indeed," Tyr croons. "While this process is surely well ingrained, even amongst our own kind, in thy case, we had to make a small exception. This practice may not yet be known unto thee, but thy form was created within thy mother's womb, and of her own design. And yet, thy features are due to thine ascension beyond this."

"Fascinating…" Thaelyn utters intriguingly.

Aerlie turns her attention to see he was deep in study of her figure, followed by glancing at her mother for comparison.

"Um, can you explain what you're looking at? Not that I'm complaining, just that I feel a little like a study project now."

"Uh, yes, well…" he coughs gently. "This would indeed represent an interesting study, but to think of the meaning…"

"My Lord," Deena inquires. "Um, what does that actually mean… of her mother's design?"

"Just as he said, this would represent a form of science well ahead of us, but if to put it in simple terms, it is to create a body based on the design of another body. We might use the term cloning here, where a sample of the former is used to create one or more copies. But in Aerlie's case, her Celestial ascension resulted in her own unique attributes, and this is reflected in her colorations."

"Wow, that's not bad, actually. So, if I understand correctly, this is what her mother might look like if lifted as a Celestial?"

"But you still need someone to do the work," Vonafel submits. "Especially if none of us would know how to do it. So, um…do I dare ask this question…who did it?"

"I am the one who brought this to pass," Tyr admits.

"Uh huh…that's what I was afraid of."

"Well, there's your male influence," Deena accedes. "Even if it is part of a science project to create a clone."

"Yeah, right," Annah intones. "But here we also have an oops moment."

"An oops moment?"

"Yeah, technically speaking, HE is her Father. And he is also HIS Father…" she points at Thaelyn.

"Oops."

"Fear not, Children," Tyr consoles. "For I understand thy cultural affinity. They may each possess a spark of mine essence within their spirits, but their bodies are of separate invention."

"So, not the same as brother and sister getting married," Annah considers. "And therefore, not as big an oops moment. All right, I get it, I think."

"But who was it that started this whole thing?" Amaree asserts. "Who was this other person, and what relation do they have?"

"A relation?" Thaelyn wonders. "Are you suggesting this was intentional?"

"Oh please! She came all this way to find you. THAT is apparently her Fate."

"Yeah," Deena adds. "And if we have a third party involved, that means she had a sponsor to do it with."

"One moment," Thaelyn issues with a finger. "Just what is this you are referring to?"

From down the aisle, a soft whispering ushers up as the people take notice of a new figure walking forward. The tall female in silver hues adds her voice to the discussion.

"The Daughter of ssSky..." Adalon offers.

The remaining audience turns to see the graceful figure sauntering along the aisle to join the conversation. Aelwyn and her group, including her male suitor, Aristan, all turn to witness this new arrival.

"Good gracious, Aelwyn," he murmurs. "This is turning out to be a truly remarkable presentation. I am beginning to wish I brought along a concept prism to record the occasion."

"Fear not, Aristan," Aelwyn whispers. "For I feel as though someone amongst the higher planes is doing exactly that."

Thaelyn and Aerlie both observe as Adalon makes her approach.

"Not you again..." he sighs and shakes his head confoundedly. "Adalon, you have the most annoying habit of showing up at moments like these."

"But if I did not arrive... At momentsss like these... We might not have... The anssswers... To sssuch quessstions as these..."

"Yes, but your answers are about as unnerving as the questions themselves. Very well, what can you offer on this occasion?"

"For thisss... I will asssk... For assssistance... From a ssselection... Of sssome very... Inquisitive... Young ladiesss..."

Adalon now turns to Vonafel and motions her over, along with the other girls. The girls look at each other and shrug tenderly before joining her.

"Vonafel," Deena offers. "After Annah finishes punching you, I want a turn at it."

"Hey! I didn't call this one."

"No, maybe not, but just for good measure…"

Adalon smiles at the girls before continuing.

"Do you have your notesss…?" she asks.

"Um, you know about that?" Vonafel muses delicately.

"I know many thingsss. You forget… I mussst pay… Clossse attention… Where our ssstudents are concerned…"

"Yeah," Deena teases. "Why are you asking HER that question."

"Well, all right," Vonafel shrugs. "It was a reflex reaction. But I don't actually have my…"

"Are you referring to thisss…" Adalon interrupts and produces Vonafel's notebook which she had been carrying discreetly in her hand.

Vonafel takes the book and glares at the woman.

"This was in my room, last I saw. How did you get hold of it?"

"I have my waysss…"

"I think we need to keep a close eye on her," Annah suggests.

"No, HE needs to keep a close eye on her," Vonafel points at Thaelyn. "We just need to be wary of her," she grins cautiously.

She opens her book to find her notes on the prophecy, and the four of them begin to read it aloud.

"The Daughter of Sky, from realms far beyond, and hardships many to number. A quest she did make to seek a lost love, as a trade for her ultimate slumber."

"What?" Thaelyn mutters silently and turns to Aerlie.

Aerlie could only return a puzzled glance as the girls continued to read.

"Through dire plights and turmoil quelled, she strove to meet with her choice. Where rebirth brings her back again, to the one who gave her a voice."

"One moment here," he interjects cautiously. "This is already building a rather curious picture. But to give her a voice…? So far, I can understand the rest of it if we are speaking of a contract of service, and this would likely represent the work involved, much like what I had in mine. But I find myself trying to associate anyone I once knew where I might assist in giving a voice…as if to say what… affording them a position of status or authority where they could speak their mind? And further, how would this relate to anyone acting as a sponsor to bring her down here?"

"I don't know, my Lord," Vonafel admits. "I'm sure these are all excellent questions to ask, but these prophecies seem to carry what we're interpreting to be private knowledge that only a select few might know anything about, and we suspect you might be one of them."

"Me?" he balks, but then pauses in contemplation. "Very well, perhaps you may be right, as the…" he coughs emphatically, "… individual who wrote them already has something of a reputation where my own history is concerned."

"Maybe so, and this next part certainly suggests you should know her. Twice around, she will come to him, the Daughter of Sky at last. We have to be talking about Aerlie here, because she arrived here twice, technically speaking. And this passage must be referring to her because the whole book talks about the same person, including the one who gave us that elixir. A potion found in a bottle of blue. According to our scholars, this has been interpreted and reinterpreted many times, not the least of which is to say the bottle itself is blue, to say nothing of the contents."

"Yeah," Deena offers. "I can only imagine how many people have been studying every blue bottle that came along just to see if it holds any relevance," she giggles.

"So, this part here, twice around she comes, the Daughter of Sky at last…to the Son of the Mountain, for in his mind, she is an echo from his past."

As Thaelyn listened to this line, he needed only to mull it for an instant, and then it hits like a load of bricks. He gasps sharply and his eyes grow wide. He falls back onto the steps and stares off into the distance, breathing rapidly and filled with shock, until finally he claps a hand over his mouth as he feels a wave of emotion taking over.

"Whatever that was," Annah mutters softly. "It got to him."

Aerlie rushes to his side and sits next to him. At this point, due to his extreme emotional output, she could actually feel his shock rippling out.

"Thaelyn, what is it? Are you alright?"

He stiffly turns to look into her eyes as tears begin welling up. He tries to speak, but there is now a prominent tremor in his voice.

"Ecco…" he whispers, and then begins weeping softly.

"My Lord," Vonafel solicits gently. "It seems clear you know what this is, but the rest of us are at a complete loss. Can you help us understand?"

"I thought she was lost," he whimpers and reaches for his kerchief. "Her name was Ecco…although spelled differently than your example. It was a type of nickname she once earned due to an aspect of her profession. She served in an institution that was part of one of the guilds there in Sigil, called the Guild of Sensations."

He looks up at Aelwyn for this point, as the woman comes out to present herself and join the others.

"I suspect you knew of this," he asserts. "I still recall those words you shared, her final words to me," he turns to gaze into Aerlie's eyes. "And you still speak those words. How curious, some part of it must have carried over."

"I knew only a small portion of it," Aelwyn responds soothingly. "It was enough to sate me that she would find that which she desired so much in life, but she bade me not to reveal her plans to you."

"Oh, did she now?" he smirks faintly. "Somehow, when I combine all this together, it does not surprise me. And I think I know now who that Sponsor must have been. Adalon…" he asserts firmly, but then takes a deep sigh. "This would have been a while ago, perhaps before you would be able to perform any deeds. So perhaps it was the Maker. Whatever the case, please pass along my deepest thanks. This was surely unexpected…and a very fine treat."

"Indeed… And I believe she knowsss…" Adalon responds softly.

"She sssaw thisss… And she knew it was… Important to you… And to her. After all…" she grins impishly. "If we are to build… A world together… We mussst have… The finessst quality… Leadership… To guide usss…"

Aerlie studies Adalon, as do the other girls. She briefly tries to recall her mother's words from the occasion of Thaelyn's visit to their home to deal with the dragons.

"A seraph…" she whispers. "Mother, you said a seraph once visited you to help with me, right?"

"Yes…" she responds. "Do you have some thoughts on this?"

"Yeah, who does she work for? Him?" she thumbs over her shoulder at Tyr. "Or the Winged Mother? Or is it Maker Kuroku? If the Maker is my Sponsor, that seraph might be hers, as she seems to be the one building this world, and I'm her latest addition. Like he said, our troubles up there were only a part of it, and now here I am being told I was made as a Celestial and directed here by someone to marry him…" she glances at Thaelyn, "…wing flutter or no," she giggles.

"Yes, about that wing flutter…" Amavain wonders. "I don't ever recall teaching you anything like that," she smiles.

"Oh Mother, I'm sure I must've picked it up from one of the other girls."

"Aerlie, I don't think ANY of the other girls in our village ever presented themselves as boldly as that!" she chuckles.

"Well, maybe it's something else that carried over. Did I have wings in my previous life?"

"Actually, no…" Thaelyn replies. "You were thoroughly grounded on that occasion. However, if it means anything, I do recall on a few occasions when I might see the seraphim during their rest periods in conversation about this or that, and behaving with some rather flirtatious manners."

"Really! So, maybe I had some experience with them. But now, as for you…" she turns to Aelwyn. "Am I supposed to know you? You seem to know me…or used to."

"Indeed," she recalls. "And we were good friends in that life, along with Nemelle here," she glances at her friend.

Aerlie gazes carefully at the other female, taking careful notice of her features.

"You're the one he spoke of, the only other Eladrin on record, right?"

Nemelle gingerly steps forward, but her bashful nature amongst such a large gathering forced her to take her defensive third-person approach.

"She admits she did hold relations with the mortal-child of the past, and she finds herself most amused over this strangely uncharacteristic manner of transition. She feels herself intrigued to reestablish her acquaintance and peruse what new sensations this curious addition to our breed may have to offer."

Aerlie winced at the bizarre behavior.

"Do you always talk like that?"

Now, Aristan steps forward with a comforting smile.

"I think you should perhaps excuse this young lady, and on occasion the other one as well. They do this sometimes. They are both strongly empathic, and they sometimes feel very self-conscious about releasing themselves openly. In fact..." he begins more energetically while waving a finger. "I could tell you a few stories about Aelwyn here..."

"Aristan!" Aelwyn interjects sternly. "I think we can refrain from that for the moment."

"Ah, but Nemelle just now expressed such fantasy over sharing new sensations..."

"Indeed, and I might share one or more with you if you should reveal any of my more embarrassing moments," she sneers at him playfully.

"Yeah..." Aerlie nods. "This should be loads of fun. So, we all knew each other in this guild? But what kind of work did I do, and how did it relate to him?" she glances at Thaelyn.

"The Guild of Sensations is one of many guilds within our city," Aelwyn explains. "Our purpose is to maintain a philosophical belief that in order to achieve true ascension of the spirit, one must discover and experience the great diversity of emotional, psychological, and intellectual sensations that may manifest within the mortal mind."

"Wow," Amaree blurts. "That goes a little over our heads down here."

"Interesting…" Aerlie muses. "And as for me?"

"You were once a student there," Aelwyn continues. "And you ascended within the ranks to an elder minister, at least until you retired. But you knew Thaelyn throughout most of your mortal life, largely though your employment within the Brothel."

"A what?!" Annah shrieks. "She actually did work in a brothel?"

"Well, that can account for some of it," Deena smirks. "Maybe also that wing flutter."

"Now, just one moment here, Children," Thaelyn asserts with a gentle smile. "This is one of the reasons I tended not to speak on this matter. It was not that sort of brothel. This is a place where a number of individuals, usually of the younger crowd, might find employment to ply their skills from their studies within the guild."

"Right…skills… Anything like what we saw in the courtyard that day?"

"Well, actually, no…" he chuckles. "She did have a strong spirit, but that demonstration would represent a rather brazen one, even for her. But then, if we consider some form of carry-over, she probably held a strong determination to achieve her goal here, and this may have manifested within her spiritual essence," he smiles. "No, in this case, you might find activities of intellectual pursuit, sensations such as argument and debate with either success or failure as a predetermined outcome, or the application of some form of emotional stimulation, and even abuse. Recall my lessons in taunting for a moment. I actually learned once from one individual who worked there how to use language as a weapon, essentially learning how to swear, but to use it as a tool."

"Oh, so this is where you got it? I sometimes wondered about that…how a guy like you, with such a goody-goody background, would ever learn to talk like that."

Aerlie found herself suddenly recalling another thought.

"Would this, in any way, apply to your conversation with the Patriarch? It seemed so carefully scripted, like you had practice."

"Indeed!" Thaelyn nods. "It was a young tiefling with a fiery temper who was my instructor. She would be the one to thank on this occasion. And by the way, you also knew her, so your demonstration following this may also apply, if only as another part of this carry-over."

"Wow, so I might not remember anything, but I seem to have brought a lot of old habits with me."

"Perhaps. But Ecco was more involved with unloading other people's burdens by using confession."

"How does this thing with the voice go?" Amaree asks. "Did you do something to give her a position of status, like maybe a political position or something?"

Thaelyn smiled gently and made a brief sigh, shaking his head as he composed himself to respond.

"You know, for all the lessons I teach in our guild, I must admit I failed in my own lectures. But then, how could one hope to anticipate such as this. This must be interpreted in a very literal sense, as Ecco suffered a tragic event once that left her mute."

"Mute?" Aerlie gushes. "I couldn't speak?"

"You once took a confession from a powerful mage, and he disclosed something to you that apparently held a deep burdening pressure. You felt as if you could not hold it to yourself, so you once shared this with another individual, I suppose another within the guild or the brothel. Unfortunately, the mage found out and returned in a rage, and he used a potent incantation to remove your ability to speak. I felt this was excessive, but could not find a proper solution to it immediately. Then, one day, I found my answer in a local curiosity shop."

"What was the answer?"

"The answer might hold meaning to those of us in the local region out there, but might not sound as pleasant to you good people down here. Then again, it did not appeal as much to Ecco either, but it worked, and that was good enough."

"Uh huh…" she grins cautiously. "Something tells me I'm going to regret this, but go ahead."

"I found a demon's tongue, and it is said they can be applied within the mouth of an individual whose original tongue was removed, as was the case here. This could restore speech, but as you might expect, a demon's tongue is a most unpleasant sort, including its form of language. To counter this, I also found a vial of deva's tears, which holds the property to soothe evil flesh. Combine these, and you have an answer."

Aerlie grimaces at the concept.

"You're right, this is better left in the Outer Planes," she chuckles.

"From that moment forward, our relationship continued until one day I returned, and she was gone. This would be the last of my memories, as I would never see her again."

"Is this that same person you once mentioned to me that day?"

"It is. But if we are speaking of the Maker getting involved, it would seem someone played a little ruse on us."

"Well, this last part sure sounds that way," Vonafel interjects. "The circle complete, the tidings revealed, together they will aspire. The wholeness of man, the oneness of world, and the birth of a proud empire. So, it would seem your Fate, Aerlie, was preordained to marry him. Congratulations, it looks like you got your prize!"

A rousing cheer ushered up from the crowd, and now swarms of gossip started stirring between them as they discussed this new revelation.

"But wait a minute," Aerlie shouts. "I still have this unfinished business, it seems. Lord Tyr," she turns again to look up at him. "What is this about that unfulfilled Favor?"

"Indeed," he intones boldly. "Thou must now choose thy Celestial gifts to complete thyself. And thou art also deserving of a formal tutoring within my court, to raise thy acumen to that more becoming of thy breed."

"Oh dear!" she gasps. "Gifts and education…on a Celestial level? Yeah, NOW I feel faint. What gifts and what education?"

"These are decisions thou must make, perhaps with the advice of thy spouse. Mine only instruction was to inform thee of thy motives to complement his, for whatever choices he once made."

Aerlie stares at Thaelyn in awe, still trying to comprehend what just happened.

"Thaelyn," she gushes breathlessly. "I'm going to need some serious consultation from you. I want to make the right choices, but wow! What kind of choices! You'll need to explain everything to me, especially if I'm going into another academy of some kind to learn all this."

"Yes, naturally… Father," he turns around to him. "I hope you will afford us a sufficient amount of time that I can bring her into alignment on these matters."

"So it will be. Bring her before me in my court when thou art ready to proceed, and we shall attend to it in due course."

Tyr pulls back, and his image begins to dissipate, vanishing from the room and allowing the natural lighting to resume. The people all returned to their former positions, but the experience of having the presence of the deity in their midst left a lasting impression on each of them. The interaction seemed so informal, as any father speaking to his son, not like that of some omnipotent being hovering over them as insects. The new direction of their religious teaching, combined with this one experience, would be enough to awaken the people that the gods are not so far away after all.

Chapter 16

THE SPELLPLAGUE

"**I** have nothing of particular noteworthiness to report on this occasion, Maker. He continues to harass the populations in that one domain, and large portions of it are being devastated by local conflicts. Meanwhile, his resource harvesting is proceeding along rhythmically, but sluggishly relating to the output product."

"Thisss affordsss usss time... But his effortsss... On that world... Make me angry... That we mussst watch... Yet another... Population sssuffer. We do not have... The meansss... To go there... On our own... And ssso we mussst... Sssimply wait... For them to come... To usss. What of our... Messsssengers...?"

"They are surviving. They are still making a last stand effort in this new domain, but unable to make any forward progress to rebuild. He is using light assault tactics simply to harry them. He does not seem immediately interested in finishing them."

"At leassst thisss much... Is tolerable. Now it is sssimply... A matter of time... For his latessst underlingsss... To find usss..."

"And then what, Maker? How do we find our way to him, if ours are not yet ready to make this leap?"

"The leap... Shall be provided... By him... With his underlingsss. We will sssimply return... Acrossss the sssame path..."

"Most interesting… He shall bring his own undoing by his actions to advance on us. But he will not know of it as he does not know of thine efforts here to create our own."

"And he will not know… How dangerousss… Oursss will be…"

"But if his side involves a superior society…"

"Sssuperior or not… I think he will choose… To run… Rather than fight. He cannot afford… To be dissscovered…"

"Of course, this does seem reasonable."

"Now… What has Tyr… Decided… For his role… In thisss new campaign…?"

"He has not, as yet. He has foreseen turmoil ahead, and is hesitant to proceed."

"It is a tragedy… But it mussst be. His participation… Is necessssary. And further…" she turns and drops her head. "I need him…"

Thaliel had been visiting Adalon in her lair for an update on Darumon. His antics had moved to another world where he was causing trouble, and at this time, it gave the appearance of gathering his resources in preparation for a future engagement, although that engagement would not likely take place anytime soon as he still needed to build his weapon for his revenge.

She was also taking notice of the local events, where Tyr and several others were planning an assault to counter a local threat with a Negative Power. Her focus had been on him lately because she also had an interest relating to her own plans.

"I suspect that aspect of it will be quite painful," Thaliel offers. "I can already feel remorse for it, and for those who will be affected by it."

"As do I…" Adalon nods. "But I may need… To visit him… Before thisss… To ensure we find… Our goal…"

⸭ ⸭ ◆ ⸭ ⸭

More than a decade has passed, and Aerlie was making routine visits to Mount Celestia to attend her special tutoring for her Celestial training. In the time since Tyr's visit in the temple after her wedding, she had made her decisions for her Celestial gifts to meet and support Thaelyn with his, as well as a selection of studies to build her own repertoire of divine wisdom. As a priestess and mage, she opted to further enhance these talents with more advanced studies in health and medicine, psychology, physiology, and physical therapy.

Her studies were scheduled to continue for quite some time, but she had already well surpassed the level of knowledge available on Tae'Eladar, and this would ultimately grant her a superior position of rank within the temple network and medical profession. She would do for them as Thaelyn and Adalon had been doing for nearly everything else.

Adalon was preparing herself to travel to Mount Celestia to meet with Tyr about his latest plans. This was a countermeasure to balance the actions that brought down Helm, but Tyr held reservations about his participation. He foresaw within this endeavor another downfall, and this one frightened him.

"Great One..." Adalon issues as she enters his court. "I feel you are troubled..."

"Maker Kuroku, thy visitation is welcome, but thy timing is grave. I have been tasked to participate in an offensive action to enforce the Measure of Balance, but my Sight has unveiled a disaster forthcoming."

"I know thisss... As I have alssso... Foressseen it..."

"Hast thou come to afford advice on this occasion?"

"In a manner of ssspeaking. But the advice... I have to offer... May not be... Sssuitable... To grant you peace... For your own troublesss..."

"It is unfortunate. Then what advice dost thou have to offer?"

"It mussst come to passss... That you participate... And it mussst come to passss... That you will sssee... Thisss end. But I will offer... Thisss to you... To consssole you... That the end... Will not be... Absssolute..."

"Not absolute? What alternative can there be if this represents..." his voice trails off.

"There is a greater need... At play here. A need where you... Can ssserve a role... Above thisss... Even after... You meet thisss end..."

"I do not understand thy meaning. Maker, thy cryptic manners can be disturbing at times."

"I am sssorry... Great One. I would have asssked... Helm... To ssserve thisss cause... But he is... No longer available..."

"Of course, and so this might be my final penance..."

"Do not dessscribe it... With sssuch woeful accord. It is unfortunate... And painful... For many... But the need... That awaitsss usss... Holdsss greater demandsss..."

"Then what need is this, and what demands dost thou suggest wait for us?"

"I need your... Participation... In my own purpossse... And for thisss... I need you... To join with me and mine..."

"But how wouldst thou suggest I invoke this, if mine own fortune follows this course?"

"Your courssse will follow... As it mussst... And you mussst make plansss... To oversssee... The dissssposition... Of what remainsss... To a sssuccessor. I would sssuggest Torm... To take your role. But then... Here is what... We cannot reveal... To the othersss... At leassst for now. You mussst donate yourssself... To my cause... To be delivered... Into a vesssssel... That will follow... My own crusssade..."

Tyr mulled the suggestion, realizing the direction of this conversation, and further reflecting on her previous statements, including those mentioned at the time Helm died, where she noted the plans she secretly made with him. He began to visualize the direction she was hinting at, and although it was disturbing to think of this as being his future, he had no other choice but to admit his path would follow its course regardless. But at least this way, it would not be a final end.

"What vessel is this thou dost offer to contain me?"

"They whom you once created… As vessssels for othersss. You will be as one… But divided by two…"

◆

Adalon had returned home, and now it was just a matter of waiting. The event was soon approaching, and she chose to perch on top of her mountain lair with a view of the city below. She knew what was coming, but this would represent a far more painful occasion than Helm's demise. This would represent a close and intimate violation that would hit many, not the least of which were those who held the tightest bond.

Aerlie was currently inside the temple giving lectures to a group of students, as was one of her duties. She was taking a day off from her Celestial studies to attend her work. Thaelyn was once again in the combat training hall giving a few of his own lessons. This was his way of sharing a little of his personal experience, as well as a means to offer distraction from the tedium of his administrative duties.

And then it hit. They both felt it.

Aerlie halted in midsentence and seemed almost dazed, as if a stunning shock had suddenly jolted her. She placed a hand against her temple as she tried to reconcile the sensation. It seemed inconceivable, but it persisted. Thaelyn also came to an abrupt standstill in his swordplay demonstration. The training sergeant had been assisting him when he noticed the sudden change in manners. His training, which was part of a long-standing habit within the Order, was to come to alert in case something bad was approaching, although it seemed unreasonable that anything might be arriving within the academy itself.

"My Lord?" he whispers urgently. "What is it?"

Thaelyn's face had gone blank by this time as he tried to account for this unnerving awareness of something being taken away from him. The pallor of his face was soon followed by his limp sword arm letting go of his weapon.

"Father…" he wheezes silently.

He turns and frantically dashes out of the room.

Aerlie had moved across the dais to Tyr's icon, where she was trying to call his spirit into focus. The other priests all gathered around, but stood there perplexed as to her behavior. She had not been able to speak since the shock hit her, but whatever it was, it registered deeply in her expression.

Thaelyn soon burst into the building and charged up to the platform to join her, and together the two of them knelt at Tyr's icon.

"Father!" he moans at the icon. "No! This cannot be! Who is responsible?!" he shouts, and then begins sobbing openly.

The priests all stared at each other, only now catching on to the meaning.

"My Lord, my Lady," ushers the high priest. "What just happened? You can't possibly mean… Not another one! Great gods above, what is happening to us here?"

Adalon could feel the anxiety, even from her mountain perch, so she lifted herself up and changed into her persona form, then used her divine skill to fold herself across space to the door of the temple, arriving on the ground and stepping inside. She then proceeded up to the dais to join the others, kneeling down and offering a hand to comfort them.

"I am ssso very sssorry… Brother Thaelyn… Sssister Aerlie. I can feel the lossss… And it ssstings…"

"Adalon," Thaelyn blubbers. "What happened? Do you know anything?"

"All I can sssay… Is he is gone. Thisss is already… Disssturbing enough for me… To reveal to you… As I know… How clossse you were…"

"I want to know why!" he affirms through his tremoring. "Such as the Powers are not meant to die, and certainly not this one!"

"You are right… But you are alssso wrong. We mussst remember… The Measure of Balance…"

"Blast the Measure of Balance! Let it take someone else!"

"Thaelyn… Calmly… You know better… Than to cursse…

The Measure of Balance. But I will admit… Thisss was a cossstly one…"

Thaelyn is silent as he returns to the vacant icon of his Father, still softly weeping along with Aerlie at his side. Adalon continues caressing them to offer them support. This wound would not likely heal anytime soon.

The priests all knelt in a moment of prayer for the fallen deity. Several tried to summon the minds of the other gods dear to them to see if they could find any word of what just happened.

The temple had also been drawing attention from outside by now, as word was slowly filtering out, declaring some new calamity. The training sergeant followed Thaelyn to the temple, along with the students from his class. This drew even more as word was circulating around the academy, and now the streets. Soon the temple was filling up with mourners.

It continued this way for a long while. Life seemed to come to a standstill. Not even Thaelyn, for all his workaholic manners, could bring himself away from his misery long enough to give any new instructions on what to do next. He and Aerlie just sat there on the floor in front of Tyr's icon. Finally, after a long while, he was able to speak.

"We must see who will follow him," he asserts tenderly. "His was too important a seat to leave empty, I should think. Perhaps someone will be assigned in his stead. Priest," he looks over his shoulder at the ranking cleric. "Do we have any word yet from any of the others?"

"I believe one of our membership was able to bring Lathander into session. He said we would be contacted soon by Lord Torm with word on this."

"Torm…yes, that might make sense. He would represent a next-in-line to Tyr. I would wish to hear what he has to offer about this. At the very least to hear a proper explanation of how one such as Tyr might ever fall for any reason."

"Then we will stay and wait for it. I only hope it will not be too much longer."

The assembly in the temple all waited and watched. Time seemed to pass slowly, until finally the temple came alive with a surreal glow. As with the previous examples, it permeated the very air, seeping out of every wall and accumulating above the dais. It did not appear to be emerging from any one altar, but instead much like with Aerdrie Faenya, simply manifested itself as an independent object, in this case, standing on the platform.

The figure appeared humanoid, but excessively tall as compared to a man. The face was smooth, as if covered by a nearly featureless porcelain mask, with slits for the eyes and mouth. The body appeared masculine and wearing a flowing magistrate's robe.

The assembly gasped at the newest arrival of a deity in their midst. The sight was curiously becoming commonplace by now, for all the recent visitations. But this one was a new sight and an unfamiliar image.

Thaelyn and Aerlie, along with the priests on the dais, all turned and bowed to offer their respects.

"Am I to assume we are in the presence of the one known as Torm?" Thaelyn inquires respectfully.

"Indeed, it is I, Torm, who now presides over the Domain of Law."

"Are you to be the successor of Tyr in this case?"

"I am."

"Then we should learn of how you would desire us to make our transition, as the Domain of Law was an important aspect of our dedication in this place."

"I will teach thee."

"I would further desire to know what became of my Father, and who is responsible."

"Tyr was given the task, in accompaniment of others, to seek and deliver jurisprudence to one who had violated the Measure of Balance. The task was completed, but Tyr was lost to us in the midst of this action. We mourn for him, as dost thee and thine own."

Thaelyn hangs his head and sighs as he realizes the duties of the Estelar can sometimes lead them into conflict, and on this occasion, it involved someone close to him. There can be no true fault applied here, as the task was simply a means to an end.

"I feel thy loss, Thaelyn," Torm continues. "And of those near to thee… I did come before thee to report these proceedings, and also to deliver a bestowment Tyr did recently bequeath unto thee."

"A bestowment?" Thaelyn puzzles. "Tyr left such instructions as these? What manner of bestowment?"

"One for which thou wilt share with thy partner in common. But the disposition of this transference must be rendered discreetly, as his wish to bestow this upon thee may invoke controversy. It is to this resolve that I must bring thee into my court where I may see to this personally."

"When?"

"Now…"

"Dear Powers, is it so imperative?"

"It is. Thou must make thyselves ready, the two of thee."

Thaelyn and Aerlie gawked at each other as the nature of this demand settled in. It was highly unusual for a god to make such a demand for a visitation within his own court.

Thaelyn motions for the priests to give way, as he and Aerlie step into a clearing on the platform. Torm then waves a hand, and the two of them are wrapped in a vortex of rippling space and whisked away.

Adalon had moved back from the dais when Torm arrived, giving the people on the platform space to conduct their meeting. When Thaelyn and Aerlie vanished from sight, much to the awe and amazement of the crowd, she could only turn and saunter slowly out of the building to return to her home. She knew what was coming, and this would finalize one last important piece of her puzzle.

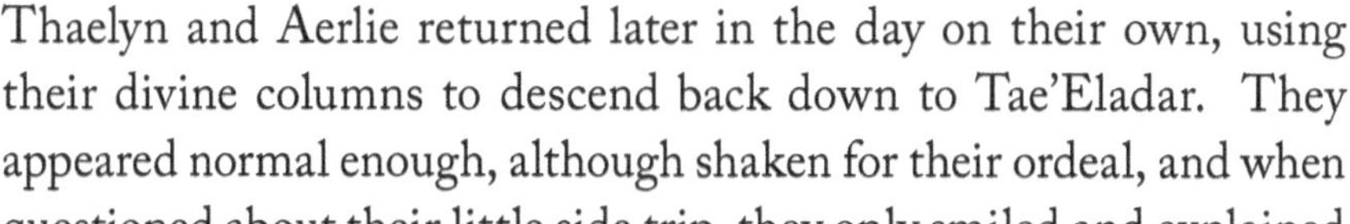

Thaelyn and Aerlie returned later in the day on their own, using their divine columns to descend back down to Tae'Eladar. They appeared normal enough, although shaken for their ordeal, and when questioned about their little side trip, they only smiled and explained how they received a special donation from Tyr to aid them in their future efforts at bringing harmony to the world.

Many did not believe them.

Although the people trusted the royal couple implicitly, many felt they were keeping a secret, if for no other reason than because Torm demanded them to return to Mount Celestia for the occasion, and it sounded urgent. But the suggestion eventually settled itself as the mention of controversy and discretion returned to mind that whatever it was, it had to be kept secret, and not simply on the level of the people, but also on the level of the gods.

Several more years passed, and life returned to normal, within reason. There were no new upsets, and Thaelyn returned to his efforts at bringing the last few nations into alignment across the primary continent of Sein'amar. He would soon be moving to the other continents, and his diplomatic efforts to the east had proven fruitful as many of them were already showing support, realizing that he was following Divine Providence, and there was no escaping it by now.

The only exception to this was to the south, where a large nation of orcs was found. There was another continent below that, but their isolation due to the orcish nation acting as a barrier imposed its own complications. Access by sea has shown little interest so far, if only due to their inherent lack of previous contact with the north, and the orcs stifling any land-based carriers.

"My Lord," his adviser explains. "So far, we've managed to establish contact with a few smallish settlements that seem open to trade, mostly along the coastline. But our information tells us there is a larger nation deeper within that might not be as friendly."

"Their isolation has kept them largely out of contact with anything this far north. This will be difficult, especially as we are limited to sea travel due to the orcs."

"At least the orcs aren't as good at building boats. This much gives us the advantage."

"Then let us make whatever footholds we can, and work from there. Trade is a good place to start, and we are certainly patient enough to see this through if we can make it peacefully. They apparently can do no better at moving north as we can south, not unless we want to fight our way through the orcish hoards."

"My Lord, at some moment, we'll need to contend with them. You know this."

"I do," he sighs. "And so far, they do not tend to care much for negotiations and peace talks. They only care to test their warriors in combat using us as sport."

"What do you think might be the final word on this? That's a big space down there."

"It is, and so we must prepare ourselves for the worst. We must ensure our troops are outfitted with the very finest, and also build fortifications along the border to ensure they hold the minimum threat potential to our people. If their only real interest is to test their younger warriors on us, eventually I would expect they will desire to find some other sport. We are moving forward nicely in our developments and should soon represent a force not simply to be reckoned with, but to be avoided at all costs."

"Aye, a fine one, that."

The meeting adjourns and Thaelyn returns to his office. Not long after, a knock comes at his door and Adalon enters inside. In his usual manner, Thaelyn rises from his chair to meet her.

"You do not need... To leap to attention... Every time we meet..." she chuckles. "I do not demand... Sssuch ssservice..."

"Indeed, perhaps so, as you do tend to behave with very mild manners, but it has become something of a habit by now. What do we have for this occasion of your visit?"

"I would like to offer... A sssuggestion..."

"A suggestion, very well, this should be interesting. What kind?"

"The lossss of Tyr... Has ssstruck deeply... In many of our heartsss. We have long... Dedicated oursssselves... To his cause... And his honor. But I think... We can do better..."

"Better? In what way? Are you suggesting we build a monument of some kind?"

"A monument indeed..." she muses. "But not of ssstone. Our

dedication… Is already a monument… To his honor… But we do not… Carry thisss… With sssuch mention… As to give it a name. I would therefore… Sssuggest… We correct thisss…"

"Adalon, if I understand you correctly, you are suggesting we give ourselves his name, is this right?"

"I did not ever… Truly desire… To be the figurehead… Of our guild. It was mossstly you… That chose thisss… Due perhapsss… To my contribution. But the time has come… When I think we have… Ssstrong enough cause… To find a sssolid icon… To ssstand behind. And it mussst… Afford itsssself… To honor that… Which givesss meaning… To our purpossse of intent…"

Thaelyn reflected on her words, which were very well spoken and demonstrated her own devotion to Tyr. He had to admit that to assign the guild a new name based on a reference to a god would give it special meaning in the eyes of all those who might look upon it in the future. It also represented a form of martyrdom, and this would carry its own expression of determination.

"Adalon," he sighs. "Your dedication to our cause is every bit as important as what he represented to us. But then again, we must not forget Shescellaie in this and her role in our society. If we are to rededicate our guild, we must give credit where credit is due, and it must reflect all of this."

"Then it would ssseem… We mussst redesign… Our emblem…" she smirks, and then turns to leave the room.

In the coming months, Thaelyn and his officers debated with artists and heraldry experts to design a new symbol to represent their guild. Finally, a pageant was held in the ceremonial hall of the guild. Both Thaelyn and Aerlie stood on the platform with their thrones, along with some of their officers, and addressed a large assembly of guild members, as well as a number of journalists.

"On this day," he announces to the audience. "We have gathered together to pay witness to a rededication of our name. In times long past, we dedicated ourselves to the great and noble purpose of uniting this world and its people into one nation, that this nation might look forward to prosperity and higher prestige. The rule of our government was enforced by the service of our men and women within our guild, and we did call ourselves the Order of the Silver Dragon, as was once a tradition within our society from time to time."

He pauses briefly to survey their reactions before continuing.

"But with the recent and most untimely death of my Father, Lord Tyr, who presided over the realm of Justice and Law, we have come to the conclusion that we should give honor to his name, that we may follow in similar ways and by similar means, with no less zeal than any other would afford in true dedication, and thereby to reflect upon his teachings, that these teachings shall become our teachings."

The crowd ushers up a round of cheers and whistles.

"Behind me," he directs to a large plaque covered by a cloth. "Is the symbol to represent our new direction. This shall represent us for now and evermore, that future generations will be born under the protection of its appeal and aspire to its cause."

He now motions to the officers to unveil the new heraldry. As the drape comes off, the gathering lets out a series of oohs and ahs of the modified design, which still involved the silver dragon head and wings in a shield background, but now with a balance and hammer running through the center as a symbol of Tyr, and vines wrapping the lower edge through the claws to represent the natural element that binds all life.

"Let it be known across the land, and wherever we may set our feet upon the soil, that we are now the most holy Order of Tyr! Long live the Order!"

The crowd now shouts a boisterous hooray and applause.

The years now turned into decades, and although the name may have changed, the direction of their travels still carried them along the same path. The nations in the far east were slowly adopting new policies to be more compatible with Thaelyn's home, and a few small relations had been developing to the far south. The orcish territories largely remained the same, but the incursions were displaying less and less favor to come too close.

It had been a couple of decades, and life was moving along predictably, but this year would be a cause for concern. Once upon a time, another prophet, native to Tae'Eladar, had made a series of predictions, describing a number of outstanding events to occur at certain moments in time, and this year was described to be dominated by waves of what he called blue fire. No one knew what he meant, and as Thaelyn would so often explain, trying to interpret such things was problematic at best. But that would soon change.

No one could have expected this day to be the one. It appeared as a typical day. The sun was shining, sweet breezes filled the air, children were at school, and the people were busy at work. But this serene setting would suddenly turn into a nightmare.

The once clear skies erupted with flashes of intense light. This was almost immediately followed by thunderous booms that reverberated through the air, and then shook the ground itself. The violence was greater than any known earthquake, and continued persistently. The skies revealed wave after wave of bluish fire tearing through the space around Tae'Eladar on all sides. No part of the land or sea was safe, everything was hit simultaneously, the entire planet. People screamed and ran in all directions as the fires descended into the atmosphere. The entire sky was filled with blue flame, long streaks of it, and with no end in sight.

Thaelyn and his people rushed outside to investigate what was happening.

"Great Powers," he shouts. "What in the names of the Almighty is going on up there?!"

Adalon also hurried outside through an exit at the top of her mountain lair. She looks up and hisses fiercely, aghast at the implications of what she saw.

"What fool was it… That caused thisss…! Who pushed the wrong button… And brought thisss down…"

Thaelyn and his men were in a frenzy on the ground.

"Captain, rally the men, fast!" he orders. "I need…" his voice falters as he begins to take notice of a curious effect.

Thaelyn raises his hand to examine himself as he feels a tingling effect ebbing through his body. He recognized the sensation, but this felt different, and much sharper.

"Dear Powers, Captain! Something is wrong with the Weave. You need to gather up as many men as you can find and order them to travel in all directions. Do NOT use magic. The Weave is failing. If we use magic, it could bring unpredictable and perhaps even catastrophic results. Spread the word, now!"

"Aye!"

"And throw off any enchanted items you might have on you, in case they backfire."

"Right…"

The bells started ringing an alarm, and soldiers were running off through the gate into the city. Thaelyn tried directing traffic through the courtyard, but he silently asked himself about the remainder of the nation. He could not be in all places at once, and without the benefit of magic, he could not send mages out through portals to investigate anything or spread the word to the far reaches. The nation would be effectively cut off by any means more sophisticated than horseback.

Adalon glared up at the sky and listened as the bells rang out. She observed the blue fires still raging across the sky, and it reminded her of that day the Primordials unleashed their weapon. This carried its own meaning, and she shuddered at the potential cause of it, but she felt powerless to do anything about it.

"Thisss sssimply cannot be…! He does not have… His weapon yet…"

She turns to examine the land down below. The fires had descended low in the sky by now, and wisps were streaming close to the ground.

"Thisss is the arcanic layer…" she considers. "Sssomething has ssset it alight…"

She considered changing into her persona form and going down with the others, but she quickly rejected the idea if the arcanic layer was burning and what repercussions this might have if she tried using any of it. Then she thought about Thaliel.

"Where are you… At thisss time…?" she asks herself. "Are you ssstill alive… And sssafe…?"

She spread her thoughts across all her servants, wondering who might still be alive and who might be lost in all this. But her primary thoughts still centered on where it came from, and she found herself cursing that she didn't see it coming.

"All my focusss… Has been on HIM…" she scorns. "And then thisss comesss up… Behind my back…"

Thaelyn had rushed down to the temple to check on things. The building had filled up with people taking refuge from the storm outside. Several injured were being brought in as the blue fires were now causing damage at ground level.

"Aerlie!" he shouts. "We need to keep ourselves from using magic. The Weave is failing, burning itself up."

"How is such a thing possible?" she shouts back across the room. "How do you set the entire Weave on fire?"

"I cannot be sure, but I would certainly like to know who or what is responsible for this. It seems entirely too coincidental from all our other recent miseries."

Across the land, the people were in a panic. Temples were harboring countless refugees trying to take shelter, and injuries were being reported as the ground shook and buildings collapsed. Soon, fires broke out, and as word began to spread through the capital city, magic was forbidden to be used to extinguish them. But this word could not reach the other cities, as the soldiers could only run through the local area. Horses would be required for the rest, but time was against them.

In other cities around the land, the people naturally tried using what they knew best to put out the fires, which in this case was a magic cantrip to dowse it, rather than traditional water. But this resulted in either nothing at all happening, or a wild backfiring of the magic at the caster. People began to vanish in puffs of bluish smoke, or become deformed by the horrific arcane backlashing. And if they happened to be standing near to another person or object, this backlashing might involve the two, melding them together in a horrid union of bodies.

Without the use of magic, the fires were getting out of control, with so many of them erupting sporadically and spreading to other buildings. The ground still shook from the rumbling of the turmoil above until finally the blast effect faded and the scene became quiet again. But the devastation it brought would leave scars for years to come.

Most of the buildings took heavy damage, leaving splinters and crushed stone layered in mounds and scattered through the streets. Homes were lost, many trade and industrial centers were crushed, and fires were burning whatever was left.

Thaelyn's officers were directing every available soldier into the city to gather up the survivors and bring them to those temples that were still standing to receive medical aid. But the priests soon found themselves overwhelmed, with stockpiles of medical supplies draining fast.

Sometime later, Thaelyn had returned to his tactical room in the guildhall, which took damage but at least was still standing. He was convening his officers for an emergency meeting.

"Our first priority must be food and shelter. We have a great many people who are without homes and other basic needs. At the very least, we must do all we can to supply them with food, and perhaps we can fabricate some manner of tent city to offer a meager form of shelter, at least until we can bring additional resources into it."

"My Lord," states the Captain. "The sheer scale of this disaster is simply unimaginable. Not only do we have our own here in B.T., but I can barely even perceive of the mayhem occurring in the other cities."

"Yes, and worst of all, it would seem the arcanic layer has almost completely burned itself out. We will not be able to use magic for a long while until the layer recharges."

"My Lord," ushers a senior academy Master. "When you say to

recharge, how do you mean? We know of the Weave, which was the creation of the goddess Mystra. But if this has been burned away, or otherwise caused to erupt in such way that it seems to be lost to us, what will replace it?"

"This is a good question. There was a time before Mystra when the arcanic energies were wild and untamed. She imposed the Weave as a layer to smooth this out so that mages and scholars could have a uniform interface to study and create our magical arts with some reliable consistency. Without this, the energies will revitalize themselves, as this is a process that occurs even without her, but they will no longer hold this uniform layer. They will revert to their natural wild condition."

"And so, this might mean our magical arts would also become wild and unpredictable. This will pose a problem for us."

"It may not be quite as bad as that, as the energies may eventually find equilibrium after a while, but it will flow like a tide, with surges and lulls."

"I see. Very well, this may not be quite as bad, but it will still demand some care in how we approach it."

"In the meantime, we must make contact with all our forces and direct them to the aid of the people."

"And clean up the mess left behind," the Captain sighs. "And then to rebuild again. But I'm already hearing of a tremendous amount of damage in just this one city, and the refuse removal alone will take months at the very least."

"I will ponder this to see if I can provide solutions, but I am already of the mind that I may need to make a few of my own movements to cut a few corners. If this was a simple natural disaster, there is no one we can blame for it. But the Weave was not a natural creation, and if it was disturbed in such a way as to cause it to whiplash against us, I want to know who is responsible. And then, I am going to file a formal complaint, accompanied by the assertion that if the

Powers are going to play such games as THIS on us, I will play a few of my own!"

+ + ◆ + +

In the days and weeks that followed, horsemen raced across the land to carry news and instructions to the local forces that struggled to clean up and reorganize the people. Horses and wagons worked continually, by day and often well into the night, to clear away the rubble.

"Much of the stone can be recycled," Thaelyn asserts. "And the wood can be mulched and used for farming and other things. Everything else…well, we will try to reuse what we can out of it, so we leave as little waste as possible."

"My Lord," the Captain infers. "With respect of course, much of this stone is reduced to small bits, and not suitable for rebuilding. We would need to quarry new stone, and this is slow enough as it is without the need to rebuild entire cities out of it."

"This is true, but we are going to begin learning a few new techniques here to expedite the process. This is one of those shortcuts I mentioned, and although it might be a leap above where we are with our current architecture, we are in such times that necessity will force our hand."

Thaelyn steps away from the table to present his thoughts.

"In past times, we used mostly quarried stone and wood supports to build our cities. This has been a traditional method of construction for as long as most of us can recall. But this must now change. We might use a form of mortar to paste together those blocks such that we seal the holes and prevent the drafts from chilling us. But now we are going to learn about a material called concrete."

"Interesting," intones an academy Master. "And how does this concrete differ from stone blocks and mortar?"

"Concrete is functionally the same as stone, very sturdy, and useful to improve our architecture to a new level. If applied with wood beams, or even iron and steel, such as with more advanced applications, you can build upwards as well as out, and create truly marvelous designs of great size. For now, however, we need function more than form, and this is where concrete will serve us best."

He steps back to the table to illustrate with gestures.

"Concrete starts out as a thick slurry, consisting of water, sand, lime, and other ingredients, such as stone bits as aggregate to help strengthen the final result. It is then poured into a mold, which can be easily built from a wooden frame, and allowed to harden. The result is a custom block of stone-like material in whatever shape you desire. Combine this with poles and beams, and you have a faster, and often better method of building manufacture with many design possibilities."

"Indeed! This could potentially save a considerable amount of time over cutting and shaping individual blocks."

"We will need to build the appropriate industry to produce this in large quantity, but we can begin with the raw ingredients in a more primitive setting to get things started. If we teach this to our people, and establish multiple worksites, we can then move more rapidly at rebuilding our homes."

"Very good, my Lord..."

Slowly, as the word spread and the necessary materials were gathered, a new industry was formed. Work crews were now producing lime and refining it to be used in the process of creating concrete, then shipping it wherever it was needed. The makeshift housing that had been reassembled from the remains of the cities was gradually being replaced with new construction of a much higher grade. The architectural designs improved as they gained experience at using this new building material, and soon the cities were showing signs of recovery.

Time progressed as the passage of years saw the slow re-establishment of the arcanic layer. And once the people had been settled somewhat, Thaelyn decided to make a trip back home, now that he had the capacity to employ magic again with some reasonable safety, but he was not at all pleased on this occasion.

"Thaelyn, thou must restrain thyself from thy outburst..." mentions one Estelar.

"Restrain, nothing!" he shouts. "Our estimates of the death toll on Tae'Eladar are insurmountable. We cannot even be sure if we can make an accurate tally with so many who simply vanished from existence, and you ask me to restrain my outburst? Mystra once promised us she would provide the Weave for our mages and scholars to study in the application of our crafts. Then, according to my consultation with Torm, she was murdered in a conspiracy. Even amongst the Estelar, you should hold murder as a crime, regardless of the Measure of Balance. This rides well outside the decrees of that principle, as theft and murder are NOT an act of any form of Balance!"

"We agree and understand thine outrage. Shar has already been punished for her involvement."

"Yes, Shar again," he glares at the assembly which had gathered at his request for a hearing. "I still recall her involvement with her sister at one time which cast a shadow over Tae'Eladar and its local star, causing it and the others to descend into that horrific ice age. I cannot be sure how many lifeforms may have perished at that time, but our studies of the fossil record show the world was apparently rich with life. The Estelar decree that life is precious, but where was this decree when Shar held her little tantrum?"

"Thaelyn, again, we ask thee to temper thy rage. She was reprimanded at that moment, and has been again. Many of her powers have now been stripped and shall remain this way, not only for the reasons thou dost describe, but for our own as well. The domains within the local folds have all taken their harm. The Great Wheel has been shattered, and many of its elements cast into disarray. Thou may declare thy people to have suffered, but thine are not the only to feel this loss."

Thaelyn could only withdraw from his outburst and take a deep sigh as he listened.

"Very well then, I shall retract some portion of my displeasure if only to consider the losses elsewhere amongst the Realms. But then

I hear this was part of a conspiracy, and I must ask myself who else was involved. If Shar had in mind to steal Mystra's Weave, who did she conspire with?"

"She admitted to us that she did ally herself with Cyric on this occasion."

"Cyric! Him again? This is intolerable! Siding with him should be beneath even HER standards. And why must I listen to so many occasions of his name coming forward recently? Where is HE in all this to take HIS punishment?"

"We have levied sanctions on him for his past transgressions, and we shall again pursue him for this occasion. The disruption caused and the losses taken cannot be ignored."

Thaelyn huffs at the insinuation that such horrendous devastation might be caused by such a trivial impetus as greed on the part of Shar, and her exploitation of Cyric and his lust for murder. But this was a matter that had to be handled by those in the appropriate positions, and he was not one of them.

"So be it, see to it then," he declares. "But know this… Despite the Measure of Balance, he is now responsible for two murders, one of these direct, the other indirect, but I will hold him responsible no less for each the same, and neither of them justifiable within the Measure of Balance. Not only this, but between him and Shar, countless others have died. Perhaps Shar can only be held accountable for her greed to take that which did not belong to her, but I will forbid her to come anywhere near my domain, or to touch anything remotely related to it. As for Cyric, if he should ever crawl out of that hole he calls home, he will feel my blade."

"Thou art not the only to declare this."

"Really! How unsurprising. Then they who declared this before should either take to my side, or take a number behind me."

He offers a curt bow, then turns and briskly leaves the Council. He departs the area and returns through his divine column back to Tae'Eladar.

On his return, he called a new meeting with his officers, scholars, and now scientists. He was pulling out a few of the stops he had traditionally placed for his evolution of the people.

"I need everyone's attention, please," he announces to the room. "I will ask you to pardon my appearance, as I just returned with word on what actually happened during the occasion we have been calling the Spellplague. Apparently, it was due to an attempt by Shar to steal away the Weave owned by Mystra in a conspiracy with Cyric to commit her murder. But it would seem Mystra had stretched the Weave so tightly that it literally snapped back once she was killed, and therefore, her control of it was released."

"My Lord," inquires the lead Professor. "Does this mean Shar actually took control of it, or did she lose it as well?"

"The snapback was so violent, it was lost completely, and we all saw the result, but the result goes well beyond our home. All the Realms, including the Great Wheel, were affected. Although it might not allow us to feel much sense of comfort, Shar has been punished, and Cyric will hopefully get his as well. But the losses are far greater than what we saw down here."

The room resounds with murmurs at the implications of such a widespread effect.

"Now, as for what I intend to do about this... If the gods are playing such tricks as these, even though it was only one god performing the deed and another who hoped to take benefit from it, the resulting chaos is driving me to take a few of my own measures to ensure we are not so dependent on them in the future. We are taking charge of our local arcanic energies and will create our own Weave from it."

"What?" the Professor gasps. "How do we accomplish that? If it took a goddess to do this before, can it be possible for us to replace her?"

"Within our local environment, I believe we can, but the knowledge to do so will be complex. Normally, I might offer knowledge quests to challenge our people to invent something new. But at this moment, I am simply going to tell you what to do, and you will do it, and along the way, we will invent our solutions, and you will learn the principles as we move forward. This will be the beginning of a new form of technology for us, so pay attention."

"Absolutely, my Lord!" he agrees energetically, and brings out his notebook and pen.

"Our first goal is to replace the original Weave with our own creation, but ours will not be formed in the same manner as Mystra's. There are ways in which to condition the natural arcanic flows that allow them to form a more consistent layer similar to the Weave, but adjusted to our needs. To do this, we must first harmonize the natural energies to a different frequency."

The Professor and the others in attendance took down notes as Thaelyn continued.

"I am envisioning a structure we shall call…oh, let us call it a Dynamistic Conditioning Spire, which will essentially appear as a tower-like housing. We will need to build a number of these evenly spaced across the land for full coverage. They will contain a system of apparatus to draw in the natural energies, convert them, and emit the adjusted form back out into the environment. This will allow us to persistently pull in only the raw energies rather than creating a looping effect of our output."

"This sounds like we will need power to permit its operation."

"Indeed, it will be one of our first official electrically powered machines since our first discovery and application of electricity during the days we studied the Sarrukhan Gate and the machinery found inside that time capsule…which brings me to my next thought. We are going to reopen that capsule for another look."

"Oh, goody! I was so hoping we might have an opportunity for this again."

"Yes, and I am sure you are not the only one. Now, the Sarrukhan technology is far more advanced than we are in our present form, and I still need to caution our need to pace ourselves for the proper development of our people. But we will begin by taking a closer look at the devices in there and see if we can pull out a few ideas from it. Specifically will be how they employ the application of these energies within their machines."

He pauses momentarily for the people to catch up with their notes.

"My next thought circles around the Gate itself. We already know how valuable our mage portals have become, but so far, they have been mostly used for the transport of special couriers and other VIP traffic. This is going to change. We are going to build our own Gateway network."

The room fills with praise and whispers at the suggestion.

"Again, the technology used in the Sarrukhan design is clearly far more than what we could hope for in our current state, but I think the experience we will gain from the Spires will afford us a new way of looking at these energies and how it works in a technological application. We will then begin with a series of hub stations connecting our major cities, but I would expect this to expand over time with local district stations for intra-city travel. We will no longer be restricted to horses and wagons travelling for days across the land. Now, if we should wish to go somewhere, it will be as simple as stepping through a door. But we shall limit ourselves to this for now, giving our people the time to grow before moving forward with other inventions."

Even though the people of Tae'Eladar had not progressed far enough technologically to develop official industrial applications that used electricity, Thaelyn's special assignment made an exception to this rule for the Spires. In the years that followed, he tutored his scientists in the inner workings of the arcanic energies, where they come from, how they are formed, and how they can be applied by machines, as opposed to a mage's mental will.

Design schematics were drawn up with several prototypes using a variety of mechanisms to induce the conversion of the natural energies, but since theirs was still a medieval society, the designs involved a bit of manual labor, rather than full automation. In addition to the mechanical wheels and levers that might be used, they incorporated more advanced electrical devices, including coils and electromagnetism. It was a curious blend, but it was uniquely Tae'Eladaran, and they were proud of it.

Thaelyn also found it necessary to teach his people how to produce custom-grown crystalline structures by using seed elements in a solution with an electric wire that was powered to attract secretions onto the growth seed. This allowed them to create crystals to be used in their new technology to channel and modulate the arcanic energies. They also employed strongly enchanted mithril disks to focus specific energies into their custom applications to simulate a mage casting a spell and directing those same energies. The result was a device that could channel the energies to produce an effect representative of a mage physically performing the act, but here in a more mechanical application, such as to create a portal and keep it open between endpoints, like with the Sarrukhan Gate.

It took many years of research and development to find their first results, but eventually the people saw the Spires going up around the land and the taming of the natural arcanic energies. Thaelyn and his people needed to allow this time to progress before installing the rest of it, as they needed to ensure they had stability with their designs before taking it to the next step. But as their experience improved, so did the technology, and soon this began to evolve over time to tolerate any irregularities in the natural flows…in case the Spires should experience trouble.

The people now had the capacity to move around much more freely than they ever did before. Horses and wagons were still used, but now trained to pass through large portal gates rather than crossing over distance between cities. Commerce and tourism began to flourish, taking the people into a new era, an even higher Golden Age than before, as now they could travel across the land from one side to the other for anything as simple as an afternoon cup of tea with friends and family. And the remarkable utility of this technology would not necessarily limit them to their own world.

Chapter 17

RETURN OF THE LICH

It had been a good twenty years since the Spellplague. The interruption it caused set back the expansion and conquest of the world by many years, as the people were largely cut off from each other with communication and access. Their focus shifted to recovery and the rebuilding of their cities and homes, and later the development and fine-tuning of this new infrastructure to govern the arcanic flows for their local use. This would allow them to return to their preferred manner of lifestyle, using magical means to achieve their goals, rather than so much slow and inefficient manual labor.

The nations occupying the continent to the east were largely compliant in joining the kingdom even before this, and most continued to follow this course. Although there was a minor note of concern for some if Thaelyn's nation still held its potential after the disaster. But once communication was reestablished, and the demonstration of their rebuilding efforts was made, they found their confidence restored.

The continent to the south was not quite as easy, however. Some progress had been made to establish trade and communication, but the sudden disruption of the Spellplague seemed to reverse a large part of it. Some of the nations blamed it as a subversive attempt to undermine their rule, while others underwent an opportunistic overthrow by hostile elements who saw the weakened grip of their old governments and chose to exploit this to drive them out. The chaos that followed led to a cascade of wars, as authoritarian bodies tried to take control of expanding territories.

Thaelyn's kingdom was trying to gain a new perspective on the events down there, sending agents to spy on local affairs and report back the latest news. It was beginning to appear that the entire continent might require a hard knock to bring it back under control.

"For all the uprisings we are seeing," he asserts at a meeting of his officers. "We may need to intervene with some portion of it, if we want to rescue anything, and likely overthrow other portions ourselves, if only to bring it under our own rule, rather than use political means, which may be impossible by now."

"We could be looking at a large oppositional force," suggests one of his advisers. "Those militant leaders have apparently gathered up a large following. I cannot be sure how it will appear in the end, but the estimates are suggesting we might be fighting in the streets against common citizens."

"I would not wish to create such havoc as to lay waste to whole populations. We should advance on those areas we might think the easiest, and perhaps encroach upon the rest more cautiously. Maybe we can find a soft underbelly somewhere."

"A coastal setting would give us a foothold. Those last few we were working with might still be somewhat compliant."

"Good, let us begin there and try to convince them to join with us, if for no other reason than their protection from the rest. We could vassalize them straight away, and establish a garrison. From there, we could reach out to the rest and see if anything presents itself."

A series of diplomatic envoys are sent out to a line of city-states along the northern coastline of the new continent, which was just across the sea from Thaelyn's nation. These were part of a grouping of small nations that were hoping to remain independent in the face of the rising tensions and rampaging hordes crisscrossing the interior of the landmass. Other than the fact of being on a seashore, they didn't have much to offer for natural resources to attract the attention of the other warring nations. But the fear of conflict was worrying.

The wars occurring deeper within continued to exchange territories, and Thaelyn's advisers made a series of visits to the coastal cities to encourage the annexation of these nearby lands, at least as much for their protection, as to simply unite them into the larger body. After a couple of years of negotiation and treaty-signing, which was in part encouraged by the encroachment of the wars close to their borders, they consented to join. Shortly after, several heavy garrisons and outposts were established on the frontier to watch the rest of it.

"I think word has started to spread to those outward territories of our arrival," advises one of Thaelyn's officers. "Whereas they didn't seem as concerned before if they made their approach, our scouts are now reporting a bit more caution."

"Good," he nods. "They know of our strength. Those coastal cities were not much of a bother before our arrival, but with our military standing guard out there, they are now having second thoughts. This might afford us a small advantage."

"It's still a mess out there. Those nations in the central part of the continent seem to be trading territories, and some of our forward scouting patrols are reporting a lot of devastated regions."

"I would imagine this will make life exceedingly hard for the populace. You must still have the opportunity to grow food and make your homes. Even the armies need this much, if not simply the people."

"They're probably taking whatever the people grow and using it for themselves. I must simply wonder how much longer they can go before everything falls apart on them."

"Do we know of any opportunities for our own movements?" Thaelyn asks. "Are there any communities that might seem open to communication, maybe negotiation for a rescue effort?"

"Nothing within convenient reach. We would likely have to wade through the rebel-controlled territories first."

"Then this might be our next course. If our purpose is to bring this world together, we cannot take no for an answer. But one problem

I can foresee already is that we have a lot of disgruntled people out there, whether militant or civilian, and they all seem ready to scrape and claw whatever they can take from the land…and each other… simply to survive. This can play a role on the mind, and some of it can be irreversible."

"That's simply a raunchy way to live, my Lord. Can any of this be reformed?"

"Perhaps, in the lesser cases. But those militants have to be coming from somewhere, and this simply takes us back to the civilian population they are drawing from."

"Aye. And some of our scouts have suggested they may be following some sort of religion that drives them."

"Do we know which one?"

"I recall where some of our scouts have tried to infiltrate their camps under a cloak to listen in on a few words. But so far, if they are following anything, it doesn't seem to fit with any of the gods we know of, either Positive or Negative."

"Could they have invented one of their own? This could be a problem."

"Aye it could!" the officer yips. "If they're not even following a proper member of the Estelar, they don't have any real guidance to teach them better. Just a fetish hung on a wall, or an idol planted on the ground, with no mind working behind it."

"This is bad. You cannot as easily kill something like that if it is based on such foundationless principles. If it were a member of the Estelar, at least we could have them tell these people this world is intended only for the righteous, as I think Maker Kuroku would have a few things to say about it."

"Right, and in the absence of that, even if we did try to take these people into our care, they might not as easily convert over to us, instead choosing their false god to anything we might have to offer, even if they did hear a voice ring out to tell them better. Good gracious, and we don't keep enough prison space to hold this many sots, as we already solved so much of it amongst our own."

"Indeed, we may need to build a large penal colony somewhere, if we cannot otherwise contain this situation. I would not wish to simply throw people away, but the peace of the world cannot tolerate they who are so clearly incompatible with our beliefs. And as I have found myself saying in the past, and I feel it must be said once again, this place must be cleansed."

✦✦✦✦✦

Somewhere across the land, not far from a small country village, was an old graveyard. It dated back perhaps centuries, as the local populace used it from time to time to inter their deceased members.

In ancient times, such places were both revered for their hallowed grounds, but sometimes also feared, as there might be occasional sightings of spirits and other shadowy figures prowling the area. Often, this was simple superstition and folklore from the old history of the place. But once in a while, the sightings were real, as restless spirits might actually return to haunt the place, perhaps even to resurrect their former bodies and rise from the ground.

These occasions would soon prompt the local guardsmen to go out and forcefully put them back where they belong, as the people found it too disturbing to see zombies and reanimated skeletons rising up and walking around. But in some ways, as unfortunate as it might seem, it was also a natural occurrence, as those restless spirits might find strength in the local arcanic energies to empower them. That, combined with a distant longing, a sense of need or desire, to return home, which might provide the impetus for their arising.

Since the advent of Thaelyn's kingdom, most of these old graveyards, cemeteries, and even a number of underground catacombs, were all thoroughly cleansed and sanctified by his higher-ranking priests, to ensure it would not happen again. And in this long time of peace and prosperity, the old superstitions and folktales began to subside into legends and children's bedside stories. Until today.

It was a small thing, really. One would hardly believe it to be a serious problem. A family of visitors were paying their respects when they saw movement emerging from a rearward row of grave markers.

Naturally, this drew their attention, thinking it was simply another family doing the same. But when they focused their attention on the bodies lumbering across the field, and coincidentally moving in their direction, they took notice of something otherworldly, and very unsettling. They were not the living sort of visitors.

The family gazed in disbelief at several bodies that were clearly heavily soiled and ratted, as if they literally rose up from a hole in the ground. And as their eyes took in the sight, it became clear this is likely where they came from.

"Bloody hell, lass…" wheezes the man. "Where in all the hells did THAT come from?"

"Gracious," emits an elder woman. "There hasn't been anything like that reported out here for longer than any of us can recall! Quick, we need to get out of here, now!"

They pick themselves up and hurry out of the cemetery, returning back to a local road. There, they rush back to the village to find a local guard.

"You there!" shouts the man. "We need help, quick like!"

The guard, along with his companions, all turned at the abrupt summons. The clear urgency of the voice made it sound like an emergency was occurring somewhere.

"What is it?" he replies. "You look like you're being chased by something. Is there a wild beast out there?"

"Nay, man! Worse! The old graveyard is haunted again. We saw several walking dead out there. They came at us, and we simply ran back here."

"Walking dead? Why, we haven't seen anything like that for… gracious, how long has it been. And surely, not since His Lordship's priesthood cleaned the place out. Are you sure of it? Mayhap it's just a few young folks out for a bit of fun?"

"I doubt it. They looked like they must've been in the ground for years, and then some. I can't believe this could be a simple playact. Go see for yourself if you don't believe it."

The man and his family now hurry off to their home and hastily lock themselves inside.

The guardsmen all looked at each other and shrugged.

"We should at least investigate. Playact or not, it shouldn't go unattended."

The group all marched out to the graveyard, unsure what to find, but hoping it was simply a ruse. But this was soon dashed when they found that same group of zombies now slogging their way along the road in the direction of the village.

"Great gods, men!" the lead guard yelps. "To arms! There's only a few of them, but we can't allow them to arrive in the village."

The guards each draw their swords and lurch to the attack. The zombies were no real match for the professional soldiers and their weapons, and the scene was quickly corrected with the dispatching of the unwanted guests.

The odd news of the arrival of zombies was a curious note in the local gossip. It was regarded by most as a one-off occurrence. Such a thing hadn't been seen for centuries, not since Thaelyn's kingdom had purified the grounds. But before the news could settle from this one event, another one was being reported.

"Guard!" calls a shout. "Come quick! We've got a problem at the old burial grounds over yon!"

Another small village, and another old cemetery, was reporting another sighting. A group of young farmers making a run to the local marketplace had passed by the village graveyard, and seen several undead moping around, but soon to turn their attention towards the village. Now, the farmers found themselves being chased...if one could call the woefully slow rate of movement the zombies made as an actual pursuit, but at least being followed along the roadway.

Once again, a group of local guards hurried out of the village to see about the disturbance, and took up action to rectify the situation back to the way they liked it. But this incident, combined with the first, was starting to echo around the region as a most curious, if not also disturbing sequence of events. It caused a few to wonder if it could be a side effect of the new Spires and this modified arcanic energy they were producing.

◆ ◆ ◆ ◆ ◆ ◆ ◆

The discord occurring in the southern continent continued as roving bands of militant troops seemed to be imposing themselves on the local inhabitants, taking toll payments, demanding tribute, confiscating property, and if nothing else of value could be found, they might even take prisoners, often young people to be used as slaves, maybe also females to be placed into forced marriage and subjugation.

"This is simply intolerable, my Lord," moans one of his officers.

"I agree," Thaelyn accedes. "We should prepare a few movements, if only to bring this under control, and deliver a bit of justice to those people. But the lands south of our recent acquisitions are rugged and mountainous. Traversing them will be difficult by ground movement. We could use gryphons to assault their positions, but you still need something on foot to take and hold territory. Therefore, we may need to advance in steps, taking one nook after another and holding it with a firm garrison. And we will need to make liberal use of portals for rapid troop movements and supply runs."

"Excellent. Then I would recommend we push out into the border areas around our holdings to create a buffer zone. If we could then circle a line around one side, at least partway, we could close in from different directions. We certainly have enough troops on our side to do the work, for all we've done up here."

"Indeed, our forces should be more than adequate on the numbers, but let us not become too confident simply for that reason alone. They know this territory, and so we will need to be prudent in our movements, and not allow ourselves to be outmaneuvered or ambushed."

As the war plans are made for the new lands to the south, more villages are awakening to shouts and cries.

"They're coming!" hollers a man as he charges into the village square. "Blast it all, it's another one coming along the road!"

A small band of young people answered the call on this occasion. The recent reports, which had been growing in number, were causing some citizens to join together, just like in the old days, as groups of mercenaries and adventurers looking to earn a few extra coins for themselves, and to help augment the guard patrols. They gathered themselves up, with their flimsy leather armor and thin swords, and rushed out to contend with the invasion.

On their arrival, they once again found a smallish number of zombies, and this time a couple of skeletons moving in the direction of the village. The two different types of opponents would require different methods to take them down, with skeletons demanding more of a crushing weapon, while swords were adequate to use on the zombies.

The group engages the undead mass, carefully slashing and swiping at them with their weapons. A young mage launched several volleys of magical projectiles, while a young cleric used her early grade holy smites and banishing spells to chip away at the abominations. The battle was a vigorous test of their skills, and made for some good exercise, but it was becoming apparent there was something at work here. The frequency of the occasions was increasing, as were the numbers, as well as the introduction of new elements into the mix.

"My Lord, have you heard of these odd reports?" a Captain advises.

"I have, and it is curious," he ponders a moment. "Did I hear it once suggested it could be an unexpected anomaly due to our new arcanic modulation techniques?"

"There were a few words going around about that, and I'm also aware of several studies to investigate, but so far, the results are inconclusive."

"I hope this is nothing serious. I would not want this to distract us from our greater goals."

"It seems to be mostly limited to the smaller villages and outward regions. This might suggest something to do with location, maybe also proximity to something, or perhaps the reverse of that, as if being away from something, like the larger population centers. If it relates to our Spires and their effect, I wonder if being near the larger cities with more people making more proficient use of magic is leaving something like a wild region, where the flows are not as well-conditioned."

"Perhaps... Maybe we made a calculation error somewhere. Pass this along to our researchers and see what they have to say about it."

The weeks passed and the reports from the smaller villages slowed down. This caused some people to breathe a sigh of relief that whatever it was had finally relented. But the reprieve would not last long.

"Gah!" shrieks a local woman as she ran along the roads. "Run for your lives! It's madness out there, I say!"

She runs through the streets, this time in a townlike setting, larger than the earlier villages, and more developed. The commotion draws the immediate attention of many onlookers, most of whom are left to wonder what the woman could be panicking over.

Several people come together to follow her with their eyes as she continues through the town to find shelter. They then turned to look out onto the road, but nothing was immediately in view. A number of town guards joined the group, although uncertain of what to look for, as the other stories had settled by now, and were only of remote villages, not towns. Then they saw it.

A large mass of bodies was coming into view from a gully some distance away. This time, it counted as dozens of individuals, once again zombies, and also skeletons.

"Great gods!" issues one guard. "Where in all the hells did they come from?"

"I'll bet they came out of those old catacombs at the base of the hill out there. But blimey! So many of them?"

"Lads!" another guard urges. "We need to take action. Sound the alarm! We need men out here in full gear!"

They split up with one of them diverting to a guard station to begin ringing an old alarm bell...the first time it had been used in generations. The others rushed back to a station to find their equipment and call the attention of even more troops. Soon, a small army of soldiers formed a line to block the invaders.

As before, the two sides met in battle, with the professional soldiers fending off the assault with reasonable ease. They had been joined by several local mages and priests to further augment their efforts, and the undead fell in sequence until all was quiet again.

"My Lord!" the Captain reports. "Another one! Bigger. This time a town to the north of us in the Merideen province."

"Any casualties?"

"No, my Lord, our people turned it away easily enough…thank the gods. But they say it held a good twenty or more undead in this one. That's a fair bit more than the others."

"Do we know where it came from?"

"They think it might have been an old catacomb to their east, at the base of some hills. But an expedition to investigate found nothing inside."

"Interesting. As if to say it rose up, marched outward, and then was dispatched by our people. Send a few of our specialists out there to take some measurements. Let us see if we can identify anything."

"Right away!" he bows and leaves the room.

A few more weeks pass, and more of these occasions are sounding out across the land. Hordes of undead, measuring twenty to thirty at a time, coming out, seemingly at random, from unknown locations, and marching in the direction of the nearest town. It was becoming as much a menace, as it was a mystery. But just as with the lesser occurrences of small groups and the villages, this too slowed down.

Thaelyn was in another meeting with his officers to review the latest reports.

"We haven't seen anything new for several days now," states one officer. "But this now troubles me."

"I think I would agree," Thaelyn nods. "First, we have these small occasions and small, otherwise remote targets. Then an increase in numbers and larger targets. I cannot believe this to be coincidence. There must be a driving factor involved here."

"Those studies made with the Spires still don't show anything unusual. Most of the reports around the nation show no abnormal activity. So, whatever it is, it still seems to be focused on specific regions. Could it be something in the local environment?"

"While this is surely a fair suggestion, the fact of observing this increase in volume is, in itself, disturbing. If it is environmental, it must be a developing condition…"

The meeting is suddenly interrupted by a messenger rushing into the room.

"My Lord! Dear gods above, another one!"

Thaelyn and his officers all jerked up to see the man arriving in a cold sweat.

"What happened?" he urges.

"The city of Springham, over in Kordaran," he pants. "I just came from there…mage portal, you know. We just suffered a large attack of creeps coming in from the local plains. But my Lord, this can't be no simple bit of nonsense of wild magic. We saw specters in this one!"

"Specters!" he shouts.

"Gods' pity, man," the Captain moans. "That's no simple bit of dead rising up. That has to be conjured!"

"Indeed!" Thaelyn asserts firmly. "This might also be our answer. Small masses, small targets. Larger masses, larger targets. And now a city… How many, and what happened out there?"

The man leaned on the table as he tried to catch his breath.

"I think most of us lost count, but it had to be a good sixty, seventy, maybe more. We had the normal bit…you know, zombies, skellies. But then we saw those spectral apparitions travelling along. And not the simple ones! These held purpose to them!"

"That can mean only one thing, and this being the one thing that disturbs me most about the Art. Necromancy."

"Aye. The city guards came out in full fare, along with a host of priests from the local temple, and several mages from the local academy. They fought hard, and we drove them back to whatever grave they crawled out of, though it was a tough one, what with the specters out there. Our weapons didn't work quite as well on them as they did the rest. Neither did the magic. And some of the priests were grousing about their smites not hitting true."

"This is a problem, and will likely need to be corrected. But if we are coming under a form of attack, I think time is against us. We have never had an occasion in this world to fight actual necromancy, as no one here ever used it to such proficiency. In fact…well…" he pauses to consider his words. "Yes, unless we are speaking of someone applying himself to a rather high level of practice, we have never had a reason to worry about it beyond those old naturally occurring occasions that once came about. And then, once we took control, we outlawed the study. And indeed, the only true studies we ever made were behind closed doors as very classified projects, in order to prevent leakage of anything unpleasant. And this was precisely to counter those natural events, and nothing more. It was simply not necessary to go any further."

"Well, my Lord," the Captain muses. "Um, with respect, of course, I think that idea may be showing its colors by now."

"Yes, I must admit, and with my own regret. But this form of study is especially distasteful to such as my kind. I would not normally expect someone to use this who might be outside this world, as this world may not represent an appropriate target for their interests. First, it may not be convenient for them, if only to say they might not care to pursue something so far from THEIR home. Second, if you involve Maker Kuroku, you have her to deal with, not simply us."

"And that would be a strong deterrent, to be sure!"

"Indeed! And third, well, I suppose I may have my enemies, but I think many of them would not be so brazen as to chase me all the way to this place, and especially after what we have created in this time."

"What this says to me is, it generally discredits anything from outside this world, leaving us with very few alternatives except to say someone from inside this world. And my Lord, the only possible direction to point a finger might be those people in that southern reach. We're starting to make a few moves here and there, so could this be their way of getting back for it?"

"It would certainly offer a possibility. All right, we should see about who, what, and where…if it is at all possible. We may need to devise a much more aggressive plan in our march to take control. If they are able to launch hidden attacks using such as this, either they are taking random potshots at us, or else someone is playing a delicate game while trying to find better targets. Perhaps they are just as unfamiliar with our lands as we are with theirs."

Another few weeks pass, and extended scouting patrols are sent, mostly under invisibility cloaks, into the warring territories looking for anyone who might be responsible for these undead invasions. Meanwhile, more cities are coming under attack with continued swarms of undead, sometimes measuring up to a hundred at a time. On each occasion, the local city guardsmen called the alarm, but this time the military was getting involved. Mages and priests, foot soldiers and archers, all outfitted with the best armor and enchanted weapons, were marching out to meet the hordes of undead. But by now, some portions of these abominations were receiving new classifications, with such as the original zombies and skeletons being described as the simpler forms, and the spectral conjurations being more advanced for the demands to bring them forth.

This stage of events continued for only a few occasions, but much like the previous ones, it was soon to escalate once again, as the focus turned from what were smaller cities to the larger ones, with the latest example being the metropolitan center of Amberdain.

Bells and whistles echoed through the streets, as guards sounded alarms from watch towers and street corners. People ran for safety, seeking shelter in temples and other city buildings. Rows of archers with enchanted bows using elemental fire projectiles lined up on the outward city walls, while lines of soldiers, mages, and priests with their holy magic, formed up outside the walls to halt the advance.

On the horizon, they saw an army, numbering in excess of a thousand, moving in their direction. The front line once again included the simple forms of zombies and skeletons. Following were numerous spectral forms, but this time appearing as the more powerful wraiths, rather than the lesser specters. And behind that was something new. It towered above the rest and didn't even appear natural.

"By the gods!" shouts one soldier. "What in the blazes is that now?" he points at the tall monstrosities.

"I can't believe what I'm looking at out there," offers a mage. "But if my eyes aren't deceiving me, I might say that looks a bit like a golem made of bone!"

"A golem of bone? Bloody hell, man! What does it take to build one of those!"

"More than anything they teach us at the academy!"

The line of undead made its advance, meeting the troops outside the city wall. Once again, weapons clash against bone and rotting flesh. Magical fire burns, and icy sprays freeze. Lightning strikes fry, and holy smites singe. And all the while, the undead horde held firm.

The zombies and skeletons were the first to fall, being the lesser forms and easier to defeat with the common methods the troops had available. The wraiths were tough, and proved mostly immune to normal weapon attacks, being largely intangible entities. Even most of the magic had a hard time of it, and the holy spells seemed weak. But given enough time, they wore through to the golems in the rear.

The golems were huge, standing much taller than any man, and composed of anything left over from all the rest. Whatever force was animating them had to be potent. And further, they seemed to be augmented with enchantments and protective wards against some of the magical and holy strikes being delivered into them. If not for the highly enchanted mithril weapons used by the troops, and their augmented bodies to provide extended durability and stamina, the golems would likely break through. But the soldiers held a solid defense, and slowly whittled away until the horrid creations were simple mounds of inert fragments.

"Thaelyn..." Aerlie asserts at the latest meeting. "This is serious. According to this report, whoever is behind this cannot be a simple man who spent too much time in a laboratory. This sounds very professional. One might even suggest on a scale like our own."

"Indeed, and all the more disconcerting to us for the implications."

"Not simply that! Dear, from my perspective, this reveals to us a very obvious weakness in our defense. And although I know how you feel about the study, it does prove one unfortunate flaw, and that being if anyone had a true intention to use this against us, we are very ill-prepared to fight back."

"Yes, Dear..." he sighs. "Of course, you are right. I had hoped we would not ever find ourselves in such a predicament, and once we found ourselves so successful in moving across this land, it did not seem important after a while, as we were essentially overpowering whatever they DID have to throw at us. But this..." he waves his hand at the most recent battle report. "Clearly, this is the work of someone with a dedicated interest."

"And the time to carry it through," she relents. "But this also makes me wonder how he is delivering it into our home territory. These things had to come from somewhere, and simply marching across the sea, or even the orcish lands, could not be it."

"Indeed. And this leaves us with only one other option...portals. But so far, I do not recall any sightings."

"They are probably being situated in hidden locations, like a staging ground, to assemble these hordes. Then unleashing them in one big mass."

"I agree. But now we need to ask where the next hit will occur. The pattern seems to be multiple strikes at some grade of target, then escalating to the next higher. So if we suggest this one at Amberdain to be the first of this grade, we might suggest there could be at least one more. Although I am asking myself how many he would unleash on this grade before taking it to the next step. This would represent a sizable effort, and depending on his resources, if he has a final goal in mind here, he should be moving towards it soon. And at this moment, I can only think of one possibility."

"Us here, I'll bet. Right?"

"Absolutely. We are the capital city, and whether we say he is simply refining his technique, or hoping to cause a bit of mischief along the way, ours would be the next most likely target."

"And likely with a BIG offensive force. We need to be ready for that, Thaelyn."

Several days pass, and another sighting is made, this time at the southern city of Fortune's Faire, in what was now the province of Menenbahd. This was the same city where Aerlie found herself held captive in the old circus, although by this time converted to Thaelyn's rule. As with the other old cities of the day, it too had a fortification wall surrounding it, and just like with Amberdain, the city was on high alert.

A sighting was made as a large invasion force was ambling its way across the hot sandy dunes of the arid landscape. Once again, the military was called in to form up a line, and again they clashed. And just like with the city of Amberdain, the battle was harsh and enduring, leaving a lot of broken heaps of undead at the feet of the soldiers.

"Thaelyn," Aerlie muses. "Although I don't want to jinx anything by saying this, but these reports are showing a great amount of success for our side against these attacks. With or without the proper countermeasures in our hands, we're holding up remarkably well. And the statistics of it seem a little too good to be true. No damage, no casualties, just a lot of weary troops after a hard workout."

"I suppose you can credit Adalon for that much," he responds. "That Draconic augmentation she gave us once must surely be showing itself on this occasion."

"Yes, but my goodness! Against some of these things, I would think we might take a little more damage. At least a few broken bones, maybe a bruise or two."

"I, uh…well, I suppose you may have a point. Could it be that for all the work they put into building these things, ours are still so much superior?"

"Do you have any of your own experience fighting such things?"

"Personally, I cannot recall any. Demons, yes. That blue Draconic once, and a variety of other things, but I think there were no actual undead in all that."

"Well, this last attack at Fortune's Faire was very similar to the one at Amberdain, and now I'm thinking, due to the size and complexity of this mix, if it were me, I wouldn't spend another on a random target just for mischief. I would say the next one should be us."

"I may need to agree, so we should call in a large deployment of troops and station them around us. These events are being spaced apart on the order of days, mostly, so we should prepare ourselves."

"I wonder where he's finding all this material to work with. Either he must have a huge supply of bodies to play with, or else he's been saving up for a long time."

Several days pass and all seems calm. A large deployment of Order troops had taken up temporary occupation around the city of Bya'an Tamoranth, giving the impression of a heavy garrison in multiple areas around the city, and making a lot of local citizens nervous for the implications. The news of these attacks was known all across the nation by now, and everyone was on edge.

Scouts were making routine runs in circular patterns around the local countryside, watching for anything to show up on any side of the city. Many of the outlying suburbs and farming areas surrounding the city were on alert to watch for anything unusual, and some of the residents had evacuated their homes to take shelter directly inside the city bounds. Thaelyn and Aerlie were also on alert, along with their officers and others. On this occasion, they would all join the fight to see to the final dissolution of this contest.

Finally, at about midday, a scout rushes in under an enhanced speed chant. The blur of his form comes to an abrupt halt near a guard post, only to dispel the chant back to his normal movement.

"Lo! A sighting!" he shouts. "Out there, across the rise on the far field. A great wall of them, by the looks of it!"

"Can you tell how many?" asks one of the guards.

"A grand many, easily in the thousands. And with all sorts, including those big beasties, and even worse!"

"Here we go!" moans another guard. "Call the alarm! We've got an invasion inbound. Send the word to His Lordship, and gather the troops out in front here. This will be our forward line.”

Soldiers now begin rushing into position. Once again, bells ring and voices shout. Calls go out to summon other troop garrisons into position to create a heavy line of defense.

A runner hurries into the guildhall to find Thaelyn.

“My Lord! They’re coming! West of the city, from out in the fields and across the farms.”

“Do we have any people out there in the line of fire?” he asks urgently.

“I think all the locals came in early this morn. Right now, we’ve got our troops moving to intercept. Word is going out to bring everyone to one point.”

“What about the other sides? Do we have any flanking assaults?”

“Nay to that, as far as I know. Only the one out in front.”

“I see, and while this is certainly convenient, it also lacks any true tactical planning. Very well, for all his skill in necromancy, maybe he is not as good at military strategies.”

Thaelyn calls in his squire to assist with his armor and sword. He sends a telepathic shot to Aerlie to let her know, and she now hurries out of the temple and up to the guildhall to find her own battle gear, which in her case involved a mithril gown and leggings, and a long battle staff.

As the word circulated around, it also caught the attention of Thaelyn’s officers, who arrived with their own accoutrements, and together they rushed out to join the rest.

Out on the field was a long line, thick with bodies, and none of them pleasant to look at. As with each time before, it involved the simple forms, then more wraiths, more golems, and even a few new additions to make life even more interesting.

“Thaelyn!” Aerlie gushes. “What in the names of the gods are those now?”

The new additions seemed to hover, or float, and appeared as more bone constructs, like the golems. But without legs to support them, they clearly had to be very magical.

"I have never seen any such as those before," he muses. "That would take talent, and dare I say it, but some small amount of artistic license."

"Oh! Do you now wish to offer him an award for Best in Show?" she smirks.

"Well…" he shrugs. "If not for the tour on the field, it might be worthy of a special mention. But you are right, THAT would be noteworthy of pursuing an active study for a countermeasure. I can only ask myself what it holds in store for us once it arrives."

The soldiers held a line in front of the outskirts of the city. Archers stood behind them with bows at the ready. Mages, including many Elder ranks, charged up their spells. And the priests were giving their prayers for extra strength.

As the first wave hit, the soldiers engaged in vigorous combat. The sheer number of them would take time to cut through. Row upon row of zombies and skeletons pressed forward, exchanging blows with the Order troops. The battle raged for a good hour before the soldiers began to see the other side diminishing. But now came the next wave.

Following the first line were the wraiths. Thaelyn and Aerlie joined the others as they laid both magical, and in Aerlie's case, divine attacks on their targets. The wraiths proved to be nearly invulnerable to the weapons, and exceptionally durable to the magic attacks. The priests, with their holy spells, sent everything they had at it, calling up their most potent chants. The soldiers in front could only hope to hold them at bay somehow, keeping them away from the priests so they could do their work. This portion of the battle was tedious, as the soldiers tried throwing their bodies into the apparitions, hoping to ram them with their living essence in the hopes the lifeforces could act as a barrier to drive the creatures back.

The wraiths seemed determined to bypass the front line to reach the priests, who were the only ones doing any real harm. The mages tried offering shielding spells to see if that could hold them back, but the incorporeal forms did not seem especially restricted behind the virtual barriers. The only option seemed to be to divide the priests into two rows, one with offensive spells, and the other with a defensive repulse chant to drive the creatures away temporarily so they could land a new hit.

"Be away with you!" Aerlie scorns as she launches an attack. "Foul creature of darkness! I swear to you, Thaelyn. These have to be some of the worst."

"I agree, and unfortunately, they are so difficult to take down. But on the brighter side, if there is one to give praise to, we are certainly learning a thing or two on how to fight them."

"Oh yes, learn on the job! Welcome to the Order, where we'll fight anything that comes our way, whether we have the means to or not."

"Yes, well, such is the way for us, it would seem."

This portion of the battle seemed to go back and forth slowly, but after a long while, the wraiths began to show signs of defeat.

"Keep at it, men!" Thaelyn encourages. "We are making progress, if only slowly. But progress is still progress."

The sun was passing overhead, going into midafternoon, as the last of these finally fell and perished into nothingness.

"Good work!" he supports. "But it looks like we are not finished yet. Keep up your guard! Soldiers to the front; this one is physical."

Now the golems begin their assault, swiping at the troops with massive limbs, and causing many to be tossed aside. The Order troops, thanks once again to the Draconic augmentations, were able to rise to their feet and charge back into the fray. The scene represented a cycling of row for row of troops taking turns to hit the large entities before being bashed to one side, only to be replaced by the next row.

"Powers pay pity," Thaelyn moans as he observes the battle. "If this should ever become a habit. Stay firm, men!" he incites. "We will not allow a few small bumps to stand in our way, right?"

"Aye!" the soldiers collectively shout in agreement.

This stage of battle stretched on as the wave of golems poured on top of them. They were proving to be tough and difficult to bring down.

By now, even with the enchantments, the troops were starting to show their limits. Thaelyn ordered his officers to cycle in fresh troops from the sidelines, hoping to replace the weary members and grant them some rest. It had become obvious, by the tactical play in use here, that the enemy line seemed linearly obsessed with forming a single row of combatants, rather than trying to circle around for any flanking maneuvers. And the next row, those strange hovering creatures, were holding back until the last in this current line was finished.

"Such a curious manner of conduct," Thaelyn murmurs. "Captain, are you taking notice of this?"

"Aye, it's like they are taking turns at us. Each one testing us to the last, then following up with the next."

"But are we speaking of the simplemindedness of these constructs, or the man behind them? Is he actually controlling them, or leaving it to whatever cognitive function they hold inherently?"

"Not a clue, my Lord. All I can say is, if this is how they fight, we'll meet them just the same."

The day was passing into the late afternoon. The many golems continued to press against Thaelyn's troops. Several of the beasts had fallen by now, with more still advancing. Thaelyn studied the sky to judge the time of day, then to measure what remained on the field.

"We still have that last one," he muses. "And whatever it holds for us, but I suspect we might see nightfall before this is done."

The continued hacking and chopping of sword against bone eventually chipped away at the constructs, causing them to fall one by one when they could no longer hold themselves upright. It was late in the day now, and the final line was approaching with the strange hovering entities.

"Be aware! We have no idea what these are capable of. But I doubt they are here for a holiday festival."

These examples appeared as a large round body made mostly of bone, including what may have once been a huge ribcage, along with several other plates anchoring to a spine with a long bony tail curving under it. It did not seem to have any proper limbs, like arms or even wings, and nothing like a head or a face. The only way to tell which way it was facing was the tail draping down behind it.

And then, they attacked.

The tail proved to be the weapon, in this case, striking and jabbing with a spiked tip. But the physical attack wasn't the only thing, and neither was it the worst of it. It also started firing off magical energy bursts. These seemed to resemble ball lightning in some ways, and as they hit, they jolted the soldiers, sending them down to the ground in a moment of numbing paralysis.

"Well, so much for not taking damage," Aerlie winces. "That might leave a mark or two."

The priests pulled the stricken soldiers away while the next line took up the front. Aerlie joined with others to examine the fallen men, removing portions of their armor to check their injuries. The skin appeared reddened, but not severely. The numbing caused the muscles to go limp, and they were unable to respond clearly to verbal interaction, as their mouths were also partially numb. The effect seemed to rocket through their bodies. But as Aerlie studied them, using her special Healer's Sight to peer inside and check for any internal injuries, she couldn't find anything critically wrong.

"This is strange," she mumbles to herself. "Is it just that you're so tough, or did that thing simply not do that much real damage to you."

She gazes into the soldier's eyes to check his reaction.

"Can you hear me alright?" she asks. "Blink for me."

The man tries blinking, and can just barely move his eyelids.

"How many fingers am I holding up. Blink to count."

Aerlie holds up three fingers, and the man attempts to blink his eyes three times.

"Good. I don't see anything life-threatening, so in the absence of anything else, all I can say is wait for the effect to wear off. Let's give it a few moments. Maybe that Draconic stuff makes you immune to electrical shock or something."

She moves to the next man and repeats the process, but each of them appeared the same.

Meanwhile, the remaining troops once again take turns striking at their opponents. Some of them take hits and go down, while others replace them on the front line. Aerlie and several of her priests continue to examine the fallen men, but the result is the same in each case.

"Thaelyn, what are those things hitting us with out there!"

Thaelyn turns to find her still studying several new examples on the ground behind the combat scene.

"It appears as an energy discharge," he responds. "What do you see over there?"

"I'm not sure. I don't see any severe burns, no tissue damage, just limp muscles, and a bit of disorientation. This looks more like a stunning effect than a harmful weapon."

"Really?" he frowns.

Thaelyn turns to examine the creatures, which were clearly behaving as hostile entities. The soldiers continued their assault, once again slowly beating them down, but it was proving to be a hard kill. And in the sky above, the sun was moving towards the horizon.

In the field behind the battle, a pile-up of dazed and limp bodies was accumulating. None of them appeared critically injured, and some of the first examples were starting to feel their bodies again.

"Are you able to move?" Aerlie inquires of one man.

"Aye, if just barely. Everything tingles, and I feel a bit weak. It's a bit like if you find yourself sleeping the wrong way, laying on an arm or some such, and you lose your feeling. Then, once you pull it back out and give it a moment, it comes back to life on you."

"Really! Are you able to stand up?"

The man glances around himself and tries to come to his feet. He wobbles a little, but soon finds his footing.

"Try a few exercises with me. Hold your arm out at length and try touching your nose with a finger."

The man complies, and was able to follow the motion, sluggishly at first, but as he seemed to limber up, it became easier.

"Can you stand on one leg?" she wonders.

He now tries balancing himself on one leg, and seems able to hold himself there.

"Now hold your arms out and jump from one foot to the other."

Again, he is able to follow the instruction, and seems to be returning to full capacity for his coordination and balance.

"Well, all right, how do you feel about going back and hitting something?" she smirks.

"Just give me a target, my Lady, and we'll see about that!"

"Good! That big round thing floating in the air," she points at one of the creatures. "Let's see if we can knock the wind out of it."

"Aye!" he shouts and rushes off.

The soldier eagerly charges forward, letting out a battle cry and raising his sword. The creature turns to face him, preparing for his assault. But before he can come within easy reach of his weapon, the creature fires another bolt at him, sending the poor man back down to the ground.

"Oops!" Aerlie winces. "Oh well, here we go again," she giggles.

Thaelyn glares at her for the impish reaction, and then at the man on the ground, who by now was being pulled once again to the rear.

"This is going to take some time, I think."

"Yes, but no one is taking any real injury," she asserts. "So, what are we suggesting these things to be?"

"Unless we are to say whoever invented them made an error in their design, that they cannot attack with such force as to cause real injury, I am at a loss. I think I dare not say what else it could be, because the only other suggestion defies my interpretation of this scenario."

"All right, but what is that other suggestion?"

"That someone is playing games on us."

"Well, while I certainly could not argue that point, I might also suggest this is definitely a good exercise for us to practice on. The only true downside is the troops are getting tired, and that's all. Just tired."

"If only for the number of foes out here. Very well, but if this is not what we originally suggested it to be, this demands us to ask who sent them and why."

"I cannot say why, but whoever it is, he must be a true master in the Art."

The sun was setting by now, and the troops were again taking turns, albeit at long intervals as they had to recover from the stunning shocks in-between. As one row went up to engage, several others were in various stages of recovery. The priests found most of their holy spells and chants to be largely useless, except for what seemed like a vague energy drain. The mages tried their best high-level spells, but being entities of an unholy design, and using what had to be a very unusual necromantic evocation to bring them to life, the common forms of elemental magic proved mostly ineffectual. Not even the archers with their elemental bows could make an impact worthy of mention. So it mostly came down to the soldiers and their mithril swords chipping away slowly, and the priests with the soft draining effect, that would ultimately bring the last of them down, and long after sunset.

"Powers behold, men," Thaelyn breathes a sigh of relief. "Let us hope we have time before the next one."

"Thaelyn," Aerlie notes. "We should see about where they came from."

"Indeed. I need scouts up here. Survey the area on that far horizon."

A group of scouts rush off across the fields to check for anything that could hold special importance.

"You know, my Lord," the Captain submits. "In this time, anything that might represent a portal or some such would be gone by now. They don't stay long, you know."

"Yes, but I am asking myself what this fellow has in mind next. He just put our people to a rather curious, if also vigorous exercise, and for what? To see how long we can remain standing against such creations that do not go down so easily? I suspect he has something more in mind...he must. This was far too elaborate for a simple exercise."

"Aye..."

Several long moments pass, and the first of the scouts reappears on the gradient rise at the edge of the farming fields. He waves to Thaelyn and shouts.

"My Lord! Lo! Over here, I found something. You need to come take a gander for yourself."

Thaelyn and his Captain, along with Aerlie and a few others who still had the strength, all begin a quick march out onto the field. They hurried out to meet the scout, now joined by the others who went out to survey the area. As they arrive, the man explains what he saw.

"Look there, just below the rise. Do you see it?"

Thaelyn and the others all gazed at a point a short way down the slope. It appeared as a single portal.

"When I came up here," the scout explains. "I first saw a row of them, a way-line, like we sometimes use for our troops. I'll bet this is where they came out. And strangely, just as I arrived, they all closed up and vanished. But then, THIS bugger shows up a moment after, all by itself out there."

"Oh dear..." Aerlie moans. "Thaelyn, that sounds like trouble, and on multiple levels."

"Multiple, yes," he nods. "And I can think of a few of those right away."

"Ehm..." the Captain wavers. "Just for the sake of asking, I suppose it might be a good one to inquire as to your thoughts on it."

Thaelyn raises his brow at the Captain, but rather than answer this himself, he passes to Aerlie.

She glares at him, with his impish smirk, and retracts with feigned surprise.

"Oh! You want ME to give the interpretation this time?"

"Well, my dearest love. As a man who holds honor and chivalry close to his heart, surely, he would yield to the lovely young lady to offer her side first."

They all share a quick laugh as Aerlie shakes her head.

"I think he's getting back at me for that bottle of blue now," she smiles. "All right, first is the portals. Just like the Captain said a moment ago, anything used as a portal would be long gone by now.

You open it up, shove something through, and then close it. Done. But now, if these things have been waiting all this time for one of our scouts to come up here and see them, THEN to close, that means we're being watched right now, and this needed a witness to see it, then to see this new one open for us. And THIS one is a source point portal. And I don't see anyone out here standing around to open it. So whoever is doing this must be using some very special techniques to open a source-end portal by remote."

"Indeed," Thaelyn nods. "And I would agree on each of those, by the way. And further to say, this portal is an invitation to us, much like saying, 'Here I am, come find me…' The trouble is, we have no idea what is on the other side waiting for us."

"Aye to that!" the Captain admits heartily. "You could find yourself neck deep in trouble with your first step out of it."

"Yes, but now this makes me wonder something. Surely, whoever is behind this, would likely suspect I would not as quickly jump to it if I also knew this. And this also causes me to wonder about our experiences back there. We may find ourselves with several issues of concern pressing against us, and our hand may also find itself being forced, if we do not actually accept this challenge. If this person is so adept at using portals, I think he would continue launching his attacks, even to open the next one inside a city. And perhaps worse, to correct for that oversight of those seemingly underpowered attacks. However…" he emphasizes with a finger.

Thaelyn pauses to again survey the lone portal in the field below.

"If this is indeed a challenge," he continues. "It might not be to step out into immediate peril. He may allow a grace period for us to assemble. Let us look at a few principles here. This is clearly a skill level that comes with knowledge and capacity. The attacks started as small groups aimed at small targets. We once speculated this was to refine a technique, as if to say he was unsure where to go or how to apply it. But if Aerlie is right, and he holds something like a Seer's Pool to view us at this time, those attacks were intentional."

"A demonstration," Aerlie muses. "But on a small scale, then to ramp it up larger and larger."

"Correct, and involving increasingly more complex apparitions, which by the way proved harder to kill."

"Oh dear, is this to say he's gloating over his capacity, or is it something else?"

"I suppose that would largely depend on his motivation for all these attacks, including this last one. You said it yourself, no one took any real injury. So, what is he actually trying to accomplish here? Is he simply playing a game with us? This here looks like he wants us to follow him, maybe also to meet with us. But regardless of this, I am not one to jump so frivolously into danger unprepared. Captain, we may need to take this offer, but we will do so with a full complement of troops, and fully prepared. And we should hurry, before this one closes, and we miss the opportunity."

"Right! Let me call up some fresh men for you. We should give the others a rest."

The Captain returns quickly to the garrison and begins shouting out orders for a new assortment of troops to gather up. Those who had taken a break during this time, as well as others who were still in reserve, all marched forward to join Thaelyn and Aerlie. As the new team assembled, Thaelyn began giving out orders.

"We are going to jump through at close timing intervals," he asserts. "We do not know what waits for us, but my suspicion is we may have just enough time before any immediate attacks. If this is true, I want everyone to take up their positions and do whatever is necessary to hold a line while we call in reinforcements. We may find ourselves in a pinch if there are hostile forces all around us, so we must try to push them back to give our people more room to move around. Beyond that, our objective will be the same as before. We must tear down whatever they throw at us, and then see who is behind it."

He makes a cursory pass around the assembly before leading them down towards the portal.

The portal was simply a swirling vortex hovering in space above the ground, much like Thaelyn's people might create with a rune stone, but here without any obvious means to do so. You could not see what was on the other side, as portals were usually a unidirectional journey from one side through to the other. There were no return energies to pass back the other way, including light to see an image of what was on the other side.

He stands there, pausing a moment to see if his Celestial senses could detect anything, but he essentially came up blank. So, with nothing else to do, he passed one final glance at his men before jumping through the hole.

His journey carried him for a strange ride, travelling through a long tunnel that seemed to take him away from Tae'Eladar. He saw the wispy vapors of ethereal travel, similar to what he might see as he used his own divine pillar, but here oriented in a different direction.

He saw the rainbow hues of the Ethereal Maelstrom, the eternal storm that circulated outside the Shell, whizzing past him. He seemed to be travelling through the storm, not outside of it, and certainly not to another location on the same planet. This journey was oriented at someplace very different.

Ahead of him, he could see a shape emerging from within the clouds of the storm. It appeared as yet another Shell! Much to his amazement, he seemed to be arriving at another star system within its own Shell, similar to the one with his home world. But before he could fully react to it, the tunnel rapidly descended down towards a body. The blurring of imagery relating to the local scenery did not allow him enough time for sightseeing before the flash of the exit point washed past him.

He found himself standing in a broad, flat expanse of what appeared initially as desolate land. It was cold and strangely dim for the lighting level. He knew his first move must be to step aside for the next person to arrive. Otherwise they might collide at the arrival zone.

The first to arrive was Aerlie, and as she struggled to find her footing after the unexpectedly long journey, she hopped to the side to allow the next one through. She looked around, and almost immediately began rubbing her arms for the harsh chill.

"Blessed Mother! Where in all Creation are we? And wow, is it cold here!"

"Fascinating…" Thaelyn muses. "Truly fascinating. Did you see it, Aerlie, as you made that final plunge? Another Shell!"

"I saw it, if only briefly. But wow! That was unexpected."

The Captain followed next, soon after by a series of soldiers, with each one trying to orient themselves after the long jump, and the peculiar sights on this side.

Thaelyn and Aerlie were still trying to interpret where they found themselves. The Captain also made a quick scan of the area. But while he was simply trying to assess the security of the situation, the two nobles were fascinated by the scenery.

"See there…" Thaelyn points up at the sky.

The others turned to find what he was pointing at. It was the local sun, but it was nothing like their own.

"Gods be blessed, man," the Captain wheezes. "What is that now. Orange, is it? And a mite small if you ask me."

"That might also be the reason for the temperature. This would be what we might describe as an orange dwarf star. They tend to be a bit cooler than the yellow one we have back home. But this now demands us to ask the most important question of all. What WORLD are we on? Because it can no longer be Tae'Eladar. Not with one of those in the sky."

"Did I see what looked like a wall or some such?"

"A Shell, yes, much like the one we have around us back home. This must be one of the other worlds created by the Estelar in our local space. I learned of this once. The story goes along with the story of our world and the Sarrukh refurbishing it. Shar once cast that shadow on our local sun. But then, I think Maker Kuroku forced her to remove it so she could restore that world. However, I believe a compromise was made along the way. Lord Ao, the over-god of the local realms, commanded two new worlds to be made, in order to give the sisters their own space. Selûne took one, and this later became the home of the Elven races. At least up until the time when they decided to travel away from it," he grins as he glances at Aerlie. "But the other one…oh, wonderful…" he moans.

"What?" the Captain asks hesitantly.

"The other would go to Shar herself, as her own little garden. And considering our recent experiences with her, I am not so sure I would wish to set foot here."

"Uh oh…should we be expecting something by about now?" he chuckles ironically.

"I will hope the answer is no. If she is paying any attention to what is occurring to us, she should know I will respond to it. And if it originates here, she had better know well enough to keep out of my way, as I do intend to defend my home against anything that might bring harm to it. However, I feel I should also be aware not to intentionally bring offence. If this world belongs to her, it is her space, not ours. And we should respect this ownership."

"Fine enough for my part. We'll simply see who's doing this to us, bring whatever might come about, and then go home. She can keep her happy little world, with all its icicles and mushrooms."

"I will admit to one thing, however, this world might make for a fascinating science review. If she would not mind at least this much, perhaps we could have a few people come over here simply to study things."

"Aye, maybe. But now what? I'm looking around us and I don't see a bloody thing out there, not that I could see much anyway, it's so dark."

"Aerlie, what do your eyes tell you?"

"Mostly the same as his, right now," she responds. "Even my infravision is telling me its dark…and cold. But I can see some mountains to that side…" she points off in one direction, "…and flat expanses down that way…" she points to the right of the first. "Although I think I might see something like plants…or something… Trees, maybe? But weird ones."

"Possibly, and in this otherwise alien environment, I would advise each of us to keep at distance from the native flora and fauna, just in case. We have no idea what is out there."

"Then, let's see," Aerlie continues. "Further along this other way…" she rotates another quarter turn, "…more land, not many features, although I think I smell something like sea water. Could there be a shoreline over there?"

"I suppose it is reasonable."

"And finally…" she reorients again another quarter turn. "Um… hmm…"

Aerlie squints through the dim lighting, trying to determine what she sees at the edge of the darkness. "Don't quote me on this, but I think I see something out there, and lots of them. But they're just on the edge of view, and they don't seem to be moving, just standing around."

"Interesting. All right, I want a portal rune to this location. Make that two. Captain, write up a note explaining where we are. I am not personally aware of an official name for this place, so we will simply call it Shar's Domain, assuming we are correct in that. We will wrap up one rune, and send it home to the guildhall for storage. I want the other one returned to our last camp so we can begin moving our people across. If we have this luxury of time to set ourselves up, we should make good use of it."

"Our ride over here seems to have closed on us," Aerlie notes as she checks the arrival zone.

"Yes, it has served its function, and now we are here. And no doubt, since we have our own, we will use that from this moment. Let us begin by importing a few defensive barriers. This will give us a little protection, and we will go from there."

The scouts move to one side and mark two portal runes. The Captain pulls out a notebook and tears out a page to write his note. He then wraps this around one of the runestones, and a scout offers a small ribbon they sometimes use for such occasions. They tie it up, and another scout pulls out a special runestone that directs him back to the guildhall.

The first scout now takes the two newly marked runestones, placing both of them in his pocket for transport. He waits for the other man to engage the return ride, and then touches the rune with his hand to be carried away.

On his arrival at the guildhall, his first duty is to find a local officer to report to.

"Sir!" he steps up to the Watch Captain. "I have a message from His Lordship on a new frontier. We need our people out on the west side to hear of his travels, just to let them know of it."

"Oh? What happened out there? I heard the ruckus about the battle. Gracious, I feel for those men."

"Aye, it was a hard one. A portal opened up for us way out in the fields, and it took us to a new bloody world!"

"A new world? Incredible! There's another one out there?"

"Aye, it seems that way. We think it's one of two the gods made once upon a time, along with the bargain to fix this one. For the moment, he's calling it Shar's Domain since we think it may belong to her. It's dark and cold, and this is full daytime with an orange sun in the sky. Anyway, we need deliveries. This is presumably where we hope to find the bloke that keeps sending his minions at us. His Lordship is first asking for defenses to be sent straight away. We have a bit of time on our hands, it seems, so we want to set ourselves up good and tidy. And I might further suggest keeping someone here at the ready in case we have more notes coming through as we move forward."

"Good to know! We'll get right on it."

"And while you do that, I need a ride out to the west side to get the men moving."

✦✦✦✦✦✦✦

The arrival of Thaelyn and his men on this strange new world would count as the first departure off Tae'Eladar, even if it was using a portal. But the local environmental conditions represented their own challenge, as they needed to call for coats, blankets, and camp facilities with firepits.

"We might as well set up a little outpost here," Thaelyn muses.

"If no one will argue our trespassing, we may find it necessary to establish a presence here, at least for the short term."

"Aye, maybe so," the Captain admits. "We might be here only to take care of the immediate business, but if you have in mind to do anything else, having a base of some sort would be in good order."

"Indeed, and this flat plain affords us a good view in all directions. I wonder who lives here. Clearly, if they are so capable of necromancy, this world might be a good staging post for it. But I do not see much in the way of habitation. So they must have brought us into an open wilderness for the occasion."

"I would expect the scouts to return soon from their run. The review they made up there to the north tells me that must be the direction of our quarry. That horde up there must be waiting for us to come to them this time, rather than coming down here to us."

"Yes, and all the more reason for me to wonder about who is behind this little game and why. They must not be very eager to assault us if they are affording us such a gracious opportunity to set up camp."

"Aye! Complete with tea and biscuits!" he laughs.

"They also mentioned seeing something like a fortress up there," Aerlie notes. "If I were to guess, I might say that must be our goal. They have a line of defense, waiting for us to gather up a sufficient force to begin our march, and then basically fight our way up to it."

"But Aerlie," Thaelyn asserts. "I must once again ask what their purpose is behind any of this. They assault us back home, putting on such a curious display, then offer this rather polite invitation to come over here, and with enough time to gather our forces, set up a sturdy foothold, and from there try once again to plow our way through what I will suggest is another of the same, simply to arrive at the doorstep of the one doing it."

"I think you were right with the word 'game'. This does actually sound like one."

As they wait for their scouts to return, they start to receive reinforcements with new camp supplies. Tents and bench seating begin to arrive, followed shortly after by kitchen facilities, and even some sleeping quarters. The outpost was quickly growing into a small garrison camp.

The scouts finally return, some of them with ragged expressions, and one of them with tattered clothes.

"Bloody hell, man!" one of them yelps. "Do NOT go near those trees down there."

"Why?" Thaelyn asks. "What did you find?"

"The blinkin' things are alive! Well, in the meaning that they come at you."

"Trees?"

"Aye! They move! Poor Sam here got his leg caught in a tangle of vines, and we thought it was just a bramble. But those things were actively reaching for us, trying to snare us and haul us in. Then we saw some of those plant things get up and advance on us. They walk! Well, sort of… But they seem mobile, and aggressive enough to pursue a person."

"Fascinating. I wonder…"

Thaelyn surveys the landscape, and then observes the sky again.

"This would suggest they could be carnivorous. Now, this is simply speculation, mind you, but I wonder if the dim sunlight here denies the traditional photosynthesis in this world. And if so, the local plant life may find it necessary to turn to alternate means to survive."

"Aye, that would be a nasty one. And further to become mobile to find better hunting grounds."

"But this naturally makes me wonder about any animal life, and how that might appear, especially if the plants are so dangerous."

"Aye! This wouldn't be a nice place to visit with your grandma!"

The camp continued to grow, with teams of workers now arriving to set up the outpost facilities, while the soldiers arranged themselves and made ready to march forward. Thaelyn oversaw the assembly of fresh troops as they took up formation.

"All right, men," he announces. "I am expecting more of the same as what we had outside of B.T. Just to the north," he directs a finger off in the distance, "we have what appears to be a broad line of opponents. We will do to them what we did to the others, and do so with the strength and tenacity that has become our tradition. After that, we see what appears as a fortress just on the horizon. We will assume this to be our target. But what waits for us inside is anyone's guess."

He waves for them to follow, and he leads the march across the field.

The distance to the front line of undead was nearly half a mile, but the terrain was easy to cover. Once they came to within clear sighting range, the undead began to form up, preparing themselves for a fight.

As with the previous times, the arrangement was very much the same, and the assortment was also similar to that which just hit the city not long before. The troops rushed forward to engage their targets, encountering the simple forms first, and working their way through. After that came the wraiths, where the troops again tried employing the tactic they used before to hold them back while the priests struggled to bring them down.

"We REALLY need to find a better way of doing this..." Aerlie moans as she conjures up one after another divine chant.

The battle again took what seemed like hours to wade through the numbers, finally arriving with the golems, where again the troops took to physical attacks to chip away at them.

"These blighters are simply too sturdy," the Captain shakes his head. "There must be a way to soften them up a bit."

After a long while, the last of these fell, and it was now down to the hovering entities. And just as before, their combination of tail spike attacks and magical shots took their toll, sending men to the ground, only to be pulled away to recover while others took a new line.

"A ward of some kind would be useful here," Thaelyn muses. "At the very least to give our people the resilience to hold up to more than one hit."

The day seemed to extend into the late hours, as the local sun passed overhead. The battle slowly pushed through the lines until finally, the last of them fell into a heap. Now it was just the fortress in the distance.

Thaelyn and his men took a sigh of relief that this much was over. But the uncertainty of their next objective was now weighing down on them.

"We should advance cautiously," Thaelyn asserts. "I do not see anything else on the field, but we should not take anything for granted. Scouts, lead us in and check for anything hidden. We will march up to that wall and hold position while we assess the next move."

They begin to move forward. All seemed calm at this point. The fortress loomed in the distance, but there did not seem to be any guards or other troops moving around. It was surrounded by a sturdy high wall, and as they arrived, they paused to study it, and further to survey the general landscape around them.

"Curious..." Thaelyn muses. "This structure seems to be all alone out here. Are there any towns or cities that anyone can see? Who would build this in what seems like the middle of nowhere?"

The scouts ran around the sides of the fortress to see if anything presented itself. They returned soon after with their report.

"My Lord! I see something like a set of smallish hamlets down the hill to the left and around the far side. So, if anyone lives here, they're found on that side. Also, there's a gate on that side. But the bugger is standing wide open. And it faces up to an inner gate leading into the keep, which again is standing bloody wide open and with no guards posted outside."

"Two of them in a row?" the Captain winces. "That's not very wise. That leaves you with only a straight run to the innards of the place. A better lay would put one to the side, thereby giving you something to circle around."

"They must not have too much to worry about then."

"With such as these things out here," Aerlie notes while glancing over her shoulder. "Who could possibly challenge them? They probably own the place."

"And with doors standing wide open," Thaelyn muses intriguingly.

"Why does that not surprise me now. We could potentially suggest they used up all their forces outside here, and if we were so successful at cutting through that, there is no further point to anything else. But at this moment, I think not. I think there is another reason here, and it must be waiting for us inside."

"Uh huh," Aerlie smirks. "And should we expect cake and beer when we arrive?"

They circled around to the west and arrived outside the gates. They carefully peeked inside, but the courtyard was indeed empty. There was nothing moving, no sounds of an alarm, no shouts, or other calls…all seemed deathly quiet.

"I don't like the looks of this, my Lord," the Captain admits.

"I must say, I am growing increasingly curious about our opponent, Captain."

The central keep represented a large building with a formal architectural design. It stood several stories high, and likely had many rooms inside. Whoever lived here liked to live in style.

Thaelyn sends the scouts in for a quick survey before entering. They make their approach to the inner keep, and again peek inside.

Inside the large wooden gates was a hallway decorated with a stylish rug and wall ornaments. Sconces lit the way, and archways led into side rooms.

Thaelyn sent his scouts to investigate the side rooms while he and the rest advanced on a set of doors at the other end of the hall. They appeared important, as if they belonged to a meeting hall or ceremonial chamber. They were only partly ajar, allowing some light to shine through, and soft noises could be heard from within.

Aerlie tapped on Thaelyn's shoulder to gain his attention.

"I hear someone inside there," she whispers.

"How many, do you think?"

"One, by the sound of it. But he must not be very active."

"Then he must be our target. But the rest of this place seems empty. Does he live here alone? Are there no servants, at the very least? Typically, if you have someone in a place like this, and with hamlets outside, you should have…"

Before Thaelyn could finish his statement, a voice suddenly echoed out of the room ahead of them.

"Do I hear the soft utterings of visitors to my humble abode?"

Thaelyn and the others turned their attention to the room ahead of them, though the doors still barred their view.

"Well, what are you waiting for?" the voice ushers. "Do come in! The door is open, I believe."

Thaelyn raises his brow at his troupe, as he reaches to push the door open to reveal the room inside.

The room is revealed to be a large study library and laboratory center, with many rows of bookshelves, and experimentation tables stocked with jars and beakers filled with unknown substances of various colors and textures. But while this might not necessarily be unexpected, not after all their other experiences, the…man…if you could call him that, sitting behind the desk in front of them, most surely was.

Thaelyn and Aerlie both grimaced as their eyes settled on the figure. The Captain felt a sense of minor revulsion, and the other soldiers who were present at the time, peeking over shoulders and around other bodies, each winced at the sight.

"A lich!" Aerlie gasps. "That's not something you see every day. And not something I would want to see, either."

"My apologies, young lady," the man accedes. "But these things tend to happen when one exceeds their natural lifespan. In my case, I simply had too many things in front of me that I felt were too important to allow such as the unfortunate mortality of my original human life to interrupt."

"Oh, how tragic!" she satirizes. "And so you do this to yourself?"

"It was necessary, as the studies I was performing held a higher priority."

He now stands up to make a formal greeting.

"So, here we are. And my goodness, are you one of the fabled Winged Folk? I thought your kind had vanished from the world."

"We almost did, but not quite. Fortunately, we found help at the last moment."

"Indeed, and so it is, our would-be king of the world, but at this time it would appear as though you have made a fair bit of good progress! I would once again offer my congratulations to you, Thaelyn, Scion of Celestia, and not simply for your success on Tae'Eladar, but for that remarkable demonstration of, as you call it, strength and tenacity."

"So..." he muses. "You were indeed watching us, I presume?"

"Oh, absolutely! I have my needs to consider too, you know. After all, if I am to represent myself as a necromancer extraordinaire, I must ensure the quality of my creations."

"Necromancer extraordinaire...?" Thaelyn ponders distantly. "Wait, do we know each other? Because I recall someone once using that term..."

"Yes, we met once before, as you were laying low those nasty Red Mages. We shared a few brief words, but I had to take my leave afterwards, as I suspected you would not care to employ my talents in any of your research laboratories. I am Master Zharaden, or whatever is left of him after that awkward conversion."

"Um, Thaelyn..." Aerlie taps him on the shoulder. "Do you know this man...and I use the term loosely. Sorry..." she smiles tenderly at the fellow.

"I will not take offence, Your Ladyship. I know you are just as much a Celestial as he is...my goodness, how the world changes. So, I would not expect my form to be at all pleasing to your eyes. Much like my talents, for that matter."

"Indeed!" Thaelyn nods. "And just like he said," he responds to Aerlie. "This was at the time we took down those Red Mages. He was inside their keep, not choosing to fight, but claiming his greater interest in pure study."

"Uh huh..." she raises her brow. "All right, but this simply begs me to ask why we are standing HERE now."

"Ah!" Zharaden croons. "Do you wish to hear a most extraordinary story? Such a grand thing! Well, you see, even as a young man, I was truly fascinated by the magical arts. But while most would invest themselves in such as the elemental studies, which seemed a bit overdone to me, and others might choose the illusionary arts, which was interesting, but a tad insubstantial for my tastes…"

Aerlie gazed at him with a blank face as he began rambling over his life's story.

"…This naturally followed with a review of several alternatives," he concedes. "But as I grew up, I began to realize the one thing that stood out more than any other, and perhaps the least understood, maybe also to say the most feared, if only due to the inherent implications of its nature…"

Aerlie briefly rolled her eyes at the Captain, who was rubbing his brow as he tried to endure the long-winded lecture.

Zharaden continues, "…Was the most-often criticized art of necromancy. Now, most people would describe this as a dark art, and I suppose I must admit, it does carry a certain overtone, as well as a number of qualities that may support this principle…"

Aerlie tried raising a finger, hoping to call his attention and interrupt his sermon, but the gesture apparently got lost in his unending oratory.

Thaelyn glanced at his young wife as she was turning restless, and he found himself becoming strangely amused as the scene unfolded.

Again, Zharaden continues, "…But of all the studies I felt were the most demanding of attention, and yet the least appreciated, if only due to the bad reputation they so often carried in the eyes of all those who held such aversions to it…I mean, just look at the history of our world, and you tell me when anyone ever actually put such as this to any GOOD use…"

Aerlie was now waving her hand, hoping to draw his attention, as he seemed lost in his thoughts while recollecting his life's experiences.

The Captain studied her, raising his brow at her futile attempts to halt the lecture. Thaelyn also gazed at her, while discreetly covering a broadening grin on his face.

Aerlie finally took notice of her husband's impish expression, so she briskly scowls at him, and elbows him in the side. She then resumes her attempt at breaking the extended monolog.

"Um, Master Zharaden? Wow! Such a truly incredible story!

But, um, what exactly is it you are doing…HERE…" she points figuratively at the ground.

"Oh that! Yes. I came here to continue my pursuits in the art of necromancy, which is unlikely to be allowed on Tae'Eladar by now, what with your husband taking over the place as he is."

"Oh! Really…" she rolls her eyes and shakes her head. "How unfortunate for that, but I guess these things happen," she titters. "But next would be all that…stuff…" she weaves her hands in front of her. "Did you have something special in mind with it?"

"Ah, but yes! As someone who desires to hold the title of Necromancer Extraordinaire, clearly, I need to demonstrate myself in the eyes of those who might recognize this level of elaborate achievement. And in the absence of anyone else residing in this world, or at least none that I have ever encountered up to now…"

"Oh no…" she covers her eyes. "Here we go again."

Zharaden continues, "…And most importantly, if I am to gain the recognition I think a man in my position might be deserving of…you know, for all my hard work and perseverance… It's not easy to be a necromancer, did you know that? My goodness, the things I could tell you about my experiences here. You need some very particular reagents for this sort of work!" he waves a finger for emphasis.

"Uh huh…"

"And then, well, a necromancer really isn't much good without bodies to work with, and this world seems not to have that many… well, not unless you consider the curious animal species they seem to have running around. Oh, I could tell you a few stories about those. Let me see…" he taps a finger to his chin.

"Wait!" she asserts abruptly, hoping to prevent a new dissertation on the flora and fauna of the world around them. "If we could try to focus ourselves on this little demonstration you put on. You know, like how you did it…maybe also WHY you did it. That is, other than for the most remarkable achievement of some of those creations of yours."

"Oh, did you like them? Yes, indeed, a few of those were truly masterpieces. You see, young Miss Ariler, your husband over here would probably not care for my form of study, and I knew this, even from before he took down those Red Mages. I do not wish to be your enemy...I never did. My interests are purely academic. But do you think a Celestial, of all people, would care to hear what a poor old necromancer like me would have to say about anything? I think the answer would be a very emphatic no. Especially, as I think I once heard him say in my Seer's Pool, his only real concern were those few random occasions of zombies and such, crawling out of some forgotten catacomb. No one else would likely care to offend you in your perfect little paradise, especially after what you built in this time. But I say, no, this is not wise."

"Good gracious..." she mutters.

"Regardless of where your travels may take you, and what you may find there, knowledge is still power, and that power might find its place one day, like it or not...even if it is a form of study you would not care to indulge in yourselves. Therefore, if YOU do not want to study it, someone else must. This is where I come in. And you already saw what that knowledge can produce. Now ask yourself, if you had a REAL opponent, with a REAL interest in offending you, even with a fraction of what I sent at you, or perhaps even worse, do you think your meager countermeasures would stand up to it? I already know the answer. I heard some of your comments out there."

"You're a dangerous one, Master Zharaden, if only for your eavesdropping," she smirks and wags a finger at him. "All right, if you already know the answer, and given what we had to go through out there, I think the point was very clearly made. But is this to say you have a proposal?"

"I do indeed. You do not permit this in your world, and I will not argue this if you are trying to align the hearts and minds of the people in one specific direction. But knowledge must still be recognized to play its role, no matter what side of the equation it comes from. I seriously doubt you would want such as me walking around your streets, and I think I would not find a comfortable place for myself by now anyway. So, I would stay here, away from you for your peace, and also for my own to continue my studies without interruption for whatever ethical and moral issues you might otherwise take along the way. One cannot study this without crossing a few lines, although I do try to hold up what little morality I possibly can. I'm not quite THAT bad as some of those examples from our old history."

"Thank goodness for that. I heard a few stories of my own on this topic."

"No doubt. But even with other forms of the Art, one might still need to cross a line or two, if only to find the limits of their capacity. Nothing can ever be said to be entirely perfect. However, my proposal to you is that I will share my results, and you may take them and study them in whatever secret labs you might have to find your countermeasures. In this way, you may keep your best while preparing for the worst."

"And as for you? Do you have anything to say for your side of it, other than the privacy to actually do it?"

"Well, I suppose there might be a few small things. Like I said, it does take some rather extraordinary reagents to perform some of this work. Just look at those golems, and then the bone wraiths I sent out there. Those were not simply masterpieces of work, but they were also rather costly to produce."

"Um, one thing, while we're on the topic. Those...bone wraiths, you call them? The magical attack seemed a little..."

"Underpowered?" he chuckles. "All of it, Your Ladyship, was engineered to be this way. Oh, I could beef it up tremendously, but then again, I didn't truly want to cause any real harm, OR damage to property. Therefore, I gave instructions to use only the basic means of attack, and simply for the demonstration. I could just as easily have them use more, and they are indeed capable of it, but I doubt you would have as many survivors to tell the tale afterwards," he grins.

"Indeed!"

She now turns to Thaelyn and the Captain, along with the others standing behind them and listening in. Both men glanced at her, and then each other, finally to examine the many soldiers who had gathered around by this time.

"This would surely benefit us, Thaelyn," Aerlie admits. "We just barely allow anything at all back home, and mostly as those top-secret projects behind some very firmly closed doors. I don't know when, or even if, we might have a true use for it, but like he said, if anyone ever did get the crazy idea to do it, we are sorely lacking in our defense."

"I suppose I must agree," he considers. "Although this is a rather curious turn of events for how it is being presented."

"How would you prefer it to be presented? Would you respond as well if he walked up to your office door and said: Hi there!" she animates her posture. "I'm a necromancer looking for a job. Do you have any openings?" she smiles cutely.

"My Lord," the Captain moans. "Are you sure you can handle this one? Between that bottle of blue she once brought forward, and a few other things, I think you may have bitten off a rather large amount."

"Perhaps," he smiles. "But I believe I have also said how much I enjoy challenges."

"Aye, a challenge is one thing, but this one would likely give a person migraines."

Thaelyn simply shrugs as he continues.

"To accept this offer might be favorable on some levels, but I am also concerned for that aspect of being a Celestial, and how this feels a little like making a deal with a devil, even though he may not be as devilish as some."

"Not everything can be perfect," Aerlie offers. "And knowledge IS power, no matter where it comes from originally. Although I would not be as permissive if it comes out of any really nasty business, and I will emphasize this with our host here. But still, if to keep it within a fair level of reason, it might be tolerable. And the end result is to enhance our studies in anti-necromantic magics, which we would not likely find anywhere else."

"I could also sweeten the deal for you, if you like," Zharaden adds.

He steps over to a nearby window and looks outside at the flat barrens. He waves for the others to come closer so he can explain his thoughts.

"Out there…" he points. "We have a lot of open space. To my knowledge, we don't have any true societies of people in this world. I've travelled a bit here and there, and found something resembling lesser forms of beings, not quite as promising as our own example, but then, maybe they're simply an early form of something. Anyway, we still have a lot of vacant territory at our disposal."

"Eh, one moment," Thaelyn urges. "Before you go too far with that idea, I am reminded of who this world likely belongs to, and we have something of a history behind us."

"I heard about that. Shar never once argued about my occupation, although granted, I'm just one person, but I took up residency here nearly a century and a half ago, and never once did she try to kick me off."

"Do you converse with her at all?"

"Admittedly, no. But in the absence of anything significant here that she might want to safeguard, I think if we were to simply ask for an easement with her, it might not be asking too much. And then, we had that little…ahem…episode with that storm she incited, and as I hear it, she might be even less interested in exerting any opposing opinions."

"Perhaps. But still, I would not wish to offend, simply out of respect. And by the way, what are these hamlets we see out here?"

"Ah, yes. They work for me. In the absence of a native population, I created my own. I can't do everything myself, so I conjured up my own population of minions to serve my needs."

"Um, dare I ask this question, but are we speaking of people with their own minds, or some form of slaves?"

"They can think and perform well enough on their own, within reason for being undead. I don't believe in slavery, any more than you. But undead can't be described in the same context as the living. They have to come from somewhere, and in this case, that means me. I attend to their needs, much like they assist me in mine. I believe that autonomous activity is much better than me micromanaging everything. And so, they may perform as people, have lives similar to people, maybe not the living example, but for what we have, they seem content with it. And they're all loyal to my attending."

"A bit like a local lord, or maybe a baron," Aerlie muses. "But my goodness, a society of undead? That would be a sight to see! Although I'm not so sure I would actually want to see it. Do you desire to interact with our people at all, even for such as trade or other forms of business?"

"We have done well enough by ourselves. They can perform and serve most of their needs to build a life here, in that form we require. And like His Lordship suggested, if we want to offer respect to the apparent owner of this world, we might not want to extend ourselves so much that we are colonizing this place with a lot of unwanted guests."

"Yes," Thaelyn nods. "And returning back to that suggestion of using this land for anything..."

"Right. But I'm not talking about taking the whole world. You could describe it as simply a few territories, and with a meaningful purpose. Listen to this. Your people will need more than just the study of these magics. They'll also need experience at fighting them. Imagine a type of training field out there where you could occasionally bring your men for a bit of exercise, as you like to call it. Here is where you can test these new studies to refine them into actual practice."

"And as for our opponents?" he raises his brow.

"You got it... I'll conjure up an army for you to bash around. It's all the same to our side...they're already dead."

"Powers help us... Aerlie, did I just mention a deal with a devil?"

"Well, Dear," she shrugs. "He DOES carry a valid point. Simply to study it on paper is not the same as going out and training it physically."

"Uh huh... Captain, you were mentioning a moment ago about biting off too much..."

"Aye," he sighs painfully. "I've got my own back home."

"And I have one other idea that came up recently," Zharaden

adds. "I'm not sure how you might feel on this, but considering a few things I overheard in my Seer's Pools…" he coughs emphatically.

"Master Zharaden!" Aerlie sets her hands on her hips and flutters her wings. "Just how often do you peek into other people's affairs?"

"Your Ladyship, this man you married carries a very prominent image, and with that image comes the command of reason. And a good part of that reason is one of his most important lessons… know your opponent. I wanted to present myself with as much a convincing argument as possible, but he will likely be a hard sell for someone like me. But if I could offer a series of suggestions, some of which to augment your people, and others to maybe solve a few of your local problems, this might prove just worthy enough to consider."

"And what problems are you speaking of?"

"The lack of any prisons for all those miscreants you're looking at in the lands of Jhanaku Karba."

Aerlie suddenly raises her brow at the mention.

"That continent to our south, where we have so many new uprisings of wars and who-knows-what-else down there. What are you thinking of, in this case?"

"A penal colony, where you can basically drop them and forget about them. This row of mountains south of us…" he glances out the window again. "I happen to know there's a large plateau…well, more or less of one, at least. With a little work, and maybe my private society of undead laborers, we could build something up there. If you're looking at so many people you might pull out, you'll need a place to put them. But by the sound of it, we're not talking about just a few hundred. It could be thousands, maybe tens of thousands, maybe more."

"We must consider a support infrastructure to maintain that many," Thaelyn notes. "Such as food, basic needs… I might wish to remove them, but not simply drop them in a wasteland to rot."

"No, I'm not thinking of that. We could be speaking of a citylike environment, enclosed by a wall… but not a prison wall," he waves a finger. "More like a fortification wall to guard against everything ELSE out there. I doubt we would need to care as much to lock them up in a place like this…there's nowhere for them to go if they want to just walk away."

"Uh oh…and I now recall our scouts and those trees out there."

"Yes, and the rest of it is as bad or worse. BUT…" he emphasizes with a finger. "While this city may be enclosed, we could involve farming plots inside for them to work their own soil, and wells to draw up water. And then you might have homes, workshops, marketplaces, and so on, to live whatever life they like until their final time comes. But you still need other natural resources, like wood, stone, minerals, and such, and for this you need to go outside. Let them harvest their own, if they want to build anything like weapons, or anything as luxurious as what you created in your world. The idea is you built your paradise, and the people are happy. No war, no crime, and whatnot. But if they don't want to live in that, they can come here instead. Life won't be convenient, maybe not even pleasant, but if they can make anything at all out of it, it's their creation. And unlike a traditional prison, they'll have the freedom to move around, and this becomes their new home for as long as they think they can survive here. And I can justify this if you consider your Maker Kuroku and HER garden project."

"He has a point, Thaelyn," Aerlie affirms. "SHE is the driving factor on our side. So, if you don't like it HER way, find your own."

"Yes, I may have to admit to this," he nods.

"And maybe," Zharaden concludes. "After they're finished in this life, I can get some new materials to work with."

Aerlie winces at the depiction, but she could only shrug again at the final conclusion.

"I suppose I must admit," Thaelyn considers. "The idea carries certain irrefutable principles. With or without the aspect of making a deal with a devil, our only real alternative, if we are speaking of anyone who might otherwise be so incompatible with our own, is that we may find ourselves in need to remove them anyway. However, this gives a chance at life, as opposed to a wartime action that would more likely result in a wasteful death. But I must once again consider Shar. Bringing so many people here, and likely both male and female examples, would ultimately lead to a true colony setting where they would grow and take over anyway."

"I have an idea…" Aerlie issues. "But it's not a polite one. However, if to keep Shar happy that we are not dumping a lot of our refuse in her backyard that would ultimately take over her garden world, what if we simply, ehm…fix them?" she smiles sheepishly.

"Oh dear gods, my Lady," the Captain groans and covers his eyes.

"Well, think of it. This is essentially a prison, not a colony to grow and prosper. It's a lifetime sentencing, and effectively no different from a death sentence in many ways, but with the only real difference being a chance at life, if you think yourself tough enough to actually do it. The only true condition here is…no babies allowed!" she wags her finger assertively.

"Um, Aerlie," Thaelyn frowns. "Just for the sake of conjecture, what if…in case of that remarkably odd occasion when we find someone who desires redemption, we choose to bring them back?"

"Hey! With the regeneration unguent, we can un-fix the fix. That's not a problem. I might also say, we could build a rehab center somewhere to do that part for us."

"Ugh…" he closes his eyes and turns away. "Why do I feel myself being backed into a corner with all these remarkable offers and suggestions?"

Thaelyn paused to stare out the window, trying to imagine how this might appear. But many aspects of it would, in fact, solve some of his own problems. On the surface, it might not go well with his Celestial perspectives, but no society could ever describe itself as perfect, not even the Estelar. Virtually every example might have its dirty underside. The study of these magics is simply the acquisition of knowledge that would ultimately benefit them if they should ever have a need to use it. And a penal colony, although not a polite solution to simply dump people somewhere, did also fit with the Measure of Balance that they are given life…somewhere…just not in the middle of their utopia where they would surely invoke so much more turmoil. This would more appropriately represent a form of exile.

"Very well, I suppose it cannot be denied," he submits. "There are many aspects which hold favorable value, and if it is kept over here, we do not necessarily have to look at it to remind ourselves of it...with respect to you, of course, Master Zharaden."

"Fine by me, I understand. I made my choice, and I need to stand by it. And then I can finally go to work for the best thing that ever came to our world back home. I just wish I knew of a few good merchants for those elaborate reagents I need to continue my studies."

"What manner of reagents are we speaking of here?"

"Well, as I found myself ascending into the higher tiers of the study, the ideas I've been developing are calling for things like body parts from extraplanar creatures, which are not so easy to come by around here. And then various fluids, oils, and ground-up components from creatures most often found in some very unsavory places."

"Hmm..." Thaelyn leans against the wall as he ponders the notion. "Most interesting. I think I might know of someone who could help. She is an old friend of mine...in a certain manner of speaking, up in the city of Sigil."

"Oh? Do you think you could direct her to me?"

"Let me go speak to her and see if she would be interested. She is a merchant, very entrepreneurial, so be aware of that, but this also causes me to ask what you may have to offer in trade. I think this place might not have the same sort of money as what we use elsewhere."

"I'm sure we can figure something out, with a little creative bargaining," he smiles. "Maybe we can form some kind of marketplace together. If she likes to exchange in odd reagents, we do have our native flora and fauna."

"Indeed, you do."

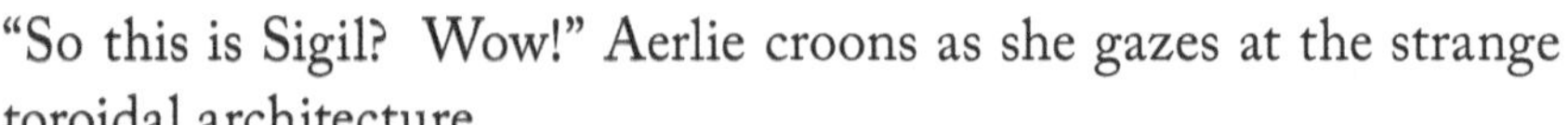

"So this is Sigil? Wow!" Aerlie croons as she gazes at the strange toroidal architecture.

Thaelyn and Aerlie were visiting the city of Sigil, to which

Thaelyn was quite familiar, but this would count as Aerlie's first visit. He was showing her around after their arrival from Mount Celestia using the local transit portals.

They were making their way to the Clerk's Ward, where both Aelwyn and Nemelle worked in the Guild of Sensations. It was also where Ecco once lived and worked. The visitation left Aerlie feeling a little unsettled as she began to realize the old association she apparently had, now feeling it more on a personal level, even though she didn't have any direct memories of it. Along the way, they stopped by the guild itself to spend some time with Aelwyn and Nemelle.

Their official destination was the little curiosity shop at the far end of the Ward, where the tanar'ri Vrischika still worked. This is the same place where Thaelyn once found that demon tongue for Ecco, and played a little game on the shopkeeper along the way. And this visit would be his first time returning since that occasion. And he had already informed Aerlie of the game.

They approached the shop, and Thaelyn took a position out of view to one side as he opened the door, thereby allowing Aerlie to enter first. He remained outside and out of view, giving her the first chance at the introduction.

Vrischika was in the back room when she heard the door open, and naturally she rushed out to greet her newest patron. But as she emerged into view, she halted, unsure if she wanted to approach any closer.

"Ehm...hmm... You look new here. But yes! Of course, you are new, and Vrischika loves new customers... Uh, are those wings real?" she points tenderly.

"Yes, they are," Aerlie smiles sweetly. "I've heard people tell me they are very lovely, but I tend to be a little more reserved," she blushes and turns away shyly.

"Oh! Really? Hmm, yes. But anyway, Vrischika welcomes you to her little shop, and she will make you a good deal! Look around, see for yourself. We have the dust from balor horns, and oils from stygian bladders…and many exotic reagents. Are you an alchemist, perhaps?"

"You know, it's funny you should ask that. My grandfather is an alchemist, and I took a bit of study with him once."

"Ah, good!" she exalts. "Yes, I can help you. Here, look at these bottles. This is special for alchemists…"

Vrischika points to a row of bottles on one of the shelves as she starts listing off the various ingredients. Aerlie plays along as if she was very interested in the subject matter.

"You know," she muses distantly. "Part of my studies also involve body parts. You know, like tails, horns, organs, maybe even tongues. Do you ever get any of those?"

"Organs, and tongues…" Vrischika pauses to consider. "Yes, I have many suppliers where I can make special requests. Do you have something in mind?"

"Actually, the tongue of a demon comes to mind. I know of this one person who might find it of special interest."

"A tongue of a demon…yes. Those are potent, and they carry special properties."

"Good, and along with that, I also have this curious need for something else… Oh, but this is probably a very rare item. I don't know if you would be able to help," she casually shrugs and turns away.

"Really. But wait, Vrischika can maybe find it for you! She knows many people who make special work. What is it you want?"

"Well, I have heard of it spoken in certain circles. One such occasion involved using it with this demon's tongue. But it's said to be so very rare, and in fact, some even question if it's real. The tears of a deva."

Vrischika's face went blank, and she suddenly felt a cold shiver run through her. And for a lesser form of demonic creature, this is a very bad thing. She already felt uncomfortable with this girl in her shop, simply for the Positive polarity aspect, as she could feel this from the moment Aerlie stepped inside. But now something new was arriving, and as the door to the shop opened, here it came.

Vrischika turned as the door swung open again, and a familiar figure strolled inside…but this was NOT that figure she wanted to see again.

She shrieked and backed away as her eyes fell on Thaelyn, with his bright smiling face, as he confidently strutted into the shop to meet with his wife.

"Ah, there you are, my Dear," he croons as the two of them gently nuzzle. "I thought for a moment you may have gotten lost. This is, after all, your first time returning to the city after that little… episode."

Vrischika glared at the two of them, now realizing what she was looking at, at least insofar as the Celestial perspective was concerned for that Positive polarity, and further that they were apparently related. She shrieked again and dashed through the door to the back room. There, she continued screeching, her discordant thudding intermixed with the sounds of glass breaking, and then followed by something heavy tipping over and falling to the floor. Eventually, she poked her head into view to again observe the couple.

"You!" she screams and points frantically. "I remember you! You, and that tongue…and then the bottle. And also that man… who was he…" she halts to recall the occasion. "No, he couldn't be related…but he had to be!" she yelps. "You cheated me!"

"Ah, but Vrischika," Thaelyn soothes. "I happen to recall that occasion, and you once said those tears were all but a myth, and probably not of any true value if someone only traded it for a simple flask of water. And I recall I did offer you a fair price for it."

"Gah!"

She shrieks again and runs back into her private room, once more stampeding into things, and knocking them over. After another moment, she reemerges back through the door.

"Oh…" Thaelyn continues, as if in afterthought. "That man was indeed unrelated. He had his needs, I had mine. Although, coincidentally, they did seem to cross paths at one point."

"GAH!!" she screams even louder and returns back to the rear of the shop.

This time, they heard the sounds of things being tossed into walls, boxes crashing to the floor, and stacks of supplies toppling over.

Aerlie gazed at Thaelyn with a wickedly mischievous smile as they both enjoyed the show.

A few moments later, Vrischika emerges back into view, staggering through the door and panting.

"I suppose I should introduce you to my lovely wife," Thaelyn issues. "This is Aerlie. I found her on the Prime world of Tae'Eladar. Such a curious place to find one such as her. But as she has so often stated, she is a Chosen One for their local goddess."

"Her?!" she points assertively at the woman. "Why? What did she do?"

"Actually, so far, she has done a few things, it would seem. One of these was to call my attention to a trio of Draconics that were harassing her people, so I had to deal with that."

"Wait, Draconics harassing them? Why would they do that?"

"In this particular case, the three of them had gone rogue and disobeyed orders from their Maker. They were launching unauthorized attacks on them. Therefore I, along with a portion of my military, had to come in to dispatch them."

"Dispatch…THREE of them? In all Creation, one is bad enough. What else after that?"

"As she said, her grandfather is an alchemist, and he had this most peculiar book in his possession, which, as it turned out, carried a very important recipe in it we found useful to solve a pressing problem. It allowed our education system to condense a considerable volume of study material into a lesser period of study time, accelerating the effort."

"That doesn't even sound possible. Not without external help. I wasn't aware those people down there held this level of expertise."

"I am sure you are right. So far, this is still a mystery to us, but it certainly came in handy. Anyway, sometime after that, I chose to marry her, since she carried such familiarity in my mind. A bit like an…echo," he smiles charmingly.

Vrischika glares at him for his curious smirk, but the meaning began to dawn on her for the earlier references. She stared at Aerlie, trying to visualize the relationship. And although the body was different, the spiritual essence did, in fact, seem familiar.

Her eyes began to bulge, and she stumbled back a step. She gasped and shrieked once again, turning and diving through the door into the back room. And on this occasion, it sounded like she was bashing her head against the wall.

"Does she do this sort of thing often?" Aerlie wonders.

"I cannot be sure. I do not visit this shop often enough to pay attention to it."

"Thank goodness!"

After several long moments of fracturing sounds, Vrischika stumbles out again, this time with bits of plaster stuck to her forehead.

"Are you finished?" Thaelyn asks politely.

The woman, whom Aerlie had been studying for her obvious features, finally seemed to settle down enough for conversation.

"You're a succubus, aren't you," Aerlie wonders.

Vrischika glares at her for a moment, then retracts and nods silently.

"You don't know?" she asserts. "You're one of them," she points at Thaelyn.

"I was born and raised on Tae'Eladar. I didn't officially join the ranks of the Celestial races until recently, when Lord Tyr came to me and informed me of my true origin. Then I went into study to learn a few things. So you might say I'm still getting used to it."

"Uh huh... And why are you here, simply to rub it in?"

"Actually no...not completely. But I will certainly thank you for the thought, back in the day when I was originally Ecco, even though I don't personally recall it. But the story sure does liven things up a bit."

"Right. Then why are you here? Do you still like those chocolate quasits?"

"Chocolate quasits?" she winces and gazes at Thaelyn.

"Yes," he affirms. "This was actually a special treat she enjoyed in the day. Would you like to try one?"

"Is it actually chocolate? And what is a quasit?"

Vrischika approaches her counter and leans over to point at a display just below her. Aerlie steps closer to examine the item on the rack.

The display showed something that appeared as a diminutive demonic form, approximating that of a bipedal arthropodal shape, with antennae and splayed feet, but small, like an oversized candy bar. And yes, it was made of chocolate.

Aerlie looked at Thaelyn and raised her brow enticingly at the idea. She then returned to Vrischika and nodded.

While Vrischika prepared the purchase, Thaelyn stepped forward with his proposal.

"Vrischika, we do actually have a serious reason for being here, and not necessarily to cause you so much suffering."

"Oh! How nice of you to tell me after the damage is done."

"Yes, well, such is the way here in the city. How would you like to enter into a business agreement with one of our people back home?"

"A business agreement…with one of YOUR people? What kind of person, who might be one of yours, would want business with me?"

"A necromancer."

Vrischika halted her motions at the pronouncing of that word. She brought her gaze up to meet with his, uncertain if she should giggle softly, or burst out in an unrestrained cackle.

"You, a Celestial, have a necromancer working for you?"

"I do now. Allow me to explain. Some while ago, as I was bringing down this guild of ruthless mages, among them was a necromancer. But he chose not to fight, instead to excuse himself and vanish. This was a century and a half ago."

"What race was he? That would be longer than most of those people would live, isn't it? And elves probably wouldn't do this in the first place," she glares at Aerlie.

"This is true, and he was human. Then, recently, we saw a series of incursions of undead appearing on our soil, growing in number and complexity for the forms they took. In the end, we found who was doing it, and it was him again, now a lich."

"Ooh, that sounds interesting."

"He was making a demonstration of his skills, and how the Art, even if it is offensive to one such as myself…and also her," he thumbs at Aerlie, "and therefore, it might not be in our favor to study, is still worthy of such for its academic value, if only to understand the appropriate countermeasures to fight it."

"Yes, this would make sense from your side."

"Therefore, he is offering himself into our service, in this case as an external agent, thereby providing us with our knowledge base for our own needs. As for him, his studies have apparently carried him to some rather high levels of expertise, such that he requires more complex, and perhaps also more precious reagents to supply him. Here is where I thought of you…" he scans the shop around him. "If you have such agents working for you that you can provide so many curious items, do you think you can assist?"

"Am I working with you, or with him? Because I don't think I would trust you, not after that demon tongue."

"Vrischika, I loved Ecco very much, and would certainly not wish to see harm brought to her, regardless of your profiteering efforts. That man needed information from her, which could only be given as a verbal response. I simply surmised you might hold a potential solution, and my teachings gave me what I needed to match it up. That is all. It was not anything personal to you…precisely," he smirks.

"Uh huh…"

"But in this case, I think it best you deal directly with this man and his needs. He is not currently residing on Tae'Eladar."

"Oh? Where is he?"

"I do not personally know if there is a name to it, but the pet world owned by Shar."

"Ah, Shadowfell. Yes, I know this one."

"Shadowfell?" Aerlie wonders. "That's what it's called?"

"Yes, I hear this before. I do not know who made it, but this is what some people use."

"I cannot be sure how you might negotiate payment," Thaelyn admits. "His occupation there is not associated with our society on

Tae'Eladar. Therefore, whatever you and he might use for currency will need to be decided independently. He does have access to a number of local resources, both flora and fauna, as well as whatever else you can find out there, and this may provide for the need. And he has created a kind of society, if you can call it that, of personal minions out of his necromantic activities. So we might say he has built a miniature colony there, complete with a local infrastructure."

"Sounds like he has been busy. This could offer a few possibilities."

"And then, I have a list of things here..." he reaches into his vest pocket and pulls out a sheet of paper, then hands it over to her. "These are some examples of things he thinks he might need at some moment. Does any of this look like something you can provide?"

Vrischika studies the paper, silently reading off the shopping list of odd elements, bizarre body parts, fluids and extracts, and other alchemical components. As she examines the list, she subtly begins nodding her head.

"Yes, this I can do."

"Excellent, then I should leave you to consider your business dealings with him. My personal suggestion might be to install a local agent of some kind, perhaps to afford more convenience. I will provide you with his location once you think you are ready."

"Good. But now, what does this mean between us? I still do not like you."

"Oh, Vrischika, pray tell that I would wish to disrupt our fine relationship. I will be sure to stop by from time to time, just as I am sure you will be delighted to throw things, break furniture, and inflict personal harm. Who am I to deny this?" he smiles brazenly.

"Oh!" Aerlie adds. "And do be sure to remind her of that fabulous offer, and how much I appreciate her thoughtfulness," she grins warmly.

"Indeed!"

As the two of them left the shop, Vrischika felt her blood beginning to boil, and she loved it. Deep down, she actually looked forward to their future meetings.

Chapter 18

THE UPRISING

The months and years progressed after their meeting with Master Zharaden. He set his undead army of laborers to work by building a new penal colony city in the eastern mountain range, calling it Haven, to symbolize the only truly safe spot in the world from all the hostile natural elements. It grew rapidly as his workforce tirelessly poured resources into it, expanding it to hold at first tens of thousands of residents, and ultimately a couple hundred thousand in densely populated communal housing blocks. Meanwhile, Thaelyn and his military began their offensive march on the southern continent to conquer it away from all the rebels and militant gangs. Those who weren't killed outright in the wartime assaults were instead captured and sent into exile…after having undergone a minor neutering procedure.

For those people who were regarded as redeemable, they were sent to a new rehabilitation facility, also located on Shadowfell. This would provide therapy, teaching, and conditioning, using such as counseling sessions and religious worship, along with trials and rituals to challenge and prove their worthiness to return to Tae'Eladar proper. With the alternative being permanent exile to Haven, which had largely turned into a free-for-all of criminal overlords and street gangs, having no local law enforcement except what the locals themselves might offer, if anything, the choice became clear after a while.

In the end, the last of the societies of Tae'Eladar had finally been united into one, with Thaelyn and Aerlie serving as the ruling family over all of it…all, except for the desert lands of the Saheen Expanse, where the orcish nations roamed.

The world was mostly at peace, except for those random, and often rare occasions of orcish impudence. The old pains and memories were largely erased, having been replaced with new insights, new perspectives, and new cultural beliefs and social values. The world had evolved gently, moving through the Ages as new knowledge was studied and new inventions engineered. Since the time when the Spellplague ravaged the world, and Thaelyn found himself in need to push several new technologies into service to effect repairs…and since the time of the discovery of the strange Sarrukhan time capsule, and the curious devices it contained, in its own day demanding of a few secret projects to thoroughly investigate…the world was now, on a more official level, coming of age to learn of these secrets on their own.

Electricity was now becoming almost a household application. Although still new, the technology was taking hold and demonstrating itself to be of immense value to promote a new way of life. Industry was developing with a modest level of automation, as an early form of Industrial Era was taking root. Mechanization was leading to the development of primitive automobiles. But in the absence of fossil fuels to power them, as such technology was generally forbidden due to its inherent polluting effects, alternatives were found based on their new hybridized form of arcanic technologies, combining magic with the common physical sciences to create something unique.

But times were starting to show a change again.

The centuries rolled by since the last of the societies merged into the kingdom. Thaelyn's overall tenure on Tae'Eladar had lasted nearly three-quarters of a millennium, and Aerlie was approaching her fourth centennial. However, in these past several decades, there had been a curious resurgence of the orcs. For unknown reasons, they had grown bolder in their ambitions, making new raids across the borders, despite the presence of guard posts and fortifications intended to frighten them away.

It all began with an occasional incursion that seemed intent to steal supplies from the smaller villages near the borders. This might include tools, food, and other materials. The townspeople were mostly ignored as the orcs knew the repercussions of attacking any of Thaelyn's citizens. But this behavior became even more brazen over the years and decades, and it seemed like an evolution of increasingly belligerent attitude and gall was taking over their society. This contradicted the rationale that Thaelyn's nation represented a powerful force, and had traditionally imposed a sense of superiority in the eyes of its opponents.

In response to this, Thaelyn and his ranking officers were in conference to discuss these matters and their reactions to it. Among these was his new senior military advisor, General Theodor Gabarleine.

"This is simply puzzling, my Lord," declares the General. "It has been so long, and they kept mostly to themselves, but this series of reports suggests a new form of leadership has taken over. What do you think?"

"Indeed," Thaelyn affirms. "This might explain the progression we are seeing in recent times. If we consider the timing, it must have arrived a few decades ago, but this already represents a problem for us, as orcish lifespans are not as long as humans, on average. Therefore, this might suggest either a young leader who happened to be successful at taking charge of his local clan, then to spread his domain to an even larger group, or perhaps a successor to an older one with a large amount of clout."

"By Blood or By Deed…as the old saying once went, to inherit one's authority from a predecessor, or to claim it by some great deed."

"Correct, but in the case of inheritance, orcish customs often contradict the idea as the younger one still needs to prove himself by a rite of passage. So this young orc, if this is indeed the case, must be from a particularly potent bloodline. Either that..." he pauses in brief contemplation. "Hmm, I wonder if..."

"My Lord?"

"General, there could be another reason that might permit the succession of generations to continue following this line of behavior."

"And what might that be?"

"A new religion..."

"By the gods...and perhaps literally," he chuckles. "Yes! That would certainly offer a clue to all this, and particularly for their sudden reversal of behavior. If they adopted a new religion, perhaps of a deity perceived to be especially powerful, such as to empower them with enough confidence that they might then challenge us after so many years of our suppressive measures..." he considers the thought. "This might very well be the one, my Lord, and then it no longer matters who the leader is if this is passed down through their shamans."

"Then, if this is the case, we have a very serious problem, General. A rogue leader with especially high ambitions is one thing. But a new religion that seems to be spreading throughout their entire culture... this demands a solution on a large scale, and the very nature of it brings dire consequences to my mind."

"Agreed! How do you kill the idea of a god in such a society that enjoys war as much as they do? Either we would need to reinforce the idea that our gods are even more powerful, or we might need to employ some especially harsh methods of containment on them to keep them in their place, and not cause any more trouble for us."

"This is true, so let us first reinforce our positions to ensure our own integrity. So far, their only true crimes are the theft of supplies and a bit of harmless mischief."

"So far, harmless..." the General intones cautiously.

"Yes, but perhaps this new religion of theirs is no more than a temporary fad to procure supplies, if for instance they have overpopulated and are running into shortages. We should investigate this. After all, it could be a fairly innocent concern. If this is all it is, we could possibly try to make some new attempts at negotiations.

If they are enduring hardships, they might actually try listening to our proposals by now."

"An interesting idea... Very well, I will send a few people to investigate the possibility, but I will do so carefully, as I am not one to trust them so quickly."

"Very well, General. But next, we should consider if this is something greater. If we are observing a transition of behavior, and if this transition continues further, we may have a serious problem. At the very least, we should try to reassert our positions of superior force and remind them to keep to their side of the fence."

The years continued with seemingly random occasions of orcish incursions. Initially, they did not seem especially focused on their direction, hitting mostly the small villages, and usually only on those occasions where they thought they could get away with it. It soon became apparent that the border towns were growing increasingly wise to these attacks, leaving the orcs to adopt new tactics. Now they were sneaking deeper inland at night to hit other locations, hiding in pockets within forested or mountainous areas, then to come out under the cover of darkness to make their raids. This brought new concern for the tactics as well as the implications that they were becoming bolder.

"My Lord," the General begins concernedly. "This is not letting up. Not only are they ignoring our attempts at negotiation, but we lost a couple of our diplomatic parties, and now they are infiltrating our border to hit us from the inside."

"General, this new leadership, or new religion, whichever it may be, is growing wearisome. Our scouts are unable to determine who is in control of these roving bands, and if these are simply raiding parties, the leadership must be further to the south. We need to find it and take it out. If this is a rogue leader of particular influence, we must remove him. But if this is a religion..." he sighs and steps back from the conference table to ponder the idea.

"If this is a religion," the General offers. "We must find their shamans, I should think. But this is problematic, as we cannot be sure who it is that proposed this religion, or if simply taking down their shamans would actually kill it. We might simply make martyrs out of them."

"Blast…" Thaelyn mutters. "This is beginning to take on proportions that do not please me for the potential outcome. This could progress to a level of all or nothing, leaving us to simply march down there and essentially conquer them…which we may need to do regardless, one of these days."

"They have been in this world for a very long time, my Lord. None of our societies have ever been able to get along with them."

"True, and this only makes matters worse for how we might need to resolve this. This would involve a large-scale war action for the sheer size of their territory. But before I commit myself to this, I need information. General, we need to understand their motivations better. Their actions continue to hint along the lines of theft, but their boldness at digging deeper into our underbelly tells me they are testing us. Where this might lead, I cannot be sure, but we need to know what this religion is about and why it brings them to take such chances against us."

"Right, then I will organize some very careful scouting forays into their territory and see if we can pick anything up."

"Just make sure our scouts come back alive to report what they find, General."

Over the coming weeks, scouting expeditions were sent deep into orcish territory; the desert wastes and savannas of the Saheen Expanse. The reports filtering back were giving rise to heightened concerns with Thaelyn and his officers. This demanded further surveillance, but this time from the air.

The orcs were primarily a land-based society, and often ill-equipped for ranged attacks, especially on flying creatures high above them. This provided relative safety to the gryphon riders, so long as they kept out of range of their primitive bows. And so, the results of these new aerial surveys reported large settlements occupying a broad area across the continent, which contradicted the historical tallies of their numbers.

"My Lord," the General notes. "These numbers are suggesting a large population, and this represents a heavy build-up of warriors over time, likely in preparation for a large-scale attack. The raids we have been seeing are probably just to find additional supplies to equip and support them."

"Our supplies, rather than theirs, as ours are likely of a much higher quality. This also represents a danger, as someone down there got the idea inside their head to steal from us and use this against us."

"We need to move quickly on this. If they should rush us, they could overrun our border towns and cause a considerable amount of harm."

"Indeed, I must agree. Then we must bring out the troops and begin assigning them to a series of outposts. But this also poses a few complications. We share an enormous border reach across our southern frontier, very literally from one side of the continent to the other. If they have so many warriors down there, they could launch from multiple incursion points, and we might find ourselves chasing this way and that trying to hold the lines. We need to approach this from a new perspective."

"Do you have something in mind?"

"For the size of their territory, the distances involved to cover it, and the demands to supply and support our troops along the way... the logistical issues present themselves rather prominently. We will need to invent some new technologies, including ways to quickly mobilize and erect outposts as we push forward and take territory. We will need to design a new type of construction method, General. This is something we have not had a need for before now, but we must rise to the occasion."

"Most interesting, and how would this appear?"

"This is a form of modular construction, where buildings can be transported as components that can be quickly assembled with minimal labor, then disassembled and transported on carts and wagons to new destinations."

"A bit like our existing tents, perhaps, but more elaborate?"

"Yes, these would represent more traditional building designs… wood or metal frames, maybe with concrete panels, locking joints, and such. Like pieces of a large puzzle to assemble onsite, as opposed to the thin cloth of tents, therefore providing better comfort and protection from the elements. We can design components for all our major buildings, including mess halls, barracks, command posts, watch towers and the like. Perhaps we could also make them interchangeable and expandable to fit the need."

"Incredible! Yes, I see it, a bit like using children's building blocks. You might have a smaller arrangement for a modest building, and then to scale it up to larger sizes."

"I would further recommend we call in our scientists to design portable versions of our gateway nodes, something simplified to point us at specific destinations, such as supply yards or military bases, and link them up for rapid returns."

"Excellent! And this would grant us a definitive advantage to move our people quickly over ground and take their territory, subduing them along the way, and bringing this to a close with a fair amount of efficiency."

"Good, we should begin making our plans and put our people to work."

Soon the kingdom began developing a new series of technologies involving this new modular building design for their military outpost structures. Several industrial centers, which included masonry and steel mills, lumber yards, and carpentry shops, were given instructions to begin producing the components necessary to be assembled into these new structures. The components were then sent to stockyards to be held until they were called into service.

The technology used by the gateway nodes found in their cities and towns, which linked the people from all locations to travel across the land, was now being reinvented with a new design for a portable version. This would be used within their military camps to link back home for easy supply runs, and it would provide their camps with quick and efficient access to deliver goods, as well as replacement troops into the field. The principle would make Thaelyn's army a formidable force able to provide new troops at the snap of the fingers.

The orcish raids continued with increasing regularity, and Thaelyn found himself pressed into sending military defense forces to make patrols along the borders and inland regions. The orcs were not ones to negotiate for anything, not ever in their history since they were first discovered in this world. They continued pressing their advance, taking even more devious tactics to find their way inside. Then one day, a new report arrived at the guildhall tactical room.

"My Lord!" the General shouts urgently as Thaelyn rushes into the room. "This just arrived," he holds up a report summary.

Thaelyn had been called in by a page from another part of the guildhall, and the news was said to be dire.

"What do we have, General?"

"We just received a new scouting report. The orcs have changed their tactics on us, and the results are sickening, to say the least. These past few weeks, as you recall, they began spreading themselves to other areas along our border, looking for openings in our defenses. But this here…" he points to the paper in his hand. "This tells me they were simply trying to fool us by diverting our attention. They hit us from the far reach, circling around that huge cavity left behind by the Spellplague in the southeast…you know, the one that nearly drained away half the Sea of Stars into the darkness below. They apparently launched a large raid on several towns over on that side. A few survivors managed to escape and found safety in the neighboring towns where they reported to the local guards, which then sent out scouting surveys to investigate."

The General examines the paper to reveal its findings.

"It says here that the towns were devastated, burned to the ground with no apparent bodies left behind, which is strange, because they said they found evidence of attack and presumably killings, leaving blood stains on the ground, and further, some of these appeared to have been dragged off."

"Dragged off? To where?"

"According to this, the scouts followed the trails, which lead well out of town and far across the land back to the orcish raiding camps. They went in under cloaks to survey the area..." he pauses to cover his mouth for the repugnancy of the report.

Thaelyn studies the man. He was a seasoned military officer, and yet he appeared queasy as he looked at the paper. Thaelyn set his hand on the General's shoulder to regain his attention.

"My pardons," the General accedes. "But I have not seen orcish behavior portrayed as grotesquely as this before. This is clearly something new and utterly intolerable. The scouts apparently found the bodies of those slain heaped onto what they described as a butcher's block, there to be carved up and the parts placed into a large stewpot."

Thaelyn's face went blank. This represented a complete alteration of their past behavioral patterns. The orcs may not have held high regard for the other races, but to attack a town so boldly, and raze it to the ground, then to carry off its citizens and make a stew out of them...this was no longer a negotiable premise. This demanded final retribution.

"My Lord," the General continues. "It goes on to say the scouts also found survivors in the camp, apparently being used as forced labor. They studied the situation for a time, trying to understand the implications, up to the moment when they saw one man collapse to the ground, apparently worked nearly to death, and then an orcish warrior came over with a heavy club and finished him. He was then added to the table with the rest."

"General," Thaelyn intones breathlessly. "This goes beyond the recklessness of any rogue leader and his maniacal ambitions, and it goes beyond any manner of religion. That these orcs would now dare assault our people for no more than their meat is unforgivable!" his voice rises. "For millennia, they harassed the nations of this world, never once attempting to live in peace and cooperation with the rest. They are fiends of the most abominable sort. Wherever they came from, and how ever they arrived here, they are no longer welcome amongst us. This one act is enough to banish them from our world entirely. And if their full society is converting to this conduct due to a religion, I must ask myself what Power would command them to insult the Children of Creation with such blasphemy!" he finishes with a shout.

"Indeed, my Lord, I must agree. How do you wish to proceed in this case?"

"General," he issues sternly. "Although I never in my life desired to take such an action as this, these orcs have crossed a line I will not forgive. Call an assembly in the Great Hall. I need my officers, my sages, my scribes, and an assortment of witnesses. And send someone to fetch my royal garb and staff."

He turns and abruptly storms out of the room, leaving the building and hurrying up to his manor house above the guildhall.

Aerlie had been in the temple during this time, but her Celestial powers had provided her with a permanent telepathic link to her husband. This gave them access to each other to share their thoughts and ideas, and it also allowed them to communicate on important matters. Thaelyn now used this, lifting a hand to his temple to summon her attention to join him as he prepared for his commencement. She rushed outside and took off in a fury to fly up to their home on top of the hillside.

The Great Hall, where they often held ceremonial events, such as the academy graduation service, was also a throne room that Thaelyn might use on occasion to give special announcements and official proclamations. It was now filling up with elder scholars and scribes, several journalists from the city news service, a variety of students and other members of his Order, and even a few citizens from the streets outside as they responded to the ringing of the bells to call the attention of the public to the special service.

Thaelyn and Aerlie had changed clothes and were now returning back downstairs for their official presentation in the throne room. This was an unusual practice, as Thaelyn most often kept to a more casual manner of dress as part of his work in the guildhall. They descended the stairs from their home and circled around to enter the Great Hall, proceeding up the carpet to the throne standing on the elevated platform, then turning to face the audience.

An attendant approached to drape Thaelyn's royal cloak over his shoulders, and place his crown on his head. It was a ceremonial dress he almost never used, but on this occasion, he had to make a very serious proclamation, and it had to be official. Aerlie also received hers as she stood next to him, and another attendant handed over a long ceremonial staff, ornately carved and crowned with an elaborate headpiece resembling the guild heraldry.

Thaelyn and Aerlie stood there stoically as the crowd came to attention. He silently pondered his words as he tried to contain his emotions.

"Good people of the kingdom," he begins boldly. "Since the earliest moments of our history, we have attempted to coexist with a nation of orcs to our south. Oft times, we had to tolerate their occupation of pockets and camps here and there, and accosting us with their belligerence and contempt for all things living. Never once, for all our efforts, would they negotiate or discuss any form of peaceful relations. And most recently, we have been receiving persistent reports of hostile acts upon our borders, despite our efforts to contain them with military defenses and retaliatory response."

He pauses to catch his breath, and again tries to contain his anger.

"We have just come into receipt of a report of their latest action, which was a large-scale assault on a set of towns to our east beyond the Great Sea. This, after a series of diversionary raids on our western frontier. Clearly, this was a premeditated effort, but this occasion was not a simple raid for goods, as so many others have been. This has seen their offence taken to new heights that cannot, and will not, be tolerated under any circumstances. Now they have taken to killing our people, and even worse is they have degraded themselves in the eyes of our gods to no less than cannibalism."

The assembly gushes with whispers and moans.

"Our scouts have confirmed this with a recent report of the bodies of those slain, and more so of survivors used as slave labor, only to meet their end as the next into the cooking pot. For this reason alone, to say nothing of our long history, I now call upon our people to bear witness to this final and absolute decree."

He takes his staff and holds it out, lifting it, and then stamping it hard on the floor. The shockingly loud clang reverberates through the Hall.

"As of this day, and by royal decree, we are now at war with the full body of the orcish nation."

He clanks the staff again to separate his statements.

"As of this day, and forevermore, no orc shall be welcome within our presence or upon our soil."

He clanks it again.

"Our history teaches us there can be no peace for as long as orcs exist alongside us. Therefore, we shall no longer make the attempt."

He clanks his staff one more time, the repeating process is simply to enforce emphasis in his statements.

"It is at this moment I must now make a grim decree, the most severe I could ever imagine. It offends my senses as a Celestial. It violates the manners of the Measure of Balance. But the greater need must overcome the lesser, and this offence must meet with an appropriate response…and this world was never intended for them."

He makes another stamp.

"By my authority, I must decree the final and absolute destruction of their kind. Let no orc remain standing upon any part of our world."

He now finishes with a set of three stamps of the staff to close his statement. The audience ushers up a murmuring of discussion at the obvious implications. This represented total war, with the full genocide of the orcs of Tae'Eladar.

On top of the mountain, Adalon rested on her perch, and looked down at the ruckus now unfolding in the streets below. She gazed at the scene within her mind's eye, which allowed her to see the ceremony inside the Hall, even though she was not physically present. She listened to the ringing of the bells and watched the assembly of the troops now forming up in the fields. She then glanced at her adult son who was lying next to her.

"And ssso it beginsss…" she mutters softly. "Sssargerasss… I come for you. The circle closesss. I will pursssue you... Acrosss worldsss... With an army... You cannot ssstop. You will know my wrath... The wrath of your ssservant... Who once played... For your amusement..."

TO BE CONTINUED